KU-178-495

The A–Z of
SCIENCE FICTION
& FANTASY FILMS

The A–Z of
SCIENCE FICTION
& FANTASY FILMS

Howard Maxford

B T Batsford Ltd London

For mum and dad, for that first trip to the cinema way back when...
For Richard Reynolds, for making it a hat trick with Batsford
And for my mate Gordon Taylor, who has seen *The Empire Strikes Back* more times than is healthy

© Howard Maxford 1997

All rights reserved. No part of this publication may be reproduced, in any form or by any means without permission from the publisher.

Printed in Singapore

for the publishers
B.T. Batsford Ltd
583 Fulham Road
London
SW6 5BY

ISBN 0 1734 8265 6

A catalogue record for this book is available
from the British Library

Cover Pictures: Kobal Collection
Interior pictures: courtesy of Joel Finler

Contents

Introduction

Having already penned *The A-Z of Horror Films*, it was perhaps inevitable that at some point I would be asked to write the follow-up, *The A-Z of Science Fiction and Fantasy Films* (we do live in the age of the sequel, after all!). Needless to say, I was more than happy to accept the kind invitation (and the advance cheque!).

As with horror, I've always been a fan of science fiction and fantasy movies (they make comfortable bedmates). Indeed, the first film I ever saw at a cinema was Walt Disney's *The Jungle Book* back in 1967 when I was just three years old. I remember being a little apprehensive about going to the cinema to see it – the old Essoldo in Stockport was a big, imposing building, after all – but was assured when my mother told me it would be just like watching a big television. However, when I asked her if it would be possible to change the channel if I didn't like the film, she simply smiled and said the other people who had paid their money might object.

That first visit went well (no screik-ing, as we say 'oop' north), so it was soon after followed by a visit to see *Lady and the Tramp* and all the other Disney releases and re-releases, both animated and live-action. We also went to see – four times in one month! – *Chitty Chitty Bang Bang*. Okay, so it's not the greatest movie ever made, yet it remains one of my all-time favourites (one of my prized possessions is a wide-screen laser disc copy of the film). Funnily enough, quite a lot of people of my generation also privately admit to loving the movie and can usually give a quick burst of *Toot Sweets* if pushed (usually after a few pints).

As a child, science fiction was deemed a little too grown-up for me. *2001: A Space Odyssey* may be one of the greatest (if not THE greatest) science fiction movies ever made, but as a four-year-old, it was a little out of my league upon its first release. Therefore, the Disney movies aside, it was on television in the 70s that I discovered many of the 50s classics and semi-classics, such as *The Day the Earth Stood Still*, *War of the Worlds* and *Destination Moon*. It was quite an education. In the early 70s there was also a cinema visit with my dad to see a re-issue of *Planet of the Apes*, shown on a double bill with its second sequel *Escape from the Planet of the Apes*, both of which impressed me greatly.

Then, of course, came *Star Wars* in 1977, the queue for which went round the entire cinema the Saturday afternoon my brother and I went to see it. Indeed, we couldn't get in to the first show, so bought tickets for the second, went home and returned two hours later. As impressed with the movie as I was – the opening shot of the giant destroyer produced a spontaneous round of applause – my overriding memory of that first of many trips to see it was the incredible amount of rubbish left on the floor by the previous audience. We practically had to wade through it to our seats! The things you remember, huh?

Star Wars was quickly followed by *Close Encounters of the Third Kind*, the double whammy of which we're still feeling the repercussions of today. A classic period at the cinema thus followed with the likes of *Superman*, *The Black Hole*, *Moonraker*, *The Empire Strikes Back* and *Raiders of the Lost Ark*. Some have survived better than others – can *Star Wars* really be over two decades old by now? – yet they all have an affectionate spot in my memory.

Of course, not all science fiction and fantasy films are of the calibre of *2001*, *Star Wars*, *Close Encounters*, *The Day the Earth Stood Still*, *The Wizard of Oz* and *Jason and the Argonauts*. Therefore what follows – a film guide cum-Who's Who – will hopefully help to put things into perspective. As with *The A-Z of Horror Films*, I will point out that, given the enormity of the task at hand, there are bound to be some omissions, be they people or films. However, as I also pointed out in the previous book, I have, unlike the writers of some guides, actually seen every film reviewed, and though my opinions about some of them may be at variance with the reader's own tastes and even received opinions – for which which I make no apologies – I hope the additional cast and credit information contained in each review will make up for any oversights or slighted feelings (people – myself included – can get very precious when one of their favourite films receives a drubbing in print!).

As before, the films included in the book are rated with saucers as follows:

no saucers	poor/disappointing (though some zero-rated films can have minor merits)
🛸	average/watchable
🛸🛸	good/well worth a look
🛸🛸🛸	excellent/among the genre's best
🛸🛸🛸🛸	a genre milestone/not to be missed

As well as plot synopses, each film entry also contains a brief paragraph of criticism followed by the relevant cast and credit lists. The credit abbreviations are as follows:

p: producer
exec p: executive producer
w: writer
d: director
ph: photographer
m: music
md: music director/conductor
ed: editor
pd: production designer

ad: art director
cos: costumes
sp: special effects
sound: sound
2nd unit d: second unit director
story, novel, make-up effects and **stunt co-ordinator** are all self-explanatory

Each entry also contains the film's country of origin (GB, USA, Ger, It, Fr, etc.), its year of release, its running time, the colour process used (Technicolor, Eastmancolor, De Luxe or black and white, etc) and, where applicable, the recording system used

(Dolby, DTS Stereo, Ultra Stereo, etc.). Also, any name recorded in the cast or credit lists in capitals denotes a stronger than usual contribution to the film from the artist involved (eg: d: STEVEN SPIELBERG means that the film was particularly well directed).

With the biographies I've attempted to provide as many contributors to the genre as possible, be they actors, directors, composers or special effects technicians. Birth and death dates, where available, have been provided, along with a career synopsis and a full credit list of their genre work, including all Oscar wins (noted AA if deserved, aa if not).

Well, that's the trailer sorted, now on to the main feature. Happy browsing!

Howard Maxford, August 1997

Top Slots

As with my previous book, *The A-Z of Horror Films*, I've decided to name my favourite science fiction and fantasy films, as well as my favourite stars and directors, along with those films and filmmakers whose work I feel has had an undeniable impact on the genre as a whole. Hopefully, this will give the reader some idea of where I'm coming from.

The Most Important and Influential Science Fiction and Fantasy Films Ever Made (In order of release)

1. *Metropolis* (1926)
2. *King Kong* (1933)
3. *Snow White and the Seven Dwarfs* (1937)
4. *The Wizard of Oz* (1939)
5. *The Day the Earth Stood Still* (1951)
6. *The War of the Worlds* (1953)
7. *The Quatermass Experiment* (1955 - aka *The Creeping Unknown*)
8. *Jason and the Argonauts* (1963)
9. *2001: A Space Odyssey* (1968)
10: *Planet of the Apes* (1968)
11. *Westworld* (1973)
12. *Star Wars* (1977)
13. *Close Encounters of the Third Kind* (1977)
15. *Alien* (1979)
16. *The Empire Strikes Back* (1980)
17. *Raiders of the Lost Ark* (1981)
18. *The Thing* (1982)
19. *The Terminator* (1984)
20. *Back to the Future* (1985)
21. *Terminator 2: Judgement Day* (1991)
22. *Beauty and the Beast* (1991)
23. *Jurassic Park* (1993)
24. *Toy Story* (1995)

The Author's Favourite Science Fiction and Fantasy Films (In order of release)

1. *King Kong* (1933)
2. *The Wizard of Oz* (1939)
3. *The Day the Earth Stood Still* (1951)
4. *The Quatermass Experiment* (1955 – aka

The Creeping Unknown)
5. *The Day the Earth Caught Fire* (1961)
6. *Jason and the Argonauts* (1963)
7. *Quatermass and the Pit* (1967 – aka *Five Million Years to Earth*)
8. *2001: A Space Odyssey* (1968)
9. *Planet of the Apes* (1968)
10. *Chitty Chitty Bang Bang* (1968)
11. *Westworld* (1973)
12. *Star Wars* (1977)
13. *Close Encounters of the Third Kind* (1977)
14. *Superman - The Movie* (1978)
15. *Invasion of the Body Snatchers* (1978)
16. *Capricorn One* (1978)
17. *Moonraker* (1979)
18. *Alien* (1979)
19. *Star Trek - The Motion Picture* (1979)
20. *The Empire Strikes Back* (1980)
21. *Raiders of the Lost Ark* (1981)
22. *The Thing* (1982)
23. *Aliens* (1986)
24. *Edward Scissorhands* (1990)
25. *Jurassic Park* (1993)

Top Science Fiction and Fantasy Film Stars
(In alphabetical order)

1. Larry "Buster" Crabbe
2. Brian Donlevy
3. Keir Dullea
4. Carrie Fisher
5. Harrison Ford
6. Michael J. Fox
7. Mark Hamill
8. Brigitte Helm
9. Leonard Nimoy
10. Christopher Reeve
11. Arnold Schwarzenegger
12. William Shatner
13. Sigourney Weaver

Top Science Fiction and Fantasy Film Directors (in alphabetical order)

1. Jack Arnold
2. John Carpenter
3. Don Chaffey
4. Roger Corman
5, Richard Fleischer
6, Val Guest
7. Byron Haskin
8. Inoshiro Honda
9. Peter Hyams
10. Stanley Kubrick
11. Fritz Lang
12. George Lucas
13. George Pal
14. Ridley Scott
15. Steven Spielberg
16. Robert Stevenson
17. Robert Wise
18. Robert Zemeckis

Other Key Contributors to the Science Fiction and Fantasy Genres
(In alphabetical order)

1. L. B. Abbott (special effects technician)
2. William Alland (producer)
3. John Barry (production designer)
4. Art Cruickshank (special effects technician)
5. Walt Disney (producer)
6. John Dykstra (special effects technician)
7. Richard Edlund (special effects technician)
8. Jerry Goldsmith (composer)
9. Ray Harryhausen (stop-motion animator)
10. Bernard Herrmann (composer)
11. Tom Howard (special effects technician)
12. Eustace Lycett (special effects technician)
13. Derek Meddings (special effects technician)
14. William Cameron Menzies (director/art director)
15. Dennis Muren (special effects technician)
16. Carlo Rambaldi (special effects technician)
17. Charles H. Schneer (producer)
18. Douglas Trumbull (special effects technician)
19. Bill Walsh (writer)
20. John Williams (composer)
21. Stan Winston (special effects technician)

A. I. P.

American production and distribution company (the initials stand for American International Productions) formed in 1955 by producers Samuel Z. Arkoff and James H. Nicholson, through which they presented all manner of low budget science fiction and horror films, several of which have taken on cult status. The company disbanded in 1980.

Genre filmography:

Terror from the Year 5000 (1958 – aka *Cage of Doom*), *Master of the World* (1961), *Panic in Year Zero* (1962), *Pajama Party* (1964), *Sergeant Deadhead* (1965 – aka *Sergeant Deadhead, the Astronaut*), *Dr. Goldfoot and the Bikini Machine* (1965 – aka *Dr. G. and the Bikini Machine*), *Dr. Goldfoot and the Girl Bombs* (1966 – aka *Le Spie Vengono dal Semifreddo/I Due Mafiosi Dell' FBI*), *Wild in the Streets* (1968), *The People That Time Forgot* (1977)

Abbott, L. B.

American special effects technician who has worked on a wide variety of films, winning Oscars for his work on *Dr Dolittle* (1967), *Tora! Tora! Tora* (1970 – with A. D. Flowers), *The Poseidon Adventure* (1972 – with A. D. Flowers) and *Logan's Run* (1976 – with Glen Robinson and Matthew Yuricich). His other credits include many for pro-

ducer Irwin Allen, among them *The Towering Inferno* and *The Swarm*.

Genre credits:

The Day the Earth Stood Still (1951 – co-sp), *Journey to the Center of the Earth* (1959 – co-sp), *The Lost World* (1960 – co-sp), *Voyage to the Bottom of the Sea* (1961 – sp), *Way, Way Out* (1966 – co-sp), *Fantastic Voyage* (1966 – co-sp), *Dr Dolittle* (1967 – sp), *Planet of the Apes* (1967 – co-sp), *Beneath the Planet of the Apes* (1969 – co-sp), *City Beneath the Sea* (1970 – aka *One Hour to Doomsday* – TVM – co-sp), *Logan's Run* (1976 – co-sp), *The Amazing Captain Nemo* (1978 – TVM – co-sp)

The Absent-Minded Professor

USA 1961 97m bw

An absent-minded professor inadvertently concocts a substance which enables him to fly.

Harmless Disney frolic, slightly better than the average. Remade in 1988 as a TV movie, and in 1997 as *Flubber*.

p: Bill Walsh for Walt Disney
w: Bill Walsh
story: Samuel G. Taylor
d: Robert Stevenson
ph: Edward Colman
m: George Bruns
song: Richard M. and Robert B. Sherman
ed: Cotton Warburton
ad: Carroll Clark
cos: Chuck Keehne, Gertrude Casey
sp: Peter Ellenshaw, Eustace Lycett, Robert A. Matey, Joshua Meador
sound: Robert O. Cook, Dean Thomas
2nd unit d: Arthur J. Vitarelli
Fred MacMurray, Nancy Olson, Tommy Kirk, Keenan Wynn, Ed Wynn, Leon Ames, Edward Andrews

The Absent-Minded Professor

USA 1988 96m colour TVM

A brilliant but forgetful professor invents a substance which enables him to fly.

Mild TV remake, cobbled together from episodes of a failed series.

p: Richard Rondell for Walt Disney
exec p: William Binn, Richard Chapman, Bill Dial
w: Richard Chapman, Bill Dial
d: Robert Sheerer
ph: King Baggott
m: Tom Scott
ed: Jerry Temple
ad: Cameron Birnie
cos: Tom Bronson
sp: Alan E. Lorimer
sound: William Teague
Harry Anderson, Cory Danziger, Mary Page Keller, David Paymer, James Noble, Bibi Osterwald, Tom Calloway

The Abyss

US 1989 DeLuxe Panavision Dolby

Divers working on an undersea oil platform move in to help a sinking nuclear submarine only to find themselves in danger, teetering on the edge of an abyss. However, help is at hand in the form of benign aliens.

Expensive, high-tech underwater actioner which plays like a cross between *Close Encounters*, *Cocoon* and the same director's *Aliens*. It certainly holds the attention while it's playing. A special edition of the film later appeared on video containing an extra 27 minutes of footage.

p: Gale Anne Hurd for TCF
w/d: James Cameron
ph: Mikael Solomon
m: Alan Silvestri
ed: Joel Goodman, Howard Smith, Conrad Buff

pd: Leslie Dilley
cos: Deborah Everton
sp: John Bruno, Dennis Muren, Hoyt Yeatman, Dennis Skotak (aa)
sound: Lee Orloff
titles: Ernest D. Farino
stunt co-ordinator: Dick Warlock
Ed Harris, Mary Elizabeth Mastrantonio, Michael Biehn, Leo Burmester, Todd Graff, John Bedford Lloyd, J. C. Quinn, Kimberly Scott

Acheson, James

British costume designer and, more recently, production designer, an Oscar winner for his costume work on *The Last Emperor* (1987), *Dangerous Liaisons* (1988) and *Restoration* (1996). His other credits include *Water*, *The Sheltering Sky*, and *Mary Shelley's Frankenstein*. He began working as a production designer in 1993 with *Little Buddha*, which he also costumed.

Genre credits:
Time Bandits (1981), *Brazil* (1985), *Highlander* (1986), *The Wind in the Willows* (1996 - pd/cos)

Adam, Ken (1921–)

Distinguished German production designer (real name Klaus Adam) best known for his stylish work on several key Bond movies, among them *Dr No*, *Goldfinger*, *Thunderball*, *Live and Let Die* and *The Spy Who Loved Me*. An Oscar winner for his work on both *Barry Lyndon* (1975) and *The Madness of King George* (1995), he began his career as an art director in 1947, working as an assistant on such films as *Queen of Spades* and *Around the World in 80 Days* before going solo with such productions as *The Trials of Oscar Wilde* and *Dr. Strangelove*. His other credits include *The Ipcress File*,

Goodbye Mr Chips, *Sleuth*, *The Seven Per Cent Solution*, *Pennies from Heaven*, *Agnes of God* and *Addams Family Values*.

Genre credits:
Dr Strangelove (1963 – aka *Dr Strangelove, or How I Learned to Stop Worrying and Love the Bomb*), *You Only Live Twice* (1967), *Chitty Chitty Bang Bang* (1968), *The Spy Who Loved Me* (1977), *Moonraker* (1979)

The Adventures of Baron Munchausen

GB/It 1989 126m Eastmancolor
Panavision Dolby
The real Baron Munchausen interrupts a play depicting his incredible adventures to explain how things really were.

Expensive, visually elaborate fantasy spectacular whose flights of fancy are frequently breathtaking to behold. Unfortunately, its astronomical budget (over $50 million) prevented it from breaking even at the box office.

p: Thomas Schuly, Ray Cooper, David Tomblin for Columbia/Prominent Features/Allied Filmmakers/Laura
exec p: Jake Eberts
w: Terry Gilliam, Charles McKeown
d: TERRY GILLIAM
ph: GIUSEPPE ROTUNNO
m: MICHAEL KAMEN
ed: Peter Hollywood
pd: DANTE FERRETTI
cos: GABRIELLA PESCUCCI
sp: Richard Conway, Adriano Pischiutta, Antonio Parra
sound: Graham V. Hartstone, Nicholas Le Messurier, Michael A. Carter, Peter Pennell
ch: Pino Penesse, Giorgio Rossi
make-up and hair: Maggie Weston
2nd unit d: Michel Soavi
JOHN NEVILLE, Sarah Polley, Jack Purvis, Eric Idle, Charles McKeown, Winston Dennis, Peter Jeffrey, OLIVER REED,

Jonathan Pryce, Robin Williams (uncredited), Bill Patterson, Sting, Valentina Cortese, Uma Thurman, Alison Steadman, Ray Cooper, Don Henderson

The Adventures of Pinocchio

GB/Fr/Ger 1996 90m Eastmancolor Dolby
A poor woodcutter carves a boy puppet from a magical tree and is astonished when he comes to life.

Good-looking (if somewhat underlit) live action version of the story with Pinocchio portrayed by a mixture of puppetry, animatronics and computer-generated animation. Charming in spots, though it eventually outstays its welcome.

p: Raju Patel, Jeffry Sneller for Polygram/Kushner-Locke/Pangaea Holdings/Twin Continental/Allied Pinocchio/Davis/Dieter Geissler
exec p: Sharad Patel, Peter Locke, Donald Kushner
w: Sherry Mills, Steve Barron, Tom Benedek, Barry Berman
novel: Carlo Collodi
d: Steve Barron
ph: Juan Ruiz Anchia
m: Rachel Portman
songs: Stevie Wonder and others
ed: Sean Barton
pd: Allan Cameron
cos: Maurizio Millenotti
sp: Jim Henson's Creature Shop
sound: Jean-Philippe Le Roux
titles: Simon Giles
2nd unit d: John Stephenson
2nd unit ph: Mike Brewster
puppeteer: Mak Wilson
Martin Landau, Jonathan Taylor Thomas, Genevieve Bujold, Rob Schneider, Udo Kier, Bebe Neuwirth, David Doyle (voice), Dawn French, Correy Carrier, Griff Rhys Jones, John Sessions

The Aftermath

USA 1980 89m CFIcolor

Astronauts returning to earth discover it to be overrun with mutants, a result of radioactive fallout from World War III.

Little more than a home movie writ large, but with a surprisingly good score.

p: Steve Barkett for Nautilus
w/d/ed: Steve Barkett
ph: Dennis Skotak, Tom Denove
m: John Morgan
pd: Robert Skotak
sp: Robert Skotak, Dennis Skotak, Jim Danforth
make-up effects: Robert Skotak and others
sound: Maurice Allen, Lynne Barkett Steve Barkett, Lynn Margulies, Sid Haig, Christopher Barkett, Alfie Martin, Forrest J. Ackerman, Jim Danforth

Agar, John (1920–)

American leading man whose first film was John Ford's *Fort Apache* in 1948, which co-starred his then-wife Shirley Temple. Since then he has appeared in all manner of routine low budgeters. His other credits include *Daughter of Dr Jekyll*, *Big Jake*, *The Amazing Mr No-Legs*, *Fear* and *The Perfect Bride*.

Genre credits:

The Rocket Man (1953), *Revenge of the Creature* (1955), *Tarantula* (1955), *The Brain from Planet Arous* (1956), *The Invisible Invaders* (1959), *Journey to the Seventh Planet* (1961), *Women of the Prehistoric Planet* (1965), *The Curse of the Swamp Creature* (1966), *Zontar – The Thing from Venus* (1966), *King Kong* (1976)

Airplane II: The Sequel

USA 1982 85m Metrocolor

Passengers on a new super jet find it out of control and careering towards the sun, but help is at hand...

Basically no more than an extension of *Airplane!*, but bright gags make it, on the whole, almost as much fun. Certainly worth a look for Shatner's cameo, which spoofs his *Star Trek* image.

p: Howard W. Koch for Paramount
w/d: Ken Finkleman
ph: Joseph Biroc
m: Richard Hazard (after Elmer Bernstein)
ed: Dennis Virkler
pd: William Sandell
cos: Rosanna Norton
Robert Hays, Julie Haggerty, Lloyd Bridges, William Shatner, Peter Graves, Chad Everett, Steven Stucker, Sonny Bono, Raymond Burr, Chuck Connors, Rip Torn, John Dehner, Kent McCord, John Vernon, Jack Jones, Herve Villechaize

Akira ✈

USA 1987 124m colour

In AD 2019, 31 years after World War Three, a young biker living in a Neo-Tokyo riddled with crime finds himself the subject of an experiment out to produce superhumans.

Slickly directed animated feature, the success of which spearheaded the new wave of *anime*, first in the East and later in the West. In itself, somewhat protracted but with many eye-catching sequences along the way.

p: Ryoshei Suzuki, Shuno Kato for Akira Committee
w: Katsuhiro Otomo, Izo Hashimoto
Comic book: Katsuhiro Otomo
ph: Katsuji Misawa
m: Shoji Yamashiro
ad: Toshiharu Mizutani

Akira Kurosawa's Dreams see Dreams

Aladdin ✈✈

USA 1992 91m Technicolor Dolby

The story of Aladdin and his magical lamp.

Stylish and pacy cartoon feature with plenty of visual flair, though best remembered for Robin Williams' star turn as the Genie of the Lamp. A box office bonanza, it was followed by two video sequels: *The Return of Jafar* (1994 – in which the Genie was voiced by Dan Castellaneta) and *Aladdin and the King of Thieves* (1997 – in which Williams returned as the Genie). There was also a television cartoon series based on the film.

p: John Musker, Ron Clements for Walt Disney
w: Ron Clements, John Musker, Ted Elliott, Terry Rossio
d: John Musker, John Clements
songs: Alan Menken (m), Howard Ashman, Tim Rice (ly)
song: *A Whole New World*, Alan Menken (m), Tim Rice (ly) (aa)
m: Alan Menken (aa)
ed: H. Lee Peterson
pd: R. S. Vander Wende
sound: Terry Porter, Mel Metcalfe, David J. Hudson, Doc Kane
voices: Scott Weinger, Linda Larkin, ROBIN WILLIAMS, Brad Kane, Lea Salonga, Jonathan Freeman, Frank Welker, Gilbert Gottfried

Alcott, John (1931–1986)

British cinematographer, an Oscar winner for his work on *Barry Lyndon* (1975). After experience at Gainsborough beginning in the 1940s, he became an assistant to Geoffrey Unsworth, for whom he shot the Dawn of Man sequence in Stanley Kubrick's *2001* when Unsworth had to leave the production to fulfil his contract to photograph *The Bliss of Mrs Blossom*. This led to three more movies with Kubrick: *A Clockwork Orange*, *Barry Lyndon* and *The Shining*. His other credits include *Little Malcolm and His Struggle Against the Eunuchs*, *March or Die*, *Who is Killing The Great Chefs of Europe?*, *Terror Train*, *Fort Apache – The Bronx*, *Under Fire*, *Greystoke – The Legend of Tarzan, Lord of the Apes* and *No Way Out*.

Genre credits:

2001: A Space Odyssey (1968 - co-ph), *A Clockwork Orange* (1971), *The Beastmaster* (1982), *Baby – Secret of the Lost Legend* (1985)

Alf's Button Afloat

GB 1938 89m bw

Six buskers inadvertently join the navy, but have an easy time of it with the help of a genie living in one of their tunic buttons.

Fast-moving fantasy-farce, adapted to suit the talents of The Crazy Gang. Hilarious in spots. There were also two previous versions in 1920 (with Leslie Henson) and 1930 (with Jimmy Nervo and Teddy Knox, who also star in this version).

p: Edward Black for Gainsborough
w: Marriott Edgar, Val Guest, Ralph Smart
novel: W. A. Darlington
d: Marcel Varnel
ph: Arthur Crabtree
md: Louis Levy
ed: Alfred Roome, R. E. Dearing
ad: Alex Vetchinsky
sound: S. Wiles
THE CRAZY GANG (BUD FLANNAGAN, CHESNEY ALLEN, JIMMY NERVO, TEDDY KNOX, CHARLES NAUGHTON, JIMMY GOLD), ALASTAIR SIM (as the genie), Wally

Patch, Peter Gawthorne

Alice in Wonderland

Lewis Carroll's 1865 nonsense story about a young girl who falls down a rabbit hole into a fantasy world has been filmed several times, though it is the 1951 Disney cartoon that is perhaps best remembered. There have also been a couple of starry versions, among them *Alice in Wonderland* (1933, which features Cary Grant as the Mock Turtle and W. C. Fields as Humpty Dumpty) and the musical *Alice's Adventure's in Wonderland* (1972, which has Peter Sellers as the March Hare, Ralph Richardson as the Caterpillar and Michael Crawford as the White Rabbit). *Dreamchild*, meanwhile, focuses on the octogenarian Alice Liddell, Carroll's inspiration for Alice. Surprisingly, Georges Méliès never tackled the subject.

Filmography:

Alice in Wonderland (1931), *Alice in Wonderland* (1933), Alice in Wonderland (1951), *Alice au Pays de Merveilles* (1951 – aka *Alice in Wonderland*), Alice (1965 – TVM), *Alice in Wonderland* (1966 – TVM), *Alice's Adventures in Wonderland* (1972), *Dreamchild* (1985), *Alice in Wonderland* (1985 – TVM), *Alice* (1988)

Alice in Wonderland

USA 1951 75m Technicolor

Alice falls down a rabbit hole and has various adventures in a world where everything is not quite what it seems.

Well crafted but finally rather tiresome animated version of a story which has never been wholly satisfactorily filmed.

p: Walt Disney
w: Winston Hibler, Bill Peet, Joe Rinaldi, Del

Connel, Joe Grant, Bill Cottrell, Erdman Penner, Milt Banta, Dick Kelsey, Dick Huemer, Tom Oreb, John Walbridge, Ted Sears
novel: Lewis Carroll
d: Ben Sharpsteen, Clyde Geronomi, Hamilton Luske, Wilfred Jackson
songs: Bob Hilliard, Sammy Fain
m: Oliver Wallace
sound: C. O. Slyfield, Robert O. Cook
voices: Kathryn Beaumont, Sterling Holloway, Ed Wynn, Jerry Colonna, Pat O'Malley, Bill Thompson, Richard Haydn, Verna Felton

---

Alice in Wonderland

GB 1966 80m bw TVM

An expensive but rather tedious adaptation of the nonsense story, done in its director-producer's usual non-conformist manner. Chiefly of curiosity value.

p: Jonathan Miller for BBC
w/d: Jonathan Miller
novel: Lewis Carroll
ph: Dick Bush
m: Ravi Shanknar, Leon Goossens
ed: Pam Bosworth
ad: Julia Trevelyan Oman
cos: Kenneth Morey
titles: Julia Brand
Anne-Marie Mallik, Alan Bennett, John Bird, Wilfred Brambell, Peter Sellers, Peter Cook, Michael Gough, Finlay Currie, John Gielgud, Wilfred Lawson, Alison Leggatt, Leo McKern, Malcolm Muggeridge, Michael Redgrave, Mark Allington, David Battley, Tony Trent, Avril Elgar, Nicholas Evans

---

Alice in Wonderland

USA 1985 2x96m colour TVM

Another all-star musical version of the story, this time from a producer better known for his disaster epics. This is pretty much a disaster too.

p: Irwin Allen for CBS Proctor and Gamble
w: Paul Zindel
novel: Lewis Carroll
d: Harry Harris
ph: Fred Koenekamp
songs: Steve Allen
m: Mort Stevens
cos: Paul Zastupnevitch
Natalie Gregory, Carol Channing, Lloyd Bridges, Imogene Coca, Red Buttons, Jonathan Winters, Ann Jillian, Sammy Davis, Jr., Louis Nye, Arte Johnson, Jayne Meadows, Harvey Korman, Anthony Newley, Martha Raye, Telly Savalas, Robert Morley, Karl Malden, Roddy McDowall

Alice's Adventures in Wonderland 🍽

GB 1972 101m Eastmancolor Todd-AO
A musical version of the Lewis Carroll story.

Initially promising but ultimately disappointing adaptation, with songs that go in one ear and out of the other. It looks good, though, and the art direction is attractive.

p: Derek Horne for TCF
exec p: Josef Shaftel
w/d: William Sterling
novel: Lewis Carroll

ph: GEOFFREY UNSWORTH
m: John Barry
ly: Don Black
ed: Peter Weatherley
pd: MICHAEL STRINGER
cos: Anthony Mendleson
ch: Terry Gilbert
make-up: Stuart Freeborn
Fiona Fullerton, Michael Crawford, Peter Sellers (who also appeared in the 1966 TV version), Robert Helpmann, Dudley Moore, Spike Milligan, Dennis Price, Flora Robson, Rodney Bewes, Peter Bull, Ralph Richardson, Michael Hordern, Patsy Rowlands, Roy Kinnear, Freddie Cox, Frank Cox, Michael Jayston, Hywel Bennett, Dennis Waterman

Alien 🍽🍽

USA/GB 1979 117m Eastmancolor Panavision Dolby
After visiting an apparently dead planet, astronauts find that their spaceship has been infiltrated by a vicious alien being whose sole intent appears to be to kill them all.

Technically arresting, genuinely frightening science fiction variation on the Bogey Man theme, with excellent art direction and effects work. A worldwide commercial success, it led to three sequels: *Aliens* (1986), *Alien 3*

(1992) and *Alien Resurrection* (1997).

p: Walter Hill, David Giler, Gordon Carroll for TCF/Brandywine
exec p: Ronald Shusett
w: Dan O'Bannon
story: Dan O'Bannon, Ronald Shusett
d: RIDLEY SCOTT
ph: Derek Vanlint
m: JERRY GOLDMSMITH
ed: Terry Rawlings, Peter Weatherley
pd: MICHAEL SEYMOUR, LES DILLEY, ROGER CHRISTIAN
cos: John Mollo
sp: CARLO RAMBALDI, H. R. GIGER, BRIAN JOHNSON, RICK ALLDER, DENYS ALING (AA), Roger Dicken
sound: Derrick Leather, Bill Rowe
titles: R. Greenberg
stunt co-ordinator: Roy Scammel
Tom Skerritt, Sigourney Weaver, John Hurt, Ian Holm, Veronica Cartwright, Harry Dean Stanton, Ian Holm, Yaphet Kotto, Helen Horton (voice only), Bolaji Badejo (credited for playing the Alien), Eddie Powell (who actually played the Alien in most scenes)

Alien Nation 🍽🍽

US 1987 86m DeLuxe Dolby
In the near future, when aliens have landed on earth and been accepted into society, a cop and his alien partner track down a gang of ruthless drug traffickers.

Despite its conventional plot contrivances, this is a buddy movie with a difference, with enough amusing detail to make it entertaining as a one-off kind. The TV series which followed was less successful.

p: Gale Anne Hurd, Richard Kobritz for TCF/American Entertainment Partnership II
w: Rockne S. O'Bannon
d: Graham Baker
ph: Adam Greenberg
m: Curt Sobel
ed: Kent Beyda, Don Brochu

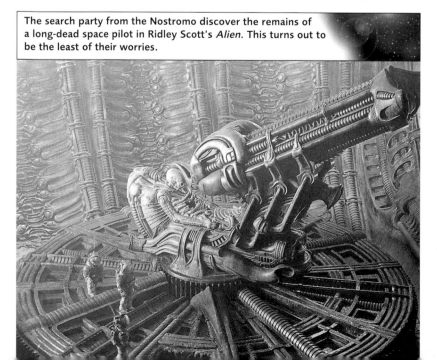
The search party from the Nostromo discover the remains of a long-dead space pilot in Ridley Scott's *Alien*. This turns out to be the least of their worries.

The cast of *Alien* in a pose for a publicity still. Left to right: John Hurt, Ian Holm, Sigourney Weaver, Veronica Cartwright, Yaphet Kotto (sitting), Harry Dean Stanton and Tom Skerritt.

pd: Jack T. Collis
cos: Erica Phillips
sp: Joseph Unsinn
sound: David MacMilton, Charles Wilborn
make-up: STAN WINSTON STUDIOS
2nd unit d/stunt co-ordinator: Conrad E. Palmisano
2nd unit ph: Frank Holgate
titles: Ernest Farino
James Caan, MANDY PATINKIN, Terence Stamp, Kevyn Major Howard, Leslie Beris, Peter Jason

Alien Resurrection

USA 1997 118m colour Dolby
Officer Ripley is cloned so that scientists can remove the alien growing inside her for experimentation and breeding purposes. Inevitably the newly bred creatures escape and run amok.

The fourth *Alien* movie is definitely an improvement on episode three, being more akin to the action-orientated second installment. Unfortunately, the story becomes increasingly foolish as it progresses and there are also some uncertain moments in the editing and continuity. Nevertheless, if one doesn't take it too seriously, it provides a certain amount of fun.

p: Gordon Carroll, David Giler, Walter Hill, Bill Badalato for Tcf/Brandywine
w: Joss Wheldon
d: Jean-Pierre Jeunet
ph: Darius Khondji
m: John Frizzel
ed: Herve Schneid
pd: Nigel Phelps
sp: Alec Gillis, Tom Woodruff Jr
sound: Richard Bryce-Goodman
Sigourney Weaver, Winona Ryder, Ron Perlman, Michael Wincott, JE Freeman, Dan Hedaya, Brad Dourif

Alien Species

USA 1995 82m colour
Research scientists working in an installation five miles beneath the earth's surface find their lives in peril from an alien, the result of an experiment gone wrong.

Dismal, low budget rip-off of elements from both *Alien* and *Species*, as its derivative title might suggest (its alternative title was *Alien Terminator!*). Leave it to gather dust in the video store (I wish I had).

p: Mike Upton, Mike Elliott for New Horizons/Calibre
exec p: Minard Hamilton, Rob Kerchner
w: Duke Lorr, Dave Payne
d: Dave Payne
ph: Michael Mickens
m: Christopher Lennertz, Nigel Holton
ed: Roderick Davies, Gene Hertel
pd: Lisa Salazar
cos: Tami Moore, Rena Moore
sp: Horror Lab/Cumberland FX, Mark Mobley
sound: Jon Ailetcher, Reggie Bryant
2nd unit d: Gene Hertel

2nd unit ph: Christopher Baffa
Maria Ford, Rodger Halston, Emile Levisetti, Bob McFarland, Cassandra Leigh, Kevin Alber

Alien Terminator

see Alien Species

Alien 3

USA/GB 1992 115m Rankcolor Panavision Dolby
Ripley unwittingly unleashes an alien on a distant planet, now being used as a prison for murderers and rapists.

Slick-looking but imperfectly scripted addition to the series, whose production problems were well publicised at the time. Something of a disappointment compared to the first two entries.

p: Gordon Carroll, David Giler, Walter Hill, Sigourney Weaver for TCF/Brandywine
exec p: Ezra Swerdlow
w: David Giler, Walter Hill, Larry Ferguson
story: Vincent Ward (the film's original director)
d: David Fincher
ph: Alex Thomson
m: Elliot Goldenthal
ed: Terry Rawlings
pd: Norman Reynolds
cos: Bob Ringwood, David Perry
sp: George Gibbs, Richard Edlund
sound: Tony Dawe, Harry Snodgrass
alien effects: Alec Gillis, Tom Woodruff, Jr.
2nd unit d: David Hogan, Martin Brierley
2nd unit ph: Paul Beeson, Nic Morris, Ken Shane, Tony Spratling
titles: John Beach
Sigourney Weaver, Charles Dance, Charles S. Dutton, Paul McGann, Brian Glover, Ralph Brown, Pete Postlethwaite, Danny Webb, Lance Henricksen, Hi Ching

Aliens

USA/GB 1986 137m Technicolor Panavision Dolby
Officer Ripley and a crew of marines are sent to destroy an army of aliens which have infiltrated a small colony.

Commercially orientated but technically adroit sequel to *Alien* which, once it gets going, provides a rollercoaster ride of shocks and thrills. A special edition was later released on video which included 17 minutes of previously unseen footage.

p: Gale Anne Hurd for TCF/Brandywine
exec p: Walter Hill, David Giler, Gordon Carroll
w: James Cameron
story: James Cameron, David Giler, Walter Hill
d: JAMES CAMERON
ph: Adrian Biddle
m: JAMES HORNER
ed: Ray Lovejoy
pd: Peter Lamont
ad: Terence Ackland Snow, Bert Davey, Fred Hole, Ken Court, Michael Lamont
cos: Emma Porteous
sp: Robert Skotak, Stan Winston, John Richardson, Suzanne Benson (aa)
sound: Roy Charman, Graham V. Hartstone, Nichola Le Messurier, Michael A. Carter
2nd unit d: Stan Winston
stunt co-ordinator: Paul Weston
Sigourney Weaver, Michael Biehn, Paul Reisner, Lance Henricksen, Carrie Henn, Bill Paxton, William Hope, Ricco Ross, Al Matthews

The Aliens Are Coming

USA 1980 96m colour TVM
Aliens land on earth and begin to possess human bodies, their intention being colonisation.

Fair science fiction hokum in the tried and tested *Invasion of the Body Snatchers* manner.

p: Quinn Martin for NBC
exec p: Philip Saltzman
w: Robert W. Lenski
d: Harvey Hart
ph: Jacques Marquette
m: William Goldstein
md: John Elizalde
ed: Richard Brockway, Jim Gross
ad: George B. Chan, Norman Newberry
cos/sp: no credits given
sound: Kirk Schuler
Tom Mason, Melinda Lee, Max Gail, Caroline McWilliams, Eric Braeden, Matthew Laborteaux, Fawne Harriman, Ed Harris, Curtis Credel, Laurence Haddon

All of Me

USA 1984 91m Technicolor
Thanks to a guru's miscalculations, a lawyer finds himself sharing his body with the soul of a client, a recently deceased eccentric millionairess.

Oddball fantasy comedy, basically an over-stretched one-joke sketch which tends to flog its central idea to death. Still, everyone tries hard and certain sequences are irresistibly amusing.

p: Stephen Friedman for Universal/Old Time/King's Road
w: Phil Alden Robinson, Henry Olek
novel: Ed Davis
d: Carl Reiner
ph: Richard H. Kline
m: Patrick Williams
ed: Bud Molin
pd: Edward Carfagno
cos: Ray Summers
sound: Willie D. Burton
Steve Martin, Lily Tomlin, Victoria Tennant, Madolyn Smith, Richard Libertini, Dana Elcar, Jason Bernard, Selma Diamond, Eric Christmas

Alland, William (1916–)

American producer with a couple of key 50s sci-fi productions to his credit.

A former actor and member of Orson Welles' Mercury Theatre troupe, he can be spotted in *Citizen Kane* as the investigative reporter. Joined the US Air Force during World War Two, after which he began writing for radio. He turned producer for Universal in 1952 and worked on many of director Jack Arnold's films. His other credits include *Look in Any Window*, which he also directed.

Genre credits:
The Creature from the Black Lagoon (1953), *It Came from Outer Space* (1953), *This Island Earth* (1954), *Revenge of the Creature* (1954), *Tarantula* (1955), *The Creature Walks Among Us* (1956), *The Mole People* (1956), *The Space Children* (1957), *The Land Unknown* (1957)

Allen, Irwin (1916–1991)

American writer, producer and director, busy in both film and television (where he was responsible for such series as *Voyage to the Bottom of the Sea*, *Lost in Space*, *Time Tunnel*, *Land of the Giants* and *The Return of Captain Nemo*). He began his career in journalism before moving into radio. Work in television followed, as did work as a literary agent (he represented P. G. Wodehouse for a while!), after which he became involved in the packaging of movies, which inevitably led to producing, his first movie being *Double Dynamite* in 1951, which he co-produced with Irving Cummings, Jr. He won an Oscar for producing the documentary feature *The Sea Around Us* (1952). His other credits during this period include *The Animal World* (another documentary feature), *The Story of Mankind* (one of the worst movies ever made) and *The Big Circus*, after which he turned to fantasy subjects in both film and television. In the 70s he produced a number of highly successful disaster movies (*The Poseidon Adventure*, *The Towering Inferno*), a genre he also exploited to less success in television (*Fire*, *Flood*, *Cave-In*, *Hanging by a Thread*). His other credits include *Five Weeks in a Balloon*, *The Swarm*, *Beyond the Poseidon Adventure* and *When Time Ran Out*.

Genre credits:
The Story of Mankind (1957 – co-w/p/d), *The Lost World* (1960 – co-w/p/d), *Voyage to the Bottom of the Sea* (1961 – co-w/p/d), *City Beneath the Sea* (1970 – aka *One Hour to Doomsday* – TVM – story/p/d), *The Time Travelers* (1976 – TVM – co-story/p), *The Return of Captain Nemo* (1978 – aka *The Amazing Captain Nemo* – TVM – exec p), *Alice in Wonderland* (1985 – TVM)

Allen, Karen (1951–)

American actress, perhaps best known for playing Marion Ravenwood opposite Harrison Ford's Indiana Jones in *Raiders of the Lost Ark*. Her other credits include *The Wanderers*, *Shoot the Moon*, *The Glass Menagerie*, *Until September* and *King of the Hill*.

Genre credits:
Raiders of the Lost Ark (1981), *Starman* (1985), *Scrooged* (1988)

Allen, Nancy (1950–)

American actress, once married to director Brian de Palma, whose films she also appeared in (*Carrie*, *Dressed to Kill*, *Blow Out*, *Home Movies*). A former model, she began her film career in 1973 with *The Last Detail*. Best known to genre fans for playing Anne Lewis in the *Robocop* movies, her other credits include *I Wanna Hold Your Hand*, *1941*, *Poltergeist III* and *Acting On Impulse*.

Genre credits:
Strange Invaders (1983), *The Philadelphia Experiment* (1984), *Robocop* (1987), *Robocop 2* (1990), *Robocop 3* (1991, released 1993)

Allen, Patrick (1919–)

Canadian actor, long in Britain, where he found much work as a voice-over artist for television commercials (most notably selling Barratt Homes from a helicopter). Also a busy supporting actor, he has popped up in a wide variety of films, among them *Dunkirk*, *Never Take Sweets from a Stranger*, *Captain Clegg* (aka *Night Creatures*), *Puppet On a Chain*, *Diamonds on Wheels*, *The Wild Geese*, *The Sea Wolves* and *Fergie and Andrew: Behind the Palace Doors* (TVM).

Genre credits:
1984 (1955), *Night of the Big Heat* (1967 – aka *Island of the Burning Damned*), *The Body Stealers* (1969 – aka *Invasion of the Body Stealers/Thin Air*), *When Dinosaurs Ruled the Earth* (1970)

Allen, Woody (1935–)

Celebrated American actor, writer and director (real name Allen Konigsberg) responsible for a string of highly acclaimed comedies, among them *Play It Again, Sam*, *Love and Death*, *Annie Hall*, *Interiors*, *Manhattan*, *Zelig*, *Hannah and Her Sisters*, *Radio Days* and *Bullets Over Broadway*. His one excursion into science fiction was with the hilarious spoof *Sleeper* (1973), which he co-wrote, directed and starred in.

Almost an Angel

USA 1990 95m DeLuxe Dolby
After a car accident, an ex-con convinces himself that he is an angel and

so sets out to do good.

Mild Runyonesque comedy, watchable but hardly inspired.

p: John Cornell for Paramount/Ironbank
w/exec p: Paul Hogan
d: John Cornell
ph: Russell Boyd
m: Maurice Jarre
ed: David Stiven
pd: Henry Bumstead
cos: April Ferry
sound: Tom Brandau
stunt co-ordinator: Spike Silver
2nd unit d: Kelly Van Horn
Paul Hogan, Elias Koteas, Linda Kozlowski, Doreen Lang, Robert Sutton, Charlton Heston, Ruth Warshawsky, Douglas Seale, Travis Venable, Joe Dallesandro

Alves, Joe (1938–)

American production designer who began his career in the theatre before moving on to television and film. He worked on three of Steven Spielberg's films in the 70s (*The Sugarland Express*, *Jaws*, *Close Encounters*) and had a stab at direction himself in 1983 with *Jaws 3D*. His other design credits include *Winning*, *Jaws 2*, *Everybody's All-American* and *Geronimo*.

Genre credits:
Pufnstuff (1970 – co-ad), *Close Encounters of the Third Kind* (1977 – pd), *Close Encounters of the Third Kind – The Special Edition* (1980 – pd), *Escape from New York* (1981 – pd), *Starman* (1984 – 2nd unit d/visual consultant), *Freejack* (1992 – pd/associate p/2nd unit d)

Always ☁

USA 1989 123m DeLuxe Dolby
A forest fire-fighter is killed when his plane explodes, but returns as a guardian angel to supervise the progress of his replacement.

Ably made and performed though rather pointless and sentimental refashioning of *A Guy Named Joe*.

p: Steven Spielberg, Frank Marshall, Kathleen Kennedy for Universal/Amblin
w: Jerry Belson
d: STEVEN SPIELBERG
ph: Mikael Salomon
m: John Williams
ed: Michael Kahn
pd: James Bissell
cos: Ellen Mirojnick
sp: Bruce Nicholson
sound: Ben Burtt
2nd unit d: Frank Marshall
Richard Dreyfuss, Holly Hunter, John Goodman, Brad Johnson, Audrey Hepburn, Keith David, Marg Helgenberger, Roberts Blossom

Alyn, Kirk (1910–)

American actor who was the screen's first *Superman* in two serials. Began his career on stage before turning to movies in the early 40s, among his credits being *My Sister Eileen*, *Little Miss Broadway* and *The Three Musketeers*. He also appeared in a handful of other serials such as *Daughter of Don Q*, *Federal Agents vs. Underworld Inc.* and *Radar Patrol vs. Spy King*.

Genre credits:
A Guy Named Joe (1944), *Superman* (1948 – serial), *Atom Man vs. Superman* (1950 – serial), *When Worlds Collide* (1951)

Amazon Women on the Moon

USA 1987 85m Technicolor
The broadcasting of a science fiction movie is continually interrupted by other programmes.

Very variable spoof in the *Kentucky Fried Movie* manner, with just a few

moments of amusement amid the dross.

p: Robert K. Weiss for Universal
w: Michael Barrie, Jim Mullholland
d: Joe Dante, John Landis, Robert K. Weiss, Carl Gottlieb, Peter Horton
ph: Daniel Pearl
ed: Bert Lovitt, Malcolm Campbell, Marshall Harvey
pd: Ivo Cristante
cos: Taryn De Chellis
sound: Susumu Tokunow
Arsenio Hall, Rosanna Arquette, Steve Guttenberg, Carrie Fisher, Paul Bartell, Lou Jacobi, Griffin Dunne, Michelle Pfeiffer, Ralph Bellamy, Andrew Dice Clay, Steve Forrest, Marc McClure, Peter Horton, Ed Begley, Jr., Sybil Danning, Howard Hesseman, Henny Youngman, Mike Mazurki, Russ Meyer

Ameche, Don (1908–1993)

American leading man who proved popular in the late 30s and early 40s in such fare as *In Old Chicago*, *Alexander's Ragtime Band*, *The Three Musketeers* (as D'Artagnan), *Swanee*, *Down Argentine Way* and *Moon Over Miami*. When his movie career faltered in middle age he turned to the theatre and television, but made a comeback in the early 80s in *Trading Places*, which he followed with *Cocoon*, which won him a best supporting actor Oscar. His final films include *Things Change*, *Folks* and *Corrina, Corrina*.

Genre credits:
Heaven Can Wait (1943), *Cocoon* (1985), *Harry and the Hendersons* (1987), *Cocoon: The Return* (1988)

An American Tail

USA 1986 81m DeLuxe Dolby
An 18th-century Russian mouse is sep-

arated from his family when they emigrate to America.

Charming, beautifully animated cartoon feature whose commercial success certainly made the Disney organisation sit up and look.

p: Don Bluth, John Pomeroy, Gary Goldman for Universal/Amblin
exec p: Steven Spielberg, Frank Marshall, Kathleen Kennedy, David Kirschner
w: Judy Freudberg, Tony Geiss
d/design: DON BLUTH
m: JAMES HORNER
songs: James Horner, Cynthia Weil, Barry Mann
sound: Bill Rowe, Ray Merrin
sound ed: Don Molina
voices: Phillip Glasser, Christopher Plummer, Dom De Luise, Madeleine Kahn, Amy Green, Erica Yohn, Nehemiah Persoff, Hal Smith, John Finnegan

An American Tail: Fievel Goes West 🛸

USA 1991 75m Technicolot Dolby
Fievel and his friends outsmart an evil cat who has persuaded his family to move out west where they are to be turned into mouse burgers.

Brilliantly animated though rather thinly plotted sequel with too much detail to dazzle the eye. Exhilarating moments, though.

p: Steven Spielberg, Robert Watts for Universal/Amblin
exec p: Steven Spielberg, Frank Marshall, Kathleen Kennedy, David Kirschner
w: Flint Dille
story: Charles Swenson
d: Phil Nibbelink, Simon Wells
m: James Horner
ly: Will Jennings
sound: Michgael C. Gaspar
voices: Phillip Glasser, James Stewart (as Wylie Burp), Dom De Luise, Amy Irving, John Cleese, Nehemiah Persoff, Cathy

Cavadini, Erica Yohn, Jon Lovitz

Ament, Don

American art director with a handful of credits at the lower budget end of the sci-fi/fantasy market.

Genre credits:
Invasion of the Saucer Men (1957 – aka *The Invasion of the Hell Creatures* – ad), *The Atomic Submarine* (1959 – co-ad), *The Underwater City* (1961 – ad)

Amicus

Production company formed in Britain in 1964 by producers Milton Subotsky and Max J. Rosenberg. Turned out many Hammer-style horror films in the 60s and 70s, including several compendium films (*Dr. Terror's House of Horrors*, *Asylum*, *Vault of Horror*, etc.) all of which were either produced or executive-produced by Subotsky and Rosenberg, with Subotsky often providing the scripts too. They also tried their hand at science fiction films, most notably with the two *Dr. Who* films. Subotsky and Rosenberg eventually went their own ways in 1977 and the company was disbanded.

Genre filmography:
Dr. Who and the Daleks (1965), *Daleks – Invasion Earth, 2150 A. D.* (1966), *The Terrornauts* (1967), *They Came from Beyond Space* (1967), *The Mind of Mr. Soames* (1969), *The Land That Time Forgot* (1974), *At the Earth's Core* (1976), *The People That Time Forgot* (1977)

And You Though Your Parents Were Weird

USA 1991 93m CFIcolor Ultra Stereo
Teenagers build a robot which houses the spirit of their dead father.

Wha...??? Ridiculous nonsense, devoid of both charm and humour.

p: Just Betzer for Trimark/Panorama
exec p: Pernille Siesbye
w/d: Tony Cookson
ph: Paul Elliot
m: Randy Miller
ed: Michael Ornstein
pd: Alexandra Kicenik
sound: Thomas M. Cunliffe, Philip Seretti
2nd unit ph: Anthony Gaudioz
robot sp: Rick Lazzarini
Marcia Strassman, Joshua Miller, Sam Behrens, A. J. Langer, Edan Gross, John Quade, Susan Gibney, Alan Thicke (voice only)

Anderson, Gerry (1929–)

British television producer who, working with his then-wife Sylvia Anderson, created such popular science fiction/fantasy series as *Supercar*, *Fireball XL5*, *Stingray*, *Thunderbirds*, *Captain Scarlet and the Mysterons*, *Joe 90* and *Secret Service*, all of which were performed by puppets and filmed in "Supermarionation". He began his television career by directing episodes of such puppet series as *The Adventures of Twizzle* and *Torchy the Battery Boy* (both created by Roberta Leigh) before setting up his own company APF (with Arthur Provis) to make his own puppet series *Four Feather Falls*. He later formed Century 21 Productions, through which he made his best series, the ever-popular *Thunderbirds*. A handful of live action series later followed, among them *UFO*, *The Protectors*, *Space: 1999* and *Space Precinct*, along with another puppet show, *Terrahawks*. Despite his success in television, Anderson's film output has been minimal, revolving chiefly round two big screen *Thunderbirds* movies, which surprisingly met with poor box office success.

Genre credits:

Thunderbirds to the Rescue (1966 – TVM – feature-length pilot for the television series – co-w/co-p), *Thunderbirds Are Go!* (1966 – co-w/co-p), *Thunderbird Six* (1968 – co-w/co-p), *Journey to the Far Side of the Sun* (1969 – aka *Doppelganger* – co-w/p), *Invasion: UFO* (1970 – TVM – exec p/co-w/co-d)

Anderson, Michael (1920–)

British director whose career has taken in such varied and variable films as *The Dam Busters*, *Around the World in 80 Days*, *Operation Crossbow*, *The Quiller Memorandum*, *The Shoes of the Fisherman* and *Conduct Unbecoming*. His work in the science fiction and fantasy genres is, unfortunately, his least interesting.

Genre credits:

Vice-Versa (1947 – assistant d), *1984* (1955), *Doc Savage, Man of Bronze* (1975), *Logan's Run* (1976), *The Martian Chronicles* (1979 – TVM), *Millennium* (1989), *20 000 Leagues Under the Sea* (1997 - TVM - d),

Android

USA 1982 80m DeLuxe

A scientist and his android assistant are visited on their spaceship by three escaped convicts.

Intelligent low budget sci-fi which elicits favourable comparisons with John Carpenter's *Dark Star*.

p: Mary Ann Fisher for New World
exec p: Rupert Harvey, Barry Opper
w: James Reigle, Don Opper
d: AARON LIPSTADT
ph: Tim Suhrstedt
m: Don Preston
ed: R. J. Kizer, Andy Aorvitch

ad: K. C. Scheibel, Wayne Springfield
cos: Merril Greene, Audrey Kasoff
sp: New World Effects
sound: Mark Uland
make-up effects: John Buechler
Klaus Kinski, DON OPPER, Brie Howard, Norbert Weisser, Crofton Hardester, Kendra Kirchner

The Andromeda Strain

USA 1970 131m Technicolor Panavision
Scientists discover a deadly microbe from outer space and work to neutralise it before it infects the world.

Cold, calculated yet thoroughly absorbing thriller, quite convincingly told.

p: Robert Wise for Universal
w: Nelson Gidding
novel: Michael Crichton
d: ROBERT WISE
ph: Richard H. Kline
m: Gil Melle
ed: Stuart Gilomore, John W. Holmes
pd: Boris Leven
cos: Helen Colvig
sp: Douglas Trumbull, James Short, Albert Whitlock
sound: Waldon C. Watson, Ronald Pierce
Arthur Hill, David Wayne, James Olsen, KATE REID, Paula Kelly, George Mitchell, Peter Hobbs

The Angel Levene
USA 1970 105m DeLuxe
An ageing Jewish tailor down on his luck is apparently helped by a black angel.

Poorish, overplayed whimsy which eventually out-stays what welcome it had.

p: Chiz Schultz for UA/Belafonte
w: Bill Gunn, Ronald Ribman
d: Jan Kadar

ph: Richard Kratina
m: Zdenek Linka
pd: George Jenkins
Zero Mostel, Harry Belafonte, Ida Kaminshka, Milo O'Shea, Eli Wallach, Anne Jackson, Gloria Foster

Angel on My Shoulder
USA 1981 96m colour TVM
A wrongly executed gangster returns to earth in the guise of a DA.

Uneasy remake of *Here Comes Mr. Jordan* which never even begins to work.

p: Barney Rosenweig for ABC/Viacom/Beowulf Productions
exec p: Mace Neufeld
w: George Kirgo after Roland Kibbee and Harry Segall
d: John Berry
ph: Gayne Rescher
m: Artie Butler
Peter Strauss, Richard Kiley, Barbara Hershey, Janis Paige, Seymour Cassell, Murray Matheson, Anne Seymour

Angels see Angels in the Outfield

Angels in the Outfield
USA 1994 102m Technicolor Dolby
A young boy prays for divine intervention so that his baseball team, which is at the bottom of the league, will win some games, and he's consequently helped by a host of angels.

Saccharine fantasy of the most squirm-inducing kind. A remake of the 1954 movie *Angels in the Outfield* (aka *Angels and the Pirates*) which starred Paul Douglas, Janet Leigh and Keenan Wynn.

p: Irby Smith, Roger Nirnbaum, Joe Roth for Walt Disney
exec p: Gary Stutman

w: Holly Goldberg Sloan, Dorothy Kingsley, George Wells
d: William Dear
ph: Matthew F. Leonetti
m: Randy Edelman
ed: Bruce Green
pd: Dennis Washington
cos: Rosanna Norton
Danny Glover, Christopher Lloyd, Tony Danza, Brenda Fricker, Jay O. Sanders, Joseph Gordon-Levitt, Matthew McConaughey, Dermot Mulroney, Jonathan Proby

---

Animal Farm
GB 1955 75m Technicolor

Farm animals unite and revolt against their cruel master, but the new regime is not without its tyrants.

Careful but cold animated version of the celebrated allegory which will no doubt please admirers of the book.

p: Louis de Rochemont for Halas and Batchelor
w: John Halas, Joy Batchelor, Lothar Wolff, Borden Mace, Philip Stapp
novel: GEORGE ORWELL
d: John Halas, Joy Batchelor
m: Matyas Seiber
narrator: Gordon Heath
voices: Maurice Denham

Animanga see Anime

Anime

Stylized Japanese animation form, taking in a wide variety of genres, though most notably science fiction, fantasy, horror and action-adventure. Rooted in Japanese comic books (or *Manga*), it took off in a major way in the early 80s with the advent of video, with many of the films made directly for the video market. More recently Anime has taken off in the West, the break-through film being *Akira* (1988), since when an increasing number of titles have become available, mostly on video.

Key filmography (English titles only):
Barefoot Gen (1983), *Urusei Yatsura - Only You* (1983), *Locke the Superman* (1984), *Warriors of the Wind* (1984), *The Dagger of Kamui* (1985), *Night on the Galactic Railroad* (1985), *Urusei Yatsura – Remember My Love* (1985), *Arion* (1986), *Laputa* (1986), *Project A-Ko* (1986), *Uresei Yatsura – Lum the Forever* (1986), *Windaria* (1986), *Dirty Pair: Project Eden* (1987), *Wings of Honneamise* (1987), *Black Magic M-66* (1987), *Neo-Tokyo* (1987), *Akira* (1988), *Grave of the Fireflies* (1988), *Legend of Galactic Heroes: Across the Sea of Stars* (1988), *My Neighbour Totoro* (1988), *Hades Project Zeorymer* (1988), *Monster City* (1988), *Patlabor* (1988), *Peacock King: Feast for the Returning Demons* (1988), *Kiki's Delivery Service* (1989), *Patlabor: The Movie* (1990), *Little Nemo* (1991), *Only Yesterday* (1991), *The Sensualist* (1991), *Great Conquest: Romance of Three Kingdoms* (1992), *Porco Rosso* (1992), *Coo of the Far Seas* (1993), *Patlabor 2* (1993), *The Wind of Amnesia* (1993), *Darkside Blues* (1994), *Ponpoko* (1994), *Catland Banipal Witt* (1995), *Memories* (1995), *Whisper of the Heart* (1995), *Fairy Princess Rain* (1996)

The Annihilator
USA 1986 104m Technicolor TVM

A newspaper editor is led to believe that passengers on a plane from Hawaii, who include his girlfriend, have been taken over by humanoids called Dynamitards.

Unremarkable variation of *Invasion of the Body Snatchers* and its various cousins which was originally intended as a pilot for a series that, thankfully, didn't appear. It begins with an interminable car chase and goes downhill from there.

p: Alex Beaton
exec p: Roderick Taylor
w: Roderick Taylor, Bruce A. Taylor
d: Michael Chapman
ph: Paul Goldsworth
m: Sylvester Levay, UDI
ed: Frank Mazzola
ad: Kirk Axtell
cos: Thomas Johnson, Marla Schlom
sound: Edwin J. Somers Jr.
2nd unit d: Tom Wright
Mark Lindsay Chapman, Susan Blakely, Lisa Blount, Brion James, Earl Boen, Geoffrey Lewis, Catherine Mary Stewart

---

Annis, Francesca (1945–)

Decorative British leading lady who scored a hit on television with *Lillie*. In films since childhood, she made her debut with *The Cat Gang* in 1959. Her other credits include *Cleopatra*, *Macbeth* and *Under the Cherry Moon*.

Genre credits:
Krull (1983), *Dune* (1986)

Antony, Lysette (1963–)

British actress working in both films and television on both sides of the Atlantic. Her credits include *Ivanhoe* (TVM), *Oliver Twist* (TVM), *Without a Clue*, *Husbands and Wives*, *Hour of the Pig* and *The Hard Truth*. She also appeared in the revival of TV's *Dark Shadows*.

Genre credits:
Krull (1983), *Switch* (1991), *Look Who's Talking Now* (1993)

APEX
USA 1994 103m Foto-Kem Sound Trip Surround Stereo

A scientist from the year 2073 is sent

back in time 100 years, but his trip causes a paradox and alters the future.

Low budget robots vs. humans sci-fi actioner, the sort of which has certainly been done often before – and often better.

p: Gary Jude Burkart for New Age/Green Communications/Republic
exec p: Talaat Captan
w: Philip J. Roth, Ronald Schmidt
story: Philip J. Roth, Gian Carlo Scandiuzzi
d: Philip J. Roth
ph: Mark W. Gray
m: Jim Goodwin
ed: Daniel Laurence
pd: Blake B. Jackson, Grant Fausey
cos: Marie Blau, Maria Hansson
sp: Altered Anatomy
sound: Bill Reinhardt
2nd unit d: Mitchell Cox, Talaat Captan, Harrison Done
2nd unit ph: Harris Done, Blake B. Jackson
stunt co-ordinator: Mitchell Cox
Richard Keats, Mitchell Cox, Brian Richard Peck, Marcus Aurelius, Adam Lawson, Lisa Russell

Arabian Adventure
GB 1979 98m Technicolor
A wicked caliph is finally deposed by a young boy and a handsome prince.

Mildly diverting fantasy adventure which should please younger audiences.

p: John Dark for Badger
w: Brian Hayles
d: Kevin Connor
ph: Alan Hume
m: Ken Thorne
ed: Barry Peters
pd: ELLIOT SCOTT
cos: Rosemary Burrows
sp: George Gibbs, Richard Conway, David Harris, Cliff Culley
sound: Dennis Nisbett, Gerry Humphreys
stunt co-ordinator: Marc Boyle

Oliver Tobias, Christopher Lee, Mickey Rooney, Milo O'Shea, Elizabeth Welch, Capucine, Peter Cushing, Emma Samms, Puneet Sira, Suzanne Danielle, Milton Reid, John Wyman, Shane Rimmer, Hal Galili, John Ratzenberger

Arabian Nights 🛸
USA 1942 86m Technicolor
A street acrobat and Scheherezade the dancer help the deposed caliph of Baghdad win back the throne from his evil half-brother.

Dated romp with amusing passages. A popular success in its day, it spawned a handful of imitations.

p: Walter Wanger for Universal
w: Michael Hogan, True Boardman
story: Michael Hogan
d: John Rawlins
ph: Milton Krasner, William V. Skall, W. Howard Greene
m: Frank Skinner
md: Charles Previn
ed: Philip Cahn
pd: Jack Otterson, Alexander Trauner
cos: Vera West
sound: Bernard B. Brown, William Fox
Jon Hall, Maria Montez, Sabu, Billy Gilbert, Leif Erickson, Thomas Gomez, John Qualen, Turhan Bey, Shemp Howard

Arcade
USA 1993 78m colour Ultra Stereo
A teenage girl attempts to rescue her boyfriend, who has been sucked into a new video game.

Poorly made blend of teenage angst (the girl's mother has committed suicide) and unremarkable effects. About par for the course for a Pyun movie. In other words, avoid.

p: Cathy Gersualdo for Full Moon
w: David S. Goyer
exec p/story: Charles Band

d: Albert Pyun
ph: George Mooradian
m/sound design: Alan Howarth
ed: Miles Wynton
pd: Don Day
cos: Cindy Rosenthal
sp: DHD Postimage
make-up effects: Bill Sturgeon
sound: Paul Coogan
Megan Ward, Peter Billingsley, John DeLancie, Sharon Farrell, Seth Green, A. J. Langer, Bryan Dattilo, Brandon Rane, Norbert Weisser, Jonathan Fuller (voice)

The Aristocats
USA 1970 78m Technicolor
A cat and her three kittens are kidnapped by an irate butler because they are set to inherit their mistress's fortune, but help is at hand in the form of an alley cat named Thomas O'Malley.

Fondly remembered cartoon feature. Not quite a classic, but ably enough put together, with a good voice cast and a couple of catchy numbers, such as the lively *Ev'rybody Wants to Be a Cat*.

p: Wolfgang Reitherman, Winston Hibler for Walt Disney
w: Larry Clemmons
story: Tom McGowan, Tom Rowe
d: Wolfgang Reitherman
ed: Tom Acosta
pd: Ken Anderson
m: George Bruns
songs: Richard M. Sherman, Robert B. Sherman, Terry Gilkyson, Floyd Huddleston, Al Rinker
voices: Eva Gabor, Phil Harris, Sterling Holloway, Paul Winchell, Scatman Crothers, Hermione Baddeley, Roddy Maude-Roxby, Pat Buttram, Nancy Kulp, Monica Evans, Carole Shelley, George Lindsey, Maurice Chevalier (singing the title song)

Arkin, Alan (1934–)
Likeable American character comedian

who, after experience on stage, made his film debut in 1957 with *Calypso Heat Wave*. Acclaimed for his work in *The Russians Are Coming, The Russians Are Coming*, *Wait Until Dark*, *The Heart Is a Lonely Hunter* and *Catch 22*, his other films include *Little Murders* (which he also directed), *Last of the Red Hot Lovers*, *Freebie and the Bean*, *The Seven Per Cent Solution* (as Sigmund Freud), *The In-Laws*, *Coupe de Ville* and *So I Married An Axe Murderer*. His attempt to take over the role of Inspector Clouseau in the film of the same name was not a success, however.

Genre credits:
The Last Unicorn (1981 – voice), *The Return of Captain Invincible* (1982 – aka *Legend in Leotards*), *Edward Scissorhands* (1990), *The Rocketeer* (1992), *North* (1994)

Arkoff, Samuel Z. (1918–)

American producer, executive producer and studio executive. Co-founded American International Pictures (AIP) in 1955 with James H. Nicholson, through which they presented dozens of low budget sci-fi, horror and exploitation pictures aimed primarily at the drive-in/teenage market, including several of Roger Corman's Poe classics, and early films by such directors as Francis Ford Coppola, Woody Allen and Martin Scorsese. Arkoff sold AIP to Filmways in 1980.

Arness, James (1923–)

American actor (real name James Aurness), familiar to TV audiences as Marshall Dillon in the long-running *Gunsmoke*. He also made a memorable alien in *The Thing* (1952). His only other genre credit is *Them* (1954).

Arnold, David (1962–)

British composer who began his career scoring the student films of his director friend Danny Cannon, whose first feature, *The Young Americans*, he scored in 1993. This in turn led to his being hired to write the music for *Stargate*, an impressive genre debut, the success of which has secured him a busy career in Hollywood. His other credits include *Last of the Dogmen* and *Tomorrow Never Dies*.

Genre credits:
Stargate (1994), *Independence Day* (1996), *Godzilla* (1998)

Arnold, Jack (1916–1992)

American director with several key 50s science fiction films to his credit, many of them in association with producer William Alland. A former actor and stage manager on both Broadway and in London's West End, he gained experience as a filmmaker in the Army Signal Corps during World War Two, working with documentary film-maker Robert Flaherty. Became a documentary maker himself after the war, turning to features in 1953 with *Girls in the Night* (aka *Life After Dark*). His other credits include *The Tattered Dress*, *Monster on Campus*, *Highschool Confidential*, *No Name on the Bullet* and *The Swiss Conspiracy*.

Genre credits:
The Creature from the Black Lagoon (1953), *It Came from Outer Space* (1953), *Revenge of the Creature* (1955), *Tarantula* (1955), *The Incredible Shrinking Man* (1957), *The Space Children* (1957), *The Monolith Monsters* (1957 – also co-story), *The Mouse That Roared* (1959), *Hello, Down There* (1969)

Arnold, Wilfred

British art director who has worked on a handful of painfully low budget British productions.

Genre credits:
Escapement (1958 – aka *The Electronic Monster*), *The Headless Ghost* (1959), *The Body Stealers* (1969 – aka *Invasion of the Body Stealers/Thin Air*)

The Arrival

USA 1996 109m Technicolor Dolby

A radio astronomer picks up a message from aliens, but later learns that the signal was broadcast from earth...

Slow starting and rather flabbily edited sci-fi actioner in the *Dark Skies* manner, with some good effects towards the end, though they seem a long time coming.

p: Thomas G. Smith, James Steele for Live Entertainment/Steelwork/Mediaworks
exec p: Ted Field, Robert W. Cort
w/d: David Twohy
ph: Hiro Narita
m: Arthur Kempel
ed: Martin Hunter
pd: Michael Novotny
cos: Mayes C. Rubeo
sp: Dreamquest, Available Light, David Allen Productions, Charles L. Finance and others
sound: David Farmer, Fernando Camara
titles: Nina Saxon
make-up effects: Todd Masters
2nd unit d/ph: Isidore Mankofsky
stunt co-ordinator: Buddy Joe Hooker, Eddie Braun

Charlie Sheen, Lindsay Crouse, Richard Schiff, Ron Silver, Shane, Teri Polo, Buddy Joe Hooker, Phyllis Applegate, Tony T. Johnson

Ashman, Howard (1951-1991)

American lyricist, most often part-nered with composer Alan Menken, with whom he wrote the cult hit musical *Little Shop of Horrors*, along with *God Bless You, Mr Rosewater*. They also collaborated on several successful animated Disney musicals before his untimely death. He is an Oscar winner for his work on *The Little Mermaid* (1989 – best song, *Under the Sea* [m: Alan Menken]) and *Beauty and the Beast* (1991 – best song, *Beauty and the Beast* [m: Alan Menken]).

Genre credits:
Little Shop of Horrors (1986 – w/play/ly), *Oliver and Company* (1988 – song), *The Little Mermaid* (1989 - co-p-ly), *Beauty and the Beast* (1991 – ly), *Aladdin* (1992 – co-ly).

Assassin

USA 1986 96m colour TVM
An agent pursues a robot which has been programmed to assassinate important people.

Flatly directed and singularly unex-citing telly fodder. Interest quickly wanes after the opening credits.

p: Neil T. Matteo
w/d: Sandor Stern
ph: Chuck Arnold
m: Anthony Guefen
ed: James Galloway
pd: Vincent J. Cresciman
Robert Conrad, Karen Austin, Richard Young, Jonathan Banks, Robert Webber

Asteroid

USA 1997 2x96m colour TVM
A lady astronomer predicts that a giant asteroid is on a collision course with earth... and it is!

Cliché-strewn disaster melodrama, all very bland save for the effects at the top of the second installment.

p: Donna Ebbs, Phil Margo, Christopher Morgan, Peter V. Ware for NBC/Davis Entertainment
exec p: John Davis, Merrill Karpf
w: Robbyn Burger, Scott Sturgeon
d: Bradford May
ph: Tom Del Ruth, David Hennings
m: Shirley Walker
ed: Bud Hayes
pd: Richard B. Lewis
cos: Kelly A. King
sp: Richard O. Helmer
sound: Bob Abbott
stunt co-ordinator: Gary Jensen
Michael Biehn, Annabella Sciorra, Jensen Daggett, Don Franklin, Zachary B. Charles, Anthony Zerbe, Carlos Gomez, Michael Weatherly, Anne-Marie Johnson

Attack of the Fifty-Foot Woman

USA 1958 69m bw
A mid-western heiress grows to gigan-tic proportions following an encounter with a radio-active flying saucer.

Lunatic grade Z schlocker which plays like distaff version of *The Amazing Colossal Man*. Worth a look for the sheer absurdity of it all. A TV remake followed in 1993.

p: Bernard Woolner for Allied Artists
exec p: James Marquette
w: Mark Hanna
d: Nathan Hertz
ph: Jacques Marquette
m: Paul Stein
ed: Edward Mann
ad/cos: no credits given
sound: Philip Mitchell
props: Richard Rubin
Allison Hayes, William Hudson, Roy Gordon, Yvette Vickers, Ken Terrell, George Douglas, Eileen Stevens, Frank Chase, Otto Waldid

Attack of the Fifty-Foot Woman

USA 1993 91m colour Dolby TVM
A woman avenges herself against her philandering husband when she grows 50 feet tall following an encounter with a spaceship.

Mildly spoofy remake of the 50s schlocker which saw theatrical release outside the States.

p: Debra Hill for HBO
w: Joseph Dougherty
d: Christopher Guest
ph: Russell Carpenter
m: Nicholas Pike
ed: Harry Keramidas
pd: Joseph T. Garrity
cos: Arianne Phillips
sp: Fantasy II
Daryl Hannah, Daniel Baldwin, Frances Fisher, William Windom, Paul Benedict, Christi Conway, O'Neal Compton, Xander Berkeley

At the Earth's Core

GB 1976 90m Technicolor
Transported to the centre of the earth, a Victorian scientist and his assistant discover the place to be inhabited by weird beings and even weirder mon-sters.

Shoddy science fiction romp, amus-ing enough for the kids, but even they may find themselves above it.

p: John Dark for Amicus
exec p: Max J. Rosenberg, Milton Subotsky
w: Milton Subotsky
novel: Edgar Rice Borroughs
d: Kevin Connor
ph: Alan Hume
m: Mike Vickers
ed: John Ireland, Barry Peters
ad: Bert Davey
cos: Rosemary Burrows
sp: Ian Wingrove
sound: George Stephenson

Peter Cushing, Doug McClure, Caroline Munro, Cy Grant, Godfrey James, Keith Barron

Austin, William

American editor with a handful of undistinguished science fiction entries to his credit.

Genre credits:
Queen of Outer Space (1958), *The Atomic Submarine* (1959), *Panic in Year Zero* (1962)

Aykroyd, Dan (1952–)

Canadian comedy actor, writer and director who rose to stardom via TV's *Saturday Night Live*, in which he regularly appeared from 1975 following work as a stand-up comedian in his homeland. Made his film debut in the Canadian low budgeter *Love at First Sight* in 1977. He then teamed up with John Belushi for a number of big screen outings, among them *1941*, *The Blues Brothers* and *Neighbors*, though it wasn't until after Belushi's death that he scored his biggest hit with *Ghostbusters*, which he also co-wrote. His other credits include *Mr. Mike's Mondo Video*, *Trading Places*, *Spies Like Us*, *Dragnet*, *Driving Miss Daisy* and *My Girl*. He also directed *Nothing But Trouble* in 1991, but it was a box office flop.

Genre credits:
It Came from Hollywood (1982), *Twilight Zone – The Movie* (1983), *Ghostbusters* (1984 – also co-w), *Indiana Jones and the Temple of Doom* (1984), *My Stepmother Is an Alien* (1988), *Ghostbusters II* (1989 – also co-w), *Coneheads* (1993-also co-w), *Rainbow* (1996)

The Iron Mole prepares to journey to the centre of the earth in *At the Earth's Core*, one of several science fiction/fantasy films produced by John Dark and directed by Kevin Connor in the mid-70s.

Babe

Australia 1995 94m Technicolor DTS
stereo

A farmer wins an orphaned piglet at a
fair and it is adopted by his sheepdog,
who trains it to competition level.

Engaging family film of the kind
they no longer often make, offering an
excellent blend of live action and animatronics to tell its tale. It quickly
became a global favourite. Bacon
sarnie, anyone? *Babe in Metropolis* followed in 1998.

p: George Miller, Doug Mitchell, Bill Miller
for Universal/Kennedy Miller
w: George Miller, Chris Noonan
novel: Dick King-Smith
d: CHRIS NOONAN
ph: Andrew Lesnie
m: Nigel Westlake
ed: Marcus D'Arcy, Jay Friedkin
pd/cos: Roger Ford
sp: SCOTT E. ANDERSON, CHARLES GIB-
SON, NEAL SCANLAN, JOHN COX (aa)
sound: Ben Osmo
animal d: Karl Lewis Miller
add d: Daphne Paris
add ph: Ken Arlidge
puppeteers: Mark Wilson, David
Greenway, Allan Trautman, Ian Tregoning
narrator: Roscoe Lee Browne
James Cromwell, Magda Szubanski,
Christine Cavanaugh (voice – as Babe),
Miriam Margolyes (voice), Danny Mann
(voice), Miriam Flynn (voice), Russie Taylor
(voice), Michael Edward-Stevens (voice),
Charles Bartlett (voice), Paul Livingston
(voice)

Babes in Toyland

USA 1934 77m bw

Two toymakers help to thwart an evil
debt collector.

Disappointing star operetta in which
flat routines alternate with tedious
songs and subplots. Of chiefly historical interest. Remakes followed in 1961
and 1986 (TVM).

p: Hal Roach
w: Nick Grindle, Frank Butler
musical book: Glen McDonough
d: Gus Meins, Charles Rogers
ph: Art Lloyd, Francis Corby
m: Victor Herbert
md: Harry Jackson
ed: William Terhune, Bert Jordan
ad/cos: no credit given
sound: Elmer Raguse
Stan Laurel, Oliver Hardy, Charlotte Henry,
Henry Brandon, Felix Dwight, Florence
Roberts, Marie Wilson, Johnny Downs

Babes in Toyland

USA 1961 105m Technicolor

A villain and his two bumbling henchmen determine to take over Toyland.

Lumbering remake, stagily and
charmlessly directed. An expensive
fiasco.

p: Walt Disney
w: Ward Kimball, Joe Rinaldi, Lowell S.
Hawley
d: Jack Donohue
ph: Edward Colman
songs: Victor Herbert, Glen McDonough,
George Bruns, Mel Leven
md: George Bruns
ed: Robert Stafford
ad: Carroll Clark, Marvin Aubrey David
cos: Bill Thomas
sp: Eustace Lycett, Robert A. Mattey, Bill
Justice, Xavier Atencio, Joshua Meador, Jim
Fetheroff
sound: Robert O. Cook
ch: Tom Mahoney
Ray Bolger, Annette Funicello, Tommy Kirk,
Gene Shelton, Henry Calvin, Ed Wynn,
Kevin Corcoran

Babes in Toyland

USA/Bavaria 1984 96m or 150m colour
TVM

After a car accident on Christmas Eve,
a young girl finds herself transported
to Toyland, which is in the grip of the
evil Barnaby Barnacle.

Another charmless remake, cheap-
looking and poorly directed, with
Toyland little more than a few pink
huts on the backlot, peopled by actors
in unconvincing animal costumes. A
must for those who have a yen to hear
Keanu Reeves sing.

p: Tony Ford, Anthony Spinner, Neil T.
Maffeo for Orion/Finnegan/Pinchuk
exec p: Pat Finnegan, Bill Finnegan, Sheldon
Pinchuk
w: Paul Zindel
d: Cliver Donner
ph: Arthur Ibbetson
songs: Leslie Bricusse, Victor Herbert
md: Ian Fraser
ed: David Saxon, Susan Heick
pd: Robert Laing
cos: Evangeline Harrison
animal cos: Vin Burnham
sp: Willi Neuner
sound: Edward Parente
ch: Eleanor Fazan
2nd unit d: Bert Batt
stunt co-ordinator: Volker J. Muller
Drew Barrymore, Keanu Reeves, Eileen
Brennan, Pat Morita, Richard Mulligan, Jill
Schoelen, Elizabeth Schot, Googy Gress,
Walter Buschoff

Baby – Secret of the Lost legend

USA 1985 95m Technicolor
Supertechnirama Dolby

Two explorers discover a family of dinosaurs in Africa.

Misconceived fantasy adventure, hard to sit through. A very poor man's *King Kong*.

p: Jonathan T. Taplin for Walt Disney/Touchstone
exec p: Roger Spottiswoode
w: Clifford Green, Ellen Green
d: B. W. L. Norton
ph: John Alcott
m: Jerry Goldsmith
ed: Howard Smith, David Bretherton
pd: Raymond G. Storey
cos: Jack Sandeen, Bill Kaiserman
sp: Roland Tantin, Philip Meador, Isidor Raponi
sound: Bob Hathaway, Kirk Francis
titles: Ed Garbert
2nd unit d/ph: Egil Woxholt
William Katt, Sean Young, Patrick McGoohan, Julian Fellowes

Back to the Future

USA 1985 116m Technicolor Dolby

An experiment in time travel sends a professor's teenage assistant back to 1955 where he meets his parents before they got married.

Phenomenally successful science fiction comedy adventure with many lively and inventive touches, though on the whole a rather typical product of the Steven Spielberg factory. Two sequels followed, along with an animated television series.

p: Neil Canton, Bob Gale for Universal/Amblin
exec p: Steven Spielberg, Kathleen Kennedy, Frank Marshall
w: ROBERT ZEMECKIS, BOB GALE

d: ROBERT ZEMECKIS
ph: Dean Cundey
m: Alan Silvestri
ed: Arthur Schmidt, Harry Keramidas
pd: Lawrence G. Paull
cos: Deborah L. Scott
sp: Kevin Pile, ILM
sound: William B. Kaplan
sound effects editing: C. L. Campbell, R. Rutledge (aa)
titles: Nina Saxon
make-up: Ken Chase
2nd unit d: Frank Marshall
2nd unit ph: Raymond Stella
ch: Brad Jeffries
MICHAEL J. FOX, CHRISTOPHER LLOYD, Lea Thompson, Crispin Glover, Claudia Wells, Thomas F. Wilson, Marc McClure, Wendie Jo Sperber, George Di Cenzo, Casey Siemaszko, Billy Zane

Back to the Future Part II

USA 1989 108m DeLuxe Dolby

Marty McFly travels into the future to get his kids out of trouble before travelling back in time to right a terrible wrong.

Clever if somewhat complex sequel with plenty of excellent ideas and touches to atone for the sag in the middle. It was filmed back-to-back with the third instalment.

p: Neil Canton, Bob Gale for Universal/Amblin
exec p: Steven Spielberg, Kathleen Kennedy, Frank Marshall
w: Bob Gale
story: Robert Zemeckis, Bob Gale
d: Robert Zemeckis
ph: Dean Cundey

Marty McFly (Michael J. Fox) travels back to the old west of 1885 to rescue Doc Brown (Christopher Lloyd) in *Back to the Future, Part III*.

m: Alan Silvestri
ed: Arthur Schmidt, Harry Keramidas
pd: Rick Carter
cos: Joanna Johnston
sp: Ken Ralston, Michael Lantieri, John Bell, Steve Gawley, ILM
sound: Charles L. Campbell, Louis L. Edeman
ch: Brad Jeffries
Michael J. Fox, Christopher Lloyd, Lea Thompson, Thomas F. Wilson, Harry Waters, Joe Flaherty, Charles Fleischer, Casey Seimaszko

Back to the Future Part III 🛸

USA 1990 118m DeLuxe Dolby
Marty McFly travels back to 1885 to rescue Doc from western badmen.

Lively finale to the series, more easily digestible plot-wise than its direct predecessor, with which it was made back to back.

p: Neil Canton for Universal/Amblin
exec p: Steven Spielberg, Kathleen Kennedy, Frank Marshall
w: Bob Gale
story: Robert Zemeckis, Bob Gale
d: Robert Zemeckis
ph: Dean Cundey
m: Alan Silvestri
ed: Arthur Schmidt, Harry Keramidas
pd: Rick Carter
cos: Joanne Johnstone
sp: Ken Ralston, Scott Farra, ILM
sound: William B. Kaplan
2nd unit d: Max Kleven
stunt co-ordinator: Walter Scott
ch: Brad Jeffries
Michael J. Fox, Christopher Lloyd, Mary Steenburgen, Richard Dysart, Lea Thompson, Thomas F. Wilson, Elizabeth Shue, Matt Clark, James Tolkan, Harry Carey, Jr.

Bad Taste

New Zealand 1987 92m colour
Humans defend themselves against cannibalistic aliens out to restock their food supplies.

Made over a period of four years, this determinedly gross splatter comedy is often energetically staged and has enough quirky touches to satisfy the late night crowd.

p: Peter Jackson for Wing Nut/New Zealand Film Commission
w: Peter Jackson, Tony Hiles, Ken Hammon
d/ph/sp: Peter Jackson
m: Michelle Scullion
ed: Peter Jackson, Jamie Selkirk
pd: no credit given
sound: Brent Burge
Mike Minett, Peter Jackson, Terry Potter, Pete O'Herne, Craig Smith, Doug Wren

Baird, Stuart (1948-)

British editor who, having worked on a handful of Ken Russell movies (*Tommy*, *Lisztomania*, *Valentino*, etc.), went to America where he worked on a number of big budget productions, among them *Gorillas in the Mist*, *Tango and Cash*, *Die Hard 2* and several for director Richard Donner, including *The Omen*, *Superman*, *Lethal Weapon*, *Lethal Weapon 2* and *Maverick*. He also occasionally acts as an associate producer (*Altered States*) and is known for having salvaged (uncredited) such films as *Predator* and *Scrooged* at the editing table. He now also directs, his debut being *Executive Decision* in 1996.

Genre credits:
Superman (1978 – ed), *Outland* (1981 – ed), *Ladyhawke* (1985 – ed/2nd unit d), *Radio Flyer* (1992 – co-ed), *Demolition Man* (1993 – ed)

Baker, Kenny

Diminutive British actor and cabaret artiste, best known for playing R2D2 in the Star Wars trilogy. He also played the Ewok Paploo in *Return of the Jedi*.

Genre credits:
Star Wars (1977), *The Empire Strikes Back* (1980), *The Time Bandits* (1981), *Return of the Jedi* (1983)

Baker, Rick (1950-)

American make-up effects artist whose innovative work on *An American Werewolf in London* won him the first official Oscar for make-up in 1981, which he later followed with a second for *Harry and the Hendersons* (1987 – aka *Big Foot and the Hendersons*), a third for *Ed Wood* (1994 – with Ve Neill and Yolanda Toussieng) and a fourth for *The Nutty Professor* (1996 – with David LeRoy Anderson. Following work on a few low budget pictures in the early 70s, he began his career in earnest as an assistant to Dick Smith working on *The Exorcist*. In 1974 he won an Emmy with Stan Winston for their old age make-up on the TV movie *The Autobiography of Miss Jane Pittman*, after which he assisted Stuart Freeborn on the celebrated Cantina sequence in *Star Wars*. His solo career finally took off with John Landis's *An American Werewolf*. His penchant for ape make-up has also seen sterling work on such films as *Greystoke* and *Gorillas in the Mist*, whilst in 1976 he both designed the make-up and played the title character in the disastrous remake of *King Kong*. His other credits include *Black Caesar*, *Live and Let Die*, *It's Alive*, *The Fury*, *Coming to America*, *Wolf* and *Baby's Day Out*.

Genre credits:
Octaman (1971), *Schlock* (1972), *Flesh Gordon* (1974), *Death Race 2000* (1975), *King Kong* (1976 – also actor, as Kong), *Star Wars* (1977 – assistant), *Tanya's Island* (1980), *The Incredible Shrinking Woman* (1981 - also actor, as an ape), *Starman* (1984 – co-sp), *Cocoon* (1985), *Harry and the Hendersons* (1987 – aka *Bigfoot and the Hendersons*), *Moonwalker* (1988), *Gremlins 2: The New Batch* (1990 – also co-p), *Batman Forever* (1995), *The Nutty Professor* (1996), *Escape from L.A.* (1996), *Men in Black* (1997), *Batman and Robin* (1997)

Baker, Roy Ward (1916-)

British director with a string of top-class 40s and 50s British productions to his credit, including *The October Man*, *The One That Got Away* and *A Night to Remember*. After experience in Hollywood his career began to decline in the 60s, so he took refuge in television, from which he was saved in 1967 by an offer to direct Hammer's third Quatermass film, *Quatermass and the Pit*, his best genre effort. After this he became a surprisingly unambitious genre director for both Hammer and Amicus, turning out such shockers as *Scars of Dracula*, *Vault of Horror* and *The Monster Club*. Returned to television in the 80s with the highly popular *Flame Trees of Thika*.

Genre credits:
Quatermass and the Pit (1967 – aka *Five Million Years to Earth*), *Moon Zero Two* (1969)

Bakshi, Ralph (1938-)

Palestinian-born animator who has eschewed the Disney style for a more adult approach. Began his film career working for the Terrytoons shorts department in the 60s before moving on to features in the 70s, the most famous of which is *Fritz the Cat*. His version of *Lord of the Rings* was intended as a two-parter, though the second episode was never made. He has also blended live action with animation in the *Roger Rabbit* manner in such films as *Streetfight* and *Cool World*, whilst in 1984 he contributed some animated sequences to the car chase comedy *Cannonball Run II*.

Genre credits:
Fritz the Cat (1972 – w/d), *Heavy Traffic* (1973 – w/d), *Streetfight* (1975 – aka *Coonskin* – w/d), *Wizards* (1977 – d), *Lord of the Rings* (1978 – d), *American Pop* (1981 – d), *Fire and Ice* (1983 – co-p/d), *Hey, Good Lookin'* (1982 – w/p/d), *Cool World* (1992 – d)

Balaban, Bob (1945-)

American supporting actor, best known to genre fans for playing the cartographer/interpreter Laughlin in Spielberg's *Close Encounters*. His other acting credits include *Midnight Cowboy*, *Prince of the City*, *Absence of Malice* and *Bob Roberts*. He has also directed *Parents*, *My Boyfriend's Back* and *The Last Good Time*.

Genre credits:
Close Encounters of the Third Kind (1977), *Close Encounters of the Third Kind – The Special Edition* (1980), *Altered States* (1981), *2010: Odyssey Two* (1984)

Bambi ☺☺

USA 1942 72m Technicolor
The adventures of Bambi, a forest deer, and his woodland friends, who include a rabbit called Thumper and a skunk called Flower.

Fondly remembered cartoon feature which may well now prove a little too sugary and soft-centred for modern tastes. There are some memorable sequences, such as the *Little April Showers* number and the forest fire finale, but the lack of plot is noticeable.

p: Walt Disney
book: Felix Salten
story: Perce Pearce, Larry Morey
supervising d: David Hand
songs: Frank Churchill, Larry Morey
m: Frank Churchill, Edward Plumb
md: Alexander Steinert
voices: Bobby Stewart, Peter Behn, Paula Winslow, Stan Alexander, Sterling Holloway, Donnie Dunagan, Sam Edwards

Band, Albert (1924-)

French-born writer, producer and director (real name Alfredo Antonini) working in both Hollywood and Europe. He began his career at Warner Bros. in the 40s as an assistant editor, before moving on to become an assistant to director John Huston, for whom he adapted *The Red Badge of Courage*. The father of producer-director Charles Band and composer Richard H. Band, his other credits include *I Bury The Living*, *The Young Guns*, *Face of Fire*, *I Pascali Rossi*, *She Came to the Valley* and *Zoltan, Hound of Dracula* (aka *Dracula's Dog*).

Genre credits:
Honey, I Blew Up the Kid (1992 – p), *Dragon World* (1993 – co-p), *Robot Wars* (1993 – d), *Prehysteria* (1993 – co-d), *Prehysteria 2* (1995 – d)

Band, Charles (1952-)

Prolific American producer, director and executive, almost entirely in the sci-fi, fantasy and horror genres. The son of director Albert Band and the brother of composer Richard H. Band, he founded Meda Home

Entertainment, an early video label, in 1978, the success of which led to the formation of both the Empire (1982) and Full Moon Entertainment (1988) production companies, through which he has presented countless low budget genre items, several of which he has directed himself. He also founded the Moonbeam and Torchlight production companies in 1994 to make films for children and adults respectively, with much of the output going directly to video. His credits as a producer, executive producer and/or studio head include *End of the World*, *Laserblast*, *Zone Troopers*, *Robot Holocaust*, *Arena*, *Robot Jox*, *Bad Channels*, *Trancers III: Deth Lives*, *Mandroid*, *Beach Babes from Beyond Infinity*, *Trancers 4: Jack of Swords*, *Test Tube Teens from the Year 2000*, *Dragonworld*, *Trancers 5: Sudden Deth* and *Prehysteria 2*. The following is a list of his directorial credits only.

Genre credits:

Dungeonmaster (1983 – co-d), *Metalstorm – The Destruction of Jared Syn* (1983), *Trancers* (1984), *Pulsepounders* (1988), *Crash and Burn* (1990), *Meridian* (1990 – aka *Kiss of the Beast*), *Trancers II: The Return of Jack Deth* (1990), *Prehysteria* (1993 – co-d)

Band, Richard H. (1953-)

American composer, son of director Albert Band and brother to producer-director Charles Band, on whose films he primarily works. He co-wrote (with Joel Goldsmith) his first film score in 1976 for *Laserblast*. His other credits include *Dr Heckyl and Mr Hype*, *Re-Animator* and *Dolls*.

Barbarella

USA 1967 98m Technicolor Panavision

In the 40th century a beautiful but sexually naive astronaut is sent on a peace-keeping mission and has various adventures in the process.

High camp, psychedelic space fantasy, delightfully dated for those in the mood, though the joke soon wears thin.

p: Dino de Laurentiis for Marianne
w: Terry Southern, Roger Vadim, Claude Brule, Vittorio Bonicelli, Clement Biddle Wood, Brian Degas, Tudor Gates, Jean-Claude Forest
book: Jean-Claude Forest
d: Roger Vadim
ph: Claude Renoir
m: Bob Crewe, Charles Fox, Michael Magne
ed: Victoria Mercanton
pd: MARIO GARBUGLIA
cos: JACQUES FONTERAY
sp: August Lohman, Charles Staffel, Gerard Cogan, Thiery Viryens-Fargo
sound: David Hildyard, Vittorio Trentino
titles: Maurice Binder
book: Jean-Claude Forest
d: Roger Vadim
ph: Claude Renoir
m: Bob Crewe, Charles Fox, Michael Magne
ed: Victoria Mercanton
pd: MARIO GARBUGLIA
cos: JACQUES FONTERAY
sp: August Lohman, Charles Staffel, Gerard Cogan, Thiery, Viryens-Fargo
sound: David Hildyard, Vittorio Trentino
titles: Maurice Binder
Jane Fonda, John Phillip Law, Anita Pallenberg, Milo O'Shea, Ugo Tognazzi, Claude Dauphin, Marcel Marceau, David Hemmings

Barb Wire

USA 1996 99m Technicolor Dolby

In 2017, a lady club owner and part time bounty hunter (!) goes in search of some much sought-after contact lenses which enable their wearers to escape the government's retina-scanning devices.

Plastic, adolescent action movie which, when it isn't accentuating its star's cleavage, is merely frenetic in the MTV manner. Teenage boys may have a ball.

p: Mike Richardson, Brad Wymany, Todd Moyer for Polygram/Dark Horse/Propaganda
exec p: Peter Heller
w: Chuck Pfarrer, Ilene Chalken
d: David Hogan

A fetishist's delight. Dildano (David Hemmings) and Barbarella (Jane Fonda) get to know each other a little better in the supercamp *Barbarella*.

ph: Rick Bota
m: Michel Colombier
ed: Peter Schink
pd: Jean-Philippe Carp
cos: Rosanna Norton
Pamela Anderson Lee, Temuera Morrison, Jack Noseworthy, Victoria Rowell, Clint Howard, Xander Berkley, Udo Kier, Steve Railsback

Baron Munchausen 🛸

Czechoslovakia 1962 81m Agfacolor
Adventures involving the world's greatest liar, Baron Munchausen.

Quirky fantasy piece, imaginatively put together for those who can adapt to its artificial look. A much-hyped multi-million dollar remake by Terry Gilliam followed in 1989 under the title *The Adventures of Baron Munchausen*. There were also two silent versions in 1911 (by Georges Méliès) and 1913, as well as a German version in 1943.

p: Ceskoslovensky Film
w/d: KAREL ZEMAN
novel: Gottfried A. Burger
ph: Jiri Tarantik
m: Zdenek Liska
Milos Kopecky, Rudolf Jelinek, Jana Becjchova, Jan Werich

Barrie, J. M. (1860-1937)

British playwright, best remembered for creating *Peter Pan*, of which several film versions have been made, most notably in 1924, 1953 (the Disney cartoon), 1976 (TVM) and 1991 (as *Hook*). There have also been several television adaptations and countless stage productions and pantomime versions. Barrie's other filmed plays include *The Admirable Crichton* and *Quality Street*.

Barron, Bebe

see Bebe, Louis

Barron, Louis (1920-)

American composer who, with his wife Bebe (1927-), created the electronic score for *Forbidden Planet* (1956), which was referred to in the credits as "electric tonalities." Over 40 years on, this groundbreaking "music" remains entirely effective.

Barron, Steve (1956-)

British director, the son of Zelda Barron, herself a director (*Secret Places*, *Shag*, *The Bulldance*, etc.). A former pop video director, he made the jump to movies in 1984 with *Electric Dreams*, though he didn't have a commercial hit until 1990 with *Teenage Mutant Ninja Turtles*, since when his career has been somewhat variable.

Genre credits:

Electric Dreams (1984), *Teenage Mutant Ninja Turtles* (1990), *The Coneheads* (1993), *The Adventures of Pinocchio* (1996)

Barry, Gene (1921-)

American actor (real name Eugene Klass) perhaps best known for his two series of *Burke's Law* (in the 60s and 90s). Much stage and film work, including *Red Garters*, *Naked Alibi*, *Thunder Road* and *Maroc 7*, though he is perhaps best known to genre fans for playing Clayton Forrester in *War of the Worlds* (1953).

Barry, John (1933–)

Popular British film composer and songwriter (real name John Barry Prendergast), best known for his James Bond scores and title songs, among them *From Russia with Love*, *Goldfinger*, *Thunderball*, *On Her Majesty's Secret Service*, *A View to a Kill*, *Diamonds Are Forever* and *The Living Daylights*. Began his career as a trumpeter before forming his own jazz band, The John Barry Seven, in 1957. Having studied orchestration with the likes of Stan Kenton (by post during his national service in Egypt!), he then became a pop arranger, working on several hits with the singer Adam Faith, who he followed into the movies with *Beat Girl* in 1959. He arranged Monty Norman's James Bond theme for the first film in the series, *Dr. No*, in 1962, after which his career as a film composer skyrocketed. He went on to win five Oscars for his work on *Born Free* (1966 – best song and score), *The Lion in Winter* (1968), *Out of Africa* (1985) and *Dances with Wolves* (1990). Among his other memorable scores are *Zulu*, *The Ipcress File*, *The Knack*, *Midnight Cowboy*, *Mary Queen of Scots*, *Monte Walsh*, *The Dove*, *Raise the Titanic*, *Body Heat* and *Chaplin*. He has also written the songs for two stage musicals, *Billy* and *Lolita*, and the title themes for a handful of television programmes, most notably *Juke Box Jury* and *The Persuaders*.

Genre credits:

You Only Live Twice (1967), *Alice's Adventures in Wonderland* (1972), *King Kong* (1976), *White Buffalo* (1977), *The Black Hole* (1979), *Moonraker* (1979), *Starcrash* (1979), *Somewhere in Time* (1980), *Peggy Sue Got Married* (1986)

Barry, John (1935-1979)

American production designer who died at the height of his career, following important contributions to both *Star Wars* (for which he won an Oscar) and *Superman*. His aspirations to become a director were scuppered when he was replaced on *Saturn Three* by the film's producer after just three days. He died during the filming of *The Empire Strikes Back*.

Genre credits:

A Clockwork Orange (1971 – pd), *Phase IV* (1973 – pd), *The Little Prince* (1974 – pd), *Star Wars* (1977 – pd), *Superman* (1978 – pd/co-2nd unit d), *Superman 2* (1980 – co-pd), *Saturn Three* (1980 – story), *The Empire Strikes Back* (1980 – co-2nd unit d)

Barrymore, Drew (1975-)

American child actress who shot to stardom as Gertie in *E. T.* Drug and alcohol abuse followed in her early teenage years, though she gradually overcame these problems and emerged as a leading lady/supporting actress in such films as *Firestarter*, *Poison Ivy*, *Wayne's World 2*, *Bad Girls* and *Scream*. She is the daughter of actor

John Barrymore, Jr., himself the son of John Barrymore of the famous Barrymore clan (Lionel, Ethel, Diana).

Genre credits:

E. T. (1982), *Babes in Toyland* (1984 – TVM), *Batman Forever* (1995)

Batman

The millionaire businessman Bruce Wayne by day and caped crusader by night was created by comic strip artist Bob Kane in 1939 and first came to the screen in two 40s serials in which he was played by Lewis Wilson and Robert Lowery respectively. A phenomenally popular television series starring Adam West as Batman and Burt Ward as his sidekick Robin followed in the mid-60s, which itself spawned a movie. In 1989, a further, much darker feature appeared starring Michael Keaton, which itself inspired several sequels in which Batman was played by Keaton,

Val Kilmer and George Clooney respectively. Aided by his loyal butler Alfred and such hardware as the Batmobile and the Batwing, Batman's flamboyant enemies include The Joker, The Penguin, The Riddler, Catwoman and Harvey Two-Face.

Filmography:

Batman (1943 – serial), *Batman and Robin* (1949 – serial), *Batman* (1966), *Batman* (1989), *Batman Returns* (1992), *Batman Forever* (1995), *Batman and Robin* (1997)

Batman

USA 1966 105m DeLuxe

The Caped Crusader discovers that his old enemies The Penguin, The Riddler, The Joker and Catwoman are behind yet another dastardly plot.

Strained movie version of the popular TV series. Some of it works, but it is never quite as funny as it thinks it is.

Lewis Wilson, the screen's first Caped Crusader, checks out his wardrobe for the 1943 serial *Batman*.

By the time Michael Keaton came to play the same role in Tim Burton's 1989 movie, the budget for filming such extravaganzas had risen somewhat. You can bet he didn't get THAT car in *Exchange and Mart*!

Kids may have a ball, however.

p: William Dozier for
TCF/Greenlawn/National Periodical
w: Lorenzo Semple, Jr.
d: Leslie H. Martinson
ph: Howard Schwartz
m: Nelson Riddle (theme: Neil Hefti)
ed: Harry Gerstad
ad: Jack Martin Smith, Serge Krizman
cos: no credit given
sp: L. B. Abbott
sound: Roy Meadows, Harry M. Leonard
titles: Richard Kuhn
2nd unit d: Ray Kellogg
2nd unit ph: Jack Marta
aerial ph: Nelson Tyler
Adam West, Burt Ward, Burgess Meredith
(as The Penguin), Cesar Romero (as The
Joker), Frank Gorshin (as The Riddler), Lee
Meriwether (as Catwoman), Neil Hamilton,
Reginald Denny

Batman

USA/GB 1989 126m Technicolor Dolby
A caped vigilante known as Batman
steps in to prevent The Joker's nefarious plan to poison the residents of
Gotham City.

Expensive, over-hyped comic strip
adventures, much darker in tone than
the hero's camper exploits in the 60s,
but worth a look for the elaborate sets
and certain key action sequences. Not
without its longeurs, the movie is more
for looking at than listening to.

p: Jon Peters, Peter Guber for Warner
exec p: Benjamin Melniker, Michael Uslan
w: Sam Hamm, Warren Skaaren
story: Sam Hamm
comic strip: Bob Kane
d: Tim Burton
ph: ROGER PRATT
m: DANNY ELFMAN
songs: Prince
ed: Ray Lovejoy
ad/set decoration: ANTON FURST, PETER
YOUNG (AA)

cos: BOB RINGWOOD
sp: Derek Meddings
sound: Bill Rowe, Tony Dawe
2nd unit d: Peter MacDonald
stunt co-ordinator: Eddie Stacey
Michael Keaton, Jack Nicholson (as The
Joker), Kim Basinger, Robert Wuhl, Pat
Hingle, Billy Dee Williams, Michael Gough,
Jack Palance, Jerry Hall

Batman and Robin

USA 1997 120m Technicolor Dolby
With the help of Robin and Batgirl,
Batman attempts to prevent arch vil-
lain Mr. Freeze's attempts to ice over
Gotham City and hold it to ransom.

Another day, another villain. The
mixture is much as before, with too
many characters and not enough plot.
The sets, costumes and special effects
are fine, however, and Uma Thurman
makes an amusing Poison Ivy. As ever,
though, there is too much dull chat
between the frenetic action highlights.

p: Peter MacGregor-Scott for Warner
exec p: Benjamin Melniker, Michael E.
Uslan
w: Akiva Goldsman
d: Joel Schumacher
ph: Stephen Goldblatt
m: Elliot Goldenthal
ed: Dennis Virkler, Mark Stevens
pd: Barbara Ling
cos: Ingrid Ferrin, Robert Turturice
sp: John Dykstra
sound: Lance Brown
make-up effects: Jeff Dawn, Rick Baker
stunt co-ordinator: Pat E. Johnson
2nd unit d: Peter MacDonald
2nd unit ph: James Anderson
George Clooney, Arnold Schwarzenegger
(as Mr. Freeze), Chris O'Donnell, Alicia
Silverstone, Uma Thurman, Michael Gough,
Pat Hingle, Elle MacPherson

Batman Forever

USA 1995 121m Technicolor Dolby
Batman has a run-in with The Riddler
and Two-Face, who want to take over

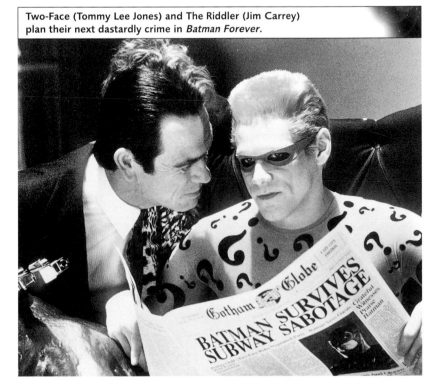

Two-Face (Tommy Lee Jones) and The Riddler (Jim Carrey) plan their next dastardly crime in *Batman Forever*.

people's brains with a special TV transmitter. But help is at hand in the form of a new sidekick called Robin.

The third Batman picture is much the same mixture as before, despite a new star and director. Great to look at, but with too many slow, talky patches between the special effects and action sequences.

p: Tim Burton, Peter Macgregor Scott for Warner
w: Lee Batchler, Janet Lee Batchler
d: Joel Schumacher
ph: Stephen Goldblatt
m: Elliot Goldenthal
ed: Dennis Virkler
pd: BARBARA LING
cos: Bob Ringwood, Ingrid Ferrin
sp: John Dykstra
make-up effects: Rick Baker
sound: Donald O. Mitchell, Frank A. Montano, Michael Herbick, Petur Hliddal
sound effects ed: John Leveque, Bruce Stambler
Val Kilmer, Jim Carrey (as The Riddler), Tommy Lee Jones (as Two-Face), Nicole Kidman, Chris O'Donnell, Michael Gough, Pat Hingle, Drew Barrymore

Batman Returns 🛸

USA 1992 115m Technicolor Dolby
Batman saves a corrupt industrialist from the wiles of Catwoman and The Penguin.

Expensive, good looking, but over-long and somewhat plotless sequel to *Batman* which, though it divided critical opinion, nevertheless made a bundle at the box office.

p: Denise Di Novi, Tim Burton for Warner
exec p: Jon Peters, Peter Guber, Benjamin Melniker, Michael E. Uslan
w: Daniel Waters
story: Daniel Waters, Sam Hamm
d: Tim Burton
ph: Stefan Czapsky

m: Danny Elfman
ed: Chris Lebenzon
pd: BO WELCH
cos: Bob Ringwood, Mary Vogt
sp: Chuck Gaspar, John Bruno and others
sound: Steve Maslow, Jeffrey L. Haboush
make-up effects: Stan Winston and others
titles: Robert Dawson
stunt co-ordinator: Max Kleven, Charlie Croughwell
2nd unit d: Max Kleven, Bill Weber
2nd unit ph: Don Burgess
Michael Keaton, Danny DeVito (as The Penguin), Michelle Pfeiffer (as Catwoman), Christopher Walken (as Max Schreck), Michael Gough, Pat Hingle, Michael Murphy, Cristi Conaway, Paul Reubens, Diane Salinger, Vincent Schiavelli

---

Batteries Not Included

USA 1987 102m DeLuxe Dolby
The residents of a condemned New York apartment building are helped by miniature flying saucers to save their home.

Sickly sweet fantasy comedy recalling Disney at its worst in the 70s. Diabetics be warned.

p: Ronald L. Schwary for Universal/Amblin
exec p: Steven Spielberg, Kathleen Kennedy, Frank Marshall
w: Brad Bird, Matthew Robbins, Brent Maddock, S. S. Wilson
story: Mick Garris
d: Matthew Robbins
ph: John McPherson
m: James Horner
ed: Cynthia Scheider
pd: Ted Haworth
cos: Aggie Guerard Rodgers
sp: Bruce Nicholson
sound: Gene Cantamessa, Bill Varney
2nd unit d: Joe Johnston
2nd unit ph: Dick Kratina
Hume Cronyn, Jessica Tandy, Frank McRae, Elizabeth Pena, Michael Carmine, Dennis Boutsikaris, Tom Aldredge, Jane Hoffman, John Disanti

---

The reptile warrior Cayman (centre) joins forces with the Kelvin twins to defend the planet Akir from the evil warlord Sador in *Battle Beyond the Stars*, an outer space update of *The Magnificent Seven* and *The Seven Samurai*. The script was penned by John Sayles, no less.

Battle Beneath the Earth

GB 1967 92m Technicolor

American scientists discover that the enemy is planning to invade by burrowing underneath the country with a giant laser.

Low budget science fiction nonsense. As foolish as it sounds, but not entirely unwatchable.

p: Charles Reynolds for MGM/Reynolds/Vetter

w: L. Z. Hargreaves

d: Montgomery Tully

ph: Kenneth Talbot

m: Ken Jones

ed: Sidney Stone

ad: Jim Morahan

sp: Tom Howard

sound: A. W. Watkins, J. B. Smith, Jerry Turner

Kerwin Matthews, Vivienne Ventura, Robert Ayres, Martin Benson, Peter Arne

Battle Beyond the Stars 🛸

USA 1980 104m Metrocolor

A young man enlists seven space mercenaries to defeat an evil warlord who is threatening his planet if certain demands are not met.

Lively space western (a remake of *The Magnificent Seven*, itself a remake of *The Seven Samurai*), brightly handled and with several perky touches in the script.

p: Ed Carlin for New World

exec p: Roger Corman

w: John Sayles

story: John Sayles, Anne Dyer

d: Jimmy T. Murakami

ph: Daniel Lacambre

m: James Horner

ed: Allan Holzman, R. J. Kizer

ad: Jim Cameron, Charles Breen

cos: Durina Rice Wood

The Android Sisters, each of whom has two mouths and four eyes, wow the punters in an outer space gambling den in the TV movie *Battlestar Gallactica*.

sp: Marcia Dripchak and others

sound: Alan S. Howarth

make-up effects: Sue Rolph, Steve Neill, Rick Stratton, Cliff Raven

Richard Thomas, Robert Vaughn, John Saxon, George Peppard, Sybil Danning, Darlanne Fluegel, Sam Jaffe, Jeff Corey, Morgan Woodward, Steve Davis

Battle for the Planet of the Apes

USA 1973 86m DeLuxe Panavision

Various ape factions fight for control of the earth.

Ho-hum tailpiece to the ape saga, redeemed by a couple of action highlights towards the end.

p: Arthur P. Jacobs, Frank Capra, Jr., for TCF/APJAC

w: John William Corrington, Joyce Hooper

story: Paul Dehn

d: J. Lee-Thompson

ph: Richard H. Kline

m: Leonard Rosenman

ed: Alan L. Jaggs

ad: Dale Hennessy

sp: Gerald Endler

sound: Herman Lewis, Don Bassman

Roddy McDowall, Claude Akins, Natalie Trundy, Severn Darden, Lew Ayres, Paul Williams, John Huston

Battlestar Gallactica 🛸

USA 1978 140m/125m Technicolor TVM

When attacked by the Cylons, a peace-loving race of humans is forced to take up arms.

Iffy *Star Wars* rip-off, spliced together from various episodes of a popular US television series and released theatrically outside America. Tolerable enough, and helped along by some excellent effects work.

p: John Dykstra for Universal/ABC

exec p: Glen Larson

w: Glen Larson, Richard A. Colla

d: Richard A. Colla
ph: Ben Colman
m: Stu Phillips, Glen Larson
ed: Robert L. Kimble, Leon Ortiz, Larry Strong
ad: John E. Chilberg III
cos: Jean-Pierre Dorleac
sp: JOHN DYKSTRA and others
sound: Jim Alexander, Robert L. Hoyt
titles: Wayne Fitzgerald
2nd unit ph: Mario Di Leo
Lorne Greene, Richard Hatch, Dirk Benedict, Maren Jensen, Jane Seymour, Patrick Macnee, Lew Ayres, John Colicos, Ray Milland, Wilfred Hyde White, Ed Begley, Jr.,

Battletruck

New Zealand 1981 92m colour
In the future after the oil wars, various parties battle it out for drums of precious fuel.

Unimaginative futuristic actioner, obviously patterned after *Mad Max*.

p: Lloyd Phillips, Rob Whitehouse for Battletruck
w: Irving Austin, John Beech, Harley Cockliss
story: Michael Abrams
d: Harley Cockliss
ph: Chris Menges
m: Kevin Peek
ed: Michael Horton
pd: Gary Hansen
Michael Beck, Annie McEnroe, James Wainwright, John Ratzenberger, Randolph Powell, Bruno Lawrence, Diana Rowan, John Bach, Kelly Johnson

Baxter, Les (1922-1996)

American composer, a graduate of the Detroit Conservatory of Music. He began his career as a dance band arranger. Several innovative albums for Capitol followed in the 50s, including *Music Out of the Moon, Perfume Set to Music* and *The Voice of the Xtabay*, which inevitably led to film offers, including several of Roger Corman's celebrated Poe films (*House of Usher, The Pit and the Pendulum, The Raven*, etc.). Other credits include *Goliath and the Barbarians, Muscle Beach Party* and *Frogs*.

Genre credits:
The Invisible Boy (1957), *Master of the World* (1961), *Panic in Year Zero* (1962), *Pajama Party* (1964), *Sergeant Deadhead* (1965 – aka *Sergeant Deadhead the Astronaut*), *Dr. Goldfoot and the Bikini Machine* (1965 – aka *Dr. G and the Bikini Machine*), *Dr. Goldfoot and the Girl Bombs* (1966 – aka *Le Spie Vengono dal Semifreddo/I due Mafiosi Dell' FBI*), *Wild in the Streets* (1968)

The Beast from 20,000 Fathoms

USA 1953 80m bw
Atomic experiments at the North Pole thaw out a prehistoric monster, which promtly goes on the rampage.

Archetypal 50s monster flick let down by inferior trick work and cardboard characters. No *King Kong*, that's for sure.

p: Bill Chester, Jack Dietz for Warner
w: Lou Morheim, Fred Friedburger
story: Ray Bradbury
d: Eugene Lourie
ph: Jack Russell
m: David Buttolph
ed/associate p: Bernard W. Burton
ad: Hal Waller
cos: Berman's
sp: Ray Harryhausen, Willis Cook
sound: Max Hutchinson
Paul Christian, Cecil Kellaway, Donald Woods, Lee Van Cleef, Kenneth Tobey, Steve Brodie

The Beastmaster

USA 1982 118m colour Dolby
A young prince, kidnapped whilst still in his mother's womb (!) by a sorceror who wishes to sacrifice him, is rescued by a peasant and grows up into muscle-bound superhero with the ability to communicate with animals.

Fairly lively sword and sorcery pic, well enough made and, on the whole, rather more fun than the more sombre *Conan the Barbarian*. Unfortunately, it goes on far longer than is necessary. A sequel, *Beastmaster 2: Through the Portals of Time*, followed in 1991.

p: Sylvio Tabet, Paul Pepperman for ECTA/Leisure Investment/Beastmaster NV/GmbH & Co
exec p: Nader Atassi, Sylvio Tabet
w: Don Coscarelli, Paul Pepperman
d: Don Coscarelli
ph: John Alcott
m: Lee Holdridge
ed: Roy Watts
pd: Conrad E. Angone
Marc Singer, Rip Torn, Tanya Roberts, John Amos, Rod Loomis, Josh Milrad

The Beast of Hollow Mountain

USA 1965 75m DeLuxe Cinemascope/Regiscope
Mexican villagers discover a monster lurking in a nearby mountain.

Cheapjack stuff which seems to consist mostly of padding.

p: William Nassour, Edward Nassour, Peliculas Rodriguez for UA/Nassour
w: Robert Hill, Jack DeWitt
story: Willis O'Brien
d: Edward Nassour, Ismael Rodriguez
ph: Jorge Stahl, Jr.
m: Raul Lavista
ed: Holbrook Todd, Mauty Wright
ad: no credit given
sp: Jack Rabin, Louis DeWitt

sound: James L. Fields, Nick Rosa
Guy Madison, Patricia Medina, Eduardo
Noriega, Carlos Rivas, Lupe Carriles, Julio
Villareal, Hal Baylor, Garcia Pena

Beaumont, Charles (1929-1967)

American writer whose credits include *The Intruder*, *Night of the Eagle* (aka *Burn, Witch, Burn*), *The Haunted Palace*, *The Masque of the Red Death*, *Mister Moses*, the hilariously inept *Queen of Outer Space* and two for George Pal.

Genre credits:
Queen of Outer Space (1958 – w), *The Wonderful World of the Brothers Grimm* (1962 – co-w), *The Seven Faces of Dr Lao* (1964 – w)

Beauty and the Beast

USA 1991 85m Technicolor Dolby
Despite first impressions, a beautiful young village girl falls in love with a monstrous beast who, in the end, turns out to be a handsome prince under a magical spell.

Smooth animated feature with memorable sequences and a lively song score. A huge commercial success, it was the first cartoon ever to be nominated for a best picture Oscar and confirmed the return to glory of Disney's animation department.

p: Don Hahn for Walt Disney/Silver Screen Partners IV
w: Linda Woolverton
d: Gary Trousdale, Kirk Wise
m: Alan Menken (aa)
songs: ALAN MENKEN (m), HOWARD ASHMAN (ly) (aa, Best Song, *Beauty and the Beast*)
ed: John Carnochan
sound: Michael Farrow, John Richards

Amateur witch Eglantine Price (Angela Lansbury) sees the contents of her wardrobe go for a walk in Disney's *Mary Poppins*-style musical *Bedknobs and Broomsticks*. For the 1979 re-release, the film was advertised with a variation on the tagline for *Superman*, "You'll believe a woman can fly!"

voices: Robby Benson, Paige o'Hara, Angela Lansbury, Jerry Orbach, David Ogden Stiers, Jesse Corti, Richard White

The Bed Sitting Room

GB 1969 91m DeLuxe
After the bomb has been dropped, people start changing into bed sitting rooms...

Pythonesque comedy by way of Lewis Carroll. Well enough made, but hard to like and even harder to laugh at, its concept and humour having dated somewhat. A box office flop, it did its director's career considerable harm at the time.

p: Richard Lester for UA
exec p: Oscar Lewenstein
w: John Antrobus, Charles Wood
play: John Antrobus, Spike Milligan
d: Richard Lester
ph: David Watkin
m: Ken Thorne

ed: John Victor-Smith
pd: Assheton Gorton
sp: Phil Stokes
sound: Peter Sutton
Ralph Richardson, Arthur Lowe, Rita Tushingham, Mona Washbourne, Michael Hordern, Peter Cook, Dudley Moore, Spike Milligan, Harry Secombe, Marty Feldman, Jimmy Edwards, Ronald Fraser, Richard Warwick, Frank Thornton

Bedknobs and Broomsticks

USA 1971 117m Technicolor
After various adventures on a flying bed, three evacuee children help an apprentice witch thwart a Nazi invasion during World War Two.

Lengthy, unimaginatively handled, not to mention somewhat variable mixture of songs, cartoon adventures and special effects which nevertheless has enough going on to keep its intended audience occupied.

p: Bill Walsh for Walt Disney

w: Bill Walsh, Don DaGradi

novel: Mary Norton

d: Robert Stevenson

ph: Frank Phillips

songs: Richard M. and Robert B. Sherman

md: Irwin Kostal

ed: Cotton Warburton, James W. Swain

ad: John B. Mansbridge, Peter Ellenshaw

cos: Bill Thomas

sp: Alan Maley, Eustace Lycett, Danny Lee (aa)

sound: Robert O. Cook, Dean Thomas

animation d: Ward Kimball

ch: Donald McKayle

titles: David Jonas

2nd unit d: Arthur J. Vitarelli
ANGELA LANSBURY, David Tomlinson, Roy Smart, Cindy O'Callahan, Sam Jaffe, Roddy McDowall, Bruce Forsythe, Tessie O'Shea, Reginald Owen, Ian Weighill, Ben Wrigley, Arthur E. Gould-Porter

Beebe, Ford L. (1888-1970)

American writer and director who helmed countless low-budget Westerns, horror films and serials, among the latter genre *The Shadow of the Eagle*, *The Adventures of Rex and Rinty*, *Ace Drummond* and *Junior G-Men*, plus *Night Monster*, *Son of Dracula* (which he also produced) *Riders of Death Valley* and *The Invisible Man's Revenge*. A former journalist and press agent, he began his film career in 1916 with *Youth of Fortune* (which also he scripted), making his directorial debut in 1920 with *The Honor of the Range*. To genre fans, however, he is perhaps best known for directing two serials involving the exploits of *Buck Rogers* and *Flash Gordon*.

Genre credits:

Buck Rogers (1939 – serial – co-d), *Flash Gordon Conquers the Universe* (1940 – serial – co-d)

Beeson, Paul (1921-)

British cinematographer who began his career as a camera assistant at Ealing in 1938. He became a camera operator in 1947 and a fully fledged cinematographer in 1955 with *West of Zanzibar*. He followed this with work on *Out of the Clouds*, *The Feminine Touch* and several films for director Leslie Norman (*The Shiralee*, *Dunkirk*, *Spare the Rod*, etc.). In the 60s he also began photographing films for Disney (*Greyfriars Bobby*, *The Prince and the Pauper*, *The Horse without a Head*), which he continued to do until the late 70s (*Escape from the Dark*, *Candleshoe*, etc.). His other credits include *Tarzan Goes to India*, *The Moon-Spinners*, *To Sir with Love* and *The Wolves of Willoughby Chase*. More recently he has also contributed additional and second unit photography to several large-scale productions, such as *Never Say Never Again* and the *Indiana Jones* films.

Genre credits:

In Search of the Castaways (1961 – ph), *The Lost Continent* (1968 – ph), *Moon Zero Two* (1969 – ph), *Beauty and the Beast* (1976 – co-ph), *The Spaceman and King Arthur* (1979 – aka *Unidentified Flying Oddball* – ph), *Alien* (1979 – co-2nd unit ph), *Hawk the Slayer* (1980 – ph), *Raiders of the Lost Ark* (1981 – add ph), *Indiana Jones and the Temple of Doom* (1984 – add ph), *Santa Claus: The Movie* (1985 – add ph), *Willow* (1988 – 2nd unit ph), *Indiana Jones and the Last Crusade* (1989 – add ph), *Alien 3* (1992 – co-2nd unit ph)

Bell, Book and Candle ☁

USA 1958 103m Technicolor

A Manhattan witch sets her sights on the publisher who lives above her shop.

Glossy but otherwise deadly dull version of a popular play, re-teaming the stars of *Vertigo* to little effect.

p: Julian Blaustein for Columbia/Phoenix

w: Daniel Taradash

play: John Van Druten

d: Richard Quine

ph: James Wong Howe

m: George Duning

ed: Charles Nelson

ad: Cary Odell

cos: Jean Louis

sound: John Livardy, Franklin Hansen, Jr.
James Stewart, Kim Novak, Jack Lemmon, ELSA LANCHESTER, Ernie Kovacs, Hermione Gingold, Janice Rule

Beneath the Planet of the Apes 🛸

USA 1969 94m DeLuxe Panavision

Another crew of astronauts lands on the ape planet to discover what happened to their predecessors and find a subterranean race who worship a live A-bomb.

Solidly crafted sequel to *Planet of the Apes* which adds a few new ideas of its own to the proceedings.

p: Arthur P. Jacobs, Mort Abrahams for TCF/APJAC

w: Paul Dehn

story: Paul Dehn, Mort Abrahams

d: Ted Post

ph: MILTON KRASNER

m: Leonard Rosenman

ed: Marion Rothman

ad: William Creber, Jack Martin Smith

cos: Morton Haack

sp: Art Cruickshank, L. B. Abbott

sound: Stephen Bass, David Dockendorf

2nd unit d: Chuck Robertson
James Franciscus, Linda Harrison, Kim Hunter, Maurice Evans, Charlton Heston, Victor Buono, Jeff Corey, Paul Richards, James Gregory, Thomas Gomez

Bennet, Spencer Gordon (1893-1987)

American director, a former actor and stuntman, who specialised in serials, the first of which, *Play Ball*, he directed in 1925. He is perhaps best known for helming the *Superman* serials. His feature films include *The Brave Warrior* and *The Bounty Killer*.

Genre credits:

The Purple Monster Strikes (1945 – serial – co-d), *Brick Bradford* (1947 – serial – d), *Bruce Gentry – Daredevil of the Skies* (1949 – serial – co-d), *Superman* (1948 – serial – co-d), *Batman and Robin* (1949 – serial – d), *Atom Man vs Superman* (1950 – serial – d), *Mysterious Island* (1950 – serial – d), *Captain Video* (1951 – serial – co-d), *The Lost Planet* (1953 – serial – d), *Atomic Submarine* (1959 – d)

Bernard, James (1925-)

British composer, one of Hammer's linchpins, his scores for their horror classics being among the genre's finest (*The Curse of Frankenstein, Dracula, The Hound of the Baskervilles, The Devil Rides Out, Frankenstein and the Monster from Hell*, etc.). Began composing during his teenage years and, after wartime service in the RAF, went to study at the Royal College of Music at the suggestion of his friend Benjamin Britten. Began his professional career scoring for BBC radio, his music for a production of *The Duchess of Malfi* leading to *The Quatermass Experiment*, his first score for Hammer. Previous to this Bernard won an Oscar in 1950 for co-authoring the story (with Paul Dehn) for the thriller *Seven Days to Noon*. His work as a composer has almost been exclusively for Hammer, exceptions being *Windom's Way, The Immortal Land, A Place for Gold, Across the Bridge, Nor the Moon by Night, The Torture Garden* (with Don Banks) and *Nosferatu*.

Genre credits:

The Quatermass Experiment (1955 – aka *The Creeping Unknown*), *X – The Unknown* (1956), *Quatermass 2* (1956 – aka *Enemy from Space*), *The Damned* (1963 – aka *These Are the Damned*), *She* (1965)

Bernds, Edward (1911-)

American writer and director, a former sound technician, with many shorts and low budget entries to his credit, among them numerous Three Stooges shorts and several entries in the Blondie series (*Blondie's Secret, Blondie's Big Deal, Beware of Blondie*, etc.). His other credits include *The Bowery Boys Meet the Monsters, Navy Wife, Joy Ride, The Three Stooges Meet Hercules* and *Highschool Hellcats*.

Genre credits:

World Without End (1956 – w/d), *Queen of Outer Space* (1958 – d), *Spacemaster X-7* (1958 – d), *Return of the Fly* (1959 – w/d), *Prehistoric Valley* (1961 – aka *Valley of the Dragons* – w/d), *The Three Stooges in Orbit* (1962 – d)

Bernstein, Elmer (1922-)

Prolific American composer who has penned a variety of memorable scores, among them *The Ten Commandments, The Man with the Golden Arm, The Sweet Smell of Success, The Magnificent Seven, To Kill a Mockingbird, The Great Escape, Thoroughly Modern Millie* (which won him an Oscar in 1967), *Airplane, Five Days One Summer* and *The Grifters*. His forays into science fiction and fantasy have only been occasional given the enormity of his output.

Genre credits:

Cat Women of the Moon (1953), *Robot Monster* (1953), *Airplane II: The Sequel* (1982 – theme only), *Saturn Three* (1980), *Heavy Metal* (1981), *Ghostbusters* (1984), *The Black Cauldron* (1986), *Slipstream* (1989), *Buddy* (1997)

Bewes, Rodney (1937-)

British comedy actor from television, best remembered for playing Bob Ferris opposite James Bolam's Terry Collier in the TV sit-coms *The Likely Lads* and *Whatever Happened to the Likely Lads?* Much TV and stage work as well as the occasional film appearance, most notably in *Billy Liar, Spring and Port Wine* and the big screen version of *The Likely Lads*.

Genre credits:

Alice's Adventures in Wonderland (1972 – as the Knave of Hearts), *Jabberwocky* (1977), *The Spaceman and King Arthur* (1979 – aka *Unidentified Flying Oddball*)

Beyond the Stars

USA 1989 91m TVCcolor Ultra Stereo
Whilst vacationing with his father, a teenager obsessed with space travel meets a celebrated astronaut who recounts his experiences to him.

Mild but not unwatchable drama with a surprising end.

p: Joseph Perez for Five Star Entertainment
exec p: Michael Plotkin
w/d: David Saperstein
ph: John Bartley
m: Geoff Levin, Chris Many
ed: Frank Irvine, Stanley Warnow, Judith Blume
pd: John J. Moore
cos: Sheila Bingham
sp: Lumeni Productions
sound: Eric Batut

stunt co-ordinator: Betty Thomas
Martin Sheen, Christian Slater, Sharon
Stone, Robert Foxworth, F. Murray Abraham,
Olivia D'Arbo

Biehn, Michael (1956-)

American actor who, after appearances
in such films as *Coach*, *Grease*, *The
Fan* and *The Lords of Discipline*,
hitched a ride to semi-stardom in director James Cameron's *The Terminator*,
in which he played Kyle Reese. Further
associations with Cameron followed,
along with leading roles in the likes of
Navy SEALS, *K-2*, *Timebomb*,
Tombstone and *Jade*. In 1978 he
appeared in the TV series *The
Runaways*.

Genre credits:

The Terminator (1984), *Aliens* (1986), *The
Abyss* (1989), *Deep Red* (1994 – TVM),
Asteroid (1997 – TVM)

Big 👽👽

USA 1988 102m DeLuxe Dolby

A 13-year-old boy wishes himself older,
only to find himself trapped inside the
body of a 30-year-old as a consequence.

Bright and agreeable age-reversal
comedy which keeps moving and provides a fair quota of easy laughs. A
popular box office success. A Broadway
musical later followed.

p: Robert Greenhut, James L. Brooks for
TCF/Gracie/American Entertainment
Partners II
w: Gary Ross, Anne Spielberg
d: PENNY MARSHALL
ph: Barry Sonnenfeld
m: Howard Shore
ed: Barry Malkin
pd: Santo Loquasto
cos: Judianna Markovsky
sound: Les Lazarowitz
titles: Saul Bass

ch: Patricia Birch
TOM HANKS, Elizabeth Perkins, Robert
Loggia, John Heard, Jared Rushton, David
Moscow, Josh Clark, Mercedes Ruehl

Big Trouble in Little China

USA 1986 103m DeLuxe Panavision Dolby

A cross-country truck driver finds himself involved in a supernatural tong
war underneath San Francisco's
Chinatown.

An expensive but relentlessly noisy
amalgam of kung fu, action and special
effects, somewhat in the vein of
Ghostbusters and *Indiana Jones*, but
much worse than either. Something of
a miscalculation on the part of its
director.

p: Larry J. Franco for
TCF/Taft/Monash/Barish
w: Gary Goldman, David Z. Weinstein, W.
D. Richter
d: John Carpenter
ph: Dean Cundey
m: John Carpenter, Alan Howarth
ed: Mark Warner, Edward A. Warschilka,
Steve Markovich
pd: John L. Lloyd
cos: April Ferry
sp: Richard Edlund
sound: Thomas Causey
sound effects: William Hartman, Arthur R.
Milch
2nd unit d: Tommy Lee Wallace
2nd unit ph: Steve Poster
stunt co-ordinator: Terry Endoso
make-up effects: Steve Johnson
underwater ph: Jack Cooperman, Barry
Herron
Kurt Russell, Kim Cattrall, Dennis Dun,
James Hong, Victor Wong, Kate Burton,
Donald Li

Bigfoot

USA 1987 96m CFIcolor TVM

Two children and an anthropologist
encounter two Sasquatches in the
Oregon mountains.

Wholly unremarkable children's
adventure. Even *Harry and the
Hendersons* is better.

p: Michael S. McLean for Walt Disney
w: John Groves
d: Danny Huston
ph: Frank Flynn
m: Bruce Rowland
ed: Howard Kunin
ad: Cameron Birnie
cos: William Ware Theiss
sound: Donald F. Johnson
make-up effects: Robert J. Schiffer, Lance
Anderson
add ph: Harry Mathias
James Sloyan, Gracie Harrison, Adam Carl,
Candace Cameron, Joseph Maher

Bigfoot and the Hendersons

see Harry and the Hendersons

Biggles

GB 1986 92m Technicolor Dolby

A new York caterer finds himself
transported back in time to help a
daredevil aviator during World War
One.

Tame, misconceived attempt to
update the comic book hero. Doesn't
work at all.

p: Kent Walwin, Pom Oliver for Compact
Yellowbill/Tambarle
exec p: Adrian Scrope
w: John Groves, Kent Walwin
stories: Captain W. E. Johns
d: John Hough
ph: Ernest Vincze
m: Stanislas
ed: Richard Trevor

pd: Terry Pritchard
cos: Darryl Bristow
sp: David Harris
sound: Peter Pardoe, Paul Le Mare, Graham V. Harstone
stunt co-ordinator: Gerry Crampton
2nd unit d: Terry Coles
Neil Dickson, Peter Cushing (his last film), Alex Hyde-White, Fiona Hutchinson, Marcus Gilbert, William Hootkins

Bill and Ted's Bogus Journey

USA 1991 93m DeLuxe Dolby
Two evil robots are sent to replace metalhead heroes Bill and Ted.

Fitfully amusing though less spontaneous sequel to *Bill and Ted's Excellent Adventure*, its best sequence revolving round a spoof of the chess game in Bergman's *The Seventh Seal*.

p: Scott Kroopf for Columbia/Tri Star/Orion/Nelson Entertainment
w: Ed Solomon, Chris Matheson
d: Pete Hewitt
ph: Oliver Wood
m: David Newman
ed: David Finfer
pd: David L. Snyder
cos: Marie France
sp: Richard Yuricich
sound: Gene S. Cantamessa
Keanu Reeves, Alex Winter, Jeff Miller, David Carrera, Joss Ackland, William Sadler, George Carlin

Bill and Ted's Excellent Adventure

USA 1988 89m Technicolor Panavision Dolby
With the aid of a time-travelling telephone booth, two dim Valley boys travel through time to research their history project.

Mildly amusing romp which contained enough quirky touches to make it a hit with its intended audience. *Bill and Ted's Bogus Journey* followed in 1991.

p: Scott Kroopf, Michael S. Murphy, Joel Soisson for De Laurentiis Entertainment/Premier
exec p: Ted Field, Robert W. Cort
w: Chris Matheson, Ted Solomon
d: Stephen Herek
ph: Timothy Suhrstedt
m: David Newman
ed: Larry Bock, Patrick Rand
pd: Roy Forge Smith
cos: Jill Ohanneson
sp: Perpetual Motion Pictures
sound: Ed White
titles: Geoffrey K. Hull
stunt co-ordinator: Dan Bradley
Alex Winter, Keanu Reeves, George Carlin, Terry Camilleri, Dan Shor, Tony Steedman, Rod Loomis, Al Leong, Jane Wiedlin, Robert V. Barron, Clifford David, Hal Landon, Jr., Bernie Casey, Amy Stock-Poynton

Binder, Maurice (1925-1991)

Celebrated American title designer, long associated with the James Bond series (*Dr No, Thunderball, Live and Let Die, Octopussy, Licence to Kill,* etc.). Credit sequences by him can also be found in such diverse films as *Indiscreet, The Mouse That Roared, Charade, Fathom, The Private Life of Sherlock Holmes* and *The Sea Wolves*.

Genre credits:
The Mouse on the Moon (1963), Barbarella (1967), You Only Live Twice (1967), The Spy Who Loved Me (1977), Moonraker (1979)

Biroc, Joseph (1903-)

Long-serving American cinematographer, an Oscar winner (1974 – with Fred Koenekamp) for his work on *The Towering Inferno*. He has worked in most genres and his credits include such diverse films as *Run of the Arrow, Bwana Devil* (in 3D), *Bye Bye, Birdie, Viva Las Vegas, Blazing Saddles, Beyond the Poseidon Adventure* and *Airplane*, along with several for director Robert Aldrich (*The Flight of the Phoenix, Hush... Hush, Sweet Charlotte, The Killing of Sister George, The Legend of Lylah Clare, Too Late the Hero, The Longest Yard, All the Marbles* [aka *California Dolls*], etc.).

Genre credits:
Red Planet Mars (1952), Unknown Terror (1957), The Amazing Colossal Man (1957), Escape from the Planet of the Apes (1971), Airplane II: The Sequel (1982)

Bishop, Ed (1942-)

American actor, long in Britain, where he has popped up in a variety of films, though he is perhaps best known for playing Commander Edward Straker in the science fiction TV series *UFO*. His other film appearances include *The War Lover, Brass Target* and *Restless Natives*.

Genre credits:
The Mouse on the Moon (1963), 2001: A Space Odyssey (1968), Journey to the Far Side of the Sun (1969 – aka Doppelganger), Saturn Three (1980)

The Bishop's Wife

USA 1947 108m bw
An angel visits a selfish bishop who is neglecting his wife because of his fundraising activities.

Sentimental whimsy of the kind only Hollywood could produce and get away with. Just the thing for a cosy afternoon by the fireside. A remake, *The Preacher's Wife*, followed in 1996.

p: Samuel Goldwyn
w: Robert E. Sherwood, Leonardo Bercovici
novel: Robert Nathan
d: Henry Koster
ph: GREGG TOLAND
m: HUGO FRIEDHOFER
md: Emil Newman
ed: Monica Collingwood
ad: George Jenkins, Perry Ferguson
cos: Irene Sharaff
sp: John P. Fulton
sound: Fred Lau
CARY GRANT, Loretta Young, David Niven, Monty Woolley, James Gleason, Gladys Cooper, Elsa Lanchester, Sara Haden, Regis Toomey

Bissell, James D. (1951-)

American production designer who has worked on a handful of fairly large-scale projects, including several for director Steven Spielberg and his Amblin company.

Genre credits:
E. T. (1982), *Twilight Zone – The Movie* (1983), *The Last Starfighter* (1984), *The Boy Who Could Fly* (1986 – also 2nd unit d), *Harry and the Hendersons* (1987 – aka *Bigfoot and the Hendersons*), *Always* (1989), *The Rocketeer* (1991)

Bissell, Whit (1909-1996)

American bit part actor, remembered chiefly for his only leading role in *I Was a Teenage Frankenstein*. His other credits include *I Was a Teenage Werewolf*, *Monster on the Campus*, *Hud*, *Seven Days in May*, *Airport* and *Casey's Shadow*. He also popped up in the 60s TV series *Time Tunnel*.

Genre credits:
Lost Continent (1951), *The Atomic Kid* (1954), *The Creature from the Black Lagoon*

(1954), *Invasion of the Body Snatchers* (1956), *The Time Machine* (1960), *City Beneath the Sea* (1970 – aka *One Hour to Doomsday* – TVM), *Soylent Green* (1973)

The Black Cauldron

USA 1985 80m Technicolor Super Technirama

In mediaeval times, a young boy called Taran fights to prevent a magical black cauldron from falling into the grasp of the evil Horned King.

Technically adroit cartoon feature, much darker than the Disney norm. Consistently visually impressive, though the narrative could have withstood more attention. Despite its virtues, the film was a commercial disappointment at the time.

p: Joel Hale for Walt Disney/Silver Screen Partners II
exec p: Ron Miller
w: David Jonas, Ted Berman, Vance Gerry, Al Wilson, Richard Rich, Peter Young, Roy Morita, Joe Hale, Art Stevens, Rosemary Anne Sisson, Roy E. Disney
novel: Lloyd Alexander
d: Ted Berman, Richard Rich
m: Elmer Bernstein
ed: Jim Koford, Jim Melton, Armetta Jackson
voices: Grant Bardsley, John Hurt, Freddie Jones, Nigel Hawthorne, Susan Sheridan, Arthur Malet, John Byner, Lindsay Rich, Eda Reiss Merin, Gregory Levinson, Brandon Call, John Huston

The Black Hole

USA 1979 98m Technicolor Technovision Dolby

Explorers in space discover an enormous space station poised on the edge of a black hole. Investigation reveals it to be manned by a long-lost scientist and his menacing robot.

Slow moving but quite enjoyable re-

working of *20,000 Leagues Under the Sea*.

p: Ron Miller for Walt Disney
w: Jeb Rosebrook, Gerry Day
story: Jeb Rosebrook, Bob Barbash, Richard Landau
d: Gary Nelson
ph: Frank Phillips
m: JOHN BARRY
ed: Gregg McLaughlin
pd: PETER ELLENSHAW
cos: Bill Thomas
sp: Peter Ellenshaw, Art Cruickshank, Eustace Lycett, Danny Lee, Harrison Ellenshaw
sound: Herb Taylor, Henry A. Maffett
Maximillian Schell, Anthony Perkins, Yvette Mimieux, Robert Forster, Ernest Borgnine, Joseph Bottoms, Roddy McDowall (voice)

Blackbeard's Ghost

USA 1967 107m Technicolor

The ghost of Blackbeard the pirate materialises to help a group of old ladies save the hotel that he built.

Unassuming family fare with familiar Disney ingredients.

p: Bill Walsh for Walt Disney
w: Bill Walsh, Ben DaGradi
novel: Ben Stahl
d: Robert Stevenson
ph: Edward Colman
m: Robert F. Brunner
ed: Robert Stafford
ad: Carroll Clark, John B. Mansbridge
cos: Bill Thomas
sp: Eustace Lycett, Peter Ellenshaw, Robert A. Mattey
sound: Robert O. Cok, Dean Thomas
2nd unit d: Arthur J. Vitarelli
Peter Ustinov, Dean Jones, Elsa Lanchester, Suzanne Pleshette, Richard Deacon

The long-lost U.S.S. *Cygnus* hovers on the edge of a black hole in Disney's *The Black Hole*, the studio's flawed big budget response to *Star Wars*, which was actually little more than an outer space remake of their own *20,000 Leagues Under the Sea*.

Blade Runner

USA 1982 117m Technicolor Panavision Dolby

In 2019 Los Angeles, a hunter of murderous "replicants" meets his match in the form of a vicious android who has developed human feelings.

Good looking but (dare one say it) overrated blend of sci-fi and film *noir* which, despite good moments, long outstays its welcome. A director's cut, which clarifies some of plot's hazier points, surfaced in 1991 to general acclaim.

p: Michael Deeley, Ridley Scott for Warner/Blade Runner Partnership
w: Hampton Fancher, David People
story: Philip K. Dick
d: Ridley Scott
ph: Jordan Cronenweth
m: Vangelis
ed: Terry Rawlings
pd: LAWRENCE G. PAULL
cos: Charles Knode, Michael Kaplan
sp: DOUGLAS TRUMBULL, RICHARD YURICICH, DAVID DRYER
sound: Bud Alper
Harrison Ford, Rutger Hauer, Sean Young, Edward James Olmos, Emmett Walsh, Daryl Hannah

Blaisdell, Paul

American special effects technician who contributed to a handful of 50s low budgeters, including a couple of Corman quickies.

Genre credits:

It Conquered the World (1956 – sp), *Not of This Earth* (1956 – sp), *The Day the World Ended* (1956 – sp), *Invasion of the Saucer Men* (1957 – aka *The Invasion of the Hell Creatures* – co-sp)

Blast Off

see Rocket to the Moon

Blithe Spirit

GB 1945 96m Technicolor

As a result of holding a seance, a novelist and his second wife find themselves being haunted by the ghost of his first wife.

Classy rendition of a classic play, discreetly mounted in rich colour and superbly played by an excellent cast. Time has in no way diminished its ability to amuse.

p: Anthony Havelock-Allan for Two Cities/Cineguild
w: NOEL COWARD from his play
adaptation: David Lean, Anthony Havelock-Allan, Ronald Neame
d: DAVID LEAN
ph: RONALD NEAME
m: RICHARD ADDINSELL
md: Muir Mathieson
ed: Jack Harris
ad: C. P. Norman
cos: Hilda Collins Rahuis
sp: Tom Howard (aa)
sound: John Cooke, Desmond Dew
ass d: George Pollock
narrator: Noel Coward
REX HARRISON, KAY HAMMOND, CONSTANCE CUMMINGS, MARGARET RUTHERFORD (as Madame Arcati), Joyce Carey, Hugh Wakefield, Jacqueline Clark

Harrison Ford as Rick Deckard in a tense moment from Ridley Scott's *Blade Runner*.

The Blob

USA 1958 83m DeLuxe

A strange jelly-like substance from outer space grows to an enormous size and threatens an American township.

Standard 50s sci-fi/monster hokum, the most surprising thing about it being that it was shot in colour. Handling strictly routine. It was remade, by the same producer, in 1988.

p: Jack H. Harris for Tonylyn
w: Theodore Simonson, Kate Phillips
story: Irvine H. Millgate
d: Irwin S. Yeaworth, Jr
ph: Thomas Spalding
m: Ralph Carmichael
title song: Burt Bacharach
ed: Alfred Hillman
ad: William Jersey, Karl Karlson
sp: Bart Sloane
sound: Gottfried Buss, Robert Clement
Steve McQueen, Aneta Corseaut, Olin Howlin, Earl Rowe, Steve Chase

The Blob

USA 1988 92m Technicolor Ultra Stereo

The small American township of Arborville is threatened by a blob-like creature from outer space which absorbs its victims on contact.

Superior remake of the 50s schlock classic, with improved effects and slick production. Ideal video viewing.

p: Jack H. Harris, Elliott Kastner for Tri-Star
w: Chuck Russell, Frank Darabont
d: Chuck Russell
ph: Mark Irwin
m: Michael Hoenig
ed: Terry Stokes, Tod Feurman
pd: Craig Stearns
cos: Joseph Porro
sp: Lyle Conway, Hoyt Yeatman, Michael Fink
sound: Wayne Heitman, Stanley Kastner, Matthew Iadarola
make-up effects: Terry Gardner

titles: Dan Curry
stunt co-ordinator: Gary Hytnes
Kevin Dillon, Shawnee Smith, Donivan Leitch, Ricky Paull Goldin, Billy Beck, Candy Clark, Jeffrey de Munn, Del Close, Beau Billingslea, Art La Fleur

Block, Irving

American special effects technician and occasional producer, involved strictly at the low-budget end of the genre.

Genre credits:

Rocketship X-M (1950 – co-sp), *Unknown World* (1951 – p/ad/co-sp), *War of the Satellites* (1957 – co-sp), *The Invisible Boy* (1957 – co-sp), *Kronos* (1957 – co-sp/associate p), *The Thirty-Foot Bride of Candy Rock* (1959 – co-sp)

The Blue Bird

USA 1940 98m Technicolor/monochrome

A poor woodcutter's two young children pursue the bluebird of happiness in the past, the future and the Land of Luxury, only to find it in their own back yard.

Comparisons with MGM's *The Wizard of Oz* are inevitable, though here the results are rather colder and harder to like. Post-production editing has also left its mark, but the production itself is fine, and there are several interesting set pieces, such as the forest fire.

p: Gene Markey for TCF
w: Ernest Pascal, Walter Bullock
play: Maurice Materlinck
d: Walter Lang
ph: ARTHUR MILLER, RAY RENNEHAN
m: ALFRED NEWMNAN
ed: Robnert Bischoff
ad: RICHARD DAY, WIARD B. IHNEN
cos: Gwen Wakeling
sp: Fred Sersen
sound: E. Clayton Ward, Roger Heman

ch: Geneva Sawyer
Shirley Temple, Johnny Russell, GALE SONDERGAARD, Eddie Collins, Nigel Bruce, Jessie Ralph, Spring Byington, Sybil Jason, HELEN ERICSON, Russell Hicks, Al Shean, Cecilia Loftus, Scotty Beckett, Ann Todd

The Blue Bird

USA/USSR 1976 99m DeLuxe

Two young children search for the bluebird of happiness only to find it is in their own back yard all along.

Much heralded as the first American-Soviet production, this misconceived remake of the 1940 film suffers both from a soggy script and non-existent direction, with the starry cast looking suitably embarrassed. The lack of imagination makes itself felt from the start. A curiosity.

p: Paul Maslansky for TCF/Lenfilm
w: Hugh Whitemore, Alfred Hayes
play: Maurice Maeterlink
d: George Cukor
ph: Frederick A. Young, Ionas Gritzus
m: Andrei Petrov
ly: Tony Harrison
md: Irwin Kostal
ed: Ernest Walter
pd: Brian Wildsmith
cos: Edith Head
Elizabeth Taylor, Jane Fonda, Cicely Tyson, Avan Gardner, Todd Lookinland, Patsy Kensit, Will Geer, Mona Washbourne, George Cole, Richard Pearson, Robert Morley, Harry Andrews, Nadejda Pavlova, Margareta Terechova, Oleg Popov, Georgi Vitzin, Leoinid Nevedomsky

Bluth, Don (1938-)

American animation director who began as an animator for Walt Disney in 1956, for whom he contributed to such films as *Sleeping Beauty* (as an in-betweener), *Robin Hood*, *Pete's Dragon* and *The Rescuers*. He eventually became disillusioned with the studio's output and left to form his own company in 1979. He now works primarily in Eire, where his studio Sullavan Bluth is based, and has had hits with the likes of *An American Tale* and *The Land Before Time*, though several of his more recent projects have been met with indifference.

Genre credits:

The Small One (1977 – short – co-songs/p/d), *Pete's Dragon* (1977 – animation d), *The Secret of Nimh* (1982 – co-w/p/d), *An American Tale* (1986 – pd/co-p/d), *The Land Before Time* (1988 – co-p/d), *All Dogs Go to Heaven* (1989 – co-pd/co-p), *Rock-a-Doodle* (1990 – co-story/co-p/d), *A Troll in Central Park* (1994 – p/co-d), *Thumbelina* (1995 – w/co-p/d), *Anastasia* (1997 – co-p/co-d)

Boam, Jeffrey (1949–)

American writer with a penchant for high voltage action films, several of which became blockbusters. His credits include *Straight Time*, *The Dead Zone*, *The Lost Boys*, *Lethal Weapon 2* and *Lethal Weapon 3*.

Genre credits:

Innerspace (1987 – actor/co-w), *Indiana Jones and the Last Crusade* (1989 – w), *The Phantom* (1996 – w/co-p)

Body Snatchers

USA 1993 87m Technicolor Dolby
A young girl discovers that the military base her father is working at has been taken over by aliens from outer space.

Third version of the Jack Finney story and a surprisingly tolerable and inexplicit one, given its director.

p: Robert H. Solo for Warner
w: Stuart Gordon, Dennis Paoli, Larry Cohen
novel: JACK FINNEY

d: Abel Ferrara
ph: Bojan Bazelli
m: Joe Delia
ed: Anthony Redman
pd: Peter Jamison
cos: Margaret Mohr
sp: Phil Cory
sound: Michael Barosky
make-up effects: Thomas R. Burman, Bari Dreiband-Berman
2nd unit d/stunt co-ordinator: Phil Neilson
2nd unit ph: Henry Link
titles: R. Greenberg
Gabrielle Anwar, Terry Kinney, Meg Tilly, Reilly Murphy, Billy Wirth, Christine Elise, R. Lee Ermey, Forest Whitaker, Kathleen Doyle

The Body Stealers

GB 1969 91m colour
Aliens kidnap parachutists out on an exercise.

Weak grade Z science fiction which wastes a good cast.

p: Tony Tenser for Tigon/Sagittarius
w: Mike St. Clair, Pete Marcus
story: Mike St. Clair
d: Gerry Levy
ph: John Coquillon
m: Reg Tilsley
ed: Howard Lanning
ad: Wilfred Arnold
sp: Tom Howard
sound: Bob Peck, Hugh Strain
George Sanders, Maurice Evans, Neil Connery, Patrick Allen, Hilary Dwyer, Robert Flemyng, Allan Cuthbertson, Lorna Wilde, Michael Culver

Bond, James (007)

The superspy, created in print by Ian Fleming, first appeared on the big screen in 1962 in *Dr No*, in which he was played by Sean Connery. An immediate success, the film was followed with *From Russia with Love*,

Goldfinger, *Thunderball*, *You Only Live Twice*, *On Her Majesty's Secret Service* (starring George Lazenby as Bond), *Diamonds Are Forever* (Connery), *Live and Let Die* (Roger Moore), *The Man with the Golden Gun*, *The Spy Who Loved Me*, *Moonraker*, *For Your Eyes Only*, *Octopussy*, *A View to a Kill*, *The Living Daylights* (Timothy Dalton), *Licence to Kill* and *Goldeneye* (Pierce Brosnan). There have also been two "rogue" Bond movies, *Casino Royale* (with David Niven, among others) and *Never Say Never Again* (Connery). The films, fairly outlandish to begind with, have occasionally strayed into the realms of science fiction and fantasy (most notably *Moonraker*), and so for the sake of completeness, reviews of the following Bonds appear within this book.

Genre filmography:
Casino Royale (1967), *You Only Live Twice* (1967), *The Spy Who Loved Me* (1977), *Moonraker* (1979)

Boren, Lamar

American cinematographer specialising in underwater photography, in which capacity he has contributed to such films as *Around the World Under the Sea*, *Thunderball* and *The Spy Who Loved Me*.

Genre credits:
Brewster McCloud (1970 – co-ph), *The Neptune Factor* (1973 – aka *The Neptune Disaster* – co-ph), *The Amazing Captain Nemo* (1978 – TVM – ph)

Borgnine, Ernest (1915-)

Bulky American actor, equally adept with heavy roles and sympathetic characters. He won a best actor Oscar for playing the title role in *Marty* (1955), after which he appeared in all manner of films, among the better ones being *The Vikings*, *The Dirty Dozen*, *Ice Station Zebra*, *The Poseidon Adventure*, *The Devil's Rain* and *The Prince and the Pauper*, whilst on television he has appeared in such series as *Future Cop* and *Air Wolf.*

Genre credits:

The Neptune Factor (1973 – aka *The Neptune Disaster*), *Future Cop* (1976 – aka *Cleaver and Haven* – TVM), *The Cops and Robin* (1978 – TVM), *The Black Hole* (1979), *Escape from New York* (1981)

Bottin, Rob (1959-)

American make-up effects designer, an Academy Award winner for his work on *Total Recall* (1990). A former assistant to Rick Baker on such films as *Squirm*, *Star Wars*, *Tanya's Island* and *The Fury*, he began his solo career with Joe Dante's *Piranha*, which led to several other collaborations with the director, including *Explorers* and *Inner Space*. It was his work on Dante's *The Howling* and, more importantly, John Carpenter's superb remake of *The Thing*, that finally confirmed his status as one of the industry's most talented and sought-after make-up effects artists. His other credits include *Rock 'n' Roll High School*, *Airplane*, *The Witches of Eastwick*, *Bugsy* and *Basic Instinct.*

Genre credits:

King Kong (1976 – assistant), *Star Wars* (1977 – assistant), *Tanya's Island* (1980 – assistant), *The Thing* (1982), *Twilight Zone – The Movie* (1983), *Legend* (1985), *Explorers* (1985), *Robocop* (1987), *Innerspace* (1987), *Total Recall* (1990), *Robocop 2* (1990), *Toys* (1992), *Robocop 3* (1993), Robocop (1994-TVM)

Bowie, David (1947-)

Highly successful British pop star and songwriter (real name David Robert Jones) who has appeared in a handful of films, most notably *Just a Gigolo*, *The Hunger*, *Merry Christmas*, *Mr. Lawrence* and *Absolute Beginners.* Perhaps his best role was as the alien Thomas Jerome Newton in *The Man Who Fell to Earth* (1976). His only other genre film is *Labyrinth* (1986).

Bowie, Les (1913-1979)

Busy British special effects technician, an Oscar winner for *Superman* (1978 – with Colin Chilvers, Denys Coop, Derek Meddings, Roy Field and Zoran Perisic). He worked on a good many of Hammer's films (*The Curse of Frankenstein*, *The Curse of the Werewolf*, *The Plague of the Zombies*, *The Mummy's Shroud*, *The Satanic Rites of Dracula*, etc.), his main task usually being to disintegrate Dracula. He also worked on a wide variety of other projects, including *The Red Shoes*, *The Assassination Bureau* and *Star Wars*. Began his career as a scenic artist, which led to his first film, *The School for Secrets* (aka *Secret Fight*) in 1946. His first Hammer film was *The Quatermass Experiment* in 1956, for which he was given a budget of just £30!

Genre credits:

The Quatermass Experiment (1955 – aka *The Quatermass Xperiment/ The Creeping Unknown* – sp), *X – The Unknown* (1956 – co-sp), *The Trollenberg Terror* (1957 – aka *The Crawling Eye* – sp), *The Day the Earth Caught Fire* (1961 – sp), *The City Under the Sea* (1965 – sp), *She* (1965 – co-sp), *Fahrenheit 451* (1966 – sp), *One Million Years B. C.* (1966 – co-sp), *Casino Royale* (1967 – co-sp), *Quatermass and the Pit* (1967 – aka *One Million Years to Earth* – sp),

Star Wars (1977 – co-sp), *Superman* (1978 – co-sp)

The Boy Who Could Fly

USA 1986 114m DeLuxe Dolby

A neighbourhood newcomer discovers that the boy next door has the ability to fly.

Long, slow, sentimental fantasy which will have most video users reaching for the fast-forward button.

p: Gary Adelson, Steve Poster for TCF
w/d: Nick Castle
ph: Adam Hollender
m: Bruce Broughton
ed: Patrick Kennedy
pd/2nd unit d: Jim Bissell
cos: Trish Keating
sp: Richard Edlund
sound: Robert Young
titles: Dan Curry
Jay Underwood, Lucy Deakins, Bonnie Bedelia, Fred Savage, Colleen Dewhurst, Fred Gwynne, Jason Priestley, Louise Fletcher

The Boys from Brazil

USA 1978 124m DeLuxe

An ageing Nazi hunter uncovers Dr. Mengele's ingenious plot to reconquer the world through the cloning of Adolf Hitler.

Smartly made and performed suspense thriller with excellent passages and intriguing plot developments.

p: Stanley o'Toole, Martin Richards for ITC/Producer Circle
exec p: Lew Grade
w: Heywood Gould
d: FRANKLIN J. SCHAFFNER
ph: Henri Decae
m: JERRY GOLDSMITH
ed: Robert E. Swink
pd: Gil Perrando

ad: Peter Lamont
cos: Anthony Mendleson
sp: Roy Wybrow
sound: Derek Ball
GREGORY PECK, LAURENCE OLIVIER , Lilli Palmer, Steve Guttenberg, Uta Hagen. Denholm Elliott, Rosemary Harris, John Dehner, John Rubinstein, Anne Meara, David Hurst, Michael Gough, Prunella Scales, Jeremy Black, Bruno Ganz, Walter Gotell, Wolf Kohler

The Boy Who Turned Yellow

GB 1972 57m colour

Whilst travelling home from school on the underground one day, a young boy suddenly turns yellow for no apparent reason.

This juvenile fantasy marked the last teaming of Powell and Pressburger and is a lamentable reduction of two major talents. Absolutely horrendous.

p: Roger Cherrill for Children's Film Foundation
w: Emeric Pressburger
d: Michael Powell
ph: Christopher Challis
ed: Peter Boita
Mark Dightman, Robert Eddison, Helen Weir, Brian Worth, Esmond Knight, Laurence Carter

The Boy with Green Hair

USA 1948 82m Technicolor

When a young boy learns that his parents have been killed in the war his hair turns green.

Sugary allegorical fantasy, poorly done and quite hard to sit through.

p: Stephen Ames for RKO
exec p: Dore Schary
w: Ben Barzman, Alfred Lewis Levitt
story: Betsy Beaton
d: Joseph Losey

ph: George Barnes
m: Leigh Harline
ed: Frank Doyle
ad: Albert S. D'Agostino, Frank Berger
Dean Stockwell, Pat O'Brien, Robert Ryan, Barbara Hale, Richard Lyon, Regis Toomey

Boyle, Peter (1933-)

Respected American character actor, memorable in such films as *Joe*, *The Candidate*, *Slither*, *Young Frankenstein* (in which he played the Monster), *FIST* and *Hammett*. He has also popped up in the occasional science fiction film, most notably as the bad guy Sheppard in Peter Hyams' *Outland*.

Genre credits:
Outland (1981), *Morons from Outer Space* (1985), *Solar Crisis* (1990), *The Shadow* (1994), *The Santa Clause* (1994)

Bradbury, Ray (1922-)

Respected science fiction and fantasy writer who began writing in 1939 with *Futuria Fantasia*, a fan magazine which he also created. Began writing short stories in 1941, the first of which was *Pendulum*. Several hundred further short stories followed, along with a handful of novels, among them *The Martian Chronicles*, *Fahrenheit 451*, *The Illustrated Man* and *Something Wicked This Way Comes*. Several of his books and stories have been adapted for film and television, though the results have been variable. He has also contributed to a small number of screenplays down the decades, including *Moby Dick*, which he co-wrote with John Huston.

Genre credits:
The Beast from 20 000 Fathoms (1953 – original story), *It Came from Outer Space* (1953 – story), *Fahrenheit 451* (1966 –

novel), *The Illustrated Man* (1969 – stories), *The Martian Chronicles* (1980 – TVM – novel), *Something Wicked This Way Comes* (1983 – w/novel), *Little Nemo: Adventures in Slumberland* (1990 – concept)

Bradley, David

American action star, familiar from the Cyborg Cop series (except for *Cyborg Cop III*).

Genre credits:
Cyborg Cop (1993), *Cyborg Cop II* (1994), *Cyborg Soldier* (1995)

Brady, Scott (1924-1985)

American general purpose actor (real name Gerald Tierney), the brother of actor Lawrence Tierney. A former boxer, he turned to acting after naval service during World War Two and made his screen debut in 1947 in *Born to Kill* (aka *Lady of Deceit*). Subsequent film work unremarkable, among them *Nightmare in Wax*, *Five Bloody Graves*, *The Night Strangler* (TVM), *The China Syndrome* and *The Winds of War* (TVM).

Genre credits:
Destination Inner Space (1966), *Journey to the Centre of Time* (1967), *Marooned* (1969), *The Mighty Gorga* (1970)

The Brain from Planet Arous

USA 1958 71m bw

A giant floating brain from outer space takes over the mind of a nuclear scientist.

Ludicrous schlocker in which initial amusement is quickly replaced by tedium.

p: Jacques Marquette for Howco/Marquette

w: Ray Buffam
d: Nathan Hertz
ph: Jacques Marquette
m: Walter Greene
ed: Irving Schoenberg
ad: no credit given
sound: Philip Mitchell
John Agar, Joyce Meadows, Robert Fuller, Tom Browne Henry, Henry Travis, Tim Graham

Brainstorm

USA 1983 101m Metrocolor Super Panavision Dolby
A scientific institution develops a process by which brain patterns can be recorded and experienced by other people – including death itself.

A promising idea, dully executed, and further hampered by the death of its female star in mid-production.

p: Douglas Trumbull for MGM/UA/JF
w: Robert Stitzel, Philip Frank Messina
story: Bruce Joel Rubin
d: Douglas Trumbul
ph: Richard Yuricich
m: James Horner
ed: Edward Warschilka, Freeman Davies
pd: John Vallone
cos: Donfeld
sp: E. E. G.
sound: Art Rochester
2nd unit ph: Robin Haagensen
Christopher Walken, Natalie Wood, Louise Fletcher, Donald Hotton, Cliff Robertson, Jordan Christopher, Bill Morey, Alan Fudge, Joe Dorsey

Brazil 🛸

GB 1985 142m Technicolor Dolby
Somewhere in the 20th century, a put-upon process worker frantically searches for the girl of his dreams.

Relentless, visually cluttered satire on Orwell's *1984* (originally to have been titled *1984 ½*). Frequently imagi-native, but too offbeat for widespread success, though now a cult item in some circles.

p: Arnon Milchan, Patrick Cassaretti for Embassy International/Handmade Films
w: Terry Gilliam, Tom Stoppard, Charles McKeown
d: Terry Gilliam
ph: Roger Pratt
m: Michael Kamen
ed/2nd unit d: Julian Doyle
pd: NORMAN GARWOOD
cos: James Acheson
sp: George Gibbs, Richard Conway
sound: Bob Doyle, Paul Carr
sound ed: Rodney Glen
stunt co-ordinator: Bill Watson
JONATHAN PRYCE, Robert de Niro, Katherine Helmond, Ian Holm, Ian Richardson, Peter Vaughan, Kini Greist, Bryan Pringle, Holly Gilliam, Don Henderson, Harold Innocent, John Grillo

Brenda Starr

USA 1987 87m CFI Dolby
A cartoonist finds himself involved in the comic strip adventures of his creation, a girl reporter out to track down a Nazi scientist who has invented a rocket.

Though completed in 1987, this spoof of 30s newspaper movies didn't see the light of day until 1992. Watching it, one can understand why. Based on a comic strip by Dale Messick, the character previously appeared in a 1945 serial (played by Joan Woodbury) and a 1976 TV movie (played by Jill St. John).

p: Myron A. Hyman for AM/PM/Brenda Starr/Tribune/Investment Empire
exec p: John D. Backe, Alan H. Lambos
w: Noreen Stone, James David Buchanan, Jenny Wolking
story: Noreen Stone, James David Buchanan

d: Robert Ellis Miller
ph: Freddie Francis
m: Johnny Mandell
ed: Mark Melnick
pd: John J. Lloyd
cos: Bob Mackie
sp: Joseph A. Unsinn
sound: Thomas Brandau
2nd unit ph: Tom Paul Hoppe
stunt co-ordinator: Victor Paul
Animation/titles: Gary Gutierrez
Brooke Shelds, Diana Scarwid, Jeffrey Tambor, June Gable, Tom Aldredge, Matthew Cowles, Charles Durning,. Eddie Albert, Henry Gibson, Ed Nelson, Tom Peck, Timothy Dalton

Bresslaw, Bernard (1933-1993)

Tall, gormless-looking British comedy actor, familiar on television in *The Army Game* (filmed as *I Only Arsked*) and in the *Carry On* films (*Carry On, Cowboy, Carry On Screaming, Carry On, Doctor, Carry On Camping, Carry On, Matron*, etc.). Occasionally popped up in cameo roles in such films as *Up Pompeii, Vampira* and *One of Our Dinosaurs is Missing*.

Genre credits:
Jabberwocky (1977), *Hawk the Slayer* (1980), *Krull* (1983)

Brewster McCloud

USA 1970 105m Metrocolor Panavision
A young man determines on flying in the Houston Astrodome, but his strange ambition leads to tragedy.

Would-be way-out fantasy which never quite hits its mark. One or two lunatic moments for Altman devotees, but the film, which followed the director's huge commercial and critical success with *M*A*S*H*, was a flop.

p: Lou Adler for MGM/Adler-Phillips

w: Doran William Cannon
d: Robert Altman
ph: Lamar Boren, Jordan Cronenweth
m: Gene Page
songs: John Phillip and others
ed: Louis Lombardo
ad: George W. Davis, Preston Ames
sound: Harry W. Tetrick, William McCaughey
wing design: Leon Erickson
2nd unit ph: Don McClendon
Bud Cort, Sally Kellerman, Shelley Duvall, Rene Auberjonois, Michael Murphy, William Windom, Margaret Hamilton, John Schuck, Stacy Keach

---

Bricusse, Leslie (1931-)

British composer, lyricist and screenplay writer, a best song Oscar winner for *Talk to the Animals* from *Doctor Dolittle* (1967) and best songscore winner for *Victor/Victoria* (1982 – with Henry Mancini). He has written the lyrics for two Bond title songs (*Goldfinger* [with Anthony Newley] and *You Only Live Twice*, along with the unused Mr. Kiss Kiss Bang Bang from *Thunderball*) and such stage and film musicals as *Charley Moon*, *Stop the World I Want to Get Off*, *Goodbye, Mr. Chips*, *Sherlock Holmes* and *Jekyll & Hyde*. He has also contributed lyrics to such films as *Revenge of the Pink Panther*, *That's Life*, *Home Alone* and *Home Alone 2: Lost in New York*.

Genre credits:
Doctor Dolittle (1967 w/songs), *You Only Live Twice* (1967 – ly), *Scrooge* (1970 – w/songs), *Willy Wonka and the Chocolate Factory* (1971 – co-songs), *Superman* (1978 – ly), *Santa Claus: The Movie* (1985 – ly), *Babes in Toyland* (1986 – TVM – co-songs), *Hook* (1991 – ly), *Tom and Jerry: The Movie* (1992 – ly)

Brigadoon ☺

USA 1954 108m Anscolor Cinemascope
Two American tourists get lost on the Scottish moors and come across a ghost village that only appears every hundred years.

Tired and flatly directed musical fantasy via a Broadway success, further hampered by artificial sets, restricted action and the cumbersome use of Cinemascope.

p: Arthur Freed for MGM
w: Alan Jay Lerner from his musical play
d: Vincente Minnelli
ph: Joseph Ruttenberg
m: FREDERICK LOWE
ly: Alan Jay Lerner
md: Johnny Green
ed: Albert Akst
ad: Cedric Gibbons, Preston Ames
cos: Irene Sharaff
sp: Warren Newcombe
sound: Wesley C. Miller
ch: Gene Kelly
Gene Kelly, Van Johnson, Cyd Charisse, Jimmy Thompson, Barry Jones, Eddie Quillan, Elaine Stewart

---

Britannia Hospital ☺☺

GB 1981 111m Technicolor
A London hospital is besieged by demonstrators on the day of a royal visit, whilst inside a mad doctor is creating the perfect being.

Savagely funny satire in which nothing is held sacred, including royalty, the government, unions and the national health service. Certainly worth a look for those who can take it. The third of Sherwin and Anderson's Mick Travis films, it was preceeded by *If...* and *O, Lucky Man!*

p: David Bellings, Clive Parsons for EMI/Filmland General
w: DAVID SHERWIN
d: LINDSAY ANDERSON
ph: Mike Fash

m: Alan Price
ed: Michael Ellis
pd: Norris Spencer
cos: Ian Hickinbotham
sp: George Gibbs
sound: Bruce White, Hugh Strain
make-up effects: Nick Malley
LEONARD ROSSITER, Brian Pettifer, John Moffatt, GRAHAM CROWDEN, Foulton Mackay, Vivian Pickles, Jill Bennett, Barbara Hicks, Peter Jeffrey, Marsha Hunt, Catherine Wilmer, Mary Maclead, Joan Plowright, Robin Askwith, MARCUS POWELL, Dave Atkins, Malcolm McDowell (as Mick Travis), Mark Hamill, Frank Grimes, Peter Machin, John Bett, Gladys Crosbie (as H. R. H. The Queen Mother), Dandy Nichols, Brian Glover, Mike Grady, Roland Culver, Arthur Lowe, Alan Bates, T. P. McKenna, Michael Medwin, Moyra Fraser

---

Broccoli, Albert R. (Cubby) (1909-1996)

Fondly regarded American producer who, with one-time partner Harry Saltzman, produced the James Bond films, going solo with the series in 1977 with *The Spy Who Loved Me*. Prior to this he was partnered with producer Irving Allen with whom he produced such movies as *The Black Knight*, *Fire Down Below* and *The Trials of Oscar Wilde* through their own independent production company Warwick.

Genre credits:
The Gamma People (1955 - co-ph), *You Only Live Twice* (1967 – co-p), *Chitty Chitty Bang Bang* (1968 – p), *Moonraker* (1979 – p)

Brodine, Norbert (1893-1970)

American cinematographer whose career began in the silent period with such films as *Almost a Husband*, *The Invisible Power* and *The Sea Hawk*.

His sound films include *Whistling in the Dark*, *Made on Broadway*, *Libeled Lady*, *The House on 92nd Street*, *Kiss of Death*, *Boomerang* and several for producer Hal Roach, including *Merrily We Live*, *Swiss Miss*, *Of Mice and Men*, *Road Show* and the Topper series. He retired in 1952.

Genre credits:
Topper (1937), *Topper Takes a Trip* (1939), *Turnabout* (1940), *One Million B.C.* (1940 – aka *Man and His Mate/The Cave Dwellers*), *Topper Returns* (1941)

Broughton, Bruce (1945-)

American composer, a graduate of USC where he studied under film composer David Raksin. Began his professional career scoring television series, including episodes of *Hawaii Five-O*, *Quincy* and *Dallas*. He began scoring films in the early 80s, his score for *Silverado* helping to move him up onto the A-list. His other credits include *The Monster Squad*, *The Presidio*, *Homeward Bound: The Incredible Journey* and *Tombstone*.

Genre credits:
Ice Pirates (1984), *Young Sherlock Holmes* (1985 – aka *Young Sherlock Holmes and the Pyramid of Fear*), *Harry and the Hendersons* (1987 – aka *Bigfoot and the Hendersons*), *Moonwalker* (1988), *The Rescuers Down Under* (1990), *Honey, I Blew Up the Kid* (1992)

Browning, Ricou (1930–)

American stuntman and second unit director, a former Olympic swimmer who specialises in underwater sequences, such as for *Flipper* and *Around the World Under the Sea*. He also played the Gill Man in Universal's three *Creature* movies.

Genre credits:
The Creature from the Black Lagoon (1954), *Revenge of the Creature* (1955), *The Creature Walks Among Us* (1956)

Bruns, George (1913-)

American composer who worked almost exclusively for Walt Disney in the 50s, 60s and early 70s. He scored many of the studio's live action films as well as a handful of their cartoon features. Non-fantasy scores include *Davy Crockett*, *Follow Me, Boys* and *The Horse in the Grey Flannel Suit*.

Genre credits:
Sleeping Beauty (1959), *One Hundred and One Dalmatians* (1960), *The Absent-Minded Professor* (1961), *Babes in Toyland* (1961), *The Sword in the Stone* (1963), *Son of Flubber* (1963), *The Jungle Book* (1967), *The Love Bug* (1967), *The Aristocats* (1970), *Robin Hood* (1973), *Herbie Rides Again* (1974)

Brynner, Yul (1915-1985)

Bald Russian-born actor, long in America, where he scored a hit playing the King of Siam in the Broadway musical *The King and I*, which won him a best actor Oscar for the 1956 film version. He also played the role on TV in the series *Anna and the King*. Memorable in such films as *Anastasia*, *The Magnificent Seven* and *The Double Man*, he is also known to genre fans for playing the killer cowboy in *Westworld* (1973), a role he revived for the sequel, *Futureworld* (1976).

Buck Rogers

USA 1939 12x20m episodes bw
Having been preserved in ice for 500 years, Captain Buck Rogers emerges to combat the evil Killer Kane.

Enjoyable serial escapades on similar lines to *Flash Gordon*, this is one of the best remembered examples of its kind. Its chapter headings include *Primitive Urge*, *Revolt of the Zuggs* and *Bodies without Minds*.

p: Barney A. Sarecky for Universal
w: Norman S. Hall, Ray Trampe
d: Saul Goodkind, Forde Beebe
ph: Jerome Ash
md: Charles Previn
ed: Alvin Todd, Louis Backlin, Joseph Glick
ad: Ralph Lacy
sound: Bernard B. Brown
Larry Buster Crabbe, Cosntance Moore, Jackie Moran, Anthony Warde, Jack Milhall

---

Buck Rogers in the 25th Century

USA 1978 96m colour TVM
Captain Buck Rogers is awakened after 500 years in suspended animation only to find himself pitted against an evil princess who wishes to take over the earth.

Lively update of the popular science fiction serial which led to a successful television series. The pilot was also released theatrically outside America with a new title sequence.

p: Richard Coffey for Universal
exec p: Glen Larson
w: Glen Larson, Leslie Stevens
d: Daniel Haller
ph: Frank Beascoechea, Leonard J. South
m: Stu Phillips
ed: John J. Dumas, Bill Martin, David Howe
ad: Paul Peters
cos: Jean-Pierre Dorleac
sp: Bud Ewing, Jack Faggard, Wayne Smith, David Garber

sound: Andrew Gilmore, John R. Carter, Clyde Sorensen
sound effects: Peter Berkos
GIL GERRARD, Pamela Hensley, Erin Gray, Henry Silva, Tom O'Connor, Joseph Wiseman, Duke Butler, Mel Blanc (voice only)

Buechler, John

American make-up effects artist working chiefly for producer Charles Band (*Ghoulies*, *Ghoulies 2*, *Demon Toys*, etc.). He has also directed several low-budget genre entries, also for *Band*.

Genre credits:
Android (1982 – sp), *Dungeonmaster* (1983 – co-d), *Zone Troopers* (1984 – sp), *Trancers* (1984-sp), *Troll* (1986 – d), *From Beyond* (1986 -co-sp), *Dinosaur Island* (1994 – sp)

The Bulldog Breed

GB 1960 97m bw
An incompetent joins the navy and ends up in outer space.
　Painful star comedy with no redeeming features.
p: Hugh Stewart for Rank
w: Jack Davies, Henry Blythe, Norman Wisdom
d: Robert Asher
ph: Jack Asher
m: Philip Green
ed: Gerry Hambling
ad: Harry Pottle
cos: Anthony Mendleson
sound: John M. Mitchell
Norman Wisdom, Ian Hunter, Liz Fraser, John le Mesurier, David Lodge, Robert Urquhart, Edward Chapman, Terence Alexander, Michael Caine, Oliver Reed, Eddie Byrne, Peter Jones, Sidney Tafler, Penny Morrell

Burns, George (1896-1996)

American comedian (real name Nathan Birnbaum) who, after experience in Vaudeville, went on to success on radio, television and in the movies, making a highly successful comeback at the age of 79, winning a best supporting actor Oscar for his work in *The Sunshine Boys* (1975). Remembered for his teaming with his wife, Gracie Allen, and for puffing on a cigar whilst telling jokes, he was one of comedy's all-time greats, and was still working just prior to his death at the age of 100. His early film credits include *The Big Broadcast*, *International House*, *The Big Broadcast of 1936* and *A Damsel in Distress*, whilst later he appeared in *Sergeant Pepper's Lonely Hearts Club Band*, *Just You and Me, Kid* and *Going in Style*, though he is perhaps best rembered for playing God in three gentle fantasies.

Genre credits:
Oh God! (1977), *Oh God – Book Two* (1980), *Oh God, You Devil* (1984), *18 Again!* (1988)

Burton, Tim (1960-)

American director with a penchant for lavish fantasy subjects. Began his career as a Disney animator after which he turned to direction with several shorts, including *Vincent* (1982), *Hansel and Gretel* (1983) and *Frankenweenie* (1984). His first feature, *Pee Wee's Big Adventure*, followed in 1985, the success of which led to *Beetlejuice* and the first *Batman* film. His other directorial credits include the delightful *Ed Wood*.

Genre credits:
The Fox and the Hound (1981 – animator), *The Black Cauldron* (1985 – conceptual artist [ideas not used]), *Hansel and Gretel* (1982 –

short – d), *Aladdin and His Wonderful Lamp* (1984 – short – d), *Batman* (1989 – d), *Edward Scissorhands* (1990 – story/d), *Batman Returns* (1992 – co-p/d), *The Nightmare Before Christmas* (1993 – aka *Tim Burton's Nightmare Before Christmas* – co-p/story), *Batman Forever* (1995 – co-p), *James and the Giant Peach* (1996 – co-p), *Mars Attacks!* (1996 – co-p/d)

Burtt, Ben

American sound designer, sound effects editor and sound effects technician (real name Benjamin Burtt, Jr.) who has won Oscars for his ground-breaking work on *Star Wars* (1977), *Raiders of the Lost Ark* (1981 – with Richard L. Anderson), *E.T.* (1982 – with Charles L. Campbell) and *Indiana Jones and the Last Crusade* (1989 – with Richard Hyams).

Genre credits:
Star Wars (1977 – sound effects), *The Empire Strikes Back* (1980 – co-sound effects), *Raiders of the Lost Ark* (1981 – co-sound effects editing), *E.T.* (1982 – co-sound effects ed), *Return of the Jedi* (1983 – sound), *Indiana Jones and the Temple of Doom* (1984 – co-sound), *Willow* (1988 – co-sound), *Indiana Jones and the Last Crusade* (1989 – co-sound/co-sound effects ed)

Butrick, Merrit (1960-1989)

American actor, best remembered for playing Captain Kirk's son David in both *Star Trek II: The Wrath of Khan* (1982) and *Star Trek III: The Search for Spock* (1984). He also appeared in such 80s films as *Zapped*, *When the Bough Breaks* and *Shy People* before succumbing to AIDS.

Caan, James (1939-)

Burly-looking American star actor, familiar from such films as *The Godfather*, *Freebie and the Bean*, *The Gambler*, *Funny Lady*, *Misery* and *Honeymoon in Vegas*. Occasional genre credits.

Genre credits:

Countdown (1968), *Rollerball* (1975), *Alien Nation* (1988), *Dick Tracy* (1990)

Cahn, Edward L. (1899-1963)

American director, a former editor at Universal, where he became their editor in chief in 1926. Turned to direction in 1931 with *Homicide Squad*. Directed several low budget sci-fi and horror films in the 50s, among them *Voodoo Woman*, *The Zombies of Mora Tau* (aka *The Dead That Walk*), *The Curse of the Faceless Man* and *The Four Skulls of Jonathan Krane*.

Genre credits:

The Creature with the Atom Brain (1955), *The She-Creature* (1956), *Invasion of the Saucer Men* (1957 – aka *The Invasion of the Hell Creatures*), *It! The Terror from beyond Space* (1958), *Invisible Invaders* (1959)

California Man

see Encino Man

Cameron, James (1954-)

Canadian writer (*Rambo: First Blood Part Two*), producer and director of high-octane action thrillers, though he began rather more humbly as an art director for Roger Corman on such films as *Battle Beyond the Stars*. His directorial debut was the much derided *Piranha II: The Flying Killers* (aka *Piranha 2: The Spawning*) in 1983, though luckily he followed this with the first *Terminator* film a year later. His other films include *True Lies*, *Titanic* and an executive producer credit on *Point Break*.

Genre credits:

Battle Beyond the Stars (1980 – co-ad), *The Terminator* (1984 – co-w/d), *Aliens* (1986 – co-w/d), *The Abyss* (1989 – w/d), *Terminator 2: Judgement Day* (1991 – co-w/d), *Strange Days* (1995 – co-w/co-p)

Cannom, Greg

American make-up effects artist, an Oscar winner for *Bram Stoker's Dracula* (1992 – with Michele Burke and Matthew W. Mungle) and *Mrs. Doubtfire* (1993 – with Ve Neill and Yolanda Toussieng). His other credits include *Curtains*, *A Nightmare on Elm Street Part 3: The Dream Warriors*, *The Lost Boys*, *The Pit and the Pendulum*, *Exorcist III*, *Hoffa*, *Heaven and Earth* and *The Man Without a Face*.

Genre credits:

Cocoon (1985), *Cocoon: The Return* (1988), *Captain America* (1989), *Meridian* (1990 – aka *Kiss of the Beast*), *Crash and Burn* (1990), *Flatliners* (1990), *Hook* (1991), *Star Trek VI: The Undiscovered Country* (1991),

Writer-director James Cameron observes the action on the set of *The Abyss*.

Forever Young (1992), *The Mask* (1994), *The Puppet Masters* (1994), *The Shadow* (1994), *Space Truckers* (1997)

Cannon, Danny (1968-)

British director who, after the very modest success of *The Young Americans* in 1993, found himself at the helm of the megabudget *Judge Dredd* (1995), which didn't quite make the waves expected of it at the box office.

The Canterville Ghost

USA 1943 95m bw

A young heiress discovers her castle ghost to be not so fierce after all.

Mild fantasy comedy, remembered chiefly for its performances rather than any sparkle in the script or handling. TV movie remakes followed in 1986 (with John Gielgud) and 1996 (with Patrick Stewart).

p: Arthur Field for MGM

w: Edwin Blum

novel: Oscar Wilde

d: Jules Dassin

ph: Robert Planck

m: George Bassman

ed: Chester W. Schaeffer

ad: Cedric Gibbons, Edward Carfagno

cos: Irene Sharaff, Valles

sound: Douglas Shearer

CHARLES LAUGHTON, MARGARET O'BRIEN, Robert Young, William Gargan, Rags Ragland, Peter Lawford, Una O'Connor, Mike Mazurki

---

Capricorn One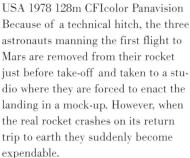

USA 1978 128m CFIcolor Panavision

Because of a technical hitch, the three astronauts manning the first flight to Mars are removed from their rocket just before take-off and taken to a studio where they are forced to enact the landing in a mock-up. However, when the real rocket crashes on its return trip to earth they suddenly become expendable.

Far-fetched but streamlined and cleverly plotted all-star action thriller with smart dialogue and plenty of pace and narrative drive.

p: Paul N. Lazarus III for ITC/Associated General/Capricorn One Associates

exec p: Lew Grade

w/d: PETER HYAMS

ph: Bill Butler

m: JERRY GOLDSMITH

ed: James Mitchell

pd: Albert Brenner

cos: Patricia Norris

sp: Henry Millar, Jr., Henry Millar, Sr., Bob Spurlock, Bruce Mattox

sound: Jerry Jost, Bill Manooch, Arthur Piantadosi, Lester Fresholtz, Michael Minkler

stunt co-ordinator: Bill Hickman

titles: Dan Perri

Elliott Gould, James Brolin, Brenda Vaccaro, Sam Waterston, O. J. Simpson, Hal Holbrook, Telly Savalas, Karen Black, David

Huddleston, David Doyler, Robert Walden, James Sikking

Capshaw, Kate (1953-)

American actress (real name Katherine Nail) who came to note as Willie Scott in *Indiana Jones and the Temple of Doom*, and went on to marry its director Steven Spielberg. Her other credits include *Black Rain* and *Love Affair*. Subsequent film appearances now more occasional.

Genre credits:

Dreamscape (1984), *Indiana Jones and the Temple of Doom* (1984), *Spacecamp* (1986)

Captain America

USA 1989 97m Eastmancolor Dolby

Frozen during World War Two, Captain America thaws out in the present day where he takes on The Red Skull.

Cheap but not cheerful comic strip adventures. In fact, pretty abysmal. It was preceeded by two unrelated but equally unmemorable TV movies: *Captain America* (1978) and *Captain America II: Death Too Soon* (1979 - aka *The Return of Captain America*), both of which starred Reb Brown.

p: Menahem Golan for 21st Century/Jadran/Castle/Marvel

exec p: Stan Lee, Joseph Calamar

w: Stephen Tolkin

story: Stephen Tolkin, Lawrence J. Block

comic strip: Joe Simon, Jack Kirby

d: Albert Pyun

ph: Philip Alan Waters

m: Barry Goldberg

ed: David Reale

pd: Douglas Leopard

cos: Heidi Kaczenski

sp: Fantasy II

sound: Pat Ciccione Jr., Frank Montalno, Ron Hitchcock

make-up effects: Greg Cannom

Matt Salinger, Darren McGavin, Ronny Cox, Ned Beatty, Michael Nouri, Melinda Dillon, Bill Mumy, Francesca Neri, Kim Gillingham

---

Captain Nemo and the Underwater City

GB 1969 106m Metrocolor Panavision

The survivors of a shipwreck are rescued by frogmen and taken to an underwater city, presided over by one Captain Nemo.

Mild fantasy adventure which needed more energy in its handling.

p: Bertram Ostrer for MGM/Omnia

exec p: Steven Pallos

w: Pip Baker, Jane Baker, R. Wright Campbell

novel: Jules Verne

d: James Hill

ph: Alan Hume

m: Walter Scott

md: Marcus Dods

ed: Bill Lewthwaite

ad: Bill Andrews

cos: Olga Lehmann

sp: Jack Mills, George Gibbs, Richard Conway

sound: A. W. Watkins, Cyril Swern, Bob Jones

underwater ph: Egil Woxholt

Robert Ryan, Chuck Connors, Nannette Newman, Bill Fraser, Kenneth Connor, John Turner, Allan Cuthbertson, Luciana Paluzzi

---

Captain Sinbad

USA/Ger 1963 88m Eastmancolor Wonderscope

Sinbad deposes a wicked sultan and saves a beautiful princess.

Lively but rather silly escapades, let down by uncertain handling and poor effects. Younger audiences may enjoy the antics.

p: Frank King, Herman King for King Brothers

w: Samuel B. West, Harry Relis
d: Byron Haskin
ph: Gunther Senftleben
m: Michel Micheley
md: Kurt Graunke
ed: Robert Swink
ad: Werner and Isabel Schlicting
cos: Harry Haynes, Tina Swanson, Ingrid Winter
sp: Tom Howard, Lee Zavitz, Audie Lohmann
sound: Walter Ruhland
ch: Gene Reed
Guy Williams, Pedro Armendariz, Heidi Bruhl, Abraham Sofaer

The Care Bears Movie

USA 1985 75m colour
In the land of Care-a-Lot, the Care Bears' attempts to make the world a happier place to live in are almost thwarted by an evil spirit.

Uninspired cartoon feature with animation on the Saturday morning level. It was followed by *The Care Bears Movie II: A New Generation* (1986) and *The Care Bears' Adventure in Wonderland* (1987).

p: Michael Hirsch, Patrick Loubert, Clive Smith for Samuel Goldwyn
exec p: Carole MacGillvcay, Robert Unkel, Jack Chojnacki
w: Peter Sauder
d: Arna Selznick, Charles Bonifacio
songs: John Sebastian, Carole King
m: Patricia Cullen
voices: Mickey Rooney, Jackie Burroughs, Harry Dean Stanton, Besen Thrasher, Georgia Engel

Carfagno, Edward C. (c 1907-1996)

American art director, long at MGM, winning Oscars for his work there on *The Bad and the Beautiful* (1952 – with Cedric Gibbons), *Julius Caesar* (1953 – with Cedric Gibbons) and *Ben-Hur* (1959 – with William A. Horning). His other credits include such major productions as *Quo Vadis?*, *The Cincinnati Kid*, *The Hindenburg* and several for director Clint Eastwood (*Sudden Impact*, *Tightrope*, *Pale Rider*, *Heartbreak Ridge*, *Bird*, *Pink Cadillac*, etc.).

Genre credits:
The Canterville Ghost (1944 – co-ad), *Neptune's Daughter* (1949 – co-ad), *The Wonderful World of the Brothers Grimm* (1962 – co-ad), *Earth II* (1971 – TVM – co-ad), *Soylent Green* (1973 – ad), *Demon Seed* (1977 – pd), *Meteor* (1979 – pd), *Time After Time* (1979 – pd), *All of Me* (1984 – pd)

Carlos, Wendy (1941-)

American composer, formerly Walter Carlos, who has provided synth scores for a couple of Stanley Kubrick pictures – *A Clockwork Orange* (1971), *The Shining* (1980) – as well as for *Tron* (1982).

Carlson, Richard (1912-1977)

American actor and occasional director (*Four Guns to the Border*, *Appointment with a Shadow* [aka *The Big Story*], etc.) who progressed from juvenile roles. Much stage work as well as appearances in such films as *The Ghost Breakers*, *The Little Foxes*, *King Solomon's Mines* and *The Maze*.

Genre credits:
Beyond Tomorrow (1940), *It Came from Outer Space* (1953), *Riders to the Stars* (1953 – also d), *The Magnetic Monster* (1953), *The Creature from the Black Lagoon* (1954), *The Power* (1967), *The Valley of Gwangi* (1969)

Carousel

USA 1956 128m DeLuxe Cinemascope 55
A shy girl marries a carnival barker who then goes to the bad trying to provide for her and their child. Killed, he is later granted leave from heaven to see how they both are doing.

Tediously flat and unimaginative fantasy musical from the stage success, with very little in the way of style or excitement to relieve the boredom. For staunch Rodgers and Hammerstein fans only.

p: Harry Ephron for TCF
w: Phoebe Ephron, Henry Ephron
play: Ferenc Molnar
d: Henry King
ph: Charles G. Clarke
m: RICHARD RODGERS
ly: Oscar Hammerstein II
md: Alfred Newman, Ken Darby
ed: William Reynolds
ad: Lyle Wheeler, Jack Martin Smith
cos: Mary Willis, Charles le Maire
sp: Ray Kellog
sound: Bernard Frederick, Harry M. Leonard
ch: Rod Alexander, after Agnes de Mille
Gordon MacRae, Shirley Jones, Cameron Mitchell, Gene Lockhart, Barbara Ruick, Robert Rounseville

Carpenter, John (1948-)

American writer, producer, composer and director who, in the late 70s, helped to establish the low budget stalk and slash genre with the hugely successful *Halloween*. A graduate of California's film school, where he made the Oscar-winning short *The Resurrection of Broncho Billy* in 1970, which led to the making of his first feature, *Dark Star*. The siege drama *Assault on Precinct 13* followed and established him as a talent to watch, though the success of *Halloween* saw him subsequently tied mostly to the horror genre. Other credits include *Elvis* (TVM), *Christine*, *Prince of Darkness* and *In the Mouth of Madness*. His remake of *The Thing*, critically reviled on its release, is now considered a genre classic.

Genre credits:

Dark Star (1974 – p/co-w/m/d), *Escape from New York* (1981 – co-w/d), *The Thing* (1982 – d), *Halloween III – Season of the Witch* (1983 – co-p/co-m), *The Philadelphia Experiment* (1984 – exec p), *Starman* (1984 – d), *Big Trouble in Little China* (1986 – m/d), *They Live* (1988 – co-m/d), *Memoirs of an Invisible Man* (1992 – d), *Village of the Damned* (1995 – co-m/d), *Escape from L.A.* (1996 – co-w/co-m/d)

Director John Carpenter (right) explains what he wants from Kurt Russell during the filming of *Escape from New York*, the second of their five films together.

Carradine, John (1906-1988)

Prolific American actor (real name Richmond Reed Carradine), known primarily for his horror roles, among them appearances in *The Invisible Man*, *The Black Cat*, *The Bride of Frankenstein*, *The Hound of the Baskervilles*, *House of Frankenstein* (as Dracula), *House of Dracula* (as Dracula) and *The Howling*, plus many more less worthy of his talents. The father of David, Keith and Robert Carradine, he made his film debut in *Tol'able David* in 1930 (using the name John Peter Richmond, which he kept for his first few films). Given his preponderance for horror films, he occasionally strayed into the realms of science fiction and fantasy. When not filming, he often toured America with a series of Shakespeare readings.

Genre credits:

The Unearthly (1957), *The Story of Mankind* (1957), *The Cosmic Man* (1958), *Invisible Invaders* (1959), *The Wizard of Mars* (1965), *The Fiend with an Electronic Brain* (1967), *The Astro-Zombies* (1968), *The Man with the Synthetic Brain* (1969), *Creatures of the Prehistoric Planet* (1970 – aka *Horror of the Blood Monsters/Horror Creatures of the Prehistoric Planet/Vampire Men of the Lost Planet*), *Moonchild* (1972), *1 000 000 A.D.* (1973), *Stowaway to the Moon* (1974 – TVM), *Missile X* (1978), *The Secret of Nimh* (1982 – voice), *Ice Pirates* (1984), *Prison Ship 20905* (1985 – aka *Prison Ship Star Slammer*), *Peggy Sue Got Married* (1986)

Carras, Anthony

American editor with many Corman horrors to his credit, among them *A Bucket of Blood*, *House of Usher* (aka *The Fall of the House of Usher*), *The Pit and the Pendulum* and *X – The Man with X-Ray Eyes*.

Genre credits:

The Last Woman on Earth (1960), *Master of the World* (1961), *Panic in Year Zero* (1962)

Carreras, Michael (1927-1994)

British producer, executive producer, writer, director and, for Hammer Films, studio head, who worked his way up through the ranks from the publicity department. Either produced or executive produced most of the studio's classic horrors (*The Curse of Frankenstein*, *Dracula*, *The Mummy*, *The Brides of Dracula*, etc.). He also wrote using the pen names Henry Younger and Michael Nash.

Genre credits:

Quatermass 2 (1957 – aka *Enemy from Space* – exec p), *The Damned* (1963 – aka *These Are the Damned* – exec p), *She* (1965 – p), *One Million Years B. C.* (1966 – w/p), *Slave Girls* (1968 – aka *Prehistoric Women* – d/w [w as Henry Younger]), *The Lost Continent* (1968 – p/d/w [w as Michael Nash]), *Creatures the World Forgot* (1970 – w/p)

Carrey, Jim (1962-)

Rubber-faced Canadian-born comic actor whose rise to stardom via such films as *Club Med*, *Finders Keepers*, *Once Bitten* and *Pink Cadillac* was somewhat slow, though he more than made up for it following the unexpected success of *Ace Ventura: Pet Detective*. Regarded by many as the new Jerry Lewis, his other credits include *Dumb and Dumber*, *Ace Ventura: When Nature Calls* and *The Cable Guy*.

Genre credits:
Peggy Sue Got Married (1986), *Earth Girls Are Easy* (1989), *The Mask* (1994), *Batman Forever* (1995 – as The Riddler), *Liar, Liar* (1997)

Carruth, Milton

American editor, long with Universal, where he cut some of their great horror classics, among them *Dracula*, *The Mummy*, *Murders in the Rue Morgue* and *Dracula's Daughter*.

Genre credits:
Francis (1949), *Francis Goes to West Point* (1952), *It Grows on Trees* (1952), *Francis in the Haunted House* (1953), *Francis in the Navy* (1955), *I've Lived Before* (1956), *The Brass Bottle* (1963 – co-ed)

Carter, Maurice

British production designer who, with art director Bert Davey, contributed to several of the fantasy films of producer John Dark and director Kevin Connor in the 70s.

Genre credits:
Mr Drake's Duck (1950 – ad), *The Land That Time Forgot* (1974 -pd), *At the Earth's Core* (1976 – pd), *The People That Time Forgot* (1977 – pd)

Carter, Rick

American production designer with several credits for director Robert Zemeckis to his name, among them *Death Becomes Her* and *Forrest Gump*.

Genre credits:
Back to the Future Part II (1989), *Back to the Future Part III* (1990), *Jurassic Park* (1993), *The Lost World: Jurassic Park* (1997)

Casino Royale

GB 1967 130m Technicolor Panavision
Sir James Bond is called out of retirement to eliminate a vast crime organisation, but does not reckon with the schemes of his nephew, Jimmy Bond.

More often silly than funny, this expensive and elaborate all-star spoof is very much a case of too many cooks and was far from the box office success its producer envisaged. Despite its excesses (which include a finale involving a flying saucer), some of it does work, and it remains of passing interest as a relic of its times.

p: Charles K. Feldman, Jerry Bresler, John Dark for Columbia/Famous Artists
w: Wolf Mankowitz, John Law, Michael Sayers
novel: Ian Fleming
d: John Huston, Ken Hughes, Val Guest, Robert Parrish, Joe McGrath
ph: JACK HILDYARD
add ph: JOHN WILCOX, NICOLAS ROEG
m: BURT BACHARACH
ly: Hal David
ed: Bill Lenny
pd: MICHAEL STRINGER
ad: John Howell, Ivor Beddoes, Lionel Couch
cos: JULIE HARRIS
sp: Cliff Richardson, Les Bowie, Roy Whybrow
sound: John W. Mitchell, Sahs Fisher, Robert Jones
2nd unit d: Richard Talmadge, Anthony Squire

ch: Tutte Lemkow
titles: RICHARD WILLIAMS
David Niven, Peter Sellers, Orson Welles, Deborah Kerr, Ursula Andress, William Holden, Charles Boyer, Joanna Pettet, Daliah Lavi, Kurt Kaszaner, Jacqueline Bisset, Derek Nimmo, George Raft, Ronnie Corbett, Peter O'Toole, Anna Quayle, Bernard Cribbins, John Wells, Richard Wattis, Jean-Paul Belmondo, Duncan Macrae, Geoffrey Bayldon, John le Mesurier, Eric Chitty

Casper

USA 1995 100m DeLuxe DTS stereo
A "ghost therapist" and his young daughter are hired by a scheming heiress to rid a mansion of ghosts so that she can search for the treasure supposedly hidden there.

Fitfully amusing spook comedy whose expensive visual effects help to compensate for the sparsity of plot. It was based on a cartoon character who had popularity in both theatrical shorts in the 40s and 50s (*The Friendly Ghost*, *Casper Comes to Clown*, *Casper's Birthday*, etc.) and a TV series in the 60s. *Casper, A Spirited Beginning* followed in 1997.

p: Colin Wilson for Universal/ Amblin/Harvey Entertainment Co
exec p: Steven Spielberg
w: Sherri Stoner, Deanna Oliver
comic strip: Joseph Oriolo
story: Joseph Oriolo, Seymour Reit
d: Brad Silberling
ph: Dean Cundey
m: James Horner
ed: Michael Kahn
pd: Leslie Dilley
cos: Rosanna Norton
sp: ILM, Dennis Murren, Michael Lantieri
sound: Gary Rydstrom, Charlie Wilborn
2nd unit ph: Ray Stella
stunt co-ordinator: Gary Hymes
Christina Ricci, Bill Pullman, Eric Idle, Cathy Moriarty, Malachi Pearson (voice, as

Casper), Dan Aykroyd, Clint Eastwood, Mel Gibson, Rodney Dangerfield

Casper – A Spirited Beginning

USA 1997 90m CFIcolor Dolby

Casper the friendly ghost goes to live with three grouchy spirits in a mansion threatened with being razed to the ground.

So-so prequel/sequel with passable effects though the script is strictly routine while the whole thing is all too obviously shot on the backlot.

p: Mike Elliott for TCF/Saban/The Harvey Entertainment Company
exec p: Haim Saban, Jeffrey A. Montgomery, Lance H. Robbins
w: Jymn Magon, Thomas Hurt
story: Thomas McClusky, Rob Kerchner
d: Sean McNamara
ph: Christian Sebalat
m: Udi Harpaz
ed: John Watts, John Gilbert
pd: Nava Arlan, Jay Vetter
sp: Ray McIntyre Jr, Scott Levy
add ph: Eric J. Swanson
Steve Guttenberg, Lori Loughlin, Rodney Dangerfield, Michael McKean. Brendon B Barrett, Richard Moll, James Earl Jones (voice) Pauly Shore (voice), Bill Farmer (voice), Jeremy Foley (voice as Casper)

Castle Keep

USA 1969 107m Technicolor Panavision

Seven American soldiers occupy a treasure-laden castle during World War Two and find themselves influenced by their surroundings.

Well enough crafted but otherwise rather pretentious and alienating fantasy which never really begins to warm one to its subject. A remake of sorts, *The Keep*, followed in 1983.

p: Martin Ransohoff, John Calley for

Columbia/Filmways
w: Daniel Taradash, David Rayfiel
novel: William Eastlake
d: Sydney Pollack
ph: Henri Decae
m: Michel Legrand
ed: Malcolm Cooke
ad: Rino Mondellini, Max Doug, Jacques Doug, Mort Rabinowitz
cos: Jacques Fonteray
sp: Lee Zavitz
2nd unit d: Ray Kellogg
titles: Phil Norman
Burt Lancaster, Peter Falk, Jean Pierre Aumont, Patrick O'Neal, Tony Bill, Al Freeman, Jr., Astrid Heeren, Bruce Dern, Scott Wilson

The Cat from Outer Space

USA 1978 103m Technicolor

A cat from outer space crash lands on earth and has to enlist human help in order to meet his mother ship in time.

'Close Encounters of the Furred Kind' might have been a better title for this mild live action romp in typical 70s Disney style. Fine for younger children.

p: Ron Miller, Norman Tokar for Walt Disney
w: Ted Key
d: Norman Tokar
ph: Charles F. Wheeler
m: Lalo Schifrin
ed: Cotton Warburton
ad: James B. Mansbridge, Preston Ames
cos: Chuck Keehne, Emily Sundby
sp: Eustace Lycett, Art Cruickshank, Danny Lee, Peter Ellenshaw
sound: Bud Maffett, Herb Taylor
2nd unit d: Arthur J. Vitarelli
2nd unit ph: Rexford Metz
stunt co-ordinator: Richard Warlock
Ken Berry, Sandy Duncan, Roddy McDowall, Harry Morgan, Jesse White, Hans Conreid, Alan Young, McLean Stevenson

Chaffey, Don (1917-1990)

British director on the international scene who began his career as an assistant in Gainsborough's art department in 1944, becoming an art director in his own right in 1946. He began directing in 1950 with the children's feature *The Mysterious Poacher*. Many more children's films followed (*Greyfriars Bobby*, *The Prince and the Pauper*, *The Magic of Lassie*, etc.), a good many of them for Disney's British arm. He also directed a couple of key fantasy films, most notably *Jason and the Argonauts*.

Genre credits:
Jason and the Argonauts (1963), *One Million Years B. C.* (1966), *Creatures the World Forgot* (1971), *Pete's Dragon* (1977), *CHOMPS* (1979)

Chain Reaction

USA 1996 102m Astrocolor Dolby

Scientists working on a top secret project to turn water into pollution-free fuel find their lives in peril, and two of them go on the run together.

Dumb, cliché-strewn star actioner with even dumber dialogue (at one point, an FBI officer says, "Police have just reported a disturbance at the science museum in front of the Neanderthal man exhibit!").

p: Arne L. Schmidt, Andrew Davis for TCF/Chicago Pacific
exec p: Richard D. Zanuck, Erwin Stoff
w: J.F. Lawton, Michael Bortman
story: Arne L. Schmidt, Rick Seaman, Josh Friedman
d: Andrew Davis
ph: Frank Tidy
m: Jerry Goldsmith
ed: Don Brochu, Dov Hoenig, Mark Stevens, Arthur Schmidt
pd: Maher Ahmad

cos: Jodie Tillen
sp: Nick Davis, Roy Arbogast, Digital Domain
sound: Robert R. Anderson, Jr.
stunt co-ordinator: Walter Scott
2nd unit d: Matt Earl Beesley
2nd unit ph: Michael A. Jones
Keanu Reeves, Rachel Weisz, Morgan Freeman, Fred Ward, Kevin Dunn, Brian Cox, Joanna Cassidy, Krzysztof Pieczynski

---

Challis, Christopher (1919-)

British cinematographer with several films for Michael Powell and Emeric Pressburger to his credit, among them *The Small Back Room*, *Tales of Hoffman*, *Gone to Earth* and *Oh, Rosalinda!* His other credits include *Sink the Bismarck*, *Those Magnificent Men in Their Flying Machines*, *Arabesque*, *Kaleidoscope*, *The Private Life of Sherlock Holmes*, *The Deep* and *Evil Under the Sun*. He began his film career in 1930 as a technician for Technicolor before becoming a fully fledged cameraman in 1947 with *End of the River*.

Genre credits:
Chitty Chitty Bang Bang (1968), *The Boy Who Turned Yellow* (1972), *The Little Prince* (1974)

Chambers, John

American make-up artist who won a special Oscar for his incredibly pliable make-up for *Planet of the Apes* (1967). He has also contributed prosthetic work to a number of other science fiction and fantasy films, as well as the horror film *Sssssss*.

Genre credits:
The Three Stooges in Orbit (1962), *The Human Duplicators* (1964), *Planet of the Apes* (1967), *Beneath the Planet of the Apes* (1969), *Escape from the Planet of the Apes* (1971), *Slaughterhouse Five* (1972 – co-make-up), *Battle for the Planet of the Apes* (1973), *The Island of Dr Moreau* (1977)

Charley & the Angel ☄

USA 1974 93m Technicolor

In 1933, a midwest store owner inadvertently defies death three times and finds an impatient angel waiting to escort him to heaven.

Pleasant period comedy, better than the mid-70s Disney norm.

p: Bill Anderson for Walt Disney
w: Roswell Rogers
novel: Will Stanton
d: Vincent McEveety
ph: Charles F. Wheeler
m: Buddy Baker
ed: Ray De Leuw, Bob Bring
ad: John B. Mansbridge, Al Roelofs
cos: Shelby Tatum
sp: Eustace Lycett, Art Cruickshank, Danny Lee
sound: Herb Taylor
2nd unit d: Christopher Heder
titles: Jack Boyd, John Jensen
Fred MacMurray, Cloris Leachman, Harry Morgan, Kurt Russell, Kathleen Cody, Liam Dunn, Barbara Nichols, Edward Andrews, Ed Begley, Jr.

Charlotte's Web

USA 1972 96m Technicolor

A spider encourages doomed farm animals to takes their destinies into their own hands (or should that be hooves?).

Tolerable animated feature with music, acceptable for younger audiences, though their parents may tend towards restlessness early on.

p: William Hanna, Joseph Barbara for Hanna Barbera/Sagittarius
w: Earl Hammer, Jr.
story: E. B. White
d: Charles Nichols, Iwao Takamoto

songs: Richard M. and Robert B. Sherman
md: Irwin Kostal
ed: Pat Foley
sound: Dick Ocean, Bill Getty, Joe Citarella
voices: Debbie Reynolds, Henry Gibson, Agnes Moorehead, Martha Scott, Paul Lynde, Rex Allen, Davy Maddern, Danny Bonaduce

---

Chew, Richard

American editor who, with Marcia Lucas and Paul Hirsch, won an Oscar for editing *Star Wars* (1977). His other genre credit is for *Late for Dinner* (1991, cut with Robert Leighton).

Children of the Damned 💩

GB 1964 91m bw

Scientific research reveals that the world's most intelligent children hail from another planet.

Acceptable follow-up to *Village of the Damned*, though the results aren't quite so effective the second time round.

p: Ben Arbeid for MGM
w: John Briley
d: Anton M. Leader
ph: Davis Boulton
m: Ron Goodwin
ed: Ernest Walter
ad: Elliot Scott
sp: Tom Howard
sound: A. W. Watkins, Dave Browne, J. B. Smith
Ian Hendry, Alan Badel, Barbara Ferris, Sheila Allen, Alfred Burke, Harold Goldblatt, Martin Miller, Ralph Michael, Bessie Love

---

Chilvers, Colin

British special effects technician, an Oscar winner for *Superman* (1978 – with Les Bowie, Denys Coop, Roy Field, Derek Meddings and Zoran Perisic). He has also co-directed one film, *Moonwalker*, and directed several episodes of the TV series *Superboy*.

Genre credits:

Moon Zero Two (1969 – co-sp), *The Rocky Horror Picture Show* (1975 – co-sp), *Superman* (1978 – co-sp), *Superman II* (1980 – co-sp), *Saturn Three* (1980 – co-sp), *Condorman* (1981 – co-sp), *Superman III* (1983 – co-sp), *Moonwalker* (1985 – co-d), *Follow That Bird* (1985 – co-sp)

Chitty Chitty Bang Bang ⏂⏂

GB 1968 145m Technicolor Super Panavision

An eccentric inventor rescues a derelict racing car for his two children, restores it and takes them on a magical adventure to a far-off land where children are forbidden.

Entertaining fantasy musical for all the family. A bit long, but bright and breezy enough to make it all very enjoyable. Harmless fun for young and old, it remains a television favourite.

p: Albert R. Broccoli for UA/Warfield/DFI
w: Roald Dahl, Ken Hughes, Richard Maibaum
novel: Ian Fleming
d: Ken Hughes
ph: CHRISTOPHER CHALLIS
songs: RICHARD M. AND ROBERT B. SHERMAN
md: IRWIN KOSTAL
ed: John Shirley
ad: KEN ADAM
cos: ELIZABETH HAFFENDEN, JOAN BRIDGE
sp: John Stears, Cliff Culley
sound: John Mitchell, Fred Hynes, Harry Miller, Les Wiggins
inventions: Rowland Emmett
ch: Marc Beaux, Dee Dee Wood
production associate: Peter Hunt
2nd unit d: Richard Taylor
2nd unit ph: Skeets Kelly, John Jordan

Dick Van Dyke (as Caractacus Potts), Sally Anne Howes (as Truly Scrumptious), ROBERT HELPMANN (as the Wicked Childcatcher), LIONEL JEFFRIES, GERT FROBE, James Robertson Justice, Benny Hill, Richard Wattis, Anna Quayle, ALEXANDER DORE, BERNARD SPEAR, Barbara Windsor, Arthur Mullard, Desmond Llewellyn, Adrian Hall (as Jeremy), Heather Ripley (as Jemima), Max Wall, Davy Kaye, Stanley Unwin, Victor Maddern, Michael Darbyshire

---

A Christmas Carol ⏂

USA 1938 69m bw

A miser reforms his ways after being visited by ghosts on Christmas Eve.

Tolerable version of tale retold many more times after this version. Also see under *Scrooge*.

p: Joseph L. Mankiewicz for MGM
w: Hugo Butler
novel: CHARLES DICKENS
d: Edwin L. Marin
ph: Sidney Wagner
m: Franz Waxman
ed: George Boemler
ad: Cedric Gibbons, John Detlie
cos: Valles
sound: Douglas Shearer
make-up: Jack Dawn
Reginald Owen, Gene Lockhart, Kathleen Lockhart, Leo G. Carroll, Lynne Carver, Terry Kilburn

---

A Christmas Carol ⏂⏂

USA/GB 1971 25m Technicolor

A miser reforms his ways after being visited by a number of ghosts on Christmas Eve.

Superior animated version of the oft told story with many points of visual interest. Alastair Sim previously played the same role in the 1951 film *Scrooge*.

p: Richard Williams for ABC (AA, BEST ANIMATED SHORT)

exec p: Chuck Jones
w: no credit given
novel: CHARLES DICKENS
d: RICHARD WILLIAMS
m: Tristam Cary
ed: Ben Rayner, Michael Crane
design: RICHARD PURDOM
sound: Malcolm Bristow
voices: Alastair Sim (as Scrooge), Michael Redgrave, Michael Hordern, Diana Quick, Joan Sims, Paul Whitsun-Jones, Melvyn Hayes

---

A Christmas Carol

USA 1984 96m Technicolor TVM Dolby

Ebenezer Scrooge repents his misely ways after a series of ghostly visitations on Christmas Eve.

Tolerable tele-version of the Yuletide favourite, though nothing special. Director Clive Donner previously edited the 1951 film *Scrooge*.

p: William F. Storke, Alfred R. Kelman for EP
exec p: Robert E. Fuisz
w: Roger O. Hirson
novel: CHARLES DICKENS
d: Clive Donner
ph: Tony Imi
m: Nick Bicat
md: Tony Britten
ed: Peter Tanner
pd: Roger Murray-Leach
cos: Evangeline Harrison
sp: Martin Gutteridge, Graham Longhurst
sound: David Crozier, Graham V. Hartstone
George C. Scott, Frank Finlay, Angela Pleasence, Edward Woodward, Michael Carter, David Warner, Susannah York, Anthony Walters

---

A Christmas Martian

Canada 1972 62m colour

Two children help a Martian whose flying saucer has broken down in their neighbourhood.

Poorly made and badly dubbed children's adventure.

p: Xerox
no other credits available

Cinderella

USA 1950 75m Technicolor

With a helping hand from her fairy godmother, Cinderella finally makes it to the palace ball.

Charming in patches, this animated version of the timeless Perrault classic fairy tale is let down chiefly by lacklustre scripting, though the wicked stepmother and the villainous cat are memorable characters. Not quite classic Disney.

p: Walt Disney
w: William Peed, Erdman Penner, Ted Sears, Winston Hibler, Homer Brightman, Harry Reeves, Ken Anderson, Joe Rinaldi
story: Charles Perrault
d: Wilfred Jackson, Hamilton Luske, Clyde Geronimi, Ben Sharpsteen
songs: Mack David, Jerry Livingston, Al Hoffman
m: Oliver Wallace, Paul J. Smith
ed: Donald Halliday
sound: C. O. Slyfield
voices: Ilene Woods, Eleanor Audley, Verna Felton, Rhoda Williams, Lucille Bliss, Luis Van Rooten, William Phipps

Cinderfella

USA 1960 91m Technicolor

A male Cinderella finally meets his princess.

Relentless star comedy which wastes a good production. For Lewis fans only.

p: Jerry Lewis for Paramount
w/d: Frank Tashlin
ph: Haskell Boggs
songs: Harry Warren, Jack Brooks
m/md: Walter Scharf
ed: Arthur P. Schmidt
ad: Hal Pereira, Henry Bumstead
cos: Edith Head, Sy Devore, Nat Wise

sp: John P. Fulton, Farciot
sound: Gene Merritt, Charles Grenzbach
ch: Nick Castle
Jerry Lewis, Judith Anderson, Ed Wynn (as the fairy godfather), Henry Silva, Robert Hutton, Maria Alberghetti, Count Basie and his Orchestra

The City Under the Sea

GB 1965 84m Eastmancolor Colorscope

A Victorian heiress is abducted by a madman who has lived in an undersea world for 100 years.

Childishly scripted but mildly endearing romp for younger viewers and their indulgent parents.

p: George Willoughby for AIP/Bruton
w: Charles Bennett, Louis M. Heyward, David Whittaker
d: Jacques Tourneur
ph: Stephen Dade
m: Stanley Black
ed: Gordon Hales
ad: FRANK WHITE
cos: Ernie Farrer
sp: Frank George, Les Bowie
sound: Ken Rawkins, C. Le Mesurier
underwater ph: John Lamb, Neil Ginger Gemmell
Vincent Price, David Tomlinson, Tab Hunter, Susan Hart, John le Mesurier, Henry Oscar, Tony Selby

City Beneath the Sea

USA 1970 96m colour TVM

In the year 2053, a planetoid threatens to wipe out a city under the Atlantic ocean.

Gaudy-looking science fiction piece which was released theatrically outside America. For confirmed addicts of this producer's hokum only.

p: Irwin Allen for Warner/Kent/Motion Picture International

w: John Meredith Lucas
d/story: Irwin Allen
ph: Kenneth Peach
m: Richard La Salle
ed: James Baiotto
ad: Roger E. Maus, Stan Jolley
cos: Paul Zastupnevich
sp: L. B. Abbott, Art Cruickshank, John C. Caldwell
sound: no credit given
Stuart Whitman, Robert Wagner, Rosemary Forsythe, Robert Colbert, Burr de Banning, Susana Miranda, Richard Basehart, Joseph Cotten, Paul Stewart, Whit Bissell, Tom Drake, Sheila Mathews, Sugar Ray Robinson, James Darren, Edward G. Robinson, Jr.

Clark, Carroll

American art director, long with RKO where he worked (often in association with department head Van Nest Polglase) on several of the Astaire-Rogers musicals, among them *Flying Down to Rio*, *The Gay Divorce*, *Top Hat*, *Roberta*, *Follow the Fleet* and *Swingtime*. He later moved to Disney, where he worked on several of their key live action films, most notably *Mary Poppins*, which earned him an Oscar nomination.

Genre credits:

King Kong (1933 – co-ad), *The Absent-Minded Professor* (1961 – ad), *Son of Flubber* (1962 – co-ad), *The Misadventures of Merlin Jones* (1963 – co-ad), *Mary Poppins* (1964 – co-ad), *The Monkey's Uncle* (1964 – co-ad)

Clarke, Arthur C. (1917–)

British scientist and science fiction novelist whose many works include *Childhood's End*, *The City and the Stars*, *The Sands of Mars*, *Rendezvous with Rama*, *The Sentinel* (the basis for *2001*, which he novelised), *2010: Odyssey Two* and *2061: Odyssey Three*. A graduate of King's College London, he helped to invent the first radar talk-down equipment whilst serving in the RAF during World War Two. He is also the inventor of the communications satellite. In the 80s he presented two TV series: *Arthur C. Clarke's Mysterious World* and *Arthur C. Clarke's World of Strange Powers*, thought it is for his story and script (which he wrote with Stanley Kubrick) for *2001: A Space Odyssey* for which he is best remembered by genre fans.

Genre credits:

2001: A Space Odyssey (1968 – novel/co-w), *2010: Odyssey Two* (1984 – novel/acting cameo [he can be spotted standing outside The White House early on in the film])

Clarke, Robert (1920-)

American actor who has also occasionally written, produced and directed. As an actor he has appeared in such films as *The Falcon in Hollywood*, *The Body Snatcher* and *Bedlam*.

Genre credits:

The Man from Planet X (1951), *3000 A.D.* (1952 – aka *Captive Women*), *The Astounding She-Monster* (1957 – aka *Mysterious Invader*), *The Hideous Sun Demon* (1959 – aka *Blood on His Lips* – also co-story/p/co-d), *Beyond the Time Barrier* (1960 – also p), *The Incredible Petrified World* (1960)

Clash of the Titans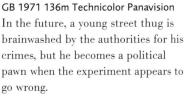

GB 1981 118m Metrocolor Dynamation Dolby

In order to win the hand of Andromeda, Perseus must first complete several tasks set for him by the goddess Thesis.

Expensive fantasy spectacular with a plethora of monsters and effects in the established Harryhausen manner. The script could certainly have stood more attention, as its elements are slackly assembled, but the trick effects make it palatable, and it went down well enough at the box office. A proposed sequel has yet to materialise.

p: Charles H. Schneer for MGM
w: Beverley Cross
d: Desmond Davis
ph: Ted Moore
m: LAURENCE ROSENTHAL
ed: Timothy Gee
pd: Frank White
cos: Emma Porteous
sp: RAY HARRYHAUSEN
sound: Robin Gregory
stunt co-ordinator: Ferdinando Poggi
Harry Hamlin, Burgess Meredith, Laurence Olivier (as Zeus), Judy Bowker, Maggie Smith, Ursula Andress, Sian Phillips, Jack Gwillim, Flora Robson, Freda Jackson, Donald Houston, Pat Roach, Tim Pigott-Smith, Susan Fleetwood

---

Cleave, Van

American composer with a handful of science fiction titles to his credit.

Genre credits:

The Conquest of Space (1955), *The Space Children* (1958), *Robinson Crusoe on Mars* (1964), *Project X* (1967)

A Clockwork Orange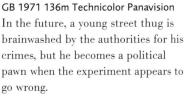

GB 1971 136m Technicolor Panavision

In the future, a young street thug is brainwashed by the authorities for his crimes, but he becomes a political pawn when the experiment appears to go wrong.

This much discussed and much banned film now seems about as dated as its view of the future and its electronic music score, whilst what points it has to make are both unsubtle and elementary. The scenes of rape and violence still leave a bad taste in the mouth, the humour is juvenile at best and the writer-director is working well below par. A tedious experience, the joke is very much on the audience.

p: Stanley Kubrick, Bernard Williams for Warner/Polaris/Kinner
exec p: Max L. Raab, Si Litvinoff
w/d: Stanley Kubrick
novel: Anthony Burgess
ph: John Alcott
m: Walter Carlos
ed: Bill Butler
pd: John Barry
cos: Milena Canonero
sound: John Jordan, Bill Rowe, Eddie Haben
sound ed: Brian Blamey
stunt co-ordinator: Roy Scammell
Malcolm McDowell, Michael Bates, Patrick Magee, Warren Clarke, Adrienne Corri, Miriam Karlin, Margaret Tyzack, Carol Drinkwater, Dave Prowse

---

The Cloning of Joanna May

GB 1991 2x74m colour TVM

A millionaire industrialist produces three clones of his former lover.

Initially intriguing but ultimately rather silly thriller, well enough made.

p: Gub Neal for Granada
exec p: Sally Head
w: Ted Whitehead
novel: Fay Weldon
d: Philip Saville
ph: Ken Morgan
m: Rachel Portman
ed: Chris Gill
pd: Stephen Fineren
cos: Catherine Cook
sound: Nick Steer, Brian Saunders
Patricia Hodge, Brian Cox, Billie Whitelaw, Siri Neal, Sarah Badel, Oliver Ford Davies,

Emma Hardy, Laura Eddy, Helen Adie

Close Encounters of the Third Kind 🛸🛸🛸

USA 1977 135m Metrocolor Panavision
Dolby

A series of UFO-related incidents in Indiana lead a surburban workman on an obsessive, intuitive trail to a pre-arranged landing site where he has a close encounter with benign aliens.

Ingeniously conceived science fiction fantasy adventure that becomes increasingly absorbing as it moves along (despite some tedious domestic sequences) and climaxes with an impressive light show in which man finally makes contact with benevolent beings from another world. An instant genre classic, it was also a box office bonanza. Not to be missed, especially in the original widescreen format.

p: Julia Phillips, Michael Phillips for Columbia/EMI
w/d: STEVEN SPIELBERG
ph: VILMOS ZSIGMOND (aa)
m: JOHN WILLIAMS
ed: MICHAEL KAHN
pd: Joe Alves, Jr.
cos: Jim Linn
sp: DOUGLAS TRUMBULL
sound: Gene Cantamessa
sound effects editing: Frank Warner (aa)
add ph: William A. Fraker, Douglas Slocombe, John Alonzo, Laszlo Kovacs, Steve Poster
stunt co-ordinator: Buddy Joe Hooker
titles: Dan Perri
RICHARD DREYFUSS, FRANCOIS TRUF-FAUT, Teri Garr, MELINDA DILLON, Bob Balaban, Lance Henriksen, Warren Kemmerling, Roberts Blossom, Phillip Dodds, CARY GUFFEY, Shawn Bishop, Adrienne Campbell, Justin Dreyfuss, Merrill Connally, George Di Cenzo, Carl Weathers

Close Encounters of the Third Kind: The Special Edition 🛸🛸

USA 1980 132m Metrocolor Panavision
Dolby

Curious attempt by Spielberg to refashion his 1977 blockbuster. Here, 16 minutes of the original footage have been excised (thus making parts of the plot confusing) and replaced by seven minutes of hitherto unused footage and a couple of extra domestic scenes (which add little to the proceedings). There's also a new ending which sees the Dreyfuss character inside the mother ship (which tends to detract from the sense of wonder and mysticism). Fans of the original may not like the changes, but first-time viewers will no doubt still enjoy the movie overall. A questionable idea, nevertheless.

new ph/sp: Robert Swarthe

Technicians and scientists wait to make their first contact with the aliens in Steven Spielberg's masterful *Close Encounters of the Third Kind*.

Clothier, William H. (1903–)

American cinematographer with several John Ford movies to his credit (*The Horse Soldiers*, *The Man Who Shot Liberty Valance*, *Cheyenne Autumn*, etc.). Began his career in 1923 as a camera assistant before going on to specialise in aerial photography, contributing to many films in this capacity throughout his career, most notably for the 1927 aerial spectacular *Wings*. His other credits include *Track of the Cat*, *The Alamo*, *Shenandoah*, *The War Wagon*, *Chisum* and *Rio Lobo*.

Genre credits:

Phantom from Space (1953), *Killers from Space* (1954), *Way, Way Out* (1966)

Cocoon 🛸🛸

USA 1985 117m DeLuxe Panavision Dolby
Aliens return to earth to retrieve several cocoons from the ocean bed, but their secret is discovered by the inhabitants of a nearby old folks' home who find the cocoons have rejuvenating properties.

Sentimental wish-fulfilment fantasy held together by strong ensemble playing and a few fresh ideas of its own.

p: Richard Zanuck, David Brown, Lili Fini Zanuck for TCF
w: Tom Benedek
story: David Saperstein
d: RON HOWARD
ph: Don Peterman
m: JAMES HORNER
ed: Michael Hill, Daniel Hanley
pd: Jack T. Collis
cos: Aggie Guerrard Rodgers
sp: Ken Ralston, Ralph McQuarrie, Scott Farrar, David Berry (aa)
sound: Richard Church
make-up effects: Greg Cannom, Rick Baker
stunt co-ordinator: Ted Grossman

Steve Guttenberg, Brian Dennehy, Don Ameche (aa), Wilford Brimley, Jessica Tandy, Hume Cronyn, Jack Gilford, Gwen Verdon, Maureen Stapleton, Herta Ware, Tahnee Welch, Barrett Oliver, Linda Harrison, Tyrone Power, Jr.

Cocoon: The Return 🛸

USA 1988 116m DeLuxe Dolby
The rejuvenated elders return with their friends from outer space to rescue some more cocoons, and some of them decide to remain on earth, even though their time left will be limited.

Pleasant sequel which, whilst not adding anything new of its own to the proceedings, passes the time quite adequately. It was, however, panned by the critics and subsequently did little business at the box office.

p: Richard Zanuck, David Brown, Lili Fini Zanuck for TCF/Zanuck-Brown
w: Stephen McPherson
story: Stephen McPherson, Elizabeth Bradley

d: Daniel Petrie
ph: Tak Fujimoto
m: James Horner
ed: Mark Roy Warner
pd: Lawrence G. Paull
cos: Jay Hurley
sp: Scott Farrar, ILM
sound: Hank Garfield, Gary Rydstrom
make-up effects: Greg Cannom
stunt co-ordinator: Artie Malesci
Don Ameche, Wilford Brimley, Jessica Tandy, Hume Cronyn, Jack Gilford, Steve Guttenberg, Maureen Stapleton, Barret Oliver, Elaine Stritch, Courtnay Cox, Gwen Verdon, Tahnee Welch, Tyrone Power, Jr., Brian Dennehy, Wendy Cooke, Herta Ware, Brian C. Smith, Mike Nomad, Linda Harrison

Colman, Edward (1905-)

American cinematographer, working almost exclusively for Disney, most notably on *Mary Poppins*. His few non-Disney credits include *Black*

Poster artwork for director Ron Howard's box office hit *Cocoon*.

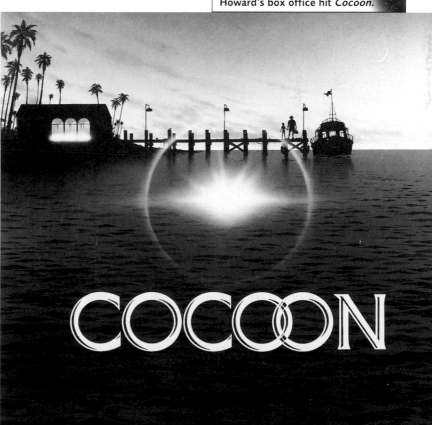

Patch and *Deadline Midnight*. Non-fantasy Disney credits include *Big Red*, *Those Calloways*, *That Darn Cat*, *The Ugly Dachshund* and *The Happiest Millionaire*.

Genre credits:
The Shaggy Dog (1959), *The Absent-Minded Professor* (1960), *Babes in Toyland* (1961), *Son of Flubber* (1962), *The Misadventures of Merlin Jones* (1963), *The Monkey's Uncle* (1964), *Mary Poppins* (1964), *The Gnome-Mobile* (1966), *The Love Bug* (1968)

Colossus: The Forbin Project
see The Forbin Project

The Colossus of New York

USA 1958 69m bw

The father of a famous scientist killed in an automobile accident transplants his son's brain into a robot.

Stupefyingly boring low budget science fiction dross.

p: William Alland for Paramount
w: Thelma Schnee
story: Willis Goldbeck
d: Eugene Lourie
ph: John F. Warren
m: Van Cleave
ed: Floyd Knudtson
ad: Hal Pereira, John Goodman
sp: John P. Fulton, Farciot Edouart
sound: John Wilkinson, Winston Leverett
Otto Kruger, Robert Hutton, Ross Martin, John Baragrey, Mala Powers

Columbia (Columbia-Tri Star)

Formed by Harry Cohn in 1924, this studio's fortunes were a little shaky at first, though in the 40s they gradually began to grow in stature. By the 50s/60s they were producing such blockbusters as *The Bridge on the River Kwai*, *Lawrence of Arabia*, *A Man for All Seasons* and *Oliver!*, all of which won Best Picture Oscars. The studio's science fiction output has been somewhat variable over the years, their crowning glory being Steven Spielberg's *Close Encounters of the Third Kind* in 1977. Their fantasy work is best represented by the films of stop-motion animator Ray Harryhausen which include such classics as *The Seventh Voyage of Sinbad*, *Mysterious Island* and *Jason and the Argonauts*.

Genre filmography:
The Lost Horizon (1937), *Mandrake the Magician* (1939 – serial), *Here Comes Mr. Jordan* (1941), *Batman* (1943 – serial), *The Monster and the Ape* (1945 – serial), *Superman* (1948 – serial), *Batman and Robin* (1949 – serial), *Atom Man vs. Superman* (1949 – serial), *Captain Video* (1951 – serial), *The 5000 Fingers of Dr. T* (1952), *The Lost Planet* (1953 – serial), *It Came from Beneath the Sea* (1955), *Earth vs. the Flying Saucers* (1956), *Twenty Million Miles to Earth* (1957), *The Seventh Voyage of Sinbad* (1958), *The Three Worlds of Gulliver* (1959), *Mysterious Island* (1961), *Jason and the Argonauts* (1963), *The First Men in the Moon* (1964), *Lost Horizon* (1973 – musical remake), *The Golden Voyage of Sinbad* (1974), *Sinbad and the Eye of the Tiger* (1977), *Close Encounters of the Third Kind* (1977), *Close Encounters of the Third Kind – The Special Edition* (1980), *Starman* (1984), *The Blob* (1988), *The Adventures of Baron Munchausen* (1989), *Last Action Hero* (1993), *Men in Black* (1997)

Coma

USA 1978 113m Metrocolor

A lady doctor discovers that patients are deliberately being put into comas so that their organs can later be sold on the black market by a sinister organisation.

Watchable variation on the frightened lady theme which, after a slowish build-up, provides its share of thrills.

p: Martin Erlichman for MGM
w/d: Michael Crichton
novel: Robin Cook (Michael Crichton)
ph: Victor J. Kemper, Gerald Hirschfeld
m: Jerry Goldsmith
ed: David Bretherton
pd: Albert Brenner
cos: Eddie Marks, Yvonne Kubis
sp: Joe Day
sound: Bill Griffith, William McCaughey, Michael J. Kohut, Aaron Rachin
Genevieve Bujold, Michael Douglas, Richard Widmark, Rip Torn, Elizabeth Ashley, Lois Chiles, Harry Rhodes, Tom Selleck, Ed Harris

Communion

USA 1990 101m DeLuxe Dolby

An account of author Whitley Streiber's supposedly true encounter with aliens on Christmas Day, 1985.

An unremarkable film which will fail to convert the sceptical. Critically mauled, it is little more than a home movie.

p: Philippe Mora, Whitley Streiber, Dan Allingham for Vestron/Pheasantry/Allied Vision/The Picture Property Co.
exec p: Paul Redshaw, Gary Barber
w: Whitley Streiber from his book
d: Philippe Mora
ph: Louis Irving
m: Eric Clapton, Allan Zavod
ed: Lee Smith
pd: Linda Pearl
cos: Melissa Daniel, Perry Ellis
sound: Bill Meredith
Christopher Walken, Lindsay Crouse, Joel Carlson, Frances Sternhagen, Andreas Katsulas, Basil Hoffman

The Computer Wore Tennis Shoes

USA 1970 91m Technicolor

A college student receives an electric shock whilst repairing a computer and gains superhuman knowledge in the process.

Artless Disney romp, rather typical of their live action output during this period.

p: Bill Anderson for Walt Disney
w: Joseph L. MacEveety
d: Robert Butler
ph: Frank Phillips
m: Robert F. Brunner
ed: Cotton Warburton
ad: John B. Mansbridge
cos: Chuck Keehne
sound: Robert O. Cook
2nd unit d: Arthur J. Vitarelli
Kurt Russell, Cesar Romero, Joe Flynn, William Schallert, Richard Bakalyan, Debbie Prine, Jon Provost, Alan Hewitt, Fritz Feld, Frank Webb, Bing Russell

Conan the Barbarian

USA 1981 124m Technicolor Todd-AO

When his parents are killed in a raid by a neighbouring clan, a young boy swears vengeance and grows up to become a great swordsman.

Good looking but overlong and stolidly handled sword and sorcery epic which also takes itself a little too seriously. Its box office success nevertheless helped to launch its muscleman star on the international scene. *Conan the Destroyer* followed in 1984.

p: Buzz Feitshans, Raffaella de Laurentiis for Dino de Laurentiis
exec p: Edward R. Pressman
w: John Milius, Oliver Stone
d: John Milius
ph: DUKE CALLAHAN
m: BASIL POLEDOURIS
ed: C. Timothy O'Meara

pd: RON COBB
cos: John Bloomfield
Arnold Schwarzenegger, James Earl Jones, Sandhal Bergman, Max Von Sydow, Ben Davidson, Cassandra Gauiola, Mako, Gerry Lopez

Conan the Destroyer

USA 1984 101m Technicolor Panavision

Conan is hired by an evil queen to escort a young princess on a dangerous journey, meeting all kinds of obstacles along the way, including a couple of monsters.

Good looking but often unintentionally funny sequel to *Conan the Barbarian*. Some of the dialogue has to be heard to be believed.

p: Raffaella de Laurentiis for Universal
exec p: Dino de Laurentiis, Edward R. Pressman, Stephen Kesten
w: Stanley Mann
story: Roy Thomas, Gerry Conway
d: Richard Flesicher
ph: JACK CARDIFF
m: Basil Poledouris
ed: Frank J. Urioste
pd: LUIGI BASILE
cos: JOHN BLOOMFIELD
sp: Carlo Rambaldi
Arnold Schwarzenegger, Grace Jones, Sarah Douglas, Wilt Chamberlain, Mako, Tracey Walter, Olivia D'Abo

Condorman

USA 1981 91m Technicolor Panavision Dolby

A comic strip artist tests out his hero's adventures in real life before putting them down on paper.

Misfiring spoof lacking any genuine originality.

p: Jan Williams for Walt Disney
exec p: Ron Miller
w: Marc Strurdivant, Glen Caron,

Mickey Rose
novel: Robert Sheckley
d: Charles Jarrott
ph: Charles F. Wheeler
m: Henry Mancini
ed: Gordon D. Brenner
pd: Albert Whitherick
cos: Kent James, Jean Zey
sp: Art Cruickshank, Colin Chilvers
sound: William Sivel
titles: Michael Sedenco
2nd unit d: Anthony Squire
2nd unit ph: Godfrey Godar
Michael Crawford, Oliver Reed, Barbara Carrera, Jean-Pierre Kalfon, James Hampton

Coneheads

USA 1993 84m DeLuxe Dolby

The Coneheads leave the planet Remulak on a mission, land on earth and find that they like the suburban lifestyle.

Fitfully amusing comedy derived from the old *Saturday Night Live* sketches. Not quite so bad as some critics would have us believe, but certainly no classic.

p: Lorne Michaels for Paramount
exec p: Michael Rachmil
w: Dan Aykroyd, Bonnie Turner, Terry Turner, Tom Davis
d: Steve Barron
ph: Francis Kenny
m: David Newman
ed: Paul Trejo
pd: Gregg Fonseca
cos: Marie France
Dan Aykroyd, Jane Curtin, Michael McKean, Jason Alexander, Laraine Newman, Lisa Jane Persky, Chris Farley, Michelle Burke, David Spade, Jan Hooks, Ellen Degeneres, Tim Meadows, Sinbad

Congo

USA 1995 107m DeLuxe Dolby

An expedition to the Congo to discover

diamonds for a telecommunications system is beset by a race of killer gorillas.

Increasingly silly variation on *King Solomon's Mines* which should have been a lot better than it is. But it passes the time for those inclined not to take it too seriously.

p: Kathleen Kennedy, Sam Mercer for Paramount
exec p: Frank Yablans
w: John Patrick Shanley
novel: Michael Crichton
d: Frank Marshall
ph: Allen Daviau
m: Jerry Goldsmith
ed: Anne V. Coates
pd: J. Michael Riva
cos: Marilyn Matthews
sp: Scott Farrar
sound: Ronald Judkins
make-up effects: Stan Winston
2nd unit d: Mikael Solomon
Dylan Walsh, Laura Linney, Ernie Hudson, Tim Curry (sporting one of the most ludicrous accents in screen history), Grant Heslow, Joe Don Baker, Mary Ellen Trainor, Bruce Campbell, Taylor Nichols, James Karen

Connery, Sean (1930-)

Scottish actor (real name Thomas Connery) who, after variable success in such films as *Hell Drivers*, *Another Time, Another Place* and *Tarzan's Greatest Adventure*, shot to stardom as the first (and many would say best) James Bond in *Dr. No* (1962). After leaving Bond in the early 70s his career dipped, though he has since returned to the box office heights with a variety of projects and remains one of the cinema's great stars, winning a best supporting actor Oscar for his work on *The Untouchables* (1987). His non-Bond films include *The Hill*, *The Molly Maguires*, *Murder on the Orient Express*, *The Man Who Would be King*, *Five Days One Summer*, *The*

Name of the Rose, *The Hunt for Red October*, *Rising Son*, *First Knight* and *The Rock*.

Genre credits:

Darby O'Gill and the Little People (1959), *You Only Live Twice* (1967), *Zardoz* (1974), *Meteor* (1979), *Outland* (1981), *Time Bandits* (1981), *Sword of the Valiant* (1983), *Highlander* (1985), *Indiana Jones and the Last Crusade* (1989), *Highlander II: The Quickening* (1990), *Dragonheart* (1996 – voice as the dragon)

Connor, Kevin (1937-)

British director, a former editor who, with producer John Dark, made a number of variable fantasy films in the 70s before turning to straight drama subjects. His other credits include *From Beyond the Grave*, *Motel Hell*, *The House Where Evil Dwells*, *The Master of the Game* (TVM) and *Great Expectations* (TVM).

Genre credits:

The Land That Time Forgot (1975), *At the Earth's Core* (1976), *Trial by Combat* (1976 – aka *Dirty Knights' Work/Choose Your Weapons*), *The People That Time Forgot* (1977), *The Warlords of Atlantis* (1978), *Arabian Adventure* (1979)

The Conquest of Space
USA 1955 80m Technicolor

An American space station is sent on a voyage to Mars.

Hilariously scripted science fiction piece which, despite being set in 1980, proves to be more dull than unintentionally funny.

p: George Pal for Paramount
w: James O'Hanlon, George Worthington Yates, Barre Lyndon, Philip Yordan
book: Chesley Bonestall, Willy Ley
d: Byron Haskin

ph: Lionel Lindon
m: Van Cleeve
ed: Everett Douglas
ad: Hal Pereira, Joseph McMillan Johnson
sp: John P. Fulton, Irmin Roberts, Paul Lerpae, Ivy Burks, Jan Domella, Farciot Edouart
sound: Harold Lewis, Gene Garvin
Eric Fleming, Walter Brooke, Mickey Shaughnessy, William Hopper, Ross Martin

The Conquest of the North Pole 🛸
Fr 1912 10m bw silent

A professor and his party fly to the North Pole where they encounter a snow monster.

Engaging trick film with many points of interest for buffs. One of its director's last films.

p: Georges Méliès
w/d: Georges Méliès

Conquest of the Planet of the Apes 🛸
USA 1972 97m DeLuxe Todd-AO 35

A talking ape leads the earth's simians in a revolt against man.

One of the better sequels to the original *Planet of the Apes*, though a noticeably more violent one.

p: Arthur P. Jacobs for TCF
w: Paul Dehn
d: J. Lee-Thompson
ph: Bruce Surtees
m: Tom Scott
ed: Marjorie Fowler, Alan Jaggs
ad: Philip Jeffries
sound: Herman Lewis, Don Bassman
Roddy McDowall, Don Murray, Ricardo Montalban, Natalie Trundy, Hari Rhodes, Severn Darden, Lou Wagner, John Randolph

Contact ☺☺☺

USA 1997 150m Technicolor Dolby

An astronomer discovers radio waves from outer space, the contents of which lead mankind to build a spaceship to take her across the galaxies for an encounter with alien life.

Long, slow-starting but increasingly absorbing slice of science fiction that, for once, treats its subject seriously, producing much for the audience to chew on, though the film isn't without its spectacular effects too.

p: Robert Zemeckis, Steve Starkey for Warner/South Side Amusement Company
exec p: Joan Bradshaw, Lynda Obst
w: James V. Hart, Michael Goldenberg
novel: Carl Sagan
d: Robert Zemeckis
ph: Don Burgess
m: Alan Silvestri
ed: Arthur Schmidt
cos: Joanna Johnston
sp: Ken Ralston
sound: Randy Thom
Jodie Foster, Matthew McConaughey, James Woods, Tom Skerritt, Angela Bassett, John Hurt, Rob Lowe, Larry King, Kathleen Kennedy

Cool World

USA 1992 102m Technicolor Dolby

A cartoonist discovers that one of his female creations wants to enter the real world so as to be able to experience sex.

Dismal blend of cartoon and live action with none of the wit, charm or technical resource of *Who Framed Roger Rabbit?* An almost unbearable experience.

p: Frank Mancuso, Jr. for Paramount
w: Michael Grais, Mark Victor
d: Ralph Bakshi
ph: John A. Alonzo
m: Mark Isham
ed: Steve Mirkovich, Annamaria Szanto

pd: Michael Corenblith
cos: Malissa Daniel
sound: James Thornton
conceptual design: Barry Jackson
titles: Dan Curry
Gabriel Byrne, Kim Basinger, Brad Pitt, Michele Abrams, Janni Brenn-Lowen, Deidre O'Connell, Carrie Hamilton, Frank Sinatra, Jr.

Coop, Denys (1920-1981)

British cinematographer (*A Kind of Loving, Billy Liar, Bunny Lake is Missing, 10, Rillington Place,* etc.) who won an Oscar for photographing the effects for *Superman* (1978). Began his career as an assistant to the great Freddie Young in 1936.

Cooper, Jackie (1921–)

American child actor who, after appearances in the *Our Gang* shorts of the late 20s, found public favour in such 30s films as *Skippy, The Champ, The Bowery* and *Treasure Island*. As an adult he successfully turned to direction, especially on television, though to genre fans he is perhaps best known as *Daily Planet* editor Perry White in the *Superman* films. He also directed several episodes of the *Superboy* TV series.

Genre credits:
Chosen Survivors (1974 – TVM – d), *The Invisible Man* (1975 – TVM – actor), *Superman* (1978 – actor), *Superman II* (1980 – actor), *Superman III* (1983 – actor), *Superman IV* (1987 – actor)

Cooper, Wilkie (1911-)

British cinematographer with many and various credits to his name, among them several for Launder and Gilliat (*The Rake's Progress, I See a Dark Stranger, Green for Danger, Captain*

Boycott, London Belongs to Me) as well as Hitchcock's *Stagefright, The Admirable Crichton* and several for effects wiz Ray Harryhausen.

Genre credits:
The Seventh Voyage of Sinbad (1958), *The Three Worlds of Gulliver* (1959 – aka *Gulliver's Travels*), *Mysterious Island* (1961), *Jason and the Argonauts* (1963), *The Mouse on the Moon* (1963), *First Men in the Moon* (1964), *One Million Years B.C.* (1966)

Cooper, Merian C. (1893-1973)

American producer, director and executive whose credits take in documentaries (*Chang, Grass*), westerns (including several with John Ford, with whom he formed Argosy Pictures in 1947) and adventure epics (*The Four Feathers, The Most Dangerous Game* [aka *The Hounds of Zaroff*]). He is best known for producing and co-directing (with Ernest B. Schoedsack) *King Kong*.

Genre credits:
King Kong (1933 – p/co-d/actor), *Son of Kong* (1933 – p), *She* (1935 – p), *Mighty Joe Young* (1949 – p)

Corigliano, John (1938-)

American composer and longtime professor of music at Lehman College, City University of New York. He has various albums to his credit, though his most notable film score has been for Ken Russell's *Altered States* (1980). His other film scores include *Revolution*.

Corman, Roger (1926-)

Legendary writer, producer, director and executive producer of horror and exploitation subjects, renowned for their low budgets and short shooting schedules (*Oklahoma Woman*, *Rock All Night*, *She Gods of Shark Reef*, *Sorority Girl*, etc.). He also directed a celebrated cycle of Poe adaptations in the 60s (*House of Usher*, *The Pit and the Pendulum*, *The Raven*, etc.). Sci-fi and fantasy work rather rarer.

Genre credits:
The Day the World Ended (1955 – p/d), *It Conquered the World* (1956 – p/d), *Not of This Earth* (1956 – p/d), *War of the Satellites* (1958 p/d), *The Last Woman on Earth* (1960 – p/d), *Gas-s-s-s!* (1970 – aka *It Became Necessary to Destroy the World in Order to Save It* – p/d), *Galaxy of Terror* (1981 – exec p), *Forbidden World* (1982 – exec p), *Not of This Earth* (1988 – exec p), *Dead Space* (1991 – exec p), *Carnosaur* (1993 – exec p)

Corri, Adrienne (1930-)

Glamorous British (Scottish) actress (real name Adrienne Riccobini) who has livened up all manner of films, among them *Lease of Life*, *Three Men in a Boat*, *The Hell-Fire Club*, *The Viking Queen*, *A Study in Terror*, *Vampire Circus* and *Madhouse*.

Genre credits:
Devil Girl from Mars (1954), *Moon Zero Two* (1969), *A Clockwork Orange* (1971)

The Cosmic Man

USA 1958 72m bw
A benign alien preaches peace and helps a crippled boy before returning to his home planet.

Hilarious low budget farrago, a woebegone attempt at something different.

p: Robert A. Terry for Futura
w: Arthur C. Pierce
d: Herbert Greene

ph: John F. Warren
m: Paul Sawtell, Bert Shefter
md: Lou Kosloff
ed: Richard C. Currier, Helen Turner
ad: no credit given
sp: Charles Duncan
sound: Phillip Mitchell
John Carradine, Bruce Bennett, Angela Greene, Paul Langton, Scott Morrow, Lyn Osborn

Cosmic Monsters

see The Strange World of Planet X

Cotten, Joseph (1905-1994)

American actor who started at the top in Orson Welles' *Citizen Kane* in which he played the reporter. A former drama critic (for the *Miami Herald*), he turned to acting in the 20s, eventually joining Welles' Mercury Theatre Company in 1937. His films include *The Magnificent Ambersons*, *Journey into Fear* (which he co-wrote with Welles), *Shadow of a Doubt*, *The Third Man*, *Duel in the Sun*, *Niagara* and, later, several horror films, among them *The Abominable Dr Phibes*, *Lady Frankenstein* and *The Hearse*.

Genre credits:
Portrait of Jennie (1948), *From the Earth to the Moon* (1958), *Ido Zero Daisakusen* (1969 – aka *Latitude Zero*), *City Beneath the Sea* (1970 – aka *One Hour to Doomsday* – TVM), *Soylent Green* (1973)

Countdown

USA 1967 101m Technicolor Panavision
America prepares to send the first men to the moon only to find themselves racing with the Russians for the honour.

Sober, unexciting science fiction which opts to be realistic rather than fantastic.

exec p: William Conrad for Warner
w: Loring Mandel
d: Robert Altman
ph: William W. Spencer
m: Leonard Rosenman
ed: Gene Milford
ad: Jack Poplin
sound: Everett A. Hughes
James Caan, Robert Duvall, Barbara Baxley, Joanna Moore, Steve Ihnat, Charles Aidman

Courage, Alexander (1919-)

American composer and arranger, best known for writing the theme music for TV's *Star Trek*, snatches of which have popped in the various movie offshoots. His other movie scores include *The Left-Handed Gun* and *Tokyo After Dark*. He has also scored much episode TV (*Voyage to the Bottom of the Sea*, *Lost in Space*, *The Waltons*, etc.). More recently he has been orchestrating scores for both John Williams and Jerry Goldsmith.

Cox, Jack (1896-1960)

Prolific British cinematographer (real name John Jaffrey Cox) who began his career as an assistant in 1913, becoming a fully-fledged cameraman in 1926. In 1928 he began a long association with Alfred Hitchcock which lasted through ten pictures over a 12-year period, among them *The Ring*, *Blackmail*, *Number Seventeen* and *The Lady Vanishes*. His other credits include *They Came by Night*, *Madonna of the Seven Moons*, *One Good Turn* and *The Square Peg*.

Genre credits:
Mr. Drake's Duck (1950), *Babes in Baghdad* (1952), *Devil Girl from Mars* (1954)

Crabbe, Larry "Buster" (1907-1983)

Athletic-looking American actor (real name Clarence Linden Crabbe), remembered not only for being the screen's first Flash Gordon, but also its first Buck Rogers. A former Olympic swimmer, he won a gold medal at the 1932 games in Los Angeles. He made his movie debut (as an extra) in 1930 in the collegiate musical *Good News*, which he followed with roles in *Maker of Men*, *The Most Dangerous Game* and *King of the Jungle* before playing Tarzan in the 1933 serial *Tarzan the Fearless* (which was also released as a feature). *Flash Gordon* followed in 1936. His other film credits include *Daughter of Shanghai*, *Red Barry* (serial), *Billy the Kid Wanted* (as Billy the Kid), *The Sea Hound* (serial) and *Arizona Raiders*, whilst in the late 50s he starred in the TV series *Captain Gallant* (aka *Foreign Legionnaire/ Captain Gallant of the Foreign Legion*). Later he turned to the swimming pool business, and was also the author of a book about fitness for the over-50s. When he died he was busy working on the planning committee for the 1984 Los Angeles Olympics, which brought his career full circle 50 years on.

Genre credits:
Island of Lost Souls (1932), *Flash Gordon* (1936 – serial), *Flash Gordon's Trip to Mars* (1938 – serial), *Buck Rogers* (1939 – serial), *Flash Gordon Conquers the Universe* (1940 – serial)

Crack in the World

USA 1965 96m Technicolor

A scientist sends a missile to the centre of the earth so that man might tap the energy contained in molten lava, but the experiment has a drastic side effect...

Chatty Saturday morning science fiction with a few lively effects sequences.

p: Bernard Glasser, Lester A. Sansom for Paramount/Security
exec p: Philip Yordan
w: Jon Manchip, Julian Halevy
story: Jon Manchip
d: Andrew Marton
ph: Manuel Berenguer
m: Johnny Douglas
ed: Derek Parsons
ad: Eugene Lourie
cos: Laure de Zarate
sp: Eugene Lourie, Alex Weldon
sound: David Hildyard, Maurice Askew
Dana Andrews, Janette Scott, Kieron Moore, Alexander Knox, Peter Damon, Cary Lasdun

Crash and Burn

USA 1990 85m colour

In the future, travellers stranded at a remote desert TV station find themselves menaced by a synthoid.

Padded, derivative thriller which picks up in the last 20 minutes or so.

p: David DeCoteau, John Schouweiler for Full Moon Entertainment
exec p: Charles Band, Debra Dion
w: J. S. Cardone
d: Charles Band
ph: Mac Ahlberg
m: Richard Band
sp: David Allen
make-up effects: Greg Cannom
Paul Ganus, Megan Ward, Bill Moseley, Eva Larue, Jack McGee, Ralph Waite

The Crater Lake Monster

USA 1977 82m colour

A crashing meteor resurrects a prehistoric monster which subsequently goes on the rampage.

Grade Z monster flick of the kind familiar in the less critical 50s.

Laughable when it isn't embarrassing.

p: William R. Stromberg for Crown International
w: William R. Stromberg, Richard Cardella
d: William R. Stromberg
ph: Paul Gentry
m: James West
ed: Nancy Grossman, Steve Neilson
pd: Roger Heisman
sp: Dave Allen, Tom Scherman
sound: Hal Scharn
Richard Cardella, Glenn Roberts, Mark Siegel, Kacey Cobb, Richard Garrison, Michael Hoover, Suzanne Lewis, Bob Hyman

The Crawling Eye

see The Trollenberg Terror

The Creature from the Black Lagoon

USA 1954 79m bw 3D

An amphibious monster threatens members of an exploration team.

Archetypal 50s monster pic, a little on the tame side, but with effective underwater sequences. It was followed by *Revenge of the Creature* (1955) and *The Creature Walks Among Us* (1956).

p: William Alland for Universal
w: Harry Essex, Arthur Ross
d: Jack Arnold
ph: William E. Snyder, James C. Havens
md: Joseph Gershenson
ed: Ted J. Kent
ad: Bernard Hertzbrun, Hilyard Brown
make-up: Bud Wesmore, Jack Kevan
Richard Carlson, Julie Adams, Richard Denning, Antonio Mereno, Nestor Pavia, Ricou Browning (as the Creature)

The Creature Walks Among Us

USA 1956 78m bw

A group of scientists capture the Gill

Man, but he escapes on goes on the rampage.

Third and last of Universal's creature features. Good underwater scenes, but otherwise the mixture is as before.

p: William Allan for Universal
w: Arthur Ross
d: John Sherwood
ph: Maury Gertsman
md: Joseph Gershenson
ed: Edward Curtiss
ad: Alexander Golitzen, Robert E. Smith
cos: Jay A. Morley, Jr.
sp: Clifford Stine
sound: Leslie I. Carey, Robert Pritchard
make-up: Bud Westmore
Jeff Morrow, Rex Reason, Leigh Snowden, Gregg Palmer, Maurice Manson, Ricou Browning (as the Creature)

Creatures the World Forgot

GB 1970 95m Technicolor
The lives and battles of a prehistoric tribe.

Dull and rather silly follow-up to Hammer's other prehistoric adventures (*One Million Years B.C.*, *When Dinosaurs Ruled the Earth*, etc.).

p: Michael Carreras for Hammer/Columbia
w: Michael Carreras
d: Don Chaffey
ph: Vincent Cox
m: Mario Nascimbene
md: Philip Martell
ed: Chris Barnes
pd: John Stoll
cos: Rosemary Burrows
sp: Sydney Pearson
sound: John Streeler
2nd unit d: Ray Sturgess
Julie Ege, Brian O'Shaughnessy, Robert John, Marcia Fox, Rosalie Crutchley

Creber, William

American art director whose genre credits take in three of the Apes films and two disaster pics for producer Irwin Allen (*The Poseidon Adventure* and *The Towering Inferno*), the latter of which earned him an Oscar nomination.

Genre credits:
The Planet of the Apes (1967 – co-ad), *Beneath the Planet of the Apes* (1969 – co-ad), *Escape from the Planet of the Apes* (1971 – co-ad), *The Flight of the Navigator* (1986 – pd/2nd unit d)

The Creeping Terror

USA 1964 100m bw
America is threatened by what appear to be man-eating carpets from outer space.

Another Golden Turkey. Good for a few laughs, but only a few.

p: Art J. Nelson for Metropolitan International
w: Robert Silliphant
d/ed: Art J. Nelson
ph: Frederick Janczak
m: Frederick Kopp
ad: Bud Raab
monster design: Jon Lackey
Vic Savage (Art J. Nelson), Shannon O'Neill, William Thourlby, John Caresio, Norman Boone, Byra Holland

The Creeping Unknown

see The Quatermass Experiment

Creepozoids

USA 1987 72m colour
In the future, five army deserters find themselves stalked by an alien creature in an abandoned installation.

Dim low budget *Alien* rip-off with

an over abundance of running around in darkly lit places.

p: David De Coteau, John Schouweiler for Titan
w: Burford Hauser, David De Coteau
d: David De Coteau
ph: Thomas Calloway
m: Guy Moon
md: Jonathan Scott Bogner
ed: Miriam L. Preissel
pd: Royce Matthew
cos: Wilma Rubble (!)
sp: Tom Calloway, John Criswell
sound: Marty Kasparian
make-up effects: Thom Floutz, Peter Carsillo
Linnea Quigley, Richard Hawkins, Joi Wilson, Michael Aranda, Kim McKamy, Ken Abraham

Crichton, Michael (1942-)

Best-selling American noveslist (*Rising Sun*, *Disclosure*), screenwriter, producer and director, a former doctor and anthropology teacher. Began writing under the name John Lange and, following the filming of several of his books, turned to direction in 1972 with the TV thriller *Pursuit*, which was based on his novel *Binary*. Directed his first theatrical feature, *Westworld*, in 1973. His other credits as a director include *The First Great Train Robbery* and *Physical Evidence*, though he is perhaps best known as the author of *Jurassic Park* and the creator of TV's *E.R.* His other pen names include Michael Douglas, Robin Cook and Jeffrey Hudson.

Genre credits:
The Andromeda Strain (1970 – novel), *Westworld* (1973 – w/d), *The Terminal Man* (1974 – novel), *Coma* (1978 – novel/w/d [novel as Robin Cook]), *Looker* (1981 – w/d), *Runaway* (1984 – w/d/exec p),

Jurassic Park (1993 – novel/co-w), *Congo* (1995 – novel), *The Lost World* (1997 – novel)

Critters

USA 1986 86m DeLuxe

A Kansas farming community finds itself prey to an invasion of man-eating critters from outer space.

Juvenile romp which is neither funny enough nor scary enough. Nevertheless, it was followed by *Critters 2* (1988), *Critters 3* (1992) and *Critters 4* (1992).

p: Rupert Harvey for New Line/SHO/Smart Egg
exec p: Robert Shaye
w: Stephen Herek, Dominic Muir
story: Dominic Muir
d: Stephen Herek
ph: Chris Tufty, Tim Suhrstedt
m: David Newman
ed: Larry Bock

> Writer, director, producer and novelist Michael Crichton poses for the cameras in a publicity shot taken during the filming of *Coma*.

pd: Gregg Fonseca
sp: Chiodo Brothers Productions
sound: Dale Johnston
titles: Ernest D. Farino
Dee Wallace Stone, M. Emmett Walsh, Scott Grimes, Billy Green Bush, Billy Zane

Cronenweth, Jordan

American cinematographer with a variety of projects to his credit, among them *The Front Page*, *Best Friends*, *Gardens of Stone* and *Final Analysis*.

Genre credits:

Brewster McCloud (1970 - co-ph), *Altered States* (1980), *Blade Runner* (1982), *Peggy Sue Got Married* (1986)

Crosby, Floyd (1889-1985)

American cinematographer, remembered for his association with Roger Corman, for whom he photographed several horror subjects in the 60s, among them *House of Usher* (aka *The Fall of the House of Usher*), *The Premature Burial*, *Tales of Terror*, *The Raven* and *X – The Man with X-Ray Eyes*. He began his career photographing documentaries for Robert Flaherty and Joris Ivens, winning an Oscar for his work on *Tabu* in 1930. His other credits include *The River*, *My Father's House* and *High Noon*.

Genre credits:

Monster from the Ocean Floor (1954), *The Snow Creature* (1954), *Attack of the Crab Monsters* (1954), *War of the Satellites* (1958), *Teenage Caveman* (1958 – aka *Out of the Darkness*), *Sergeant Deadhead* (1965 – aka *Sergeant Deadhead the Astronaut*)

Cross, Beverley

British screenwriter and playwrite whose stage musical *Half a Sixpence*

(with songs by David Heneker) was filmed in 1967 with a script by himself. His other screenplays have mostly been for the fantasy films of Ray Harryhausen and Charles Schneer, though he did contribute (uncredited) some sequences to David Lean's *Lawrence of Arabia*.

Genre credits:

Jason and the Argonauts (1963 – co-w), *Sinbad and the Eye of the Tiger* (1977 – co-story/w), *Clash of the Titans* (1981 – w)

Crossworlds

USA 1996 87m CFIcolor Dolby

Good and evil warriors from another galaxy travel to earth to retrieve a magical crystal which is in the possession of an unsuspecting art student.

Slackly handled adventures which could have made better use of the possibilities at hand. A few sequences work, such as a fist fight through various time zones and a scene in a disintegrating elevator, but on the whole the results are tedious rather than exciting.

p: Rupert Harvey, Lloyd Segan for Trimark
exec p: Mark Amin, Stephen Hopkins
w: Krishna Rao, Raman Rao
d: Krishna Rao
ph: Christopher Walling
m: Christophe (sic) Beck
ed: Anita Brandt-Burgoyne
pd: Aaron Osborne
cos: Tammy Mor
sp: Wendy Grossberg, Joseph Grossberg, Shockwave Entertainment
sound: Cameron Hamza
titles: Rick Weis
stunt co-ordinator: Don Ruffin
Rutger Hauer, Josh Charles, Stuart Wilson, Andrea Roth, Perry Anzilotti, Jack Black, Richard McGregor

Cruickshank, Art

American special effects technician and effects photographer, an Oscar winner for his effects work on *Fantastic Voyage* (1966). Long with Disney, where he has often collaborated with Eustace Lycett and Danny Lee.

Genre credits:
Fantastic Voyage (1966), *Planet of the Apes* (1967 – co-sp), *Beneath the Planet of the Apes* (1969 – co-sp), *City Beneath the Sea* (1970 – aka *One Hour to Doomsday* – TVM – co-sp), *Earth II* (1971 – TVM – co-sp), *The World's Greatest Athlete* (1973 – co-sp), *Herbie Rides Again* (1974 – co-sp), *The Island at the Top of the World* (1974 – co-sp), *Charley and the Angel* (1974 – co-sp), *Escape to Witch Mountain* (1974 – co-sp), *The Strongest Man in the World* (1975 – co-sp), *Freaky Friday* (1976 – co-sp), *The Shaggy D.A.* (1976 – co-sp), *Herbie Goes to Monte Carlo* (1977 – co-sp), *Return from Witch Mountain* (1978 – co-sp), *The Cat from Outer Space* (1978 – co-sp), *The Black Hole* (1979 – co-sp), *Herbie Goes Bananas* (1980 – co-sp), *Condorman* (1981 – co-sp), *The Devil and Max Devlin* (1981 – co-sp), *The Watcher in the Woods* (1982 – co-sp)

Cundey, Dean

American cinematographer who hitched a ride to the top with director John Carpenter (*Halloween*, *The Fog*, *The Thing*, etc.) before moving on to even bigger things with Robert Zemeckis and Steven Spielberg. His other credits include *Roller Boogie*, *Psycho II*, *Romancing the Stone*, *Warning Sign* and *Big Business*. In 1996 he turned to direction with *Honey, We Shrunk Ourselves*, the third instalment in the series.

Genre credits:
Galaxina (1980), *Escape from New York* (1981), *The Thing* (1982), *Halloween III: Season of the Witch* (1983), *Back to the Future* (1985), *Project X* (1987), *Who Framed Roger Rabbit?* (1988), *Back to the Future Part II* (1989), *Back to the Future Part III* (1990), *Hook* (1991), *Death Becomes Her* (1992), *Jurassic Park* (1993), *The Flintstones* (1994 – also actor), *Casper* (1995), *Honey, We Shrunk Ourselves!* (1996 - d)

Curry, Tim (1946-)

Extrovert British comedy character actor, best known for playing Frank N. Furter in *The Rocky Horror Picture Show* (1974). He also made a convincing Devil in *Legend*, under all of Rob Bottin's brilliant make-up. His other credits include *Annie*, *It* (TVM), *Home Alone 2: Lost in New York* and *Three Musketeers*.

Genre credits:
Legend (1985), *Ferngully: The Last Rainforest* (1992 – voice), *The Shadow* (1994), *Congo* (1995)

Curse of the Fly

GB 1965 83m bw Cinemascope
The Delambre family continue their teleportation experiments, this time in England.

Low budget attempt to continue the series at a British studio. It's nothing special.

p: Robert L. Lippert, Jack Parsons for TCF
w: Harry Spalding
d: Don Sharp
ph: Basil Emmott
m: Bert Shefter
ed: Robert Winter
ad: Harry White
sound: Jockm May
make-up effects: Harold Fletcher
Brian Donlevy, George Baker, Carole Gray, Michael Graham, Rachel Kempson, Yvette Rees, Burt Kwouk, Jeremy Wilkin, Mary Manson

Cushing, Peter (1913-1994)

British actor who, along with Christopher Lee, came to personify Hammer Films, most notably as Baron Frankenstein and Van Helsing. Though known primarily for his horror work (*The Curse of Frankenstein*, *Dracula*, *The Mummy*, *Horror Express*, *From Beyond the Grave*, etc.) he has also had a handful of brushes with the science fiction and fantasy genres, most notably with the two Dr. Who movies in the 60s and as Grand Moff Tarkin in *Star Wars*.

Genre credits:
She (1965), *Dr. Who and the Daleks* (1965 – as Dr. Who), *Daleks – Invasion Earth, 2150 A. D.* (1966 – as Dr. Who), *Night of the Big Heat* (1967 – aka *Island of the Burning Damned*), *At the Earth's Core* (1976), *Trial by Combat* (1976 – aka *Dirty Knights' Work/Choose Your Weapons*), *Star Wars* (1977), *Arabian Adventure* (1979), *Biggles* (1986)

Cyberjack

USA 1995 93m Kodak color Dolby
In the future, an ex-cop, now a janitor for a computer firm following the death of his partner, helps prevent a group of terrorists from planting a virus in an aerial guidance system.

The science fiction trimmings are mostly irrelevant, for this is little more than a low rent variation on *Die Hard*, but with none of that film's energy.

p: John A. Curtis for Catalyst/Prism/Everest Entertainment/Fuji Eight
exec p: Barry L. Collier, Masao Takiyama, John A. Curtis
w: Eric Poppen
d: Robert Lee
ph: Allan Trow
m: George Blondheim
ed: Derek Whelen

Behind you! Peter Cushing as the big screen's first (and so far only) Dr. Who in a posed publicity still for *Daleks - Invasion Earth, 2150 A.D.*

pd: Richard Paris, Linda De Rosario
cos: Suzanne Magee
sp: The Magic Camera Company, Gary Paller, Paller Special Effects
sound: Lindsay Bucknell
2nd unit d: John Curtis
stunt co-ordinator: Marc Akerstream
Michael Dudikoff, Suki Kaiser, Brion James, John Cuthbert, James Thom, Topaz Hasfal-Schou, Garvin Cross

Cyborg

USA 1989 84m Technicolor
In the future, a female cyborg trans-ports vital information about a cure for the plague across America, and is accompanied by a martial arts expert whose skills come in handy in protect-ing her from violent gangs.

Little more than a thin excuse for the star to show off his skills, this routine-ly made actioner is an archetypal Cannon/Pyun movie (ie: not very good) and presents the usual depress-ing post-apocalyptic view of the future. A reasonable success on video, it spawned two sequels which Van Damme wisely avoided: *Cyborg II: Glass Shadow* (1993) and *Cyborg III*

(1994). Other films during this period also took up the cyborg theme, among them *Cyberchick* (1990), *Cybernator* (1991), *Cybertracker* (1993), *Cybereden* (1993) and *Cyborg Cop* (1993).

p: Menahem Golan, Yoram Globus for Cannon
w: Kitty Chalmers
d: Albert Pyun
ph: Philip Alan Walters
m: Kevin Bassinson
ed: Scott Stevenson, Rozanne Zingale
pd: Douglas Leonard
sp: Fantasy II
make-up effects: Greg Cannom
Jean-Claude Van Damme, Deborah Richter, Alex Daniels, Rolf Muller, Vincent Klyn, Dayle Haddon

Cyborg Cop

USA/South Africa 1993 94m Technicolor
An ex-cop learns that his brother has been turned into a cyborg by a wealthy drug dealer and so sets out, and so sets out to rescue him from the Caribbean island where he is being held.

Bog standard low budget action fod-der of the type found gathering dust in video stores. Incredibly, it was followed by *Cyborg Cop II* (1994), *Cyborg Cop III* (1995) and *Cyborg Soldier* (1995). Enough already!

p: Danny Lerner for New World/Nu Image
w: Gregg Latter
d: Sam Firstenberg
ph: Joseph Wein
m: Paul Fishman
ed: Alan Patillo
pd: John Rosewarne
sp: Image Animation
David Bradley, Alona Shaw, Todd Jensen, John Rhys Davies

D'Agostino, Albert S. (1893-1970)

American art director, with RKO for over 20 years. Working mostly in collaboration, he designed such films as *Werewolf of London*, *Dracula's Daughter*, *Cat People*, *The Magnificent Ambersons*, *Mr and Mrs Smith*, *I Walked with a Zombie*, *Notorious*, *Clash by Night*, *The Spiral Staircase*, *I Remember Mamma* and *Androcles and the Lion*. Began his film career at the age of 21 following experience as a set designer for the theatre.

Genre credits:

The Invisible Ray (1936 – ad), *The Boy with Green Hair* (1948 – co-ad), *The Thing* (1951 – aka *The Thing from Another World* – co-ad)

Dahl, Roald (1916–1990)

Norwegian novelist and screenwriter, adept at both macabre books for children and twist-in-the-tale thrillers for adults. Also famous for the TV series *Roald Dahl's Tales of the Unexpected* which he introduced for several years from 1979.

Genre credits:

You Only Live Twice (1967 – w), *Chitty Chitty Bang Bang* (1968 – co-w), *Willy Wonka and the Chocolate Factory* (1971 – w/novel), *The Witches* (1990 – novel), *The BFG* (1990 – TVM – w/novel), *James and the Giant Peach* (1996 – novel)

Daleks – Invasion Earth, 2150 A. D.

GB 1966 84m Technicolor Techniscope

Dr. Who travels to the year 2150 where he discovers a desolated London in the grip of the Daleks.

Enjoyably dated, reasonably cheerful low budget science fiction romp from the popular BBC TV series, a sequel to *Dr. Who and the Daleks*.

p: Milton Subotsky, Max J. Rosenberg for Aaru
exec p: Joe Vegoda
w: Milton Subotsky, David Whitaker
d: Gordon Flemyng
ph: John Wilcox
m: Bill McGuffie, Barry Gray
ed: Ann Chegwidden
ad: George Provis
cos: Jackie Cummins
sp: Ted Samuels
sound: A. Ambler, John Cox

Peter Cushing, Bernard Cribbins, Ray Brooks, Andrew Keir, Jill Curzon, Roberta Tovey, Eddie Powell, Bernard Spear, Philip Madoc, Sheila Steafel, John Wreford

D'Amato, Joe (1936-)

Italian director (real name Aristide Massaccesi) with a penchant for exploitation, including horror (*The Anthropophagous Beast*, *Buried Alive*) and pornography (the Black Emanuelle series). His many pseudonyms include Kevin Mancuso, Steve Benson, Michael Wotruba and David Hills.

Genre credits:

Ator the Fighting Eagle (1982 – as David Hills), *Ator the Invincible* (1983 – aka *The Blade Master/Cavedwellers* – as David Hills), *Texas 2000* (1984 – aka *2020 Texas Gladiators* – as Kevin Mancuso), *Ator III: The Hobgoblin* (1990 – aka *Quest for the Mighty Sword* – as David Hills)

Danforth, Jim

American special effects technician and stop motion animator, not quite in the same league as Ray Harryhausen, whom he helped animate several sequences for *Clash of the Titans*.

Genre credits:

The Seven Faces of Dr Lao (1964 – co-sp), *When Dinosaurs Ruled the Earth* (1970 – co-sp), *Flesh Gordon* (1974 – co-sp – billed as Mij Htrofnad [!]), *Dark Star* (1974 – co-sp), *The Day Time Ended* (1979 – co-sp), *The Aftermath* (1980 – co-sp), *Clash of the Titans* (1981 – assistant sp)

Daniels, Anthony

British character actor known primarily for playing C3PO in the *Star Wars* movies, a role he has also played on radio.

Genre credits:

Star Wars (1977), *Lord of the Rings* (1978 – voice), *The Empire Strikes Back* (1980), *The Return of the Jedi* (1983)

Danning, Sybil (1950-)

Curvaceous Austrian-born actress with many low budget exploitation films to her credit (*Swedish Love Games*, *Loves of a French Pussycat*, *The Howling II: Your Sister Is a Werewolf*, *Chained Heat*, *Reform School Girls*, *The Tomb*, etc.), though she has also appeared in supporting roles in bigger international films, such as *Bluebeard*, *The Three Musketeers* and *The Prince and the Pauper*.

Genre credits:

Meteor (1979), *Battle Beyond the Stars* (1980), *Hercules* (1983), *The Seven Magnificent Gladiators* (1983), *Jungle Warriors* (1983), *Amazon Women on the Moon* (1987), *Warrior Queen* (1987)

Dante, Joe (1947-)

American director with a penchant for big budget fantasy films crammed with cameos from old time actors such as Dick Miller, Kenneth Tobey and Kathleen Freeman. Following experience as a journalist he began his film career making trailers for Roger Corman, for whom he made his directorial debut in 1977 with *Hollywood Boulevard*, which he co-directed with Allan Arkush and also co-edited. He had a hit with the *Jaws* rip-off *Piranha* in 1978, which he followed with *The Howling* and *Gremlins* and many more mainstream successes. He has also appeared as an actor in *Sleepwalkers*.

Genre credits:

Twilight Zone – The Movie (1983 – co-d), *Gremlins* (1984 – d), *Explorers* (1985 – d), *Amazon Women on the Moon* (1987 – co-d), *Innerspace* (1987 – d), *Gremlins 2: The New Batch* (1990 – d), *Matinee* (1993 – d), *The Phantom* (1996 – co-exec p), *Small Soldiers* (1998 – d)

Darby O'Gill and the Little People

USA 1959 90m Technicolor

An ageing Irish caretaker falls down a well and is befriended by leprechauns.

Surprisingly tedious fantasy which only really comes to life when the trick effects are on screen. An overdose of Blarney doesn't help matters much, either.

p: Walt Disney
w: Lawrence Edward Watkin
novel: H. T. Kavanagh
d: Robert Stevenson
ph: Winton C. Hoch
m: Oliver Wallace
ed: Stanley Johnson
ad: Carroll Clark
sp: PETER ELLENSHAW, JOSHUA MEADOR, USTACE LYCETT

Albert Sharpe, Jimmy O'Dea, Sean Connery, Estelle Windwood, Janet Munro, Kieron Moore, Denis O'Dea, Jack McGowran, Walter Fitzgerald, J. G. Devlin

Dark Angel

USA 1990 92m DeLuxe

A Houston vice cop and his partner track down a vicious drugs killer who, it turns out, is in fact an alien from another world.

Violent actioner which produces just as many unintentional laughs as it does intentional ones. Quite slickly made for all that.

The director gets directed. Joe Dante (right) puts Steven Spielberg through his paces for his gag cameo in *Gremlins*.

Anthony Daniels (right) in an archetypal pose as See Threepio in *Star Wars*, here accompanied by Kenny Baker as Artoo-Detoo.

p: Jeff Young for Vision

exec p: Mark Damon, David Saunders

w: Jonathan Tydor, Leonard Maas, Jr.

d: Craig R. Baxley

ph: Mark Irwin

m: Jan Hammer

ed: Mark Helrich

pd: Phillip M. Leonard

cos: Joseph Porro

sp: Bruno Van Zeebroek

sound: Bud Maffett

stunt co-ordinator: Paul R. Baxley, Jr.

Dolph Lundgren, Brian Benben, Betsy Brantley, Joan Bilas, Matthias Hues, Michael J. Pollard, Sam Anderson, Jim Haynie

The Dark Breed

USA 1995 92m Foto-Kem Stereo Surround

Astronauts returning from a secret mission turn out to have been infected by an alien virus which mutates them into monstrous killers.

Predictable sci-fi actioner in the *Dark Skies* manner, with distant echoes of *The Quatermass Experiment*. Well enough done, but its formulaic plot contains few surprises.

p: Joseph Merhi, Richard Pepin for PM

w: Richard Preston, Jr.

d: Richard Pepin

ph: Ken Blakey

m: Louis Febre

ed: Paul G. Vollk

pd: Steve Ramos

cos: Amber Lyne Garcia

sp: Encore Visual Effects, Michael Taylor

make-up effects: Criswell Productions

sound: Lionel Ball, Mikle Hall, M.R. Allen

stunt co-ordinator: Cole S. McKay

2nd unit d: Scott McAboy, Cole S. McKay

puppeteer: Michael V. McFarlane

Jack Scalia, Lance Le Gault, Donna W. Scott, Robin Curtis, Carlos Carrasco, Felton Perry, Jonathan Banks, Eddie Frierson (voice)

The Dark Crystal

GB 1982 94m Technicolor Panavision Dolby

Two young Gelflings combat evil in order to restore a shard to an enormous crystal whose power can rejuvenate life.

Conceptually arresting fantasy containing many original ideas, though the end results are perhaps a little too frightening for children. Discerning adults may have a ball, however.

p: Gary Kurtz for Universal/ITC

exec p: Lew Grade, Jim Henson, David Lazer

w: David Odell

d: JIM HENSON, FRANK OZ

ph: Oswald Morris

m: Trevor Jones

ed: Ralph Kemplen

pd: HARRY LANGE

conceptual design/creature design/cos: BRIAN FROUD

sp: Roy Field, Brian Smithies

sound: Bill Rowe

2nd unit d: Gary Kurtz

voices: Stephanie Garlick, Lisa Maxwell, Billie Whitelaw, Percy Edwards, Barry Dennen, Brian Muehl, Joseph O'Conor

Dark Skies

USA 1996 96m Technicolor TVM

In the early 1960s, a young government agent investigates a series of alien encounters and discovers the stories to be all too true.

Entertaining feature-length pilot for another *X Files*-style series.

p: Bruce Kerner for Columbia

exec p: Brent V. Friedman, Joseph Stern, Bryce Zabel

w: Bryce Zabel, Brent V. Friedman

d: Tobe Hooper

ph: Bill Butler

m: Mark Snow

ed: Andrew Cohen

pd: Curtis A. Schnell

cos: Jennifer Parsons

sp: Joe Rayner

sound: Marty Bolger

make-up effects: Todd Masters

stunt co-ordinator: John Moio

Eric Close, Megan Ward, J. T. Walsh, John W. Jackson, Conor O'Farrell, Francis Guinan, Scott Allan Campbell

Dark Star

USA 1974 83m Metroclor

The crew of a small starship roving the universe destroying unstable stars become bored with their mission and are finally destroyed by one of their talking bombs which thinks it is God.

Delightfully imaginative black comedy, inventively made on a low budget. A cult classic, it helped to establish its director as a talent to watch.

p: John Carpenter for Jack H. Harris

w: JOHN CARPENTER, DAN O'BANNON

d: JOHN CARPENTER

ph: Douglas Knapp

m: John Carpenter

ed/pd/sp: DAN O'BANNON

Brian Narelle, Andreijah Pahich, Dan O'Bannon, Carl Kuniholm, Joe Sanders

Darkdrive

USA 1996 80m colour

In 2001, a death machine used to execute criminals keeps their memories in a special electronic databank, but when this starts to show signs of criminal activity someone has to enter it to sort things out.

The premise is ingenious. Unfortunately, the handling is strictly routine and the budget obviously low, whilst the inside of the machine, after a few moments of computer graphics, seems to consist mostly of a run-down industrial estate.

p: Ken Olandt, Jim Hollensteiner, Gian Carlo Scandiuzzi, Phillip Roth for UFO/Agate/SR
w: Alec Carlin
d: Phillip Roth
ph: Andres Garreton
m: Jim Goodwin
ed/add ph: Christian McIntire
pd: Linda Kennedy
cos: Maggie Brown
sp: Andrew Hofman
Ken Olandt, Claire Stansfield, Julie Benz, Gian Carlo Scandiuzzi, Brian Faker, Brian Finney, Brenda Mathers (voice)

D. A. R. Y. L.

USA/GB 1985 99m TVCcolor Panavision Dolby

A family discovers that the mysterious young boy they have adopted is in fact a robot...

Passable romp for younger audiences.

p: John Heyman, Burtt Harris, Gabrielle Kelly for Paramount
w: David Ambrose, Allan Scott, Jeffrey Ellis
d: Simon Wincer
ph: Frank Watts
m: Marvin Hamlisch
ed: Adrian Carr
pd: Alan Cassie
cos: Shay Cunliffe
sp: Michael Fink
sound: Simon Kaye
stunt co-ordinator: John Moio
Mary Beth Hurt, Michael McKean, Barret Oliver (as Daryl), Kathryn Walker, Colleen Camp

Davey, Bert

British art director with a handful of interesting 70s credits.

Genre credits:
The Land That Time Forgot (1974 – ad), *Toomorrow* [sic] (1970 – co-ad), *The People That Time Forgot* (1977 – co-ad), *Aliens*

(1986 – co-ad)

Daviau, Allen

American cinematographer who has photographed several films for Steven Spielberg, including *The Color Purple* and *Empire of the Sun*. His other credits include *The Falcon and the Snowman*, *Avalon*, *Bugsy* and *Fearless*.

Genre credits:
E. T. (1982), *Twilight Zone – The Movie* (1983 – co-ph), *Harry and the Hendersons* (1987 – aka *Bigfoot and the Hendersons*), *Defending Your Life* (1991)

Davis, George W. (1914-)

American art director, long at 20th Century Fox, where he won Oscars for designing *The Robe* (1953 – with Lyle Wheeler) and *The Diary of Anne Frank* (1959 – also with Wheeler). His

other credits include *All About Eve*, *The Egyptian*, *The Seven-Year Itch*, *How the West Was Won* and *Wild Rovers*.

Genre credits:
The Ghost and Mrs Muir (1947 – co-ad), *The Time Machine* (1960 – co-ad), *Atlantis – The Lost Continent* (1960 – co-ad), *The Wonderful World of the Brothers Grimm* (1960 – co-ad), *The Seven Faces of Dr Lao* (1964 – co-ad), *The Power* (1968 – co-ad), *Brewster McCloud* (1970 – co-ad), *Earth II* (1971 – TVM – co-ad)

Davis, Warwick

Diminutive British actor who came to fame as the title character in *Willow*. His other credits include the Leprechaun films. He now also runs Willow Management, a casting agency which caters for actors and actresses who, like himself, are 'vertically challenged'.

The heat is on. Edward Judd asks for directions in Val Guest's sobering *The Day the Earth Caught Fire*.

Genre credits:
Return of the Jedi (1983), *Willow* (1988), *Gulliver's Travels* (1995 – TVM)

The Day of the Dolphin

USA 1973 104m Technicolor Panavision
A marine biologist discovers that a super-intelligent dolphin he has trained may be used to try and blow up the president's yacht.

Good looking but finally rather pretentious "realistic fantasy" which takes itself much too seriously to be entertaining. A curious project for the talents involved.

p: Robert E. Relyea for Avco-Embassy/Icarus
w: Buck Henry
novel: Robert Merle
d: Mike Nichols
ph: WILLIAM A. FRAKER
m: Georges Delerue
ed: Sam O'Steen
pd: Richard Sylbert
cos: Anthea Sylbert
sp: Albert Whitlock
sound: Laurence O. Jost
George C. Scott, Trish Van Devere, Paul Sorvino, Fritz Weaver

The Day of the Triffids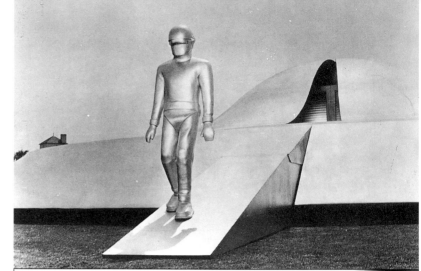

GB 1962 Eastmancolor Cinemascope
Man-eating plants from outer space take over the earth, and a handful of humans battle to survive.

Elementary science fiction thriller which now comes across as rather dated. Ripe for remaking.

p: George Pitcher for Philip Yordan
w: Philip Yordan
novel: John Wyndham
d: Steve Sekely
ph: Ted Moore
m: Ron Goodwin

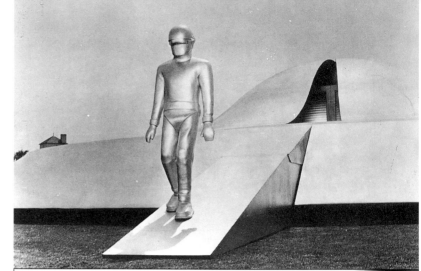

The imposing Gort (Lock Martin) makes his presence known in Robert Wise's *The Day the Earth Stood Still*, one of the best science fiction movies to come out of the 50s. All together now: "Klaatu barada nikto!"

ed: Spencer Reeve
ad: Cedric Dawe
cos: Bridget Sellars
sp: Wally Veevers
sound: Bert Ross, Maurice Askew
Howard Keel, Nicole Maurey, Kiron Moore, Janette Scott, Alexander Knox

The Day the Earth Caught Fire

GB 1961 99m bw Dyaliscope
Simultaneous nuclear tests by both the Russians and the Americans knock the earth off its axis and send it heading for the sun.

Imaginatively scripted slice of science fiction prophecy with its newspaper background an added bonus. Fast-talking and riveting throughout.

p: Val Guest for British Lion/Pax
w: WOLF MANKOWICZ, VAL GUEST
d: VAL GUEST
ph: Harry Waxman
m: Monty Norman
md: Stanley Black
ed: Bill Lenny
ad: Tony Masters
cos: Beatrice Dawson
sp: Les Bowie
sound: Buster Ambler

cam op: Moray Grant
technical advisor: Arthur Christiansen
EDWARD JUDD, Janet Munro, Leo McKern, Arthur Christiansen, Michael Goodliffe, Bernard Braden, Reginald Beckwith, Renee Asherson

The Day the Earth Stood Still

USA 1951 92m bw
An alien and his robot land in Washington D. C. in an attempt to stop the nations of the world from using atomic weaponry.

Regarded as a genre classic, this remains an intelligent, sharply made and often eerie piece which conveys its anti-war message with style and conviction.

p: Julian Blaustein for TCF
w: EDMUND H. NORTH
story: Harry Bates
d: ROBERT WISE
ph: LEO TOVER
m: BERNARD HERRMANN
ed: William Reynolds
ad: Lyle Wheeler, Addison Heher
cos: Charles Le Maire, Travilla, Perkins Bailey
sp: Fred Sersen

sound: ARTHUR L. KIRBACH, HARRY M. LEONARD
MICHAEL RENNIE, PATRICIA NEAL, Hugh Marlowe, Sam Jaffe, Billy Gray, Francis Beaver, Lock Martin (as Gort)

The Day the World Ended

USA 1956 81m bw Superscope
Survivors of a nuclear war find themselves threatened by mutants.

Grade Z schlock, for Corman completists only.

p: Roger Corman for Golden State
exec p: James H. Nicholson, Samuel Z. Arkoff, Alex Gordon
w: Lou Rusoff
d: Roger Corman
ph: Jock Feindel
m: Ronald Stein
ed: Ronald Sinclair
ad: no credit given
cos: Gertrude Reai
sp: Paul Blaisdell
sound: Jean Speak
Richard Denning, Lori Nelson, Adele Jergens, Touch (Mike) Connors, Paul Birch, Raymond Hatton, Paul Dubov, Paul Blaisdell, Jonathan Haze

Death Machine

GB 1994 111m Eastmancolor Dolby
A mad scientist working for the Chaank Corporation creates a killer robot which (inevitably) goes on the rampage.

Slick low budget amalgam of *The Terminator*, *Robocop* and *Hardware* (among others), let down only by overlength and the familiarity of its premise.

p: Dominic Anciano for Entertainment/Victor/Fugitive Features
exec p: Jim Beach
w/d: Stephen Norrington

ph: John De Borman
m: Crispin Merrell
ed: Paul Endacott
pd: Chris Edwards
cos: Stephanie Collie
sp: Dave Elsey and Creature Effects, Nik Williams, Animated Extras, Roy Scott, Christian Hogue, Peter Hutchinson
sound: Nainita Desai
2nd unit d: Chris Baker
Brad Dourif, Ely Pouget, William Hootkins, John Sharian, Martin McDougall, Andreas Wisniewski, Richard Brake, Stephen Norrington

The Death of the Incredible Hulk

USA 1990 96m colour TVM
Dr David Banner yet again tries to cure himself of his propensity for turning into a green giant when angered.

Desperate attempt to continue a franchise which had long passed its sell-by date.

p: Hugh Spencer-Phillips, Robert Ewing for New World/Bixby-Brandon
exec p: Bill Bixby
w: Gerald Di Pego
d: Bill Bixby
ph: Chuck Colwell
m: Lance Rubin
ed: Janet Ashikaga
pd: Douglas Higgins
cos: Trish Keating
sp: Dean Lockwood
sound: Lars Ekstrom
stunt co-ordinator: Ed Urlich
Bill Bixby, Lou Ferrigno, Carla Ferrigno, Elizabeth Gracen, Philip Sterling, Andreas Katsulas

Death Race 2000

USA 1975 78m Technicolor
In the year 2000, various competitors take part in the annual televised Transcontinental Death Race in which

they score points by running down people.

Raw but often quite vigorous low budget exploitation piece of the blackest variety. Now very much a cult item, its success at the time provoked a slew of imitations, among them *Deathsport* and *Cannonball* (aka *Carquake*).

p: Roger Corman for New World
w: Robert Thom, Charles Griffith
story: Ib Melchior
d: Paul Bartel
ph: Tak Fujimoto
m: Paul Chihara
ed: Tina Hirsch
ad: Robin Royce, B.B. Neel
sp: Richard McLean
David Carradine, Sylvester Stallone, Simone Griffeth, Mary Woronov, Roberta Collins, Martin Kove, Don Steele

De Laurentiis, Dino (1919-)

Italian producer and executive, a former extra and assistant director, with many big budget international spectaculars to his credit, among them *War and Peace*, *Barabbas*, *The Bible*, *Waterloo*, *Hurricane*, *Ragtime* and *The Bounty*. His attempts to break into the science fiction blockbuster market have met with variable success, though he keeps on trying. His other credits include such diverse films as *La Strada*, *Cabiria*, *Serpico*, *Death Wish*, *Silver Bullet*, *Year of the Dragon*, *Blue Velvet* and *Kuffs*.

Genre credits:
Barbarella (1968), *King Kong* (1976), *White Buffalo* (1977), *Flash Gordon* (1980), *Conan the Barbarian* (1981), *Conan the Destroyer* (1984), *Dune* (1984), *Red Sonja* (1985), *King Kong Lives* (1986), *Maximum Overdrive* (1986), *Earth Girls Are Easy* (1988)

De Witt, Louis

American special effects technician with many low budgeters to his credits, including several horror films, among them *The Black Sleep*, *Macabre* and *The Monster from Green Hell*.

Genre credits:

The Beast of Hollow Mountain (1956 – co-sp), *War of the Satellites* (1957 – co-sp), *The Invisible Boy* (1957 – co-sp), *The Thirty-Foot Bride of Candy Rock* (1959 – co-sp)

Deathsport

USA 1978 83m Metrocolor

In the future, gladiators do combat with murderous motorcyclists.

Tedious exploitation piece, lamentably short on imagination.

p: Roger Corman for New World
w: Henry Suso, Donald Stewart
d: Henry Suso, Allan Arkush
ph: Gary Graver
m: Andrew Stein

David Carradine, Claudia Jennings, William Smithers, Richard Lynch

Deep Red

USA 1994 85m DeLuxe TVM

A private eye is hired to help protect a young girl whose blood has been infected by an alien organism which prolongs life.

Slow moving but quite tolerable blend of Sam Spade-style film noir and *X Files*-style sci-fi.

p: Timothy Marx for MTE/DBA
exec p: Dave Bell
w: D. Brent Mote
d: Craig R. Baxley
ph: Joao Fernandes
m: Gary Chang
ed: Jeff Freeman
pd: Garreth Stover

Michael Biehn, Joanna Pacula, Steven

Williams, Lisa Collins, Tobin Bell, Lindsay Haun, John de Lancie

Deepstar Six

USA 1988 100m Metrocolor Dolby

Undersea workers inadvertently release a monster from the depths.

Routine underwater shocker somewhere in the wake of *The Abyss*.

p: Sean S. Cunningham, Patrick Markey for Carolco
exec p: Andrew Vajna, Mario Kassar
w: Lewis Abernathy, Geoff Miller
d: Sean S. Cunningham
ph: Mac Ahlberg
m: Harry Manfredini
ed: David Handman
pd: John Reinhart
cos: Amy Endries
sp: James Isaac
make-up effects: Mark Shostrom
sound: Hans Roland
underwater ph: Pete Romano, Al Giddings
titles: Burke Mattson

Taurean Blacque, Nancy Everhard, Greg Evigan, Miguel Ferrer, Marius Weyers, Nia Peeples, Matt McCoy, Cindy Pickett

Defending Your Life

USA 1991 112m Technicolor

An advertising executive is killed in an accident whilst driving his new car and finds himself in Judgement City where he has to defend his earthly actions.

Amusing comedy in the *Here Comes Mr Jordan / Heaven Can Wait* manner, with plenty of well observed sideswipes at American consumerism. Its best joke, however, features Shirley MacLaine as the hostess of a show presenting people with views of their former lives. Unfortunately, the film was a commercial disappointment.

p: Michael Grillo for Warner/Geffen
exec p: Herbert S. Nanas

John Spartan (Sylvester Stallone) totes his gun in the futuristic thriller *Demolition Man*.

w/d: Albert Brooks
ph: Allen Daviau
m: Michael Gore
ed: David Finfer, Spencer Gross
pd: Ida Random
cos: Deborah L. Scott
sound: Thomas Causey

Albert Brooks, Meryl Streep, Rip Torn, Lee Grant, Buck Henry, Shirley MacLaine, Michael Durrell, Julie Cobb

Dehn, Paul (1912–1976)

British writer and lyricist, an Oscar winner for co-authoring the story (with James Bernard) for *Seven Days to Noon* (1951). Began his career as a journalist in 1936, working primarily as a film critic. Turned out a series of top notch screenplays (often in collaboration) in the 60s and 70s, among them *Goldfinger*, *The Spy Who Came in from the Cold*, *The Deadly Affair*, *The Taming of the Shrew* and *Murder on the Orient Express*. His genre work was solely for the *Planet of the Apes* films.

The astronauts unload their luggage after their long journey in *Destination Moon*, the first of many science fiction movies produced by George Pal in the 50s.

D

Genre credits:

Beneath the Planet of the Apes (1970 – co-story/w), *Escape from the Planet of the Apes* (1971 – w), *Conquest of the Planet of the Apes* (1972 – w), *Battle for the Planet of the Apes* (1973 – story)

Demolition Man

USA 1993 114m Technicolor Dolby
In 1996, a cop is frozen in a Cryo Penetentiary for committing involuntary manslaughter and is thawed out in 2032 so as to track down a former adversary.

Frenetic futuristic actioner, strictly for star fans.

p: Joel Silver, Michael Levy, Howard Kazanjian for Warner/Silver
w: Daniel Waters, Robert Reneau, Peter M. Lenkov
story: Peter M. Lenkov, Robert Reneau
d: Marco Brambilla
ph: Alex Thomson
m: Elliot Goldenthal
ed: Stuart Baird
pd: David L. Snyder
cos: Bob Ringwood
sound: Robert G. Henderson
Sylvester Stallone, Wesley Snipes, Sandra Bullock, Nigel Hawthorne, Benjamin Bratt, Bob Gunton

Demon Seed

USA 1977 95m Metrocolor Panavision
Whilst he is away on business, the wife of a scientist is raped and impregnated by his super-intelligent computer, Proteus.

Odd little fantasy-thriller, well enough done for its purpose, but much too long.

p: Herb Jaffe for MGM
w: Robert Jaffe, Roger O. Hirson
novel: Dean R. Koonitz
d: Donald Cammell

ph: Bill Butler
m: Jerry Fielding
ed: Francisco Mazzola
pd: Edward Carfagno
cos: Sandy Cole
sp: Tom Fisher, Glen Robinson
sound: Jerry Jost
Julie Christie, Fritz Weaver, Gerritt Graham, Barry Kroeger, Lisa Lu

Destination Moon

USA 1950 91m Technicolor
The Americans finally get to the moon in a rocket financed by private backers.

A naive and somewhat out-of-date movie with a limited imagination. It's a mildly amusing in retrospect.

p: George Pal for Universal
w: Rip Van Ronkel, Robert Heinlan, James O'Hanlon
d: Irving Pitchel
ph: LIONEL LINDON
m: Leith Stevens
ed: Duke Goldstone
ad: Ernst Fetge
sp: Lee Zavitz
animation: Walter Lantz
Warner Anderson, John Archer, Tom Powers, Dick Wesson

Devlin, Dean

American writer and producer, often in collaboration with director Roland Emmerich, with whom he had great success with both *Stargate* and *Independence Day*. A former actor, he met Emmerich whilst performing in *Moon 44*.

Genre credits:

Moon 44 (1989 – actor), *Universal Soldier* (1989 – co-w), *Stargate* (1994 – co-w/co-p), *Independence Day* (1996 – co-w/p), *Godzilla* (1988 – co-w/p)

Dexter, Anthony (1919-)

American actor (real name Walter Fleischmann) who, after stage experience, made his film debut in 1951 in the title role in *Valentino*. Other credits include *The Brigand*, *Captain John Smith and Pocahontas*, *The Parson and the Outlaw* and *Thoroughly Modern Millie*.

Genre credits:

Fire Maidens from Outer Space (1954), *The Story of Mankind* (1959), *Twelve to the Moon* (1959), *The Phantom Planet* (1962)

Dick, Philip K. (1917-1982)

Prolific American author (36 novels, over 100 short stories), three of whose science fiction stories have been adapted for the screen, most notably *Blade Runner* (1982 [from *Do Androids Dream of Electric Sheep?*]). The others are *Total Recall* (1990 [from *We Can Remember It for You Wholesale*]) and *Screamers* (1995 [from *Second Variety*]). First published in 1952, he died the same year as his greatest success.

Genre credits:

Blade Runner (1982), *Total Recall* (1990), *Blade Runner: The Director's Cut* (1991), *Screamers* (1995)

Dick Tracy

USA 1990 103m Technicolor Dolby
Super cop Dick Tracy finally brings to justice gangster boss Big Boy Caprice and his assorted henchmen.

Elaborate big screen version of the Chester Gould comic strip, of note chiefly for its production design (which uses only the seven primary colours featured in the comic strip) and its roster of famous guest stars in heavy make-up.

p: Warren Beatty for Touchstone/Silver Screen Partners IV

exec p: Barrie M. Osborn, Art Linson, Floyd Mutrux

w: Jim Cash, Kack Epps, Jr.

comic strip: Chester Gould

d: Warren Beatty

ph: VITTORIO STORARO

m: Danny Elfman

songs: STEPHEN SONDHEIM (aa, best song, *Sooner or Later*)

ed: Richard Marks

pd/set decoration: RICHARD SYLBERT, RICK SIMPSON (AA)

cos: Milena Canonero

sp: Michael Lloyd, Harrison Ellenshaw

sound: Thomas Causey

character make-up: JOHN CAGLIONE, DOUG DREXLER (AA)

ch: Jeffrey Hornaday

stunt co-ordinator: Billy Burton

titles: Wayne Fitzgerald

Warren Beatty, Madonna, Al Pacino, Mandy Patinkin, Dustin Hoffman, Glenne Headley, Charlie Korsmo, Dick Van Dyke, Charles Durning, James Caan, Michael J. Pollard, Estelle Parsons, Mike Mazurki, Kathy Bates, Catherine O'Hara, William Forsyth, Seymour Cassel, John Schuck, Charles Fleischer, R. G. Armstrong, Paul Sorvino, Henry Jones, Bert Remsen, Ed O'Ross, Allen Garfield

Dicken, Roger

British special effects technician whose credits include *The Blood Beast Terror*, *Witchfinder General* and *Scars of Dracula*. Began his career as an assistant on TV's *Thunderbirds*.

Genre credits:

When Dinosaurs Ruled the Earth (1969 – co-sp), *The Land That Time Forgot* (1974 – co-sp), *The Warlords of Atlantis* (1978 – co-sp), *Alien* (1979 – co-sp)

Digby: The Biggest Dog in the World

GB 1973 88m Technicolor

An old English sheepdog accidentally eats a new serum which makes it grow to an enormous size.

Undemanding fantasy comedy for younger children. Surprisingly, it wasn't made by Disney.

p: Walter Shenson for TCF

w: Michael Pertwee

novel: Ted Kay

d: Joseph McGrath

ph: Harry Waxman

m: Edwin T. Astley

sp: Tom Howard

Jim Dale, Spike Milligan, Angela Douglas, Milo O'Shea, Dinsdale Landen, Garfield Morgan, Bob Todd, Victor Spinetti, Victor Maddern, Norman Rossington

Dilley, Leslie

British art director who has won Oscars for *Star Wars* (1977 – with John Barry and Norman Reynolds) and *Raiders of the Los Ark* (1981 – with Norman Reynolds). His other credits include *The Last Remake of Beau Geste*, *An American Werewolf in London* and *What About Bob?*

Genre credits:

Star Wars (1977 – co-ad), *Superman* (1978 – co-ad), *Alien* (1979 – co-ad), *The Empire Strikes Back* (1980 – co-ad), *Raiders of the Lost Ark* (1981 – co-ad), *Invaders from Mars* (1986 – ad), *The Abyss* (1989 – co-ad), *Honey, I Blew Up the Kid* (1993 – ad)

Dillman, Bradford (1953-)

American actor who, after stage experience in the mid-50s, turned to movies in 1958 with *A Certain Smile*. His many credits include *Compulsion* (as Artie Straus), *The Way We Were*, *Gold*,

Piranha, *The Swarm* and *Sudden Impact*.

Genre credits:

Escape from the Planet of the Apes (1971), *Chosen Survivors* (1974), *The Disappearance of Flight 412* (1974 – TVM), *Bug* (1975)

Dinosaurus!

USA 1960 85m DeLuxe Cinemascope

A caveman and two dinosaurs are revived on a remote tropical island.

Amateur low budgeter with dismal effects.

p: Jack H. Harris for Universal

w: Jean Yeaworth, Dan E. Weisburd

story: Jack H. Harris

d: Irwin S. Yeaworth, Jr.

ph: Stanley Cortez

m: Ronald Stein

ed: John H. Bushelman

ad: Jack Senter

cos: Bill Edwards

sp: Tim Baar, Wan Chang, Gene Warren

sound: Vic Appel

underwater ph: Paul Stader

Ward Ramsey, Paul Lukather, Alan Roberts, Kristina Hanson

The Disappearance of Flight 412

USA 1974 74m colour TVM

Two USAF jets mysteriously disappear whilst in pursuit of a UFO.

Unsurprising anecdote which fails to convince or excite as it should.

p: Gerald L. Adler for Cinemobile

w: George Simpson, Neal Burger

d: Jud Taylor

m: Morton Stevens

Glenn Ford, Bradford Dillman, David Soul, Robert F. Lyons, Guy Stockwell, Kent Smith

Disney, Walt (1901–1966)

Legendary American animator, producer and studio head whose animated features remain the best the cinema has ever produced. Trained as an artist in Kansas before going to France in 1917 as an ambulance driver for the Red Cross during the last few months of World War One. Became a commercial artist upon his return home, turning to animated ads and shorts (Laugh-O-Grams) soon after, though his attempts to set up his own company at this stage ended in financial disaster. He went to Hollywood in 1923 and set up his own studio with his brother Roy and churned out countless "Alice" cartoons with former Laugh-O-Gram partner Ub Iwerks (*Alice's Day at the Sea*, *Alice's Spooky Adventure*, *Alice the Lumberjack*, etc). A series of Oswald the Rabbit shorts followed (*Harem Scarem*, *Ozzie of the Mounted*, *Hot Dog*, etc), then in 1927 came Mickey Mouse and Disney never looked back. The first two Mickey cartoons (*Plane Crazy*, *Gallopin' Goucho*) were silent and in black and white, though the third, *Steamboat Willie*, had sound, the voice of Mickey being provided by Walt himself. Much Mickey Mouse merchandising followed, as did the Silly Symphonies series (*The Skeleton Dance*, *Cannibal Capers*, *Monkey Melodies*, *Three Little Pigs*, etc). This series also included the first colour cartoon, *Flowers and Trees*. Many shorts featuring Disney's other creations appeared in the 30s (Donald Duck, Goofy, Pluto, Minnie Mouse) whilst in 1937 he gave the world the first feature-length cartoon, *Snow White and the Seven Dwarfs*. Despite industry fears, the film was a commercial smash, and Disney followed it with several other equally classy ventures, among them *Pinocchio*, *Fantasia* and *Bambi*. In 1950 he turned to live action with an adaptation of *Treasure Island* (though live action had been interspersed with his "Alice" cartoons and a handful of 40s titles such as *The Reluctant Dragon*, *Saludos, Amigos* and *Song of the South*). Wildlife documentaries also became a speciality (*The Living Desert*, *Nature's Half Acre*, *Bear Country*, etc), whilst in 1954 Disney also successfully broke into television (*Davy Crockett*, *The Mickey Mouse Club*, etc). Disneyworld opened in 1955, whilst in 1964 he had one of his greatest commercial successes with the live action/animated musical *Mary Poppins*. Following Disney's death in 1966, the studio went through a period of artistic uncertainty which was reflected in its product, which included bland live action comedies and cartoon features which failed to live up to their illustrious predecessors. Since the late 80s, however, the company has turned around completely, producing top-line live action films and animated features. The studio's recent successes include *The Lion King* and *The Hunchback of Notre Dame*. In all, Disney collected a staggering 29 Oscars for his work.

Genre credits (features only):
Snow White and the Seven Dwarfs (1937), *Pinocchio* (1940), *Fantasia* (1940), *The Reluctant Dragon* (1940), *Dumbo* (1941), *Bambi* (1942), *Saludos, Amigos* (1943), *The Three Caballeros* (1944), *Make Mine Music* (1946), *Song of the South* (1946), *Fun and Fancy Free* (1947), *Melody Time* (1948), *So Dear to My Heart* (1949), *The Adventures of Ichabod and Mr Toad* (1949), *Cinderella* (1950), *Alice in Wonderland* (1951), *Peter Pan* (1953), *20,000 Leagues Under the Sea* (1954), *Lady and the Tramp* (1955), *The Shaggy Dog* (1959), *Sleeping Beauty* (1959), *Darby O'Gill and the Little People* (1959), *One-Hundred-and-One Dalmatians* (1961), *The Absent-Minded Professor* (1961), *Babes in Toyland* (1961), *Moon Pilot* (1962), *In Search of the Castaways* (1962), *Son of Flubber* (1963), *The Sword in the Stone* (1963), *The Misadventures of Merlin Jones* (1964), *Mary Poppins* (1964), *Winnie the Pooh and the Honey Tree* (1966)

Genre credits following Disney's death:
The Jungle Book (1967), *The Gnome Mobile* (1967), *Blackbeard's Ghost* (1967), *Winnie the Pooh and the Blustery Day* (1968), *The Love Bug* (1968), *The Computer Wore Tennis Shoes* (1970), *The Aristocats* (1970), *Bedknobs and Broomsticks* (1971), *Million Dollar Duck* (1971), *Now You See Him, Now You Don't* (1972), *Charley and the Angel* (1973), *Robin Hood* (1973), *Herbie Rides Again* (1974), *Winnie the Pooh and Tigger Too* (1974), *The Island at the Top of the World* (1974), *Escape to Witch Mountain* (1974), *The Strongest Man in the World* (1975), *The Shaggy D.A.* (1976), *The Rescuers* (1977), *Freaky Friday* (1977), *The Many Adventures of Winnie the Pooh* (1977), *Herbie Goes to Monte Carlo* (1977), *Pete's Dragon* (1977), *Return from Witch Mountain* (1978), *The Cat from Outer Space* (1978), *The Spaceman and King Arthur* (1979 – aka *Unidentified Flying Oddball*), *The Black Hole* (1979), *Herbie Goes Bananas* (1980), *Popeye* (1980), *Dragonslayer* (1980), *The Fox and the Hound* (1981), *Condorman* (1981), *The Watcher in the Woods* (1981), *Tron* (1982), *Winnie the Pooh and a Day for Eeyore* (1983), *Mickey's Christmas Carol* (1983), *Something Wicked This Way Comes* (1983), *Splash!* (1984), *Baby, Secret of the Lost Legend* (1985), *The Black Cauldron* (1985), *My Science Project* (1985), *Return to Oz* (1985), *Basil: The Great Mouse Detective* (1986 – aka *The Great Mouse Detective*), *Flight of the Navigator* (1986), *Fourteen Going on Thirty* (1987 – TVM), *Who Framed Roger Rabbit?* (1988), *Oliver and Company* (1988), *The Absent-Minded Professor* (1988 – TVM), *The Little Mermaid* (1989), *Duck Tales: The Movie* (1990 – aka *Duck Tales: The Movie – Treasure of the Lost Lamp*), *The Rescuers Down Under* (1990), *Beauty and the Beast* (1991), *Aladdin* (1992), *The Lion King* (1994), The Return of Jafar (1994

Talk to the animals. Rex Harrison has a chat with one of his co-stars during the filming of the fantasy musical *Doctor Dolittle*.

– video), *Pocahontas* (1995), *A Goofy Movie* (1995), *The Hunchback of Notre Dame* (1996), *Honey, We Shrunk Ourselves* (1996), *James and The Giant Peach* (1996), *Aladdin, King of Thieves* (1997 – video), *Hercules* (1997), *The Legend of Mulan* (1998)

Doc Savage, Man of Bronze

USA 1975 100m Technicolor

A superhero flies to South America to avenge the death of his father.

Feeble comic strip nonsense, lacking both the wit and style needed to carry it off.

p: George Pal for Warner
w: George Pal, Joe Morhaim
novel: Kenneth Robeson
d: Michael Anderson
ph: Fred J. Koenekamp
m: John Philip Sousa
md: Frank de Vol
ly: Don Black
ed: Thomas McCarthy
ad: Fred Harpman
cos: Patrick Cummings
sp: Howard A. Anderson, Sass Bedig, Robert MacDonald
sound: Harlan Riggs
stunt co-ordinator: Tonu Eppers
Ron Ely, Paul Gleason, Bill Lucking, Michael Miller, Eldon Quick

Dr. Cyclops

USA 1940 76m Technicolor

In the jungles of Brazil a research scientist miniaturises five of his colleagues for experimentation.

Routine mad doctor stuff, ineptly scripted and acted, but with good use of colour. Effects work variable.

p: Dale Van Every for Paramount
w: Tom Kilpatrick
d: Ernest B. Shoedsack
ph: HENRY SHARP, WINTON C. HOCH
m: Ernst Toch, Gerard Carbonara, Albert Hay Malotte
ed: Ellsworth Hoagland
ad: Hand Dreier, Earl Hedrick
sp: Farciot Edouart, Wallace Kelley
sound: Harry Lindgren, Richard Olson
Albert Dekker, Janice Logan, Victor Kilian, Thomas Coley, Charles Halton, Paul Fix

Dr. Dolittle

USA 1967 152m DeLuxe Todd-AO

A doctor with the ability to talk to animals sets forth on a voyage to discover the whereabouts of the Great Pink Sea Snail.

Ham-fisted fantasy musical with variable songs and performances. Bright moments survive, but children will probably find the length taxing.

p: Arthur P. Jacobs for TCF/APJAC
w/m/ly: Leslie Bricusse
novel: Hugh Lofting
d: Richard Fleischer
ph: Robert Surtees
song: *Talk to the Animals*, m/ly: Leslie Bricusse (aa)
md: Lionel Newman, Alexander Courage
ed: Samuel E. Beetley, Marjorie Fowler
pd: Mario Chiari, Jack Martin Smith, Ed Graves
cos: Ray Aghayan
sp: L. B. Abbott (aa), Art Cruickshank, Emil Kosa, Jr., Howard Lydecker
sound: Murray Spivack
titles: Don Record
ch: Herbert Ross
Rex Harrison, Samantha Eggar, Anthony Newley, William Dix, RICHARD ATTENBOROUGH (singing *I've Never Seen Anything Like It in My Life*), Peter Bull, Geoffrey Holder

I don't think we're in Kansas anymore! Dr. Who (Peter Cushing), Ian (Roy Castle), Barbara (Jennie Linden) and Susan (Roberta Tovey) find themselves on the planet Skaro in *Dr. Who and the Daleks*, the first of the two big screen Dr. Who movies starring Cushing.

Dr. Who

Canada/USA/GB 1996 96m colour TVM
The Doctor is regenerated in San Francisco in 1999 and encounters his old enemy, The Master.

Fairly slick update of the much-loved long running BBC television series, though it nevertheless drew critical flak for being something of a mid-Atlantic compromise, finally satisfying neither old admirers nor new converts.

p: Peter V. Ware for BBC/MCA/Universal
exec p: Alex Beaton, Philip David Segal, Jo Wright
w: Matthew Jacobs
d: Geoffrey Sax
ph: Glen MacPherson
m: John Debney, John Sponsler, Louis Serbe
pd: Richard Hudolin
cos: Jori Woodman
sp: North West Imaging
sound: Gordon W. Anderson
Paul McGann, Eric Roberts, Daphne Ashbrook, Sylvester McCoy, Yee Jee Tso, John Novak, Michael David Simms

Dr. Who and the Daleks

GB 1965 Technicolor Techniscope
Dr. Who, his two granddaughters and one of their friends are transported through time to a post-nuclear planet ruled by the deadly Daleks.

Cheerful low budget science fiction romp for younger children, based on the long-running television serial.

p: Max J. Rosenberg, Milton Subotsky for British Lion/Regal/Aaru
exec p: Joe Vegoda
w: Milton Subotsky
series: Terry Nation
d: Gordon Flemyng
ph: John Wilcox
m: Malcolm Lockyer, Barry Gray
ed; Oswald Hafenrichter
ad: Bill Constable
cos: Jackie Cummins
sp: Ted Samuels, Les Hillman
sound: Buster Ambler, John Cox
Peter Cushing, Roy Castle, Jennie Linden, Roberta Tovey, Barrie Ingham, Michael Coles

Donaggio, Pino (1941-)

Italian composer (real name Giuseppe Donaggio) with a penchant for fantasy and thriller scores, including several for director Brian de Palma (*Carrie*, *Home Movies*, *Dressed to Kill*, *Blow Out*, *Body Double*, *Raising Cain*). His other credits include *Don't Look Now*, *Piranha*, *The Howling*, *Two Evil Eyes* and *Trauma*. He also composed the hit song *You Don't Have to Say You Love Me*.

Hercules (1983), *Hercules II* (1985), *Meridian* ('1990 – aka *Kiss of the Beast*)

Donati, Danilo

Italian production and costume designer with a couple of fantasy films for producer Dino de Laurentiis to his credit.

Genre credits:
Flash Gordon (1980 – pd/cos), *Red Sonja* (1985 – pd/cos)

Don Bluth's Thumbelina see Thumbelina

Donlevy, Brian (1899–1972)

Burly-looking Irish-American character actor, long in Hollywood, where he appeared in such films as *Beau Geste*, *Brigham Young*, *The Great McGinty* and *The Glass Key*. In the 50s he came to England to portray Professor Quatermass in two films for Hammer.

Genre credits:
The Quatermass Experiment (1955 – aka *The Creeping Unknown*), *Quatermass 2* (1957 aka *Enemy from Space*), *The Curse of the Fly* (1965)

Donner, Richard (1939–)

American director and producer with a penchant for slick action movies, among them the *Lethal Weapon* series. Following acting experience in New York, he began his career in Hollywood in the late 50s, first as a commercials director, then in series television, among his credits being episodes of *Wanted Dead or Alive*, *The Banana Splits* (the *Danger Island* segments) and *Kojak*. His first film as a director was *X-15* in 1961. Two more movie assignments followed in the 60s, *Salt and Pepper* and *Twinky*, neither of them successes. However, in 1976 he had a major commercial success with *The Omen*, which he followed with *Superman* two years later, since when he has remained one of Hollywood's most sought-after directors. Other credits: *Inside Moves*, *The Toy* and *Maverick*.

Genre credits:
X-15 (1961 – d), *Superman* (1978 – d), *Superman 2* (1980 – directed some uncredited sequences), *Ladyhawke* (1985 – co-p/d), *The Goonies* (1985 – co-p/d), *Scrooged* (1988 – co-p/d)

Donovan's Brain

USA 1953 81m bw
A scientist keeps alive the brain of a dead business tycoon only to find himself increasingly dominated by it.

Silly but not entirely unengaging sci-fi horror which at least has the courage of its own convictions.

p: Tom Gries for UA/Dowling
w: Felix Feist, Hugh Brook
novel: Curt Siodmak
d: Felix Feist
ph: Joseph Biroc
m: Eddie Dunstedter
ed: Herbert L. Strock
pd: Boris Leven

cos: Chuck Keehne
sp: Harry Redmond, Jr.
sound: Earl Snyder
Lew Ayres, Nancy Davis (later Reagan), Gene Evans, Steve Brodie, Lisa K. Howard, Tom Powers, Victor Sutherland, Michael Colgan

Doppelganger

see Journey to the Far Side of the Sun

Double, Double, Toil and Trouble

USA 1993 90m colour Ultra Stereo
During Halloween, twin sisters win a magic wand at a fancy dress party and use it to keep their aunt, who just happens to be a witch, in check.

Exceptionally mild family entertainment for the kind of family that probably no longer exists.

p: Adria Later, Mark Lacino for Dual Star/Warner
exec p: Jim Green, Allen Epstein
w: Jurgen Wolff
d: Stuart Margolin
ph: Richard Leiterman
m: Richard Bellis
ed: George Appleby
pd: David Fischer
cos: Jane Still
sp: Roy Cutler, Fantasy II
sound: Rick Patton
stunt co-ordinator: Ken Kirzinger
Mary Kate Olsen, Ashley Olsen, Cloris Leachman, Phil Fondarano, Eric McCormack, Kelli Fox, Wayne Robson, Meshach Taylor

Double Dragon

USA 1994 95m CFIcolor DTS Stereo
In New Angeles in 2007, after the big 'quake, two teenage brothers fight to protect half of a magical medallion from falling into the hands of a megalomaniac who possesses the other half.

Another videogame-to-movie transfer, and not that good a one, though one sequence involving a boat chase across a flooded Los Angeles is well enough staged.

p: Sunil R. Shah, Ash R. Shah, Alan Schechter, Jan Hamsher, Don Murphy for Imperial/Scanbox/Greenleaf
exec p: Sundip R. Shah, Anders P. Jensen
w: Michael Davis, Peter Gould
story: Paul Dini, Neal Shusterman
d: James Yukich
ph: Gary Kibbe
m: Jay Ferguson
ed: Florent Retz
pd: Mayne Berke
cos: Fiona Spence
sp: Pacific Data Images, Illusion Arts Inc., Joe Lombardi
sound: Patrick Hanson
stunt co-ordinator/2nd unit d: Jeff Imada
add ph: Michael O'Shea, Tony Mitchell
make-up effects: Chiodo Brothers
Robert Patrick, Mark Dacasos, Scott Wolf, Kristina Malandro, Alyssa Milano, Julia Nickson, George Hamilton, Vana White, Jeff Imada

Dourif, Brad (1950–)

American character actor with a liking for offbeat roles, particularly psychotics. He is also known for voicing the killer doll Chucky in the *Child's Play* movies. His other credits include *One Flew Over the Cuckoo's Nest*, *Wise Blood*, *The Eyes of Laura Mars*, *Blue Velvet*, *Exorcist III* and *Trauma*.

Genre credits:
Dune (1984), *Wild Palms* (1993 – TVM), *Death Machine* (1994), *Phoenix* (1995), *Alien Resurrcetion* (1997)

Dragonheart

USA 1996 103m colour DTS stereo
A young prince turns to the bad and so

one of his knights teams up with a dragon to free the land from his tyrannical rule.

The computer-animated dragon is well enough done, but this otherwise unimaginative sword and sorcery romp has totally the wrong look and atmosphere. A real disappointment.

p: Raffaella de Laurentiis for Universal
exec p: David Rotman, Patrick Read Johnson
w: Charles Edward Pogue
d: Rob Cohen
ph: David Eggby
m: Randy Edelman
ed: Peter Amundson
pd: Benjamin Fernandez
sp: Scott Squires, Phil Tippett, ILM
Dennis Quaid, David Thewlis, Julie Christie, Sean Connery (voice as the dragon), Pete Poslethwaite

Dragonslayer

USA 1981 110m Metroclor Panavision Dolby

A young sorcerer helps to rid a small township of a marauding dragon.

Good looking but rather slow moving and dimly lit fantasy, at its best when the special effects take over.

p: Hal Barwood for Paramount/Walt Disney
exec p: Howard W. Koch
w: Hal Barwood, Matthew Robbins
d: Matthew Robbins
ph: Derek Vanlint
m: Alex North
ed: Tony Lawson
pd: Elliot Scott
sp: Thomas Smith, ILM
Peter MacNichol, Ralph Richardson, Caitlin Clarke, Peter Eyre, John Hallam, Albert Salmi

Dreamchild

GB 1985 93m Technicolor
In 1932, Alice Hargreaves, Lewis

Carroll's inspiration for the "Alice" stories, is invited to American to receive an honourary degree in celebration of Carroll's 100th anniversary, and finds herself haunted by images from the past.

Pleasantly literary concoction of fantasy and actual events, nicely put together, but not entirely sure of its own motives.

p: Rick McCallum, Kenith Trodd for Thorn EMI/PFH
exec p: Dennis Potter, Verity Lambert
w: Dennis Potter
d: Gavin Millar
ph: BILLY WILLIAMS
m: Stanley Myers
ed: Angus Newton
pd: Roger Hall
cos: Jane Robinson
sp: Lyle Conway, Jim Henson's Creature Shop
sound: Godfrey Kirby, Jon Blunt
CORAL BROWNE, Ian Holm, Peter Gallagher, Nicola Cowper, Jane Asher, Amelia Shankley, Emma King, Imogen Boorman and the voices of Fulton Mackay, Alan Bennett, Julie Walters, Frank Middlemass, Tony Haygarth, Ken Campbell

Dreams

Japan/USA 1990 119m Technicolor
A collection of stories based on dreams experienced by Akira Kurosawa.

Not all art is great art, and though Kurosawa is undeniably a great artist, this isn't one of his masterpieces, though there are striking visual touches along the way.

p: Hisao Kurosawa, Mike Y. Inoue for Warner/Akira Kurosawa USA
exec p: Steven Spielberg
w/d: Akira Kurosawa
ph: Takaeo Saito
m: Shinichiro Ikebe
ed: Tome Minami
ad: Yoshiro Muraki, Akira Sakuragi
cos: Emi Wada
sp: ILM
sound: Kenichi Benitani
Akira Terao, Mitsunori Isak, Martin Scorsese (as Vincent Van Gogh), Chisu Ryu, Mieko Harada

Dreamscape

USA 1984 100m CFIcolor Dolby
A young man with telepathic powers is recruited by a scientific institution to help them with their experiments with dreams.

Fairish fantasy thriller, at its liveliest during the dream sequences themselves.

p: Bruce Cohn Curtis, Jerry Tokofsky for Bella/Zupnik-Curtis
w: David Loughery, Chuck Russell, Joseph Ruben
story: David Loughery
d: Joseph Ruben
ph: Brian Tufano
m: Maurice Jarre
ed: Richard Halsey
pd: Jeff Staggs, Clifford Searcy
cos: Linda M. Bass
sp: Peter Kuran
sound: Kirk Francis, Susumu Tokonow
make-up effects: Craig Reardon
titles: Dale Tate
stunt co-ordinator: Jim Arnett
Dennis Quaid, Max Von Sydow, Christopher Plummer, Kate Capshaw, Eddie Albert, David Patrick Kelly, George Wendt, Larry Gelman, Larry Cedar

Dreyfuss, Richard (1947-)

American star actor, a best actor Oscar winner for *The Goodbye Girl* (1977). He came to prominence in the 70s with such hits as *American Graffiti, The Apprenticeship of Duddy Kravitz,*

Infinity beckons astronaut Dave Bowman (Keir Dullea) in Stanley Kubrick's masterful *2001: A Space Odyssey*.

Jaws and *Close Encounters*, having made his film debut in 1969 with a small part in *The Graduate*. Drug abuse saw the gradual collapse of his career, though he made a successful comeback in 1985 with *Down and Out in Beverly Hills*, since when he has appeared in such movies as *Stakeout*, *Tin Men*, *Postcards from the Edge* and *What About Bob?*

Genre credits:
Close Encounters of the Third Kind (1977 – as Roy Neary), *Close Encounters of the Third Kind – The Special Edition* (1980), *Always* (1989), *James and the Giant Peach* (1996 – voice)

Du Prez, John

British composer whose output includes all three *Teenage Mutant Ninja Turtle* movies as well as such titles as *Monty Python's Meaning of Life*, *Personal Services*, *A Fish Called Wanda* and, er, *Carry On, Columbus*.

Genre credits:
Teenage Mutant Ninja Turtles (1990), *Teenage Mutant Ninja Turtles II: The Secret of the Ooze* (1991), *Teenage Mutant Ninja Turtles III: The Turtles Are Back... In Time!* (1992), *The Wind in the Willows* (1996 – co-songs/m)

Duck Dogers in the 24 1/2 Century

USA 1953 6m Technicolor
Daffy Duck is sent to Planet X to get some Aludium Phosdex (the shaving cream atom) and encounters a Martian on a similar mission.

Superior cartoon short, as memorable for its design as for its gags.

p: Warner
story: Michael Maltese
d: Chuck Jones
md: Carl W. Stalling
voices: Mel Blanc

Duck Tales: The Movie Treasure of the Lost Lamp

USA/Fr 1990 74m Technicolor Dolby
Scrooge McDuck, accompanied by Huey, Dewey and Louie, searches for a genie's lamp and crosses paths with an evil magician called Merlock.

Mild *Indiana Jones*-style cartoon japes which should please young viewers of the *Duck Tales* series on which it is based.

p: Bob Hatchcock for Walt Disney/Movietoons
w: Alan Burnett
d: Bob Hathcock
m: David Newman
ed: Charles King
sound: Nick Ash, Nick Alphin, Dean A. Zupancic
voices: Alan Young, Christopher Lloyd, June Foray, Rip Taylor, Richard Libertini, Chuck McCann, Russi Taylor, Joan Gerber, Terence McGovern

Dullea, Keir (1936-)

American actor, best known for playing astronaut Dave Bowman in *2001: A Space Odyssey*. He began his acting career on stage in stock, reaching Broadway in 1959 and films in 1961 with *Hoodlum Priest*. His other film credits include *David and Lisa*, *Bunny Lake is Missing*, *De Sade*, *Black Christmas*, *Full Circle* and *Brainwaves*.

Genre credits:
2001: A Space Odyssey (1968), *The Starlost: Deception* (1982 – TVM), *2010: Odyssey Two* (1984)

Dumbo

USA 1941 64m Technicolor
A baby circus elephant with enormous ears discovers that he can fly.

Marvellously stylish and inventive cartoon feature with a heartwarming story and such memorable set pieces as the crow's song and the pink elephant nightmare. A triumph in the art of animation.

p: Walt Disney
story: Helen Aberson, Harold Pearl
d: Ben Sharpsteen
m: FRANK CHURCHILL, OLIVER WALLACE (AA)
ly: NED WASHINGTON
voices: Edward Brophy, Herman Bing, Verna Felton, Sterling Holloway, Cliff Edwards

Dunlap, Paul

American composer working at the low budget end of the sci-fi/fantasy/horror market.

Genre credits:
The Lost Continent (1951), *Target Earth* (1954), *The Angry Red Planet* (1959), *The Three Stooges in Orbit* (1962), *Castle of Evil* (1966), *Cyborg 2087* (1966), *Destination Inner Space* (1966),

Dune

USA/Mexico 1984 148m Technicolor Todd-AO Dolby
Two feuding houses battle over a desert planet valuable for the life-giving spice mined there.

A long, slow, rather reverential version of the cult novel which, despite occasional unpleasantness and a confusing narrative, is consistently good to look at, though viewers expecting a variation on *Star Wars* will be disappointed. At a cost of $45m, its failure at the box office was almost unprecedented at the time.

p: Raffaella de Laurentiis for Dino de Laurentiis
w/d: David Lynch
novel: Frank Herbert
ph: FREDDIE FRANCIS
m: Toto, Brian Eno, Daniel Lanois, Roger Eno
md: Mary Paich, Allyn Ferguson
ed: Anthony Gibbs
pd: TONY MASTERS
cos: BOB RINGWOOD
sp: BARRY NOLAN, ALBERT WHITLOCK, KIT WEST, Carlo Rambaldi
sound: Alan Splet, Nelson Stoll
sound ed: Les Wiggins, Leslie Shatz, Teresa Eckton, Bill Varney, Steve Maslow, Kevin O'Connell
titles: Robert Schaefer

Kyle MacLachlan, Francesca Annis, Jose Ferrer, Max Von Sydow, Sian Phillips, Sting, Linda Hunt, Richard Jordan, Freddie Jones, Kenneth McMillan, Dean Stockwell, Brad Dourif, Silvano Mangano, Leonardo Cimino, Virginia Madsen, Everett McGill, Jack Nance, Jurgen Prochnow, Paul Smith, Patrick Stewart, Sean Young, Alicia Roanne Witt

Duvall, Robert (1931-)

Distinguished American character actor, a best actor Oscar winner for *Tender Mercies* (1983). Began his career on stage in the late 50s following military service in Korea. Made his movie debut in 1962 in *To Kill a Mockingbird*, since when he has played key roles in such movies as *The Godfather* (as Tom Hagen), *The Godfather, Part Two*, *The Seven Per Cent Solution*, *Network*, *Apocalypse Now* (as Lieutenant Colonel Kilgore) and TV's *Lonesome Dove*.

Genre credits:

Countdown (1967), *THX-1138* (1971 – as THX-1138), *Invasion of the Body Snatchers* (1978 – cameo), *Phenomenon* (1996)

Dykstra, John (1947-)

American special effects technician who began his film career as an assistant to Douglas Trumbull. In 1975 he joined forces with producer-director

George Lucas to create Industrial Light and Magic to handle the effects for *Star Wars*, for which he won an Oscar (with John Stears, Richard Edlund, Grant McCune and Robert Blalack). Soon after he left and created his own company, Apogee. His other credits include *Avalanche Express*, *Caddyshack* and *Firefox*.

Genre credits:

The Andromeda Strain (1969 – assistant sp), *Silent Running* (1971 – assistant sp), *Voyage to Outer Space* (1973 – short – sp), *Star Wars* (1977 – co-sp), *Battlestar Galactica* (1979 – TVM – sp/p), *Star Trek: The Motion Picture* (1979 – co-sp), *Starflight One* (1987 – TVM – sp), *Lifeforce* (1986 – sp), *Invaders from Mars* (1987 – sp), *My Stepmother is an Alien* (1988 – sp), *Batman Forever* (1995 – co-sp), *Batman and Robin* (1997 – sp)

From left to right: Dr. Keynes (Max Von Sydow), Gurney Halleck (Patrick Stewart), Paul Atreides (Kyle MacLachlan) and Duke Leto Atreides (Jurgen Prochnow) in a moment from the underrated *Dune*.

E. T. 🛸🛸

USA 1982 115m Technicolor Dolby

A friendly alien stranded on earth is helped by a young boy.

When released, this modern-day fairy tale captured the hearts of millions, making it the most financially successful movie of all time. As a piece of filmmaking it could have been sharper, and it is emotionally manipulative, but as an experience it has its rewards. Only time will tell if it is a truly great movie.

p: Steven Spielberg, Kathleen Kennedy for Universal/Amblin
w: Melissa Mathison
d: Steven Spielberg
ph: Allen Daviau
m: JOHN WILLIAMS (AA)
ed: Carol Littleton
pd: James D. Bissell
cos: Deborah Scott
sp: CARLO RAMBALDI, Dennis Murren, Kenneth F. Smith (aa)
sound: Gene Cantamessa
sound effects editing: Robert Knudson, Robert Glass, Don Digirolamo, Gene Cantamessa (aa)
2nd unit d: Glenn Randall
Dee Wallace, Henry Thomas (as Elliott), Peter Coyote, Robert MacNaughton, DREW BARRYMORE (as Gerty), K. C. Martell, Sean Frye, C. Thomas Howell

---

Earth Angel 🛸

USA 1991 96m CFIcolor TVM

In 1962, a teenage girl dies in a car crash on the way to her highschool prom only to find her ghostly body transported 30 years through time, where she has to sort out the love life of her former boyfriend, now a teacher, as well as that of another teenage girl.

Mild but not unpleasant variation on themes from *Back to the Future* and *Peggy Sue Got Married*.

p: Roy Gilbert for Leonard Hill Films
exec p: Leonard Hill, Joel Fields
w: Nina Shengold
d: Joe Napolitano
ph: Stan Taylor
m: Kevin Klinger
ed: James Coblentz
pd: Shay Austin
cos: Betty Madden
sound: Steve Nelson
Cathy Podewell, Mark Hamill, Roddy McDowall, Cindy Williams, Erik Estrada, Rainbow Harvest, Brian Krause, Alan Young

---

Elliott (Henry Thomas) and his extraterrestrial pal get ready for a tearful farewell in Steven Spielberg's blockbuster *E.T.*

The Earth Dies Screaming ☺

GB 1964 62m bw

The earth is invaded by aliens from outer space, and survivors in a small village take stock of the situation.

Low budget sci-fi quickie, tolerable enough as a programmer and interesting for its credits.

p: Robert L. Lippert, Jack Parsons for Lippert
w: Henry Cross
d: Terence Fisher
ph: Arthur Lavis
m: Elizabeth Lutyens
ed: Robert Winter
ad: George Provis
cos: Jean Fairlie
sound: Buster Ambler
sound ed: Spencer Reeve
Willard Parker, Virginia Field, Dennis Price, Thorley Walters, Vanda Godsell, David Spenser, Anna Palk

Earth Girls Are Easy ☺

USA 1988 100m Technicolor Panavision

Three aliens crash land in a hairdresser's swimming pool and she teaches them about the California lifestyle.

Determinedly kitsch comedy with musical numbers. Brainless fun for those in the mood.

p: Tony Garnett for Fox/De Laurentiis/Kestrel
w: Julie Brown, Charles Coffey, Terrence E. McNally
d: Julien Temple
ph: Oliver Stapleton
md: Nile Rodgers
ed: Richard Halsey
pd: Dennis Gassner
cos: Linda Bass
sp: Dream Quest
Geena Davis, Jeff Goldblum, Jim Carrey, Damon Wayans, Julie Brown, Michael McKean, Rick Overton, Larry Linville,

Charles Rocket

Earth vs. the Flying Saucers

USA 1956 83m bw

America makes a stand against invading flying saucers from another world.

Juvenile romp in the 50s manner, not entirely unwatchable, though at its liveliest during the effects sequences. A low budget *Independence Day* of it time.

p: Charles H. Schneer for Columbia
exec p: Sam Katzman
w: George Worthington Yates, Raymond T. Marcus
story: Curt Siodmak, Donald Keyhos
d: Fred F. Sears
ph: Fred Jackman, Jr.
md: Constantin Bakaleinikoff
ed: Danny D. Landres
ad: Paul Palmentola
sp: Ray Harryhausen
sound: Josh Westmoreland
Hugh Marlowe, Joan Taylor, Morris Ankrum, Donald Curtis

Earth vs. the Spider

USA 1958 70m bw

A giant spider threatens a small isolated township.

Grade Z 50s schlock with poor effects work.

p: Bert I. Gordon for AIP
exec P: James H. Nicholson, Samuel Z. Arkoff
w: Lazslo Gorog, George Worthington Yates
d/sp/story: Bert I. Gordon
ph: Jack Marta
m: Albert Glasser
ed: Ronald Sinclair
ad: Walter Keller
sound: Al Overton
Ed Kemmer, June Kenney, Gene Persson, Gene Roth, Hal Torey, Mickey Finn, Sally

Fraser, Troy Patterson

Ebirah – Horror of the Deep

Japan 1966 86m Eastmancolor Tohoscope

Godzilla battles a giant lobster which is guarding his island, whilst onlookers escape with the help of Mothra.

Pretty juvenile, even for a Godzilla movie, which is saying something! It looks good though, despite the inanity of it all.

p: Tomoyuki Tanaka for Toho
w: Shinichi Seyizawa
d: Jun Fukuda
ph: Kazuo Yamada
m: Masaru Sato
ed: no credit given
ad: Takeo Kita
sp: Eiji Tsuburaya
sound: Shoichi Yoshizawa
Akira Takarada, Toru Watanabe, Hideo Sunazuka, Kumi Mizuno, Jun Tazaki

Edlund, Richard (1940-)

Highly acclaimed American special effects technician, photographer and producer who first came to note for his photographic work on *Star Wars*, which won him his first Oscar (1977 – with John Stears, John Dykstra, Grant McCune and Robert Blalack). A graduate of the Naval Photographic School, he subsequently became one of the linchpins of George Lucas's Industrial Light and Magic effects unit, winning further Oscars for his work on *The Empire Strikes Back* (1980 – with Brian Johnson, Dennis Murren and Bruce Nicholson), *Raiders of the Lost Ark* (1981 – with Kit West, Bruce Nicholson and Joe Johnston) and *Return of the Jedi* (1983 – with Dennis Murren, Ken Ralston and Phil Tippet). In 1983 he split from ILM and formed his own effects house, Boss. His other credits include *The China Syndrome*, *Poltergeist*, *Fright Night*, *Poltergeist II: The Other Side*, *The Monster Squad*, *Die Hard*, *Big Top Pee-Wee* and *Air Force One*.

Genre credits:

Star Wars (1977 – effects ph), *Battlestar Galactica* (1978 – effects ph), *The Empire Strikes Back* (1980 – co-sp), *Raiders of the Lost Ark* (1981 – co-sp), *Return of the Jedi* (1983 – co-sp), *2010: Odyssey Two* (1984 – sp), *Masters of the Universe* (1985 – sp), *Big Trouble in Little China* (1986 – sp), *Solarbabies* (1986 – aka *Solar Wariors* – sp), *The Boy Who Could Fly* (1986 – sp), *Masters of the Universe* (1987 – co-sp), *Vibes* (1988 – sp), *Ghost* (1990 – sp), *Alien 3* (1992 – sp), *Solar Crisis* (1992 – sp), *Species* (1995 – sp), *Multiplicity* (1996 – sp)

Edouart, Farciot (1895-1980)

American special effects technician, long with Paramount. An Oscar winner for his work on *Spawn of the North* (1938 – with Gordon Jennings, Jan Domela, Dev Jennings, Irmin Roberts, Art Smith and Loyal Griggs), *I Wanted Wings* (1941 – with Gordon Jennings and Louis Mesenkop) and *Reap the Wild Wind* (1941 – with Gordon Jennings, William L. Pereira and Louis Mesenkop). His other credits include *Lives of a Bengal Lancer*, *Sullivan's Travels*, *Ace in the Hole* (aka *The Big Carnival*) and *The Mountain*.

Genre credits:

Alice in Wonderland (1933 – co-sp), *Dr Cyclops* (1939 – co-sp), *When Worlds Collide* (1951 – co-sp), *Conquest of Space* (1955 – co-sp), *The Space Children* (1958 – co-sp)

Edward Scissorhands

USA 1990 98m DeLuxe Dolby

A young man who has shears for hands is invited down from his lonely castle to live with a suburban family, but his integration is far from easy.

Generally delightful variation on the Frankenstein story with just the right touch in all departments.

p: Denise di Novi, Tim Burton for TCF
exec p: Richard Hashimoto
w: Caroline Thompson
story: Tim Burton, Caroline Thompson
d: TIM BURTON
ph: STEFAN CZAPSKY
m: DANNY ELFMAN
ed: Richard Halsye
pd: BO WELCH
cos: Coleen Atwood
sound: Peter Hliddal
make-up effects: Stan Winston
titles: Robert Dawson
JOHNNY DEPP, Winona Ryder, DIANNE WEIST, Alan Arkin, Anthony Michael Hall, Kathy Baker, Vincent Price (his last film)

18 Again!

USA 1988 99m DeLuxe

As a result of a car accident, an 81-year-old man finds he has swapped bodies with his 18-year-old grandson.

Amiably performed comedy using a theme suddenly popular in 1988 (also see *Big*, *Like Father Like Son*, *Vice-Versa* and *Fourteen Going on Thirty*).

p: Walter Coblenz, Jonathan Prince, Josh Goldstein for New World
w: Jonathan Prince, Josh Goldstein
d: Paul Flaherty
ph: Stephen M. Katz
m: Billy Goldenberg
ed: Danford B. Greene
pd: Dena Roth
cos: John Buehler
sp: Howard Jensen

sound: Russell Williams
George Burns, Charlie Schlatter, Tony Roberts, Red Buttons, Anita Morris, Miriam Flynn, Jennifer Runyon

Eisenmann, Ike (1962-)

American actor who, as a child, became familiar through TV's *Fantastic Journey*, along with a couple of 70s Disney films in which he played one of two children with supernatural powers.

Genre credits:

Escape to Witch Mountain (1974), *Return to Witch Mountain* (1978), *Powder* (1995 – voice)

Elfman, Danny (1954-)

American composer with a penchant for dark fantasy themes. A singer, songwriter and performer with the rock group Oingo Boingo, he began scoring films in the early 80s and linked himself to the career of director Tim Burton, scoring *Pee-Wee's Big Adventure*, *Beetlejuice*, *Batman*, *Edward Scissorhands*, *Batman Returns*, *The Nightmare Before Christmas* (singing the role of Jack Skellington) and *Mars Attacks!* Other credits include *Scrooged*, *Darkman*, *Nightbreed*, *Sommersby*, *Black Beauty* and *Dolores Claiborne* as well as the TV themes for *Sledgehammer*, *The Simpsons* and *Tales from the Crypt*. He is the brother of director Richard Elfman.

Genre credits:

Beetlejuice (1988), *Batman* (1989), *Dick Tracy* (1990), *Edward Scissorhands* (1990), *Batman Returns* (1992), *The Nightmare Before Christmas* (1993 – aka *Tim Burton's The Nightmare Before Christmas*), *Mars Attacks!* (1996), *Men in Black* (1997)

Ellenshaw, Peter (1914-)

British art director, production designer and special effects technician, a noted matte artist long associated with the Disney studio, for whom he won a Best Special Effects Oscar for *Mary Poppins* (1964 – with Hamilton Luske and Eustace Lycett). Began his career as a special effects technician in the mid-30s for Alexander Korda's London Films, working on such films as *Victoria the Great*, *The Drum* and *The Red Shoes* before being taken on by Disney's British arm in the early 50s. His son Harrison Ellenshaw is also a noted matte artist. His other credits include *Treasure Island*, *The Sword and the Rose*, *Rob Roy – The Highland Rogue*, *Westward Ho the Wagons*, *Johnny Tremain* and *Perri*.

Genre credits:

Things to Come (1936 – ass sp), *20,000 Leagues Under the Sea* (1954 – co-sp), *Darby O'Gill and the Little People* (1959 – co-sp), *The Absent-Minded Professor* (1961 – co-sp), *In Search of the Castaways* (1961 – co-sp), *Mary Poppins* (1964 – co-sp), *Blackbeard's Ghost* (1967 – co-sp), *The Love Bug* (1968 – co-sp), *The Island at the Top of the World* (1974 – pd/co-sp), *The Shaggy DA* (1976 – co-sp), *The Man Who Fell to Earth* (1976 – co-sp), *Herbie Goes to Monte Carlo* (1977 – co-sp), *Star Wars* (1977 – co-sp), *The Black Hole* (1979 – pd/co-sp), *The Empire Strikes Back* (1980)

Elliott, Denholm (1922–1992)

British character actor, remembered by genre fans for playing Marcus Brody in two of the Indiana Jones films. He made his stage debut in 1945 and began making films in 1949 with *Dear Mr. Prohack*. His other credits include *The Sound Barrier* (aka *Breaking the Sound Barrier*), *The Cruel Sea*, *Alfie*

(as the abortionist), *Percy*, *A Bridge Too Far*, *Trading Places*, *Defence of the Realm* and *Noises Off*. He died from AIDS.

Genre credits:

Quest for Love (1971), *Watership Down* (1978 – voice), *The Boys from Brazil* (1978), *Raiders of the Lost Ark* (1981), *Indiana Jones and the Last Crusade* (1989)

Emmerich, Roland

German writer, director and producer, often in collaboration with writer-producer Dean Devlin. He trained at the Munich Film School, where he studied production design and directed his first film, *The Noah's Ark Principle*. *Making Contact* (aka *Joey*) and *Ghost Chase* followed, along with experience as a producer on *Eye of the Storm*. He began his association with big budget special effects pictures with *Moon 44*, which eventually led to box office gold with both *Stargate* and *Independence Day*. Emmerich also has his own production company, Centropolis, through which he has produced much of his output.

Genre credits:

Making Contact (1985- aka Joey – d), *Moon 44* (1989 – co-p/co-story/d), *Universal Soldier* (1992 – d), *Stargate* (1994 – co-w/d), *Independence Day* (1996 – co-w/co-exec p/d), *Godzilla* (1998 – co-w/d)

The Empire Strikes Back ☁☁☁☁

USA 1980 124m Eastmancolor Panavision Dolby

With help from The Force, the Rebel Alliance continue their inter-gallactic fight against Darth Vader, first on the ice planet of Hoth and later in the cloud city of Bespin.

Technically accomplished sequel to

Star Wars, with plenty of narrative drive, superior effects and a plethora of exhiliratingly staged action sequences, including an epic battle in the snowy wastes of Hoth and a memorable chase through an asteroid field. There are also new characters in the form of Lando Calrissian and the wizened Jedi master Yoda. A genuine classic. As with *Star Wars* and *Return of the Jedi*, a special anniversary re-issue appeared in 1997 with improved sound and effects and a couple of minor new sequences.

p: Gary Kurtz for TCF/Lucasfilm
exec p: George Lucas
w: Leigh Brackett, Lawrence Kasdan
story: George Lucas
d: IRVIN KERSHNER
ph: PETER SUSCHITZKY
m: JOHN WILLIAMS
ed: PAUL HIRSCH
pd: NORMAN REYNOLDS
ad: Leslie Dilley, Harry Lange, Alan Tomkins
cos: John Mollo, Tiny Nicholls, Eileen Sullivan
sp: BRIAN JOHNSON, RICHARD EDLUND, DENNIS MUREN, BRUICE NICHOLSON (AA)
sound: Bill Varney, Steve Maslow, Gregg Landaker, Peter Sutton (aa)
sound effects: Ben Burtt, Randy Thom
make-up effects: Stuart Freeborn
2nd unit d: Harley Cockliss, John Barry, Peter MacDonald
2nd unit ph: Chris Menges, Geoff Glover Mark Hamill, HARRISON FORD, Carrie Fisher, Billy Dee Williams, Alec Guinness, Anthony Daniels, Dave Prowse, James Earl Jones (voice, as Darth Vader), Peter Mayhew, Kenny Baker, Frank Oz (voice, as Yoda), John Hollis, Jeremy Bulloch, Julian Glover, Michael Sheard, Denis Lawson, John Ratzenberger, Norman Chancer, Clive Revill (voice)

Luke Skywalker (Mark Hamill) rides his Tauntaun across the ice planet of Hoth in *The Empire Strikes Back*, the superb sequel to *Star Wars*.

Encino Man

USA 1992 88m Technicolor

Two airheads unearth a caveman in their back yard, resuscitate him and introduce him to the 20th century.

Mild teenage japes in the Bill and Ted manner.

p: George Zaloom for Warner/Hollywood/Touchwood Pacific Partners
w: Shawn Schepps
story: George Zaloom, Shawn Schepps
d: Les Mayfield
ph: Robert Brickman
m: J. Peter Robinson
ed: Eric Sears, Jonathan Siegel
pd: James Allen
cos: Marie France
sound: Robert Allan Ward

Sean Astin, Pauly Shore, Brendan, Robin Tunney, Michael DeLuise, Frank Van Horn

Enemy from Space

see Quatermass 2

Enemy Mine ☁

USA/Ger 1985 98m DeLuxe Dolby

During an interplanetary war, an earthling finds himself stranded on a desolate planet with one of the aliens he has been fighting, but they eventually come to trust and depend on each other.

Basically no more than a variation on *Hell in the Pacific* in an outer space setting, but sufficiently engaging, with the emphasis on character rather than

the hardware for once.

p: Stephen Friedman for King's Road Entertainment
exec p: Stanley O'Toole
w: Edward Khmara
story: Barry Longyear
d: Wolfgang Petersen
ph: Tony Imi
m: Maurice Jarre
ed/2nd unit d: Hannes Nikel
pd: Rolf Zehetbauer
sound: Milan Bor, Christopher Schubert, Christopher Price, Ed Perente
sound ed: Mike le Maire
DENNIS QUAID, LOUIS GOSSETT, JR., Brion James, Richard Marcus, Carolyn McCormick, Bumper Robinson

Erik the Viking

GB/Sweden 1989 108m Technicolor Dolby

A group of dim-witted Norsemen decide to lay off rape and pillage so as to sail to the end of the world in search of Valhalla.

A few mildly amusing moments fail to save this Pythonesque romp in which a good cast is mostly left high and dry.

p: John Goldstone for Prominent Features/AB Svenks Filmindustri/Erik the Viking Productions
exec p: Terry Glinwood
w/d: Terry Jones
book: Terry Jones
ph: Ian Wilson
m: Neil Innes
ed: George Akers
pd: John Beard
cos: Pam Tait
sp: Richard Conway
sound: Bob Doyle
2nd unit d: Julian Doyle
titles: Trevor Bond
Tim Robbins, John Cleese, Imogen Stubbs, Mickey Rooney, Eartha Kitt, John Gordon

Sinclair, Tim McInnerny, Gary Cady, Tsutomu Sekine, Anthony Sher, Charles McKeown, Jim Broadbent, Samantha Bond, Freddie Jones, Richard Ridings, Danny Schiller

Escape from L.A.

USA 1996 91m DeLuxe Dolby

In 2013, when America has become a totalitarian state and L.A. has been turned into an island prison following an earthquake, Snake Plisskin is sent in to assassinate the president's daughter, who has taken up with a revolutionary.

Big budget sequel to *Escape from New York*, all very predictable and silly (the car/surfboard chase was a first), but passable enough as video fodder, despite some variable effects. Certainly not the blockbuster its makers were expecting, though.

p: Debra Hill, Kurt Russell for Paramount/Rysher Entertainment
w: John Carpenter, Debra Hill, Kurt Russell
d: John Carpenter
ph: Gary K. Kibbe
m: Shirley Walker, John Carpenter
ed: Edward A. Warschilka
pd: Lawrence G. Paull
cos: Robin Michel Bush
sp: Kimberly K. Nelson

make-up effects: Rick Baker
sound: Thomas Causey, John Pospisil
stunt co-ordinator: Jeff Imada
titles: Nina Saxon
Kurt Russell, Stacy Keach, Cliff Robertson, George Corraface, Peter Fonda, Steve Buscemi, Robert Carradine, Pam Grier, Valeria Golino, Paul Bartel, William Pena, Jeff Imada

Escape from New York

USA 1981 99m Metrocolor Panavision

In 1997, the U.S. president's plane crash lands in New York, now an enormous prison, and a convict is offered his freedom if he will go in and rescue him.

Futuristic action thriller which moves briskly enough but is let down by an overdose of brutal detail. A sequel, *Escape from L. A.*, followed in 1996.

p: Debra Hill, Larry Franco for Avco Embassy/Barber/Goldcrest/IFI
w: John Carpenter, Nick Castle
d: John Carpenter
ph: Dean Cundey
m: John Carpenter, Alan Howarth
ed: Todd Ramsey
pd: Joe Alves

cos: Steven Loomis
sp: Pat Patterson, Eddie Surkin, Gary Zink, Roy Arbogast
sound: Tommy Causey
stunt co-ordinator: Dick Warlock
Kurt Russell (as Snake Plisskin), Ernest Borgnine, Lee Van Cleef, Donald Pleasence (as the president), Isaac Hayes, Adrienne Barbeau, Charles Cyphers, Season Hubley, Harry Dean Stanton, Tom Atkins

Escape from the Planet of the Apes

USA 1971 97m DeLuxe Panavision

Three apes travel from the future to escape the destruction of the earth.

Elementary third entry in the Apes series which passes the time well enough.

p: Arthur P. Jacobs, Frank Capra, Jr. for TCF/APJAC
w: Paul Dehn
d: Don Taylor
ph: Joseph Biroc
m: Jerry Goldsmith
ed: Marion Rothman
ad: Jack Martin Smith, William Creber
sp: Howard A. Anderson
sound: Dean Vernon, Theodore Soderberg
Roddy McDowall, Kim Hunter, Bradford Dillman, Ricardo Montalban, Natalie Trundy, Eric Braeden, William Windom, Sal Mineo

Escape to Witch Mountain

USA 1974 97m Technicolor

Two children with mysterious powers are chased across America by a scheming millionaire.

Condescending science fiction adventure for undemanding children. All rather tame by today's standards, and further hampered by poor special effects. *Return from Witch Mountain* followed in 1978.

Snake Plissken (Kurt Russell) takes to the air during the climax to John Carpenter's *Escape from L.A.*, the long-delayed big budget sequel to his earlier hit, *Escape from New York*.

p: Jerome Courtland for Walt Disney

w: Robert Malcolm Young

novel: Alexander Key

d: John Hough

ph: Frank Phillips

m: Johnny Mandell

cos: Chuck Kheene, Emily Sundby

sp: Art Cruickshank, Danny Lee

sound: Frank Regula

Eddie Albert, Donald Pleasence, Kim Richards, Ray Milland, Walter Barnes, Reta Shaw, Denver Pyle, Ike Eisenmann

---

Essex, Harry (1910-1997)

American screenplay writer whose credits include *The Killer That Stalked New York*, *Kansas City Confidential* and *The Sons of Katie Elder*, though to genre fans he is best known for scripting *It Came from Outer Space* (1953) from the Ray Bradbury story. He also directed two films: *I, the Jury* and *Mad at the World*.

Evans, Maurice (1901-1989)

British (Welsh) actor, remembered by genre fans for playing the ape Dr. Zaius in *Planet of the Apes* and its first sequel. Much stage experience, including stints in the West End and on Broadway. His other film credits include *White Cargo*, *The Story of Gilbert and Sullivan*, *Macbeth* and *Rosemary's Baby*. He also popped up regularly in the TV sitcom *Bewitched*.

Genre credits:

Scrooge (1935), *Planet of the Apes* (1967), *Beneath the Planet of the Apes* (1969), *The Body Stealers* (1969 – aka *Invasion of the Body Stealers*)

Event Horizon

USA/GB 1997 96m colour Dolby

A team of astronauts is sent to investigate the mysterious return of a spaceship which has been missing for seven years. However, upon boarding it, they discover themselves prey to a force which plays deadly games with their psyches.

Derivative, wholly predictable shocker which borrows freely from a variety of genre movies, among them *Alien*, *The Black Hole*, *The Shining* and *The Exorcist*. Peopled with two-dimensional characters and containing little more than a series of aural and visual shock effects, it stands as a monument to the imaginative bankruptcy to which genre films have fallen in the 90s. We settle for so little, we fans, and it really shouldn't be this way.

p: Lawrence Gordon, Lloyd Levin, Jeremy Bolt for Paramount/Golar/Impact Pictures

exec p: Nick Gillot

w: Philip Eisner

d: Paul Anderson

ph: Adrian Biddle

m: Michael Kamen

ed: Martin Hunter

pd: Joseph Bennett

cos: John Mollo

sp: Richard Yuricich

sound: Chris Munro

Laurence Fishburne, Sam Neill, Kathleen Quinlan, Joely Richardson, Sean Pertwee

---

Evolver

USA 1994 88m Foto-Kem Dolby

A teenage boy wins a prototype robot in a video game competition, but the robot, intended for military use, evolves and goes on a killing spree.

Tame juvenile variation on *The Terminator*, with a robot that couldn't look less threatening. Wholly unremarkable.

p: Jeff Geoffray, Walter Josten, Henry Seggerman for Trimark/Blue Rider

exec p: Mark Amin

w/d: Mark Rosman

ph: Jacques Haitkin

m: Christopher Tyng

ed: Brent Schoenfeld

pd: Ken Aichele

sp: Steve Johnson, XFX Inc.

sound: Mary Jo Devenney, David Lewis Yewdall

2nd unit d: Rob Melntant

stunt co-ordinator: John Stewart

Evolver concept design: Jim Salvati

Ethan Randall, John DeLancie, Cindy Pickett, Paul Dooley, Nassira Nicola, Chance Quinn, Cassidy Rae, W. H. Macy (voice)

Explorers

USA 1985 110m Technicolor Dolby

Three schoolboys build their own spaceship in which they rendezvous with friendly aliens.

Unbearably tedious fantasy adventure with absolutely nothing at all new to offer. Script and performances are similarly glutinous. The public stayed away in droves.

p: Edward S. Feldman, David Bombyk for Paramount/Blue Dolphin/ILM

exec p: Michael Finnell

w: Eric Luke

d: Joe Dante

ph: John Hora

m: Jerry Goldsmith

ed: Tina Hirsch

pd: James D. Bissell

cos: Rosanna Norton

sp: ILM

make-up effects: Rob Bottin

Ethan Hawke, River Phoenix, Jason Presson, Amanda Peterson, Dick Miller, Robert Piccardo, Leslie Rickert, James Cromwell, Dana Ivey, Bobby Fite

Fahrenheit 451

GB 1966 112m Technicolor

In the future it is a capital offence to be found reading, and firemen go about burning all the books.

Curiously ineffective futuristic drama in the manner of Orwell's *1984*. It strives for a sense of style, but looks very much of its period. The title alludes to the temperature at which paper begins to burn.

p: Lewis M. Allen for Rank/Anglo Enterprise/Vineyard
w: Francois Truffaut, Jean-Louis Richard
novel: Ray Bradbury
d: François Truffaut
ph: Nicolas Roeg
m: Bernard Herrmann
ed: Thom Noble
ad: Syd Cain, Tony Walton
Oskar Werner, Julie Christie, Cyril Cussack, Anton Diffring, Jeremy Spenser

Fantasia

USA 1940 135m Technicolor Fantasound

A programme of classical music as interpreted by the animators of the Walt Disney studio.

Highly ambitious animated feature which won't be to everyone's taste (least of all children waiting for Mickey Mouse to appear). There are also several lapses in both taste and pace, though the film's frequent flashes of brilliance are undeniable and it rightly stands as a landmark in the field of animation.

p: WALT DISNEY
d: Samuel Armstrong, James Algar, Bill Roberts, Paul Scatterfield, T. Hee, Hamilton Luske, Jim Handley, Forde Beebem, Norm Ferguson, Wilfred Jackson
md: Leopold Stokowski (who also appears)
narrator: Deems Taylor

Fantastic Voyage

USA 1966 100m DeLuxe Cinemascope

A group of doctors are miniaturised and injected into the bloodstream of a dying scientist in order to operate on his brain.

Silly but good looking and generally engaging escapade, later remade unofficially as *Inner Space*. A kitsch classic.

p: Saul David for TCF
w: Harry Kleiner, David Duncan
story: Otto Klement, Jay Lewis Bixby
d: RICHARD FLEISCHER
ph: ERNEST LASZLO
m: Leonard Rosenman
ed: William B. Murphy
as/set decoration: Jack Martin Smith, Dale Hennessy, Walter M. Scott, Stuart A. Reiss (aa)
sp: Art Cruickshank (aa), L. B. Abbott, Emil Kosa, Jr.
sound: Bernard Freericks, David Dockendorf
titles: Richard Kuhn
Stephen Boyd, Raquel Welch, Edmond O'Brien, Donald Pleasence, Arthur Kennedy, Arthur O'Connell, William Redfield, James Brolin, Brendan Fitzgerald

La Fatiche di Ercole

see Hercules (1958)

Feitshans, Fred

American editor working at the low budget end of the genre.

Genre credits:

The Man from Planet X (1950 – ed), *Two Lost Worlds* (1950 – ed), *The Indestructible Man* (1955 – ed), *Pajama Party* (1964 – ed), *Dr. Goldfoot and the Bikini Machine* (1965 – aka *Dr. G and the Bikini Machine* – co-ed), *Sergeant Deadhead* (1965 – aka *Sergeant Deadhead the Astronaut* – co-ed), *Wild in the Streets* (1968 – ed)

Female Space Invaders

see Starcrash

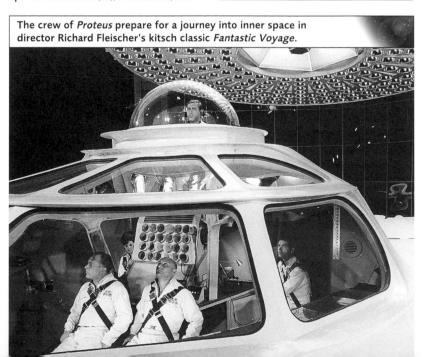

The crew of *Proteus* prepare for a journey into inner space in director Richard Fleischer's kitsch classic *Fantastic Voyage*.

Ferngully: The Last Rainforest

Denmark/Canada/GB/Korea/Thailand
1992 76m DeLuxe Dolby

A forest fairy helps a miniaturised lumberjack destroy an evil tree spirit before returning him to his normal size.

Eco-friendly cartoon feature, more than passable for youngsters, though some of it (particularly the tuneless songs) may irritate adults.

p: Wayne Young, Peter Faiman for FAI/Youngheart
exec p: Ted Field, Robert W. Cort
w: Jim Cox
story: Diana Young
d: Bill Kroyer
m: Alan Silvestri
songs: various
ed: Gillian Hutshing
ad: Susan Kroyer
sound: Jon Johnston, Hari Ryatt, Bruce Stubblefield
voices: Samantha Mathis, Robin Williams, Tim Curry, John Cleese, Grace Zabriskie, Christian Slater, Jonathan Ward, Cheech Marin, Tommy Chong, Kathleen Freeman, Sheena Easton, Elton John

Ferrari, William

American art director, an Oscar winner for his work on *Gaslight* (1944 – with Cedric Gibbons). Spent much of his early career at MGM.

Genre credits:

Gog (1954 – ad), *The Lost Missile* (1958 – ad), *Atlantis, The Lost Continent* (1960 – co-ad), *The Time Machine* (1960 – co-ad)

Fiedel, Brad (1951-)

American composer with a penchant for synth scores. A former songwriter (for Paul Simon's DeShufflin' Music), he broke into features in 1975 with the unreleased *Apple Pie* following experience scoring educational films. His credits include *Compromising Positions*, *Desert Bloom*, *The Accused*, *Fright Night 2*, *Blink*, *The Real McCoy* and *True Lies*.

Genre credits:

The Terminator (1984), *Plymouth* (1990 – TVM), *Terminator 2: Judgement Day* (1991), *Johnny Mnemonic* (1995)

Field of Dreams

USA 1989 106m DeLuxe Dolby

An Iowa farmer hears a voice which tells him to build a baseball pitch in one of his corn fields so that ghosts of The White Sox can play on it.

Well made but increasingly lunatic fantasy which doesn't seem to have any discernible point. Americans took it to their hearts without question; however, elsewhere the reaction was mostly that of bemusement.

p: Lawrence Gordon, Charles Gordon for Universal/Carolco/Gordon Company
exec p: Brian Frankish
w/d: Phil Alden Robinson
novel: W. P. Kinsella
ph: John Lindley
m: James Horner
ed: Ian Crafford
pd: Dennis Grassner
cos: Linda Bass
sp: Bruce Nicholson, Robbie Knott
sound: Russell Williams III
titles: Dan Perri
Kevin Costner, Amy Madigan, James Earl Jones, Burt Lancaster, Ray Liotta, Gaby Hoffman, Timothy Busfield, Frank Whalley, Dwier Brown

The Fifth Element

GB/Fr 1997 127m Technicolor Dolby

In 2214, a New York cab driver finds himself involved in a mission to save earth from an all-consuming globe of evil, his task being to bring together four magical stones and a young girl – the fifth element.

Initially intriguing big budget epic which unfortunately turns into a rather dumb comedy at the halfway mark thanks to the introduction of a high camp radio DJ (played by Chris Tucker) whose presence is totally superfluous and totally annoying. The sets, costumes and special effects are well up to par for this kind of thing, however.

p: Patrice Ledoux for Gaumont
w: Luc Besson, Robert Kamen
d/story: Luc Besson
ph: Thierry Arbogast
m: Eric Serra
ed: Sylvie Landra
pd: Dan Weil
cos: JEAN-PAUL GAULTIER
sp: Mark Stetson
make-up effects: Nick Dudman
sound: Daniel Brisseau
Bruce Willis, Gary Oldman, Luke Perry, Lee Evans, Ian Holm, Milla Jovovich, Chris Tucker, Julie T. Wallace

Fire in the Sky

USA 1993 110m DeLuxe Dolby

In 1975, a lumberjack is apparently kidnapped by aliens in a wood near Arizona. His friends, who witnessed the event, are subsequently accused of his murder.

Supposedly based on an actual incident, this alien abduction drama spends more time with the disappearance investigation than it does with the close encounter, but it passes the time adequately enough for those willing to suspend disbelief.

p: Joe Wizan, Todd Black for Paramount
exec p: Wolfgang Glattes
w: Tracy Torme

book: Travis Walton
d: Robert Lieberman
ph: Bill Pope
m: Mark Isham
ed: Steve Mirkovich
pd: Laurence Bennet
cos: Joe I. Tompkins
sp: Michael Owens, ILM
sound: Henry Garfield
titles: Nina Saxon
D. B. Sweeney, Robert Patrick, Craig Sheffer, Peter Berg, Henry Thomas, Bradley Gregg, James Garner, Noble Willingham, Kathleen Wilhoite, Georgia Emelin, Scott MacDonald, Kenneth White

Fire Maidens from Outer Space

GB 1956 80m bw

An expedition to Jupiter's 13th moon discovers it to be inhabited entirely by nubile young women.

Hilariously then dismayingly inept grade Z schlocker which has to be seen to be believed.

p: Criterion Films/Eros
w/d: Cy Roth
ph: Ian Struthers
m: Borodin, Monia Liter, Trevor Duncan
ed: A. C. T. Clair
ad: Scott MacGregor
cos: Cynthia Tingey
sound: no credit given
Susan Shaw, Anthony Dexter, Sidney Tafler, Harry Fowler, Paul Carpenter, Owen Barry

Firebird 2015 A. D.

USA 1980 96m colour

In the future, oil shortages cause cars to be banned, but a few enthusiasts still manage to keep their battered vehicles running.

Dismal low budget actioner, a long, long way from *Mad Max*.

p: Glen Ludlow for Mara

exec p: Harold Sobel
w: Maurice Hurley, Biff McGuire, Barry Pearson
d: David Robertson
ph: Robert Fresco
m: Paul Hoffert, Lawrence Stragge
ed: Michael MacKowert
ad: Richard Hudolin
cos: Wendy Patridge
sp: Neil Trifunovich
sound: Ralph Parker
stunt co-ordinator: Keith Wardlow
Darren McGavin, Doug McClure, George Touliatos, Barbara Williams, Robert Wisden

The First Men in the Moon ☁

GB 1964 103m Lunacolor Panavision Dynamation

A Victorian scientist and two friends journey to the moon where they discover a subterranean civilisation.

Acceptable fantasy adventure, not quite so zestful as some of the other Harryhausen effects spectaculars, but with a few inventive touches here and there which may endear it to younger audiences.

p: Charles H. Schneer for Columbia/Ameran
w: Nigel Kneale, Jan Read
novel: H. G. Wells
d: Nathan Juran
ph: Wilkie Cooper
m: Laurie Johnson
ed: Maurice Rootes
ad: John Blezard
sp/associate p: Ray Harryhausen
technical staff: Les Bowie, Kit West
sound: Buster Ambler, Red Law
titles: Sam Sulman
Edward Judd, Martha Hyer, LIONEL JEFFRIES, Miles Malleson, Erik Chitty, Betty McDowall, Norman Bird, Gladys Henson, Hugh McDermott, Peter Finch (unbilled cameo)

Fisher, Carrie (1956-)

American actress, the daughter of Debbie Reynolds and Eddie Fisher, best known to genre fans for playing Princess Leia in the *Star Wars* films. On stage from the age of 12 (in her mother's Vegas act), she made her film debut in 1975 in *Shampoo*. She has since successfully turned her hand to writing novels (*Postcards from the Edge* [based on her own drugs problems], *Surrender the Pink*, *Delusions of Grandma*) and screenplays (*Postcards from the Edge*). Her other credits as an actress include *The Blues Brothers*, *Hannah and Her Sisters*, *The Burbs*, *When Harry Met Sally* and *Soapdish*.

Genre credits:
Star Wars (1977), *The Empire Strikes Back* (1980), *Return of the Jedi* (1983), *The Time Guardian* (1987), *Amazon Women on the Moon* (1987), *Drop Dead Fred* (1991)

The Fisher King

USA 1991 137m Technicolor Dolby

A has-been disc jockey and a New York tramp join forces to track down the Holy Grail.

Long, loud and rather infuriating modern-day fantasy which very quickly outstays its welcome, though some found things to admire in it.

p: Debra Hill, Linda Obst for Tri-Star/Hill-Obst
w: Richard LaGravenese
d: Terry Gilliam
ph: Roger Pratt
m: George Fenton
ed: Lesley Walker
pd: Mel Bourne
cos: Beatrix Paszdor
Robin Williams, Jeff Bridges, Mercedes Ruehl (aa), Amanda Plummer, Christian Clemenson, Michael Jeter

Fisher, Terence (1904-1980)

British director, mostly associated with Hammer Horror (*The Curse of Frankenstein*, *Dracula*, *The Mummy*, *The Man Who Could Cheat Death*, *The Phantom of the Opera*, *The Devil Rides Out*, *Frankenstein and the Monster from Hell*, etc.). Began his film career as a clapper boy in 1928 after experience in the navy and as a window dresser. Worked his way up to become an apprentice editor, his first solo credit being *Brown on Resolution* in 1935. After editing for several years he became a trainee director with Rank, his first credit being for *Colonel Bogey* in 1947, which he followed with *Portrait from Life*, *Marry Me*, *The Astonished Heart* and *So Long at the Fair*. His first film for Hammer/Exclusive was the 1952 B thriller *The Last Page* which he followed with several more undistinguished programme fillers (*Wings of Danger*, *Face the Music* and *The Stranger Came Home*, etc.) before being given *The Curse of Frankenstein* to direct as he was owed a picture by Hammer on his contract.

Genre credits:
Stolen Face (1952), *Four-Sided Triangle* (1953), *Spaceways* (1953), *The Earth Dies Screaming* (1964), *Night of the Big Heat* (1966 – aka *Night of the Burning Damned*)

Five Million Years to Earth see Quatermass and the Pit

The Five-Thousand Fingers of Dr. T

USA 1953 88m Technicolor

A young boy has a curious dream about his much-hated piano teacher.

Marvellously imaginative fantasy which unfortunately proved too far ahead of its time for popular success and is probably a little too nightmarish for younger children anyway. Discerning adults may have a ball, however.

p: STANLEY KRAMER for Columbia
w: Dr. Seuss (Theodore Geisel), Allan Scott
d: Roy Rowland
ph: FRANZ PLANER
m: FREDERICK HOLLANDER
ly: Dr. Seuss (Theodore Geisel)
md: Morris Stoloff
ed: Harry Gerstad, Al Clark
pd: RUDOLPH STERNAD
cos: Jean Loius
sound: Russell Malmgren
HANS CONREID, Tommy Rettig, Peter Lind Hayes, Mary Healey, John Heasley, Robert Heasley

Flash Gordon

USA 1936 13x20m bw serial

Superhero Flash Gordon, his girlfriend Dale Arden and Professor Zarkov travel to the planet Monmgo to thwart Emperor Ming's plans to destroy earth.

Lively but wildly dated serial exploits which still provide a fair measure of fun (and unintentional laughter). The archetypal adventure serial, it now has something of a cult following. Chapter titles include *The Planet of Peril*, *The Tunnell of Terror* and *Captured by Shark Men*. It was followed by *Flash Gordon's Trip to Mars* (1938) and *Flash Gordon Conquers the Universe* (1940). Also see below.

p: Henry MacRae for Universal
w: Frederick Stephani, George Plympton, Basil Dickey, Ella O'Neill
cartoon strip: Alex Raymond
d: Frederick Stephani
ph: Jerry Ash, Richard Fryer
m: no credit given
ed: Saul Goodkind, Edward Todd, Louis Sacklin

Larry 'Buster' Crabbe as the screen's first Flash Gordon, here in a cliffhanging moment from 'Tournament of Death', chapter eight of the original 1936 *Flash Gordon* serial. He is flanked by Jean Rogers (as Dale Arden) and Charles Middleton (as the Emperor Ming).

ad: Ralpg Berger
sp: Norman Dewes, Elmer A. Johnson
sound: no credit given
Buster Crabbe, Jean Rogers, Priscilla Lawson, Charles Middleton (as Ming), Frank Shannon (as Zarkov), Richard Alexander, John Lipson

Flash Gordon

GB 1980 115m Technicolor Todd-AO

Superhero Flash Gordon has to battle against the ever-evil Emperor Ming to save the world from destruction.

Witless and often quite smutty revamping of the old serial, with just one or two 'flashes' of interest (mostly involving the sets and costumes) along the way, though not nearly enough to justify the obviously large budget.

p: Dino de Laurentiis for EMI/Starling
exec p: Bernard Williams
w: Lorenzo Semple, Jr., Michael Allin
cartoon strip: Alex Raymond
d: Mike Hodges
ph: Gilbert Taylor
songs: Queen

m/md: Howard Blake
ed: Malcolm Cooke
pd/cos: DANILO DONATI
sp: Frank Van Der Veer, Barry Nolan
sound: Ivan Sharrock, Gerry Humphreys, Robin O'Donoghue
titles: Robert Greenberg
2nd unit d: William Kronick
add ph: Harry Waxman
Sam J. Jones, Melody Anderson, Topol, Max Von Sydow (as Ming), Timothy Dalton, Ornella Muti, Brian Blessed, Peter Wyngarde, Suzanne Danielle, Peter Duncan, Richard O'Brien

Flash Gordon Conquers the Universe

USA 1940 12x20m bw serial
Flash Gordon again encounters Ming the Merciless, who is using a deadly dust to conquer the earth.

Fairish tailpiece to the trilogy of serials with thrills in the by now established manner.

p: Henry MacRae for Universal
w: George H. Plympton, Barry Shipman, Basil Dickey
d: Forde Beebe, Ray Taylor
ph: Jerome Ash
Buster Crabbe, Carol Hughes, Charles Middleton (as Ming), Frank Shannon, Anne Gwynne, Beatrice Roberts

Flash Gordon's Trip to Mars

USA 1938 15x20m bw serial
Flash Gordon and his friends prevent the Emperor Ming from destroying the earth with a ray gun planted on Mars.

Second of the three fondly remembered Flash Gordon serials which supplies plenty of dated fun for addicts. Chapter titles include *New Worlds to Conquer*, *The Living Dead*, *Queen of Magic* and *Tree Men of Mars*.

p: Barney A. Sarecky for Universal
w: Wyndham Gittens, Norman S. Hall, Ray Trampe, Herbert Dalmas
d: Forde Bebe, Robert Hill
ph: Jerome Ash
ed: Saul A. Goodkind, Alvin Todd, Joe Gluck, Louis Sackin
ad: Ralph de Lacy
Buster Crabbe, Jean Rogers, Frank Shannon, Charles Middleton (as Ming), Beatrice Roberts, Wheeler Oakman, Kane Richmond, Kenneth Duncan, Warner Richmond, Ben Lewis, Lane Chandler, Jack Mulhall

Fleischer, Richard (1916-)

American director who, after stage experience (he founded The Arena Players in 1937), entered films in 1942 as an assistant in RKO's Pathe Newsreel unit. He then graduated to the shorts unit, making his directorial debut in 1944 with *Memo for Joe*. Subsequently directed many episodes of the studio's *This Is America* and *Flicker Flashbacks* series (the latter of which he originated) before turning to features in 1946 with *Child of Divorce*. Several hard-edged thrillers followed, among them *The Armored Car Robbery* and *Narrow Margin*. In 1954 he was hired by Walt Disney to direct the studio's major live action feature *20,000 Leagues Under the Sea*, an assignment that raised some eyebrows, as Fleischer's father was Max Fleischer, Disney's main rival in the field of animation (he produced the *Popeye* and *Betty Boop* series and such features as *Gulliver's Travels* and *Mr. Bugs Goes to Town*). Fleischer's subsequent credits include such wide-ranging films as *The Vikings*, *The Boston Strangler*, *10*, *Rillington Place*, *Amityville 3D* and *Million Dollar Mystery* (aka *Money Mania*).

Genre credits:
20,000 Leagues Under the Sea (1954), *Fantastic Voyage* (1966), *Doctor Dolittle* (1967), *Soylent Green* (1973), *Conan the Destroyer* (1984), *Red Sonja* (1985)

Flemyng, Gordon (1934–)

British director who helmed the two theatrical Dr. Who features in the 60s. His other credits include *Solo for Sparrow*, *Great Catherine* and *The Last Grenade*.

Genre credits:
Dr. Who and the Daleks (1965), *Daleks – Invasion Earth, 2150 A.D.* (1966)

Flesh Gordon

USA 1974 78m colour
Earth is threatened by a sex ray transmitted by the nefarious Emperor Wang, but Flesh Gordon comes to the rescue.

Fairly feeble soft porn farce (originally intended as a hard core sex romp) peppered with just one or two hilarious moments. Worth a look for the penisaurus.

p: Howard Ziehm, William Osco for Graffitti
w: Michael Benveniste
d: Howard Ziem, Michael Benveniste
ph: Howard Ziehm
m: Ralph Ferraro
ed: Abbas Amin
ad: Donald Harris
sp: Tom Scherman, David Allen, Rick Baker, Jim Danforth (billed backwards as Mij Htrofnad)
Jason Williams, Suzanne Fields, Joseph Hudgins, William Hunt (as Wang), Candy Samples, John Hoyt

Flight of the Navigator

USA 1986 90m DeLuxe Dolby
A teenage boy disappears for eight

years only to return home completely unchanged and unaged, and the authorities try and figure out where he's been.

Mildly diverting family film which quickly settles down into an old-fashioned fantasy adventure.

p: Robby Wald, Dimitri Villard, David Joseph for PSO/Viking/New Star Entertainment
w: Matt MacMannus, Michael Burton
story: Mark H. Baker
d: Randall Kleiser
ph: James Glennon
m: Alan Silvestri
ed: Jeff Gourson
pd/2nd unit d: William J. Creber
cos: Mary Lou Bird
sp: Peter Donen
sound: Robert Wald
Joey Cramer, Veronica Cartwright, Cliff de Young, Sarah Jessica Parker, Matt Adler, Howard Hesseman, Paul Mall (Paul Reubens – voice)

The Flintstones

USA 1994 91m Technicolor Dolby
Fred Flinstone is promoted to vice-president of his company only to find himself being used as a patsy by his scheming boss in an embezzlement plot.

Expensive live action version of the classic TV cartoon series (presented by "Steven Spielrock"). Patches amuse, but the plot is much too wispy to support an entire feature.

p: Bruce Cohen for Amblin/Hanna-Barbera
exec p: William Hanna, Joseph Barbera, Kathleen Kennedy, David Kitschner, Gerald R. Molen
w: Tom S. Parker, Jim Jennewien, Steven E. de Souza
d: Brian Levant
ph: Dean Cundey
m: David Newman
ed: Kent Beyda

pd: William Sandell
cos: Rosanna Norton
sp: ILM, Jim Henson's Creature Shop
sound: Charles Wilborn
titles: Jay Johnston
stunt co-ordinator: Gary M. Hymes
John Goodman, Elizabeth Perkins, Rick Moranis, Rosie O'Donnell, Kyle MacLachlan, Halle Berry, Elizabeth Taylor, Dann Florek, Richard Moll, Jonathan Winters, Harvey Korman (voice), Jay Leno, Sam Raimi, Dean Cundey, Joe Barbera, Bill Hanna

The Fly ☁

USA 1958 93m Eastmancolor Cinemascope
A scientist working on the transmission of matter finds himself turning into a giant fly when the experiment goes wrong.

Routinely presented science fiction horror in the 50s manner, surprisingly shot in colour and wide screen. Regarded with affection in certain quarters, it was followed by *The Return of the Fly* (1959), and *Curse of the Fly* (1965) and was remade in 1986, which itself was followed by a sequel, *The Fly II* (1989).

p: Kurt Neumann for TCF
w: James Clavell
story: George Langelaan
d: Kurt Neumann
ph: Karl Struss
m: Paul Sawtell
ed: Merrill G. White
ad: Lyle Wheeler, Theobald, Holsopple
cos: Charles Le Maire, Adele Balkan
sp: L. B. Abbott
sound: Eugene Grossman, Harry M. Leonard
make-up effects: Ben Nye
Vincent Price, David Hedison, Herbert Marshall, Patricia Owens, Kathleen Freeman, Betty Lou Gerson, Charles Herbert, Eugene Borden, Torben Meyer

The Fly ☁

USA/Canada 1986 96m DeLuxe Dolby
A scientist experimenting with teleportation fails to notice a fly in the compartment when he tries the gadget out on himself and begins to mutate into a giant insect.

Slick-looking remake with improved script and production values, as well as a pretty high gross-out factor.

p: Stuart Cornfield, Marc-Ami Boyman, Kip Ohman for TCF/Brooks films
w: Charles Edward Pogue, David Cronenberg
story: George Langelaan
d: DAVID CRONENBERG
ph: Mark Irwin
m: Howard Shore
ed: Ronald Sanders
pd: Carl Spier
sound: Bryan Day, Michael Lacrois, Gerry Humphreys, Robin O'Donoghue
make-up effects: CHRIS WALAS, STEPHEN DUPUIS (aa)
stunt co-ordinator: Wayne McLean
titles: Wayne Fitzgerald
Jeff Goldblum, Geena Davis, John Getz, Joy Boushel, Les Carlson, George Chuvalo, Michael Copeman, Carol Lazare, David Cronenberg (in a cameo, delivering a pupae!)

The Fly II

USA 1989 105m DeLuxe Dolby
Martin Brundle begins to show signs that he might be about to follow in his father's footsteps.

Slick but rather leisurely paced sequel to a remake which fails to add anything new to the formula. An adequate time filler for horror addicts.

p: Steven-Charles Jaffe for TCF/Brooksfilsm
exec p: Stuart Cornfield
w: Mick Garris, Jim Wheat, Ken Wheat, Frank Darabont
story: Mick Garis

d: Chris Walas
ph: Robin Vidgeon
m: Christopher Young
ed: Sean Barton
pd: Michael S. Bolton
sp: Chris Walas, Jon Berg, Stephen Dupuis
sound: Leslie Shatz, John Wardlow
titles: Sam Alexander
Eric Stoltz, Daphne Zuniga, Lee Richardson, Ann Marie Lee, Gary Chalk, Harley Cross, Frank C. Turner, John Getz

Folk, Robert (1950-)

American composer, a graduate of the New York's Juilliard School. In films from 1984 with *The Slayer*, he went on to score all of the *Police Academy* comedies. His other credits include *Bachelor Party*, *Miles from Home*, *Toy Soldiers*, *Can't Buy Me Love* and *Trapped in Paradise*.

Genre credits:
The Never Ending Story II: The Next Chapter (1990), *Tremors* (1990), *Beastmaster 2: Through the Portal of Time* (1991), *The Troll in Central Park* (1993), *Arabian Knight* (1994 – aka *The Thief and the Cobbler*), *Lawnmower Man 2: Beyond Cyberspace* (1995), *Theodore Rex* (1996)

Follow That Bird

USA 1985 87m Tecnicolor Dolby
Big Bird leaves Sesame Street to live with a family of dodos, but finally realises that there's no place like home.

Well mounted comedy adventure featuring all the regular Muppets from the popular children's television series *Sesame Street*. It's ideal for younger viewers.

p: Tony Garnett for Warner/Children's Television Workshop
exec p: Joan Ganz Cooney
w: Tony Geiss, Judy Freudberg
d: Ken Kwapis

ph: Curtis Clark
m: Van Dyke Parks, Lennie Niehaus
md: Steve Buckingham
ed: Stan Warnow
ad: Carol Spier
cos: Mary Jane McCarthy
sp: Colin Chilvers
sound: Bryan Day, Michael Lacrois
John Candy, Chevy Chase, Waylon Jennings, Carroll Spinney (as Big Bird), Jim Henson, Frank Oz, Richard Hunt, Kathryn Mullen, Jerry Nelson, Dave Thomas, Sandra Bernhard, Joe Flaherty

Forbidden Planet

USA 1956 98m Eastmancolor
Cinemascope
In the year 2200, a space cruiser lands on the planet Altair 4 to investigate the disappearance of a spaceship only to find its sole survivor living with his daughter and their robot in the remains of a previous civilisation.

This genre classic is basically a clever re-working of *The Tempest* in science fiction terms, backed by good production and special effects. The pace may occasionally slacken, but the early use of electronic music and the creation of a monster from the protagonist's own id are certainly interesting. The film also introduced Robby the Robot to the world.

p: Nicholas Nayfack for MGM
w: CYRIL HUME
story: Irving Black, Allen Adler

d: FRED M. WILCOX
ph: George Folsey
m: Louis Barron, Bebe Barron
ed: Ferris Webster
ad: Cedric Gibbons, Arthur Lonergan
cos: Helen Rose, Walter Plunkett
sp: A. Arnold Gillespie, Warren Newcombe, Irving G. Ries, Joshua Meador
sound: Wesley C. Miller
Walter Pidgeon, Anne Francis, Leslie Nielsen, Warren Stevens, Jack Kelly, Earl Holliman, George Wallace, Richard Anderson, James Drury, Bob Dix

The Forbin Project

USA 1969 100m Technicolor Panavision
An indestructable computer is installed to take over the defence system of the United States, but it teams up with the Russian one and holds the world to ransom.

Persuasive and intellectually exciting thriller. A brilliant premise, superbly executed.

p: Stanley Chase for Universal
w: JAMES BRIDGES
novel: D. F. Joneas
d: JOSEPH SARGENT
ph: Gene Polito
m: Michel Colombier
md: Stanley Wilson
ed: Folmar Blangsted
ad: Alexander Golitzen, John L. Lloyd
sp: Albert Whitlock
Eric Braeden, Gordon Pinsent, William

Dr. Morbius (Walter Pidgeon – centre) and Robby the Robot welcome their visitors in *Forbidden Planet*, a clever futuristic update of Shakespeare's *The Tempest*.

Schallert, Susan Clark

Ford, Harrison (1942-)

American actor who has starred in two of the cinema's most successful franchises: *Star Wars* and *Indiana Jones*. He made his stage debut during his college years, which led to a season in summer stock with The Belfry Players in 1964. Not long after, an appearance at the Laguna Beach Playhouse led to Ford being contracted to Columbia Pictures as part of their talent programme. This involved taking part in acting classes and posing for publicity photos, with the occasional bit part in a movie thrown in for good measure, such as his debut in 1966 in *Dead Heat on a Merry-go-Round*. A handful of other films followed (*Luv*, *A Time for Killing [*aka *The Long Ride Home]*), but nothing of note. Leaving Columbia dissatisfied, Ford signed a contract with Universal, which produced plenty of TV guest shots for him on such shows as *The Virginian*, *Gunsmoke*, *Kung Fu* and *The Partridge Family*. Another movie, *Journey to Shiloh*, followed, along with loan-outs to appear in *Zabriskie Point* and *Getting Straight*. There was also a TV movie western *The Intruders*, after which Ford took up carpentry (originally to renovate his house) and quit acting, so frustrated was he that his career was failing to take off. He did actually appear in a handful of TV shows and films during this period, but it wasn't until he was offered the role of Bob Falfa in George Lucas's *American Graffiti* that things slowly started looking up for Ford, though it wouldn't be until 1976 when he landed the role of Han Solo in *Star Wars* that stardom finally beckoned, following further bit parts in such films as *The Conversation* and such TV movies as *Dynasty* and *The Possessed*. Since the *Star Wars* and *Indiana Jones* films, Ford has diversified quite successfully, his other credits including *Witness*, *Frantic*, *Working Girl*, *Presumed Innocent*, *The Fugitive* and the Jack Ryan series (*Patriot Games*, *Clear and Present Danger*). He is the husband of *E.T.* screenwriter Melissa Mathison.

Genre credits:

Star Wars (1977), *The Empire Strikes Back* (1980), *Raiders of the Lost Ark* (1981), *Blade Runner* (1982), *Return of the Jedi* (1983), *Indiana Jones and the Temple of Doom* (1984), *Indiana Jones and the Last Crusade* (1989)

Harrison Ford looking suave in his DJ as Indiana Jones in *Indiana Jones and the Temple of Doom*.

Forever Young

USA 1992 102m Technicolor Dolby
In 1939, a test pilot agrees to be frozen alive in an experiment following the apparent death of his girlfriend, and wakes up in 1992 to find the world much changed.

Reasonably likeable variation on an increasingly familiar theme, with the star a little too confident of his own charisma.

p: Bruce Davey for Warner/Icon
exec p: Edward S. Feldman, Jeffrey Abrams
w: Jeffrey Abrams
d: Steve Miner
ph: Russell Boyd
m: Jerry Goldsmith
ed: Jon Poll
pd: Gregg Fonsecca
cos: Aggie Guerard Rodgers
sound: Jim Tanenbaum
special make-up: Dick Smith
Mel Gibson, Jamie Lee Curtis, Elijah Wood, George Wendt, Isabel Glasser, David Marshall Grant

Fortress

USA 1993 85m CFIcolor
In the near future, a young couple find themselves incarcerated in a high-tech underground prison for attempting to have a second child.

Violent actioner which, despite its short running time, bores well before the expected bid for escape.

p: John Davis, Stuart Gordon for Columbia/Tri Star
exec p: Graham Burke, Grey Coote
w: Steve Feinberg, Troy Neighbors, Terry Curtis Fox
d: Stuart Gordon
ph: David Eggby
m: Frederick Talghorn
ed: Timothy Wellburn
pd: David Copping
cos: Terry Ryan
sp: Paul Gentry and others
sound: Paul Clark
make-up effects: Bob Clark
stunt co-ordinator: Glenn Boswell
Christopher Lambert, Kurtwood Smith, Loryn Locklin, Lincoln Kilpatrick, Clifton Gonzalez Gonzalez, Jeffery Combs, Tom Towles, E. Briant Wells, Vernon Wells, Heidi Stein

Fourteen Going on Thirty

USA 1987 906m colour TVM

A teenage wiz invents a machine which speeds up the ageing process, and his best friend acts as his first guinea pig.

Mild age-reversal comedy, one of several made during this period, of which this is probably the weakest.

p: Susan B. Landau for Walt Disney
exec p: James Orr, Jim Cruickshank
w: Richard Jefferies
story: James Orr, Andrew Cruickshank
d: Paul Schneider
ph: Fred J. Koenekamp
m: Lee Holdridge
ed: Richard A. Harris
ad: Raymond G. Storey
cos: Tom Brosnon
sp: Isadoro Raponi, Allen Gorzales
sound: John Glascock

Steve Eckholdt, Daphne Ashbrook, Rick Rossovich, Gabey Olds, Loretta Swit, Patrick Duffy

Fowler, Hugh S. (1904-1975)

American editor, an Oscar winner for his work on *Patton* (1970). His other credits include *Gentlemen Prefer Blondes*, *The List of Adrian Messenger* and *The Life and Times of Judge Roy Bean*.

Genre credits:
The Lost World (1960), *Way, Way Out* (1966), *Planet of the Apes* (1967)

The Fox and the Hound

USA 1981 83m Technicolor

A fox and a hound, though friendly as youngsters, become increasingly antagonistic towards each other as they grow older.

Solidly crafted cartoon feature. Not quite classic Disney, but it passes the time well enough, though a little more humour in the script might have helped.

p: Wolfgang Reitherman, Art Stevens for walt Disney
exec p: Ron Miller
w: Larry Clemmons, Ted Berman, Peter Young, Steve Hulett, David Michener, Burney Mattinson, Earl Kress, Vance Gerry
novel: Daniel P. Mannix
d: Art Stevens, Ted Berman, Richard Rich
m: Buddy Baker
ed: James Melton, Jim Koford
voices: Mickey Rooney, Kurt Russell, Jack Albertson, Pearl Bailey, Jeanette Nolan, Sandy Duncan, John Fiedler, Paul Winchell, Corey Feldman

Fox, Michael J. (1961-)

Diminutive Canadian actor who shot to stardom first on television as Alex P. Keaton in the sitcom *Family Ties* and then on the big screen as Marty McFly in the *Back to the Future* trilogy. He made his television debut in 1980 with *Palmerstown USA*. His film debut in *Mignight Madness* followed the same year, which itself was followed by an appearance in *Class of 1984* in 1982. Since the end of the *Back to the Future* series, his career has undulated somewhat. His other credits include *Teen Wolf*, *The Secret of My Success*, *Doc Hollywood*, *The Hard Way* and the TV sitcom *Spin City*.

Genre credits:
Back to the Future (1985), *Back to the Future II* (1989), *Back to the Future III* (1990), *Mars Attacks!* (1996)

Francis

USA 1949 91m bw

A second lieutenant befriends a talking mule.

Laboured fantasy comedy which pleased at the time and led to six sequels: *Francis Goes to the Races* (1951), *Francis Goes to West Point* (1952), *Francis Covers Big Town* (1953), *Francis Joins the WACS* (1954), *Francis in the Navy* (1955) and *Francis in the Haunted House* (1956).

p: Robert Arthur for Universal
w: David Stern from his novel
d: Arthur Lubin
ph: Irving Glassberg
m: Frank Skinner
ed: Milton Carruth
ad: Bernard Herzbrun, Richard H. Reidel
cosa: Rosemary Odell
sp: David Horsley
sound: Leslie I. Carey, Corson Jowett

Donald O'Connor, Patricia Medina, Zasu Pitts, Ray Collins, John McIntire, Frank Feylen, Tony Curtis, Chill Wills (as the voice of Francis)

Francis, Freddie (1917-)

Celebrated British cinematographer, an Oscar winner for both *Sons and Lovers* (1960) and *Glory* (1989), whose other credits include *A Hill in Korea*, *Room at the Top* and *The Innocents*. Turned to direction in 1962 with *Two and Two make Six* and *Vengeance*, then slipped into the horror genre with such films as *Paranoiac* and *Dracula Has Risen from the Grave*. He returned to cinematography in 1981 with *The French Lieutenant's Woman*, which was followed by sterling work on *The Elephant Man*, *Glory*, *Cape Fear* and *The Princess Caraboo*, etc. He is the father of producer Kevin Francis.

Genre credits:
Tales of Hoffman (1951 – cam op), *They Came from Beyond Space* (1966 – d), *Dune* (1984 – ph), *Brenda Starr* (1986 – released 1992 – ph)

Franco, Larry

American producer, often associated with the films of director John Carpenter, for whom he began as an assistant director on *The Fog*. His other assistant director credits include *Straight Time*, *The Rose*, *Apocalypse Now* and *Black Sunday*. His producing credits take in *Christine*, *Prince of Darkness* and *Tango and Cash*.

Genre credits:

Escape from New York (1981 – co-p), *The Thing* (1982 – associate p/ass d/actor), *Starman* (1984 – p), *Big Trouble in Little China* (1986 – p), *They Live* (1988 – actor/p), *The Rocketeer* (1991 – exec p), *Batman Returns* (1992 – co-p), *Jumanji* (1995 – exec p)

Frankenstein Unbound

USA 1990 87m DeLuxe Ultra Stereo

A scientist from the 21st century finds himself transported back in time to 19th-century Switzerland where he encounters Dr. Frankenstein, Byron, Shelley, the Monster and the young Mary Shelley.

Agreeable mixtures of genres, silly certainly, but most of it comes off quite well. It was Corman's first film as a director for 19 years, his previous effort being *Von Richtofen and Brown*, 1971.

p: Roger Corman, Thom Mount, Kobi Jaeger for Warner/Mount
w: Roger Corman, F. X. Sweeney, Ed Neumeier
novel: Brian W. Aldiss
d: Roger Corman
ph: Armando Nannuzzi, Michael Scott
m: Carl Davis
ed: Jay Cassidy
pd: Enrico Tovaglieri
cos: Franca Zucchelli
sp: Renato Agostini, Bill Taylor, Syd Dutton
make-up effects: Nick Dudman

sound: Gary Alper
2nd unit d: Thierry Notz
John Hurt, Raul Julia, Bridget Fonda, Jason Patric, Michael Hutchence, Nick Brimble, Catherine Rabett, Bruce McGuire, Grady Clarkson

Freaky Friday

USA 1976 100m Technicolor

A teenage girl and her mother wish to swap bodies for the day only to find their wish granted...

Messy Disney farce, rather typical of their live action product in the 1970s. A TV remake followed in 1995.

p: Ron Miller for Walt Disney
w: Mary Rodgers from her novel
d: Gary Nelson
ph: Charles F. Wheeler
m: Johnny Mandel
song: Ala Kasha, Joel Hirschhorn
ed: Cotton Warburton
ad: John B. Mansbridge, Jack Senter
cos: Chuck Keehne, Emily Sundby
sp: Eustace Lycett, Danny Lee, Art Cruickshank
sound: Herb Taylor, Ron Roncorn
titles: John Jensen, Art Stevens
Jodie Foster, Barbara Harris, John Astin, Patsy Kelly, Dick van Patten, Sorrell Booke, Marie Windsor, Ruth Buzzi, Marc McClure

Freddie as F.R.O.7

GB 1992 91m Technicolor

A French frog prince turns secret agent and attempts to discover who's behind a plan involving the theft of Britain's tourist attractions

Dim animated adventures with echoes off James Bond but a plot too foolish to engage one's attention for long. The proposed sequels were abandoned following box office indifference

p: Jon Acevski, Norman Priggen for Hollywood Road/Rank

w: Jon Acevski, David Ashton
d: Jon Acevski
m: Davis Dundas, Rick Wentworth
ly: Don Black, Jon Acevski, David Ashton
ed: Alex Rayment
ad: Paul Sharedlow
sound: John Bateman
Voices: Ben Kingsley, Jenny Agutter, Nigel Hawthorne, Brian Blessed, Phyllis Logan, Michael Hordern, Jonathan Pryce, Billie Whitelaw, Prunella Scales, John Sessions, David Ashton

Freeborn, Stuart

Distinguished British make-up artist, remembered chiefly by genre fans for creating the creatures for the Cantina Bar sequence in *Star Wars*. He began his career in 1936 at Denham Studios. Other credits include *Oliver Twist*, *The Bridge on the River Kwai*, *The Wind and the Lion*, *Murder on the Orient Express*, *The Elephant Man* and *Company of Wolves*.

Genre credits:

The Thief of Baghdad (1940), *The Mouse That Roared* (1959), *Dr. Strangelove* (1963), *2001: A Space Odyssey* (1968), *Alice's Adventures in Wonderland* (1972), *Star Wars* (1977), *Superman* (1978), *Superman 2* (1980), *The Empire Strikes Back* (1980), *Return of the Jedi* (1983)

Frog Dreaming

Australia 1985 90m Colorfilm Dolby

A teenage boy discovers the true nature of the monster lurking at the bottom of Donkegin Hole.

Pleasant but overlong children's fare.

p: Barbi Taylor, Everett de Roche for UAA/Middle Reef/Western
w: Everett de Roche
d: Brian Trenchard-Smith
ph: John McLean
m: Brian May

ed: Brian Kavanaugh
pd: Jon Dowding
cos: Aphrodite Kondos
sp: Brian Pearce
sound: Craig Carter, Mark Lewis
underwater ph: Ron Taylor
Henry Thomas, Rachel Freind, Tamsin West, Tony Barry, John Ewart, Dennis Miller, Katy Manning

From Beyond

USA/It 1986 88m DeLuxe Ultra Stereo
A scientist experiments with sensory equipment which results in murder and madness.

Gory fantasy horror whose plot loses its way about halfway through.

p: Brian Yuzna, Roberto Bessi for Empire/Tarvin
exec p: Charles Band
w: Brian Yuzna, Dennis Paoli, Stuart Gordon
novel: H. G. Lovecraft
d: Stuart Gordon
ph: Mac Ahlberg
m: Richard Band
ed: Lee Percy
ad: Giovanni Natalucci
cos: Angee Beckett
sp: John Beuchler, Mark Shostrom, John Naulin, Anthony Doublin
titles: Robert Dawson
Jeffrey Combs, Barbara Crampton, Ted Sorel, Ken Foree, Carolyn Purdey-Gordon, Bunny Summers

Fulton, John P. (1902-1965)

Pioneering American special effects technician, long with Universal, where he worked on many of their key horror films, most notably *The Invisible Man* and its sequels. A former camera assistant and cinematographer (*Hell's Harbour*, *Eyes of the World*, *The Great Impersonation*) he switched to effects in 1930 with his move to Universal. His other credits include *Frankenstein*, *The Mummy*, *Son of Dracula*, *The Ghost Catchers*, *Elephant Walk*, *Rear Window* and *The Disorderly Orderly*. He won Oscars for his work on *Wonder Man* (1945), *The Bridges at Toko-Ri* (1954) and *The Ten Commandments* (1956).

Genre credits:
Ali Baba and the Forty Thieves (1943), *Wonder Man* (1945), *The Conquest of Space* (1955), *The Search for Bridey Murphy* (1956), *I Married a Monster from Outer Space* (1958), *The Colossus of New York* (1958), *The Space Children* (1958), *Visit to a Small Planet* (1960), *The Bamboo Saucer* (1967)

Furlong, Edward (1977-)

American actor who made his screen debut as the young John Connor in *Terminator 2: Judgement Day* (1991). His other credits include *A Home of Our Own* and *Little Odessa*.

Future Cop

USA 1976 96m Technicolor TVM
A middle-aged cop discovers that his new partner is an android.

Dim action fare, one of several TV films to employ this gimmick at the time (*The Cops and Robin*, *Holmes and Y Yo*, *The Six Million Dollar Man*, etc.). *Robocop* it ain't.

p: Anthony Wilson
exec p: Gary Damsker
w: Jud Taylor
ph: Terry Meade
m: Billy Goldenberg
ed: Ronald J. Fagan, Steven C. Brown
ad: Jack De Shields
cos: Phyllis Garr, Dick Bruno
sp/titles: Howard A. Anderson
sound: Howard Beals
stunt co-ordinator: George Savage

Ernest Borgnine, Michael Shannon, John Amos, John Larch

Future Cop (1984) see Trancers

Futureworld

USA 1976 106m Metrocolor Panavision
At a futuristic holiday resort peopled by robots, the head of the organisation invites influential guests whom he plans to replace with duplicates.

A bigger budgeted but less imaginative sequel to *Westworld*. Watchable but not very exciting.

p: James T. Aubrey, Paul Lazarus III for American International
exec p: Samuel Z. Arkoff
w: Mayo Simon, George Schenk
d: Richard T. Heffron
ph: Howard Schwarz, Gene Polito
m: Fred Karlin
md: Bodie Chandler
ed: James Mitcherl
ad: Trevor Williams
cos: Jimmy George
sp: Gene Grigg, Brent Sellstrom
sound: Charlie Knight
2nd unit d: Robert Jessup
titles: Michael Hamilton
Peter Fonda, Blythe Danner, Arthur Hill, Yul Brynner, John Ryan, Stuart Margolin, Jim Antonio

Gale, Bob (1952-)

American screenwriter, often in collaboration with director Robert Zemeckis, with whom he penned the *Back to the Future* trilogy. His other credits include *I Wanna Hold Your Hand*, *1941* and *Used Cars*, all of them with Zemeckis.

Genre credits:
Back to the Future (1985 – co-w/co-p), *Back to the Future II* (1989 – w/co-story/co-p), *Back to the Future III* (1990 – w/co-p)

Gargoyles

USA 1972 74m Technicolor TVM
In Mexico to research a new book, a demonologist and his daughter discover a secret race of gargoyles.

Silly fantasy thriller which could have been better. It passes the time, though.

p: Bob Christiansen, Rick Rosenberg for Tomorrow Entertainment
exec p: Norman Gimbel
w: Elinor Karpf, Stephen Karpf
d: B. W. L. Norton
ph: Earl Rath
m: Robert Prince
ed: Frank P. Keller
sp: Milt Rice, George Peekman
gargoyle make-up: Ellis Burman, Stan

Winston, Ross Wheat
Cornel Wilde, Jennifer Salt, Grayson Hall, Scott Glenn

Garland, Beverly (1926-)

American actress (real name Beverly Fessenden), in films from 1950 with *D. O. A.* Many 50s B movies followed, a good deal of them for Roger Corman (*The Gunslinger, Swamp Women, Thunder Over Hawaii,* etc.). Her early genre work aside, however, she is perhaps best known for her roles in such TV series as *Decoy, My Three Sons* and *The Scarecrow and Mrs. King.* Her other film credits include *The Glass Web, The Joker is Wild, Pretty Poison, Airport '75, Roller Boogie* and *It's My Turn.*

Genre credits:
The Rocket Man (1954), *It Conquered the World* (1956), *Not of This Earth* (1956), *The Alligator People* (1959)

Garland, Judy (1922-1969)

American singer and actress. One of the 20th century's great entertainers, she will always be remembered for playing Dorothy Gale in *The Wizard of Oz* (1939) which won her a special Oscar. Her other credits include *Babes in Arms, Meet Me in St. Louis, Easter Parade, A Star is Born* and *I Could Go On Singing.*

Garris, Mick

American writer and director who got his big break as the story editor on Spielberg's *Amazing Stories* TV series. His other credits include *Critters 2: The Main Course, Psycho IV* (TVM)

and *Sleepwalkers.*

Genre credits:
Batteries Not Included (1987 – story), *The Fly II* (1987 – story), *The Stand* (1995 – d)

Gawain and the Green Knight

GB 1973 93m Technicolor Panavision
A mysterious knight with supernatural powers challenges King Arthur's knights to kill him, but only one of them has the courage to do so.

Quite lively mediaeval fantasy which uses it low budget fairly imaginatively. Remade, more or less, by the same director in 1984 under the title *Sword of the Valiant.*

p: Philip Breen for UA/Sancrest
w: Philip Breen, Stephen Weeks
d: Stephen Weeks
ph: Ian Wilson
m: Ron Goodwin
ed: John Shirley
ad: Anthony Woolard
cos: Ashura Cohn
titles: Richard Williams
Murray Head, Ciaran Madden, Nigel Green, Anthony Sharp, Robert Hardy, Murray Melvin, Geoffrey Bayldon

Genesis II

USA 1972 74m Technicolor TVM
When a time travel experiment goes wrong, a scientist finds himself transported to the 21st century where he discovers that much has changed.

Dreary attempt by writer-producer Roddenberry to launch another *Star Trek*-style series. Two more attempts followed (*Planet Earth* and *Strange New World*), each of which displayed a similar lack of imagination.

p: Gene Roddenberry for Warner/Norway
w: Gene Roddenberry
d: John Lewellyn Moxey
ph: Gerald Perry Finnerman
m: Harry Sukman
ed: George D. Watters
ad: Hilyard Brown
cos: William Ware Theiss
sound: Jack Solomon
make-up effects: Tom Burman
Alex Cord, Mariette Hartley, Ted Cassidy, Titos Vandis, Percy Rodrigues, Liam Dunn

George, Roger

American special effects technician working at the low budget end of the sci-fi genre.

Genre credits:
The Amazing Transparent Man (1959), *Beyond the Time Barrier* (1960), *Pajama Party* (1964), *Sergeant Deadhead* (1965 – aka *Sergeant Deadhead the Astronaut*), *Dr Goldfoot and the Bikini Machine* (1965 – aka *Dr G and the Bikini Machine*), *Castle of Evil* (1966), *Destination Inner Space* (1966), *Dimension 5* (1966)

Gershenson, Joseph (1904-)

Russian-born music director, in films from 1920 as a musician. From 1941 he headed Universal's music department, conducting many of the studio's genre pictures, often uncredited. His credited scores include *Abbott and Costello Meet the Invisible Man*, *The Deadly Mantis* and *The Thing That Couldn't Die*.

Genre credits:
Abbott and Costello Go to Mars (1953), *It Came from Outer Space* (1953), *This Island Earth* (1954), *The Creature from the Black Lagoon* (1954), *Revenge of the Creature* (1955), *The Creature Walks Among Us* (1956), *The Mole People* (1956), *The*

Monolith Monsters (1957), *The Incredible Shrinking Man* (1957), *The Land Unknown* (1957)

Ghost

USA 1990 126m Technicolor Dolby
The ghost of a murdered stockbroker returns from the dead, and with the help of a fake medium and his girl-friend helps to bring his killer to book.

Curious but generally entertaining mish-mash of fantasy, comedy, drama, thrills, romance and detection. *Topper* did it better, but this still found a huge paying audience.

p: Lisa Weinstein for Paramount
exec p: Steven-Charles Jaffe
w: Bruce Joel Rubin (aa)
d: Jerry Zucker
ph: Adam Greenberg
m: Maurice Jarre
ed: Walter Murch
pd: Jane Musky
cos: Ruth Morley
sp: Richard Edlund
sound: Jeff Wexler
Patrick Swayze, Demi Moore, Whoopi Goldeberg (aa), Tony Goldwyn, Stanley Lawrence, Christopher J. Keene, Susan Breslau, Martina Degnan

Ghostbusters

USA 1984 105m Technicolor Panavision Dolby
When a series of hauntings take New York by surprise, three unemployed parapsychologists open a ghost dispos-al business and find themselves faced with saving the world.

Lively supernatural farce which, despite a couple of lapses in pace, pro-vides a fair amount of harmless enter-tainment. It also made a pot of money at the box office. Who you gonna call?

p: Ivan Reitman for Columbia-Delphi/Black

Rhino
exec p: Bernie Brillstein
w: Dan Aykroyd, Harold Ramis
d: Ivan Reitman
ph: LASZLO KOVACS
m: Elmer Bernstein
song: RAY PARKER, JR.
ed: Sheldon Kahn, David Blewitt
pd: John de Cuir
cos: Theoni V. Aldrege
sp: RICHARD EDLUND
sound: Richard Beggs, Tom McCarthy, Jr., Gene Cantamessa
stunt co-ordinator: Bill Couch
titles: R. Greenberg
BILL MURRAY, Dan Aykroyd, Harold Ramis, Sigourney Weaver, Ernie Hudson, Rick Moranis, Annie Potts, William Atherton, David Margulies

Ghostbusters II

USA 1989 103m DeLuxe Panavision Dolby
When New York is again menaced by monsters from the spirit world, the Ghostbusters come to the rescue.

Expensive but unimaginative and much delayed sequel which does little other than to regurgitate the plot of the first film – and to much less effect. A prime example of 80s take-the-money-and-run filmmaking.

p: Ivan Reitman for Columbia
w: Harold Ramis, Dan Aykroyd
d: Ivan Reitman
ph: Michael Chapman
m: Elmer Bernstein
ed: Sheldon Kahn, Donn Cambern
pd: Bo Welch
cos: Gloria Gresham
sp: Dennis Murren
sound: Gene Cantamessa
2nd unit d: Michael Moore
Bill Murray, Dan Aykroyd, Sigourney Weaver, Harold Ramis, Rick Moranis, Ernie Hudson, Peter MacNicol, Kurt Fuller, David Margulies, Annie Potts

111

The Giant Spider Invasion

USA 1975 76m Eastmancolor

Strange crystals from outer space hatch spiders which grow to a giant size and threaten a small township.

Abysmal low budget farago with absolutely nothing going for it.

p: Bill Rebane, Richard L. Ruff for Transcentury/Cinema Group 75
w: Richard L. Huff, Robert Easton
d: Bill Rebane
ph: Jack Willoughby
ed: Barbara Pokras
ad: Ito Rebane
Barbara Hale, Steve Brodie, Leslie Parrish, Alan Hale, Robert Easton, Bill Williams

---

Gibbons, Cedric (1893-1960)

American art director, long at MGM, where he headed the art department. A multiple Oscar winner, he won the award (which he also designed) for *The Bridge of San Luis Rey* (1929), *The Merry Widow* (1934 – with Frederic Hope), *Pride and Prejudice* (1940 – with Paul Groesse), *Blossoms in the Dust* (1941 – with Urie McCleary), *Gaslight* (1944 – with William Ferrari), *The Yearling* (1946 – with Paul Groesse), *Little Women* (1949 – with Paul Groesse), *An American in Paris* (1951 – with Preston Ames), *The Bad and the Beautiful* (1952 – with Edward Carfagno), *Julius Caesar* (1953 – with Edward Carfagno) and *Somebody Up There Likes Me* (1959 – with Malcolm F. Brown). He began his career in 1915 at the Edison Studios. After a brief time with the Goldwyn Studio, he moved to MGM in 1924 and stayed there for the rest of his career. He also co-directed one film, *Tarzan and His Mate*, with Jack Conway, and won a further honorary Oscar in 1950.

Genre credits:
Mysterious Island (1929 – ad), *The Wizard of Oz* (1939 – co-ad), *The Canterville Ghost* (1944 – co-ad), *Forbidden Planet* (1956 – co-ad)

Gibson, Mel (1956-)

American actor, long in Australia, where he made his film debut in *Summer City* in 1977. He followed this with *Tim* and *Mad Max* in 1979, the latter of which established him as a star. He began making films in America in the mid-80s, among them the *Lethal Weapon* series, *Air America*, *Bird on a Wire*, *Hamlet* and *Maverick*. He now also produces and directs; his credits in this area so far include *The Man Without a Face* and *Braveheart* (1995), the latter winning him two Oscars, one for best direction and one for best picture (with Alan Ladd, Jr and Bruce Davey).

Genre credits:
Mad Max (1979), *Mad Max 2* (1981 – aka *The Road Warrior*), *Mad Max Beyond Thunderdome* (1985), *Forever Young* (1992), *Pocahontas* (1995 – voice)

Gibbs, George

British special effects technician, later at ILM, where he won Oscars for his work on *Indiana Jones and the Temple of Doom* (1984 – with Dennis Muren, Michael McAlister and Lorne Peterson) and *Who Framed Roger Rabbit?* (1988 – with Ken Ralston, Richard Williams and Edward Jones).

Genre credits:
Warlords of Atlantis (1978 – co-sp), *Britannia Hospital* (1981 – sp), *Brazil* (1985 – co-sp), *Labyrinth* (1986 – co-sp), *Who Framed Roger Rabbit?* (1988 – co-sp), *Indiana Jones and the Last Crusade* (1989 – co-sp), *Alien 3* (1992 – co-sp), *101 Dalmations* (1996 – co-sp)

Gillespie, A. Arnold (1899-1978)

American special effects technician who began his career as an art director in 1922 with *Manslaughter*. He moved to MGM in 1924 and designed such films as *Ben-Hur*, *London After Midnight* and *Mutiny on the Bounty* before turning to special effects in 1935, winning Oscars for his work on *Thirty Seconds Over Tokyo* (1944 – with Donald Jahraus and Warren Newcombe), *Green Dolphin Street* (1947, with Warren Newcombe) and *Ben-Hur* (1959, with Robert MacDonald). His other effects credits include *Command Decision*, *The Bad and the Beautiful*, *North by Northwest*, *Mutiny on the Bounty* (remake) and *The Greatest Story Ever Told*.

Genre credits:
The Wizard of Oz (1939 – co-sp), *Forbidden Planet* (1956 – co-sp), *Atlantis, The Lost Continent* (1961- co-sp)

Gilliam, Terry (1940-)

American director, actor and animator, long in Britain, first known as a member of the Monty Python team, for whom he animated sequences for their TV series. He also co-wrote and appeared in all the Python movies (*And Now for Something Completely Different*, *Monty Python and the Holy Grail*, *Monty Python's Life of Brian*, *Monty Python's Meaning of Life*, *Monty Python Live at the Hollywood Bowl*) as well as co-directing *Holy Grail* with Terry Jones. He also provided the opening title credits for the 1970 horror film *Cry of the Banshee*.

Genre credits:
Jabberwocky (1977 – also actor), *Time*

Bandits (1981 – also cop-w), *Brazil* (1985), *The Adventures of Baron Munchausen* (1988), *The Fisher King* (1991), *Twelve Monkeys* (1996)

Gilling, John (1912–1985)

British writer, producer and director remembered primarily for his thrillers and horror films, which include *The Flesh and the Fiends*, *The Shadow of the Cat*, *The Plague of the Zombies*, *The Reptile* and *The Mummy's Shroud*. In films from 1947 with his screenplay for *Black Memory*. He turned to direction the following year with *Escape from Broadmoor*.

Genre credits:
The Gamma People (1955 – co-w/d), *The Night Called* (1965 – aka *Blood Beast from Outer Space* – d)

Glasgow, William

American art director whose credits include several for director Robert Aldrich (*Whatever Happened to Baby Jane?*, *Hush… Hush, Sweet Charlotte*, *The Killing of Sister George*, *The Legend of Lylah Clare*, etc) as well as a handful of low budget 50s sci-fi pics.

Genre credits:
Cat-Women of the Moon (1953, *It! The Terror from Beyond Space* (1958), *Invisible Invaders* (1959)

Glass, Jack

American special effects technician, mostly associated with the films of producer Ivan Tors.

Genre credits:
Two Lost Worlds (1950), *The Magnetic Monster* (1953), *Riders to the Stars* (1954)

A Gnome Named Gnorm see Upworld

Godzilla

This prehistoric monster with radioactive breath has appeared in countless Japanese monster marathons, the first of which was 1954's *Godzilla* (original title *Gojira*). As with the sequels, Godzilla was played by a man in a rubber monster suit so as to save on the expense of stop motion animation. The film climaxes with the destruction of Tokyo, also a feature of many of the sequels. A dubbed American version of this first film, with extra scenes involving Raymond Burr as a reporter, was released the following year. In the sixties, sequels came thick and fast with Godzilla, originally the aggressor, often the hero. Teamed at various stages with King Kong, Megalon and Mothra, the films became more childish. A big budget Hollywood remake appeared in 1998.

Key filmography:
Godzilla (1954/5 – aka *Godzilla, King of the Monsters/Gojira*), *Gigantis the Fire Monster* (1955 – aka *The Return of Godzilla/Godzilla's Counterattack/Gojira No Gyakushyu*), *King Kong vs. Godzilla* (1962 – aka *Kingu Kongu Tai Gojira*), *Godzilla vs. the Thing* (1964 – aka *Godzilla vs. Mothra/Gojira Tai Mosura*), *Ghidrah – The Three-Headed Monster* (1965 – aka *Ghidorah/Sandai Kaiju Chikyu Saidai No Kessen*), *Invasion of the Astro Monster* (1965 – aka *Monster Zero/Kaiju Daisenso*), *Godzilla vs. the Sea Monster* (1966 – aka *Ebirah, Horror of the Deep/Nankai No Dai Ketto*), *Son of Godzilla* (1967 – aka *Gojira No Musuko*), *Destroy All Monsters* (1968 – aka *Kaiju Soshingeki*), *Godzilla's Revenge* (1969 – aka *Oro Kaiji Daishingeki*), *Godzilla vs. the Smog Monster* (1971 – aka *Gojira Tai Hedora*), *Godzilla vis. Gigan* (1971 – aka *Godzilla on Monster Island/Gojira Tai Gaigan*), *Godzilla vs. Megalon* (1973 – aka *Gojira Tai Megaro*), *Godzilla vs. Mechagodzilla* (1974 – aka *Godzilla vs. the Cosmic Monster/Godzilla vs. the Bionic Monster/Gojira Tai Meka-Gojira*), *Terror of Mechagodzilla* (1975 – aka *The Terror of Godzilla/Meka-Gojira No Gyakushyu*), *Godzilla 1984* (1984 – aka *Godzilla 1985/Gojira*), *Godzilla vs. Biollante* (1989 – aka *Gojira Tai Biollante*), *Godzilla vs. King Ghidrah* (1991 – aka *Gojira Tai Kingu Ghidorah*), *Godzilla vs. Queen Mothra* (1992 – aka *Gojira Tai Mosura*), *Godzilla vs. Mechagodzilla* (1993 – aka *Gojira Tai Meka-Gojira*), *Godzilla vs. Space Godzilla* (1995), *Godzilla the Destroyer* (1995), *Godzilla* (1998)

Godzilla on Monster Island see Godzilla vs. Gigan

Godzilla vs. Gigan
Japan 1971 89m colour
Godzilla teams up with Angurus to save the world from Ghidra and Gigan and a bunch of cockroach aliens (no kidding!).
Hilarious rubber-suited nonsense. Good for a laugh, but not for long.

p: Tomoyuki Tanaka for Toho
w: Shinichi Sekizawa
d: Jun Fukuda
ph: Kiyoshi Hasegawa
sp: Shokei Nakano
Hiroshi Ichikawa, Yuriko Hishimi, Tomoko Umeda, Kunio Murai, Minoru Takashima

Godzilla vs. Megalon
Japan 1973 86m colour
Godzilla joins forces with Jet Jaguar to destroy the Seatopians and the monsters they have under their control.
Ludicrous monster epic, indistinguishable from all the others.

p: Tomoyaki Tanaka for Toho
w: Jun Fukuda, Shinichi Sekizawa

story: Shunichi Sekizawa
d: Jun Fukuda
ph: Yuzuru Aizawa
m: Riichiro Manabe
ed: Michiko Ikeda
ad: Yoshibum Honda
sp: Akiyoshi Nakano
sound: Teishiro Hayashi
Katsuhiko Sasakli, Hiroyuki Kawase, Ytaka
Hayshi, Kotaro Tomita

Godzilla vs. the Sea Monster

see Ebirah – Horror of the Deep

Goldblum, Jeff (1952-)

Offbeat American actor who began his
career off Broadway and in
Shakespeare in the Park. After brief
appearances in such films as
California Split, *Death Wish* and
Nashville he gradually grew to leading
man status via appearances in the likes
of *The Big Chill*, *Silverado* and *Into
the Night*. His other credits include
Beyond Therapy, *The Tall Guy* and
Deep Cover.

Genre credits:
Invasion of the Body Snatchers (1978), *The
Fly* (1987 – as Seth Brundle), *Earth Girls Are
Easy* (1988), *Vibes* (1988), *Jurassic Park*
(1993), *Powder* (1995), *Independence Day*
(1996), *The Lost World: Jurassic Park* (1997)

The Golden Voyage of Sinbad 🍲

GB 1973 105m Eastmancolor Dynarama
Sinbad races with an evil magician to
the fountain of destiny, but is hampered by various monsters on the way.

Flatly directed and dully acted fantasy adventure, helped along by its special effects. The second of
Harryhausen and Schneer's Sinbad
movies, it was preceeded by *The*

Seventh Voyage of Sinbad (1958) and
followed by *Sinbad and the Eye of the
Tiger* (1977). A proposed fourth film,
*Sinbad and the Seven Wonders of the
World*, was never made.

p: Charles H. Schneer, Ray Harryhausen for
Columbia/Morningside
w: Brian Clemens
story: Brian Clemens, Ray Harryhausen
d: Gordon Hessler
ph: Ted Moore
m: Miklos Rozsa
ed: Roy Watt
pd: John Stoll
cos: Verena Coleman, Gabriella Falk
sp: RAY HARRYHAUSEN
sound: George Stephenson, Doug Turner
masks: Colin Arthur
ass ed: Jeremy Thomas
John Philip Law, Caroline Munro, Tom Baker,
Douglas Wilmer, Gregoire Aslan, Martin

Shaw, John D. Garfield, Aldo Sambrell

Goldsmith, Jerry (1929-)

Prolific American composer (real name
Jerrold Goldsmith), comfortable with
most genres, though with a predelic-
tion for sci-fi and action themes. He
studied music at USC (under Miklos
Rozsa) before beginning his career
scoring for radio and television in the
50s following experience as a music
clerk at CBS. He broke into films in
1957 with *Black Patch*. Other early
credits include *City of Fear*, *Studs
Lonigan* and *Freud*. In the 60s he contributed scores to such movies as *The
Prize*, *Von Ryan's Express*, *Our Man
Flint*, *The Blue Max* and *The Sand
Pebbles*. In the 70s he scored, among
others, *The Wild Rovers*, *Papillon*,

Sinbad (John Philip Law) and Margiana (Caroline Munro) arrive on the
island of Lemuria to find the Fountain of Destiny in *The Golden Voyage
of Sinbad*, the second of Ray Harryhausen's three Sinbad adventures.

Chinatown, *The Wind and The Lion* and *The Omen* (1976), the last of which finally won him an Oscar. His more recent scores include the three *Rambo* films, *Hoosiers*, *The Russia House*, *Sleeping with the Enemy*, *Basic Instinct* and *Air Force One*. His TV work includes themes for *Dr Kildare*, *The Man from UNCLE*, *The Waltons* and *Star Trek – The Next Generation*. He makes a cameo appearance in director Joe Dante's *Gremlin's 2: The New Batch*, most of whose other films he has also scored.

Genre credits:

Planet of the Apes (1968), *The Illustrated Man* (1969), *Escape from the Planet of the Apes* (1971), *The Reincarnation of Peter Proud* (1975), *Damnation Alley* (1977), *Capricorn One* (1978), *Coma* (1978), *The Boys from Brazil* (1978), *Alien* (1979), *Star Trek* (1979), *Outland* (1981), *The Secret of Nimh* (1982), *Twilight Zone – The Movie* (1983), *Gremlins* (1984), *Supergirl* (1984), *Innerspace* (1987), *Leviathan* (1989), *Star Trek V: The Final Frontier* (1989), *Gremlins 2: The New Batch* (1990), *Total Recall* (1990), *Mom and Dad Save the World* (1992), *Forever Young* (1992), *The Shadow* (1993), *Congo* (1995), *Powder* (1995), *Star Trek: First Contact* (1996 – co-m)

Goldsmith, Joel

American composer and synth player, the son of Jerry Goldsmith. His credits include *The Man with Two Brains* and *Jobman*. His first score (with Richard Band) was for *Laserblast* in 1976.

Genre credits:

Laserblast (1976 – co-m), *Star Trek* (1979 – co-sound effects), *Runaway* (1984 – synth programmer), *Moon 44* (1989 – m), *Star Trek: First Contact* (1996 – co-m), *Kull the Conqueror* (1997 – m)

Golitzen, Alexander (1907-)

Russian art director, in America from 1923. Began his film career in 1933 as an illustrator before graduating to art director in 1935 with *The Call of the Wild*. He has won Oscars for his work on *The Phantom of the Opera* (1943 – with John B. Goodman), *Spartacus* (1960 – with Eric Orbom) and *To Kill a Mockingbird* (1962 – with Henry Bumstead). His other credits include *Foreign Correspondent*, *The Climax*, *Letter to an Unknown Woman*, *Man of a Thousand Faces*, *Cape Fear*, *Thoroughly Modern Millie* and *Earthquake*.

Genre credits:

Abbott and Costello Go to Mars (1953 – co-ad), *Francis in the Navy* (1955 – co-ad), *This Island Earth* (1955 – co-ad), *The Mole People* (1956 – co-ad), *Francis in the Haunted House* (1956 – co-ad), *The Incredible Shrinking Man* (1957 – co-ad), *The Monolith Monsters* (1957 – co-ad), *The Land Unknown* (1957 – co-ad), *The Brass Bottle* (1963 – co-ad), *The Forbin Project* (1969 – aka *Colossus: The Forbin Project* – co-ad), *Slaughterhouse Five* (1972 – co-ad)

Goodwin, Ron (1925-)

British composer, equally adept with action scores as with comedy. A graduate of London's Guildhall School of Music, he began his career as a copyist and arranger before forming his own orchestra in 1951. He began his film career in 1958 with *Whirlpool*, since when he has scored such films as the *Miss Marple* series, *Lancelot and Guinevere*, *633 Squadron*, *Operation Crossbow*, *Those Magnificent Men in Their Flying Machines*, *Monte Carlo or Bust* (aka *Those Daring Young Men in Their Jaunty Jalopies*), *Where Eagles Dare*, *The Trap*, *The Battle of Britain* (replacing a rejected score by

William Walton) and *Frenzy* (replacing a rejected score by Henry Mancini). He also scored several films for Disney's British arm in the 70s (*One of Our Dinosaurs is Missing*, *Candleshoe*, etc.).

Genre credits:

Village of the Damned (1960), *The Day of the Triffids* (1962 – co-m), *Children of the Damned* (1963), *The Happy Prince* (1974), *The Spaceman and King Arthur* (1979 – aka *Unidentified Flying Oddball*)

Gordon, Bert I. (1922-)

American writer, producer, director and effects technician with numerous low budgeters to his credit (*The Cyclops*, *Attack of the Puppet People*, *War of the Colossal Beast*, etc.), though few of them are of outstanding merit. Came to films in 1957 via television and commercials.

Genre credits:

King Dinosaur (1957 – co-story/co-p/d), *The Beginning of the End* (1957 – co-w/p/sp/co-d), *St. George and the Seven Curses* (1962 – aka *The Magic Sword* – story/co-sp/p/d), *Village of the Giants* (1965 – co-sp/p/d)

Gough, Michael (1917-)

Distinguished looking and sounding British character actor, on stage from 1936 and in films from 1947 with *Blanche Fury*. Though he has appeared in many quality productions (*Anna Karenina*, *The Small Black Room*, *Richard III*, *Julius Caesar*, *The Go-Between*, *Out of Africa*), he is also equally at home in horror films (*Dracula*, *Horrors of the Black Museum*, *Konga*, *The Phantom of the Opera*, *Trog*, *Horror Hospital*, *The Legend of Hell House*). More recently has has found a new audience as Alfred the Butler in the Batman movies.

Genre credits:
They Came from Beyond Space (1967),
Arthur the King (1985 - aka *Merlin's Sword* -
TVM), *Batman* (1989) *Batman Returns*
(1992), *Batman Forever* (1995), *Batman and
Robin* (1997)

Grant, Arthur (1915–1972)

British cinematographer, long with
Hammer, for whom he photographed
such films as *The Abominable
Snowman*, *Captain Clegg* (aka *Night
Creatures*), *Phantom of the Opera*,
The Plague of the Zombies, *The Devil
Rides Out* and *Taste the Blood of
Dracula*. Began his career in 1929 as a
camera assistant at the Cecil Hepworth
studios before becoming an operator in
1947 with *When You Came*. Became a
director of photography in 1950 with
The Dragon of Pendragon Castle.

Genre credits:
The Dragon of Pendragon Castle (1950),
The Angel Who Pawned Her Harp (1954),
The Damned (1963 – aka *These Are the
Damned*), *Quatermass and the Pit* (1967 –
aka *Five Million Years to Earth*)

Graves, Peter (1925-)

American actor (real name Peter
Aurness) in films from 1950 with
Rogue River following experience as a
radio announcer. His other credits
include *Fort Defiance*, *Black Tuesday*,
Wolf Larsen, *Disaster in the Sky*
(TVM) and *Airplane*, in which he
played the pilot. He is also familiar
from TV's *Mission: Impossible*.

Genre credits:
Red Planet Mars (1952), *It Conquered the
World* (1956), *The Beginning of the End*

(1957), *Airplane 2: The Sequel* (1982)

Gray, Barry (1925-1984)

British composer best known for his
scores and themes for Gerry Anderson's
television puppet series, which began in
1956 with *Twizzle* and continued on
through *Torchy the Battery Boy*,
Supercar, *Fireball XL5*, *Stingray*,
Thunderbirds, *Captain Scarlet*, *Joe 90*,
The Secret Service and the live action
UFO and *Space 1999*. Began his career
as an arranger in variety.

Genre credits:
Dr Who and the Daleks (1965 – co-m),
Daleks Invasion Earth, 2150 A.D. (1966 – co-
m), *Thunderbirds to the Rescue* (1966 –
TVM – series pilot), *Thunderbirds Are Go!*
(1966), *Thunderbird Six* (1968), *Journey to
the Far Side of the Sun* (1969 – aka
Doppelganger), *Invasion: UFO* (1970 –
TVM)

The Great Muppet Caper 😋😋

GB 1981 97m Technicolor
Kermit, Fozzie and Gonzo become
reporters and travel to England to discover who was behind the robbery of
some priceless jewels.

Bright and agreeable caper spoof
with Hellzapoppin'-style gags and a
technically imaginative use of the
famous puppets. Good fun for young
and old alike.

p: David Lazer, Frank Oz for ITC
w: Ton Patchett, Jay Tarses, Jerry Juhl, Jack
Rose
d: JIM HENSON
ph: Oswald Morris
m/ly: JOE RAPOSO
pd: Harry Lange
cos: Julie Harris, Claista Hendrickson
Diana Rigg, Charles Grodin, John Cleese,

Peter Ustinov, Jack Warden, Trevor Howard,
Robert Morley, Michael Robbins

Gremlins

USA 1984 106m Technicolor Dolby
A quiet American town is threatened
by hordes of destructive creatures
which multiply when they come into
contact with water.

An enjoyable harkback to the monster movies of the 1950s, this black
fantasy has a good smattering of
humour, thrills, in-jokes and gag
cameos.

p: Michael Finnell for Warner/Amblin
exec p: Steven Spielberg, Kathleen
Kennedy, Frank Marshall
w: Chris Columbus
d: JOE DANTE
ph: John Hora
m: Jerry Goldsmith
ed: Tina Hirsch
pd: James H. Spencer
cos: Norman Burza, Linda Matthews
gremlin design/sp: CHRIS WALAS
sound: Ken King, Bill Varney, Steve Maslow,
Kevin O'Connell
stunt co-ordinator: Terry Leonard
Zach Galligan, Hoyt Axton, Frances Lee
McCain, Phoebe Cates, Polly Holliday, Scott
Brady, Dick Miller, Keye Luke, Chuck Jones,
Edward Andrews, Kenneth Tobey, Judge
Reinhold, Steven Spielberg and the voices of
Howie Mandell, Frank Walker and Fred
Newman

Gremlins 2: The New Batch 😋

USA 1990 105m Technicolor Dolby
The gremlins take over a Donald
Trump-style skyscraper in Manhattan.

Zany, Hellzapoppin'-like sequel in
which anything goes. It tends to outstay its welcome, but buffs will have a
field day spotting all the in-jokes and
gag cameos.

Billy Peltzer (Zach Galligan) has a chat with his pal Gizmo in *Gremlins 2: The New Batch*, director Joe Dante's *Hellzapoppin'*-like sequel to *Gremlins*.

p: Michael Finnell, Rick Baker for Warner/Amblin
exec p: Steven Spielberg, Frank Marshall, Kathleen Kennedy
w: Charles Haas
d: Joe Dante
ph: John Hora
m: Jerry Goldsmith
ed: Kent Beyda
pd: James Spencer
cos: Rosanna Norton
sp: Doug Beswick, Dennis Michelson
sound: Ken King, Douglas Vaughan
sound effects: Mark Mangini, David Stone
gremlin effects: Rick Baker
2nd unit d: James Spencer
stunt co-ordinator: Mike McGaughy
Zach Galligan, Phoebe Cates, John Glover, Robert J. Prosky, Christopher Lee, Robert Picardo, Kathleen Freeman, John Astin, Kenneth Tobey, Dick Miller, Joe Dante, Jerry Goldsmith, Paul Bartell, Hulk Hogan, Henry Gibson, Leonard Maltin, Haviland Morris, Jackie Joseph, Keye Luke, Don Stanton, Dan Stanton, Charlie Haas, Dick Butkus, Bubba Smith and the voices of Howie Mandell, Tony Randall, Frank Walker and Jeff Bergman

Groundhog Day

USA 1993 101m Technicolor Dolby
A self-absorbed television weatherman finds himself living through his least-liked day of the year again and again.

Amusingly scripted high concept comedy which manages to sustain itself surprisingly well.

p: Trevor Albert, Harold Ramis for Columbia
exec p: C. O. Erickson
w: DANNY RUBIN, HAROLD RAMIS
story: Danny Rubin
d: HAROLD RAMIS
ph: John Bailey
m: George Fenton
ed: Pembroke J. Herring
pd: David Nichols
cos: Mike Butler
sp: Tom Ryba
sound: Les Lazarowitz
2nd unit d: Steve Boyum
2nd unit ph: James Blandford, George Kohut
BILL MURRAY, Andie MacDowell, Chris Elliott, Stephen Tobolowsky, Harold Ramis, Brian Doyle-Murray, Angela Patton, Marita Geraghty, Rick Overton

Guest, Val (1911-)

Prolific British actor, writer, producer, director and lyricist, a former trade journalist who began his film career as a writer on a number of classic British comedies (*Good Morning, Boys*, *Oh, Mr. Porter*, *The Frozen Limits*, etc.). He made his directorial debut on the Arthur Askey comedy *Miss London Ltd.*, which he followed with all manner of comedies and lightweight musicals (*Mr. Drake's Duck*, *The Runaway Buss*, *Penny Princess*, etc.). It was *The Quatermass Experiment*, which he made for Hammer, that altered the course of his career, however, leading to further genre entries. Subsequent non-genre films include *The Camp on Blood Island*, *Up the Creek*, *Expresso Bongo*, *Jigsaw*, *Casino Royale*, *Confessions of a Window Cleaner* and TV's *Shillingbury Tales*.

Genre credits:

Alf's Button Afloat (1938 – co-w), *The Quatermass Experiment* (1955 – aka *The Creeping Unknown* – co-w/d), *Quatermass 2* (1957 – aka *Enemy from Space* – co-w/d), *The Day the Earth Caught Fire* (1962 – co-w/p/d), *When Dinosaurs Ruled the Earth* (1970 – w/d)

Gulliver's Travels

There have been several film versions of Jonathan Swift's satirical novel down the decades, the first being a Georges Méliès trick film in 1902. The most faithful, however, has been the most recent, the two-part television version made in 1995, which found great favour on both sides of the Atlantic. Dave Fleischer's 1939 animated version is also of note.

Filmography:

Le Voyage de Gulliver à Lilliput et Chez les Géants (1902 – aka *Gulliver's Travels*), *Gulliver's Travels* (1939), *The Three Worlds of Gulliver* (1960), *Gulliver's Travels* (1976),

Gulliver's Travels

USA 1939 74m Technicolor

In 1699, a shipwrecked sailor finds himself washed ashore in a land where the inhabitants are only an inch high.

Superbly managed cartoon feature, with excellent comic detail and solidly etched characters. A delight for young and old.

p: Max Fleischer for Paramount
w: Edmond Seward, Dan Gordon, Cal Howard, Ted Pierce, I. Sparger
novel: Jonathan Swift
d: Dave Fleischer
ph: Charles Schettler
songs: Ralph Rainger, Leo Robin
m: Victor Young

Gulliver's Travels

GB 1976 81m Eastmancolor

Following a shipwreck, a sailor finds himself washed ashore in a cartoon land where all the inhabitants are no more than an inch high.

Tame version of the Swift novel with half-hearted animation. Youngsters will no doubt enjoy themselves, however.

p: Josef Shaftel for EMI
w: Don Black
d: Peter Hunt
ph: Alan Hume
m: Michel Legrand
ly: Don Black
pd: Michael Stringer
Richard Harris, Norman Shelley, Catherine Schell

Gulliver's Travels

GB 1995 2x96m colour TVM

Eighteenth-century ship's surgeon Lemuel Gulliver returns home after eight years' absence and recalls his fantastical adventures in a land of little people, a land of giants and on a floating island. But no one believes him and he is put into an asylum.

The best adaptation yet of the Jonathan Swift satire, complemented by excellent special effects.

p: Duncan Kenworthy for Hallmark/Channel Four/Jim Henson Productions
exec p: Robert Halmi, Sr., Brian Henson
w: Simon Moore
novel: Jonathan Swift
d: Charles Sturridge
ph: Howard Atherton
m: Trevor Jones
ed: Peter Coulson
pd: Roger Hall
cos: Shirley Russell
sp: Tim Webber
sound: Simon Kaye, Paul Hamblin
2nd unit ph: Trevor Brooker
titles: Chris Allies
Ted Danson, Mary Steenburgen, James Fox, Peter O'Toole, Edward Woodward, Warwick Davis, Nicholas Lyndhurst, Thomas Sturridge, Ned Beatty, Geraldine Chaplin, Kristin Scott Thomas, John Gielgud, Graham Crowden, Robert Hardy, Shashi Kapoor, Edward Petherbridge, Omar Shariff, Richard Wilson, Navin Chowdhry, Phoebe Nicholls, Karyn Parsons, John Standing, John Wells, Alfre Woodard, Isabelle Huppert (voice)

Guinness, Sir Alec (1914-)

Celebrated British actor of stage, screen and television. He has a penchant for disguise, as his roles in *Oliver Twist* (as Fagin), *Kind Hearts and Coronets* (as eight members of the Ascoyne-D'Ascoyne family) and others will attest. An Oscar winner for his performance as the misguided Colonel Nicholson in David Lean's *The Bridge on the River Kwai* (1957), some of his other noteworthy films include *The Lavender Hill Mob*, *The Man in the White Suit*, *The Card*, *Murder by Death* and *Little Dorrit*, six films for for David Lean and the television series *Tinker, Tailor, Soldier, Spy* and *Smiley's People*. To genre fans, however, he is best known for playing the Jedi knight Obi-Wan (Ben) Kenobi in the *Star Wars* trilogy, the first of which earned him an Oscar nomination as best supporting actor. Following training at The Fay Compton Studio, Guinness began his acting career in 1933 with a walk-on part in the film *Evensong*. He made his debut in 1934 in *Libel*, after which he joined the Old Vic Company. He went on to become one of the leading stage actors of his generation and, later, a top film star, especially after his success in *Kwai*.

Genre credits:

Scrooge (1970), *Star Wars* (1977), *The Empire Strikes Back* (1980), *The Return of the Jedi* (1983)

Guttenberg, Steve (1958-)

American comedy actor, perhaps best known for playing Mahoney in the first four *Police Academy* films. His other hits include *Diner* and *Three Men and a Baby*, though they were outnumbered by his duds, which take in *Can't Stop the Music* and *Bad Medicine*. He began his career in various off-Broadway productions before turning to film in 1977 with *The Chicken Chronicles*.

Genre Credits:

The Boys from Brazil (1978), *The Man Who Wasn't There* (1982), *Cocoon* (1985), *Short Circuit* (1986), *Amazon Women on the Moon* (1987), *High Spirits* (1988), *Cocoon: The Return* (1988), *Casper, A Spirited Beginning* (1997)

Haley, Jack (1899-1979)

American comedy actor who, despite appearances in such films as *Alexander's Ragtime Band, Moon Over Miami* and *Beyond the Blue Horizon*, is remembered chiefly for playing the Tin Man in *The Wizard of Oz* (1939).

Hall, Kevin Peter (1955-1991)

Tall (7' 2") African American actor who suited up to play the creatures in *Predator* (1987), *Harry and the Hendersons* (1987 – aka *Bigfoot and the Hendersons*) and *Predator II* (1990). He also played Harry in the TV sit-com version of *Harry and the Hendersons*.

Haller, Daniel (Dan) (1929-)

American art director and, later, director. A former stage designer, he also worked on commercials before beginning his Hollywood career in 1955. Created many atmospheric sets for Roger Corman's Poe films in the 60s, including *House of Usher* (aka *The Fall of the House of Usher*), *The Pit and the Pendulum, The Premature Burial* and *The Raven*. He turned to direction in 1965 with *Die, Monster,*

Die! (aka *The Monster of Terror*) after which he helmed such movies as *Devil's Angels, The Wild Racers, The Dunwich Horror* and *Follow That Car.*

Genre credits:
Teenage Caveman (1958 – aka *Out of the Darkness* – ad), *War of the Satellites* (1958 – ad), *The Ghost of Dragstrip Hollow* (1959 – ad), *Master of the World* (1961 – ad), *Panic in Year Zero* (1962 – ad), *City Under the Sea* (1965 – aka *Wargods of the Deep* – ad), *Buck Rogers in the 25th Century* (1979 – TVM – d)

Halloween III: Season of the Witch 🛸

USA 1983 99m Technicolor Panavision

A mysterious industrialist plans a nasty surprise for the children of America on Hallow'en.

Murdered Micahel Myers can be spotted only briefly in a walk-on cameo in this complete change of direction for the *Halloween* series, which centres round killer masks and magical stones. Fairly good fun on the whole, though the fashionable gore is a reret, on which count Kneal had his name removed from the credits.

p: John Carpenter, Debra Hill for Moustapha Akaad Productions
w/d: Tommy Lee Wallace
original w: NIGEL KNEALE
ph: Dean Cundey
m: John Carpenter, Alan Howarth
ed: Peter Coulson
pd: Peter Jamison
cos: Jane Riehm, Francis Aubrey
sp: John G. Belyeu
sound: Bill Varney, Steve Maslow, James Carvarette, Jr
2nd unit ph: Trevor Brooker
titles: John Walsh
masks: John Post
Tom Atkins, Stacey Nelkin, DAN O'HERLIHY, Michael Currie, Ralph Strait, Judeen Barber,

Gary Stephens, Dick Warlock

Hamill, Mark (1951-)

American actor best known for playing Luke Skywalker in the *Star Wars* trilogy. Began his professional career in television in 1970, among early appearances being *General Hospital* and *The Texas Wheelers*. His other credits include *Corvette Summer, The Big Red One* and *In Exile*.

Genre credits:
Wizards (1977 – voice), *Star Wars* (1977), *The Empire Strikes Back* (1980), *Britannia Hospital* (1982), *Return of the Jedi* (1983), *Slipstream* (1989), *Earth Angel* (1991 – TVM), *Batman: Mask of the Phantasm* (1994 – voice), *When Time Expires* (1997 – TVM)

Hamilton, Linda (1956-)

American actress who, after experience on television (in the soap opera *Secrets of Midland Heights*), broke into movies and shot to fame as Sarah Connor in the two *Terminator* films. She also appeared in the cult TV series *Beauty and the Beast*.

Genre credits:
The Terminator (1984), *King Kong Lives* (1986), *Terminator 2: Judgement Day* (1991)

Hamilton, Margaret (1902-1985)

Hatchet-faced American comedy character actress, best remembered for playing the Wicked Witch of the West in *The Wizard of Oz*. A former kindergarten teacher, she turned to acting in the late 20s, and after stage experience she went to Hollywood in 1933, making her debut in *Another Language*. Her other credits include *The Adventures of Tom Sawyer, The Invisible Woman,*

Mad Wednesday, *Thirteen Ghosts* and *The Anderson Tapes*.

Genre credits:
The Wizard of Oz (1939), *Brewster McCloud* (1970), *Journey Back to Oz* (1974 – voice)

Hammer Films

British production company, synonymous with the making of horror films (*The Curse of Frankenstein*, *Dracula*, *The Mummy*, *The Phantom of the Opera*, *The Devil Rides Out*, etc.), though they first broke onto the international scene with the science fiction thriller *The Quatermass Experiment* in 1955. Formed in 1935 by William Hinds (aka Will Hammer) and his partner Enrique Carreras, the original Hammer films produced a handful of light comedies and dramas in the mid-30s before going bankrupt during World War Two. They re-emerged in 1947, however, and entered the quota quickie market, churning out countless thrillers and no-budgeters, many of them based on popular radio series. During the 50s, Hammer's quota policy became more adventurous and downward-sliding American stars were brought in to make the films more appealing to American audiences and distributors. Then, in 1955, almost accidentally they stumbled on *The Quatermass Experiment*, a top-rated television serial by Nigel Kneale and decided to make a film version, the success of which astonished the industry and provoked Hammer into remaking the Frankenstein and Dracula legends. This led to a successful series of horror outings, with the occasional foray into science fiction and fantasy along the way.

Genre credits:
Stolen Face (1952), *Spaceways* (1953), *Four-Sided Triangle* (1953), *The Quatermass Experiment* (1955 – aka *The Quatermass Xperiment/The Creeping Unknown*), *X – The Unknown* (1956), *Quatermass 2* (1957 – aka *Enemy from Space*), *She* (1965), *One Million Years B. C.* (1966), *Quatermass and the Pit* (1967 – aka *Five Million Years to Earth*), *The Vengeance of She* (1968), *Moon Zero Two* (1969), *Slave Girls* (1968 – aka *Prehistoric Women*), *The Lost Continent* (1968), *When Dinosaurs Ruled the Earth* (1970), *Creatures the World Forgot* (1971)

Hannah, Daryl (1960-)

American actress who came to attention as the acrobatic android in *Blade Runner*, though prior to this she had made brief appearances in such films as *The Fury* (her debut) and *Hard Country*. Her other credits include *Wall Street*, *Legal Eagles*, *Roxanne*, *Steel Magnolias* and *The Little Rascals*.

Genre credits:
Blade Runner (1982), *Splash!* (1984), *Clan of the Cave Bear* (1986), *High Spirits* (1988), *Memoirs of an Invisible Man* (1992), *Attack of the Fifty-Foot Woman* (1993 – TVM)

Hans Christian Andersen 💩

USA 1952 112m Technicolor
A cobbler leaves his home village to try his luck in Copenhagen and finds himself making shoes for a ballerina with whom he falls in love.

Stolid, unimaginative fantasy musical whose tuneful score deserves a better framework. Today's youngsters will find themselves quickly bored.

p: Samuel Goldwyn
w: Moss Hart
d: Charles Vidor
ph: Harry Stradling
songs: FRANK LOESSER
md: Walter Scharf
ed: Daniel Mandell
ad: Richard Day, Clave
cos: Clave
sp: Clarence Slifer
Danny Kaye, Farley Granger, Zizi Jeanmaire, John Qualen, Joey Walsh

Harburg, E. Y. (1896-1981)

American lyricist who, with composer Harold Arlen, wrote the songs for *The Wizard of Oz* (1939). His other hits include *Lydia the Tattooed Lady*, *April in Paris*, *The Man That Got Away* and *How Are Things in Glocca Morra?* (from *Finian's Rainbow*, which was filmed in 1968).

Hardware

GB 1990 92m Technicolor
Post-apocalypse mercenaries attempt to destroy an android whose job it is to modulate the population.

Flashy pot-pourri of *Mad Max*, *Blade Runner*, *Alien* and *The Terminator*, with a noisy soundtrack and plenty of gratuitous violence and gore. It has its admirers, though the film ran into legal problems for allegedly ripping off its story from a *2000 AD* comic strip without permission.

p: Joanne Sellar, Paul Trybits for Wicked Films
w/d: Richard Stanley
ph: Steven Chivers
m: Simon Boswell
ed: Derek Trigg
pd: Joseph Bennett
cos: Michael Baldwin
sp: Image Imagination, Barney Jeffrey
sound: Jonathan Miller, Kate Hopkins
Dylan McDermott, Stacey Travis, John Lynch, William Hootkins, Iggy Pop (voice), Mark Northover, Oscar James, Paul McKenzie, Carl McCoy

Whilst diving, Neb (Dan Jackson), Captain Cyrus Harding (Michael Craig) and Herbert Brown (Michael Callan) encounter Ray Harryhausen's stop-motion giant squid in *Mysterious Island*.

Harline, Leigh (1907-1969)

American composer and songwriter who won two Oscars for *Pinocchio* (1940), one for best score (with Paul J. Smith and Ned Washington) and one for best song, *When You Wish Upon a Star* (with Ned Washington). A conductor for radio in the late 20s and early 30s, he joined the Disney studio in 1932 as a composer/conductor and worked on many of their shorts before co-writing the music for the studio's first animated feature, *Snow White and the Seven Dwarfs*. He left Disney in 1941 and went on to work on such films as *Pride of the Yankees*, *The Sky's the Limit*, *The Road to Utopia* and *Monkey Business*.

Genre credits:
Snow White and the Seven Dwarfs (1937 – co-m), *Pinocchio* (1940 – co-m/co-songs), *The Boy with Green Hair* (1948 – m), *Visit to a Small Planet* (1959 – m), *The Wonderful World of the Brothers Grimm* (1962 – m), *The Seven Faces of Dr Lao* (1964 – m)

Harris, Jack H.

American producer, a former distributor, whose credits include various versions of *The Blob*.

Genre credits:
The Blob (1958 – p), *Beware! The Blob* (1971 – aka *Son of Blob* – exec p/co-story), *The Blob* (1988 – co-p), *Blobermouth* (1990 – p [re-dub of the 1958 movie by comedy group L.A. Connection])

Harryhausen, Ray (1920-)

American special effects wiz, known for his stop-motion effects which have graced a number of spectacular fantasy adventures. Began experimenting with stop-frame animation after seeing *King Kong* in 1933, which eventually led to work with George Pal on his *Puppetoon* series in the early 40s. Worked with his hero Willis O'Brien on *Mighty Joe Young* in 1949. Then, in the 50s, he teamed up with producer Charles H. Schneer, with whom he has worked almost exclusively since. He is also the inventor of the effects process Superdynamation.

Genre credits:

Mighty Joe Young (1949 – co-sp), *The Beast from 20,000 Fathoms* (1953), *It Came from Beneath the Sea* (1955), *Earth vs. the Flying Saucers* (1956), *Twenty-Million Miles to Earth* (1957), *The Seventh Voyage of Sinbad* (1958), *The Three Worlds of Gulliver* (1960), *Mysterious Island* (1961), *Jason and the Argonauts* (1963), *The First Men in the Moon* (1963 – also associate p), *One Million Years B. C.* (1966), *The Valley of Gwangi* (1968), *The Golden Voyage of Sinbad* (1973 – also co-story/co-p), *Sinbad and the Eye of the Tiger* (1977 – also co-p), *Clash of the Titans* (1981 – also co-p)

Haskin, Byron (1899-1984)

American director, cinematographer and special effects technician with a handful of key 50s science fiction films to his credit. After experience as a cartoonist he began his film career in 1919 as a camera assistant, graduating to cinematographer proper in 1922. He began directing as early as 1927 with *Matinee Ladies*, though he continued to work as a photographer and effects technician. His other directorial credits include *Treasure Island* for Disney, *The Naked Jungle*, *Jet Over the Atlantic* and *September Storm*.

Genre credits:

A Midsummer Night's Dream (1935 – co-sp), *War of the Worlds* (1953 – d), *Conquest of Space* (1954 – d), *From the Earth to the Moon* (1958 – d), *Captain Sinbad* (1963 – d), *Robinson Crusoe on Mars* (1964 – d), *The Power* (1967 – d)

Hawk the Slayer

GB 1980 93m Technicolor Dolby

A young prince and his friends destroy an evil warlord.

Cliché-strewn sword and sorcery adventure for younger audiences.

p: Harry Robertson for ITC/Chips/Marcel-Robertson
exec p: Jack Gill
w: Terry Marcel, Harry Robertson
d: Terry Marcel
ph: Paul Beeson
m: Harry Robertson
ed: Eric Boyd-Perkins
ad: Michael Pickwoad
cos: Ken Lewington
sp: Effects Associates
John Terry, Jack Palance, Bernard Bresslaw, Ray Charleson, Annette Crosbie, Peter O'Farrell, Cheryl Campbell, Harry Andrews, Catriona McColl, Graham Stark, Roy Kinnear, Shane Briant, Patrick Magee, Ferdy Mayne, Morgan Sheppard, Christopher Benjamin, Ken Parry

Hayes, Alison (1930-1977)

American actress (real name Mary Jane Hayes) best remembered for playing Nancy Archer in *Attack of the Fifty-Foot Woman*. She appeared in a number of low budget genre pictures in the 50s, among them *The Undead*, *Zombies of Mora Tau*, *The Crawling Hand* and *The Disembodied*.

Genre credits:

Francis Joins the WACS (1954), *The Unearthly* (1957), *Attack of the Fifty-Foot Woman* (1958), *The Hypnotic Eye* (1960)

Heart Condition

USA 1990 100m DeLuxe

A bigoted white vice cop has a heart attack and receives a donor heart from a black lawyer, who subsequently

haunts him.

Dismal fantasy-comedy which tackily exploits the most basic racial issues in its bid to preach harmony. It might have got by 30 years ago, but not in 1990.

p: Steve Tisch for Enterprise/New Line
exec p: Robert Shaye
w/d: James D. Parriott
ph: Arthur Albert
m: Patrick Leonard
ed: David Finfer
pd: John Muto
cos: Louise Frogley
Bob Hoskins, Denzel Washington, Chloe Webb, Lisa Stahl, Robert Apisa, Jeffrey Meek, Frank R. Roach

Heaven Can Wait

USA 1943 112m Technicolor

A recently deceased playboy recounts his life to Satan, who promptly sends him up to heaven.

Engaging period comedy with a touch of fantasy and brush strokes typical of its director.

p: Ernst Lubitsch for TCF
w: SAMSON RAPHAELSON
play: Lazlo Bus Fekete
d: ERNST LUBITSCH
ph: EDWARD CRONJAGER
m: Alfred Newman
ed: Dorothy Spencer
ad: James Basevi, Leland Fuller
cos: Rene Hubert
sp: Fred Sersen
sound: Eugene Grossman, Roger Heman
DON AMECHE, GENE TIERNEY, LAIRD CREGAR, CHARLES COBURN, MARJORIE MAIN, EUGENE PALLETTE, ALLYN JOSLYN, Spring Byington, Signe Hasso, Louis Calhern

Heaven Can Wait

USA 1978 100m Movielab

A football player is sent back down to earth in a different body after being

Brigitte Helm (as Maria) awaits to be robotised in director Fritz Lang's 1926 silent classic *Metropolis*. The film made Helm a star.

taken to heaven too soon by accident.

Agreeable, likeably performed update of *Here Comes Mr. Jordan*. One of the biggest box office draws of its year.

p: Warren Beatty, Elaine May
play: Harry Segall
d: Warren Beatty, Buck Henry
ph: William A. Fraker
m: Dave Grusin
ed: Robert C. Jones, Don Zimmermann
pd: Paul Sylbert
cos: Theadora Van Runkle, Richard Bruno
sp: Robert MacDonald
sound: John K. Williamson, Tommy Overton
titles: Wayne Fitzgerald
WARREN BEATTY, Julie Christie, JAMES MASON, Jack Warden, JAMES BROLIN, DYAN CANNON, Buck Henry, Vincent

Gardenia, Joseph Maher

Heavenly Pursuits 🛸
GB 1986 92m Technicolor
A sceptical schoolmaster discovers that he may have the power to perform miracles.

Mildly amusing anecdote which whiles away the time.

p: Michael Relph for Island/Film Four/NFFC/SKREBA
w/d: Charles Gormley
ph: Michael Coulter
m: B. A. Robertson
ed: John Gow
pd: Rita McGurn
cos: Lindy Hemming
sound: Louis Kramer, Peter Maxwell,

Nicholas Gaster
Tom Conti, Helen Mirren, David Hayman, Brian Pettifer, Jennifer Black, Dave Anderson, Gordon Jackson

Helm, Brigitte (1907-1996)
German actress (real name Gisele Eve Schittenhelm) remembered chiefly for playing the robot in Fritz Lang's *Metropolis*. Her other credits include *Am Rande der Welt*, *Alraune*, *Die Herrin von Atlantis* and *Gold*.

Hennesey, Dale
American art director, an Oscar winner for *Fantastic Voyage* (1966 – with Jack Martin Smith). His many credits take in such diverse films as *Everything You Always Wanted to Know About Sex But Were Afraid to Ask*, *Young Frankenstein* and *Annie*.

Genre credits:
Fantastic Voyage (1966 – co-ad), *Battle for the Planet of the Apes* (1973 – ad), *Logan's Run* (1976 – ad), *Sleeper* (1973 – pd)

Henriksen, Lance
American character actor, often in villainous roles, though he is perhaps best known for playing Bishop the android in *Aliens*. His other credits include *Dog Day Afternoon*, *The Right Stuff*, *Jennifer Eight*, *Boulevard*, *Color of Night* and the TV series *Millennium*.

Genre credits:
Close Encounters of the Third Kind (1977), *Close Encounters of the Third Kind – The Special Edition* (1980), *The Terminator* (1984), *Aliens* (1986), *Alien 3* (1992), *Super Mario Bros.* (1993), *No Escape* (1994), *Powder* (1995)

Henson, Brian

American puppeteer, producer and director who has inherited the mantle of his late father, Jim Henson.

Genre credits:

The Muppet Christmas Carol (1992 – puppeteer/co-p/d), *Muppet Treasure Island* (1996 – puppeteer/co-p/d), *Buddy* (1997 - co-exec p)

Henson, Jim (1936-1990)

American producer, director and puppeteer, the creator of the world famous Muppets, who have appeared on television, in films and as an attraction at Disney's MGM Studio Park in Florida. He began his career in 1954 as a puppeteer on the *Junior Good Morning Show* for several weeks, after which he went to the University of Maryland where he studied studio art. In 1955 he got his first long-running TV slot with a show called *Sam and Friends* which featured Kermit the Frog and several other creations. This ran until 1961, during which time Henson also made many hundreds of commercials featuring his evolving cast of Muppets. *Tales of the Tinkerdee* followed in 1962, along with guest spots on such programmes as *The Jimmy Dean Show*, *The Ed Sullivan Show* and *The Jack Paar Show*, along with the occasional special, such as *Tales from Muppetland – The Frog Prince*, *Hey, Cinderella!* and *The Muppet Musicians of Bremen*. Then, in 1969, came *Sesame Street* which introduced a whole slew of Muppet characters, among them Big Bird, Oscar the Grouch, the Cookie Monster and Ernie and Bert. Further specials followed, along with regular guest spots on *The Julie Andrews Hour*, all of which led up to *The Muppet Show* in 1976 and the establishing of such characters as Fozzie Bear, Gonzo, Miss Piggy and Statler and Waldorf. The show ran until 1981 and produced a movie offshoot in 1979. This in turn led to further movies featuring not only the Muppets from the television series, but new characters in new stories, such as *The Dark Crystal*, Henson's second film as a director (with long-time collaborator Frank Oz). Further television series followed, such as *Fraggle Rock*, *Mother Goose Stories* and *The Storyteller*, along with the establishing of The Creature Shop, a special effects facility which has provided animatronic creatures for such movies as *Dreamchild*, *Labyrinth*, *The Witches* and the *Teenage Mutant Ninja Turtle* series. Following Henson's untimely death in 1990, his son Brian has taken over his father's mantle, directing such movies as *Muppet Christmas Carol* and *Muppet Treasure Island*. A new television show also appeared in 1996 titled *Muppets Tonight*. Like Walt Disney before him, Henson's legacy is just as strong following his death.

Genre credits:

The Muppet Movie (1979 – puppeteer/p), *The Great Muppet Caper* (1981 – puppeteer/d), *The Dark Crystal* (1982 – co-d), *The Muppets Take Manhattan* (1984 – puppeteer/exec p), *Labyrinth* (1986 – co-w/d)

Herbie Goes Bananas

USA 1980 100m Technicolor
Herbie and his two new owners foil a plot to smuggle priceless Inca treasures out of Brazil.

Tired, rather belated tailing-off of Disney's Herbie series.

p: Ron Miller, Kevin Corcoran for Walt Disney
w: Don Tait
d: Vincent McEveety
ph: Frank Phillips
m: Frank de Vol
ed: Gordon D. Brenner
ad: Rodger Maus, John B. Mansbridge
cos: Jack Sandeen
sp: Art Cruickshank, Danny Lee
sound: Herb Taylor, Henry A. Maffett
2nd unit d: Charles Dymytryk
add ph: Mike Sweeten
Cloris Leachman, Charles Martin Smith, Stephen W. Burns, John Vernon, Harvey Korman, Richard Jaekel, Alex Rocco, Fritz Feld, Joaquin Garay III, Elyssa Davalos

Herbie Goes to Monte Carlo

USA 1977 105m Technicolor
Herbie enters the car race at Monte Carlo and rounds up some jewel thieves in the process.

Tame third instalment in Disney's ongoing Herbie series.

p: Ron Miller for Walt Disney
w: Arthur Alsberg, Don Nelson
d: Vincent McEveety
ph: Leonard J. South
m: Frank de Vol
ed: Cotton Warburton
ad: John B. Mansbridge, Perry Ferguson
cos: Chuck Keehne, Emily Sundby
sp: Eustace Lycett, Art Cruickshank, Danny Lee, Peter Ellenshaw
sound: Herb Taylor, Hal Etherington
2nd unit d: Arthur J. Vitarelli
add ph: Charles F. Wheeler
Dean Jones, Don Knotts, Julie Sommers, Roy Kinnear, Bernard Fox, Eric Braeden, Xavier Saint McCary, Jacques Marin, François Lelande

Herbie Rides Again

USA 1974 88m Technicolor
An old lady whose home is under threat by a corrupt property developer is helped by her magical car.

Fairish follow-up to *The Love Bug*

which generated two further sequels.

p: Bill Walsh for Walt Disney
w: Bill Walsh
story: Gordon Buford
d: Robert Stevenson
ph: Frank Phillips
m: George Bruns
ed: Cotton Warburton
ad: John B. Mansbridge, Walter Tyler
cos: Chuck Keehne, Emily Sundby
sp: Eustace Lycett, Art Cruickshank, Danny Lee, Alan Maley
sound: Herb Taylor
2nd unit d: Arthur J. Vitarelli
Helen Hayes, Stefanie Powers, Ken Berry, John McIntire, Huntz Hall, Keenan Wynn

Hercules

It 1958 105m Eastmancolor Dyaliscope
After various adventures in which his mighty strength proves useful, Hercules helps Jason in his quest to find the golden fleece.

The sword and sandal romp that produced an industry, on which count it deserves a footnote in cinema history. Its endearingly shoddy production values, skimpy costumes, unconvincing effects and poor dialogue and dubbing are typical of the films that followed.

p: Federico Teti for Oscar/Galatea
exec p: Ferruccio De Martino
exec p (American release): Joseph E. Levine
w: Ennio De Concini, Pietro Francisi, Galo Fratini
d/story: Pietro Francisi
ph/sp: Mario Bava
m: Enzo Masetti
md: Carlo Savina
ed: Mario Serandrei
ad: Flavio Mogherini
cos: Giulio Coltellacci
sound: Giulio Tagliacozzo, Renato Cadueri
ch: Gisa Geert
Steve Reeves, Fabrizio Mione, Gianna Maria Canale, Sylva Koscina

Hercules

USA 1997 91m Technicolor Dolby
Aided by his flying horse Pegasus, the demi-god Hercules becomes an earthly hero and goes on to thwart the plans of Hades to take over Mount Olympus.

The narrative is somewhat predictable (and Disneyfied) and the songs rather thin, but otherwise this is a stylishly designed cartoon feature with plenty for the eye if not the ear.

p: Alice Dewey, John Musker, Ron Clements for Walt Disney
d: John Musker, Ron Clements
songs: Alan Menken (m), David Zippel (ly)
m: Alan Menken
pd: GERALD SCARFE
sound: Gary Rydstrom
voices: Tate Donovan, Susan Egan, James Woods, Rip Torn, Samantha Eggar, Danny DeVito, Bobcat Goldthwaite, Paul Shaffer, Charlton Heston

Hercules in New York

USA 1969 90m Eastmancolor
Bored with life on Mount Olympus, Hercules ventures forth into modern-day New York.

Hilariously cheap and inept "comedy", of note only for Schwarzenegger's first film appearance, here billed as Arnold Strong and dubbed very badly.

p: Aubrey Wisberg for RAF Industries
exec p: Lewis G. Chapin, Jr., Murray M. Kaplan
w: Aubrey Wisberg
d: Arthur J. Seidelman
ph: Leo Leobowitz
m: John Balamos
ed: Donald Finamore
ad: Perry Watkins
cos: Charles D. Tomlinson
sound: Abe Seidman
Arnold Strong (Schwarzenegger), Arnold Stang, Deborah Loomis, James Karen, Ernest Graves, Michael Lipton

Hercules – The Movie (1969) see Hercules in New York

Hercules Goes Bananas
see Hercules in New York

Hercules Unchained

It/Fr 1959 105m Eastmancolor Dyaliscope
Hercules falls foul of the evil Queen Lidia.

Foolish sword and sandal adventure which was bought and heavily promoted by the American producer Joseph E. Levine. Subsequently, it made a lot of money.

p: Bruno Vialati for Lux/Galatea
exec p: Feruccio de Martino
exec pc (American release): Joseph E. Levine
w: Pietro Francisci, Ennio de Concini
d: Pietro Francisci
ph: Mario Bava
m: Enzo Maseti
md: Carlo Savina
ed: Mario Seraudrei, Misa Gabrini
ad: Flavio Mogherini
cos: Maria Baroni
sound: Giulio Tagliacozzo
ch: Johnny Blysdael
Steve Reeves, Sylva Koscina, Sylvia Lopez, Primo Carnera

Herrmann, Bernard (1911-1975)

Celebrated American composer and conductor, remembered for his productive association with director Alfred Hitchcock (*The Trouble with Harry*, *The Man Who Knew Too Much*, *The Wrong Man*, *Vertigo*, *North By*

Northwest, *Psycho*, *The Birds*, *Marnie*). Trained at Juilliard, after which he began composing for CBS radio, where he became a member of Orson Welles' Mercury Theatre group, working on a variety of programmes, including *War of the Worlds*. When Welles went to Hollywood in 1941 to direct *Citizen Kane*, Herrmann followed. He won an Oscar the following year for scoring *All That Money Can Buy*, worked with Welles again on *The Magnificent Ambersons*, then contributed a string of standout scores to a variety of productions. He is also noted for his associations with producer Charles H. Schneer and effects wiz Ray Harryhausen (*The Seventh Voyage of Sinbad*, *The Three Worlds of Gulliver*, *Mysterious Island*, *Jason and the Argonauts*), François Truffaut (*Fahrenheit 451*, *The Bride Wore Black*) and Brian de Palma (*Sisters*, *Obsession*). Other credits include *Jane Eyre*, *The Snows of Kilimanjaro*, *Twisted Nerve*, *It's Alive* and *Taxi Driver*.

Genre credits:
The Ghost and Mrs Muir (1947), *The Day the Earth Stood Still* (1951), *The Seventh Voyage of Sinbad* (1958), *Journey to the Centre of the Earth* (1959), *The Three Worlds of Gulliver* (1960), *Mysterious Island* (1961), *Jason and the Argonauts* (1963), *Fahrenheit 451* (1966)

Heston, Charlton (1924-)

Virile American leading man (real name John Charlton Carter), a best actor Oscar winner for playing the title role in *Ben-Hur* (1959). In the 50s and early 60s he seemed to be typed in epics, such as *The Ten Commandments* (in which he played Moses), *El Cid*, *55 Days at Peking*, *The Greatest Story Ever Told* and *Khartoum*, though he

has displayed a wider range in such films as *Touch of Evil*, *The Big Country*, *Julius Caesar* and *Antony and Cleopatra* (which he also directed). To science fiction fans, though, he is perhaps best known for playing the astronaut Taylor in *Planet of the Apes*. He made his movie debut in 1950 with *Dark City*, since when he has appeared in such films as *The Greatest Show on Earth*, *Will Penny*, *Skyjacked*, *Earthquake*, *Airport '75*, *The Three Musketeers*, *The Four Musketeers*, *The Prince and the Pauper*, *Treasure Island* (TVM), *The Crucifer of Blood* (TVM – as Sherlock Holmes) and *In the Mouth of Madness*.

Genre credits:
Planet of the Apes (1967), *Beneath the Planet of the Apes* (1969), *The Omega Man* (1971), *Soylent Green* (1973), *Solar Crisis* (1990), *Almost an Angel* (1990 – as God), *Hercules* (1997 – voice)

High Desert Kill

USA 1989 96m DeLuxe TVM

Four friends on a hunting expedition in the New Mexico badlands find their minds affected by a supernatural entity.

Fairish science-fiction thriller utilising elements from *Invasion of the Body Snatchers* and *Deliverance*. It passes the time, but the denouement is not great shakes.

p: G. Warrren Smith, Barry Greenfield for Universal/Lehigh Entertainment
exec p: T.S. Cook, Jon Epstein
w: T.S. Cook Ferguson
story: Mike Marvin, Darnell Fry
d: Harry Falk
ph: Michel Hugo
m: Dana Kaproff
ed: David Byron Lloyd
pd: Roger Holzberg

cos: Lynn Bernay
sp: Jack Faggard
sound: Bayard Carey
Anthony Geary, Marc Singer, Chuck Connors, Micah Grant, Vaughn Armstrong, Lori Birdsong, Deborah Anne Mansy

Highlander

GB 1986 117m Technicolor Panavision Dolby

An immortal travels through time in search of the ultimate prize: mortality.

Relentlessly flashy and noisy fantasy which plays like a two-hour pop video. Occasional visual pleasures, but it really doesn't amount to much. It was followed by two sequels, *Highlander II: The Quickening* (1990), *Highlander III: The Sorcerer* (1994 – aka *Highlander: The Final Dimension*) and a short-lived television series.

p: Peter S. Davis, William N. Panzer for Thorn EMI/Highland Productions/Davis-Panzer
w: Gregory Widen, Peter Bellwood, Larry Ferguson
d: Russell Mulcahy
ph: Gerry Fisher
m: Michael Kamen, Queen
ed: Peter Honess
pd: Allan Cameron
cos: Jim Acheson
Christopher Lambert (as Conor McCloud), Sean Connery, Roxanne Hart, Clancy Brown, Beatie Edney, Alan North, Sheila Gish, Jon Polito, Celia Imrie

Highlander II: The Quickening

USA 1990 100m Eastmancolor Dolby

Following the disintegration of the ozone layer in 1999, a shield is put in place to protect man from the sun, under which Conor McCloud battles it out with a space warrior from the planet Zeist for the control of the earth.

Flashy but confused and confusing sequel which contradicts much of what has gone before it – not that many will care. Another weak sequel, *Highlander III, The Sorceror*, appeared in 1994 directed by Andy Morahan.

p: Peter S. Davis, William Panzer for Lamb Bear/Davis/Panzer
exec p: Ziad El-Khoury, Jean Luc Detait, Guy Collins, Mario Sotela
w: Peter Bellwood
story: Brian Clemens, William Panzer
d: Russell Mulcahy
ph: Phil Meheux
m: Stewart Copeland
ed: Hubert C. de la Bouillerie, Anthony Redman
pd: Roger Hall
cos: Deborah Everton
sp: John Richardson, Sam Nicholson
sound: Ed White
Christopher Lambert, Sean Connery, Virginia Madsen, Michael Ironside, John C. McGinley, Allan Rich

High Spirits

GB 1988 96m Technicolor
The owner of a crumbling Irish castle fakes a haunting so as to attract the tourists, only to find himself with some real ghosts on his hands.

Raucous supernatural comedy which quickly outstays its welcome, though the effects aren't too bad.

p: Stephen Woolley, David Saunders for Palace/Vision PDG
w: Peter Bellwood
story: Brian Clemens, William Panzer
w/d: Neil Jordan
ph: Alex Thomson
m: George Fenton
ed: Michael Bradsell
pd: Anton Furst
sp: Derek Meddings
Peter O' Toole, Steve Guttenberg, Beverly D'Angelo, Donald McCann, Peter Gallagher,

Mary Koughlan, Daryl Hannah, Liam Neeson, Ray McAnally, Jennifer Tilly

Hill, Debra

American producer and screenwriter who came to attention through her association with director John Carpenter, with whom she collaborated on such films as *Halloween*, *The Fog* and *Escape from New York*. Her other credits since include *The Dead Zone*, *Clue* and *Big Top Pee-Wee*.

Genre credits:
Escape from New York (1981 – co-p), *The Fisher King* (1991 – co-p), *Attack of the Fifty-Foot Woman* (1993 – TVM – p), *Escape from L. A.* (1996 – co-w/co-p)

Hinds, Anthony (1922-)

British producer and writer (always using the pseudonym John Elder), son of Hammer founder William Hinds (aka Will Hammer). Long associated with Hammer/Exclusive himself, he joined Exclusive for a brief period in 1939 as a bookings clerk before war service in the RAF. He re-joined Exclusive in 1946, gaining experience overseeing the quota quickies made on their behalf for distribution and became a fully fledged producer when Hammer/Exclusive turned to production themselves, producing 37 of the studio's first 50 features/programmers. He went on to produce many of Hammer's classic horror films including *The Curse of Frankenstein*, *Dracula*, *The Hound of the Baskervilles*, *The Brides of Dracula* and *The Phantom of the Opera*. He left Hammer in 1969, though continued to write for both them and Tyburn.

Genre credits:
Stolen Face (1952), *The Quatermass*

Experiment (1955 – aka *The Creeping Unknown*), *X – The Unknown* (1957), *Quatermass 2* (1957 – aka *Enemy from Space*), *The Damned* (1963 – aka *These Are the Damned*)

Hirsch, Paul

American editor who won an Oscar for editing *Star Wars* (1977 – with Marcia Lucas and Richard Chew). His other credits include *Creepshow*, *Footloose*, *Ferris Bueller's Day Off* and *Steel Magnolias*, along with several for director Brian de Palma (*Sisters*, *Phantom of the Paradise*, *Carrie*, *Obsession*, *Raising Cain*, etc).

Genre credits:
Star Wars (1977 – co-d), *The Empire Strikes Back* (1980 – ed)

Hirsch, Tina

American editor who, after experience as an assistant on *Greetings*, *Hi, Mom*, *Putney Swope* and *Woodstock*, went solo in 1972 with *Cornucopia Sexualis*. Since then she has worked on such films as *Big Bad Mamma*, *The Driver*, *More American Graffiti* and several for director Joe Dante.

Genre credits:
Death Race 2000 (1975 – ed), *Xanadu* (1980 – co-ed), *Heartbeeps* (1981 – ed), *Twilight Zone – The Movie* (1983 – co-ed), *Gremlins* (1984 – ed), *Explorers* (1985 – ed)

Hodges, Mike (1932-)

British writer and director who, after directing a couple of television films in the late 60s (*Suspect* and *Rumour*) turned to features in 1971 with *Get Carter*. His other credits include *Pulp*, *A Prayer for the Dying* and *Black Rainbow*.

Genre credits:

Toddler on the rampage! Adam (Joshua Shalikar) does a Godzilla in Las Vegas during the climax of *Honey, I Blew Up the Kid*.

Genre credits:

The Terminal Man (1974 – w/p/d), *Flash Gordon* (1980 – d), *Morons from Outer Space* (1985 – d)

Holsopple, Theodore

American art director working at the bin end of the genre market. His other credits include *She Devil*.

Genre credits:

Rocketship X-M (1950), *Captive Women* (1952 – aka *3000 A. D.*), *The Indestructible Man* (1955), *Kronos* (1957), *The Bamboo Saucer* (1967 – aka *Collision Course*)

Honda, Inoshiro (1911-1993)

Prolific Japanese director, long associated with the Godzilla series and its various offshoots, all of them featuring men sweating it out in rubber monster suits. 1964 seems to have been a busy year for him.

Genre credits:

Godzilla, King of the Monsters (1954 – aka *Gojira* – also co-w), *Half Human* (1955 – aka *Jujin Yukiotako*), *Rodan* (1957), *The H-Man* (1958 – aka *Uomini H/Bijyo to Ekitainingen*), *Mothra* (1962 – aka *Mosura*), *King Kong vs Godzilla* (1962 – aka *Kingu Kongu Tai Gojira*), *Godzilla vs Mothra* (1964 – aka *Godzilla vs the Thing/Gojira Tai Mosura*), *Attack of the Mushroom People* (1964 – aka *Curse of the Mushroom People/Matango, the Fungus of Terror* – co-d), *Dagora the Space Monster* (1964 – aka *Uchu Daikaiju Dogora*), *Frankenstein Conquers the World* (1964 – aka *Fuharankenshutain Tai Baragon*), *Ghidrah, the Three-Headed Monster* (1965 – aka *Sandai Kaiji Chikyu Saidai No Kessen*), *Godzilla vs Monster Zero* (1967 – aka *Invasion of the Astro-Monsters/Invasion of Planet X/Monster Zero*), *King Kong Escapes* (1968), *Godzilla's*

Hey! We're down here! Ron (Jared Rushton), Amy (Amy O'Neill) and Russ (Thomas Brown) attempt to gain the attention of Professor Wayne Szalinski (Rick Moranis) in the hit comedy *Honey, I Shrunk the Kids*.

Revenge (1969 – aka *Ord Kaiju Daishingeki* – also co-w), *Destroy All Monsters* (1969 – aka *Kaiju Soshingeki*), *The War of the Gargantuas* (1970 – aka *Sanda Tai Gailah* – also co-w), *Yog, Monster from Space* (1971), *Monsters from an Unknown Planet* (1971)

Honey, I Blew Up the Kid

USA 1992 89m Technicolor Dolby
Having shrunk his kids, a madcap inventor now proceeds to enlarge his youngest son.

Unremarkable follow-up to *Honey, I Shrunk the Kids*, which basically reverses the premise of the first film to variable effect. It was followed by *Honey, I Shrunk the Audience* (which can only be seen at Disney's Epcot Centre), and *Honey, We Shrunk Ourselves*.

p: Dawn Steel, Edward S. Feldman for Walt Disney
exec p: Albert Band, Stuart Gordon

w: Thom Eberhardt, Peter Elbling, Garry Goodrow
story: Garry Goodrow
d: Randall Kleiser
ph: John Hora
m: Bruce Broughton
ed: Michael A. Stevenson
pd: Leslie Dilley
cos: Tom Bronson
sp: Thomas G. Smith
Rick Moranis, Marcia Strassman, Robert Oliveri, Daniel Shalikar, Joshua Shalikar, John Shea, Lloyd Bridges

Honey, I Shrunk the Kids 🍸

USA 1989 90m Metrocolor Dolby
A suburban scientist accidentally shrinks his kids, who subsequently have to trek across their back garden in order to get home.

Slow starting comedy variation on *The Land of the Giants* and *The Incredible Shrinking Man*. Quite lively once it gets going, and helped along by

good effects work and large-scale sets. It was followed by *Honey, I Blew Up the Kid*, *Honey I Shrunk the Audience* and *Hone.y We Shrunk Ourselves*.

p: Penney Finkleman Cox for Walt Disney/Buena Vista/Silver Screen Partners III/Doric
exec p: Thomas G. Smith
w: Ed Naha, Tom Schulman
story: Stuart Gordon, Brian Yunza, Ed Naha
d: Joe Johnston
ph: Hiro Narita
m: James Horner
ed: Michael A. Stevenson
pd: Gregg Fonseca
cos: Carol Brolaski
sp: Michael Muscai, David Allen, Phil Tippett
sound: Wylie Stateman, Fernando Camera
2nd unit d: James Douglas Cox
2nd unit ph: Henner Hofmann
Rick Moranis, Matt Frewer, Kristine Sutherland, Thomas Brown, Jarea Rushton, Amy O'Neal, Robert Oliver

Honey, We Shrunk Ourselves!

USA 1996 71m Foto-Kem Dolby
Professor Wayne Szalinski, his wife, his brother and sister-in-law find themselves accidentally miniaturised, and have to try and gain the attention of their children to help reverse the process.

The effects are quite reasonable, but otherwise this is a rather tame and pointless addition to a series which had already run its course.

p: Barry Bernardi for Walt Disney
w: Karey Kirkpatrick, Nell Scovell, Joel Hodgson
d: Dean Cundey
ph: Raymond N. Stella
m: Michael Tavera
ed: Charles Bornstein
pd: Carol Winstead Wood

sp: Cliff Wenger
make-up effects: John Chambers, Dan Striepeke, Tom Burman
sound: David Hildyard
stunt co-ordinator: Erik Cord
2nd unit ph: Ronnie Taylor
Burt Lancaster, Michael York, Barbara Carrera, Nigel Davenport, Richard Basehart, Nick Cravat, Bob Ozman, Gary Baxley, John Gillespie, David Cass

The Island of Dr. Moreau

USA 1996 94m DeLuxe Dolby

A lone shipwreck survivor finds himself stranded on an island where a scientist has been genetically experimenting with animals and part-turning them into humans.

Good looking but increasingly silly version of a story which has never been satisfactorily filmed. The movie's original director, Richard Stanley, was fired after just three days and replaced by the once brilliant Frankenheimer (*The Manchurian Candidate*, *Seven Days in May*, *Seconds*, *Grand Prix*) whose recent track record of duds (*The Holcroft Covenant*, *Dead Bang*, *Year of the Gun*) hardly qualified him for the project. The best thing about this version is the stunning main title sequence.

p: Edward R. Pressman for New Line
exec p: Tim Zinnemann, Claire Rudnick Polstein
w: Richard Stanley, Ron Hutchinson
novel: H.G. Wells
d: John Frankenheimer
ph: William A. Fraker
m: Gary Chang
ed: Paul Rubell
pd: Graham Grace Walker
cos: Norma Moriceau
sp: Digital Domain, Michael Z. Hanan
make-up effects: Stan Winston
sound: David Lee

Many actresses reacted like this after appearing in one of Roger Corman's 50s quickies! This shot comes from *It Conquered the World*

stunt co-ordinator: Glenn Boswell
Marlon Brando, Val Kilmer, David Thewlis, Fairuza Bale, Daniel Rigney, Temuera Morrison, Nelson de la Rosa, Ron Perlman, Marco Hofschneider, William Hootkins

Island of Lost Souls

USA 1932 74m bw

On a remote South Sea island, a mad scientist transforms animals into humans for scientific purposes. Inevitably, they revolt.

Once highly regarded but now rather dated version of the H. G. Wells novel, of occasional interest for Laughton's ranting.

p: Paramount
w: Waldemar Young, Philip Wylie
novel: H. G. Wells
d: Erle C. Kenton
ph: Karl Struss

sp: Gordon Jennings
Charles Laughton, Bela Lugosi, Richard Arlen, Leila Hyams, Kathleen Burke, Stanley Fields, Arthur Hohl, Bob Kortman, Randolph Scott, Buster Crabbe, Alan Ladd, Duke York

It Came from Beneath ther Sea

USA 1955 79m bw

An atomic-powered submarined disturbs a giant octopus which subsequently goes on the rampage and destroys half of San Francisco.

Hackneyed low budget monster flick in the 50s tradition. Close inspection reveals the beast to have only six tentacles owing to the restricted budget.

p: Charles H. Schneer for Columbia
exec p: Sam Katzman
w: George Worthington Yates, Hal Smith
story: George Worthington Yates

d: Robert Gordon
ph: Henry Freulich
md: Mischa Bakaleinikoff
ed: Jerrome Thoms
ad: Paul Palmentola
sp: Ray Harryhausen
sound: Josh Westmoreland
Kenneth Tobey, Faith Domergue, Ian Keith, Donalds Curtis, Harry Lauter, Chuck Griffiths

It Came from Hollywood

USA 1982 80m bw/colour

A selection of clips from some of the worst science fiction and horror movies ever made.

Initially amusing pot-pourri of awfulness which eventually outstays its welcome.

p: Susan Strausberg, Jeff Stein for Paramount
w: Diana Olsen
d: Malcolm Leo, Andrew Solt
introduced by: Dan Aykroyd, John Candy, Cheech and Chong, Gilda Radner

It Came from Outer Space ☄

USA 1953 80m bw 3D

When a spaceship is seen to land in the Arizona desert, an astronomer decides to investigate.

A science fiction thriller rather typical of its period, containing such now familiar elements as a desert setting and aliens with the ability to take over human bodies. Fairly gripping, nevertheless, with a couple of good shock effects along the way to help keep things bubbling nicely.

p: William Alland for Universal
w: Harry Essex
story: Ray Bradbury
d: JACK ARNOLD
ph: Clifford Stine

m: Herman Stein
md: Joseph Gershenson
ed: Paul Weatherwax
ad: Bernard Herzbrun, Robert Boyle
sp: David S. Horsley
Richard Carlson, Barbara Rush, Charles Drake, Kathleen Hughes, Joe Sawyer, Russell Johnson

It Conquered the World

USA 1956 71m bw

With the help of a misguided scientist, a carrot creature with lobster claws from Venus attempts to conquer earth.

Fitfully amusing but otherwise quite tedious and inept low budgeter with echoes of *Invasion of the Body Snatchers*. For Corman completists only. *Zontar, the Thing from Venus*, a remake by other hands, appeared in 1968.

p: Roger Corman for Sunset
w: Lou Rusoff
d: Roger Corman
ph: Frederick E. West
m: Ronald Stein
ed: Charles Gross
ad: no credit given
sp: Paul Blaisdell
sound: Al Overton
Peter Graves, Lee Van Cleef, Beverly Garland, Sally Fraser, Russ Bender, Charles B. Griffith

It! The Terror from Beyond Space

USA 1958 69m bw

In 1973 (!) astronauts returning from Mars are picked off one by one by an alien which thrives on blood.

Hilariously dated yet fairly endearing shocker whose premise resurfaced 20 years later in *Alien*.

p: Robert E. Kent for Vogue
w: Jerome Bixby

d: Edward L. Cahn
ph: Kenneth Peach
m: Paul Sawtell, Bert Shefter
ed: Grant Whytock
ad: William Glasgow
cos: Jack Masters
sp: Robert Carlisle
sound: Al Overton
Marshall Thompson, Shawn Smith, Paul Langton, Ann Doran, Kim Spalding, Dabbs Greer, Richard Hervey, Tom Carney, Ray "Crash" Corrigan (as It)

Ray "Crash" Corrigan sweats it out in a rather ill-fitting rubber suit in this publicity pose for *It! The Terror from Beyond Space*.

Jabberwocky

GB/USA 1977 101m Technicolor
In the Middle Ages a cooper's apprentice manages to slay a monster.

Mediaeval romp which can now be seen to be very typical of its director's pictorially cluttered style, with the usual emphasis on schoolboy scatology.

p: Sandy Lieberson for Umbrella Entertainment Productions
exec p: John Goldstone
w: Charles Alverson, Terry Gilliam
d: TERRY GILLIAM
ph: Terry Bedford
m: De Wolfe
ed: Michael Bradsell
pd: ROY SMITH
cos: Hazel Pethig, Charles Knode
sp: John Brown
sound: Garth Marshall
Michael Palin, Max Wall, Warren Mitchell, Harry H. Corbett, Deborah Fallender, John Le Mesurier, Bernard Bresslaw, Rodney Bewes, Annette Badland, Brenda Cowling, Dave Prowse, Peter Cellier, Derek Francis, Bryan Pringle, Simon Williams, Frank Williams, Terry Gilliam, Brian Glover, Graham Crowden, Gordon Kaye, Neil Innes, Janine Duvitsky

Jack

USA 1996 108m Technicolor Dolby
Owing to a rare medical condition, a baby's cells multiply at four times their natural rate, so that by the age of ten he has the body of a 40-year-old man.

Indulgent, ickily sentimental star vehicle, a would-be comedy trading in the most obvious of age gap jokes. A major step into murky waters for its once respected director, particularly in its use of farting to gain cheap laughs during one embarrassing sequence. Painful.

p: Richard Mestres, Fred Fuchs, Francis Ford Coppola for Hollywood/American Zoetrope/Great Oaks
exec p: Doug Claybourne
w: James DeMonaco, Gary Nadeau
d: Francis Ford Coppola
ph: John Toll
m: Michael Kamen
ed: Barry Malkin
pd: Dean Tavoularis
cos: Aggie Guerard Rodgers
sp: Gary Gutierrez
sound: Agamemnon Andrianos
2nd unit d: Roman Coppola
Robin Williams, Diane Lane, Jennifer Lopez, Brian Kerwin, Fran Drescher, Bill Cosby, Michael McKean, Don Novello, Allan Rich, Adam Zolotin, Todd Bosley, Seth Smith, Mario Yedida, Bria Neuenschwander (!)

Jack and the Beanstalk

USA 1952 78m Supercinecolor/Sepiatone
A babysitter falls asleep and dreams that he is in the story of *Jack and the Beanstalk*.

Embarrassing star comedy in sickly colour.

p: Alex Gottlieb for Warner
exec p: Pat Costello
w: Nat Curtis
story: Pat Costello
d: Jean Yarborough
ph: George Robinson
songs: Bob Russell, Lester Lee
m: Heinz Roemheld
md: Raoul Kraushaar
ed: Otho Lovering
ad: McClure Capps
cos: Albert Deare, Jack Mosser, Lloyd Lambert
sp: Carl Lee
sound: William Randall, Joel Moss
ch: Johnny Conrad
Bud Abbott, Lou Costello, Buddy Baer, William Farnum, Dorothy Ford, James Alexander, Barbara Brown

Jack the Giant Killer

USA 1961 94m Technicolor
When a Cornish princess is captured by an evil magician, a brave farm hand comes to the rescue.

Lively fantasy with colourful characters and excellent trick work, including a gallery of grotesque monsters. Very enjoyable film of its type.

p: Robert E. Kent for Zenith
exec p: Edward Small
w: Orville Hampton, Nathan Juran
d: NATHAN JURAN
ph: DAVID S. HORSLEY
m: Paul Sawtell, Bert Shefter
ad: FERNANDO CARRERE, FRANK MCCOY
sp: HOWARD ANDERSON
Kerwin Mathews, Judi Meredith, TORIN THATCHER, WALTER BURKE, Barry Kelley, Don Beddoe, Anna Lee

Jacobs, Arthur P. (1918-1973)

American producer, a former publicist for Twentieth Century-Fox. Said by some to have helped whitewash the murder of Marilyn Monroe in the press. Through his company APJAC (geddit?) he produced the Apes series for Fox. His other credits include *What a Way to Go*, *The Chairman*, *Goodbye, Mr. Chips*, *Tom Sawyer* and *Huckleberry Finn*.

Genre credits:

Dr. Dolittle (1967), *Planet of the Apes* (1968), *Beneath the Planet of the Apes* (1969), *Escape from the Planet of the Apes* (1971), *Conquest of the Planet of the Apes* (1972), *Battle for the Planet of the Apes* (1973 – co-p)

James and the Giant Peach

USA 1996 80m Technicolor Dolby
When his parents are eaten by a rhinoceros, a young boy called James goes to live with his two evil aunts, but salvation is at hand when a mysterious stranger gives him a bagful of magical crocodile tongues which lead to adventures inside a giant peach.

Fitfully amusing blend of live action and animation, not quite in the same league as *The Nightmare Before Christmas*, some of the animated characters being a little too grotesque.

p: Denise Di Novi, Tim Burton for Walt Disney/Allied Filmmakers/Skellington
exec p: Jake Eberts
w: Karen Kirkpatrick, Steve Bloom, Jonathan Roberts
book: Roald Dahl
d: Henry Selick
ph: Pete Kozachik, Hiro Narita
m/songs: Randy Newman
ed: Stan Webb
pd: Harley Jessup
concept design: Lane Smith
cos: Julie Slinger
sp: Pete Kozachik
make-up: Richard Snell
animation supervisor: Paul Berry
sound: Agamemnon Andrianos, Gary Rydstrom, Gary Summers
Miriam Margolyes, Joanna Lumley, Paul Terry, Pete Postlethwaite, Mike Starr; voices: Richard Dreyfuss, Simon Callow, Jane Leeves, Susan Sarandon, David Thewlis

Jarre, Maurice (1924-)

French composer best known for his long-standing association with director David Lean, for whom he scored *Lawrence of Arabia, Doctor Zhivago, Ryan's Daughter* and *A Passage to India*, winning Oscars for *Lawrence* (1962), *Zhivago* (1965) and *India* (1982). Studied composition at the Paris Conservatoire, after which he became the conductor for the Jean Louis Barrault Theatre Company and, not long after, the music director for the Theatre National Populaire, which is where he began scoring plays. He scored his first film, *Hotel des Invalides*, in 1952, which he followed with many more home-grown films, most notably *Sundays and Cybele* (aka *Cybele ou les Dimanches de Ville d'Avray*) which not only earned him an Oscar nomination, but brought him to the attention of David Lean. His other scores – and there are many of them –

James and his insect friends hitch a lift off a passing mechanical shark in the animated version of the popular Roald Dahl fantasy *James and the Giant Peach*.

include *Eyes without a Face* (aka *Les Yeux Sans Visage*), *The Longest Day*, *Grand Prix*, *The Professionals*, *The Damned*, *Jesus of Nazareth* (TVM), *The Prince and the Pauper* (aka *Crossed Swords*), *The Year of Living Dangerously*, *The Bride*, *Gorillas in the Mist* and *Dead Poets Society*. He is the father of recording artist Jean-Michel Jarre.

Genre credits:
Barbarella (1967), *The Island at the Top of the World* (1974), *Mr. Sycamore* (1975), *Dreamscape* (1983), *Mad Max – Beyond Thunderdrome* (1985), *Enemy Mine* (1985), *Solarbabies* (1986 – aka *Solar Warriors*), *Almost an Angel* (1990), *Ghost* (1990), *Jacob's Ladder* (1990)

Jason and the Argonauts 😑😑😑

GB 1963 104m Technicolor
Jason travels to the end of the world in search of a magical golden fleece and has to combat several monsters along the way.

Spectacular fantasy adventure with some of the best stop motion effects since *King Kong*. A thoroughly professional piece of genre entertainment with many memorable moments, including a bronze giant and a hydra.

p: CHARLES H. SCHNEER for Columbia
w: JAN READ, BEVERLEY CROSS
d: DON CHAFFEY
ph: WILKIE COOPER
m: BERNARD HERRMANN
ed: MAURICE ROOTES
pd: Geoffrey Drake
ad: Herbert Smith, Jack Maxted, Tony Sarzi Braga
sp: RAY HARRYHAUSEN
sound: CYRIL COLLICK, RED LAW, ALFRED COX
titles: James Wines
Todd Armstrong, Honor Blackman, Niall

MacGinnis, Andrew Faulds, Laurence Naismith, Nigel Green (as Hercules), Nancy Kovak

---

Jetsons: The Movie

USA 1990 83m CFIcolor
Much to their concern, the Jetson family's asteroid looks set to become a mining factory.

Poor transfer to the big screen of a popular cartoon sit-com. The animation is variable at best.

p: William Hanna, Joseph Barbera for Universal/Hanna Barbera/Wang/Cuckoo's Nest
w: Dennis Marks, Carl Sautter
d: William Hanna, Joseph Barbera
m: John Debney
voices: George O'Hanlon, Mel Blanc, Penny Singleton, Patric Zimmerman, Don Messick, Jean Vanderpyl, Tiffany

---

Johnny Mnemonic

USA/Canada 1995 98m colour Dolby
In 2021, an information courier journeying from Asia to America finds his life in danger when various factions vie for the top secret information held in a special micro chip in his brain.

Dim-witted blend of frenetic action and virtual reality, a major step backwards for its star whose previous film was the commercial smash *Speed*. Painful when it isn't laughable.

p: Don Carmody for TCF/Alliance
w: William Gibson from his comic strip
d: Robert Longo
ph: Francois Protat
m: Brad Fiedel
ed: Ronald Sanders
pd: Nilo Rodis Jamero
cos: Olga Dimitros
sp: Fantasy II, Sony Pictures Imageworks and others
Keanu Reeves, Dolph Lundgren, Ice T., Dina

Meyer, Takeshi Kitano, Henry Rollins, Udo Kier, Denis Akiyama

---

Johnson, Laurie (1927-)

British composer and conductor, trained at the Royal College of Music. Best known for his TV themes and scores for *The Avengers*, *The Professionals* and *The New Avengers*, as well as such stage musicals as *The Four Musketeers* and *Lock Up Your Daughters*. His film credits include *Tiger Bay*, *And Soon the Darkness*, *Captain Kronos – Vampire Hunter*, *Hedda* and *It's Alive 2*.

Genre credits:
Dr. Strangelove (1963), *The First Men in the Moon* (1963)

Johnston, Joe

American director. A former effects designer and illustrator with ILM, he contributed effects designs to *Star Wars* and co-supervised the optical photography for *The Empire Strikes Back*, going on to win an Oscar for his effects work on *Raiders of the Lost Ark* (1981 – with Richard Edlund, Kit West and Bruce Nicholson). He then designed a couple of films before turning to direction with the box office smash *Honey, I Shrunk the Kids*. He also directed the aerial effects sequences for Spielberg's *Always* (1989).

Genre credits:
Star Wars (1977 – co-effects design), *Battlestar Galactica* (1979 – TVM – co-effects design), *The Empire Strikes Back* (1980 – co-effects supervisor), *Raiders of the Lost Ark* (1981 – co-sp), *Return of the Jedi* (1983 – co-sp), *The Ewok Adventure: Caravan of Courage* (1984 – TVM – pd), *Ewoks: The Battle for Endor* (1985 – co-pd), *Batteries Not Included* (1987 – 2nd unit d),

Honey, I Shrunk the Kids (1989 – d), *Always* (1989 – aerial effects d), *The Rocketeer* (1991 – d), *The Pagemaster* (1994 – live action d), *Jumanji* (1995 – d)

Jones, Dean (1931-)

American actor, the ideal leading man in several inoffensive Disney films of the 60s and 70s, most notably *The Love Bug*. A former blues singer, he has also appeared in a handful of TV series, among them *Ensign O'Toole* and *Herbie the Love Bug*. His other film credits include *Tea and Sympathy*, *Jailhouse Rock*, *Under the Yum Yum Tree*, *That Darn Cat*, *The Ugly Dachshund*, *Snowball Express*, *Born Again* and *Beethoven* (in a rare villanous role).

Genre credits:
Blackbeard's Ghost (1967), *The Love Bug* (1969), *Million Dollar Duck* (1971), *Mr. Superinvisible* (1976), *The Shaggy D.A.* (1976), *Herbie Goes to Monte Carlo* (1977)

Dean Jones (left) seemed to turn up in practically every one of Disney's live action features during the late 60s and early 70s. This scene is from *The Shaggy D.A.*, the studio's sequel to *The Shaggy Dog*.

Jones, Freddie (1927-)

British character actor, now on the international scene. Long on stage before making his film debut in *Marat/Sade* in 1966, he is also familiar to TV audiences via such series as *The Ghosts of Motley Hall*. His other film credits take in *Otley* (as one of the screen's campest villains), *Frankenstein Must Be Destroyed* (as the Monster), *The Satanic Rites of Dracula*, *Juggernaut*, *The Elephant Man* and *Cold Comfort Farm* (TVM).

Genre credits:
Krull (1983), *Dune* (1985), *Young Sherlock Holmes* (1985 – aka *Young Sherlock Holmes and the Pyramid of Fear*), *Eric the Viking* (1989)

Jones, James Earl (1931-)

Commanding African-American actor, on stage from 1957. He came to screen stardom in 1970 in *The Great White Hope* in a role that he'd played on Broadway to great acclaim, though he had actually made his movie debut back in 1964 with a brief role in *Dr. Strangelove*. His other screen credits include *The Bingo Long Travelling All Stars and Motor Kings*, *Jesus of Nazareth* (TVM), *Exorcist II: The Heretic*, *Gardens of Stone*, *Grim Prairie Tales*, *The Hunt for Red October*, *Patriot Games*, *Sneakers* and *Clear and Present Danger*. To genre fans, however, he will always be the voice of Darth Vader. His velvety vocals also provide the sting for CNN.

Genre credits:
Dr Strangelove (1964), *Star Wars* (1977 - voice), *The Empire Strikes Back* (1980 - voice), *Conan the Barbarian* (1982), *Return of the Jedi* (1983 – voice), *Aladdin and His Wonderful Lamp* (1984 – short – voice), *Pinocchio and the Emperor of Night* (1987 – voice), *Field of Dreams* (1989), *Meteor Man* (1993), *The Lion King* (1994 – voice), *Judge Dredd* (1995 – voice/narrator), *Casper, A Spirited Beginning* (1997 – voice)

Jones, Jeffrey (1947-)

American comedy actor who came to prominence as the headmaster in John Hughes' *Ferris Bueller's Day Off*, since when he has popped up in all manner of films, most notably as Criswell in Tim Burton's *Ed Wood*. He has also appeared in *Amadeus* (as Emperor Joseph III, telling Mozart that his music suffers from "too many notes"), *Transylvania 6-5000*, *Without a Clue*, *The Hunt for Red October* and *Enid is Sleeping*.

Genre credits:
Howard the Duck (1986 – aka *Howard – A New Breed of Hero*), *Beetlejuice* (1988), *Mom and Dad Save the World* (1992), *Stay Tuned* (1992)

Jones, Trevor (1949-)

South African-born composer working on the international scene. Studied at London's Royal Academy of Music, after which he went to work for the BBC. Began scoring student films before finally turning to features. His other credits include *Runaway Train*, *Angel Heart*, *Mississippi Burning*, *Sea of Love*, *Arachnophobia* and *Cliffhanger*.

Genre credits:
Excalibur (1981), *The Dark Crystal* (1982), *Labyrinth* (1986), *Murder on the Moon* (1989 – TVM), *Freejack* (1992), *Loch Ness* (1995)

Journey to the Center of the Earth

USA 1959 132m DeLuxe Cinemascope
A Victorian professor and his friends set out on an incredible journey to the centre of the earth.

Slow starting and now somewhat dated fantasy adventure which, once the expedition itself finally begins, does pick up a little speed and resource. Some charming sequences remain, though the effects are variable and the Scottish accents atrocious.

p: Charles Brackett for TCF
w: Walter Reisch, Charles Brackett
novel: JULES VERNE
d: Henry Levin
ph: Leo Tover
m: BERNARD HERRMANN
songs: James Van Heusen, Sammy Cahn
md: Lionel Newman
ed: Stuart Gilmore, Jack W. Holmes
ad: Lyle Wheeler, Franz Bachelin
cos: David Ffolkes
sp: L. B. Abbott, James B. Gordon, Emil Kosa, Jr.
sound: Bernard Fredericks, Warren B. Delaplain
James Mason, Pat Boone, Arlene Dahl, Peter Ronson, Diane Baker, Thayer David, Robert Adler, Alan Napier, Alex Finlayson, Ben Wright

Journey to the Far Side of the Sun

GB 1969 99m DeLuxe Cinemascope
Two astronauts are sent on a mission to a newly discovered planet on the far side of the sun, which turns out to be a mirror image of the earth.

Frequently imaginative science fiction story which does tend to play like a live action version of one of its producer's television puppet shows.

p: Gerry Anderson, Sylvia Anderson for Universal/Century 21
w: Gerry Anderson, Sylvia Anderson, Donald James
story: Gerry Anderson, Sylvia Anderson
d: Robert Parrish
ph: John Read
m: Barry Gray
ed: Len Walter
ad: Bob Bell, Reg Hill
cos: Elsa Fennell
sp: Derek Meddings
sound: Ken Rawkins, Ted Karnon
effects ph: Harry Oakes
Roy Thinnes, Ian Hendry, Patrick Wymark. Herbert Lom, Ed Bishop, George Sewell, Lynn Loring, Vladek Sheybal

Magic mushrooms, anyone? Professor Oliver Lindenbrook (James Mason) and company pause for breath in *Journey to the Center of the Earth*, a film just begging for the remake treatment.

Judd, Edward (1932-)

British actor who popped up in a number of mainstream genre offerings in the 60s, most notably as the reporter Peter Stenning in the *Day the Earth Caught Fire*. His other credits include *The Long Ships*, *Living Free*, *Universal Soldier*, *Vault of Horror* and *The Kitchen Toto*.

Genre credits:

The Day the Earth Caught Fire (1961), *The First Men in the Moon* (1964), *Invasion* (1966), *Island of Terror* (1966), *The Vengeance of She* (1967)

Judge Dredd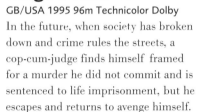

GB/USA 1995 96m Technicolor Dolby

In the future, when society has broken down and crime rules the streets, a cop-cum-judge finds himself framed for a murder he did not commit and is sentenced to life imprisonment, but he escapes and returns to avenge himself.

Slick but empty hardware show which, even at this length, seems padded by scenes of tedious chat. The action is reasonably well staged, though the film failed to live up to its box office expectations.

p: Andrew Vajna, Beau Marks, Charles L. Lippincott for Cinergi/Hollywood
w: William Wisher, Stephen E. De Souza
story: Michael de Luca, William Wisher
comic strip: John Wagner, Carlos Ezquerra
d: Danny Cannon
ph: Adrian Biddle
m: Alan Silvestri
ed: Alex Mackie, Harry Keramidas
pd: Nigel Phelps
cos: Emma Porteous, Gianni Versace
sp: Joss Williams and others
sound: Leslie Shatz, Chris Munro
make-up effects: Nick Dudman
narrator: James Earl Jones
2nd unit d: Beau Marks
titles: Susan Bradley

Sylvester Stallone, Armand Assante, Max Von Sydow, Diane Lane, Joan Chen, Jurgen Prochnow, Rob Schneider, Ian Dury

Jules Verne's Rocket to the Moon see Rocket to the Moon

Jumanji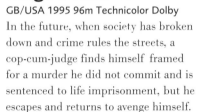

USA 1995

A young boy discovers a magical game called Jumanji which unleashes all manner of horrific consequences on those who dare play it.

Fairly amusing and imaginative fantasy adventure with excellent special effects and a handful of memorable set pieces, including a stampede by elephants and rhinos through a town centre. Younger children may find it a little on the scary side, however.

p: Scott Kroopf, William Teitler for Columbia/Tri Star
exec p: Ted Field, Robert W. Cort, Larry J. Franco
w: Jonathan Hensleigh, Greg Taylor, Jim Strain
story: Greg Taylor, Jim Strain, Chris Van Allsburg
book: Chris Van Allsburg
d: Joe Johnston
ph: Thomas Ackerman
m: James Horner
ed: Robert Dalva
pd: James Bissell
cos: Martha Wayne Snetsinger
sp: ILM
sound: Randy Thom, Gary Rydstrom
animatronics/make-up effects: Tom Woodruff, Jr., Alec Gillis

Robin Williams, Jonathan Hyde, Kristen Dunst, Bradley Pierce, Bonnie Hunt, Bebe Neuwirth, David Alan Grier, Patricia Clarkson, Adam Hann-Byrd, Laura Bell Bundy, James Handy

The Jungle Book

GB 1942 109m Technicolor

An Indian waif brought up in the jungle by wolves later saves his village from a man-eating tiger.

Well mounted presentation of the Kipling stories, with the excellent colour photography compensating for any longueurs.

p: Alexander Korda for London Films
w: Laurence Stallings
books: Rudyard Kipling
d: Zolta Korda
ph: LEE GARMES, W. HOWARD GREENE
m: MIKLOS ROZSA
ed: William Hornbeck
pd: Vincent Korda
ad: Jack Okey, J. McMillan Johnson
sp: Lawrence Butler
sound: William A. Wilmarth
2nd unit d: Andre de Toth
Sabu, Joseph Calleia, John Qualen, Frank Puglia, Rosemary de Camp, Patricia O'Rourke, Noble Johnson, Ralph Byrd, John Mather, Faith Brook

The Jungle Book

USA 1967 78m Technicolor

A young boy, raised in the jungle by animals, is saved from the wiles of an evil tiger by a friendly panther and a life-loving bear.

Engaging cartoon feature with memorable characters and songs. A long-standing Disney favourite. It was remade by Disney as a live action feature in 1995.

p: Walt Disney
w: Larry Clemmons, Ralph Wright, Ken Anderson, Vance Gerry
books: Rudyard Kipling
d: Wolfgang Reitherman
songs: Richard M. and Robert B. Sherman, Terry Gilkyson
m: George Bruns
ed: Tom Acosta, Norman Carlisle

sound: Robert O. Cook
voices: Bruce Reitherman (as Mowgli), PHIL HARRIS (as Baloo), Sebastian Cabot (as Bagheera), GEORGE SANDERS (as Shere Khan), Sterling Holloway (as Kaa), Louis Prima, J. Pay O'Malley, Verna Felton, Clint Howard, Darleen Carr, John Abbott, Ben Wright, Chad Stuart, Lord Tim Hudson

---

The Jungle Book

USA 1994 111m Technicolor Dolby
An Indian boy, brought up in the jungle by wolves, later returns to civilisation to claim his true love.

Colourful, good-looking live action remake, let down by overlength and the fact that the animals don't talk, which puts a strain on the narrative.

p: Raju Patel, Edward S. Feldman for Buena Vista/Walt Disney/Baloo/Vegahom Europe NV
exec p: Rajendra Kumar, Shared Patel, Mark Damon, Lawrence Mortorff
w: Stephen Sommers, Ronald Yanover, Mark D. Geldman
book: Rudyard Kipling
story: Ronald Yanover, Mark D. Geldman
d: Stephen Sommers
ph: Juan Ruiz Anchia
m: Basil Poledouris
ed: Bob Ducsay
pd: ALLAN CAMERON
cos: JOHN MOLLO
sp: Peter Montgomery, Buena Vista Visual Effects
sound: Joseph Geisinger
stunt co-ordinator: Gerry Crampton, David Ellis, Tim Davison
2nd unit d: Greg Michael, David Ellis
2nd unit ph: Peter Robertson
titles: Susan Bradley
Jason Scott Lee, Lena Headey, John Cleese, Sam Neill, Cary Elwes, Jason Flemyng, Ron Donachie

---

Junior

USA 1993 110m DeLuxe DTS stereo
With the help of a miracle drug and a stolen egg, a male scientist manages to get himself pregnant.

Fitfully amusing but generally rather desperate umbilical comedy which should have made more of the situations available, especially given the talent involved.

p: Ivan Reitman for Universal/Northern Lights
exec p: Joe Medjuck, Daniel Goldberg, Beverly Camhe
w: Kevin Wade, Chris Conrad
d: Ivan Reitman
ph: Adam Greenburg
m: James Newton Howard
ed: Sheldon Kahn
pd: Stephen Lineweaver
cos: Albert Wolsky
sound: Gene Steven Cantamessa
Arnold Schwarzenegger, Danny DeVito, Emma Thompson, Frank Langella, Pamela Reed, Judy Collins, James Eckhouse, Aida Turturro, Phyllida Law

---

Juran, Nathan (1907-)

Austrian art director, an Oscar winner (with Richard Day) for *How Green Was My Valley* (1941). In 1952 he turned to direction with *The Black Castle*, which he followed with such films as *The Golden Blade*, *Good Day for a Hanging* and *The Boy Who Cried Werewolf*. He also helmed several stop motion monster pictures, including three for Ray Harryhausen.

Genre credits:
Harvey (1950 – ad), *The Deadly Mantis* (1957 – d), *Twenty Million Miles to Earth* (1957 – d), *The Seventh Voyage of Sinbad* (1958 – d), *Jack the Giant Killer* (1962 – d), *The First Men in the Moon* (1963 – d)

Jurassic Park

USA 1993 122m Eastmancolor Dolby
A billionaire invites a group of experts to view his new theme park, a tropical island on which real dinosaurs have been cloned.

Expensive but poorly adapted screen version of a thrilling book, redeemed by its brilliant effects work and memorable set pieces, on which count it broke all box office records. Despite the Oscar win for sound, much of the dialogue is inaudible. A sequel, *The Lost World: Jurassic Park*, followed in 1997.

p: Kathleen Kennedy, Gerald R. Molen for Universal, Amblin
w: Michael Crichton, David Koepp
novel: MICHAEL CRICHTON
d: Steven Spielberg
ph: Dean Cundey
m: JOHN WILLIAMS
ed: Michael Kahn
pd: Rick Carter
cos: Sue Moore, Eric Sandberg
sp: DENNIS MUREN, STAN WINSTON, PHIL TIPPET, MICHAEL LANTIERI (AA)
sound: Gary Summers, Gary Rydstrom, Shawn Murphy, Ron Judkins (aa)
sound effects editing: Gary Rydstrom, Richard Hyams (aa)
animation: Bob Kurtz
stunt co-ordinator: Gary Hymes
Sam Neill, Laura Dern, Richard Attenborough, Jeff Goldblum, Bob Peck, Martin Ferrero, B. D. Wong, Samuel L. Jackson, Joseph Mazzello, Ariana Richards, Wayne Knight, Jerry Molen, Dean Cundey, Richard Kiley (voice)

Kahn, Michael

American editor long associated with the films of director Steven Spielberg, winning Oscars for his work on *Raiders of the Lost Ark* (1981) and *Schindler's List* (1993). His other Spielberg credits include *1941*, *The Color Purple* and *Empire of the Sun*. Non-Spielberg films include *The Devil's Rain*, *The Return of a Man Called Horse*, *Table for Five*, *Fatal Attraction* and *Toy Soldiers*. He began his career as a 19-year-old at the Desilu television studios in the late 60s editing episodes of *Hogan's Heroes*.

Genre credits:
Close Encounters of the Third Kind (1977), *Close Encounters of the Third Kind – The Special Edition* (1980), *Raiders of the Lost Ark* (1981), *Indiana Jones and the Temple of Doom* (1984), *Indiana Jones and the Last Crusade* (1989), *Always* (1989), *Hook* (1991), *Jurassic Park* (1993), *The Lost World: Jurassic Park* (1997)

Kamen, Michael (1948-)

American composer with a penchant for high-octane action scores, among them the *Die Hard* and *Lethal Weapon* series, *Licence to Kill*, *The Last Boy Scout* and *Robin Hood: Prince of Thieves* (for which he penned the popular song *Everything I Do I Do For*

You). His other credits include *Polyester*, *The Krays*, *Let Him Have It*, *The Three Musketeers* and *Mr Holland's Opus*.

Genre credits:
Lifeforce (1985 – co-m), *Brazil* (1985), *Highlander* (1985), *The Adventures of Baron Munchausen* (1989), *The Last Action Hero* (1993), *Jack* (1996), *101 Dalmations* (1996), *Event Horizon* (1997)

Katz, Gloria

American screenplay writer who, with her regular partner Willard Huyck, penned *American Graffiti*.

Genre credits:
Indiana Jones and the Temple of Doom (1984 – co-w), *Howard the Duck* (1986 – aka *Howard, A New Breed of Hero* – co-w)

Kaye, Danny (1908-1987)

American comedy actor (real name David Daniel Kaminsky) who gained enormous popularity in the 40s and 50s in such vehicles as *Up in Arms*, *White Christmas* and *The Court Jester*, though his appeal is now something of an acquired taste. He also appeared in a number of equally popular light fantasies.

Genre credits:
Wonder Man (1945), *The Secret Life of Walter Mitty* (1947), *Hans Christian Andersen* (1952), *Peter Pan* (1975 – TVM – as Captain Hook), *Pinocchio* (1976 – TVM – as Gepetto)

Kazaam

USA 1996 89m Technicolor Dolby
A 14-year-old boy accidentally discovers a 5,000-year-old genie in a derelict building and can't get rid of him until

he's made his pre-requiste three wishes.

Wholly predictable but reasonably lively fantasy with enough slapstick and effects to keep youngsters amused.

p: Paul Michael Glaser, Scott Kroopf, Bob Engelman for Touchstone/Interscope Communications/Polygram
exec p: Ted Field, Leonard Armato, Shaquille O'Neal, Robert W. Cort
w: Christian Ford, Roger Soffer
d/story: Paul Michael Glaser
ph: Charles Minsky
m: Christopher Tyng
ed: Michael E. Polakow
pd: Donald Burt
cos: Hope Hanafin
sp: Charles Gibson
sound: Robert Janiger, Lance Brown, Victor Iorillo
stunt co-ordinator: Jeff Imada
Shaquille O'Neal, Francis Capra, Ally Walker, James Acheson, John Costelloe, Marshall Manesh, Fawn Reed

Keaton, Michael (1951-)

American comedy actor (real name Michael Douglas) who, surprisingly, was chosen by director Tim Burton to play Batman in the 1989 blockbuster. In television from 1972 as a technician, he later turned to improv, making his television debut in front of the cameras in 1977 in *All's Fair*. More television work followed, after which he made his film debut in 1982 in the comedy *Night Shift*. His other credits include *Mr. Mom* (aka *Mr. Mum*), *Johnny Dangerously*, *Gung Ho*, *Clean and Sober*, *Pacific Heights*, *Much Ado About Nothing*, *My Life* and *The Paper*.

Genre credits:
Beetlejuice (1988), *Batman* (1989), *Batman Returns* (1992), *Multiplicity* (1996)

Keir, Andrew (1926-)

British (Scottish) character actor, a memorable Professor Quatermass in Hammer's *Quatermass and the Pit*. His other credits include *The Maggie, Dracula – Prince of Darkness, Blood from the Mummy's Tomb, The Viking Queen, The Thirty-Nine Steps* and *Rob Roy*.

Genre credits:

Daleks – Invasion Earth, 2150 A. D. (1966), *Quatermass and the Pit* (1967 – aka *Five Million Years to Earth*), *Dragonworld* (1994)

Kelley, DeForest (1920-)

American actor known primarily for playing Dr "Bones" McCoy in the *Star Trek* films and TV series. In movies from the early 40s, his other credits include *Fear in the Night, The Man in the Grey Flannel Suit, Gunfight at the O.K. Corral* and *Raintree County*.

Genre credits:

Night of the Lepus (1972), *Star Trek* (1979), *Star Trek II: The Wrath of Khan* (1982), *Star Trek III: The Search for Spock* (1984), *Star Trek IV: The Voyage Home* (1986), *Encounter at Farpoint* (1987 – TVM [feature length pilot for *Star Trek: The Next Generation*]), *Star Trek V: The Final Frontier* (1989), *Star Trek VI: The Undiscovered Country* (1991)

Kemper, Victor J. (1927-)

American cinematographer who began his career in television in 1949 as an engineer and, later, technical supervisor. Turned to cinematography in the 70s and worked on such important pictures as *Husbands, The Hospital, The Candidate* and *Dog Day Afternoon*. His other credits include *Stay Hungry, Slap Shot, The Four Seasons, Crazy People, F/X 2: The Deadly Art of Illusion* and *Beethoven*.

Genre credits:

The Reincarnation of Peter Proud (1975), *Oh, God!* (1977), *Coma* (1978), *The Final Countdown* (1980), *Xanadu* (1980)

Kennedy, Kathleen (1954-)

American producer, married to Frank Marshall, with whom she produced many of director Steven Spielberg's movies in the 80s, including *The Color Purple* and *Empire of the Sun*. Her other credits include *Poltergeist, The Money Pit, Alive* and *Twister*.

Genre credits:

E.T. (1982 – co-p), *Twilight Zone – the Movie* (1983 – co-p), *Gremlins* (1984 – co-p), *Back to the Future* (1985 – co-exec p), *Young Sherlock Holmes* (1985 – aka *Sherlock Holmes and the Pyramid of Fear* – co-exec p), *An American Tail* (1985 – co-exec p), *Innerspace* (1987 – co-exec p), *Batteries Not Included* (1987 – co-exec p), *The Land Before Time* (1988 – co-exec p), *Who Framed Roger Rabbit?* (1988 – co-exec p), *Always* (1989 – co-p), *Back to the Future Part III* (1990 – co-exec p), *Gremlins II: The New Batch* (1991 co-exec p), *The Flintstones* (1994 – co-exec p), *Congo* (1995 – co-exec p), *The Indian in the Cupboard* (1995 – co-p), *The Lost World: Jurassic Park* (1997 – exec p), *Contact* (1997 – actress)

Kershner, Irvin (1923-)

American director who, after helming such comedies as *A Fine Madness, The Flim Flam Man* (aka *One Born Every Minute*), *Loving, Up the Sandbox* and *S*P*Y*S* went on to direct the second *Star Wars* movie, *The Empire Strikes Back*. His other credits since include the rogue Bond film *Never Say Never Again*. A former commercial artist and book illustrator, he began his film career in 1950 making documentaries. He directed his first feature, *Stakeout on Dope Street* (which he also co-wrote), in 1958. His other credits include *The Hoodlum Priest, The Return of a Man Called Horse* and *The Eyes of Laura Mars*.

Genre credits:

The Empire Strikes Back (1980), *Robocop 2* (1990), *To Be or Not to Be* (1993 – TVM [feature-length pilot for *SeaQuest DSV*])

Khambatta, Persis (1950-)

Glamorous-looking Indian-born actress in a variety of international films, among them *The Wilby Conspiracy* and *Nighthawks*. To genre fans, however, she will always be remembered as the bald-headed Ilia in the first *Star Trek* movie.

Genre credits:

Star Trek (1979), *Megaforce* (1982), *Warrior of the Lost World* (1984), *Phoenix the Warrior* (1988), *Lois and Clark: The New Adventures of Superman* (1993 - TVM)

Kidder, Margot (1948-)

Canadian actress, best known for playing Lois Lane in the four Christopher Reeve *Superman* movies. Much television work in the late 60s was followed by her film debut in 1969 in the comedy *Gaily, Gaily* (aka *Chicago, Chicago*). Her other credits include *Quackser Fortune Has a Cousin in the Bronx, The Great Waldo Pepper, The Amityville Horror, Willie and Phil* and *To Catch a Killer* (TVM).

Genre credits:

Superman (1978), *Superman II* (1980), *Superman III* (1983), *Gobots: Battle of the Rock Lords* (1986 – voice), *Superman IV:*

Ilia (the stunning Persis Khambatta) leads Mr. Spock (Leonard Nimoy), Commander Willard Decker (Stephen Collins), Admiral James T. Kirk (William Shatner) and Dr. Leonard "Bones" McCoy (DeForest Kelley) across an outer space pathway for an encounter with the mysterious V'ger in the underrated *Star Trek: The Motion Picture*.

The Quest for Peace (1987)

A Kid in King Arthur's Court

USA 1995 89m Technicolor Dolby

A teenage boy finds himself transported back in time to King Arthur's court where his baseball and skateboarding skills come in handy.

Tedious teenage variation on *A Connecticut Yankee*, with the jokes on the obvious side.

p: Robert L. Levy, Peter Abrams, J.P. Guerin for Disney/Trimark/Tapestry
exec p: Mark Amin
w: Michael Part, Robert L. Levy
d: Michael Gottlieb
Thomas Ian Nicholas, Joss Ackland, Art Malik, Ron Moody, Kate Winslet, Daniel Craig, Paloma Baeza, David Tysall

Kiel, Richard (1939-)

Giant (7' 2") American actor, best known for playing Jaws in two James Bond films, *The Spy Who Loved Me* and *Moonraker*, prior to which he appeared mostly in villainous or monstrous roles. His other credits include *House of the Damned*, *Roustabout*, *Silver Streak*, *Force Ten from Navarone*, *Pale Rider* and *Hysterical*.

Genre credits:

The Magic Sword (1961 – aka *St. George and the Seven Curses*), *The Phantom Planet* (1961), *Eegah!* (1962), *The Human Duplicators* (1965), *The Spy Who Loved Me* (1977), *The Humanoid* (1979), *Moonraker* (1979), *War of the Wizards* (1983)

Kilmer, Val (1959-)

Handsome American actor who played Batman once in *Batman Forever*. His other credits include *Top Secret*, *Real Genius*, *Kill Me Again*, *The Doors* (as Jim Morrison) and *Tombstone*.

Genre credits:

Willow (1988), *Batman Forever* (1995), *The Island of Dr Moreau* (1996)

King Kong ☺☺☺☺

USA 1933 100m bw

An adventurous film producer follows a map to a mysterious island where prehistoric monsters still roam and a giant ape wanders the jungle.

Without doubt the most famous monster movie of all time, with some of the most brilliant trick effects ever put on film. A fast moving, exciting, thrill-a-minute mixture of action, suspense, romance and adventure, climaxing with the now legendary sequence atop the Empire State Building. An absolute must. *Son of Kong* followed later the same year.

p: Merian C. Cooper for RKO
exec p: David O. Selznick
w: JAMES CREELMAN, RUTH ROSE
story: Edgar Wallace, Merian C. Cooper
d: MERIAN C. COOPER, ERNEST B. SHOEDSACK
ph: Edward Linden, Vernon L. Walker, J. O. Taylor
m: MAX STEINER
ed: TED CHEESMAN
ad: Carroll Clark, Al Herman, Van Nest Polglase
cos: Walter Plunkett
sp: WILLIS O'BRIEN
sound: Earl A. Wolcott
sound effects: MURRAY SPIVACK
FAY WRAY, ROBERT ARMSTRONG (as Carl Denham), BRUCE CABOT, FRANK REICHER, Sam Hardy, Noble Johnson, James Flavin, Victor Wong, Paul Porcasi, Russ Powell, Merian C. Cooper (cameo), Ernest B. Shoedsack (cameo, as the pilots who gun down Kong)

King Kong

USA 1976 137m Metrocolor Panavision

Members of an expedition searching for oil on a remote Pacific island discover it to be inhabited by a giant ape, which they subsequently capture and bring back to New York.

Enjoyably and hilariously awful big budget remake of the 1933 classic whose Oscar-winning (!) effects mostly consist of Rick Baker romping about in a monkey suit. An enormous publicity campaign guaranteed it an audience, most of whom no doubt wished they'd stayed at home. Some of the dialogue has to be heard to be believed. A sequel, *King Kong Lives*, appeared in 1986.

p: Dino de Laurentiis for Paramount
exec p: Federico de Laurentiis, Christian Ferry
w: Lorenzo Semple, Jr.
ph: Richard H. Kline
m: John Barry
ed: Ralph E. Winters
pd: Dale Hennesy, Mario Chiari
cos: Moss Mabry
sp: Carlo Rambaldi, Glen Robinson, Frank Van Der Veer (aa)
sound: Jack Solomon
2nd unit d: William Kronick
stunt co-ordinator: Bill Couch
Jeff Bridges, Charles Grodin, Jessica Lange, Rene Auberjonois, Julius Harris, John Randolph, Ed Lauter, Jack O'Halloran, Rick Baker (as Kong)

King of the Rocket Men

USA 1944 12x20m bw serial

A scientist develops a suit that enables him to fly, and so sets out to thwart the evil Dr. Vulcan.

Standard Monogram serial with predictable plot developments but surprisingly well done flying sequences. Chapter titles include *Dangerous Evidence*, *Plunging Death*, *High Peril* and *Fatal Dive*.

p: Franklin Adreon for Monogram
w: Royal Cole, William Lively, Sol Shor
d: Fred Brannon
ph: Ellis W. Carter
m: Stanley Wilson
ed: Cliff Dell, Sam Starr
ad: Fred Ritter
sp: Howard and Theodore Lydecker
sound: Earl Crain, Sr.
Tristram Coffin, Mae Clarke, Don Haggerty, House Peters, Jr., James Craven, I. Stanford Jolley, Ted Adams, Stanley Price

Kinski, Klaus (1926-1991)

Intense-looking, often explosive German actor (real name Claus Gunther Nakszynski) in international films, often as a support. In movies from 1948 after experience as a cabaret artiste, he has often appeared in roles unworthy of his talents, though he has made several memorable pictures with director Werner Herzog, including *Aguirre Wrath of God*, *Nosferatu* (memorable in the title role), *Fitzcarraldo* and *Cobra Verde*. The father of actress Nastassja Kinki, he also wrote and directed one film, the disastrous biopic *Paganini*.

Genre credits:

Android (1982), *Titan Find* (1986 – aka *Creature*)

Kline, Richard H. (1926-)

American cinematographer who photographed a number of major science fiction and fantasy productions in the 70s and 80s. His other credits include *The Boston Strangler*, *The Fury*, *The Competition*, *Body Heat* and *Death Wish II*.

Genre credits:

Camelot (1967), *The Andromeda Strain* (1970), *Soylent Green* (1973), *Battle for the Planet of the Apes* (1973), *The Terminal Man* (1974), *King Kong* (1976), *Star Trek* (1979), *All of Me* (1984), *Howard the Duck* (1986 – aka *Howard, A New Breed of Hero*), *My Stepmother is an Alien* (1988)

Kneale, Nigel (1922-)

Manx-born writer who became a staff writer for the BBC just after the war. Created such television classics as *The Quatermass Experiment* (originally written to fill an unexpected gap in the schedules), *Quatermass 2*, *Quatermass and the Pit*, *The Creature* and, later, *The Sex Olympics*, *Beasts*, *Kinvig* and a fourth *Quatermass* series (for Thames/Euston). The first three *Quatermass* series were filmed at various stages by Hammer, the first of which launched the studio on the international scene. Kneale's other screen credits include *The Abominable Snowman*, *Look Back in Anger*, *The Entertainer*, *The Witches* and *The Woman in Black* (TVM). He had his name removed from the credits of *Halloween III: Season of the Witch*.

Genre credits:

The Quatermass Experiment (1955 – aka *The Creeping Unknown* – original series only), *Quatermass 2* (1957 – aka *Enemy from Space* – co-w), *The First Men in the Moon* (1964 – w), *Quatermass and the Pit* (1967 – aka *Five Million Yerars to Earth* – w), *Halloween III: Season of the Witch* (1983 – w)

Knight Rider

USA 1982 96m Technicolor TVM

A young man is given a computerised car with the ability to talk (among many other things) so that he may use it to combat crime.

Mild pilot for a popular series which

got into its stride as it went along, offering a blend of *Herbie* and *The Six Million Dollar Man*.

p: Harker Wade for NBC/Universal
w/exec p: Glen A. Larson
d: Dan Haller
ph: Frank P. Beascoechea
m: Stu Phillips (theme: Stu Phillips, Glen A. Larson)
ed: William Morton, David Hare
ad: Charles R. Davis, Seymour Klate
cos: Jean-Pierre Dorleac
sound: John R. McDonald, Alan Bernard
stunt co-ordinator: Robert Bralver, Jerry Summers
David Hasselhoff, Edward Mulhare, Richard Basehart, Vince Edwards, Phyllis Davis, Richard Anderson

Knightriders

USA 1981 146m colour
A group of modern-day knights stage a series of jousting contests on motorcycles.

Silly fantasy which might have been more tolerable at a less elephantine length.

p: Richard P. Rubinstein for Laurel
exec p: Sahah M. Hassanein
w/d: George A. Romero
ph: Michael Gornick
m: Donald Rubinstein
ed: Pasquale Buba, George A. Romero
pd: Cletus Anderson
sound: Michael Gornick
stunt co-ordinator: Gary Davis
Ed Harris, Gary Lahti, Amy Ingersoll, Tom Savini, Patricia Tallman, Brother Blue, Christine Forrest, Warner Shook, Stephen King, Ken Hixon

Korda, Alexander (1893-1956)

Celebrated Hungarian producer, director and executive producer (real name Sandor Corda) who worked in Hungary, France, Germany, Britain and America. Directing from 1914 with *The Duped Journalist*, he proved to be one of British cinema's most influential filmmakers in the 1930s, producing and/or directing such classics as *The Private Life of Henry VIII*, *Rembrandt*, *The Scarlet Pimpernel*, *Sanders of the River*, *Knight Without Armour* and *The Four Feathers*. He also created a studio at Denham and the production company London Films. His other credits include *That Hamilton Woman* (aka *Lady Hamilton*), *To Be or Not to Be*, *The Third Man*, *The Sound Barrier* and *Richard III*. Genre-wise, his most important contribution was to have produced *The Thief of Baghdad*.

Genre credits:
The Ghost Goes West (1935 – p), *Things to Come* (1936 – p), *The Man Who Could Work Miracles* (1937 – p), *The Thief of Baghdad* (1940 – p), *The Jungle Book* (1942 – p), *Tales of Hoffman* (1951 – exec p)

Korda, Vincent (1896-1979)

Hungarian art director, the brother of producer Alexander Korda, on whose films he mostly worked, winning an Oscar for *The Thief of Baghdad* (1940). His other credits include *The Private Life of Henry VIII*, *The Four Feathers*, *The Third Man* and *The Sound Barrier*.

Genre credits:
The Man Who Could Work Miracles (1936), *Things to Come* (1936), *The Thief of Baghdad* (1940), *The Jungle Book* (1942)

Kosa, Jr, Emil

American special effects technician, an Oscar winner for his work on *Cleopatra* (1963). His other work has often been in association with L. B. Abbott and Art Cruickshank.

Genre credits:
The Day the Earth Stood Still (1951 – co-sp), *Journey to the Center of the Earth* (1959 – co-sp), *The Lost World* (1960 – co-sp), *Way, Way Out* (1966 – co-sp), *Fantastic Voyage* (1966 – co-sp), *Planet of the Apes* (1967 – co-sp)

Kostal, Irwin (1911-1994)

American composer and musical director who won Oscars for adapting *West Side Story* (1961 – with Saul Chaplin, Johnny Green, Sid Ramin) and *The Sound of Music* (1965). Long associated the work of songwriters Richard M. and Robert B. Sherman, he began his career as a Dixieland pianist before becoming an orchestrator for NBC in Chicago. Moved to New York in 1946 where he orchestrated many Broadway shows before breaking into television and films. His other credits include *Half a Sixpence* and *The Magic of Lassie*.

Genre credits:
Mary Poppins (1964 – md), *Chitty Chitty Bang Bang* (1968 – md), *Bedknobs and Broomsticks* (1971 – md), *Charlotte's Web* (1972 – md), *The Blue Bird* (1976 – md), *Pete's Dragon* (1977 – md), *Mickey's Christmas Carol* (1983 – m)

Kraushaar, Raoul (1908-)

American composer and music director whose credits include *Melody Ranch*, *Bride of the Gorilla*, *Back from the Dead* and *Mustang* as well as a handful of 50s sci-fi and fantasy films.

Genre credits:

Jack and the Beanstalk (1952 – md), *Invaders from Mars* (1953 – m), *Unknown Terror* (1957 – m), *The Thirty-Foot Bride of Candy Rock* (1959 – m)

Krull

GB 1983 118m Metrocolor Panavision Dolby

A warrior prince fights the force of an evil warlord in order to rescue his bride, who is being held captive.

Visually pleasing mega-buck action fantasy which quickly resolves itself into a series of predictable set pieces in the *Star Wars*/*Robin Hood* manner.

p: Ron Silverman for Columbia/Barclays Mercantile
exec p: Ted Mann
w: Stanford Sherman
d: Peter Yates
ph: PETER SUSCHITZKY
m: JAMES HORNER
ed: Ray Lovejoy
pd: STEPHEN GRIMES
cos: Anthony Mendleson
sp: Derek Meddings
sound: Ivan Sharrock, Bill Rowe
sound effects: Winston Ryder
2nd unit d/additional d: Derek Cracknell
stunt co-ordinator: Vic Armstrong
Ken Marshall, Freddie Jones, Lysette Anthony, Alun Armstrong, Francesca Annis, David Battley, Bernard Bresslaw, Liam Neeson, Todd Carty, John Welsh, Robbie Coltrane

---

Kubrick, Stanley (1928-)

Celebrated American director, producer and screenwriter whose films include such classics as *Paths of Glory*, *Spartacus* and *Barry Lyndon*. He won a special Oscar for his groundbreaking effects work on *2001: A Space Odyssey*. Began his career as a stills photographer for *Look* magazine in 1945. He started directing in 1950 with the short *Fear of the Fight*, which he followed with his first feature, *Fear and Desire*, in 1951. *2001* remains one of the genre's key films.

Genre credits:

Dr. Strangelove, or How I Learned to Stop Worrying and Love the Bomb (1963 – co-w/p/d), *2001: A Space Odyssey* (1968 – co-w/co-sp/exec p/d), *A Clockwork Orange* (1971 – w/p/d)

Kurtz, Gary (1940-)

American producer, a graduate of USC, where he gained experience working on public health films. He followed this with a variety of jobs on more than 30 Roger Corman films. He went to Vietnam in the 60s with the Marines as part of their film unit, after which he gained further professional experience on such films as *Two Lane Blacktop* and *Chandler* before teaming up with George Lucas for *American Graffiti* and the first two *Star Wars* movies.

Genre credits:

Star Wars (1977 – p), *The Empire Strikes Back* (1980 – p), *The Dark Crystal* (1982 – p/2nd unit d), *Return to Oz* (1985 – exec p), *Slipstream* (1989 – p)

Director Stanley Kubrick lines up a shot on the set of *Dr. Strangelove*.

Labyrinth

USA/GB 1986 100m Technicolor Dolby

The Goblin King kidnaps a young girl's baby stepbrother, and in order to get him back she must wend her way through an elaborate maze.

Expensive but charmless fantasy which generates no sympathy for its heroine's plight.

p: Eric Rattray for Tri-Star/Labyrinth/The Henson Organization
exec p: George Lucas, David Lazer
w: Terry Jones
story: Dennis Less, Jim Henson
d: Jim Henson
ph: Alex Thomson
m: Trevor Jones
songs: David Bowie
ed: John Grover
pd: ELLIOT SCOTT
cos: Brian Froud, Ellis Fyfe
sp: George Gibbs
sound: Peter Sutton
conceptual design: Brian Froud
2nd unit d/ph: Peter MacDonald
3rd unit d/ph: Jimmy Devis
model ph: Paul Wilson
David Bowie, Jennifer Connelly, Toby Froud, Shelley Thompson, Christopher Malcolm, Natalie Finald

Lady and the Tramp

USA 1955 76m Technicolor Cinemascope

The adventures of a suburban house dog and her mongrel friend.

Sugary, rather talkative cartoon feature with pleasant enough passages for older children and a couple of good songs.

p: Walt Disney
story: Erdman Penner, Joe Rinaldi, Ralph Wright, Don da Gradi
book: Ward Green
d: Hamilton Luske, Clyde Geronimi, Wilfred Jackson
m: Oliver Wallace
songs: Peggy Lee, Sonny Burke
ed: Don Halliday
sound: C. C. Shyfield, Harold Steck, Robert O. Cook
voices: Peggy Lee, Barbara Luddy, Larry Roberts, Bill Thompson, Verna Felton, Bill Ballcom

Ladyhawke

GB/It 1985 118m Technicolor Technovision Dolby

A young pickpocket helps a mysterious knight thwart an evil priest who has turned his true love into a hawk.

Good-looking if somewhat predictably plotted fantasy adventure. Nice locations, but occasionally underlit.

p: Richard Donner, Lauren Shuler for Warner/TCF
exec p: Harvey Bernhard
w: Edward Khmara, Michael Thomas, Tom Mankiewicz
d: Richard Donner
ph: VITTORIO STORARO
m: ANDREW POWELL
ed/2nd unit d: Stuart Baird
pd: WOLF KROEGER
cos: Nana Cecchi
sp: John Richardson, Richard A. Greenberg
Matthew Broderick, Rutger Hauer, Michelle Pfeiffer, Leo McKern, John Wood, Ken Hutchison

Lahr, Bert (1895-1967)

American vadevillian, best remembered for playing the Cowardly Lion in *The Wizard of Oz* (1939). His other credits include *Faint Heart*, *Rose Marie* and *The Night They Raided Minsky's*.

Lambert, Christophe(r) (1957-)

French actor (also known as Christophe Lambert) who, after a couple of films in his homeland, rose to stardom in the title role of *Greystoke: The Legend of Tarzan, Lord of the Apes* in 1984, though he is better known to genre fans as Connor MacLeod in the three *Highlander* films. His other credits include *Subway*, *The Sicilian*, *To Kill a Priest* and *Knight Moves*.

Genre credits:
Highlander (1986), *Highlander II: The Quickening* (1991), *Fortress* (1993), *Highlander III: The Sorcerer* (1994), *Mortal Kombat* (1995)

The Land Before Time

USA 1988 70m Technicolor Dolby

Adventures of a small dinosaur, separated from his family after an earthquake.

Well made but overly cute animated feature which nevertheless found great box office favour, despite not quite being in the same league as the same team's *An American Tail*. Several video sequels followed: *The Land Before Time II: The Great Valley Adventure* (1994), *The Land Before Time III: The Time of the Great Giving* (1995) and *The Land Before Time IV* (1996).

p: Don Bluth, Gary Goldman, John Pomeroy for Universal/Amblin
exec p: Steven Spielberg, George Lucas, Frank Marshall, Kathleen Kennedy
w: Stu Krieger
story: Tony Geiss, Judy Freudberg
d/pd: Don Bluth
m: James Horner
voices: Gabriel Damon, Helen Shaver, Bill Erwin, Will Ryan, Juduth Barsi, Pat Hingle, Burke Barnes, Candice Houston

---

The Land That Time Forgot 🛸

GB 1974 91m Technicolor

During World War One, a German U-boat picks up survivors from a torpedoed cargo ship and takes them to a long forgotten Arctic island where the climate is hot and dinosaurs still rule.

Livelies, most entertaining effort in a string of low budget fantasy adventures made by this producer and director.

p: John Dark for Lion International/Amicus
exec p: Max J. Rosenberg, Milton Subotsky, Robert H. Greenberg
w: Michael Moorcock, James Cawthorne
novel: Edgar Rice Burroughs
d: KEVIN CONNOR
ph: Alan Hume
m: Douglas Gamley
ed: John Ireland
pd: MAURICE CARTER
ad: Bert Davey
cos: Julie Harris
sp: Derek Meddings, Roger Dicken, Charles Staffell
sound: George Stephenson, Bob Jones
Doug McClure, Susan Penhaligon, John McEnery, Keith Baron, Anthony Ainley, Godfrey James, Ben Howard, Roy Holder, Bobby Parr, Declan Mulholland, Colin Farrell

---

Lang, Fritz
(1890-1976)

Distinguished German director, a for-
mer newspaper sketch artist, working in film in Germany from 1917 as a writer, his first filmed screenplay being *Die Hochzeit in Ekzentrik Klub*. He made his directorial debut in 1919 with *Halbbut*. He married screenwriter Thea Von Harbou in 1922, with whom he worked on all his films until 1932, after which he moved first to France and then America, where he helmed such movies as *Fury*, *You Only Live Once*, *The Woman in the Window*, *Ministry of Fear* and *The Big Heat*. His other German silent credits include *Destiny*, *Inferno*, *Dr. Mabuse der Spieler* and *The Spy*. His first sound film was *M* in 1931. He returned to Germany in the 50s and directed such films as *Der Tiger Von Ischnapur* and *The Thousand Eyes of Dr. Mabuse*. To genre fans he is best known for directing *Metropolis*, however, which remains the key science fiction film of the silent period.

Genre credits:

Die Nibelungen (1923 – Part One: Siegfried/Siegfrieds Tod, Part Two: Kriemhilds Rache/Kriemhild's Revenge – co-w/d [co-w uncredited]), *Metropolis* (1926 – d), *Die Frau Im Mond* (1929 – aka *The Woman in the Moon/Rocket to the Moon* – co-w/p/d)

Lantieri, Michael

American special effects technician who began as an assistant on such films as *Flashdance*, *Fright Night* and *The Woman in Red* before moving into the science fiction and fantasy genres, where he won an Oscar for his work on *Jurassic Park* (1993 – with Dennis Muren, Stan Winston and Phil Tippett). His other credits include *Twins*, *The Witches of Eastwick*, *Amistad* and *Saving Private Ryan*.

Genre credits:

Indiana Jones and the Temple of Doom (1983 – co-sp), *The Last Starfighter* (1984 – co-sp), *My Science Project* (1985 – co-sp), *Star Trek IV: The Voyage Home* (1986 – co-sp), *Who Framed Roger Rabbit?* (1988 – co-sp), *Back to the Future, Part II* (1989 – co-sp), *Back to the Future, Part III* (1990 – co-sp), *Hook* (1991 – co-sp), *Death Becomes Her* (1992 – co-sp), *The Flintstones* (1994 – co-sp), *Casper* (1995 – co-sp), *Congo* (1995 – co-sp), *Matilda* (1996 – co-sp), *Mars Attacks!* (1996 – co-sp), *The Lost World: Jurassic Park* (1997 – co-sp)

Larson, Glen A.

American writer, producer, director and composer working primarily in television, where he has produced and/or created such series as *McCloud*, *The Six Million Dollar Man*, *The Fall Guy*, *Cover Up* and *Magnum P.I.* Some of the movie-length pilots for these series were released theatrically outside America.

Genre credits:

Battlestar Galactica (1978 – TVM – co-w/co-m/exec p), *Buck Rogers in the 25th Century* (1978 – co-w/co-m/exec p), *Knightrider* (1982 – w/exec p/co-theme m)

Last Action Hero

USA 1993 126m Technicolor Panavision Dolby

With the aid of a magic ticket, a young boy finds himself co-starring in a movie with his favourite action hero.

Expensive but far from consistently amusing action comedy which provided its star with his first real flop.

p: Steve Roth, John McTiernan for Columbia/Tri-Star
exec p: Arnold Schwarzenegger
w: Shane Black, David Arnott
story: Zak Penn, Adam Leff

d: John McTiernan
ph: Dean Semler
m: Michael Kamen
ed: John Wright
pd: Eugenio Zanetti
cos: Gloria Gresham
sp: Richard Greenberg, John Sullivan and others
sound: Lee Orloff
stunt co-ordinator: Fred M. Waugh, Joel Kramer, Vic Armstrong
2nd unit d: Fred M. Waugh
2nd unit ph: David B. Nowell
Arnold Schwarzenegger, Austin O'Brien, Charles Dance, Anthony Quinn, F. Murray Abraham, Art Carney, Frank McRae, Tom Noonan, Robert Prosky, Mercedes Ruehl, Ian McKellern, Joan Plowright, Tina Turner, Sharon Stone, Robert Patrick, Jean-Claude Van Damme

The Last Days of Pompeii

USA 1935 96m bw

A blacksmith becomes a famous gladiator in the last days of Pompei and helps several people escape the eruption of Vesuvius.

Stilted historical melodrama from the makers of *King Kong*. Badly written and acted, it bores well before the end when even the climax of death and destruction fails to rise to the occasion.

p: Merian C. Cooper for RKO
w: Ruth Rose, Boris Ingster
story: James Ashmore Creelman, Melville Baker
d: Ernest B. Shoedsack
ph: Eddie Linden, Jr., J. Roy Hunt
m: Roy Webb (using large chunks of Max Steiner's score from *King Kong*)
ed: Archie Marshek
ad: Van Nest Polglase, Al Herman
cos: Aline Bernstein
sp: Willis O'Brien, Vernon L. Walker, Harry Redmond
sound: Clem Portman, Walter Elliott
Preston Foster, Basil Rathbone, Alan Hale, Dorothy Cooper, Louis Calhern, Wyrley Birch

The Last Starfighter

USA 1984 100m Technicolor Panavision Dolby

A boy with a penchant for video games is recruited by aliens to help save their planet.

Amusing, tongue-in-cheek adventures with a generally perky script.

p: Gary Adelson, Edward O. Denault for Universal/Lorimar
w: JONATHAN BETUEL
d: Nick Castle
ph: King Baggott
m: Craig Safan
ed: C. Timothy O'Meara
pd: Ron Cobb
ad: James D. Bissell
cos: Robert Fletcher
sp: Kevin Pike, Michael Lantieri, Darrell D. Pritchett, James Dale Camomile, Joseph C. Sasgen
sound: Jack Solomon
make-up effects: Terry Smith
Lance Guest, Robert Preston, Dan O'Herlihy, Catherine Mary Stewart, Barbara Bosson, Norman Snow, Kay E. Kuter, Dan Mason, Chris Herbert, John O'Leary

Alex (Lance Guest) gets to meet his co-pilots in the engaging *Last Starfighter*. Just in case you were wondering, the aliens are played by John Maio (left) and Scott Dunlop (right).

Laszlo, Ernest (1905-1984)

American cinematographer of Hungarian descent. A former camera operator, he began working as a cinematographer in the mid-40s with such films as *The Hitler Gang* and *Two Years Before the Mast*. In the 60s he photographed a number of films for director Stanley Kramer, among them *Judgement at Nuremberg*, *Inherit the Wind* and *It's a Mad, Mad, Mad, Mad World*. His other credits include *Vera Cruz*, *Star!* and *Airport*.

Genre credits:

The Space Children (1958), *Fantastic Voyage* (1966), *Logan's Run* (1976)

Late for Dinner

USA 1991 93m DeLuxe Dolby

In 1962, two friends on the run for a crime they did not commit are frozen by a doctor looking for guinea pigs for his experiment, only to wake up in 1991.

Likeable fantasy adventure which for once doesn't concentrate on the hardware.

p: Dan Lupovitz, W. D. Richter for Castle Rock/New Line
w: Mark Andrus
d: W. D. Richter
ph: Peter Sova
m: David Mansfield
ed: Richard Chew, Robert Reighton
pd: Lilly Kilvert
cos: Aggie Guerard Rodgers
sp: Stan Parks and others
sound: Art Rochester
Brian Wimmer, Peter Berg, Marcia Gay Harden, Colleen Flynn, Peter Gallagher, Kyle Secor, Michael Beach

The Lawnmower Man

US/GB 1992 108m DeLuxe Dolby
GB 1992 108m DeLuxe

A mentally retarded gardener is given a new lease of life when his employer, a doctor, uses him as a guinea pig for his experiments with virtual reality computer technology and drug therapy. However, though the experiments at first have a positive effect, he later becomes a megalomaniac.

Though no more than mildly diverting in itself, the surprise commercial success of this virtual reality adventure produced a number of tame immitations (*Johnny Mnemonic*, *Virtuosity*, etc.) as well as two sequels of its own: *Lawnmower Man 2: Beyond Cyberspace* (1995) and *Lawnmower Man 3: Jobe's War* (1998). Under the circumstances, the effects aren't too bad at all.

p: Gimel Everett, Milton Subotsky for Allied Vision/Fuji Eight/Lane-Pringle
exec p: Edwards Simons, Steve Lane, Robert pringle, Clive Turner
w: Brett Leonard, Gimel Everett
story: Stephen King
d: Brett Leonard
ph: Russell Carpenter
m: Dan Wyman
ed: Alan Baumgarten
pd: Alex McDowell
cos: Mary Jane Fort
sp: Xaoz
sound: Russell Fager
Pierce Brosnan, Jeff Fahey (as Jobe Smith), Jenny Wright, Jeremy Slate, Geoffrey Lewis, Dean Norris, Mark Gringleson, Rosalee Mayeux, Austin O'Brien

Lawnmower Man 2: Beyond Cyberspace

USA 1995 92m DeLuxe Dolby

In LA in the future, Jobe Smith finds himself reconstituted – thanks to virtual reality – by a ruthless businessman who wants to take over the world's computer network, but things don't go according to plan...

Twice as expensive but half as entertaining as its predecessor, this vacuous sequel fails to engage, despite some good effects sequences.

p: Edward Simons, Keith Fox for Allied Entertainment/Fuji Eight/August
exec p: Steve Lane, Robert Pringle, Peter McRae, Clive Turner, Avram Butch Kaplan
w/d: Farhad Mann
story: Farhad Mann, Michael Miner
ph: Ward Russell
m: Robert Folk
ed: Peter Berger, Joel Goodman
pd: Ernest Roth
cos: Deborah Everton
sp: Farhad Mann, Cinesite, Todd-AO Digital Images, Sessumus Engineering
sound: Richard Schexnayder
2nd unit d: Spiro Razatos
2nd unit ph: John Connor, Sr.
stunt co-ordinator: Spiro Razatos, Ken Bates
Patrick Bergin, Matt Frewer, Kevin Conway, Austin O'Brien, Ely Pouget, Camille Cooper, Crystal Celeste Grant, Patrick La Brecque, Richard Fancy, Sean Parhm

Leakey, Phil (1908-1992)

British make-up artist who, having trained at Shepperton Studios in the mid-40s, joined Hammer/Exclusive in 1947, where he worked on many of their second-feature thrillers/programmers (*Meet Simon Cherry*, *Room to Let*, *Someone at the Door*, etc.) as well as several of their key 50s horror films (*The Curse of Frankenstein*, *Dracula*, *The Revenge of Frankenstein*, etc.). His other credits include *Only Two Can Play*, *Sammy Going South*, *The Ipcress File* and *The Belstone Fox*.

Genre credits:

The Quatermass Experiment (1955 – aka *The Creeping Unknown*), *X – The Unknown* (1956), *Quatermass 2* (1957 – aka *Enemy from Space*)

Lebenzon, Chris

American editor who has worked on several films for Tim Burton, including *Ed Wood*. His other credits, among them many for director Tony Scott, include *Top Gun*, *Beverly Hills Cop 2*, *Revenge*, *Days of Thunder*, *The Last Boy Scout* and *Crimson Tide*. He has also worked on the likes of *Wolfen*, *Midnight Run*, *Josh and Sam* and *Weeds*.

Genre credits:

Batman Returns (1992 – co-ed), *The Nightmare Before Christmas* (1993 – aka *Tim Burton's The Nightmare Before Christmas* – co-ed), *Mars Attacks!* (1996 – ed)

Lee, Christopher (1922-)

British actor whose prolific output has mostly been in the horror genre, often in partnership with Peter Cushing. Regarded by many as the definitive screen Dracula, he began his career after military service during the war, winning a seven-year contract with Rank in 1947. However, his height proved a restriction, and he subsequently found himself playing bit parts in all manner of films (*Corridor of Mirrors*, *Hamlet*, *Prelude to Fame*, *A Tale of Two Cities*, *Valley of Eagles*, etc.) until, ironically, his height did win him the role of the Creature in Hammer's *The Curse of Frankenstein* in 1956, after which it was but a short step to the title roles in *Dracula* and *The Mummy* and international fame. His appearances in science fiction and fantasy have been rare,

whilst in the 70s, dissatisfied with the horror genre, he attempted to break away by appearing in the likes of *The Three Musketeers*, *The Man with the Golden Gun* (as Scaramanga), *The Four Musketeers* and *1941*.

Genre credits:

Hercules in the Centre of the Earth (1961 – aka *Hercules in the Haunted World/Vampires vs. Hercules*), *She* (1965), *Night of the Big Heat* (1967 – aka *Island of the Burning Damned*), *Starship Invasions* (1977), *End of the World* (1977), *Return from Witch Mountain* (1978), *Arabian Adventure* (1979), *Gremlins 2: The New Batch* (1990)

Lee, Danny

American special effects technician, long with Disney, where he won an Oscar for his work on *Bedknobs and Broomsticks* (1971 – with Alan Maley and Eustace Lycett). Often works in collaboration with Eustace Lycett and Art Cruickshank.

Genre credits:

The Love Bug (1968 – co-sp), *Now You See Him, Now You Don't* (1972 – co-sp), *The World's Greatest Athlete* (1973 – co-sp), *Charley and the Angel* (1974 – co-sp), *Escape to Witch Mountain* (1974 – co-sp), *Herbie Rides Again* (1974 – co-sp), *The Island at the Top of the World* (1974 – co-sp), *Freaky Friday* (1976 – co-sp), *Herbie Goes to Monte Carlo* (1977 – co-sp), *The Shaggy DA* (1976 – co-sp), *Return from Witch Mountain* (1978 – co-sp), *The Cat from Outer Space* (1978 – co-sp), *The Black Hole* (1979 – co-sp), *Herbie Goes Bananas* (1980 – co-sp), *The Devil and Max Devlin* (1981 – sp)

Legend

GB 1985 94m Technicolor Panavision Dolby

Darkness is thwarted by a princess and

her friends when he tries to kill the earth's two remaining unicorns.

Produced at enormous expense, this extremely thin fairy tale makes the fatal error of jettisoning story and character in favour of sumptuous visuals which, though gorgeous to look at, a movie do not make. Something of a box office disaster.

p: Tim Hampton for Arnon Milchan
w: William Hjortsberg
d: Ridley Scott
ph: ALEX THOMSON
m: JERRY GOLDSMITH (Tangerine Dream for the US release)
ed: Terry Rawlings, William Gordean
pd: ASSHETON GORTON
cos: Charles Knode
sp: Nick Allder
sound: Roy Charman
make-up effects: ROB BOTTIN
stunt co-ordinator: Vic Armstrong
titles: Peter Govey
add ph: Max Mowbray, Harry Oakes
Tom Cruise, Mia Sara, Tim Curry, David Bennett, Alice Playten, Billy Barty, Cork Hubbert, Peter O'Farrell, Kiran Shah, Annabelle Lanyon, Robert Picardo

Legend in Leotards
see The Return of Captain Invincible

Leonetti, Matthew

American cinematographer whose many and varied credits take in *Bat People* (aka *It Lives by Night*), *Breaking Away*, *Raise the Titanic*, *Fast Times at Ridgemont High*, *Poltergeist*, *Jagged Edge*, *Dragnet* and *Another 48 Hrs*.

Genre credits:

Ice Pirates (1984), *Weird Science* (1985), *Angels in the Outfield* (1994 – aka *Angels*), *Strange Days* (1995)

Leviathan

USA/It 1989 98m Technicolor Dolby
Miners working from a station based
on the ocean floor find themselves prey
to a genetically created monster.

Tolerable underwater variation on
Alien and *The Thing*. It passes the
time.

p: Luigi de Laurentiis, Aurelio de Laurentiis
for Fox/Gordon/Filmauro
exec p: Lawrence Gordon, Charles Gordon
w: David Peoples, Jeb Stuart
story: David Peoples
d: George Pan Cosmatos
ph: Alex Thomson
m: Jerry Goldsmith
ed: Robert Silvi, John F. Burnett
pd: Ron Cobb
cos: April Ferry
sp: Stan Winston, Barry Nolan
sound: Robin Gregory
Peter Weller, Richard Crenna, Amanda Pays,
Michael Carmine, Daniel Stern, Ernie
Hudson, Hector Elizondo, Lisa Eilbacher,
Meg Foster

Liar Liar

USA 1997 86m DeLuxe DTS stereo
A lawyer who lies compulsively finds
himself able to tell nothing but the
absolute truth for a day after his five-
year-old son makes a birthday wish.

A one-joke film which nevertheless
has some genuinely hilarious sequences
(as well as the usual mugging expected
from this star).

p: Brian Grazer for Universal/Imagine
exec p: James D. Brubaker, Michael Bostick
w: Paul Guay, Stephen Mazur
d: Tom Shadyac
ph: Russell Boyd
m: John Debney, James Newton Howard
(theme)
ed: Don Zimmerman
pd: Linda DeScenna
cos: Judy Ruskin

sp: Jon Fargat
sound: Jose Antonio Garcia
stunt co-ordinator/2nd unit d: Mickey
Gilbert
Jim Carrey, Maura Tuerney, Justin Cooper,
Cary Elwes, Anne Haney, Swoozie Kurtz,
Jennifer Tilly, Amanda Donohoe, Jason
Bernard, Mitchell Ryan, Chip Mayer

Lifeforce

USA/GB 1985 97m Technicolor
London is devastated by vampires from
outer space able to suck the lifeforce
out of people.

Risible nonsense with expensive but
variable effects. A box office disaster –
deservedly so.

p: Menaham Golan, Yoram Globus for
Cannon/Easerdam
w: Dan O'Bannon, Don Jakoby
novel: Colin Wilson
d: Tobe Hooper
ph: Alan Hume
m: Henry Mancini, Michael Kamen, James
Gutrie
ed: John Grover
pd: John Graysmark
cos: Carin Harris, Tiny Nicholls
sp: John Dykstra, John Grant
make-up effects: Nick Malley
Steve Railsback, Peter Firth, Frank Finlay,
Mathilda May, Patrick Stewart, Michael
Gothard, Nicholas Ball, Aubrey Morris

Lifepod

USA 1993 96m colour TVM
Survivors of a spaceship explosion
escape in a lifepod, but there is a killer
among them.

Credited outer space remake of
Alfred Hitchcock's *Lifeboat*. Not quite
so effective this time round, but it
passes the time well enough, especially
if you haven't seen the original.

p: Mark Stern, Tim Harbert for Fox
West/Trilogy/RHI
exec p: Richard B. Lewis, John Watson, Pen
Densham, Scott Brazil
w: M. Jay Roach, Pen Densham
story: Pen Densham
d: Ron Silver
ph: Robert Steadman
m: Hanz Zimmer, Mark Mancina
ed: Alan Baumgarten
pd: Curtis R. Schnell
cos: Katherine Dover
sp: Starlight Films, Sam Nicholson
sound: Richard Lightstone
Robert Loggia, Ron Silver, C. C. H. Pounder,
Kelli Williams, Adam Storke, Stan Shaw,
Jessica Tuck

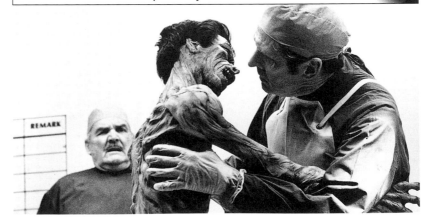

A space vampire gets ready to suck the soul from an unsuspecting
doctor in director Tobe Hooper's truly dreadful *Lifeforce*.

Like Father, Like Son

USA 1987 98m Technicolor

A middle-aged doctor and his high-school son swap bodies after drinking a mysterious Indian potion.

Mildly amusing age reversal comedy, one of several released during this period (*Vice-Versa*, *18 Again*, *Big*, etc.).

p: Brian Grazer, David Valdes for Tri-Star/Imagine

w: Lorne Cameron, Steven L. Bloom

story: Lorne Cameron

d: Rod Daniel

ph: Jack N. Green

m: Miles Goodman

ed: Lois Freeman-Fox

pd: Dennis Gassner

cos: Robert Turtrice

sp: John Frazier

Dudley Moore, Kirk Cameron, Margaret Colin, Catherine Hicks, Patrick O'Neal, Sean Astin, Cami Cooper, Bill Morrison

Lindenlaub, Karl Walter

German cinematographer whose work has added a certain visual flair to the films of director Roland Emmerich these include *Ghost Chase*.

Genre credits:

Moon 44 (1989), *Universal Soldier* (1992), *Stargate* (1994), *Independence Day* (1996), *Godzilla* (1998)

Ling, Barbara

American production designer whose credits take in the two Batman films directed by Joel Schumacher, for whom she also designed *Falling Down*.

Genre credits:

Making Mr. Right (1987), *Batman Forever* (1995), *Batman and Robin* (1997)

Link

GB 1986 103m Technicolor Dolby

An educated chimpanzee goes on the rampage at an isolated research institute.

Overlong gimmick thriller with interesting touches to compensate for its far-fetched plot.

p: Richard Franklin, Richard McCallum for Cannon/EMI

exec p: Verity Lambert

w: Everett de Roche

story: Lee Zlotoff, Tom Ackerman

d: Richard Franklin

ph: Mike Malloy

m: JERRY GOLDSMITH

ed: Andrew London

pd: Norman Garwood

cos: Catherine Cook

sp: John Gant

sound: David Stephenson

animal trainer: Ray Berwick

2nd unit ph: Gale Tattersall, Mike Proudfoot

Elisabeth Shue, Terence Stamp, Steve Pinner, Richard Garnett, Joe Belcher, Kevin Lloyd

The Lion King

USA 1994 90m Technicolor Dolby

A young African lion cub is reared to be the next king, but reckons without the schemes of his wicked uncle.

Brilliantly animated cartoon feature in Disney's very best modern manner.

p: Don Hahn for Walt Disney

exec p: Thomas Schumacher

w: Irene Mecchi, Jonathan Roberts, Linda Woolverton

d: Roger Allers, Rob Minkoff

songs: Elton John (m), Tim Rice (ly) (aa, best song, "*Can You Feel the Love Tonight?*")

m: Hans Zimmer (aa)

ed: Ivan Bilancio

sound: Terry Porter, Mel Metcalfe, David J. Hudson, Doc Kane

titles: Burke Mattson, Susan Bradley

voices: Jonathan Taylor Thomas, Matthew Broderick, JEREMY IRONS, Whoopi Goldberg, Rowan Atkinson, James Earl Jones, Moira Kelly, Niketa Calame, Nathan Lane, Ernie Sabella, Robert Guillaume, Cheech Marin, Jim Cummings, Madge Sinclair

Lippert, Robert L. (1909-1976)

American producer, director and exhibitor of low budget exploitation films.

Genre credits:

Rocketship X-M (1950 – exec p), *Lost Continent* (1951-exec p)

Liquid Sky

USA 1982 112m TVCcolor

A lesbian alien from outer space pursues victims for the substance they produce in their brains upon achieving orgasm.

Would-be outrageous sci-fi comic, amateurishly presented on a painfully low budget. Considered a cult item in some circles.

p: Slava Tsukerman for Z Films

w: Slava Tsukerman, Anne Carlisle, Nina V. Kerova

d: Slava Tsukerman

ph/sp: Yuri Neyman

m: Slava Tsukerman, Brenda I. Hutchinson, Clive Smith

ed: Slava Tsukerman, Sharyn Leslie Ross

pd/cos: Marina Levikova-Neyman

sound: Ed Novick, Phoebe Bendiser

Anne Carlisle, Paula E. Sheppard, Bob Brady, Susan Doukas, Elaine C. Grove

Lithgow, John (1945-)

American star character actor with several Brian de Palma films to his credit (*Obsession*, *Blow Out*, *Raising Cain*).

His other credits include *The World According to Garp* (as a transsexual), *Terms of Endearment*, *At Play in the Fields of the Lord*, *Cliffhanger*, *The Princess Caraboo* and the TV sci-fi comedy *Third Rock from the Sun* .

Genre credits:

Twilight Zone: The Movie (1983), *The Adventures of Buckaroo Banzai Across the Eighth Dimension* (1984), *2010: Odyssey Two* (1984), *Santa Claus: The Movie* (1984), *Harry and the Hendersons* (1987 – aka *Bigfoot and the Hendersons*)

Little Bigfoot

USA 1995 94m colour stereo

A family vacationing in the mountains come across a baby bigfoot and help to protect its environment from the schemes of a ruthless tycoon out to redevelop the area.

Overly cute romp with a message (look after the environment, kids) which makes *Harry and the Hendersons* look like *Gone with the Wind*.

p: Richard Pepin, Joseph Merhi for PM
w: Richard Preston, Jr.
story: Scott McAboy
d: Art Camacho
ph: Ken Blakey
m: Louis Febre
ed: Chris Worland
pd: Zeev Tankus
cos: Amber Lyne Garcia
Ross Malinger, P. J. Soles, Kenneth Tigar, Kelly Packard, Don Stroud, Matt McCoy

---

The Little Convict

Australia 1979 74m colour TVM

Jake the Peg tells the story of how convicts were transported to Australia.

Poor amalgam of live action and animation aimed at younger audiences, who deserve better.

p: Yorram Gross for Australian Film Commission/Little Convict Syndicate
w: John Palmer
d: Yorram Gross
ph: Chris Ashbrook, Frank Hammond
m: Bob Young
ed: Rod Hay
cos: Judith Dorsman
Rolf Harris

The Little Mermaid

USA 1989 82m Technicolor Dolby

A young mermaid falls in love with a handsome prince and trades her voice with a wicked sea witch so as to be able to follow him onto dry land.

Charming animated feature with some virtuoso passages. Ideal family viewing, it marked a renaissance in Disney animation.

p: Howard Ashman, John Musker for Walt Disney/Silver Screen Partners IV
w/d: John Musker, Ron Clements
story: Hans Christian Andersen
m: Alan Menken (aa)
songs: Alan Menken (m), Howard Ashman (ly) (aa best song, *Under the Sea*)
ed: John Carnochan
ad: Michael A. Perza, Jr., Donald A. Towns
sound: Terry Porter, Mel Metcalfe, David J. Hudson
voices: Jodi Benson, Rene Auberjonois, Buddy Hackett, Paddi Edwards, Christopher Daniel, Pat Carroll, Jason Marin, Kenneth Mars, Ben Wright, Samuel E. Wright

---

Lloyd, Christopher (1938-)

American actor with a penchant for quirky roles, most notably that of Doc Emmett Brown in the *Back to Future* trilogy. After much stage work he made his film debut in 1975 in *One Flew Over the Cuckoo's Nest*. He became a star via the TV sit-com *Taxi* (as

Reverend Jim), which helped to gain him larger film roles. His other credits include *Goin' South*, *Schizoid*, *Clue*, *The Dream Team*, *The Addams Family* and *Addams Family Values* (the latter two as Uncle Fester).

Genre credits:

Star Trek III: The Search for Spock (1984 – as a Klingon), *The Adventures of Buckaroo Banzai Across the Eighth Dimension* (1984), *Back to the Future* (1985), *Who Framed Roger Rabbit?* (1988 – as Judge Doom), *Back to the Future, Part II* (1989), *Back to the Future, Part III* (1990), *Duck Tales: The Movie – Treasure of the Lost Lamp* (1990 – voice), *Suburban Commando* (1991), *Angels in the Outfield* (1994 – aka *Angels*), *The Pagemaster* (1994), *Anastasia* (1997 – voice)

Loch Ness

GB 1996 101m Metrocolor Dolby

An American zoologist travels to Scotland in search of the Loch Ness monster and has a romance with the landlady of his hotel, whose daughter has often sighted the "kelpie".

Mild in all departments, this fumbled effort makes it neither as a comedy, a romance nor a fantasy. A real disappointment given the opportunities at hand.

p: Tim Bevan, Eric Fellner, Stephen Ujlaki for Polygram/Working Title
w: John Fusco
d: John Henderson
ph: Clive Tickner
m: Trevor Jones
ed: Jon Gregory
pd: Sophie Becher
cos: Nic Ede
sp: Jim Henson's Creature Shop, Peerless Camera Company
sound: Mark Auguste
Ted Danson, Joely Richardson, Kirsty Graham, Ian Holm, Nick Brimble, Harris

Yulin, James Frain, Keith Allen, Richard Vernon, Brian Pettifer

Logan's Run

USA 1976 118m Metrocolor Todd-AO
In the year 2274, society dooms those over the age of 30 to death so as to control the population growth, but a policeman defies the rules and goes on the run.

Flatly handled, studio-bound adventure with some very obvious model work (which actually won an Oscar) and some very dated set and costume design (the usual 70s view of the future as a kind of antiseptic EPCOT). A few flashes of imagination in the script make it just about watchable.

p: Saul David for MGM
w: David Zelag Goodman
novel: William F. Nolan, George Clayton Johnson
d: Michael Anderson
ph: Ernest Laszlo
m: Jerry Goldsmith
ed: Bill Wyman
ad: Dale Hennesy
cos: Bill Thomas
sp: L.B. Abbott, Glen Robinson, Matthew Yuricich (aa)
Michael York, Jenny Agutter, Richard Jordan, Roscoe Lee Browne, Farrah Fawcett-Majors, Peter Ustinov, Michael Anderson, Jr.

Lohman, Augie

American special effects technician who began his career at the low budget end of the genre before securing projects of greater importance later on.

Genre credits:
Lost Continent (1951 – sp), *Captain Sinbad* (1963 – co-sp), *Barbarella* (1967 – sp), *Soylent Green* (1973 – sp)

EPCOT lives! A dated, mid-70s view of the future as seen in *Logan's Run*.

Lois and Clark: The New Adventures of Superman

USA 1993 74m Technicolor TVM
In the guise of Clark Kent, Superman joins *The Daily Planet* and, with the help of fellow reporter Lois Lane, brings to book criminal mastermind Lex Luthor.

Reasonable feature-length pilot for a series which consequently did much better in the ratings than anyone had dared expect.

p: Mel Efros for Warner/Gangbuster/Roundelay
exec p: David Jacobs, Robert Butler
w/cr: Deborah Joy Levine
d: Robert Butler
ph: Chuck Minsky
m: Jay Gruska
ed: John Duffy
pd: Mayling Chen
cos: Brad Loman
sp: Richard Stutman, Elan Soltes

sound: Kenn Michael Fuller
Dean Cain, Teri Hatcher, Lane Smith, Michael Landes, Tracy Scoggins, Elizabeth Barondes, John Shea, Persis Khambatta

Lom, Herbert (1917-)

Czech-born character actor (real name Herbert Charles Angelo Kuchacevich ze Schluderpacheru), equally adept at comic or sinister roles, though perhaps best known for playing Inspector Dreyfus in the Pink Panther films. His other credits include *The Seventh Veil*, *The Ladykillers*, *Northwest Frontier*, *El Cid*, *The Phantom of the Opera* (title role), *The Lady Vanishes*, *The Sect* and *Son of the Pink Panther*.

Genre credits:
Mysterious Island (1961 – as Captain Nemo), *Journey to the Far Side of the Sun* (1969 – aka *Doppelganger*)

Look Who's Talking

USA 1989 96m Technicolor Dolby

A single pregnant woman is helped in her hour of need by a streetwise cab driver, but her new-born son has one or two things to say about their ensuing romance.

Agreeably performed umbilical comedy which took off in a big way at the box office. It was followed by two less satisfactory sequels: *Look Who's Talking, Too* (1990) and *Look Who's Talking Now* (1993).

p: Jonathan D. Krane Tri-Star/MCEG
w/d: Amy Heckerling
ph: Thomas del Ruth
m: David Kitay
ed: Debra Chiate
ad: Reuben Freed, Graeme Murray
cos: Molly Maginnis
sound: Ralph Parker
John Travolta, Kirstie Alley, Bruce Willis (voice, as Mikey), Olympia Dukakis, George Segal, Abe Vigoda, Twinl Caplan, Joan Rivers (voice)

Look Who's Talking Now

USA 1993 97m Technicolor Dolby

The Umbriacco's two dogs now comment upon their daily lives.

A few amusing one-liners enliven a film that otherwise should not really have been allowed.

p: Jonathan D. Krane for Tri-Star/MCEG
w: Tom Ropelewski, Leslie Dixon
d: Tom Ropelewski
ph: Oliver Stapleton
m: William Ross
ed: Michael A. Stevenson, Harry Hitner
pd: Michael Bolton
cos: Molly Maginnis, Mary E. McLeod
John Travolta, Kirstie Alley, Lysette Anthony, Olympia Dukakis, George Segal, Danny de Vito (voice), Diane Keaton (voice), David Gallagher, Tabitha Lupien, Charles Barkley,

John Stocker

Look Who's Talking, Too

USA 1990 81m Technicolor Dolby

Little Mikey gets a baby sister.

Virtually plotless regurgitation of the first film, though not without its amusing moments.

p: Jonathan D. Krane, Bob Gray for Tri-Star/MCEG
w: Amy Heckerling, Neal Israel
d: Amy Heckerling
ph: Thomas Del Ruth
m: David Kitay
ed: Debra Chiate
pd: Reuben Freed
cos: Molly Maginnis
sp: Chris Walas
sound: Ralph Parker
John Travolta, Kirstie Alley, Olympia Dukakis, Elias Koteas, Twink Kaplan, Bruce Willis (voice), Roseanne Barr (voice), Damon Wayans (voice), Mel Brooks (voice – as Mr. Toilet Man), Gilbert Gottfried, Lorne Sussman, Megan Milner

Looker

USA 1981 90m Technicolor Panavision Dolby

A plastic surgeon investigates a series of strange murders involving his clients.

Glitzy thriller with plenty of surface gloss but a central premise too silly for words.

p: Howard Jeffrey for Warner/Ladd
w/d: Michael Crichton
ph: Paul Lohmann
m: Barry de Vorzon
ed: Carl Kress
pd: Dean Edward Mitzner
cos: Betsy Cox
sp: Joe Day
sound: Chuck Wilborn, Robert J. Litt, David

Kimball, Andrew Patterson
stunt co-ordinator: Fred Waugh
Albert Finney, James Coburn, Susan Dey, Leigh Taylor-Young, Dorian Harewood, Tim Ros5sovich, Kathryn Witt, Terri Welles

Lord of the Rings

USA 1978 133m DeLuxe Dolby

A young Hobbit prevents an evil lord from obtaining a all-powerful ring.

Elaborate animated adaptation of the popular books, generally skillful and certainly less taxing than reading the stories. A sequel was planned but never made, hence the rather abrupt ending.

p: Saul Zaentz for UA/Fantasy
w: Chris Conkling, Peter S. Beagle
book: J. R. R. Tolkein
d: Ralph Bakshi
ph: Timothy Galfas
m: Leonard Rosenman
ed: Donald W. Ernst
sound: Bill Varney, Bob Minkler, Bill Mumford
titles: Wayne Fitzgerald
voices: Christopher Guard, John Hurt, William Squire, Michael Scholes, Norman Bird, Michael Graham-Cox, David Cox, Anthony Daniels, Peter Woodthorpe, Michael Deacon, Dominic Guard, Fraser Kerr, Philip Stone

The Lost Continent

GB 1968 98m Technicolor

Passengers on a tramp steamer in the Sargasso Sea come across a strange island governed by the Spanish Inquisition.

Preposterous adventure yarn with a few absurd monsters thrown in for good measure. One or two lively moments, but the results are mostly tedious.

p: Michael Carreras for Hammer

w: Michael Nash (Michael Carreras)

novel: Dennis Wheatley

d: Michael Carreras

ph: Paul Beeson

m: Gerard Schurmann

md: Philip Martell

ed: James Needs, Chris Barnes

ad: ARTHUR LAWSON

cos: Carl Toms

sp: Robert A. Mattey, Cliff Richardson

sound: Denis Whitlock

Eric Porter, Hildegarde Neff, Suzanna Leigh, Tony Beckley, Nigel Stock, Jimmy Hanely, Michael Ripper, Victor Maddern, James Cossins, Eddie Powell, Neil McCallum, Dana Gillespie, Alf Joint

---

Lost Horizon

USA 1937 118m bw

Four travellers escaping a Far East revolution by plane find themselves kidnapped and taken to an isolated Tibetan valley whose equable climate induces great longevity in its people.

Classic wish-fulfilment fantasy whose story still manages to compel. Production, acting and direction all make themselves felt, though the philosophising is a little trite.

p: Frank Capra for Columbia

w: Robert Riskin

novel: JAMES HILTON

d: FRANK CAPRA

ph: Joseph Walker

m: DMITRI TIOMKIN

md: Max Steiner

ed: Gene Havlick, Gene Milford (aa)

ad: STEPHEN GOOSSON (AA)

cos: Ernest Dryden

sp: E. Roy Davidson, Ganahl Carson

aerial ph: Elmer Dyer

Ronald Colman, H. B. WARNER, THOMAS MITCHELL, Edward Everett Horton, SAM JAFFE, Isabel Jewell, Jane Wyatt, John Howard, Margo

---

Lost Horizon

USA 1972 143m Technicolor Panavision

Western travellers escaping from a Chinese revolution are taken to a mystical valley high in the Tibetan mountains.

Overlong and ill-advised musical remake with none of the charm (or even technical resource) of the original.

p: Ross Hunter for Columbia

w: Larry Kramer

novel: JAMES HILTON

d: Charles Jarrott

ph: Robert Surtees

m/md: Burt Bacharach

ly: Hal David

ed: Mary Winetrobe

pd: Preston Ames

ch: Hermes Pan

PETER FINCH, Liv Ullman, Michael York, Bobby Van, Sally Kellerman, JOHN GIELGUD, George Kennedy, Olivia Hussey, James Shigeta, Charles Boyer

---

The Lost World

USA 1960 98m DeLuxe Cinemascope

Professor Challenger leads an expedition to an Amazon plateau where prehistoric monsters and tribes of cannibals are discovered.

Preposterous adventure lacking both style and invention, not to mention convincing monsters and art direction. Enjoyably awful for lovers of the ludicrous.

p: Irwin Allen for TCF/Saratoga

w: Irwin Allen, Charles Bennett

novel: Arthur Conan Doyle

d: Irwin Allen

ph: Winton C. Hoch

m: Bert Shefter, Paul Sawtell

ed: Hugh S. Fowler

ad: Duncan Cramer, Walter Simonds

cos: Paul Zastupnevitch

sp: Willis O'Brien, L.B. Abbott, Emil Kosa, James B. Gordon

sound: E. Clayton Ward, Harry M. Leonard

CLAUDE RAINS, Michael Rennie, Jill St. John, RICHARD HAYDN, David Hedison, Fernando Lamas, Ray Stricklyn, Jay Novello

---

The Lost World: Jurassic Park

USA 1997 122m DeLuxe DTS stereo

Billionaire John Hammond sends a special team to Isla Sorna, a second island off the Costa Rican coast which was used as a breeding area for his Jurassic Park dinosaurs, his hope being to make a record of the creatures in their natural environment. However, the arrival of a group of hunters out to catch the animals for a zoo in San Diego quickly sends the mission haywire.

If one doesn't expect too much of it, this is a reasonably enjoyable sequel to *Jurassic Park* with some dazzling effects, though as before the plot isn't without its inconsistencies, and the thing does become rather silly towards the end. As expected, it made a heap of money.

p: Gerald R. Molen, Colin Wilson for Universal/Amblin

exec p: Kathleen Kennedy

w: David Koepp

novel: Michael Crichton

d: Steven Spielberg

ph: Janusz Kaminski

m: John Williams

ed: Michael Kahn

pd: Rick Carter

cos: Sue Moore

sp: DENNIS MUREN, STAN WINSTON, MICHAEL LANTIERI

sound: Gary Rydstrom

2nd unit d: David Koepp

stunt co-ordinator: M. James Arnett, Gary Hymes

Jeff Goldblum, Julianne Moore, Pete Postlethwaite, Arliss Howard, Richard

Attenborough, Vince Vaughn, Peter Stormare, Harvey Jason, Bernard Shaw, Joseph Mazello, Ariana Richards

Lourie, Eugene (1905-1991)

French designer and special effects technician who, after working in France for director Jean Renoir on such films as *Les Bas-Fonds*, *La Grande Illusion* and *La Règle du Jeu*, went to America with him in 1943. Here he not only continued to work with Renoir (*This Land Is Mine*, *The Southerner*), but also designed such films as Chaplin's *Limelight*, *Battle of the Bulge*, *Krakatoa*, *East of Java*, *What's the Matter with Helen?*, *Burnt Offerings* and *Bronco Billy*. Turned to direction in 1953 with *The Beast from 20 000 Fathoms*.

Genre credits:

The Beast from 20 000 Fathoms (1953 – d), *The Colossus of New York* (1958 – d), *The Giant Behemoth* (1959 – aka *Behemoth – The Sea Monster* – w/co-d), *Gorgo* (1961 – co-story/d), *Crack in the World* (1965 – ad/co-sp), *The Amazing Captain Nemo* (1978 – co-ad), *Supertrain* (1979 - TVM 2nd unit d)

The Love Bug

USA 1968 107m Technicolor

A racing driver discovers that his Volkswagen has a mind of its own.

Lively Disney frolic which proved to be one of the studio's most successful live action features. It was followed by three sequels: *Herbie Rides Again* (1974), *Herbie Goes to Monte Carlo* (1977) and *Herbie Goes Bananas* (1980).

p: Bill Walsh for Walt Disney
w: Bill Walsh, Don da Gradi
story: Gordon Buford

d: Robert Stevenson
ph: Edward Colman
m: George Bruns
ed: Cotton Warburton
ad: Carroll Clark, John B. Mansbridge
cos: Bill Thomas
sp: Eustace Lycett, Alan Maley, Peter Ellenshaw, Howard Jensen, Danny Lee
sound: Robert O. Cook, Dean Thomas
2nd unit d: Arthur J. Vitarelli
stunt co-ordinator: Carey Loftin
Dean Jones, Michele Lee, DAVID TOMLIN-SON, Buddy Hackett, Joe Flynn, Benson Fong, Joe E. Ross

Lucas, George (1944-)

American writer, producer, director and executive producer, the father of contemporary screen science fiction via his celebrated *Star Wars* movies. A graduate of the University of Southern California's Film School (where he made his first short, *Look at Life*, in 1965), he was among the first generation to make their way into the movie industry via this route, first working as a camera assistant to title designer Saul Bass and then as an assistant to editor Verna Fields (who would later edit Steven Spielberg's first two theatrical features). In 1967 he returned to the University of Southern California as an assistant teacher of camera, during which time he also made his first science fiction film, a short entitled *Electronic Labyrinth:THX 1138: 4EB*. This led to documentaries about the making of *MacKenna's Gold* and *The Rain People*, on the latter of which he also acted as Francis Ford Coppola's assistant. In 1969 he also helped to photograph the Rolling Stones concert film *Gimme Shelter* (released in 1970), after which he began work on his first theatrical feature *THX 1138*, an expansion of his 1967 short, co-produced by Francis Ford Coppola through his American Zoetrope studio. This led to

a second film for Coppola, *American Graffiti*, which went on to gross over $55m at the box office, earning Lucas best writer and director Oscar nominations in the process. The struggle to get *Star Wars* onto the screen followed, with Lucas eventually placing the project at Fox. So as to achieve the highest possible standard of special effects for the production he formed his own effects house, Industrial Light and Magic, which he set up with effects wiz John Dykstra. He also formed his own production company, Lucasfilm, through which he has since produced all of his films. The huge commercial success of *Star Wars*, not to mention the merchandising bonanza attached to it, made Lucas a very wealthy man, thanks to the canny contract he had worked out for himself for the movie and its sequels. The film also earned him further best writer and director Oscar nominations. The *Star Wars* franchise aside, Lucas is also the brains behind the equally successful *Indiana Jones* franchise, whilst ILM has gone from strength to strength as an effects house facility, winning many Oscars in the process. Lucas's non-*Star Wars* and *Indiana Jones* projects have met with variable success, however, and include such titles as *Howard the Duck*, *Tucker: The Man and His Dream* and *The Radioland Murders*. Meanwhile, in 1997, rejuvenated versions of the *Star Wars* trilogy, with additional footage and improved effects, appeared by way of celebrating *Star Wars'* 20th anniversary and as a curtain raiser to the second trilogy of films.

Genre credits:

THX 1138 (1970 – co-w/story/ed/d), *Star Wars* (1977 – aka *Star Wars IV: A New Hope* – exec p/w/d), *The Empire Strikes Back* (1980 – story/exec p), *Raiders of the Lost Ark* (1981 – co-story/co-exec p), *Twice*

George Lucas (left) and Steven Spielberg take a break during the filming of *Raiders of the Lost Ark*, the first of their many successful collaborations.

Upon a Time (1982 – exec p), *Return of the Jedi* (1983 – story/exec p), *The Ewok Adventure: Caravan of Courage* (1984 – TVM – story/exec p), *Indiana Jones and the Temple of Doom* (1984 – story/co-exec p), *Ewoks: The Battle for Endor* (1985 – TVM – story/exec p), *Labyrinth* (1986 – exec p), *Howard the Duck* (1986 – aka *Howard, A New Breed of Hero* – exec p), *Captain Eo* (1986 – w/exec p [Disneyworld short]), *Willow* (1988 – story/exec p), *The Land Before Time* (1988 – co-exec p), *Indiana Jones and the Last Crusade* (1989 – co-story/co-exec p)

Lungdren, Dolph (1959-)

Muscle-bound Swedish actor, now in American action films. Began his film career in 1985 with a featured walk-on role in *A View to a Kill*, after which he played the Russian boxer Ivan Drango in *Rocky IV*. Stardom consequently beckoned. His master's degree in chemical engineering belies his screen image, though. His other credits include *The Punisher*, *Red Scorpion*, *Cover Up* and *Meltdown*.

Genre credits:
Masters of the Universe (1987 – as He-Man), *Dark Angel* (1990 – aka *I Come in Peace*), *Universal Soldier* (1992), *Johnny Mnemonic* (1995)

Lutyens, Elizabeth (1906-1983)

British composer, trained at the Royal College of Music. The daughter of architect Sir Edward Lutyens, she composed for film, television, radio and the concert platform. Her other credits include *Never Take Sweets from a Stranger*, *The Skull* and *The Psychopath*.

Genre credits:
The Earth Dies Screaming (1964), *Spaceflight IC-1* (1965), *The Terrornauts*

(1967)

Lycett, Eustace

American special effects technician, long with Disney, winning Oscars for his work on *Mary Poppins* (1964 – with Peter Ellenshaw and Hamilton Luske) and *Bedknobs and Broomsticks* (1971 – with Alan Maley and Danny Lee). Often works in collaboration with Danny Lee and Art Cruickshank.

Genre credits:
Darby O'Gill and the Little People (1959 – co-sp), *One-Hundred-and-One Dalmatians* (1961 – co-sp), *The Absent-Minded Professor* (1961 – co-sp), *Babes in Toyland* (1961 – co-sp), *Moon Pilot* (1961 – sp), *Son of Flubber* (1962 – co-sp), *The Monkey's Uncle* (1964 – co-sp), *Mary Poppins* (1964 – co-sp), *The Gnome Mobile* (1967 – co-sp), *Blackbeard's Ghost* (1967 – co-sp), *The Love Bug* (1968 – co-sp), *Million Dollar Duck* (1971 – sp), *Now You See Him, Now You Don't* (1972 – co-sp), *The World's Greatest Athlete* (1973 – co-sp), *Charley and the Angel* (1974 – co-sp), *Herbie Rides Again* (1974 – co-sp), *Freaky Friday* (1976 – co-sp), *The Shaggy DA* (1976 – co-sp), *Herbie Goes to Monte Carlo* (1977 – co-sp), *Return from Witch Mountain* (1978 – co-sp), *The Cat from Outer Space* (1978 – co-sp), *The Black Hole* (1979 – co-sp), *Herbie Goes Bananas* (1980 – co-sp)

Lydecker, Howard and Theodore

American special effects technicians working at the lower budget end of the genre.

Genre credits:
Tobor the Great (1954 – co-sp), *The Atomic Kid* (1954 – co-sp), *The Underwater City* (1961 – co-sp [Howard only]), *Way, Way Out* (1966 – co-sp [Howard only])

McCarthy, Kevin (1914-)

American character actor, best known for playing Miles Bennel in *Invasion of the Body Snatchers* and reprising the role in cameo form for the remake. His other credits include *The Misfits*, *The Prize*, *Piranha*, *The Howling*, *Ghoulies III* and *The Distinguished Gentleman*.

Genre credits:

Invasion of the Body Snatchers (1956), *Invasion of the Body Snatchers* (1978), *Captain Avenger* (1979), *Twilight Zone: The Movie* (1983), *Innerspace* (1987), *Eve of Destruction* (1990), *Matinee* (1993)

McClure, Doug (1935-1995)

American general purpose actor, perhaps best known for his role in TV's *The Virginian*. In films from 1957, he appeared in mainly routine productions. However, in the mid-70s, he came to Britain, where he appeared in a number of low budget fantasy adventures for producer John Dark and director Kevin Connor. His other films include *The Unforgiven*, *Shenandoah*, *Beau Geste*, *Humanoids from the Deep* (aka *Monster*), *Cannonball Run II* and *Maverick*.

Roddy McDowall spent most of the 70s in ape make-up for the *Planet of the Apes* film and TV series. Here he is playing Caesar, leader of the apes, in *Battle for the Planet of the Apes*, the fifth and last episode in the film series.

Genre credits:

The Land That Time Forgot (1975), *At the Earth's Core* (1976), *The People That Time Forgot* (1977), *Warlords of Atlantis* (1978)

McClure, Marc

American actor, perhaps best known for playing cub reporter Jimmy Olsen in the *Superman* movies. His other credits include *I Wanna Hold Your Hand*, and *Grim Prairie Tales*.

Genre credits:

Superman (1978), *Superman 2* (1980), *Superman 3* (1983), *Supergirl* (1984), *Back to the Future* (1985), *Amazon Women on the Moon* (1987), *Superman IV: The Quest for Peace* (1987)

MacDonald, Richard (1919-1993)

British production designer who worked on many of director Joseph

Losey's films, among them *The Sleeping Tiger*, *The Servant* and *Modesty Blaise*. His other credits include several for director John Schlesinger (*Far from the Madding Crowd*, *Day of the Locust*, *Marathon Man*, etc) and *Jesus Christ, Superstar*, *Swashbuckler*, *Altered States*, *Plenty*, *The Russia House* and *The Addams Family*.

Genre credits:

Something Wicked This Way Comes (1983), *Supergirl* (1984), *Electric Dreams* (1984), *Spacecamp* (1986)

McDowall, Roddy (1928-)

British actor (real name Roderick Andrew Anthony Jude McDowall) who, after appearing in a few British films in the 30s (*Scruffy*, *Murder in the Family*, *Poison Pen*, etc.), was evacuated to America in 1940 to escape the

McDowell, Malcolm (1943-)

British actor perhaps best known for playing Mick Travers in Lindsay Anderson's *If, O, Lucky Man* and *Britannia Hospital*. Also for playing Alex in Stanley Kubrick's *A Clockwork Orange*. In films from 1968 with a small part in *Poor Cow*, his other credits include *The Raging Moon*, *Aces High*, *Caligula* (title role), *Cat People*, *The Player* and *Bopha*! He was also responsible for killing off Captain Kirk in *Star Trek: Generations*.

Genre credits:
Time After Time (1979 – as H.G. Wells), *Britannia Hospital* (1982), *Class of 1999* (1989), *Moon 44* (1989), *Tank Girl* (1994), *Star Trek: Generations* (1994)

If looks could kill! Malcolm McDowell as Alex De Large in Stanley Kubrick's dated but still-controversial *A Clockwork Orange*.

London Blitz. There, he became a noted child star in such Hollywood films as *How Green was My Valley*, *My Friend Flicka* and *Lassie, Come Home*. After experience on Broadway he returned to the screen as an adult in a wide variety of roles in such films as *Cleopatra*, *The Poseidon Adventure*, *The Legend of Hell House*, *Evil Under the Sun* and, of course, four of the five *Planet of the Apes* films (and the TV series) in which he usually played Cornelius. A celebrated stills photographer, he has also directed one (unsuccessful) film, *Tam Lin* (aka *The Devil's Widow*).

Genre credits:
Planet of the Apes (1967), *Escape from the Planet of the Apes* (1971), *Conquest of the Planet of the Apes* (1972), *Battle for the Planet of the Apes* (1973), *Laserblast* (1978), *The Thief of Baghdad* (1978 – TVM), *Alice in Wonderland* (1985 – TVM), *Earth Angel* (1991 – TVM)

McEveety, Vincent

American director, long with Disney. He is the brother of producer Joseph L. McEveety and director Bernard McEveety. His credits include *Firecreek*, *The Biscuit Eater*, *Superdad*, *Gus*, *The Apple Dumpling Gang Rides Again*, *The Watcher in the Woods* and *Amy*.

Genre credits:
Million Dollar Duck (1971), *Charley and the Angel* (1973), *Wonder Woman* (1974 – TVM), *Herbie Goes to Monte Carlo* (1977), *Herbie Goes Bananas* (1980)

McMurray, Fred (1908-1991)

American star actor who, after success in such films as *Double Indemnity*, *The Caine Mutiny* and *The Apartment*, took up with Disney and appeared in such films as *The Absent-Minded Professor* (as Ned Brainard), *Bon Voyage*, *Follow Me, Boys* and *The Happiest Millionaire*.

Genre credits:
The Shaggy Dog (1959), *The Absent-Minded Professor* (1961), *Son of Flubber* (1962), *Charlie and the Angel* (1973), *Beyond the Bermuda Triangle* (1976 – TVM)

McQuarrie, Ralph

American production illustrator, design consultant, matte painter and conceptual artist, formerly an illustrator for the Boeing Company, Kaiser Graphics and CBS News (illustrating the Apollo missions) among others. Began his film career as an illustrator/storyboard artist on *Star Wars* and went on to win an Oscar for his effects work on *Cocoon* (1985 – with Ken Ralston, Scott Farrar and David Berry).

Genre credits:
Star Wars (1977 – concept artist/illustrator), *Close Encounters of the Third Kind* (1977 – illustrator), *Battlestar Galactica* (1979 – TVM – illustrator), *Close Encounters of the Third Kind – The Special Edition* (1980 – illustrator), *The Empire Strikes Back* (1980 – illustrator), *Raiders of the Lost Ark* (1981 – illustrator), *Return of the Jedi* (1983 – illustrator), *Cocoon* (1985 – co-sp)

Mad Max

Australia 1979 100m Eastmancolor Todd-AO 35

In a future dominated by violent motor cycle gangs, a lone cop avenges the running-down of his wife and baby son.

Very much a cult item, this low budget exploitation piece has a certain rough-hewn style to it and plenty of excitingly choreographed action sequences. Its success helped to launch both its director and star on the international scene.

p: Byron Kennedy for Mad Max

PTY/Kennedy-Miller

w: James McCausland, George Miller

d: GEORGE MILLER

ph: David Eggby

m: Brian May

ed: Tony Paterson, Cliff Hayes

ad: Jon Dowding

cos: Clare Griffin

sp: Chris Murray

sound: Gary Wilkins

stunt co-ordinator: Grant Page

2nd unit ph: Tim Stuart

titles: Bill Owen

Mel Gibson (who was dubbed for the American release), Joanne Samuel, Steve Bisley, Hugh Keays-Byrne, Tim Burns, Stephen Clark, Max Fairchild, Sheila Florence

---

Mad Max 2

Australia 1981 96m Colorfilm Panavision Dolby

In a future starved of fuel, an ex-road cop helps to protect an oil well from a vicious gang of bikers.

Slick, action-orientated sequel with plenty going on. A huge hit in America under the title *Road Warrior*.

p: Byron Kennedy for Kennedy Miller

w: Terry Hayes, George Miller, Brian Hannant

d: George Miller

ph: Dean Semler

m: Brian May

ed: David Stiven, Timm Wellburn, Michael Balson

ad: Graham Walker

cos: Norma Moriceau

sp: Jeffrey Clifford

sound: Lloyd Carrick, Roger Savage, Bruce Lamshed, Byron Kennedy

stunt co-ordinator: Max Aspin

make-up effects: Bob McCarron

Mel Gibson, Bruce Spence, Vernon Wells, Emil Minty, Max Phipps

---

Mad Max – Beyond Thunderdome ☁

Australia 1985 106m Technicolor Panavision Dolby

After deadly adventures in Batertown, Mad Max is cast out into the desert where he discovers a tribe of children whom he helps to escape to freedom.

Third and most commercially orientated of the Mad Max movies. Thinly plotted but visually arresting, with some well staged action sequences.

p: George Kennedy for Kennedy Miller

w: Terry Hayes, George Kennedy

d: GEORGE KENNEDY, GEORGE OGILVIE

ph: DEAN SEMLER

m: MAURICE JARRE

ed: Richard Francis-Bruce

pd: Graham "Grace" Walker

cos: Norma Moriceau

sp: Mike Wood

sound: Roger Savage, Lloyd Carrick

Mel Gibson, Tina Turner, Frank Thring, Bruce Spence, Helen Buday, Angelo Rossitto, Rob Grubb

---

Made in Heaven

USA 1987 103m Metrocolor Dolby

A young man dies, meets his ideal woman in heaven who is yet to be born, then tries to find her back on earth when he himself is reincarnated.

Misconceived, ill-shapen and uninteresting romantic fantasy.

p: Raynold Gideon, David Blocker, Bruce A. Evans for Lorimar

w: Bruce A. Evans, Raynold Gideon

d: Alan Rudolph

ph: Jan Kiesser

m: Mark Isham

ed: Tom Walls

pd: Paul Peters

cos: April Ferry

sound: Ron Judkins, Robert Jackson

Timothy Hutton, Kelly McGillis, Debra Winger (as a male guardian angel), Maureen Stapleton, Don Murray, Marj Dusay, Amanda Plummer, Mare Winningham, Timothy Daly, Tom Petty, Neil Young, Ellen Barkin, Tom Robbins, Ric Ocasek, Gary Larson

---

The Magic of Dr. Snuggles

Holland 1984 70m colour TVM

Dr. Snuggles enters a balloon race and helps repair an ailing rainbow.

Poorly animated feature-length version of the children's television series.

p: Joseph Adelman for Kiddpix/De Patie-Freleng

d: Jim Terry

m: Bullets

The Magic Toyshop

GB 1986 107m colour TVM

Two young children go to stay with their mysterious uncle at his toyshop.

Curious concoction of mystery, magic and special effects from the writer of *The Company of Wolves*. Very nicely made in parts, though whom it is aimed at is anyone's guess.

p: Steve Morrison for Granada

w: Angela Carter from her novel

d: David Wheatley

ph: Ken Morgan

m: Bill Connor

ed: Anthony Ham

pd: Stephen Fineren

Tom Bell, Caroline Milmoe, Kilian McKenna, Patricia Kerrigan, Lorcan Cranitch

---

Magical Mystery Tour

GB 1967 50m colour TVM

Passengers on a mystery tour find themselves involved in a series of increasingly surreal adventures.

Half-successful musical fantasia which plays like an early pop video. Fans of the Fab Four may find patches of it of interest, whilst others may find it all rather amateurish.

p: The Beatles, Denis O'Del, Gavrik Losey for Apple
w/d: The Beatles
ph: Aubrey Denar, Tony Busbridge, Daniel Lacamore, Mike Sarason
songs: The Beatles
md: George Martin
ed: Roy Benson
ad: Roger Graham, Keith Liddiard
sound: Michael Lax
The Beatles, Victor Spinetti, Jessie Robbins, Nat Jackley, Jan Carson, George Claydon, Derek Royce, Mandy Weet

The Magnetic Monster

USA 1953 75m bw
A radio-active element draws energy to itself causing a series of implosions of increasing size.

Brisk though now rather dated low budget sci-fi entry, one of the better examples of its kind.

p: Ivan Tors for UA
w: CURT SIODMAK, IVAN TORS
d: Curt Siodmak
ph: Charles Van Enger
m: Blaine Sanford
ed: Herbert L. Strock
pd: George Van Marter
Richard Carlson, King Donovan, Byron Foulger, Jean Byron

Mainwaring, Daniel (1902-1977)
American writer who also occasionally used the pseudonym Geoffrey Homes. Remembered chiefly for penning the original *Invasion of the Body Snatchers* (with an uncredited Sam Peckinpah). His other credits include *The Big Steal*, *The Gun Runners* and *The George Raft Story*.

Genre credits:
Invasion of the Body Snatchers (1956 – co-w), *Spacemaster X-7* (1958 – co-w), *Atlantis, the Lost Continent* (1960 – w)

Majors, Lee (1940-)
American actor (real name Harvey Lee Yeary II) known primarily for playing Steve Austin in TV's *The Six Million Dollar Man*. His other credits include *Will Penny*, *The Norseman*, *Killer Fish* and such TV series as *The Big Valley* and *The Fall Guy*.

Genre credits:
The Six Million Dollar Man (1973 – TVM), *Starflight One* (1983 – TVM), *The Return of the Six Million Dollar Man and the Bionic Woman* (1987 – TVM), *Scrooged* (1988), *Bionic Showdown* (1989 – TVM)

Making Mr. Right
USA 1987 98m Technicolor Dolby
A lady public relations officer is hired to help promote an android only to find herself falling in love with the prototype.

What might have made an amusing half hour is instead stretched to snapping point. Everyone tries hard, but beyond the central concept the movie has no substance.

p: Mike Wise, Joel Tuber for Orion
exec p: Susan Seidelman, Dan Enright
w: Laurie Frank, Floyd Byars
d: Susan Seidelman
ph: Edward Lachman
m: Chaz Jankel
ed: Andrew Mondshein
pd: Barbara Ling
cos: Rudy Dillon, Adelle Lutz
sp: Bran Ferren
sound: Howard Warren, Lee Dichter
make-up effects: John Caglione, Carl Fullerton, Doug Drexier
John Malkovich, Ann Magnuson, Polly

Bergen, Laurie Metcalfe, Hart Bochner, Glenne Headly, Ben Masters

The Man Called Flintstone
USA 1966 87m Technicolor
Fred Flintstone finds himself mistaken for a lookalike spy.

Reasonably amusing cartoon feature expanded from the popular TV show. It should please its intended audience, and is certainly more fun than the later live action version.

p: William Hanna, Joseph Barbera for Columbia/Hanna Barbera
w: Harvey Bullock, Ray Allen
story: William Hanna, Joseph Barbera, Warren Foster, Alex Lovy
d: William Hanna, Joseph Barbera
m: Marty Patch, Ted Nichols
songs: Doug Goodwin, John McCarty
voices: Alan Reed, Mel Blanc, Jean Vander Pyl, Gerry Johnson, Don Messick, June Foray, Harvey Korman, John Stephenson, Janet Waldo

Man in the Moon
GB 1960 99m bw
A man who earns his living as a human guinea pig is trained to be Britain's first astronaut.

Promising comedy which gradually peters out after a good start at a common cold research centre.

p: Michael Relph for Allied Film Makers/Excalibur
w: Bryan Forbes, Michael Relph
d: Basil Dearden
ph: Harry Waxman
m: Philip Green
ed: John D. Guthridge
pd: Don Ashton
sound: C. C. Stevens, Bill Daniels
2nd unit d: Norman Harrison
Kenneth More, Shirley Anne Field, Charles

Gray, Michael hordern, John Phillips, John Glyn-Jones, Norman Bird, Richard Pearson, Jeremy Lloyd

The Man in the Santa Claus Suit ☁

USA 1980 96m colour TVM

Santa Claus comes to earth in the guise of a fancy dress shop proprietor and helps various people have a happy Christmas.

Quite enjoyable venture into Damon Runyon country. Just what the season ordered.

p: Lee Miller for NBC
exec p: Dick Clark
w: George Kirgo
novel: Leonard Gershe
d: Corey Allen
ph: Woody Omens
m: Peter Matz
ed: Lovell Ellis
Fred Astaire, Gary Burghoff, John Byner, Bert Convy, Nanette Fabray, Harold Gould, Danny Wells, David Greenberg, Andre Gower, Carlo Imperato

The Man Who Fell to Earth ☁

GB 1976 138m Technicolor Panavision

An alien in search of water for his dying planet takes humanoid form in order to achieve his mission, but becomes an alcoholic in the process.

An immensely long and flashily tedious piece of pseudo science fiction with a confusing story made even more so by a barrage of alienating directorial tricks. Something of a cult item in some circles, nevertheless.

p: Michael Deely, Barry Spikings for British Lion
w: Paul Mayersburg

novel: Walter Trevis
d: Nicolas Roeg
ph: Anthony Richmond
md: John Phillips
ed: Graeme Clifford
pd: Brian Eatwell
sp: Peter Ellenshaw
David Bowie, Candy Clark, Rip Torn, Buck Henry, Bernie Casey, Jackson D. Kane

The Man Who Fell to Earth

USA 1986 96m Metrocolor TVM

An alien crashlands on earth and attempts to secure help for his ailing home planet which is suffering from a catastrophic drought.

Dismal TV remake of the David Bowie/Nicolas Roeg film, apparently intended as a pilot for a projected series which mercifully never materialised.

p: Lewis Chesler, Christopher Chulack for MGM
exec p: David Gerber
w: Richard Kletter
novel: Walter Trevis
d: Robert J. Roth
ph: Frederick Moore
m: Doug Timm
ed: John Carnochan, Gail Yasunaga
pd: John Mansbridge
cos: Marianna Elliott
sp: Charles E. Dolan
make-up: Tom Burman
sound: Bruce Bisenz, David Caldwell
stunt co-ordinator: John A. Moio
Lewis Smith, James Laurenson, Robert Picardo, Bruce McGill, Wil Wheaton, Annie Potts, Beverly D'Angelo

Mancini, Henry (1924–1994)

American composer/songwriter, best remembered for his *Pink Panther* scores and for the song *Moon River*, which won him an Oscar (1961 – with Johnny Mercer). He also won Oscars for his score for *Breakfast at Tiffany's* (1961), for the song *Days of Wine and Roses* (1962 – with Johnny Mercer, from the film of the same name) and for his song score for *Victor/Victoria* (1982 – with Leslie Bricusse). A graduate of the Juilliard School of Music, Mancini began his professional career after the war as a pianist and arranger for the Glenn Miller Orchestra. His film career began in 1952 when he became a staff composer at Universal, working (often annonymously) on countless low budget efforts, such as *Abbott and Costello Meet the Mummy* and *The Creature from the Black Lagoon*. In 1954 he came to attention when he earned an Oscar nomination for his music direction for *The Glenn Miller Story*, which he followed up with *The Benny Goodman Story* in 1955. Orson Welles' *Touch of Evil* followed in 1958, after which Universal terminated Mancini's contract, along with many other staff composers/arrangers/orchestrators. Luckily, he was hired by writer-director Blake Edwards to score his new television series *Peter Gunn*, the success of which led to a long-term association with the director, including such films as *The Pink Panther*, *A Shot in the Dark*, *The Great Race*, *Darling Lili*, *The Return of the Pink Panther*, *10*, *Blind Date* and *Son of the Pink Panther*. His other scores include *Charade*, *Hatari*, *Arabesque*, *Two for the Road*, *Silver Streak*, *Nightwing*, *Mommie Dearest* and *Without a Clue*.

Genre credits:
It Came from Outer Space (1953 – co-m), *The Creature from the Black Lagoon* (1954 – co-m), *Tarantula* (1955 – co-m), *Condorman* (1981), *Lifeforce* (1985 - co-m), *Santa Claus: The Movie* (1985), *The Great Mouse Detective* (1986 – aka *Basil, the Great Mouse Detective*), *Ghost Dad* (1990), *Switch* (1991),

Tom and Jerry: The Movie (1992)

Manga see Anime

Mannequin ☁

USA 1986 90m DuArt

A window dresser's dummy comes to life and falls in love with her creator.

Mildly agreeable comedy with bright patches between the flotsam and jetsam. The rather more dire *Mannequin Two: On the Move* followed in 1991.

p: Art Levinson for Gladden
exec p: Edward Rugoff, Joseph Farrell
w: Edward Rugoff, Michael Gottlieb
d: Michael Gottlieb
ph: Tim Suhrstedt
m: Sylvester Levay
ed: Richard Halsey
pd: Josan Russo
cos: Lisa Jensen
sp: Phil Cory
sound: Jay Brodin
2nd unit d: Buddy Joe Hooker
ANDREW MCCARTHY, Kim Catrall, Estelle Getty, G. W. Bailey, James Spader, Christopher Maher, Stephen Vinovich, Mesach Taylor

---

Mansbridge, John B.

American art director who spent most of his career at Disney, where he worked on several of their key live action fantasies.

Genre credits:
Blackbeard's Ghost (1967 – co-ad), *The Love Bug* (1968 – co-ad), *Million Dollar Duck* (1971 – co-ad), *Bedknobs and Broomsticks* (1971 – co-ad), *Now You See Him, Now You Don't* (1972 – co-ad), *The World's Greatest Athlete* (1973 – co-ad), *Herbie Rides Again* (1974 – co-ad), *Charley and the Angel* (1974 – ad), *Escape to Witch Mountain* (1974 – co-ad), *The Island at the Top of the World* (1974 – co-ad), *The Strongest Man in the World* (1975 – co-ad), *The Shaggy D.A.* (1976 – co-ad), *Freaky Friday* (1976 – co-ad), *Herbie Goes to Monte Carlo* (1977 – ad), *Return from Witch Mountain* (1978 – co-ad), *The Cat from Outer Space* (1978 – co-ad), *The Black Hole* (1979 – co-ad), *Herbie Goes Bananas* (1980 – co-ad), *The Man Who Fell to Earth* (1986 – TVM – pd)

M.A.N.T.I.S.

USA 1994 85m colour

A crippled scientist turns himself into M.A.N.T.I.S. (Mechanically Augmented Neuro-Transmitter Interceptor System), a superhero who conquers Ocean City's criminals with special paralysing darts.

Dim variation on *Robocop* with rather too much dull chat between the action and effects.

p: Steve Ecclesine for Universal
exec p: Sam Hamm, Sam Raimi, Robert Tapert
w: Sam Hamm
story: Sam Raimi, Sam Hamm
d: Eric Laneuville
ph: William Dill
m: Joseph LoDuca
ed: Steve Polivka
pd: Mick Strawn
cos: Winnie Brown
sp: Dean Robinson, KNB EFX Group
M.A.N.T.I.S. design: Denys Cowan
sound: Russell Williams
stunt co-ordinator: Bob Minor
Carl Lumbley, Bobby Hosea, Gina Torres, Steve James, Obba Babbatunde, Marcia Cross, Alan Fudge, Sam Raimi (as a student from Venus!)

The March of the Wooden Soldiers

see Babes in Toyland (1934)

Margheriti, Antonio (1930-)

Prolific Italian director who often works under the pseudonym Anthony M. Dawson. In films from 1950 as an assistant editor, he graduated to directing documentaries and travelogues in 1953 with *Vecchia Roma*. He began directing special effects in 1954 and writing screenplays in 1955, which led to his first feature film as a director in 1960. This was *Assignment: Outer Space* (aka *Spacemen*) which he also co-wrote. A mixture of science fiction, action and horror followed, among his credits being *Castle of Blood* (aka *La Danza Macabre*), *The Long Hair of Death* (aka *I Lunghi Capelli della Morte*), *Mr. Superinvisible*, *The Commander* and *Killer Fish*.

Genre credits:
La Notte Che la Terra Tremo (1959 – aka *The Night the Earth Shook* – sp), *Assignment: Outer Space* (1960 – aka *Spacemen* – co-w/d), *Battle of the Worlds* (1961 – aka *Il Pianeta degli Uomini Spenti* – d), *The Golden Arrow* (1962 – aka *La Freccia D'oro* – d), *Hercules, Prisoner of Evil Terror* (1964 – aka *Ursus il Terrore dei Kirghisi* – d), *Anthar the Invincible* (1964 – aka *The Devil of the Desert Against the Son of Hercules/Anthar L'invincible* – co-w/d), *The Giants of Rome* (1964 – aka *I Giganti di Roma* – d), *Wild, Wild Planet* (1965 – aka *I Criminali della Galassia* – co-p/d), *War of the Planets* (1965 – aka *I Diafinoidi Portano La Morte/I Diafanoidi Vengono da Marte* – co-p/d), *Snow Devils* (1965 – aka *I Diavoli dello Spazio* – co-p/d), *War Between the Planets* (1965 – aka *Planet on the Prowl/Missione Pianeta Errante/Il Pianeta Errante* – co-p/d), *The Unnaturals* (1969 – aka *Contronatura* – co-w/co-p/d), *The Humanoid* (1978 – aka *L'Umanoide* – d), *Yor, the Hunter from the Future* (1983 – aka *Il Mondo di Yor* – d), *Treasure Island in Space* (1986 – aka *La Isola del Tessoro* – TVM – d), *Aliens from the*

Abyss (1989 – aka *Alieni degli Abissi* – d)

Mars Attacks! 🛸

USA 1996 106m Technicolor Dolby

Martians arrive on earth and begin a plan of mass destruction, but salvation comes from the unlikeliest of sources.

Kitschy sci-fi spoof with excellent special effects and some undeniably funny sequences. The narrative is patchy at best, however, and the film eventually outstays its welcome. The starry cast also has little to do, save for Nicholson in dual roles. Despite its faults, certainly more fun than *Independcence Day*.

p: Tim Burton, Larry Franco for Warner
w: Jonathan Gems
story source: Topps Trading Cards
d: Tim Burton
ph: Peter Suschitzky
m: Danny Elfman
ed: Chris Lebenzon
pd: Wynn Thomas

cos: Colleen Attwood
sp: James Mitchell, Michael Fink, David Andrews, Michael Lantieri
sound: Randy Thom, Dennis L. Maitland, Sr
stunt co-ordinator: Joe Dunne

Jack Nicholson, Glenn Close, Annette Benning, Pierce Brosnan, Danny DeVito, Tom Jones, Lukas Haas, Martin Short, Sarah Jessica Parker, Michael J. Fox, Rod Steiger, Natalie Portman, Jim Brown, Sylvia Sidney, Lisa Marie, Paul Winfield, Pam Grier, Jack Black, Janice Rivera, Ray J, Joe Don Baker, Brandon Hammond, O-Lan Jones, Jerzy Skolimowski, Frank W. Welker (voice)

Marshall, Frank (1947-)

American producer, executive producer and director, often in association with his wife Kathleen Kennedy, with whom he produced many of Steven Spielberg's films in the 80s through their Amblin company. He began his career as an assistant to director Peter Bogdanovich, appearing in *Targets* and *The Last Picture Show*. He was also Bogdanovich's associate producer on *Paper Moon*, *Daisy Miller* and *Nickelodeon*. His directorial credits include *Arachnophobia* and *Alive*.

Genre credits:

Raiders of the Lost Ark (1981 – actor/p), *E.T.* (1982 – production supervisor only), *Twilight Zone: The Movie* (1983 – exec p), *Indiana Jones and the Temple of Doom* (1984 – co-exec p/co-2nd unit d), *Gremlins* (1984 – exec p), *The Goonies* (1985 – co-exec p), *Back to the Future* (1985 – co-exec p/2nd unit d), *An American Tail* (1986 – co-exec p), *Innerspace* (1987 – co-exec p), *Batteries Not Included* (1987 – co-exec p), *Who Framed Roger Rabbit?* (1988 – co-p), *Indiana Jones and the Last Crusade* (1989 – co-exec p/co-2nd unit d), *Back to the Future II* (1989 – co-exec p), *Always* (1989 – co-p/2nd unit d), *Back to the Future III* (1990 – co-exec p), *Gremlins 2: The New Batch* (1990 – co-exec p), *An American Tale: Fievel Goes West* (1991 – co-exec p), *Hook* (1991 – co-p), *The Indian in the Cupboard* (1995 – co-p)

Take that! The Martian ambassador takes Congress by surprise in director Tim Burton's sci-fi comedy *Mars Attacks!*

Mary Poppins

USA 1964 139m Technicolor Panavision
The fantastic adventures of two
Edwardian children, their magical
nanny and a chimney sweep named
Bert.

Though a little old-fashioned and
sweet to the tooth now, this is a generally lively and agreeable musical fantasy for children and their indulgent parents, with an array of excellent special
effects, cartoon elements, tricks and
songs to hold one's attention, despite
overlength and Dick Van Dyke's truly
horrendous attempt at Cockney.

p: Bill Walsh for Walt Disney
w: Bill Walsh, Don da Gradi
book: P. L. Travers
d: Robert Stevenson
ph: Edward Colman
songs: RICHARD M. AND ROBERT B.
SHERMAN (AA – also aa best song, *Chim
Chim Cheree*)
md: Irwin Kostal
ed: Cotton Warburton (aa)
ad: CARROLL CLARK, WILLIAM H. TUN-
TKE, TONY WALTON
cos: Bill Thomas, Tony Walton
sp: EUSTACE LYCETT (AA), PETER ELLEN-
SHAW, ROBERT A. MATTEY
sound: Robert O. Cook, Dean Thomas
animation d: Hamilton Luske
2nd unit d: Arthur J. Vitarelli
ch: Marc Breaux, Dee Dee Wood
Julie Andrews (aa), Dick Van Dyke (in two
roles), David Tomlinson, Glynis Johns,
Reginald Owen, Ed Wynn, Karen Dotrice,
Matthew Garber, Arthur Treacher, Jane
Darwell, Hermione Baddeley, Elsa
Lanchester

The Mask

USA 1994 101m Foto-Kem Dolby
A shy bank clerk is transformed into a
cartoon-like superhero when he dons a
mysterious mask he has found.

Comic book hokum, at its best dur-

ing the incredible effects sequences, on
which count it became a box office hit.

p: Bob Engelman for New Line/Dark Horse
w: Mike Werb
story: Michael Fallon, Mark Verheiden
d: Charles Russell
ph: John R. Leonetti
m: Randy Edelman
ed: Arthur Coburn
pd: Craig Stearns
sp: ILM, Ken Ralston, Scott Squires, Steve
Williams
make-up effects: Greg Cannom
Jim Carrey, Cameron Diaz, Peter Riegart,
Peter Greene, Amy Yasbeck, Richard Jeni,
Nancy Fish, Johnny Williams, Tim Bagley,
Orestes Matacena

Masters of the Universe

USA 1987 106m Metrocolor
He-Man battles the evil Skeletor for the
title of Master of the Universe.

Juvenile fantasy spectacular based
on a popular children's toy. Not too
bad for a Cannon film, but that's not
really saying much.

p: Evzen Kolar, Michael Flynn, Elliot Schick
for Cannon/Golan-Globus
exec p: Edward R. Pressman
w: David Odell
d: Gary Goddard
ph: Hanania Baer
m: Bill Conti
ed: Anne V. Coates
pd: William Stout
cos: Julie Weiss
sp: Richard Edlund
sound: Ed Novick
sound effects: John Paul Fasel
make-up effects: Michael Westmore
stunt co-ordinator: Walter Scott, Loren
Janes
titles: Wendell K. Baldwin, Kyle
Seidenbaum
Dolph Lungdren (as He-Man), Frank

Langella (as Skeletor), Meg Foster, Billy
Barty, Courtney Cox, Robert Duncan
McNeill, Jon Cypher, Chelsea Field

Masters, Tony

British art director/production designer whose most notable contribution to
the science fiction genre was the sets
he designed for *2001: A Space
Odyssey*, on which he worked with
Harry Lange, Ernest Archer and John
Hoesli.

Genre credits:
The Day the Earth Caught Fire (1961 – ad),
2001: A Space Odyssey (1968 – co-pd),
Zero Population Growth (1971 – aka
Z.P.G./The First of January – pd)

Matheson, Richard (1926-)

American novelist and short story
writer with many genre credits to his
name, including several of Roger
Corman's celebrated Poe adaptations
(*House of Usher*, *The Pit and the
Pendulum*, *The Raven*, etc.). He made
his screenplay debut in 1957 with *The
Incredible Shrinking Man*. His other
credits include *The Comedy of
Terrors*, *The Devil Rides Out*, *The
Legend of Hell House*, *Dracula*
(TVM), *Jaws 3D* and *Loose Cannons*.

Genre credits:
The Incredible Shrinking Man (1957 –
w/novel), *Master of the World* (1961 – w),
The Last Man on Earth (1964 – novel/co-w
[as William P. Leicester]), *The Omega Man*
(1971 – novel), *Somewhere in Time* (1980 –
w/novel), *The Incredible Shrinking Woman*
(1981 – based on *The Incredible Shrinking
Man*), *Twilight Zone – The Movie* (1983 –
co-w)

Mathews, Kirwin (1926-)

American leading man, a former teacher, perhaps best remembered for playing Sinbad in *The Seventh Voyage of Sinbad*. He made his movie debut in 1956 in *Five Against the House*. His other credits include *Maniac*, *The Pirates of Blood River*, *The Boy Who Cried Werewolf* and *Nightmare in Blood*.

Genre credits:

The Seventh Voyage of Sinbad (1958), *The Three Worlds of Gulliver* (1960), *Jack the Giant Killer* (1961), *Battle Beneath the Earth* (1968), *Octaman* (1971)

Mathison, Melissa

American screenwriter whose greatest success has been *E.T.* Her other credits include *The Black Stallion* and *The Escape Artist*. She is also married to actor Harrison Ford, whose second wife she is.

Genre credits:

E.T. (1982), *Twilight Zone: The Movie* (1983 – co-w [as Josh Rogan]), *The Indian in the Cupboard* (1995)

Matilda 🍦

USA 1996 90m Technicolor Dolby
A young girl with a passion for reading learns that she posesses magical powers, which she uses to usurp her evil headteacher Miss Trunchbull.

Engaging children's fantasy with enough humour and incident to endear it to parents as well.

p: Danny DeVito, Michael Shamberg, Stacey Sher, Liccy Dahl for Tri-Star/Jersey
exec p: Michael Peyser, Martin Bergman
w: Nicholas Kazan, Robin Swicord
novel: Roald Dahl
d: Danny DeVito

ph: Stefan Czapsky
m: David Newman
pd: Bill Brzeski
cos: Jane Ruhm
Mara Wilson, Danny DeVito, Rhea Perlman, Pam Ferris, Embeth Davidtz, Paul Reubens, Tracey Walter

Matinee

USA 1993 100m DeLuxe Dolby
During the Cuban missle crisis, a young boy besotted with horror films gets to meet his favourite producer who is premiering his latest picture in town.

Coming-of-age comedy drama offering an engaging blend of youth nostalgia and movie spoof.

p: Michael Finnell for Universal
w: Charles Haas
story: Jerico Haas, Charles Haas
d: Joe Dante
ph: John Hora
m: Jerry Goldsmith
ed: Marshall Harvey
pd: Steven Legler
cos: Isis Mussenden
sound: Howard Warren
John Goodman, Cathy Moriarty, Simon Fenton, Omri Katz, Kellie Martin, Lisa Jakub, Dick Miller, John Sayles, Jesse Lee

Matter of Life and Death, A 🍦🍦🍦🍦

USA 1946 104m Technicolor
After bailing out of his plane, a British airman discovers himself apparently caught between this world and the next and on trial for his life.

One of the Archers' finest achievements, this celebrated fantasy has just the right touch in all departments: rich colour, well judged performances and a perfect blend of humour, drama and audacity.

p: MICHAEL POWELL, EMERIC PRESS-BURGER for GTFD/The Archers
w/d: MICHAEL POWELL, EMERIC PRESSBURGER
ph: JACK CARDIFF
m: ALLAN GRAY
ed: REGINALD MILLS, JOHN SEABOURNE
cos: HEIN HECKROTH
sound: SC.C. Stevens
cam op: Geoffrey Unsworth
DAVID NIVEN, ROGER LIVESEY, KIM HUNTER, MARIUS GORING, RAYMOND MASSEY, ABRAHAM SOFAER, Richard Attenborough, Joan Maude, Kathleen Byron, Bona Colleano

Mattey, Robert A.

American special effects technician and effects photographer, perhaps best known for creating Bruce, the shark for *Jaws*. He began his career at Disney, after which he went independent.

Genre credits:

The Absent-Minded Professor (1961 – co-sp), *Son of Flubber* (1962 – co-sp), *Mary Poppins* (1964 – co-sp), *The Monkey's Uncle* (1964 – co-sp), *The Lost Continent* (1968 – co-sp)

Maximum Overdrive

USA 1986 97m Technicolor
A passing comet causes all things mechanical to go haywire in a North Carolina township.

Sometimes lively though mainly silly excuse for a series of destructive episodes.

p: Martha Schumacher for Dino de Laurentiis
w/d: Stephen King
ph: Armando Nannuzzi
m: AC-DC
ed: Evan Lottman
pd: Giorgio Postiglione
cos: Clifford Capone
Emilio Estevez, Pat Hingle, Yeardley Smith,

Laura Harrington, John Short, Ellen McElduff

Mayhew, Peter

Towering British actor, a former hospital porter who made his film debut in *Sinbad and the Eye of the Tiger*, in which he played the Minotaur. However, he is better known for playing Chewbacca in the *Star Wars* trilogy.

Genre credits:

Sinbad and the Eye of the Tiger (1977), *Star Wars* (1977), *The Empire Strikes Back* (1980), *Return of the Jedi* (1983)

Mazes and Monsters 🛸

USA 1983 96m colour TVM

Four college friends who play a fantasy role-playing game find that one of their number has been taken over by the game.

Odd but engaging drama with fantasy elements, a nice change from the usual cops and robbers TV movies.

p: Tom McDermott, Richard A. Briggs for CBS/Procter and Gamble/McDermott Productions
w: Tom Lazarus
novel: Rona Jaffe
d: Steven H. Stern
ph: Laszlo George
m: Hagood Hardy
ed: Bill Parker
ad: Trevor Williams
cos: Christopher Ryan, Aleida MacDonald
sound: Owen Langevin
Tom Hanks, Wendy Crewson, David Wallace, Chris Makepeace, Lloyd Bochner, Peter Donat, Anne Francis, Murray Hamilton, Vera Miles, Louise Sorel, Susan Strasberg, Chris Wiggins

Meddings, Derek (1931–1995)

British special effects technician, an Oscar winner for his work on *Superman* (1978 – with Les Bowie, Colin Chilvers, Denys Coop, Roy Field and Zoran Perisic). He began his film career as a title artist following training as an artist. He then went to make models at Anglo Scottish Pictures, after which he started doing matte paintings for effects man Les Bowie, working on a variety of pictures, including *The Trollenberg Terror* and several Hammer horrors. Then in 1957 he began what proved to be a lengthy association with producers Gerry and Sylvia Anderson, working on their TV series *The Adventures of Twizzle*, which in turn led to *Torchy the Battery Boy* and *Four Feather Falls*. Gradually, the Anderson's programmes became more ambitious, as did Meddings' effects for them, leading to such classic series as *Fireball XL5*, *Stingray* and

Former hospital porter Peter Mayhew made a big hit as the towering Chewbacca in *Star Wars*. Here he is accompanied by a disguised Luke Skywalker (Mark Hamill) on the right.

Thunderbirds, for which Meddings designed all the model work. Film work with the Andersons followed (*Thunderbirds Are Go*, *Thunderbird Six*, etc), as did a long association with the Bond films beginning with *Live and Let Die* and culminating with Meddings' last film *Goldeneye*. His other credits include *Aces High*, *The Man with the Golden Gun*, *For Your Eyes Only*, *Spies Like Us*, *Hudson Hawk* and *Cape Fear*.

Genre credits:

The Trollenberg Terror (1958 – aka *The Crawling Eye* – assistant sp), *Thunderbirds to the Rescue* (1966 – TVM – feature-length pilot for the television series – sp), *Thunderbirds Are Go!* (1966 – sp), *Thunderbird Six* (1968 – sp), *Journey to the Far Side of the Sun* (1969 – aka *Doppelganger* – sp), *Invasion: UFO* (1970 – TVM – sp), *Zero Population Growth* (1971 – aka *Z.P.G./The First of January* – sp), *The Land That Time Forgot* (1974 – co-sp), *The Spy Who Loved Me* (1974), *Superman* (1978 – co-sp), *Moonraker* (1979 – sp), *Superman 2* (1980 – co-sp), *Superman 3* (1983 – co-sp), *Krull* (1983 – sp), *Santa Claus* (1985 – co-sp), *High Spirits* (1988 – sp), *Batman* (1989 – co-sp), *The Never Ending Story II: The Next Chapter* (1990 – co-sp)

Medea

It/Fr/Ger 1969 118m Eastmancolor
Panavision

Jason takes as his wife the high priestess Medea, guardian of the magical golden fleece, a gift from the gods.

Sometimes visually arresting but otherwise deadly dull version of Euripides' play, which also served as the basis for the rather more fantasmagorical *Jason and the Argonauts*. Even culture vultures will tire of this well before the end, whilst fans of the legendary opera star Maria Callas will be dismayed to learn that not only does she not sing, but that she is also

dubbed.

p: Franco Rossellini for San Marco/Janus/Number One
w/d: Pier Paolo Pasolini
play: Euripides
ph: Ennio Guarnieri
m: Elsa Morante
ed: Nino Baragli
pd: Dante Ferretti, Nicolas Tamburro
cos: Piero Tosi
sound: Carlo Tarchi
Maria Callas, Giuseppe Gentile, Massimo Girotti, Laurent Terzieff, Franco Jacobbi, Piera Degli Esposti, Anna Maria Chio

---

Meet the Feebles

New Zealand 1989 96m colour

A temperamental hippo resorts to massacre when she is ousted from a variety show.

Determinedly outrageous puppet show which plays like the Muppets on acid. Its adults-only humour quickly palls, however.

p: Jim Booth, Peter Jackson for Wingnut
w: Daniel Muleron, Frances Walsh, Stephen Sinclair, Peter Jackson
d: Peter Jackson
ph: Murray Milne
m: Peter Dasent
ed: Jamie Selkirk
pd: Michael Kane
puppet design: Cameron Chittock
cos: Glenis Foster
sound: Grant Taylor
titles: Sue Rogers
voices: Donna Akersten, Stuart Devenie, Mark Hadlow, Ross Jolly, Peter Vere Jones, Mark Wright, Brian Sergent

---

Megaforce

USA 1982 95m colour

A secret force, headed by Ace Hunter, combats crime with the aid of souped-up motorcycles.

TV-like futuristic drivel with the usual array of tired stunts expected from this director.

p: Albert S. Rudy for Golden Harvest
w: James Whittaker, Albert S. Rudy, Andre Morgan, Hal Needham
d: Hal Needham
ph: Michael Butler
m: Jerrold Immel
ed: Patrick T. Roark
ad: Joel Schiller
Barry Bostwick, Michael Beck, Persis Khambatta, Edward Mulhare, George Furth, Henry Silva

---

Melchior, Ib (1917-)

Danish writer and director, a former stage actor who went to America in the early 40s where he continued to act on radio. He also designed sets for Radio City Music Hall. Began working for television in the 50s as an actor, writer and director, which led to his first feature film assignment, *Live Fast, Die Young*, in 1958.

Genre credits:

The Angry Red Planet (1959 – co-w/d), *Journey to the Seventh Planet* (1960 – co-w/montage sequences), Reptilicus (1962 – co-w), *The Time Travellers* (1964 – w/co-story/d), *Robinson Crusoe on Mars* (1964 – co-w), *Planet of the Vampires* (1965 – aka *Terror en el Espacio/Terrore nello Spacio* – co-w English language version only), *Death Race 2000* (1975 – original short story only)

Méliès, Georges (1861-1938)

Pioneering French director, a stage magician who began making simple "trick" films, such as *A Vanishing Lady*, as early as 1896, which he followed with an incredible 78 short films that same year. He built his own studio at Montreuil by 1897 where, under the

Star Films banner, he made 20 to 30 films a year. His most famous early film is the elaborate *Voyage to the Moon*, which provided the cinema with its first iconographic image. Business began to decline in 1908, yet Méliès persisted in churning out the same kind of production, though by this time the cinema had moved on. He retired from the movies in 1912 to pursue other interests, but never with the same degree of success. After years of obscurity, he was rediscovered in 1929, when he was named the father of fantasy film.

Selected genre credits:

The Vanishing Lady (1896), *The Fakir* (1896), *Conjuring* (1896), *The Cabinet of Mephistophiles* (1897), *The Bewitched Inn* (1897), *The Astronomer's Dream* (1898), *The X-Ray Novice* (1898), *Fantastical Illusions* (1898), *The Man with Four Heads* (1898), *She* (1899), *Cinderella* (1900), *One-Man Band* (1900), *The Bewitched Dungeon* (1900), *Little Red Riding Hood* (1901), *The Dream of a Hindu Beggar* (1901), *Indiarubber Head* (1901), *The Magician's Cavern* (1901), *The Human Fly* (1902), *Gulliver's Travels* (1902), *Voyage to the Moon* (1902 – aka *A Trip to the Moon*), *Jupiter's Thunderbolts* (1902), *The Animated Statue* (1903), *The Kingdom of the Fairies* (1903), *The Magic Lantern* (1903), *The Untamable Whiskers* (1904), *The Impossible Voyage* (1904), *The Chloroform Fiends* (1905), *The Legend of Rip Van Winkle* (1905), *Tunneling the English Channel* (1906), *20 000 Leagues Under the Sea* (1907), *The Living Doll* (1908), *The Indian Sorceror* (1908), *Baron Munchausen* (1911), *The Conquest of the Pole* (1912), *Cinderella* (1912)

Melle, Gil (1935-)

American composer, mostly for television. His film scores have generally been undistinguished and include *Frankenstein: The True Story* (TVM), *Embryo*, *Blood Beach* and *Restless*.

Genre credits:

The Andromeda Strain (1970), *The Ultimate Warrior* (1975), *Starship Invasions* (1977)

Memoirs of a Survivor

GB 1981 115m Technicolor

In the corrupt future, a woman escapes the violence around her by passing through time into a Victorian house.

Odd but overlong mixture of *Alice in Wonderland* and *1984*. A few points of interest, but it doesn't work because it doesn't go anywhere.

p: Michael Medwin, Penny Clark for EMI/Memorial
w: Kerry Crabbe, David Gladwell
novel: Doris Lessing
d: David Gladwell
ph: Walter Lassally
m: Mike Thorn
ed: William Shapter
pd: Keith Wilson
Julie Christie, Christopher Guard, Debbie Hutchings, Leonie Mellinger, Nigel Hawthorne, Pat Keen, John Comer

Men in Black 😕😕

USA 1997 90m Technicolor Dolby

A New York cop is invited to work for a top secret government agency which acts as an immigration regulator for aliens living on earth, only to find himself the planet's saviour.

Highly entertaining comedy which keeps moving and, for a change, doesn't outstay its welcome. Great fun, helped immeasurably by engaging performances from Smith and Jones.

p: Walter F. Parkes, Laurie MacDonald for Columbia/Amblin/MacDonald-Parkes Productions
exec p: Steven Spielberg
w: Ed Solomon
d: Barry Sonnenfeld
ph: Don Peterman
m: Danny Elfman
ed: Jim Miller
pd: Bo Welch
cos: Mary E. Vogt
sp: Eric Brevig, ILM
make-up effects: Rick Baker
sound: Peter F. Kurland
2nd unit d: Eric Brevig
2nd unit ph: Keith Peterman, David M. Dunlap
stunt co-ordinator: Gregg Smrz (sic)
titles: Open Films
TOMMY LEE JONES, WILL SMITH, Linda Fiorentino, Vincent D'Onofrio, Rip Torn, Tony Shalhoub, Siobhan Fallon, Mike Nussbaum, Jon Gries, Sergio Calderon, Michael Goldfinger (!), David Cross, Tim Blaney (voice), Mark Setrakian (voice), Brad Abrell (voice)

Menken, Alan (1950-)

American composer and songwriter who, with his former partner, lyricist Howard Ashman (1950-1991), wrote the stage musicals *God Bless You*, *Mr. Rosewater* and *Little Shop of Horrors* before going on to conquer Disney in the late 80s. He is an Oscar winner for his work on *The Little Mermaid* (1989 – best score and best song, *Under the Sea* [ly: Howard Ashman]), *Beauty and the Beast* (1991 – best score and best song, *Beauty and the Beast* [ly: Howard Ashman]), *Aladdin* (1992 – best score and best song, *A Whole New World* [ly: Tim Rice]) and *Pocahontas* (1995 – best score and best song, *Colors of the Wind* [ly: Stephen Schwartz]). His other credits include *Rocky V* (song), *Newsies* (aka *The Newsboys* – songscore), *Life with Mikey* (score) and *Home Alone 2: Lost in New York* (song).

Genre credits:

Little Shop of Horrors (1986 – m/co-songs), *The Little Mermaid* (1989 – m/co-songs), *Beauty and the Beast* (1991 – m/co-songs), *Aladdin* (1992 – m/co-songs), *The Return of Jafar* (1994 – TVM – co-songs), *Pocahontas* (1995 – m/co-songs), *The Hunchback of Notre Dame* (1996 – m/co-songs), *Hercules* (1997 – m/co-songs)

Menzies, William Cameron (1896-1957)

Celebrated American art director, an Oscar winner for his work on *The Tempest* (1928), *The Dove* (1928) and *Gone with the Wind* (1939 – special award). Began his career as an illustrator for advertisements and children's books before turning to art direction in 1918, his debut film being *The Naulahka*. He became one of Hollywood's top designers with such films as *Robin Hood*, *Bulldog Drummond*, *The Adventures of Tom Sawyer* and *Foreign Correspondent*. He also directed a handful of films, among them *Always Goodbye*, *The Green Cockatoo*, *Things to Come* and *The Maze*.

Genre credits:

The Thief of Baghdad (1923 – co-ad), *Chandu the Magician* (1932 – ad/co-d), *Alice in Wonderland* (1933 – co-w/ad), *Things to Come* (1936 co-ad/d), *The Thief of Baghdad* (1940 – associate p/co-ad/co-d), *Invaders from Mars* (1953 – ad/d)

Meteor

USA 1979 107m Technicolor Panavision

When the earth is threatened by a mammoth meteor, America and Russia have to combine their nuclear forces to repel it.

Lukewarm disaster melodrama which came too near the end of a fashionable cycle. The actors look suitably uncomfortable with their dialogue.

p: Arnold Orgolini, Theodore Parvin for Warner/Palladium
exec p: Sandy Howard, Gabriel Katzka, Sir Run Run Shaw
w: Stanley Mann, Edmund H. North
story: Edmund H. North
d: Ronald Neame
ph: Paul Lohmann
m: Laurence Rosenthal
ed: Carl Kress
pd: Edward Carfagno
cos: Albert Wolsky
sp: Margo Anderson, William Cruse
sound: Jack Solomon
stunt co-ordinator: Roger Creed
Sean Connery, Natalie Wood, Brian Keith, Trevor Howard, Henry Fonda, Martin Landau, Sybil Danning, Joseph Campanella, Richard Dysart, Bibi Besch

---

Metro Goldwyn Mayer (MGM/UA)

From the heyday of the silents through to the late 50s, MGM was the dominant Hollywood studio, churning out top quality musicals and dramas, though their record with science fiction, as with horror, has been fairly patchy, their crowning glories being *Forbidden Planet* in 1956 and Stanley Kubrick's *2001: A Space Odyssey* in 1968. They also produced one of the cinema's most enduring fantasies, *The Wizard of Oz*, in 1939. MGM began life in the 20s as Loewe's Inc., an exhibition company first merged with Metro Pictures, then with Goldwyn Productions to produce the world-famous logo.

Genre filmography:

Mysterious Island (1929), *Babes in Toyland* (1934 – aka *March of the Wooden Soldiers*), *The Wizard of Oz* (1939), *Anchors Aweigh* (1945), *The Next Voice You Hear* (1950), *Invitation to the Dance* (1956), *Forbidden Planet* (1956), *The Time Machine* (1960), *Village of the Damned* (1960), *Atlantis – The Lost Continent* (1960), *The Wonderful World of the Brothers Grimm* (1963), *Captain Sinbad* (1963), *Children of the Damned* (1963), *Hercules, Samson and Ulysses* (1965), *Around the World Under the Sea* (1966), *2001: A Space Odyssey* (1968), *Battle Beneath the Earth* (1968 – aka *Battle Beneath the Sea*), *Captain Nemo and the Underwater City* (1969), *The Phantom Tollbooth* (1969), *Brewster McCloud* (1970), *Earth II* (1971 – TVM), *The Tales of Beatrix Potter* (1971 – aka *Peter Rabbit and the Tales of Beatrix Potter*), *Soylent Green* (1973), *Westworld* (1973), *Logan's Run* (1976), *Demon Seed* (1976), *Clash of the Titans* (1981), *Brainstorm* (1983), *2010: Odyssey Two* (1984), *The Ice Pirates* (1984), *Solar Warriors* (1986 – aka *Solar Babies*), *Spaceballs* (1987), *Willow* (1988), *Species* (1995)

Metropolis

Ger 1926 75m, 120m, 128m, 139m, 182m, bw silent

In the future dissatisfed workers who are made to labour underground are coaxed into revolting by a robot version of a saintly girl they trust, which has been created by a mad scientist.

Important for its design, its themes (workers unite!) and its ground-breaking special effects, this much re-edited epic production is something of a slog to sit through yet it remains important viewing.

p: Erich Pommer for UFA
w: Thea Von Harbour, Fritz Lang
novel: Thea Von Harboul
d: Fritz Lang
ph: KARL FREUND, GUNTHER RITTAU
ad: OTTO HUNTE, ERICH KETTELHUT, KARL VOLBRECHT
cos: Aenne Willkom
sp: EUGENE SCHUFFTAN
BRIGITTE HELM, Gustav Frolich, Alfred Abel, Fritz Rasp, RUDOLF KLEIN-ROGGE,

Theodor Loos, Olaf Storm, Heinrich George, Grete Berger, Helene Weignel

Meyer, Nicholas (1945-)

American writer, director and novelist who made his way into movies via Paramount's publicity department. He then became a story editor at Warner, during which time he wrote his first script, *Invasion of the Bee Girls*, and his first novel, *The Seven per Cent Solution*, which was published in 1974. A screen version followed in 1976, for which Meyer wrote the script, earning himself an Oscar nomination into the bargain. Further novels followed (*Target Practice*, *The West End Horror*, etc). Meyer made his directorial debut in 1979 with *Time After Time* which in turn led to *Star Trek II: The Wrath of Khan*. His other directorial credits include *Volunteers*, *The Deceivers* and *Company Business*.

Genre credits:

Invasion of the Bee Girls (1973 – w), *Time After Time* (1979 – w/d), *The Night That Panicked America* (1975 – TVM – story/co-w), *Star Trek II: The Wrath of Khan* (1982 – d), *Star Trek IV: The Voyage Home* (1986 – co-w), *Star Trek VI: The Undiscovered Country* (1992 – co-w/d)

Michael ☺

USA 1996 92m Technicolor Dolby

Three tabloid journalists travel to mid-America where a motel owner claims she has an angel staying with her as a guest, and after her death he travels back to Chicago with them by car.

The plot may not sound up to much, but this is a surprisingly effective fantasy comedy-cum-road movie in which the three journalists find their lives enriched because of their experiences. It also doesn't outstay its welcome like

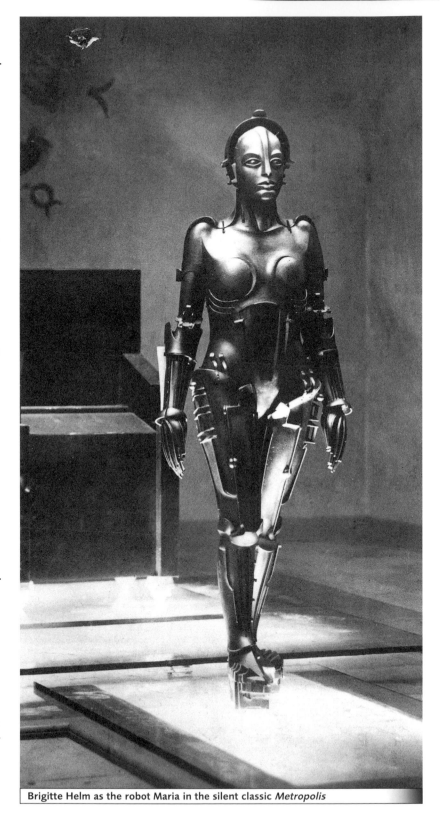

Brigitte Helm as the robot Maria in the silent classic *Metropolis*

so many films do today.

p: Sean Daniel, Nora Ephron, James Jacks for Turner/Alphaville
exec p: Delia Ephron, Jonathan D. Krane
w: Nora Ephron, Delia Ephron, Pete Dexter, Jim Quinlan
story: Pete Dexter, Jim Quinlan
d: Nora Ephron
ph: John Lindley
m: Randy Newman
ed: Geraldine Peroni
pd: Dan Davis
cos: Elizabeth McBride
sp: Ken Ralston, Alec Gillis, Tom Woodruff, Jr., Sony Pictures Imageworks
sound: Geoffery Lucius Patterson, Lee Dichter
ch: Juann Fregalette Jansen
stunt co-ordinator: Charlie Croughwell
John Travolta, Andie McDowell, William Hurt, Teri Garr, Bob Hoskins, Robert Pastorelli, Jean Stapleton, Joey Lauren Adams, Carla Gugino

Mickey's Christmas Carol 😕😕

USA 1983 26m Technicolor
Having been visited by three ghosts on Christmas Eve, Ebeneezer Scrooge is persuaded into being more charitable and less miserly.

Thoroughly charming animated version of the Dickens classic featuring all the famous Disney characters.

p: Burney Mattinson for Walt Disney
w: Burney Mattinson, Tony L. Marino, Ed Crombert, Don Griffith, Alan Young, Alan Dinehart
novel: CHARLES DICKENS
d: Burney Mattinson
m: Irwin Kostal
ly: Frederick Searles
ed: James Melton
ad: Don Griffith
voices: Alan Young, Clarence Nash, Wayne Allwine

Mighty Joe Young 😕

USA 1949 94m bw
A girl befriends a giant gorilla which she takes to New York, where it first causes panic, but later saves the day by rescuing orphans from their burning home (aah).

Predictable semi-sequel to *King Kong*, with tired dialogue and situations, though it does build to a pretty exciting climax followed, for once, by a happy ending.

p: Merian C. Cooper for RKO/Arko
exec p: John Ford, Merian C. Cooper
w: Ruth Rose
story: Merian C. Cooper
d: Ernest B. Schoedsack
ph: J. Roy Hunt
m: Roy Webb
md: Constantin Bakaleinikoff
ed: Ted Cheesman
ad: James Basevi, Howard Richmond
cos: Adele Balkan
sp: Willis O'Brien (aa), Ray Harryhausen, Peter Peterson
photographic effects: Harold Stine, Bert Willus
sound: Walter Elliott
Terry Morse, Robert Armstrong, Ben Johnson, Frank McHugh, Lora Lee Michel, Douglas Fawley, Regis Toomey

Mighty Morphin Power Rangers – The Movie

USA/Australia/Japan 1995 95m DeLuxe Dolby
Six teenagers with special powers usurp a gelatinous villain called Ivan Ooze.

Slick, fast-moving, action-packed kiddie fare which will make little sense to anyone unfamiliar with the phenomenally popular TV series on which it is based. A merchandising bonanza. *Mighty Morphin Power Rangers 2* followed in 1998.

p: Haim Saban, Shuki Levy, Suzanne Todd for TCF/Saban/Toei
w: Arne Olsen
story: John Kamps, Arne Olsen
d: Brian Spicer
ph: Paul Murphy
m: Graeme Revell
ed: Wayne Wahrman
pd: Craig Stearns
cos: Joseph Porro
sp: various
sound: Bob Clayton
2nd unit d: Gary Hymes
2nd unit ph: Ian Jones
stunt co-ordinator: Rocky McDonald
Karen Ashley, Johnny Yong Bosch, Steve Cardenas, Jason David Frank, Amy Jo Johnson, David Yost, Paul Schrier, Jason Narvy, Paul Freeman (as Ivan Ooze), Gabrielle Fitzpatrick, Nicholas Bell, Peta-Maree Rixon, Kerry Casey, Peter Mochrie

Millennium

USA 1989 108m DeLuxe
Time travellers return from the future to avert a catastrophe, but complications follow.

Dated time travel story whose central gimmick fails to convince. Adequate effects.

p: Douglas Leiterman, Robert Vince for Rank/Gladden
w: John Varley
d: Michael Anderson
ph: Rene Ohashi
m: Eric N. Robertson
ed: Ron Wisman
pd: Gene Rudolf
cos: Olga Dimitrov
sp: Sam Nicholson, Albert Whitlock
sound: Douglas Ganton, Paul Coombe, Don White, Marvin Berns
2nd unit ph: John Harris
make-up effects: Bob Laden
Kris Kristofferson, Cheryl Ladd, Daniel J. Travanti, Robert Joy, Lloyd Bochner, Berni Carver

Miller, Dick (1928-)

American actor, a long-time fixture of the Roger Corman school, now known for his cameo shots in the films of Joe Dante. Prior to acting he was, at various times, a disc jockey, TV talk show host, semi-pro footballer and psychologist. He made his film debut in 1955 in Corman's *Apache Woman*. His other credits include *Bucket of Blood*, *Little Shop of Horrors*, *The Premature Burial*, *The Dirty Dozen*, *TNT Jackson* (which he also co-scripted), *Piranha*, *The Howling*, *Chopping Mall* (aka *Killbots*), *After Hours*, *Pulp Fiction* and *Demon Knight*.

Genre credits:

It Conquered the World (1956), *Attack of the Crab Monsters* (1956), *Not of This Earth* (1957), *War of the Satellites* (1958), *Heartbeeps* (1981), *Twilight Zone: The Movie* (1983), *The Terminator* (1984), *Gremlins* (1984), *Night of the Creeps* (1986), *Innerspace* (1987), *Gremlins 2: The New Batch* (1990), *Evil Toons* (1991), *Matinee* (1993), *Batman: Mask of the Phantasm* (1994 – voice)

Miller, George (1945-)

Australian writer, producer and director, a former doctor, best known for helming the *Mad Max* films, the first two of which he made with his then partner Byron Kennedy, with whom he formed the production company Kennedy Miller. Sadly, Kennedy was killed in a helicopter crash in 1983. Miller's other films include *The Witches of Eastwick* and *Lorenzo's Oil*. (He is not to be confused with the other director George Miller (1943-) who was born in Scotland and works in Australia. His credits include *The Man from Snowy River*, *The Aviator*, *Anzacs* [TVM] and *The Never Ending Story II: The Next Chapter*).

Genre credits:

Mad Max (1979 – co-w/d), *Mad Max 2* (1981 – aka *The Road Warrior* – co-w/d), *Mad Max Beyond Thunderdome* (1985 – co-w/p/co-d), *Babe* (1995 – co-w/co-p)

Miller, Ron (1933-)

American producer and executive producer who joined the Walt Disney company in 1957, first working as an assistant director, then as an associate producer for the company's TV arm. Disney's son-in-law, he oversaw the majority of the studio's live action product in the 70s. He later became the company's president in 1979, a post he held until his resignation in 1984.

Non-fantasy credits include *Bon Voyage*, *That Darn Cat*, *The Boatniks*, *Candleshoe*, *Tex* and *Never Cry Wolf*.

Genre credits:

Moon Pilot (1961 – associate p), *The Misadventures of Merlin Jones* (1963 – assoc p), *The Monkey's Uncle* (1964 – co-p), *Now You See Him, Now You Don't* (1972 – p), *The Small One* (1977 – short – exec p), *Freaky Friday* (1976 – p), *Pete's Dragon* (1977 – p), *The Rescuers* (1977 – exec p), *Herbie Goes to Monte Carlo* (1977 – p), *The Cat from Outer Space* (1978 – co-p), *The Spaceman and King Arthur* (1979 – aka *Unidentified Flying Oddball* – p), *The Black Hole* (1979 – p), *Herbie Goes Bananas* (1980 – co-p), *The Fox and the Hound* (1981 – exec p), *Condorman* (1981 – exec p), *Splash!* (1984 – exec p), *The Black Cauldron* (1985 – exec p)

Million Dollar Duck

USA 1971 92m Technicolor

A mixture of apple sauce and radioactivity make a professor's duck lay eggs with solid gold yolks.

Undemanding Disney romp, rather typical of their live action output during this period.

p: Bill Anderson for Walt Disney
w: Roswell Rogers
story: Ted Key
d: Vincent McEveety
ph: William Snyder
m: Buddy Baker
ed: Lloyd L. Richardson
ad: John B. Mansbridge, Al Roelofs
cos: Chuck Keehne, Emily Sundby
sp: Eustace Lycette
sound: Robert O. Cook, Dean Thomas
titles: Ward Kimball, Ted Berman
2nd unit d: Arthur J. Vitarelli
Dean Jones, Sandy Dennis, Joe Flynn, Tony Roberts, Jack Kruschen, Lee Harcourt-Montgomery, James Gregory, Virginia Vincent, Jack Bender, Billy Bowles, Arthur Hunnicutt

The Mind Benders

GB 1963 113m bw

Scientists experiment on one of their colleagues with a sensory deprivation tank.

Glum but interesting scientific melodrama with engrossing passages.

p: Michael Relph for Anglo Amalgamated/Novus
w: James Kennaway
d: Basil Dearden
ph: Denys Coop
m: Georges Auric
ed: John D. Guthridge
ad: James Morahan
DIRK BOGARDE, John Clements, Mary Ure, Michael Bryant, Wendy Craig

Miracle on 34th Street

USA 1947 94m bw

Macy's Santa Claus claims that he is the real thing.

Sentimental whimsy which gets by on its star's performance rather than any ingenuity in the handling, though it is often pleasantly amusing along the way.

p: William Perlberg for TCF
w: George Seaton (aa)
story: Valentine Davies (aa)
d: George Seaton
ph: Charles Clarke, Lloyd Ahern
m: Cyril Mockridge
md: Alfred Newman
ed: Robert Simpson
ad: Richard Day, Ernest Lansing
cos: Kay Nelson, Charles Le Maire
sp: Fred Sersen
sound: Roger Heman, Arthur L. Kirbach
EDMUND GWENN (aa), Maureen O'Hara, John Payne, Natalie Wood, Gene Lockhart, Porter Hall, William Frawley, Jerome Cowan, Thelma Ritter

---

Miracle on 34th Street

USA 1994 114m DeLuxe
A department store Santa Claus claims to be the real thing and ends up in court as a consequence.

Slick-looking remake of the overrated 1947 Christmas favourite, let down by overlength, but made tolerable by Attenborough's cheery performance as Kris Kringle.

p: John Hughes for TCF
w: John Hughes (after George Seaton)
d: Les Mayfield
ph: Julio Macat
m: Bruce Broughton
ed: Raja Gosnell
pd: Doug Kraner
cos: Kathy O'Rear
RICHARD ATTENBOROUGH, Dylan McDermot, Elizabeth Perkins, Mara Wilson, Robert Prosky, J. T. Walsh, William Windom, James Remar, Joss Ackland, Simon Jones

---

Mollo, John

British costume designer, an Oscar winner for his work on *Star Wars* (1977) and *Gandhi* (1982 – with Bhanu Athaiya). His other credits include *Greystoke: The Legend of Tarzan, Lord of the Apes, Cry Freedom* and *Chaplin*.

Genre credits:

Star Wars (1977 – cos), *Alien* (1979 – cos), *The Empire Strikes Back* (1980 – co-cos), *Outland* (1981 – cos), *The Jungle Book* (1994 – aka *Rudyard Kipling's The Jungle Book* – cos), *Event Horizon* (1997 – cos)

The Monster from Green Hell

USA 1957 71m bw/colour
A rocket launched into space to chart the effect on various insects crash lands in Africa where the cargo grows to giant proportions.

Ludicrous grade Z schlocker which seems to consist mostly of stock footage from *Stanley and Livingstone.*

p: Al Zimbalist for Gross-Krasne
exec p: Jack J. Gross, Philip N. Krasne
w: Louis Vittes, Andre Bohen
d: Kenneth Crane
ph: Ray Flin
m: Albert Glasser
ed: Kenneth G. Krane
ad: Ernst Fetge
cos: Joe Dimmutt
sp: Jess Davidson, Jack Brabin, Louis de Witt
sound: Stanley Codey, Robert W. Roderick
Jim Davis, Barbara Turner, Eduardo Ciannelli, Robert E. Griffin, Joel Fluellen

---

The Monster That Challenged the World

USA 1957 83m bw
A giant caterpillar (!) threatens an isolated Californian military base.

Dim monster pic, very much of its period.

p: Arthur Gardner, Jules V. Levy for UA/Levy-Gardner-Laven
w: Pat Fielder
story: David Duncan
d: Arnold Laven
ph: Lester White
m: Heinz Roemheld
ed: John Faure
ad: James Vance
sp: August Lohman
sound: Charles Althaus, Joel Moss
underwater d: Paul Stader
underwater ph: Scotty Welborn
Tim Holt, Audrey Dalton, Hans Conreid, Harlan Warde, Casey Adams, Gordon Jones, Mimi Gibson

---

Moon 44

Germany 1989 99m Technicolor
Panavision Dolby
In the future, a troubleshooter is sent to a remote moon to discover who is sabotaging expensive mining equipment.

Derivative and unsavoury space thriller, sometimes good to look at, but sabotaged by hackneyed and cliché-ridden scripting.

p: Dean Heyde, Roland Emmerich for Spectrum/Centropolis
exec p: Michael A. P. Scording
w: Dean Heyde, Roland Emmerich
d: Roland Emmerich
ph: Karl Walter Lindenlaub
m: Joel Goldsmith
ed: Tony Wigland
pd: Oliver Scholl
cos: Ha Nguyen
Michael Pare, Lisa Eichhorn, Malcolm McDowell, Brian Thompson, Dean Devlin, Stephen Geoffreys, Leon Rippy, John March, Roscoe Lee Browne

---

Moon Pilot

USA 1961 99m Technicolor
An American astronaut is helped on his mission by a mysterious girl from

another planet.

Mild romp in the expected Disney live action style – ie: not too much style at all.

p: Ron Miller, Bill Anderson for Disney
w: Maurice Tombragel
story: Robert Buckner
d: James Neilson
ph: William Snyder
m: Paul Smith
songs: Richard M. and Robert B. Sherman
ed: Cotton Warburton
ad: Carroll Clark, Marvin Aubrey Davis
cos: Bill Thomas
sp: Eustace Lycett
sound: Robert O. Cook, Harry M. Lindgren

The future, 1969-style. Warren Mitchell, Bernard Bresslaw and Neil McCallum in a scene from Hammer's endearingly awful *Moon Zero Two*, which was billed as the first space western. Until *Battle Beyond the Stars* came along 11 years later, it was also the last.

Tom Tyron, Edmond O'Brien, Brian Keith, Dany Saval, Kent Smith, Tommy Kirk, Bob Sweeney

Moon Zero Two

GB 1969 100m Technicolor
On the moon, a crook hires a salvage operator to gain control of an asteroid made of sapphire.

Dim, over-talkative "space western" which muffs what few opportunities it has. *2001* it ain't.

p: Michael Carreras for Hammer
w: Michael Carreras
d: Roy Ward Baker
ph: Paul Beeson
m: Don Ellis
md: Philip Martell
ed: Spencer Reeve
ad: Scott MacGregor
sp: Les Bowie, Kit West, Colin Chilvers
James Olson, Catherina von Schell (later Catherine Schell), Warren Mitchell, Adrienne Corri, Ori Levy, Bernard Bresslaw, Michael Ripper, Dudley Foster, Neil McCallum

Moonraker

GB/FR 1979 126m Technicolor Panavision Dolby
James Bond prevents an industrialist's plans to take over the world from a space station.

Expensive, camped up, rather far-fetched Bond adventure which very quickly resolves itself into a series of set pieces. Not everybody's idea of a Bond movie, but good fun for those in the mood and put together with a certain degree of professionalism. The space station set is dazzling.

p: Albert R. Broccoli for UA/Eon/Les Productions Artistes Associés
w: Christopher Wood
novel: Ian Fleming
d: Lewis Gilbert
ph: Jean Tournier
m: JOHN BARRY
ly: Hal David
ed: John Glen
pd: KEN ADAM
cos: Jacques Fanteray
sp: DEREK MEDDINGS
sound: Daniel Brisseau, Gordon K. McCallum
titles: MAURICE BINDER
2nd unit d: John Glen, Ernest Day
2nd unit ph: Jacques Renoir
Roger Moore, Lois Chiles (as Holly Goodhead), Michael Londsale (as Hugo Drax), Corrine Clery, Bernard Lee, Desmond Llewellyn, Richard Kiel (as Jaws), Lois Maxwell, Walter Gotell, Toshiro Susa, Geoffrey Keen, Alfie Bass

Moontrap

USA 1988 92m colour
Two space shuttle astronauts discover an ancient craft orbiting the earth, and closer investigation reveals it not to be as derelict as they first thought.

Low budget schlocker, obviously inspired by *Alien*, but with none of that film's style or imagination.

p: Robert Dyke, John Cameron for Shapiro Glickenhaus Entertainment
w: Tex Ragsdale
d: Robert Dyke
ph: Peter Klein

m: Joseph LoDuca
pd: B. K. Taylor
sp: Gary Jones
Walter Koenig, Bruce Campbell, Leigh Lombardi, Tom Case, Judy Levitt, Robert Kurcz, John J. Saunders, Reavis Graham

Moonwalker

USA 1988 97m Technicolor Dolby
A fantasia of music, dance and special effects featuring Michael Jackson, resolving itself with an episode in which he prevents kids from becoming drug addicts.

More of an ego trip than a movie. A hit with Jackson fans on video, though it will send regular moviegoers running for cover.

p: Dennis E. Jones, John Romeyn, Jerry Kramer for Lorimar
exec p: Michael Jackson, Frank Dileo
w: David Newman
story: Michael Jackson
d: Colin Chilvers, Jerry Kramer
ph: John Hora, Tom Ackerman, Bob Collins, Fred Elmes, Crescenzo Notarile
songs: various
m: Bruce Broughton
ed: David E. Blewitt, Mitchell Sinoway, Dale Beldin
pd: Michael Ploog
ad: John Walker, Bryan Jones
cos: Betty Madden
sp: Dream Quest
sound: Bruce Bisenz, Don Lusby
ch: Michael Jackson, Vincent Paterson, Jeffrey Daniel
stunt co-ordinator: John Moid, Jack Gill
Michael Jackson, Joe Pesci, Sean Lennon, Kellie Parker, Brandon Adams

Moore, Ted (1914-1987)

Distinguished South African cinematographer, living in Britain from 1930. Became a camera assistant in

1932 and joined the RAF's Film Unit during the war. He became a camera operator in the 50s on such major films as *Outcast of the Islands*, *The African Queen* and *Genevieve*, becoming a cinematographer proper in 1955 with *Prize of Gold*. He worked with directors Terence Young and John Gilling most often during this period of his career and with Young later advanced onto the Bond films, of which he eventually photographed seven, including *Dr No*, *From Russia with Love*, *Goldfinger* and *Diamonds Are Forever*. He won an Oscar for *A Man for All Seasons* (1966). His other credits include *How to Murder a Rich Uncle*, *The Trials of Oscar Wilde*, *The Prime of Miss Jean Brodie*, *Psychomania*, *Orca – Killer Whale* and *Priest of Love*.

Genre credits:
The Gamma People (1955), *The Day of the Triffids* (1962), *The Golden Voyage of Sinbad* (1973), *Sinbad and the Eye of the Tiger* (1977), *Clash of the Titans* (1981)

Moranis, Rick (1954-)

Canadian comedy actor, perhaps best known for playing Louis Tully in the two *Ghostbusters* movies and Professor Wayne Szalinski in *Honey, I Shrunk the the Kids* and its two sequels (as well as the Disneyworld attraction *Honey, I Shrunk the Audience*). He first came to attention with his then partner Dave Thomas in the Canadian comedy show *SCTV* (*Second City Television*) which led to a spin-off movie called *Strange Brew* in 1983. This marked Moranis's movie debut (he also co-wrote and co-directed the movie). His other credits include *Brewster's Millions*, *Parenthood*, *My Blue Heaven* and *Splitting Heirs*.

Genre credits:

Ghostbusters (1984), *Streets of Fire* (1984), *Little Shop of Horrors* (1986 - as Seymour Krelbourne), *Spaceballs* (1987 – as Dark Helmet), *Ghostbusters 2* (1989), *Honey, I Shrunk the Kids* (1989), *Honey, I Blew Up the Kid* (1992), *The Flintstones* (1994 - as Barney Rubble), *Honey, We Shrunk Ourselves* (1996)

Moroder, Giorgio (1940-)

Italian composer on the international scene. He has won Oscars for *Midnight Express* (1978 – score), *Flashdance* (1983 – for the title song, with Keith Forsey and Irene Cara) and *Top Gun* (1986 – for the song *Take My Breath Away* with Tom Whitlock). His other scores include *American Gigolo*, *Cat People* and *Over the Top*.

Genre credits:

Superman III (1983 – co-m), *The Never Ending Story* (1984 – co-m), *Electric Dreams* (1984 – m), *Metropolis* (1985 – new score), *Never Ending Story II: The Next Chapter* (1990 – co-songs), *Cybereden* (1993 – m)

Morons from Outer Space

GB 1985 92m Technicolor

Three aliens crash land on the M1, are taken in hand by the government and turned into media stars.

Indulgent and rather juvenile comedy which quickly descends into a series of sketches, none of them particularly funny.

p: Barry Hanson for Thorn EMI
exec p: Verity Lambert
w: Mel Smith, Griff Rhys Jones
d: Mike Hodges
ph: Phil Meheux
m: Peter Brewis
ed: Peter Boyle

pd: Brian Eatwell
cos: May Routh
sp: David Speed
Mel Smith, Griff Rhys Jones, James B. Sikking, Jimmy Nail, Dinsdale Landen, Paul Brown, Joanne Pearce, Tristra, Jellinek, George Innes, Shane Rimmer, Ronnie Stevens, Leslie Grantham, Jimmy Mulville

---

Morris, Oswald (1915-)

Distinguished British cinematographer, an Oscar winner for his work on *Fiddler on the Roof* (1971). Began his career in 1932 as a camera assistant on quota quickies. After the war he graduated to camera operator and worked on such films as *Green for Danger*, *Oliver Twist* and *The Passionate Friends*. Became a fully fledged cinematographer in 1950 with *The Golden Salamander*. In 1952 he photographed *Moulin Rouge* for director John Huston, which led to several more pictures with the director, including *Moby Dick*, *Heaven Knows, Mr. Alison*, *Reflections in a Golden Eye* and *The Man Who Would Be King*. His other credits include *Look Back in Anger*, *The Entertainer*, *The Taming of the Shrew*, *Oliver!*, *Lady Caroline Lamb*, *The Man with the Golden Gun* (co-ph), *The Seven Per Cent Solution* and *Equus*.

Genre credits:

Scrooge (1970), *The Wiz* (1978), *The Great Muppet Caper* (1981), *The Dark Crystal* (1982)

Morrow, Jeff (1913–1993)

American actor, perhaps best remembered by genre fans for playing Exeter in *This Island Earth*. His other credits include *The Robe*, *The Story of Ruth* and *Harbour Lights*.

Genre credits:

This Island Earth (1955), *The Creature Walks Among Us* (1956), *The Giant Claw* (1957), *Octaman* (1973)

Mortal Kombat

USA 1995 101m Foto-Kem Dolby

Various martial artists are invited to a remote island for a fight tournament presided over by an evil sorceror who wants to take over the world.

Surprisingly well made blend of action and effects, all of which makes this the best of the video-game-to-movie transfers (also see *Super Marios Bros.*, *Streetfighter*, *Double Dragon*, etc.). Needless to say, one could write the story on the back of a stamp. (NB: Among the credits is one for Cappuccino Service!)

p: Lawrence Kasanoff for New Line/Threshold
exec p: Bob Engelman, Danny Simon
w: Kevin Dorney
d: Paul Anderson
ph: John R. Leonetti
m: George S. Clinton
ed: Martin Hunter
pd: JONATHAN CARLSON
cos: Ha Nguyen
sp: Daniel Lester, Alison Savitch, Kim Lavety and others
make-up effects: Alec Gillis, Tom Woodruff, Jr.
sound: Steve Nelson, David Farmer
stunt co-ordinator/fight ch: Pat E. Johnson
Christopher Lambert, Robin Shou, Bridgette Wilson, Cary Hiroyuki-Tagawa, Linden Ashby, Talisa Soto, Chris Casamassa, Gregory McKinney

---

Mosquito

USA 1994 85m colour

Mosquitos grow to an enormous size having fed off the blood of an alien whose spaceship has crashlanded near a woodland campsite. Naturally, the campers become prey to the giant insects.

Silly but lively low budget update of the giant bug movies of the 50s, with added 90s gore. An adequate late night schlocker for the uncritical.

p: David Thiry, Eric Pascarelli for Hemdale Communications/Acme/Excalibut/Antibes
exec p: Andre Blay, Larry Magid, Marc Schulman, Alan Kaplan
w: Gary Jones, Steve Hodge, Tom Chaney
d/story: Gary Jones
ph: Tom Chaney
m: Allen Lynch, Randall Lynch
ed: Tom Ludwig, Bill Shaffer
pd: Jeff Ginyard
sp: Richard Jake Jacobsen
sound: Jeffrey Caruana, Eric Pascarelli
Gunnar Hansen (who gets to use his trademark chainsaw at one point to destroy the bugs), Ron Ashton, Steve Dixon, Rachel Loiselle, Tim Lovelace, Mike Hard, Kenny Mugwump, John Reneaud

The Mouse on the Moon

GB 1963 85m Eastmancolor
Grand Fenwick launches its own space programme with a rocket powered by the country's explosive home-made wine.

Unimaginative sequel to the slightly more enjoyable *The Mouse That Roared*. One or two good jokes, but that's about it.

p: Walter Shenson for UA/Walter Shenson Productions
w: Michael Pertwee
novel: Leonard Wibberley
d: Richard Lester
ph: Wilkie Cooper
m: Ron Grainer
ed: Bill Lenny
ad: John Howell

cos: Anthony Mendleson
sound: Dudley Messenger, Bill Daniels
titles: Maurice Binder
Margaret Rutherford, Ron Moody, Bernard Cribbins, David Kossoff, Terry-Thomas, Michael Crawford, John le Mesurier, Graham Stark, Eric Barker, Robin Bailey, Clive Dunn, Frankie Howerd

Multiplicity

USA 1996 112m Technicolor Dolby
A building contractor harassed by work agrees to be cloned so as to ease his workload, but complications follow when his clone is cloned...

Would-be frantic farce, a high-concept movie which crashes and burns early on, unlike the same makers' *Groundhog Day*, the success of which it tries and fails to emulate. A disappointment.

p: Trevor Albert, Harold Ramis for Columbia
exec p: Lee R. Maves
w: Chris Miller, Mary Hale, Lowell Ganz, Babaloo Mandel
story: Chris Miller
d: Harold Ramis
ph: Laszlo Kovacs
m: George Fenton
ed: Pam Henning, Craig Henning
pd: Jackson De Govia
cos: Shay Cunliffe
sp: Richard Edlund
sound: Dennis L. Maitland, Sandy Berman
stunt co-ordinator: Mike Cassidy
Michael Keaton, Andie McDowell, Harris Yulin, Richard Masur, Eugene Levy, Anne Cusack, John De Lancie, Obba Babatunde

Munro, Caroline (1951-)

British horror starlet and game show hostess (on British TV's *3,2,1*) who has appeared as glamorous support in a variety of films, including *The Abominable Dr. Phibes*, *Dracula A. D.*

1972, *Captain Kronos – Vampire Hunter*, *The Last Horror Film*, *Don't Open Till Christmas*, *The Black Cat* and *Night Owl*.

Genre credits:

The Golden Voyage of Sinbad (1973), At the Earth's Core (1976), Starcrash (1979 – as Stella Starr), The Spy Who Loved Me (1977)

The Muppet Christmas Carol 🎩🎩

GB 1992 86m Technicolor Dolby
A miser is visited by three ghosts on Christmas Eve and is persuaded to mend his ways.

Delightful version of the Dickens favourite with all the famous characters played by the Muppets (Kermit as Bob Cratchit, Miss Piggy as Emily Cratchit, etc.).

p: Brian Henson, Martin G. Baker, Jerry Juhl for Walt Disney/Jim Henson Productions
exec p: Frank Oz
w: Jerry Juhl
novel: CHARLES DICKENS
d: BRIAN HENSON
ph: John Fenner
songs: Paul Williams
m: Miles Goodman
ed: Michael Jablow
pd: Val Strazovac
cos: Polly Smith
sound: Bobby Mackston
ch: Pat Garrett
Michael Caine (as Scrooge), Steven Mackintosh, Meredith Braun, Donald Austen, Robin Weaver; puppeteers/voices: Frank Oz, Jerry Nelson, Steve Whitmire, David Rudman, David Goelz, Brian Henson

The Muppet Movie 🎩🎩

GB/USA 1979 97m Eastmancolor Dolby
Kermit, Fozzie and Miss Piggy travel to Hollywood to become movie stars and have various adventures along the way.

Tim Curry's Long John Silver and Kevin Bishop's Jim Hawkins join Sam the Eagle, Kermit the Frog and Gonzo the Great aboard *The Hispaniola* for the lively *Muppet Treasure Island*, the fifth of the popular Muppet movies.

Captain Nemo (Herbert Lom) and company prepare to take on the monsters in Ray Harryhausen's effects spectacular *Mysterious Island*.

Rather enjoyable big screen romp featuring, for the first time, television's favourite puppets, with *Hellzapoppin'*-like gags and plenty of invention. A box office hit.

p: Jim Henson, David Lazer for ITC
exec p: Lew Grade
w: Jerry Juhl, Jack Burns
d: James Frawley
ph: ISIDORE MANKOFSKY
songs: Paul Williams, Kenny Ascher
ed: Chris Greenberg
pd: Joel Schiller
Charles Durning, Edgar Bergen, Elliott Gould, Telly Savalas, James Coburn, Milton Berle, Mel Brooks, Dom De Luise, Cloris Leachman, Orson Welles, Charles Sand, Bob Hope, Steve Martin; puppeteers/voices: Jim Henson, Frank Oz

The Muppets Take Manhattan 👒

USA 1984 94m Technicolor
The Muppets go to New York with the intention of staging their college revue on Broadway.

Generally entertaining addition to the Muppet cycle which, despite a few longueurs, has a sufficiency of lively moments, though the guest stars are given too little to do.

p: David Lear for Tri-Star
exec p: Jim Henson
w: Frank Oz, Tom Patchett
story: Tom Patchett, Jay Tarses
d: Frank Oz
ph: Robert Paynter
songs: Jeff Moss
m: Ralph Burns
ed: Evan Lottman
ad: Stephen Hendrickson
cos: Karen Rosion, Calista Hendrickson, Polly Smith
sp: Ed Drohan
sound: Les Lazarowitz
ch: Chris Chadman
Art Carney, James Coco, Elliott Gould, Dabney Coleman, Joan Rivers, Brooke Shields, Gregory Hines, Linda Lavin, Liza Minnelli, Juliana Donald, Lonny Price, Louis Zorich; puppeteers/voices: Jim Henson, Frank Oz

Muppet Treasure Island 👒

USA/GB 1996 99m Technicolor
The Muppets set off for the Caribbean in search of buried treasure.

Lively musical spoof of the much-filmed Robert Louis Stevenson classic, with plenty of gags to buoy the familiar story.

p: Brian Henson, Martin G. Baker for Buena Vista/Jim Henson
exec p: Frank Oz
w: Jerry Juhl, James V. Hart, Kirk R. Thatcher
novel: Robert Louis Stevenson
d: Brian Henson
ph: John Fenner
songs: Barry Mann, Cynthia Weil
m: Hans Zimmer
ed: Michael Jablow
pd: Val Strazovec
cos: Polly Smith
sp: Jim Henson's Creature Shop, Thomas G.

Smith, Nick Alklder and others
sound: Peter Lindsay
2nd unit d: David Lane, Selwyn Roberts
2nd unit ph: Tony Spratling
ch: Pat Garrett
Tim Curry, Kevin Bishop, Jennifer Saunders, Billy Connolly, voices: Dave Goelz, Steve Whitmore, Jerry Nelson, Kevin Clash, Bill Barretta, Frank Oz

---

Murder on the Moon

GB 1989 96m colour TVM
In 2015, the body of an American is found in the Russian sector of the moon. A politically fraught investigation follows.

The lunar setting fails to add anything special to this wholly routine murder mystery.

p: Tamara Asseyev for LWT/Viacom International
exec p: Nick Elliott
w: Carla Jean Wagner
d: Michael Lindsay-Hogg
ph: David Watkin
m: Trevor Jones
ed: Robert K. Lambert, Ralph Sheldon
pd: Austin Spriggs
cos: Jane Robinson
sp: Grahame Longhurst, Dave Watkins
sound: David Crozier
titles: Louis Schwartzberg
stunt co-ordinator: Rocky Taylor
Brigitte Nielsen, Julian Sands, Jane Lapotaire, Brian Cox, Gerald McRaney, Celia Imrie, David Yip, Georgina Hale, Michael J. Shannon

---

Muren, Dennis

American special effects technician, long with ILM, where he began as a second cameraman on *Star Wars*. He is now the company's senior visual effects supervisor and has won Oscars for his work on *The Empire Strikes Back* (1980 – with Brian Johnson, Richard Edlund and Bruce Nicholson), *E.T.* (1982 – with Carlo Rambaldi and Kenneth F. Smith), *Return of the Jedi* (1983 – with Richard Edluund, Ken Ralston and Phil Tippet), *Indiana Jones and the Temple of Doom* (1984 – with Michael McAlister, Lorne Peterson and George Gibbs), *Innerspace* (1987 – with William George, Harley Jessup and Kenneth Smith), *The Abyss* (1989 – with John Bruno, Hoyt Yeatman and Dennis Skotak), *Terminator 2: Judgement Day* (1991 – with Stan Winston, Robert Skotak and Gene Warren, Jr.) and *Jurassic Park* (1993 – with Stan Winston, Phil Tippet and Michael Lantieri). Phew!

Genre credits:
Willy Wonka and the Chocolate Factory (1971 – co-sp), *Star Wars* (1977 – co-sp), *Close Encounters of the Third Kind* (1977 – co-sp), *Battlestar Galactica* (1979 – TVM – co-sp), *The Empire Strikes Back* (1980 – co-sp), *Close Encounters of the Third Kind – The Special Edition* (1980 – co-sp), *E.T.* (1982 – co-sp), *Return of the Jedi* (1983 – co-sp), *Young Sherlock Holmes* (1985 – aka *Young Sherlock Holmes and the Pyramid of Fear* – co-sp), *Innerspace* (1987 – co-sp), *Willow* (1988 – co-sp), *Ghostbusters II* (1989 – sp), *The Abyss* (1989 – co-sp), *Terminator 2: Judgement Day* (1991 – co-sp), *Jurassic Park* (1993 – co-sp), *Casper* (1995 – co-sp), *The Lost World: Jurassic Park* (1997 – co-sp)

My Stepmother is an Alien

USA 1988 107m Technicolor
A scientist accidentally imperils another planet with one of his experiments, and a beautiful alien is sent to help him put things right.

Generally embarrassing comedy with a few mild laughs for the simpleminded.

p: Franklin R. Levy, Ronald Parker for Weintraub Entertainment
exec p: Laurence Mark, Art Levinson
w: Jerico Weingrod, Herschel Weingrod, Timothy Harris, Jonathan Reynolds
d: Richard Benjamin
ph: Richard H. Kline
m: Alan Silvestri
ed: Jacqueline Cambas
pd: Charles Rosen
cos: Aggie Guerard Rodgers
sp: John Dykstra
sound: Jerry Jost
Dan Aykroyd, Kim Basinger, Jon Lovitz, Alyson Hannigan, Joseph Maher, Seth Green, Adrian Sparks, Wesley Mann, Ann Prentiss (voice)

Mysterious Island

USA 1961 100m Technicolor
Superdynamation
In 1865 Americna soldiers escaping capture by balloon land on an uncharted island where they encounter various monsters and are later saved froma volcanic erruption by Captain Nemo.

Generally engaging mixture of adventure, thrills and trick photography for children of all ages.

p: Charles H. Schneer for Columbia/Ameran
w: John Prebble, Dan Ullman, Crane Wilbur
novel: Jules Verne
d: Cy Endfield
ph: Wilkie Cooper
m: BERNARD HERRMANN
ed: Frederick Wilson
ad: Bill Andrews
sp: RAY HARRYHAUSEN
sound: John Cox, Bob Jones, Peter Handford
underwater ph: Egil Woxholt
titles: Bill Gill
Joan Greenwood, Michael Craig, Herbert Lom (as Captain Nemo), Michael Callan, Gary Merrill, Nigel Green, Percy Herbert, Beth Ryan

Nader, George (1921-)

American actor with a penchant for action roles. In films from 1952 with *Monsoon*, his genre work has been mostly undistinguished. His other credits include *Four Guns to the Border*, *Congo Crossing* and *Four Girls in Town*. He was also familiar to TV audiences in the 50s in such shows as *Ellery Queen* and *The Man and the Challenge*.

Genre credits:
Robot Monster (1953 – aka *Monster from the Moon*), *The Human Duplicators* (1965), *Beyond Atlantis* (1973)

Naha, Ed

American screenplay writer, a former fanzine journalist and author (*The Making of Dune*, *The Films of Roger Corman – Brilliance on a Budget*, etc.).

Genre credits:
Troll (1986 – w), *C.H.U.D. II: Bud the C.H.U.D.* (1989 – w), *Honey, I Shrunk the Kids* (1989 – co-w), *Matinee* (1992 – co-w)

Nascimbene, Mario (1916-)

Italian composer, trained at Milan's Giuseppe Verdi Conservatory. Perhaps best known for his sword-and-sandal scores, which include *Alexander the Great*, *Solomon and Sheba*, *Barabbas* and, of course, *The Vikings*. Also scored several of Hammer's prehistoric epics.

Genre credits:
One Million Years B. C. (1966), *The Vengeance of She* (1968), *When Dinosaurs Ruled the Earth* (1970), *Creatures the World Forgot* (1971)

Nash, Michael

see Carreras, Michael

The Navigator: A Medieval Odyssey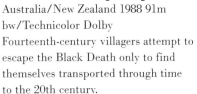

Australia/New Zealand 1988 91m bw/Technicolor Dolby
Fourteenth-century villagers attempt to escape the Black Death only to find themselves transported through time to the 20th century.

Curious fantasy, more interesting for its concept than for its execution, which tends to be a little on the flashy side.

p: John Maynard, Gary Hannam for Recorded Releasing/Arenafilm
w: Vincent Ward, Kely Lyons, Geoff Chapple
d/story: Vincent Ward
ph: Geoffrey Simpson
m: Davood A. Tabrizi
ed: John Scott
pd: Sally Campbell
cos: Glenys Jackson
sp: Ken Durey, Paul Nichola
sound: Dick Reade, Phil Judd
stunt co-ordinator: Timothy Lea
Bruce Lyons, Hamish McFarlane, Marshall Napier, Chris Heywood, Mark Wheatley, Tony Herbert, Noel Appleby, Sarah Pierse, Paul Livingstone

Needs, James

Busy British editor and editorial supervisor, a Hammer mainstay until the mid-70s. He seems to have had a hand in practically every film the studio made, including a good deal of their non-horrors. He cut practically every one of Hammer's horror classics (*The Curse of Frankenstein*, *Dracula*, *The Mummy*, *The Devil Rides Out*, etc.).

Genre credits:
The Quatermass Experiment (1955 – aka *The Creeping Unknown* m – ed), *X – The Unknown* (1956 – ed), *Quatermass 2* (1957 – aka *Enemy from Space* – ed), *The Damned* (1963 – aka *These Are the Damned* – co-ed), *One Million Years B. C.* (1966 – co-ed), *Quatermass and the Pit* (1967 – aka *Five Million Years to Earth* – co-ed), *Slave Girls* (1968 – aka *Prehistoric Women* – co-ed), *The Lost Continent* (1968 – co-ed)

Neil, Ve

Award-winning make-up artist who has won Oscars for *Beetlejuice* (1988 – with Steve La Porte and Robert Short), *Mrs Doubtfire* (1993 – with Greg Cannom and Yolanda Toussieng) and *Ed Wood* (1994 – with Rick Baker and Yolanda Toussieng). Has worked much with director Tim Burton.

Genre credits:
Laserblast (1976 – co-make-up), *The Day Time Ended* (1979 – make-up), *Star Trek* (1979 – co-make-up), *The Incredible Shrinking Woman* (1981 – co-make-up), *Beetlejuice* (1988 – co-make-up), *Edward Scissorhands* (1990 – co-make-up), *Batman Returns* (1992 – co-make-up)

Nemec III, Joseph

American production designer with many large-scale movies to his credit, among them *Patriot Games* and *The Getaway* (remake). Studied to be an architect before turning to theatre and film design.

Genre credits:
Terminator 2: Judgement Day (1992), *The Shadow* (1994)

Nemesis
USA 1992 94m colour
In 2027 Los Angeles a part-cyborg cop battles with a group of androids whose intention is to take over the world by imitating its leaders.

Another low budet re-hash of themes lifted from *Robocop*, *Blade Runner* etc. As with most of its director's films, routine in practically every way, though it was still followed by two sequels.

p: Ash R Shah, Eric Karson, Tom Karnowski for Imperial/Shah-Jensen
w: Rebecca Charles
d: Albert Pyun
ph: George Mooradian
m: Michael Rubini
ed: David Kern, Mark Conte
pd: E. Colleen Saro
sp: Fantasy II, Gene Warren Jr
Oliver Gruner, Tim Thomerson, Merel Kennedy, Marjorie Monaghan, Deborah Shelton, Brion James, Nicholas Guest, Jackie Earle Haley

Neuman, Kurt (1906/8 – 1958)
German writer, producer and director, in American from 1925. He began his career directing shorts. He has a handful of Tarzan credits to his name (*Tarzan and the Amazons*, *Tarzan and the Leopard Woman*, *Tarzan and the Huntress*, etc.) as well as such low budgeters as *The Secret of the Blue Room*, *Ellery Queen – Master Detective* and *Circus of Love*.

Genre credits:
Rocketship X-M (1950 – w/p/d), *Kronos* (1957 – p/d), *She Devil* (1957 – co-w/p/d), *The Fly* (1958 – p/d)

The Never Ending Story
Ger 1984 95m Technicolor Technovision
A young boy becomes involved in the fairy tale he is reading and is thus able to save a magical kingdom.

Expensive fantasy adventure which, despite occasional pleasing visuals, fails to involve one in its story, such that it is. It was followed by *The Never Ending Story II: The Next Chapter* (1990) and *The Never Ending Story III* (1994).

p: Bernd Eichinger, Dieter Geissler for Warner/Bavaria/WDR
exec p: Neu Constantin, Mark Damon, John Hyde
w/d: Wolfgang Petersen
novel: Michael Ende
ph: Jost Vacano
m: Klaus Doldinger, Giorgio Moroder
ed: Jane Seitz
pd: ROLF ZEHETBAUER
sp: Brian Johnson
sound: Mike Le Mare
conceptual artist: Ul de Rico
Barrett Oliver, Gerald McRaney, Moses Gunn, Patricia Hayes, Noah Hathaway

A New Hope
see Star Wars

Nichols, Nichelle (1933-)
African-American actress, singer, dancer and cabaret artiste, remembered for playing Uhura in the *Star Trek* television and film series (she also provided Uhura's voice for the animated television series of *Star Trek* in 1973). Trained as a ballet dancer before starting her career in revue. Made her movie debut in *Porgy and Bess* in 1959. Her television debut followed in 1964 in an episode of *The Lieutenant*, which was created by future *Star Trek* creator and producer Gene Roddenberry. Her other films include *Made in Paris* and *Mr. Buddwing*.

Genre credits:
Star Trek – The Motion Picture (1979), *Star Trek II: The Wrath of Khan* (1982), *Star Trek III: The Search for Spock* (1984), *Star Trek IV: The Voyage Home* (1986), *Star Trek V: The Final Frontier* (1989), *Star Trek VI: The Undiscovered Country* (1991)

Nicholson, Bruce
American special effects technician and effects supervisor, long with ILM, where he began as an optical camera assistant on *Star Wars*. He has won Oscars for his work on *The Empire Strikes Back* (1980 – with Richard Edlund, Dennis Muren and Brian Johnson) and *Raiders of the Lost Ark* (1981 – with Richard Edlund, Kit West and Joe Johnston). He now heads ILM's optical department.

Genre credits:
Star Wars (1977 – co-sp), *Close Encounters of the Third Kind* (1977 – co-sp), *Battlestar Galactica* (1979 – TVM – co-sp), *The Empire Strikes Back* (1980 – co-sp), *Close Encounters of the Third Kind – The Special Edition* (1980 – co-sp), *Raiders of the Lost Ark* (1981 – co-sp), *Return of the Jedi* (1983 – co-sp), *Starman* (1984 – co-sp), *Field of Dreams* (1989 – co-sp), *Village of the Damned* (1995 – sp)

Nicholson, James H. (1916-1972)

American producer and executive producer, long in association with his partner, Samuel Z. Arkoff, with whom he founded American International Pictures (AIP) in 1955, which produced a number of Roger Corman's films, along with dozens of sci-fi and exploitation items, including *I Was a Teenage Frankenstein*, *Blood of Dracula*, *How to Make a Monster*, *House of Usher*, *Tales of Terror*, *The Abominable Dr. Phibes*, etc.

Genre credits:

It Conquered the World (1956 – exec p), *Invasion of the Saucer Men* (1957 – co-p), *Terror from the Year 5000* (1958 – aka *Cage of Doom* – co-exec p), *Teenage Caveman* (1958 – aka *Out of the Darkness* – co-exec p), *Night of the Blood Beast* (1958 – co-exec p), *Master of the World* (1961 – co-p), *Panic in Year Zero* (1962 – co-exec p), *Sergeant Deadhead the Astronaut* (1965 – aka *Sergeant Deadhead* – co-p), *Dr. Goldfoot and the Bikini Machine* (1965 – aka *Dr. G. and the Bikini Machine* – co-p), *Wild in the Streets* (1968 – co-p)

The Night Caller

GB 1965 84m bw

Scientists find themselves in danger from a curious orb from outer space.

Straightforward low budgeter with moments of style. An adequate late night offering.

p: Ronald Liles for Armitage/New Art
exec p: John Phillips
w: Jim O'Connolly
novel: Frank Crisp
d: John Gilling
ph: Stephen Dade
m: Johnny Gregory
ed: Philip Barnikel
ad: Harry White
cos: Duncan McPhee

sound: John Cox, Kevin Sutton
John Saxon, Maurice Denham, Patricia Haines, John Carson, Jack Watson, Alfred Burke, Warren Mitchell, Aubrey Morris, Ballard Berkeley, Marianne Stone

Night of the Big Heat

GB 1967 94m Eastmancolor

In order to survive, aliens make a remote Scottish island unbearably hot.

Unremarkable lower berth genre pic, not that dissimilar to the same makers' *Island of Terror*.

p: Ronald Liles for Planet
exec p: Tom Blakeley
w: Ronald Liles, Pip Barker, Jane Barker
novel: John Lymington
d: Terence Fisher
ph: Reg Wyer
m: Malcolm Lockyer
ed: Rod Keys
ad: Alex Vetchinsky
cos: Kathleen Moore
sound: Dudley Messenger, E. Karnon
Christopher Lee, Patrick Allen, Peter Cushing, Sarah Lawson, Jane Merrow, William Lucas, Kenneth Cope

Night of the Comet

USA 1984 96m Technicolor

Two sisters have to fend for themselves when a comet turns the earth's population into carnivorous zombies.

Amusing low budget science fiction horror piece in the B picture manner.

p: Wayne Crawford, Andrew Wayne for Atlantic
w/d: Thom Eberhardt
ph: Arthur Albert
m: David Richard Campbell
md: Don Perry
ed: Fred Stafford
pd: John Muto
cos: Linda Linn
sp: Court Wizard, John Muto

sound: Steve Nelson
titles: Mark Sawicki
Catherine Mary Stewart, Kelli Maroney, Robert Beltran, Mary Woronov, John Achorn, Sharon Farrell, Michael Bowen

The Night That Panicked America

USA 1975 96m colour TVM

An account of the unexpected reaction to Orson Welles' famous 1938 radio broadcast of *The War of the Worlds*.

Entertaining recreation of the actual broadcast, let down only by an over abundance of domestic drama.

p: Anthony Wilson, Joseph Sargent for Paramount
w: Nicholas Meyer, Anthony Wilson
story: Nicholas Meyer
d: Joseph Sargent
ph: Jules Brenner
m: Frank Comstock
ed: Bud S. Isaacs, Tony Rudecki
ad: Monty Elliott
sound: Neiman-Tillas Associates
Vic Morrow, Cliff de Young, Paul Shenar (as Orson Welles), Tom Bosley, Will Geer, Meredith Baxter, Walter McGinn, Michael Constantin, Eileen Brennan

The Night They Saved Christmas

USA 1984 96m colour TVM

The arrival of an oil company near the North Pole threatens not only the existence of Santa Claus, but of Christmas itself.

Sugary seasonal confection, hard to take.

p: Robert Halmi for ABC
w: James C. Moloney, David Niven, Jr.
d: Jackie Cooper
ph: David Worth
m: Charles Gross
pd: George Costello

cos: Andy Hylton
sp: Intravision
sound: Jan Brodin
2nd unit d: David Kappes, Skott Snider
titles: Kenneth Hunter
Jaclyn Smith, Art Carney, Paul LeMat, Mason Adams, June Lockhart, Paul Williams

The Nightmare of the Submarine Tunnel ☺

Fr 1907 20m bw silent

President Falliers of France and King Edward VII of England dream about linking their two countries together with a Channel tunnel, but the project ends in disaster.

Archetypal Méliès fantasy with several amusing touches, especially given the course history has since taken.

p: Georges Méliès for Star
w/d: Georges Méliès
Georges Méliès , Fernande Albany

Nimoy, Leonard (1931-)

American actor and director, known the world over for playing the Vulcan Mr. Spock in the *Star Trek* television series (1966-1968) and movie franchise. This has been both a blessing and blight to his career, causing him to write a book entitled *I Am Not Spock* in 1975, which he followed with *I Am Spock* 20years later, when he had come to terms with the fact that he would be forever identified with the character. On stage from the age of eight (in a production of *Hansel and Gretel*), Nimoy later studied acting at the Pasadena Playhouse at the age of 19, breaking into films at the age of 20 with the lead in the low budget boxing drama *Kid Monk Baroni*. Further films, such as *Queen for a Day*, *Rhubarb*, *Satan's Satellites*, *Old Overland Trail* and *The Brain Eaters*, followed, along with much television

work, including guest appearances in *Dragnet*, *Laramie*, *The Man from UNCLE* and *Get Smart*. Following the cancellation of the *Star Trek* television series, Nimoy joined the cast of *Mission: Impossible* (as Paris) from 1969-1971, after which he appeared in all manner of movies and TV movies, among them *Assault on the Wayne* (TVM), *Catlow*, *The Alpha Caper* (TVM – aka *Inside Job*), *The Missing Are Deadly* (TVM) and *Invasion of the Body Snatchers*. There were also many television guest spots, a brief return to Spock, whom he voiced for Filmation's 17-part animated series *Star Trek* in 1973, and much stage work, including *Fiddler on the Roof* (as Tevye), *Oliver!* (as Fagin), *Caligula*, *The Man in the Glass Booth*, *Equus* and *The King and I* (as the King of Siam). He returned to the role of Spock again in 1979 for the big budget feature *Star Trek: The Motion Picture*, which led to appearances in the following five movies and a guest spot on the television series, *Star Trek: The Next Generation*. Nimoy began his directing career in 1970 (by which time he'd already co-produced a low budget movie called *Deathwatch* in 1966) with an episode of television's *Night Gallery* titled *Death on a Barge*. He went on to direct episodes of *Mission: Impossible*, *The Powers of Matthew Starr* and *T. J. Hooker* (which starred his *Star Trek* co-star William Shatner). His first theatrical features as a director were episodes two and three in the *Star Trek* movie series, the success of which led to other directorial assignments, including the blockbuster *Three Men and a Baby*, *The Good Mother*, *Funny About Love* and *Holy Matrimony*, etc. He is also a poet, several collections of his work having been published (*You and I*, *I Think of You*, *We Are All Children Searching for Love*) and a

keen amateur photographer.

Genre credits:
Francis Goes to West Point (1952 – actor), *Invasion of the Body Snatchers* (1978 – actor), *Star Trek: The Motion Picture* (1979 – actor), *Star Trek II: The Wrath of Khan* (1982 – actor), *Star Trek III: The Search for Spock* (1984 – actor/d), *Star Trek IV: The Voyage Home* (1986 – actor/co-story/d), *The Transformers* (1986 – aka *Transformers: The Movie* – voice), *Star Trek V: The Final Frontier* (1989 – actor), *Star Trek VI: The Undiscovered Country* (1991 – actor/co-story/exec p), *The Pagemaster* (1994 – voice)

1984 ☺

GB 1984 110m Eastmancolor

In the fascist state of Oceania, the proletariat are de-humanised and continually watched by Big Brother, and a rebellious worker who questions why is tortured into seeing the truth.

Relentlessly gloomy and depressing adaptation of Orwell's terrifying vision, murkily photographed and verbosely scripted. The acting is of occasional note, but the torture scenes alienate and the length and pace are self-defeating.

p: Al Clark, Robert Devereaux, Simon Perry for Virgin/Rosenblum/Umbrella
w/d: Michael Radford
novel: George Orwell
ph: Roger Deakins
m: Dominic Muldowney, Eurythmics
ed: Tom Priestley
pd: Allan Cameron
cos: Emma Porteouse
sp: Ian Scoones, Ray Caple
sound: Bruce White
John Hurt, Richard Burton, Suzanna Hamilton, Cyril Cussack, Shirley Stelfox, Bob Flag (as Big Brother)

The Nightmare Before Christmas 😴😴

USA 1993 75m Technicolor Dolby

No longer satisfied with simply being the king of Halloween, Jack Skellington determines on taking over Christmas as well, with ghoulish results.

A novelty item in which the novelty wears thin before the end. But there is much to appreciate in the design and humour of this grotesque animated musical.

p: Tim Burton, Denise DiNovi for Touchstone/Buena Vista
w: Caroline Thompson, Michael McDowell
story: Tim Burton
d: Henry Selick
ph: Pete Kozachik
m/songs/associate p: Danny Elfman
ed: Stan Webb, Chris Lebenzon
ad: Deane Taylor
animation supervisor: Eric Leighton
visual consultant: Rick Heinriche
sound: Terry Porter, Shawn Murphy, Greg Russell
voices: Chris Sarandon, Danny Elfman, Catherine O'Hara, William Hickey, Glenn Shadix, Paul Reubens

No Escape

USA 1994 118m Eastmancolor

In 2022, a con is sent to Absolom, an open-air prison on a remote tropical island, and discovers it is populated by two rival factions.

Well made but derivative and finally rather overlong adventure with echoes of *Devil's Island*, *Escape from New York* and *Mad Max*. The sci-fi elements are practically redundant after the opening scenes.

p: Gale Anne Hurd for Allied Filmmakers/Savoy/Pacific Western/Platinum
exec p: Jake Eberts
w: Michael Gaylin, Joel Gross

novel: Richard Herley
d: Martin Campbell
ph: Phil Meheux
m: Graeme Revell
ed: Terry Rawlings
pd: Allan Cameron
cos: Norma Moriceau
Ray Liotta, Lance Henriksen, Kevin J. O'Connor, Don Henderson, Kevin Dillon, Jack Shepherd, Michael Lerner, Ernie Hudson, Ian McNiece, Cheuk-Fai Chan, Russell Kiefel, Brian M. Logan

North 😴

USA 1994 Technicolor Dolby

Believing that he isn't loved, an eight-year-old boy leaves home and goes in search of new parents.

Engaging fantasy comedy which starts on a very high note but ultimately fails to sustain itself, though moments stay in the mind.

p: Rob Reiner, Alan Zweibel for Castle Rock
exec p: Jeffrey Scott, Andrew Scheinman
w: Alan Zweibel, Andrew Scheinman
novel: Alan Zweibel
d: Rob Reiner
ph: Adam Greenber
m: Marc Shaiman
md: Artie Kane
ed: Alan Edward Bell
pd: J. Michael Riva
cos: Chuck Velasco, Margo Baxley
sp: Terry Frazee
sound: Bob Eber
ch: Pat Birch
titles: R. Greenber
stunt co-ordinator: R. A. Rondell
Elijah Wood, Jason Alexander, Julia Louis-Dreyfus, Bruce Willis (as a pink bunny rabbit), Mathew McCurley, Jon Lovitz, Dan Aykroyd, Alan Arkin, Alan Rachins, Reba McEntire, Graham Greene, Kathy Bates, Abe Vigoda, Kelly McGillis, Alexander Godunov, John Ritter, Scarlett Johanssen, Alan Zweibel, Marc Shaiman

Norton, Rosanna

American costume designer who has worked several times for director Joe Dante.

Genre credits:
Airplane 2: The Sequel (1982), *Explorers* (1985), *Innerspace* (1987), *Gremlins 2: The New Batch* (1990), *Angels in the Outfield* (1994 – aka *Angels*), *The Flintstones* (1994), *Casper* (1995), *Barb Wire* (1996)

The Nutty Professor

USA 1963 107m Technicolor

A bumbling college professor discovers a potion that transforms him into a crooner.

For those who can tolerate his mugging, this is one of the star's better vehicles, though that isn't really saying much (unless you live in France).

p: Ernest Gluckman for Paramount
exec p: Jerry Lewis
w: Jerry Lewis, Bill Richmond
d: Jerry Lewis
ph: W. Wallace Kelley
m: Walter Scharf
ed: John Woodcock
ad: Hal Pereira, Walter Tyler
cos: Edith Head, Sy Devore, Nat Wise
sp: Paul K. Lerpae
sound: Hugo Grenzbach, Charles Grenzbach
make-up: Wally Westmore
JERRY LEWIS, Stella Stevens, Howard Morris, Kathleen Freeman, Henry Gibson, Marvin Kaplan, Buddy Lester, Skip Ward, Les Brown

The Nutty Professor

USA 1996 95m Technicolor Dolby

An overweight college professor discovers a miracle slimming potion, but there are side effects...

Fitfully hilarious update of the Jerry Lewis comedy (especially for those who like fart jokes), helped immeasurably by its brilliant make-up effects. Some of the dialogue is unintelligable, however.

p: Brian Grazer, Russell Simmons for Imagine
exec p: Jerry Lewis
w: Tom Shadyac, David Sheffield, Barry W. Blausteuin, Steve Oedekerk
d: Tom Shadyac
ph: Julio Macat
m: David Newman
ed: Don Zimmerman
pd: William Elliott
make-up effects: RICK BAKER, DAVID LEROY ANDERSON (AA)
EDDIE MURPHY, Jada Pinkett, James Coburn, Larry Miller, John Ales, Dave Chappelle

Two scenes from the highly-stylised stop-motion feature *A Nightmare Before Christmas*. Top: Santa Claus finds his cargo of presents hijacked by three trick or treaters. Bottom: Sally the rag doll looks on as Jack Skellington makes plans to take over Christmas.

O'Bannon, Dan (1946-)

American writer who has also directed a couple of genre films, including *The Return of the Living Dead* and *The Resurrected*. His other screenplay credits include *Dead and Buried* and *Blue Thunder*. He also contributed to the computer animation in *Star Wars* (1977).

Genre credits:
Dark Star (1974 – co-w/pd/ed/co-sp), *Alien* (1979 – w/design consultant), *Lifeforce* (1985 – co-w), *Invaders from Mars* (1986 – co-w), *Total Recall* (1990 – co-w), *Screamers* (1995 – co-w)

O'Brien, Edmond (1915-1985)

American actor working on both sides of the Atlantic. A best supporting actor Oscar winner for *The Barefoot Contessa* (1954), he was also memorable as the slowly dying poison victim Frank Bigelow in *D.O.A.* After amateur experience he turned professional in 1937 and joined Orson Welles' Mercury Players. He made his film debut in 1938 with *Prison Break*, which he followed with *The Hunchback of Notre Dame* later the same year. His other credits include *The Killers*, *Julius Caesar*, *Pete Kelly's Blues*, *The Birdman of Alcatraz* and *Seven Days in May*. He also directed two films,

Shield for Murder (with Howard Koch) and *Mantrap*, the latter of which he also co-produced (with Stanley Frazen).

Genre credits:
1984 (1955 – as Winston Smith), *Moon Pilot* (1961), *Fantastic Voyage* (1966)

O'Brien, Willis H. (1886–1962)

Pioneering American special effects wiz, a stop motion expert whose work on *King Kong* was and still is an industry milestone. He didn't turn to film until later in life after experience as a rancher, poultry farmer, draughtsman and cartoonist. An experiment with stop motion in 1914 led to a film contract, however, the result being the short film *The Dinosaur and the Missing Link*, made in 1915 and released in 1917. Further shorts followed, all of which led to his first feature film, *The Lost World*, in 1925. He was working on a film called *Creation*, which was never completed, when he got the call to work on *King Kong*. A sequel quickly followed, and in 1949 O'Brien received an Oscar for his effects work on the Kong-like *Mighty Joe Young*, on which he was assisted by the young Ray Harryhausen, who eventually inherited his crown. Sadly, O'Brien's subsequent work never quite matched his achievements on *Kong*.

Genre credits:
The Dinosaur and the Missing Link (1915 – short), *R. F. D. 10 000 B. C.* (1917 – short), *Prehistoric Poultry* (1917 – short), *Curious Pets of Our Ancestors* (1917 – short), *The Ghost of Slumber Mountain* (1919 – short), *The Lost World* (1925), *Creation* (1931 – uncompleted), *King Kong* (1933), *Son of Kong* (1933), *Mighty Joe Young* (1949), *The Animal World* (1956), *The Beast of Hollow Mountain* (1956 – story only), *The Black Scorpion* (1957), *The Giant Behemoth* (1958

– aka *Behemoth the Sea Monster*), *The Lost World* (1960 – advisor only)

O'Herlihy, Dan (1919-)

Irish actor with much stage (Dublin's Abbey Theatre) and radio experience. His film roles have mostly been as a supporting actor, though this hasn't prevented him from leaving his mark in such films as *Hallowe'en III: Season of the Witch*, *The Last Starfighter* and *Robocop*. His other credits include *Odd Man Out*, *The Adventures of Robinson Crusoe* (as Crusoe), *The Virgin Queen*, *Fail Safe*, *QB VII* (TVM) and *The Dead*.

Genre credits:
Hallowween III: Season of the Witch (1983), *The Last Starfighter* (1984), *Robocop* (1987), *Robocop 2* (1990)

Oh, God! 🛸

USA 1977 104m Technicolor
God appears to an assistant supermarket manager and tells him to spread the word.

Elementary fantasy comedy which proved unexpectedly popular, but is otherwise rather flatly handled. It was followed by *Oh, God! Book II* (1980) and *Oh, God! You Devil!* (1984).

p: Jerry Weintraub for Warner
w: Larry Gelbart
novel: Avery Corman
d: Carl Reiner
ph: Victor J. Kemper
m: Jack Elliott
ed: Bud Mollin
ad: Jack Senter
GEORGE BURNS, JOHN DENVER, Teri Garr, Ralph Bellamy, Donald Pleasence, William Daniels, Barnard Hughes, Paul Sorvino, Barry Sullivan, Dinah Shore, Jeff Corey, David Ogden Stiers, George Furth

Oh, God! Book II

USA 1980 94m Technicolor

God chooses a young schoolgirl to help
him convince the world that he still
exists.

Sentimental sequel with one or two
mild laughs.

p: Gilbert Cates for Warner
w: Josh Greenfield, Hal Goldman, Fred S.
Fox, Seaman Jacobs, Melissa Miller
story: Josh Greenfield
d: Gilbert Cates
ph: Ralph Woolsey
m: Charles Fox
ed: Peter E. Berger
pd: Preston Ames
cos: Vicki Sanchez
sound: Don Sharpless, Vern Poole, Dick
Alexander, Andy MacDonald
titles: Phil Norman
GEORGE BURNS, Louanne, Suzanne
Pleshette, David Birney, Howard Duff, Hans
Conreid, Wilfred Hyde White

Oh, God! You Devil!

USA 1984 96m Technicolor

A songwriter sells his soul to the Devil
for a hit, but help is at hand...

Unremarkable conclusion to the *Oh,
God!* series in which George Burns this
time plays both God and the Devil.

p: Robert M. Sherman for Warner
exec p: Irving Fein
w: Andrew Bergman
d: Paul Bogart
ph: King Baggott
m: David Shire
ed: Andy Zall
pd: Peter Wooley
cos: Liza Stewart
sp: Ray Klein
sound: Richard I. Burnbaum
George Burns, Ted Wass, Ron Silver, Eugene
Roche, Roxanne Hart

Oliver and Company

USA 1988 74m Metrocolor

A homeless kitten is taken in by a gang
of city dogs who make a living through
petty crime.

A cartoon version of *Oliver Twist* in
animals terms. Not a brilliant idea, but
it should satisfy younger audiences.
Has a dated 70s feel, but luckily Disney
revitalised their animation output with
their next feature, *The Little Mermaid*,
since when the studio has been on
something of a roll cartoon-wise.

p: (none given) for Walt Disney/Silver
Screen Partners
w: Timothy J. Disney, Jim Cox, James
Mangold
story: Vance Gerry, Joe Ranft, Mike Gabriel,
Jim Mitchell, Kirk Wise, Chris Bailey, Dave
Michener, Roger Allers, Gary Trousdale, Kevin
Lima, Michael Cedeno, Leon Joosen, Pete
Young, Gerrit Graham, Samuel Graham, Steve
Hulett, Chris Hubbel, Danny Mann (phew!)
novel: Charles Dickens
d: George Scribner
m: J.A.C. Redford
songs: Howard Ashman, Dan Hartman,
Charlie Midnight, Dean Pitchford, Tom
Snow, Barry Manilow, Jack Feldman, Bruce
Sussman, Rob Minkoff, Ron Rocha
ed: Jim Melton, Mark Hester
ad: Dan Hansen
voices: Joey Lawrence, Billy Joel, Sheryl Lee
Ralph, Cheech Marin, Richard Mulligan,
Roscoe Lee Brown, Bette Midler, Robert
Loggia, Dom DeLuise

Oliver, Barrett (1973-)

American child actor who popped up
in a number of 80s fantasy films.

Genre credits:
Knight Rider (1982 – TVM), *The Never
Ending Story* (1984), *D.A.R.Y.L.* (1985),
Cocoon (1985), *Cocoon: The Return* (1988)

Olson, James (1930-)

American actor whose credits take in
such wide-ranging films as *The
Sharkfighters*, *Crescendo*, *Wild Rovers*,
Ragtime and *Amityville II: The
Possession*.

Genre credits:
Moon Zero Two (1969), *The Andromeda
Strain* (1970), *The Groundstar Conspiracy*
(1972)

The Omega Man

USA 1971 98m Technicolor Panavision

After germ warfare has devastated the
world, the only survivor battles for his
life against plague-carrying zombies.

Lacklustre science fiction with an
over-plus of talk, lethargically handled.

p: Walter Seltzer for Warner
w: John William Corrington, Joyce M.
Corrington
novel: Richard Matheson
d: Boris Sagal
ph: Russell Metty
m: Ron Grainer
ed: William Ziegler
ad: Arthur Loel, Walter M. Simonds
cos: Margo Baxley
sound: Bob Martin
Charlton Heston, Rosalind Cash, Anthony
Zerbe, Paul Koslo, Lincoln Kilpatrick

On a Clear Day You Can See Forever

USA 1970 120m Technicolor

A New York girl reveals herself to be
the reincarnation of an 18th-century
Englishwoman whilst being hypnotised
to stop smoking.

Overlong and dully handled fantasy
musical via a successful Broadway
show. Unfortunately most of the songs
add little but length and the modern-
day psychological angle is at variance
with the period flashbacks.

p: Howard Koch for Paramount

w: Alan Jay Lerner from his musical book

d: Vincent Minnelli

ph: Harry Stradling

m: Burton Lane

ly: Alan Jay Lerner

md: Nelson Riddle

ed: David Bretherton

pd: John De Cuir

cos: CECIL BEATON, Arnold Scaasi

sound: Benjamin Winkler, Elden Rubers

ch: Howard Jeffrey

titles: Wayne Fitzgerald

time lapse ph: John Ott

Barbra Streisand, Yves Montand, Jack Nicholson, Bob Newhart, Simon Oakland, Larry Blyden, John Richardson, John le Mesurier, Roy Kinnear, Leon Ames, Irene Handl

---

One-Hundred-and-One Dalmatians 🛸🛸

USA 1961 79m Technicolor

An arch villainess kidnaps dalmatian puppies for their skins, but she reckons without the intervention of the dogs of London, who organise a rescue.

Slow starting but very popular cartoon feature which picks up speed as it moves along, though adults may enjoy the exploits of its villainess, Cruella de Vil, more than the dogs.

p: Walt Disney

story: Bill Peet

novel: Dodie Smith

d: Wolfgang Reitherman, Hamilton S. Luske, Clyde Geronimi

m: George Bruns

songs: Mel Leven

ed: Donald Halliday, Roy M. Brewer, Jr

pd/ad: Ken Anderson

sp: Ub Iwerks, Eustace Lycett

sound: Robert O. Cook

voices: Rod Taylor, J. Pat O'Malley, Cate Bauer, Betty Lou Gerson (as Cruella de Vil), Lisa Davis

---

One-Hundred-and-One Dalmatians 🛸

USA/GB 1996 103m Technicolor
Panavision Dolby

An evil businesswoman plots to kidnap dalmation puppies for their fur...

Fairly cheerful live action remake of the Disney cartoon, given some adult appeal by Glenn Close's high camp as Cruella de Vil.

p: John Hughes, Ricardo Matres for Walt Disney/Great Oaks

exec p: Edward S. Feldman

w: John Hughes

novel: Dodie Smith

d: Stephen Herek

ph: Adrian Biddle

m: Michael Kamen

ed: Trudy Ship

pd: Assheton Gorton

cos: Anthony Powell, Rosemary Burrows

sp: Michael Owens, George Gibbs, ILM, Jim Henson's Creature Shop

sound: Clive Winter, Tim Chau, Donald J. Malouf

GLENN CLOSE, Jeff Daniels, Joely Richardson, Hugh Laurie, Joan Plowright, Mark Williams, John Shrapnel, Tim McInnery

---

One Million B.C. 🛸

USA 1940 81m bw

In prehistoric times a warrior is befriended by a peaceful tribe and shows them how to defend themselves from dinosaurs.

Dated, anachronistic monster pic, of interest chiefly for the talent involved.

p: Hal Roach

w: Mickell Novak, George Baker, Joseph Frickert, Grover Jones

d: Hal Roach, Hal Roach, Jr., (and, some say, D. W. Griffith)

ph: Norbert Brodine

m: Werner B. Heyman

ed: Ray Snyder

ad: Charles D. Hall, Nicolai Remisoff

cos: Harry Black

sp: Roy Seawright

sound: William Randall

narrator: Conrad Nagel

Victor Mature, Carole Landis, Lon Chaney, Jr., Nigel de Brulier, Conrad Nagel, John Hubbard

---

One Million Years B.C. 🛸🛸

GB 1966 100m Technicolor

In prehistoric times, a cave girl abandons her tribe to look for a mate.

Lively remake of the 1940 Hal Roach film *One Million B.C.*, here benefitting from lively action sequences and excellent effects work.

p: Michael Carreras for Hammer

w: Michael Carreras

d: DON CHAFFEY

ph: Wilkie Cooper

m: MARIO NASCIMBENE

md: Philip Martell

ed: James Needs, Tom Simpson

ad: Robert Jones

cos: Carl Toms

sp: RAY HARRYHAUSEN, Les Bowie

sound: Bill Rowe, Len Shilton

2nd unit ph: Jack Mills

Raquel Welch, John Richardson, Robert Brown, Martine Beswick, Percy Herbert, Lisa Thomas, Malya Nappil

---

On the Beach 🛸

USA 1959 134m bw

In 1964, when the world has been decimated by atomic war, an American captain and his crew set out in a submarine from Australia, the last place to be contaminated by fallout, to see if life exists elsewhere.

Earnest but overlong, overtalkative and inevitably depressing doomsday scenario, well made and acted, but a little too concerned with the lives of its central characters (one of whom takes part in an irrelevant auto race) rather than the whole picture. The scenes set in a deserted San Francisco and San Diego are memorable, however.

p: Stanley Kramer for UA
w: John Paxton, James Lee Barrett
novel: Nevil Shute
d: Stanley Kramer
ph: Giuseppe Rotunno
m: Ernest Gold
ed: Frederic Knudtson
pd: Rudolph Sternad
ad: Fernando Carrere
cos: Fontana Sisters, Joe King
sp: Lee Zavitz
sound: Hans Wetzel
sound effects: Walter Elliott
2nd unit ph: Daniel L. Fapp
Gregory Peck, Ava Gardner, Anthony Perkins, Fred Astaire, John Tate, Donna Anderson, Lola Brooks, Guy Doleman

Orlando

GB/Fr/It/Russia/Netherlands 1992 93m Eastmancolor Dolby

From 1600 to the late 20th-century, the various experiences, romantic and otherwise, of an English nobleman, including his transformation into a woman.

Witty exploration of gender attitudes down the ages which met with a certain degree of critical acclaim.

p: Christopher Sheppard for Sigma/British Screen/Mikado/Adventure Pictures/Lenfilm
w/d: Sally Potter
novel: Virginia Woolf
ph: Alexsei Rodionov
m: David Motion, Sally Potter
md: Bob Last
ed: Herve Schneid
pd: Ben Van Os, Jan Roelfs
cos: Sandy Powell, Dien Van Straedlen
sound: Jean-Louis Ducarme, Dominic O'Donoghue
Tilda Swinton, Billy Zane, Quentin Crisp (as Elizabeth I), John Wood, Lothaire Bluteau,

Charlotte Vladrey, Heathcote Williams, Peter Eyre, Anna Healy, Ned Sherrin, Thom Hoffman, Dudley Sutton, Jimmy Somerville

Orphée

Fr 1950 112m bw

Death falls in love with a handsome poet and dies whilst trying to help him.

Acclaimed fantasy, regarded by many as its writer-director's finest achievement. However, despite effective touches (such as the passing through of mirrors to reach the nether world) its narrative drive now seems rather lacklustre, and modern audiences may wonder what all the fuss was about. A sequel, *Le Testament D'Orphée*, followed in 1950.

p: Andre Paulve for Films du Palais Royal
w/d: Jean Cocteau from his play
ph: Nicolas Hayer
m: Georges Auric
md: Jacques Metehen
ed: Jacqueline Sadoul
pd: Jean d'Eaubonne
cos: Marcel Escoffier
sound: Calvet
narrator: Jean Cocteau
Jean Marais, Francois Perier, Maria Cesares, Marie Dea, Juliette Greco, Edouard Dermithe

Outland

GB 1981 105m Technicolor Panavision Dolby

The marshall of a mining colony on Jupiter's third moon investigates a series of suicides and uncovers a drugs ring.

Fairly slick re-working of *High Noon* in an outer space setting. A film very much typical of its writer-director's output.

p: Richard A. Roth for Ladd/Outland
exec p: Stanley O'Toole
w/d: Peter Hyams
ph: Stephen Goldblatt

m: Jerry Goldsmith
ed: Stuart Baird
pd: Philip Harrison
cos: John Mollo
sp: John Stears, Roy Field
sound: Robin Gregory
sound ed: Gordon Davidson
Sean Connery, Peter Boyle, FRANCES STERNHAGEN, James B. Sikking, Kika Markham, Clarke Peters, John Ratzenberger, Steven Berkoff, Norman Chancer

Oz, Frank (1944-)

British-born actor, writer, producer, director and puppeteer (real name Frank Oznowicz), long associated with Jim Henson's Muppets, for which he provided the voices of Miss Piggy, Fozzie Bear and Animal among others. He began in television with *Sesame Street* and *The Muppet Show* before graduating to movies with Henson. He is also known for operating and providing the voice of Yoda in *The Empire Strikes Back* and *Return of the Jedi*. His work as a director includes *Dirty Rotten Scoundrels*, *What About Bob?* and *Housesitter*. Performance-wise he has popped up in several of director John Landis's films, among them *The Blues Brothers* and *Spies Like Us*.

Genre credits:

The Muppet Movie (1979 – voice/puppeteer), *The Empire Strikes Back* (1980 – voice/puppeteer), *The Great Muppet Caper* (1981 – co-p/voice/puppeteer), *The Dark Crystal* (1982 – co-d), *Return of the Jedi* (1983 – voice/puppeteer), *The Muppets Take Manhattan* (1984 – co-w/d/voice/puppeteer), *Follow That Bird* (1985 – voice/puppeteer), *Labyrinth* (1986 – actor), *Little Shop of Horrors* (1986 – d), *The Muppet Christmas Carol* (1992 – exec p/voice), *The Indian in the Cupboard* (1995 – d), *Muppet Treasure Island* (1996 – exec p/voice)

The Pagemaster

USA 1994 75m Technicolor Dolby

A teenage boy finds himself transported to an animated fantasy world where he encounters various villains from the world of literature.

Tame animated feature with live action bookends. The concept is sound enough; unfortunately, the production lacks the required imagination to make the most of the situations.

p: Paul Gertz, David Kirschner for TCF/Turner
w: David Casci, Ernie Contreras, David Kirschner
d: Joe Johnston (live action), Maurice Hunt (animation)
ph: Alexander Gruszynski
m: James Horner
ed: Jeffrey Patch, Kaja Fehr
pd: Roy Forge Smith, Gay Lawrence, Valerio Ventura
Macaulay Culkin, Christopher Lloyd, Ed Begley, Jr., Mel Harris, Alexis Kirschner, Jessica Kirschner, voices: Whoopi Goldberg, Leonard Nimoy, Patrick Stewart, Frank Welker, George Hearn, Dorian Harewood, Phil Hartman, Robert Piccardo

---

Pal, George (1908–1980)

Hungarian-born writer, producer, director, animator and special effects technician who made a number of key

Producer George Pal (right) watches as director Michael Anderson sets up a shot during the filming of *Doc Savage, Man of Bronze.*

science fiction and fantasy films in the 50s, most notably *Destination Moon*, *The War of the Worlds* and *The Time Machine*. He began his film career as a title writer in Budapest in the late 20s. In 1931 he became a cartoon animator at UFA in Berlin after which he moved to Paris where he made animated commercials. Turning to stop frame animation, he began making "puppetoons" in Holland, an idea he took to Hollywood in 1940 where he made 40 shorts, among them *Dipsy Gypsy*, *Western Daze*, *Jasper and the Haunted House* and *Tubby the Tuba*, several of which were animated by the young Ray Harryhausen. Pal won a special Oscar for his puppetoons in 1943. He turned to feature length production in 1949 with *The Great Rupert*, and five of his subsequent sci-fi/fantasy films won Oscars for their special effects, all of which Pal oversaw. Many of the films he produced were directed by Byron Haskin. His few non-genre films include *Houdini* and *The Naked Jungle*.

Genre credits:

The Great Rupert (1949 – p), *Destination Moon* (1950 – p), *When World Collide* (1951 – p), *War of the Worlds* (1953 – p), *The Conquest of Space* (1955 – p), *Tom Thumb* (1958 – p/d), *The Time Machine* (1960 – p/d), *Atlantis, the Lost Continent* (1960 – p/d), *The Wonderful World of the Brothers Grimm* (1962 – p/co-d), *The Seven Faces of Dr. Lao* (1964 – p/d), *The Power* (1968 – p), *Doc Savage – Man of Bronze* (1975 – co-w/p), *The Puppetoon Movie* (1987 – puppetoon compilation)

Palance, Jack (1920-)

Intense-looking American character actor (real name Walter Palanuik), best remembered for his western roles, particularly as the bad guy in *Shane*. A best supporting actor Oscar winner for his role in *City Slickers*, his other credits include such diverse films as *The Big Knife*, *Barabbas*, *The Professionals*, *Torture Garden*, *Monte Walsh*, *Dracula* (TVM – title role), *Bagdad Cafe* and *City Slickers II: The*

Legend of Curly's Gold.

Genre credits:

The Shape of Things to Come (1979 – TVM), *Hawk the Slayer* (1980), *Gor* (1987), *Outlaw of Gor* (1988), *Batman* (1989), *Cyborg 2* (1993), *The Swan Princess* (1994 – voice)

Paramount

Formed in 1912 by Adolf Zukor, Paramount first went by the name Famous Players, then Famous Players Lasky before becoming Paramount Pictures in 1914 following a series of mergers and takeovers. In the 30s they were known for their slick, sophisticated comedies, whilst later came the biblical epics of director Cecil B. de Mille. Their major contribution to the science fiction and fantasy genres have been *War of the Worlds* and the *Star Trek* and *Indiana Jones* franchises.

Genre filmography:

Dr. Cyclops (1939), *When Worlds Collide* (1951), *The War of the Worlds* (1953), *The Conquest of Space* (1955), *The Little Prince* (1974), *Star Trek – The Motion Picture* (1979), *Raiders of the Lost Ark* (1981), *Star Trek II: The Wrath of Khan* (1982), *Indiana Jones and the Temple of Doom* (1984), *Star Trek III: The Search for Spock* (1984), *Star Trek IV: The Voyage Home* (1986), *Star Trek V: The Final Frontier* (1989), *Indiana Jones and the Last Crusade* (1989), *Star Trek VI: The Undiscovered Country* (1991), *Star Trek: Generations* (1994), *Congo* (1995), *Star Trek: First Contact* (1996)

Paré, Michael (1959-)

American actor with a penchant for low budget actioners and sci-fi. Began his film career in 1983 with *Eddie and the Cruisers.*

Genre credits:

The Philadelphia Experiment (1984), Space Rage (1986), World Gone Wild (1988), Moon 44 (1990), Solar Force (1994), Village of the Damned (1995)

Paynter, Robert (1928-)

British cinematographer, familiar for his work with the directors Michael Winner (*Hannibal Brooks*, *The Games*, *Chato's Land*, *The Mechanic*, *The Nightcomers*, *The Big Sleep*, *Firepower*, etc.) and John Landis (*An American Werewolf in London*, *Trading Places*, *Spies Like Us*, *Into the Night*). His other credits include *Scorpio*, *The Final Conflict* and *National Lampoon's European Vacation.*

Genre credits:

Saturn 3 (1980 – add ph only), *Superman 2* (1980), *Superman 3* (1983), *The Muppets Take Manhattan* (1984), *Little Shop of Horrors* (1986), *The Secret Garden* (1987 – TVM)

Peggy Sue Got Married

USA 1986 105m DeLuxe Dolby

At her 25th high-school reunion, a middle-aged woman dreams herself back to 1960 and tries to change her destiny.

Fairly engaging fantasy-nostalgia piece, hingeing on a charming central performance. On the whole, more effective than the rather noisier *Back to the Future*, of which this is a distaff version.

p: Paul R. Gurain for Tri-Star/Delphi IV/Zoetrope
exec p: Barrie M. Osborne
w: Jerry Leichtling, Arlene Sarner
d: Francis Ford Coppola
ph: Jordan Cronenweth
m: John Barry
ed: Barry Malkin

pd: Dean Tavoularis
cos: Theodora Van Runkle
sp: Larry Cavanaugh
sound: Richard Bryce Goodman, Lee Dichter, Tom Fleischman
KATHLEEN TURNER, Nicolas Cage, Barry Miller, Catherine Hicks, Maureen O'Sullivan, Leon Ames, John Carradine, Helen Hunt, Don Murray, Barbara Harris, Kevin J. O'Connor, Joan Allen, Jim Carrey

The People That Time Forgot

GB 1977 90m Technicolor

Backed by a London newspaper, Major McBride searches for the lost continent of Caprona, where two of his friends disappeared in 1916.

Silly but quite lively sequel to *The Land That Time Forgot*. Okay for younger audiences, but the effects are hardly convincing.

p: John Dark for AIP/Amicus
exec p: Samuel Z. Arkoff, Max J. Rosenberg
w: Patrick Tilley
novel: Edgar Rice Borroughs
d: Kevin Connor
ph: Alan Hume
m: John Scott
ed: John Ireland, Barry Peters
pd: Maurice Carter
sp: John Richardson, Ian Wingrove
Patrick Wayne, Sarah Douglas, Doug McClure, Tony Britton, Thorley Walters, Dana Gillespie, Shane Rimmer

Peppard, George (1928–1994)

American actor who made his film debut in 1957 in *The Strange One* following experience on stage, radio and television. His other credits include *Breakfast at Tiffany's*, *How the West Was Won*, *The Carpetbaggers*, *Operation Crossbow*, *The Blue Max* (as a German fighter pilot with an

American accent) and *The Groundstar Conspiracy*, not to mention such popular TV series as *Banacek* and *The A-Team*. He also produced and directed one film, *Five Days from Home* (1978).

Genre credits:

The Groundstar Conspiracy (1972), *Damnation Alley* (1978), *Battle Beyond the Stars* (1980 – as Space Cowboy)

Pereira, Hal (1905-1983)

American art director, an Oscar winner for *The Rose Tattoo* (1955 – with Tambi Larsen). A former stage designer, he began his film career at Paramount in 1942, where he later became the studio's supervising art director. His credits include such wide-ranging projects as *Double Indemnity*, *Ace in the Hole* (aka *The Big Carnival*), *Roman Holiday*, *White Christmas*, *To Catch a Thief*, *The Trouble with Harry*, *The Man Who Knew Too Much*, *The Ten Commandments*, *King Creole*, *Vertigo*, *Hatari*, *The Spy Who Came in from the Cold* and *The Odd Couple*. He also designed several of Paramount's key 50s science fiction films.

Genre credits:

When Worlds Collide (1951 – co-ad), *War of the Worlds* (1953 – co-ad), *The Conquest of Space* (1955 – co-ad), *The Search for Bridey Murphy* (1956 – co-ad), *The Colossus of New York* (1958 – co-ad), *The Space Children* (1958 – co-ad), *Visit to a Small Planet* (1959 – co-ad), *I Married a Monster from Outer Space* (1958 – co-ad), *Robinson Crusoe on Mars* (1964 – co-ad), *Project X* (1967 – co-ad)

Perinal, Georges (1897–1965)

Distinguished French cinematograph-er, filming documentaries from 1923. His early credits in his homeland include Jean Cocteau's *Le Sang d'un Poète* (aka *Blood of a Poet*) and several for director Réné Clair, among them *Sous les Toits de Paris*, *Le Million*, *A Nous la Liberté* and *Quatorze Juillet*. In 1932 he photographed *The Girl from Maxim's* for Alexander Korda, which led to a long association with the producer/director in Britain, where he photographed such classics as *The Private Life of Henry VIII*, *Catherine the Great*, *Rembrandt*, *The Four Feathers*, *The Life and Death of Colonel Blimp* and *Oscar Wilde*.

Genre credits:

Things to Come (1935), *The Thief of Bagdad* (1940), *Satellite in the Sky* (1956), *Tom Thumb* (1958)

Perrine, Valerie (1944-)

American actress, perhaps best known to genre fans for playing Eve Teschmacher in the first two *Superman* films. She made her film debut in 1972 in *Slaughterhouse Five*, since when she has appeared in such films as *Lenny*, *W.C. Fields and Me*, *The Electric Horseman*, *Can't Stop the Music*, *The Border* and *Water*.

Genre credits:

Slaughterhouse Five (1972), *Superman* (1978), *Superman 2* (1980)

Peter Pan

USA 1953 76m Technicolor

A boy with the ability to fly whisks three London children away to Never Never Land where they have various magical adventures and encounter the villainous Captain Hook.

Fondly remembered cartoon feature with all the Disney virtues.

p: Walt Disney

w: Ted Sears, Bill Peat, Erdman Penner, Joe Rinaldi, Winston Hibler, Ralph Wright, Milt Banta

play: J. M. Barrie

d: Hamilton Luske, Clyde Geronimi, Wilfred Jackson

songs: Sammy Cahn, Sammy Fain, Oliver Wallace, Erdman Penner, Ted Sears, Winston Hibler, Jack Lawrence

m: Oliver Wallace

voices: Bobbie Driscoll (as Peter Pan), Kathryn Beaumont, Hans Conreid (as Captain Hook), Tom Conway, Bill Thompson, Paul Collins, Heather Angel, Tommy Luske, Candy Candido

Pete's Dragon

USA 1977 127m Technicolor Dolby

At the turn of the century, a young boy runs away from home with Elliot, his pet dragon which only he can see.

The least of Disney's 70s offerings, this poorly conceived, directed and performed fantasy musical shows just how far the studio had fallen following Walt's death a decade earlier. A real chore to sit through.

p: Ron Miller, Jerome Courtland for Walt Disney

w: Malcolm Marmonstein

story: Seton I. Miller, S. S. Field

d: Don Chaffey

ph: Frank Phillips

songs: Al Kasha, Joel Hirschhorn

md: Irwin Kostal

ed: Gordon D. Brenner

ad: John B. Mansbridge, Jack Martin Smith

cos: Bill Thomas

sp: Peter Ellenshaw, Eustace Lycett, Art Cruickshank, Danny Lee

sound: Herb Taylor, Frank C. Regula

ch: Oona White

animation d: Don Bluth

Sean Marshall (as Pete), Shelley Winters, Mickey Rooney, Helen Reddy, Jim Dale, Red

Buttons, Jim Backus, Ben Wrigley

The Phantom

USA 1996 100m Technicolor Dolby

In the 30s, a superhero called The Phantom attempts to prevent an American tycoon from gaining possession of three magical skulls which, when placed together, wield enormous power.

Mild superheroics based on a comic strip first seen in *The New York Journal American* in 1936 (pre-empting both *Superman* and *Batman*). Formulaic certainly, but more tolerable than most similar romps.

p: Robert Evans, Alan Ladd, Jr for Paramount/The Ladd Company/Village Roadshow
exec: Richard Vane, Joe Dante, Graham Burke, Greg Coote, Peter S. Joquist, Bruce Sherlock
w: Jeffrey Boam
comic strip: Lee Falk
d: Simon Wincer
ph: David Burr
m: David Newman
ed: O. Nicholas Brown
pd: Paul Peters
sp: Buena Vista Visual Effects
Billy Zane, Treat Williams, Kristy Swanson, Catherine Zeta Jones, James Remar, Patrick McGoohan

Phase IV

GB 1973 85m Technicolor

Scientists investigating the behaviour patterns of ants in the Arizona desert find themselves isolated and under attack.

Silly but visually arresting thriller, to be avoided by haters of creepy crawlies.

p: Paul Radin for Paramount/Alced
w: Mayo Simon

Superheroes come in all shapes and sizes. Here The Phantom (Billy Zane) protects Diana Palmer (Kristy Swanson) from the bad guys in *The Phantom*. Given the film's lukewarm reception at the box office, sequels in this case seem unlikely.

P

d: SAUL BASS
ph: Dick Bush
m: Brian Gascoyne
ed: Willy Kemplen
pd: John Barry
sp: John Richardson
2nd unit ph: Jack Mills
ant ph: KEN MIDDLEHAM
Nigel Davenport, Michael Murphy, Lynne Frederick, Alan Gifford, Robert Henderson, Helen Horton

Phenomenon
USA 1996 124m Technicolor Dolby
On his 37th birthday a car mechanic is struck by a mysterious bolt of light which greatly increases his mental powers. Inevitably, government agents soon become interested in him.

Sentimental blend of romance and fantasy, this mild star vehicle passes the time amiably enough, though it is never less than predictable and is fairly short on actual character development.

p: Barbara Boyle, Michael Taylor for Touchstone
exec p: Charles Newirth, Jonathan Krane
w: Gerald DiPego
d: John Turteltaub
ph: Phedon Papamichael
m: Thomas Newman
ed: Bruce Green
pd: Garreth Stover
cos: Betsy Cox
sp: Ken Ralston
sound: Ronald Judkins
John Travolta, Kyra Sedgwick, Forest Whitaker, Robert Duvall, Jeffrey DeMunn, Richard Kiley

The Philadelphia Experiment 🛸
USA 1984 101m CFIcolor
In 1943, an experiment to make a warship radar-invisible goes wrong and sends two sailors into the future to 1984.

Neatly packaged time warp adventure, briskly and competently handled. A sequel followed in 1993.

p: Joel B. Michaels, Douglas Curtis for New World/Cinema Group Ventures/New Pictures
exec p: John Carpenter
w: William Gray, Michael Janover
story: Wallace Bennett, Don Jakoby
d: Stewart Raffill
ph: Dick Bush
m: Ken Wannberg
ed: Neil Travis
ad: Chris Campbell
cos: Joanne Palace
sp/2nd unit d: Max W. Anderson
sound: Bob Gravenor, David Lewis Yewdall
sound effects: Dick Le Grand, Chuck Smith
stunt co-ordinator: Fernando Celib
titles: Duane Swafford
Michael Pare, Nancy Allen, Bobby Di Cicco, Eric Christmas, Louise Latham

Philadelphia Experiment 2
USA 1993 93m Foto-Kem Dolby
A navy pilot finds himself transported to a parallel 1993 when an experiment involving the transportation of a war plane through time goes wrong.

Dreary follow-up to an engaging original, with little to connect it to its predecessor.

p: Mark Levinson, Doug Curtis for Trimark/Alternative Pictures
exec p: Mark Amin
w: Kevin Rick, Nick Paine
d: Stephen Cornwell
ph: Ronn Schmidt
m: Gerald Gouriet
ed: Nina Gilberti
pd: Armin Ganz
cos: Eileen Kennedy
sp: Janet Muswell
sound: Ed White
2nd unit ph: Doyle Smith

Brad Johnson, Marjean Holden, Gerrit Graham, Geoffrey Blake, John Christian Graas, Lisa Robbins, David Wells

Phoenix
USA 1995 86m Foto-Kem
In the future, anroids run amok on the mining planet of Titus 4 and a felon and his team are sent in to save the day, only to find themselves being manipulated by the powers that be.

Tired variation on an old theme. Script, direction, acting and action sequences alike are lacklustre.

p: Jimmy Lifton, Dan Bates, Troy Cook, Billy Drago for Triad
exec p: Morton Salkind
w: Jimmy Lifton, Troy Cook
d: Troy Cook
ph: T. Alexander
m: Lisa Bloom
ed: Paulette Renee Victort
pd: James Scanlon
cos: Susan Wachsler
sp: Stargate Films
sound: James Einoff
stunt co-ordinator: Chuck Borden
2nd unit ph: James Shepphird
add ph: James Lebovitz, Mark Melville
Brad Dourif, Billy Drago, Stephen Nichols, Denice Duff, Peter Murnick, William Sanderson

Pidgeon, Walter (1897-1984)
Canadian actor long in Hollywood, making his debut in *Mannequin* in 1925 after experience on the stage. His credits include *Man Hunt, Blossoms in the Dust, Mrs Miniver, Madame Curie, Executive Suite, Advise and Consent, Funny Girl* (as Florenz Ziegfeld), *Harry in Your Pocket* and *Sextette*, though to genre fans he is best known for playing Dr. Morbius in *Forbidden Planet* and Admiral Nelson

in *Voyage to the Bottom of the Sea*.

Genre credits:

The Glass Slipper (1955), *Forbidden Planet* (1956), *Voyage to the Bottom of the Sea* (1961), *The Neptune Factor – An Undersea Odyssey* (1973 – aka *The Neptune Disaster*)

Pierce, Arthur C.

American writer who was prolific at the low budget end of the genre market in the 60s. He also directed one of his scripts, *Women of the Prehistoric Planet*.

Genre credits:

The Cosmic Man (1958), *Beyond the Time Barrier* (1960), *Invasion of the Animal People* (1960 – aka *Terror in the Midnight Sun*), *Mutiny in Outer Space* (1964), *The Human Duplicators* (1964), *Women of the Prehistoric Planet* (1965 – also d), *Cyborg 2087* (1966), *Destination Inner Space* (1966), *Dimension 5* (1966)

Pink, Sid (Sidney) (1916-)

American writer, producer and director who, after making *The Angry Red Planet* in 1959, made a handful of low budget genre pictures in Europe. His other credits include *Pyro*, *The Sweet Sound of Death*, *Finger on the Trigger* and *The Tall Women*. He began his career as a movie theatre manager and projectionist.

Genre credits:

The Angry Red Planet (1959 – co-story/co-p), *Journey to the Seventh Planet* (1961 – story/co-w/p/d), *Reptilicus* (1962 – story/co-w/p/d), *Operation Atlantis* (1965 – p)

Pinocchio

USA 1940 77m Technicolor
A wooden puppet is brought to life by the Blue Fairy and has many misadventures with his sidekick Jiminy Cricket before being turned into a real boy.

Delightful, beautifully crafted cartoon feature which has lost none of its gaiety and charm and contains several bravura sequences.

p: Walt Disney
w: Ted Sears, Otto Englander, Webb Smith, William Cottrell, Joseph Sabo, Erdman Penner, Aurelius Battaglia
story: Collodi
supervising d: Ben Sharpsteen, Hamilton Luske
m: LEIGH HARLINE, PAUL J. SMITH, NED WASHINGTON (AA)
song: *When You Wish Upon a Star*
m: LEIGH HARLINE (m), NED WASHINGTON (ly) (AA)
voices: Dickie Jones (Pinocchio), CLIFF EDWARDS (Jiminy Cricket), Charles Judels, Christian Rub, Frankie Darro

Plan 9 from Outer Space

USA 1959 79m bw
Invaders from another world threaten to take over the earth by raising the dead to help them.

Judged by many to be the worst movie ever made, this zero budget schlock science fiction entry is at least worth seeking out for its considerable unintentional hilarity, which includes cardboard gravestones, which not only wobble but fall over, and hub cap flying saucers. Notable also for being Lugosi's last film; he died after only three days of filming and was subsequently replaced by an actor not only shorter than him, but who spends most of his time hiding behind a cape to disguise the fact that he looks nothing like Lugosi. Now a cult item, it has to be seen to be believed. A stage musical followed in the 90s.

p: Edward D. Wood, Jr. for Criswell
exec p: S. Edward Reynolds
w/d/ed: Edward D. Wood, Jr.
ph: William G. Thompson
md: Gordon Zahler
ad: no credit given
cos: Dick Chaney
sp: Charles Duncan, Jim Woods
sound: Dale Knight
Bela Lugosi, Gregory Walscott, Mona McKinnon, Duke Moore, Tom Keene, Vampira, Tor Johnson, Lyle Talbot, Criswell, Dudley Manlove, John Beckinridge, Joanna Lee

Planet Earth

USA 1974 colour TVM
A suspended animation accident sees an astronaut transported into the future where society is ruled by women.

Dismal attempt by its writer-producer to find another *Star Trek*.

exec p: Gene Roddenberry for Warner/Norway
w: Gene Roddenberry, Juanita Bartlett
story: Gene Roddenberry
d: Marc Daniels
ph: Arch R. Delzell
m: Harry Sukman
ed: George Walters
ad: Robert Kinosluta
cos: William Ware Theiss
sound: no credit given
John Saxon, Diana Muldaur, Ted Cassidy, Janet Margolin, Christopher Cary

Planet of the Apes

USA 1968 119m DeLuxe Panavision
Astronauts find themselves trapped on a planet where Man has regressed and apes now dominate.

Seminal science fiction adventure, intelligently written and crafted, with the final twist an added bonus to an

George Taylor (Charlton Heston), Nova (Linda Harrison),
Zira (Kim Hunter) and Cornelius (Roddy McDowall) take stock
of the situation towards the end of the excellent *Planet of the Apes*.

already fine entertainment. The flexible ape make-up also adds immeasurably. It was followed by four sequels, *Beneath the Planet of the Apes* (1969), *Escape from the Planet of the Apes* (1970), *Conquest of the Planet of the Apes* (1972) and *Battle for the Planet of the Apes* (1973). There were also two television series, one live action (1974), the other animated (1975).

p: Mort Abrahams for TCF/APJAC
w: MICHAEL WILSON, ROD SERLING
novel: Pierre Boulle
d: FRANKLIN J. SCHAFFNER
ph: LEON SHAMROY
m: JERRY GOLDSMITH
ed: HUGH S. FOWLER
pd: Jack Martin Smith, William Creber
cos: Marion Haack
sp: L. B. Abbott, Art Cruickshank, Emil Kosa, Jr.
sound: Herman Lewis, David Dockendorf
make-up: JOHN CHAMBERS (special AA)
CHARLTON HESTON, RODDY MCDOWELL, KIM HUNTER, MAURICE EVANS, James Whitmore, James Daly, Linda Harrison

Pleasence, Donald (1919-1995)

British actor who, though best known for his horror films, has also made a couple of key science fiction films, most notably *Fantastic Voyage* in which he played the sinister Dr. Michaels, and *THX 1138* in which he played *SEN 5241*. He began his acting career in rep in Jersey, making his West End debut in 1939. He joined the RAF during World War Two, during which he was a POW. He made his film debut in *The Beachcomber* in 1954 and was familiar to TV audiences in the 50s as Prince John in *Robin Hood*. His other credits include *A Tale of Two Cities*, *Hell is a City*, *The Great Escape*, *The Caretaker*, *The Greatest Story Ever Told*, *Soldier Blue*, *Outback*, *The Black Windmill*, *The Eagle Has Landed* (as Himmler), *Telefon*, *Hannah's War* and *Shadows and Fog*. His countless horror films include the *Halloween* series, *Death Line*, *Tales That Witness Madness*, *Dracula* (as Dr. Seward), *Phenomena* (aka *Creepers*), *Prince of Darkness* and *The Raven*.

Genre credits:
Fantastic Voyage (1966), *You Only Live Twice* (1967 – as Blofeld), *THX 1138* (1970), *The Pied Piper* (1971), *Oh God* (1977), *Escape from New York* (1981 – as the U.S. President)

Plummer, Christopher (1927-)

Distinguished Canadian actor with much stage experience, especially in Shakespeare, though to film audiences he shall forever be known as Captain Von Trapp in *The Sound of Music* (which he himself later labelled 'The Sound of Mucus'). He began his career on stage in Canada in 1950, making his film debut in 1958 in *Stage Struck*. His other credits include *The Fall of the Roman Empire*, *The Night of the Generals*, *Waterloo*, *The Man Who Would Be King* (as Rudyard Kipling), *The Return of the Pink Panther*, *International Velvet*, *Murder by Decree* (as Sherlock Holmes), *Dragnet*, *Where the Heart Is* (as a character called Shitty) and *Wolf*. He is also the father of actress Amanda Plummer (*The World According to Garp*, *Static*, *The Fisher King*, *Freejack*, *Pulp Fiction*, *Nostradamus*, etc.).

Genre credits:
Starcrash (1978), *Somewhere in Time* (1980), *Dreamscape* (1984), *An American Tail* (1986 – voice), *Star Trek VI: The Undiscovered Country* (1991), *Rock-a-Doodle* (1992 – voice), *Harrison Bergeron* (1995), *Twelve Monkeys* (1995)

Plymouth
USA 1990 96m Technicolor TVM
When their town is rendered uninhabitable following a toxic accident, its inhabitants are transported to a colony on the moon by the company responsible, but life there proves to be just as dangerous.

A promising idea is frittered away via a series of dull domestic dramas. Like its lunar setting, the whole thing lacks atmosphere.

p: Ian Sander for Touchstone/Lotoff/RAI Uno
exec p: Ralph Winter, Lee David Zlotoff
w/d: Lee David Zlotoff
ph: Hiro Narita
m: Brad Fiedel
ed: John W. Wheeler
pd: Michael Baugh
cos: Tom Brosnan
sp: Perpetual Motion Pictures
sound: Steve Nelson
Cindy Pickett, Dale Midkiff, Richard Hamilton, Jerry Hardin, Matthew Brown, Perrey Reeves, Brent Fraser

Pocahontas
USA 1995 81m Technicolor Dolby
In 1607, seaman John Smith travels to the New World, where he falls in love with an Indian girl called Pocahontas.

Though historically inaccurate and somewhat sanitised, this cartoon feature is nevertheless made with a certain amount of flair, and includes several well-staged musical sequences in the best Disney manner (though there is perhaps a little too much posing on rocky promontories from its two central characters). At least none of the obligatory animals speak this time round.

p: James Pentecost for Walt Disney
w: Carl Binder, Susannah Grant, Philip Lazebnik
d: Mike Gabriel, Eric Goldberg
m: Alan Menken (aa)
songs: Alan Menken (m), Stephen Schwartz (ly) (aa, best song, *The Colors of the Wind*)
ed: H. Lee Patterson
ad: Michael Giamo
voices: Irene Bedard, Mel Gibson, Billy Connolly, Christian Bale, David Ogden Stiers, Russell Means, Linda Hunt, John Kassir, Danny Mann, Joe Baker, Gordon Tootoosis

Poledouris, Basil (1945-)

American composer who began his career in 1973 with *Extreme Close-Up* following training at The University of Southern California. A wide variety of projects have followed since, among them *Big Wednesday*, *The Blue Lagoon*, *Iron Eagle*, *Farewell to the King*, *The Hunt for Red October*, *Hot Shots, Part Deux*, *Free Willy*, *Serial Mom* and *Lonesome Dove* (TVM).

Genre credits:
Conan the Barbarian (1982), *Conan the Destroyer* (1984), *Flesh and Blood* (1985), *Robocop* (1987), *Robocop 3* (1993), *The Jungle Book* (1994 – aka *Rudyard Kipling's The Jungle Book*), *Starship Troopers* (1997)

Popeye

USA 1980 114m Metrocolor Technovision
After a long absence, Popeye returns to Sweethaven to look for his long-lost father.

Ill-conceived live action musical version of the popular cartoon character. Hard to tolerate for long, particularly given its director's penchant for having everyone talk at once, though the cast do look their parts.

p: Robert Evans for Paramount/Disney
exec p: C. O. Erickson
w: Jules Feiffer
comic strip: E. C. Segar
d: Robert Altman
ph: Giuseppe Rotunno
songs: Harry Nilsson
m/md: Tom Pierson
ed: Tony Lombardo
pd: Wolf Kroeger
cos: Scott Bushell
sp: Allen Hall
sound: Bob Gravenor, Michael Minkler
ch: Sharon Kinney, Lou Wills, Hovey Burhess
titles: Patty Ryan
Robin Williams, Shelley Duvall, Paul Dooley, Ray Walston, Linda Hunt, Richard Libertin, Wesley Ivan Hurti

Powder

USA 1995 112m Technicolor Dolby
An albino teenager with what seem to be supernatural powers is discovered living in the basement of his grandparents' house, from whence he is placed in care and sent to the local high school, where the pupils react to him in the expected manner.

A teenage angst movie with a difference, this affecting inevitably sentimental drama exudes a curious power of its own which keeps one watching until the final moving pay off. Well worth seeking out.

p: Roger Birnbaum, Daniel Grodnik for Hollywood/Caravan
exec p: Riley Kathryn Ellis, Robert Snukal
w/d: Victor Salva
ph: Jerzy Zielinski
m: JERRY GOLDSMITH
ed: Dennis M. Hill
pd: Waldemar Kalinowski
cos: Betsy Coxl
sp: Stephanie Powelll
sound: Steve C. Aaron
make-up: Thomas R. Burman, Bari

Dreidband-Bruman
Sean Patrick Flannery, Jeff Goldblum, Mary Steenburgen, Lance Henricksen, Susan Tyrell, Brandon Smith, Bradford Tatum, Missy Crider, Tom Tarantini, Chad Cox, Ike Eisenmann (voice)

Powell, Eddie (1927-)

British stunt man, long associated with Hammer, where he often doubled for Christopher Lee. A despatch rider for the Grenadier Guards during World War Two, he turned to stunt work in 1948, his largest role being that of Prem the Mummy in Hammer's *The Mummy's Shroud*. His other credits include *Dracula – Prince of Darkness*, *Dracula Has Risen from the Grave*, *The Devil Rides Out*, *Where Eagles Dare*, *The Omen* and *The Keep*.

Genre credits:
Daleks – Invasion Earth, 2150 A. D. (1966), *The Lost Continent* (1968), *Alien* (1979 – uncredited work as the alien), *Flash Gordon* (1980), *Krull* (1983), *Legend* (1985)

Pratt, Roger (1947-)

British cinematographer who began his career filming documentaries before moving on to such films as *Mona Lisa*, *High Hopes*, *Shadowlands* and *Mary Shelley's Frankenstein*. He also photographed several episodes of TV's *The Storyteller* for Jim Henson.

Genre credits:
Brazil (1985), *Batman* (1989), *The Fisher King* (1991), *Twelve Monkeys* (1995)

Prayer of the Roller Boys

USA 1991 90m colour
In the future, when society as we know it has ceased to exist, a group of rollerblading teenagers take to the street

The cast of *Predator* take time out to pose for the cameras during filming. Left to right: Shane Black (future screenwriter of *Lethal Weapon*), Sonny Landham, Arnold Schwarzenegger, Richard Chaves (kneeling), Carl Weathers, Bill Duke (future director of *A Rage in Harlem*) and Jesse Ventura.

to pedal a drug called Royal Mist.

Lame futuristic trash of the kind already dated in the 70s.

p: Robert Mickelson for Gaga/JVC/TV Tokyo/Fox Lorber
w: Peter Iliff
d: Rick King
ph: Phedon Papamichael
m: Stacy Widelitz
ed: Daniel Leowenthal
pd: Thomas A. Walsh
cos: Marrily Murray-Walsh
sound: Craig Felburg
Corey Haim, Patricia Arquette, Christopher Collet, J. C. Quinn, Julius Harris, Devin Clark, Mark Pellegrino, Morgan Weisser, G. Smokey Campbell

Predator

USA 1987 115m DeLuxe
Mercenaries on a secret mission in the jungle are picked off one by one by a

chameleon-like creature from outer space.

Relentlessly elongated actioner with ridiculous dialogue which very quickly outstays its welcome. However, it made a pot of money and produced a sequel, *Predator 2*, that appeared in 1990.

p: Laurence Pereira, Jim Thomas for TCF
exec p: Lawrence Gordon, Joel Silver, John Davis
w: Jim Thomas, John Thomas
d: John McTiernan
ph: Donald McAlpine
m: Alan Silvestri
ed: John F. Link, Mark Helfrich
pd: John Vallone
cos: Marilyn Vance Straker
sp: R. Greenberg, Joel Hynek
sound: Kevin Carpenter, Don Bassman,

Kevin Cleary, Richard Overton
make-up effects: Stan Winston
2nd unit d/stunt co-ordinator: Craig R. Baxley
2nd unit ph: Frank E. Johnson
Arnold Schwarzenegger, Carl Weathers, Kevin Peter Hall (as the Predator), Shane Black, Sonny Landham, Jesse Ventura, Bill Duke, Elpidia Carrillo

Predator 2

USA 1990 107m DeLuxe Dolby
In 1997, a second predator treats Los Angeles as its own private game park.

Sickeningly expensive follow-up in which plot and character take second place to the relentless action, special effects, noise and foul language. It caters to the lowest possible denominator – and then some.

p: Lawrence Gordon, Joel Silver, John Davis for TCF
w: Jim Thomas, John Thomas
d: Stephen Hopkins
ph: Peter Levy
m: Alan Silvestri
ed: Mark Goldblatt
pd: Lawrence G. Paul
cos: Marilyn Vance-Straker
sp: R. Greenberg
sound: Richard Raguse
make-up effects: Stan Winston
stunt co-ordinator: Gary Davis
Danny Glover, Gary Busey, Maria Conchita Alonso, Ruben Blades, Bill Paxton, Robert Davi, Adam Baldwin, Kevin Peter Hall (as the Predator), Ken McCord, Morton Downey, Jr., Calvin Lockhart, Steve Kahan

---

Pressman, Edward R. (1943-)

Busy American producer whose output includes a good selection of science fiction and horror titles, as well as more mainstream productions, among them *Badlands*, *Paradise Alley*, *Plenty*, *Wall Street*, *Talk Radio*, *Reversal of Fortune* and *Storyville*.

Genre credits:
Conan the Barbarian (1981 – exec p), *Masters of the Universe* (1987 - exec p), *Cherry 2000* (1988 - co-p), *Martians, Go Home* (1990 - exec p), *The Crow* (1994 - p), *Judge Dredd* (1995 - co-exec p), *The Crow: City of Angels* (1996 - p), *The Island of Dr Moreau* (1996 - p)

Price, Vincent (1911-1993)

American actor known primarily for his horror roles, most notably in *House of Wax*, *Fall of the House of Usher* (aka *House of Usher*), *The Pit and the Pendulum*, *The Raven*, *The Tomb of*

Ligeia, *Witchfinder General*, *The Abominable Dr. Phibes* and *Theatre of Blood*. On stage from 1935 and in films from 1938 with *Service DeLuxe*, his non-horror credits include *The Song of Bernadette*, *Laura*, *The Three Musketeers*, *The Ten Commandments* and *The Whales of August*.

Genre credits:
Master of the World (1961), *City Under the Sea* (1965 – aka *Wargods of the Deep*), *Dr. Goldfoot and the Bikini Machine* (1965 – aka *Dr. G and the Bikini Machine*), *Dr. Goldfoot and the Girl Bombs* (1966 – aka *Le Spie Vengono del Semifreddo/I Due Mafiosi dell' FBI*), *The Great Mouse Detective* (1986 – aka *Basil, The Great Mouse Detective* – voice, as Professor Ratigan), *Edward Scissorhands* (1990)

The Princess and the Goblin

GB/Wales/Hungary 1992 79m
Technicolor
A princess and a young miner join forces to usurp a goblin intent on overthrowing the throne.

Wholly unremarkable animated feature with litttle interest opprovided by the vocals or the visuals.

p: Robin Lyons for Siriol/Pannonia/ NHK/SC4
exec p: Steve Walsh, Marietta Dardai
w: Robin Lyons
novel: George MacDonald
d: Jozef Gemes
m: Istvan Lerch
sound: Imre Andras Nyerges, Clive Pendry, John Griffiths
voices: Joss Ackland, Claire Bloom, Sally Ann Marsh, Roy Kinnear, Peggy Mount, Rik Mayall, Peter Murray, Mollie Sugden, Victor Spinetti, William Hootkins, Maxine Howe

---

The Princess Bride ☁

USA 1987 98m DeLuxe Dolby
A swashbuckling farm boy rescues his true love from a dastardly prince.

Haltingly handled spoof fairy story with compensations in the script.

p: Andrew Scheinmann, Rob Reiner for Act III/Princess Bride
exec p: Norman Lear
w: WILLIAM GOLDMAN from his novel
d: Rob Reiner
ph: Adrian Biddle
m: Mark Knopfler
ed: Robert Leighton
pd: Norman Garwood
cos: Phyllis Dalton
sp: Nick Allder
sound: David John
2nd unit ph: Ray Andrew
stunt co-ordinator: Peter Diamond
Cary Elwes, Mandy Patinkin, Chris Sarandon, Christopher Guest, Peter Falk, Robin Wright, Andre the Giant, Peter Cook, Billy Crystal, Fred Savage, Wallace Shawn, Carol Kane, Mel Smith

---

Project Shadowchaser

GB/Canada 1992 93m Fujicolor Dolby
In the near future, a convict given a life sentence in a cryogenic freezer is thawed out in the mistaken belief that he was the architect of a hospital where the president's daughter is being held hostage by a group of terrorists, one of whose number is an android.

Lacklustre blend of *Demolition Man*, *The Terminator* and *Die Hard*, routinely handled and further compromised by its obviously low budget.

p: John Eyres, Geoff Griffiths for EGM/NAR/Prism Entertainment/Shadowchase
w: Stephen Lister
d: John Eyres
ph: Alan M. Trow
m: Gary Pinder

ed: Delhak Wreen
pd: Mark Harris
cos: Philip Crichton
sp/2nd unit d: Brian Smithies
sound: Paul Davies, Steve Stockford
stunt co-ordinator: Terry Plummer
make-up effects: Chrissie Overs
Martin Kove, Meg Foster, Joss Ackland,
Frank Zagarino, Paul Koslo, Ricco Ross,
Raymond Evans, Robert Freeman

Project X

USA 1968 97m Technicolor

In the future, scientists brainwash a man into thinking he is living in the 1960s in order to recover some vital information.

Entertaining little thriller with rather more intelligence to it than one usually associates with the films of this producer-director.

p: William Castle for Paramount
w: Edmund Morris
novels: Leslie P. Davies
d: William Castle
ph: Harold Stine
m: Van Cleave
ed: Edwin H. Bryant
ad: Hal Pereira, Walter Tyler
sp: Paul K. Lerpae
titles/effects: Hanna-Barbera
2nd unit d: Wally Burr
Christopher George, Henry Jones, Harold Gould, Greta Baldwin, Monte Markham

The Projected Man

GB 1966 90m Technicolor Techniscope

A scientist working on the transmission of matter subjects himself to an experiment only to turn into a monster with the ability to kill on contact.

Fitfully diverting low budgeter with the expected clichés to hand.

p: John Croydon, Maurice Foster for MLC
w: John C. Cooper, Peter Bryan

story: Frank Quattrocchi
d: Ian Curteis
ph: Stan Pavey
m: Kenneth V. Jones
ed: Derek Holding
ad: Peter Mullins
cos: Kathleen Meore
sp: Flo Nordhoff, Robert Hedges, Mike Hope
sound: S. G. Rider, Red Law
Bryant Halliday, Mary Peach, Norman Wooland, Derek Farr, Ronald Allen, Derrick de Marney, Sam Kydd

Proteus

GB 1995 92m Technicolor Dolby

Survivors of a boat wreck take refuge on a seemingly deserted oil rig where a scientist's experiments with genetic engineering have produced a murderous creature which has the ability of taking over humans.

Or, in other words, *Alien* on an oil rig which had more or less been done with *The Intruder Within*. Both derivative and predictable, this is little more than the usual batch of tired clichés, tediously strung together by make-up effects artist-turned director Keen.

p: Paul Brooks for Polygram/Metrodome/Victor/Bestsellers/Wonderful Films (!)
exec p: Barry Barnholtz, Alan Martin, Alasdair Waddell
w: John Brosnan
novel: Harry Adam Knight
d: Bob Keen
ph: Adam Rodgers
m: David A. Hughes, John Murphy
ed: Liz Webber
pd: Mike Grant
cos: John Krausa
sp: Image Imagination
sound: Andy Kennedy, Aiden Hobbs
stunt co-ordinator: Rod Woodruff
Craig Fairbrass, Toni Barry, William Marni, Jenifer Calvert, Robert Firth, Margot

Steinberg, Ricco Ross, Doug Bradley

Prototype

USA 1982 96m Technicolor TVM

A scientist's experiments produce the first humanoid, and everything goes well until the military show an interest.

What could have been an intriguing update of *Frankenstein* all too quickly comes to rely on formula.

p: Robert A. Papazian for CBS
w/exec p: Richard Levinson, William Link
d: David Greene
ph: Harry May
m: Billy Goldenberg
ed: Parkie Singh
ad: Bill Ross
cos: Jacqueline Saint Anne
sp: Marty Bresin
sound: Robert Miller
Christopher Plummer, David Morse, Frances Sternhagen, Arthur Hill, Stephen Elliott, James Sutorius

Prowse, Dave

Tall (6'7") British actor and stunt man, best remembered for playing Darth Vader in the *Star Wars* trilogy (though Vader's voice was actually provided by James Earl Jones). He has also played the Frankenstein Monster three times in *Casino Royale* (as a gag cameo), *Horror of Frankenstein* and *Frankenstein and the Monster from Hell*, as well as the Green Cross Code Man in a TV ad campaign. His other film credits include *Up the Chastity Belt*, *White Cargo*, *Blacksnake* and *Vampire Circus*.

Genre credits:
Casino Royale (1967), *Jabberwocky* (1977), *Star Wars* (1977), *The Empire Strikes Back* (1980), *Return of the Jedi* (1983)

Pufnstuff

USA 1970 98m Technicolor

A young boy is transported to a comic book land and is helped by a friendly dragon to thwart a wicked witch.

Cheeseparing children's fantasy, very little of which works. Based on the popular television series *H. R. Pufnstuff*.

p: Si Rose for Universal/Krofft Enterprises
w: John Fenton Murray, Si Rose
d: Hollingsworth Morse
ph: Kenneth Peach
m: Charles Fox
ly: Norman Gimbel
ed: David Rawlins
ad: Alexander Golitzen, Walter Scott Herndon
ch: Paul Godkin
Jack Wilde, BILLIE HAYES, Martha Raye (as Witchiepoo), Mama Cass, Johnny Silver, Billy Barty, Angelo Rossitto

The Puppet Masters

USA 1994 109m DeLuxe Dolby

An alien spaceship crash-lands near a small American township and the creatures within begin to take over the local populace at an alarming rate. Consequently, the army are brought in to contain the situation before it reaches national importance.

The Tommyknockers meets *Invasion of the Body Snatchers* meets *Aliens* meets *Invaders from Mars* meets *Outbreak*. Slickly enough done for those who don't mind (or perhaps enjoy spotting) clichés.

p: Ralph Winter for Hollywood
exec p: Michael Engelberg
w: Ted Elliott, Terry Rossio, David S. Gayer
novel: Robert A. Heinlein
d: Stuart Orme
ph: Clive Tickner
m: Colin Towns
ed: William Goldenberg
pd: Daniel Lomino
cos: Tom Brosnan
sp: Buena Vista Visual Effects, Roy Arbogast
sound: Robert Anderson, Jr., John Pospisil
make-up effects: Greg Cannom
stunt co-ordinator: Jeffrey Danshaw
Donald Sutherland, Eric Thal, Julie Warner, Keith David, Will Patton, Yaphet Kotto, Richard Belzer

The Purple Rose of Cairo ☺

USA 1984 82m DeLuxe/bw

During the Depression, a star-struck waitress finds her life changed when an actor in a third-rate movie she is watching walks off the screen and into reality because he loves her.

An engaging concept which might have made a good sketch is unfortunately stretched to the limit. Despite good production, the results are only fitfully amusing.

p: Robert Greenhut for Orion
exec p: Jack Rollins, Charles H. Joffe
w/d: Woody Allen
ph: Gordon Willis
m: Dick Hyman
ed: Susan E. Morse
pd: Stuart Wurtzel
cos: Jeffrey Kurland
sp: R. Greenberg
sound: James Sabat, Frank Graziadei, Richard Dior
Mia Farrow, Jeff Daniels, Danny Aiello, Dianne Weist, Stephanie Farrow, Van Johnson, Milo O'Shea, Irving Metzman, David Keiserman, Edward Herrmann, John Wood, Zoe Caldwell

Pyun, Albert

American director and occasional writer working at the low budget exploitation end of the genre market, mostly turning out undistinguished direct-to-video fodder. His other credits include *Dangerously Close*, *Down Twisted* and *Kickboxer 2*.

Genre credits:

The Sword and the Sorcerer (1982 – co-w/d), *Radioactive Dreams* (1986 -d), *Alien from LA* (1987 – w/d), *Cyborg* (1989 – d), *Spiderman* (1989 – d), *Arcade* (1993 – d), *Nemesis* (1994 – d), *Nemesis 2: Nebula* (1994 – d), *Nemesis 3: Time Lapse* (1995 - d)

R.K.O. Radio Pictures

Reknowned in the 30s for its glossy musicals starring Ginger Rogers and Fred Astaire and in the 40s for its Val Lewton-produced horrors, R.K.O. was founded in 1921 as an adjunct to the Keith Orpheum circuit and produced top quality family entertainment for almost three decades before running into financial difficulties, after which it was bought by Lucille Ball and Desi Arnaz's Desilu TV production outfit in 1953. Perhaps the studio's greatest contribution to the fantasy genre was the 1933 effects spectacular *King Kong*.

Genre filmography:
King Kong (1933), *Son of Kong* (1933), *The Boy with Green Hair* (1948), *Mighty Joe Young* (1949)

Rabin, Jack

American special effects technician working at the low budget end of the science fiction and horror genres. Also an occasional writer, producer and art director. His other credits include *The Neanderthal Man*, *The Pharoah's Curse*, *The Black Sleep* and *Macabre*.

Genre credits:
Rocketship X-M (1950 – co-sp), *Unknown World* (1951 – co-ad/co-p/co-sp), *Robot Monster* (1953 – aka *Monster from the Moon* – co-sp), *Cat Women of the Moon*

(1953 – co-story/c□
Hollow Mountain (□
de la Montana Hu□
from Green Hell (1□
Invisible Boy (1957□
Satellites (1957 – □
Giant Behemoth (1□
Sea Monster – co□
Submarine (1959 □
The Thirty-Foot B□
co-story/co-sp), D□
co-sp)

Raggedy □ Andy

USA 1977 85m □

A little girl's d□ into all kinds □

Well made h□ charming carto□ action bookene□

p: Richard Horn□ Gold/ITT/Bobb□
exec p: Lester □
w: Patricia Thac□
story: Johnny □
d: Richard Willi□
ph: Dick Minga□
songs/m: Joe □
ed: Harry Char□ McIlwainew, M□
pd: Corny Col□
ad: William Mi□
sound: Dick V□
voices: Didi C□ Stuthman, Nik□ Silver, Sheldor□

Raiders □ Ark □

USA 1981 11□
Dolby

Adventurer □
Jones races □
the long-los□

Technica□

Q see Q: The Winged Serpent

Q: The Winged Serpent 🛸

USA 1982 100m colour

A flesh-eating prehistoric serpent threatens New York city.

Quirky monster pic which at least keeps moving for the most part.

p: Larry Cohen for UFD
exec p: Dan Sandburg, Richard de Bona
w/d: Larry Cohen
ph: Fred Murphy
m: Robert O. Ragland
ed: Armand Lebowitz
ad: no credit given
cos: Tim D'Arcy
sp: David Allen, Randy Cook, Peter Kuram
sound: Jeff Hayes

Michael Moriarty, David Carradine, Candy Clark, Richard Roundtree, James Dixon

---

Quaid, Dennis (1954-)

American actor, brother of Randy Quaid, who made his movie debut in 1975 in *Crazy Mama*, since when he has appeared in all manner of mainstream films, among them *The Long Riders*, *Jaws 3D*, *The Right Stuff*, *The Big Easy*, *D.O.A.*, *Postcards from the Edge* and *Wyatt Earp*.

Genre credits:
Caveman (1980), *Dreamscape* (1985), *Innerspace* (1987), *Dragonheart* (1996)

Quaid, Randy (1953-)

American actor, brother of Dennis Quaid, who tends to play affable hicktype characters. Began his movie career as a supporting actor in a handful of films for director Peter Bogdanovich (*Targets*, *The Last Picture Show*, *What's Up, Doc?*, *Paper Moon*) after which he scored a personal success in *The Last Detail*. Since then he has appeared in all manner of movies, among them *The Apprenticeship of Duddy Kravitz*, *Bound for Glory*, *The Long Riders*, *Parents*, *Texasville* (for Bogdanovich), *Days of Thunder*, *Quick Change* and *Major League II*.

Genre credits:
Martians, Go Home (1984), *Freaked* (1993), *Independence Day* (1996)

Quarantine

Canada 1989 99m colour Ultra Stereo

In the future, victims of a virus find themselves quarantined by a fascist regime.

Tedious low budgeter exploiting the cliched totalitarian view of the future to little effect.

p: Charles Wilkinson for Apple Pie/Atlantis/Beaco/BC/Telefilm Canada
exec p: Stephen Cheikes
w/d: Charles Wilkinson
ph: Tobias Schliessler
m: Graeme Coleman
ed: Raymond Hall
ad: Robert Logevall
cos: Tracey Boulton, Phillip Low
sp: Randy Shimkew
sound: Michael McGee, Paul Sharpe

Beatrice Beopple, Garwin Sanford, Jerry Wasserman, Tom McBeath, Michele

---

Goodger, Kaj-Erik Eriksen, Cynthia Wong (voice)

Quatermass and the Pit 💩💩

GB 1967 87m Technicolor

During extension work on London's underground, an impenetrable spacecraft is unearthed and a mysterious force makes itself felt.

Intellectually exciting and compulsively watchable big screen transferral of the TV series with many gripping moments, only occasionally let down by unconvincing effects and dated terminology. Certainly the best in the Quatermass films.

p: Anthony Nelson Keys for Hammer/Associated British
w: NIGEL KNEALE, from his TV series
d: ROY WARD BAKER
ph: Arthur Grant
m: Tristam Carey
md: Philip Martell
ed: James Needs, Spencer Reeve
ad: Bernard Robinson
cos: Rosemary Burrows
sp: Les Bowie
sound: Sash Fisher

ANDREW KEIR, JAMES DONALD, BARBARA SHELLEY, Julian Glover, Duncan Lamont, Edwin Richafield, Peter Copley, Sheila Steafel, Brian Marshall

---

The Quatermass Experiment 💩💩💩

GB 1955 82m bw

The only surviving member of a space expedition begins to mutate once back on earth and is later cornered in Westminster Abbey having been on the rampage.

Though the script and concept have now dated somewhat, this nevertheless remains an eerily effective and sometimes quite frightening science fiction horror whose success in both Britain and America helped to put Hammer films on the map. Required viewing for genre addicts.

p: Anthony Nelson Keys for Hammer/Exclusive
w: Richard Landau, Val Guest
TV series: NIGEL KNEALE
d: VAL GUEST
ph: Jimmy Harvey
m: JAMES BERNARD.
md: John Hollingsworth
ed: James Needs
ad: J. Elder Wills
cos: Molly Arbuthnot
sp: Les Bowie
sound: H. C. Pearson
Brian Donlevy, Jack Warner, Margia Dean, RICHARD WORDSWORTH, David King Wood, THORA HIRD, Gordon Jackson, Lionel Jeffries, Harold Lang, Maurice Kauffmann, Sam Kydd, Jane Asher

Quatermass 2 🛸🛸

GB 1957 85m bw
Professor Quatermass discovers that an industrial plant supposedly making synthetic food is in fact harbouring aliens from outer space.

Imaginatively plotted follow-up to *The Quatermass Experiment*, betrayed only by its low budget, general scientific naivety and a monster that looks like a walking mud pie. Plenty of interest for genre addicts.

p: Anthony Hinds for Hammer
w: Nigel Kneale, Val Guest
TV series: NIGEL KNEALE
d: Val Guest
ph: Gerald Gibbs
m: James Bernard
md: John Hollingsworth
ed: James Needs
ad: Bernard Robinson
cos: Rene Cooke
sp: Bill Warrington, Henry Harris,

Frank George
sound: Cliff San
Brian Donlevy, Jo
Bryan Forbes, W
Ripper, Charles
Tom Chatto

Queen o

USA 1958 79m
Astronauts or
tion are diver
discover is ru

Hilariously
must for devo
The dialogue
believed (des

p: Ben Schwal
w: Charles Be
story: Ben He
d: Edward Ber
ph: William W
m: Marlin Skil
ed: William A
ad: David Mil
sp: Milt Rice
Zsa Zsa Gabo

A mome
Zsa Zsa G

Genre credits:
Star Wars (1977 – co-sp), *The Empire Strikes Back* (1980 – co-sp), *Return of the Jedi* (1983 – co-sp), *Star Trek III* (1984 – sp), *Cocoon* (1985 – co-sp), *Star Trek IV: The Voyage Home* (1986 – sp), *Back to the Future, Part II* (1989 – co-sp), *Who Framed Roger Rabbit?* (1988 – co-sp), *Back to the Future, Part III* (1990 – co-sp), *The Rocketeer* (1991 – co-sp/co-2nd unit d), *The Mask* (1994 – co-sp), *Phenomenon* (1996 – sp), *Michael* (1996 - sp), *Contact* (1997 – sp)

Rambaldi, Carlo

Italian special effects technician now working mostly in Hollywood. So far he has won three Oscars for his effects work for, incredibly, *King Kong* (1976 – with Glen Robinson, and Frank Van Der Veer), *Alien (*1979 – with H.R. Giger, Brian Johnson, Nick Allder and Denys Ayling), and *E. T.* (1982 – with Dennis Murren and Kenneth F. Smith). His other credits include *Deep Red* (aka *Profundo Rosso/The Hatchet Murders*), *Possession*, *The Hand* and *Primal Rage*.

Genre credits:
King Kong (1976 – co-sp), *Alien* (1979 – co-sp), *E. T.* (1982 – co-sp), *Dune* (1984 – co-sp), *King Kong Lives* (1986 – sp)

Rats Night of Terror

It/Fr 1983 80m Telecolor Technovision
In 225 AB (after the bomb!), a new breed of "primitives" have to fend for themselves against a plague of man-eating rats.

Poorly dubbed post-apocalyptic nonsense with just a couple of well-staged rat attack sequences in its favour.

p: (no producer credit given) for Beatrice/Imp
w: Claudio Fragasso, Herve Piccini
story: Bruno Mattei

d: Vincent Dawn, Clyde Anderson
ph: Franco Delli Colli
m: Luigi Ceccarelli
ed: Gilbert Kikione
ad: Maurizio Mammi, Charles Fimelli
cos: Elda Chinellato
sound: no credit given
Richard Raymond, Janna Ryann, Richard Crost, Alex McBride, Ann Gisel Glass, Tony Lombardo

Ray, Fred Olen (1954-)

Prolific American producer and director, a former TV station engineer and make-up man who works at the low budget end of the exploitation/horror market, much of his output going straight to video. His other credits include *Commando Squad*, *Hollywood Chainsaw Hookers*, *Evil Toons*, *Teenage Exorcist*, *Biohazard*, *Biohazard II*, *Hollywood Scream Queen*, *Hot Tub Party*, *Terminal Force*, *Bulletproof* and *Mob Boss*.

Genre credits:
Alien Dead (1979 – aka *It Fell from the Sky*), *The Halloween Planet* (1982), *Phantom Empire* (1987), *Deep Space* (1988), *Demon Sword* (1990), *Bad Girls from Mars* (1991), *Empire of the Dark* (1991), *Wizards of the Demon Sword* (1992), *Dark Universe* (1993), *Dinosaur Island* (1994)

The Red Balloon 🛸🛸

Fr 1955 35m Technicolor
A small boy finds a red balloon on the streets of Paris, and it becomes his sole playmate.

Charming if somewhat overrated fantasy short.

p: Montsouris
w: Albert Lamorisse (aa)
d: Albert Lamorisse
ph: Edmond Sechan
m: Maurice Le Roux

ed: Pierre Gillette
Pascal Lamorisse, George Seiner, Wladimir Popt, Paul Perry

Red Planet Mars

USA 1952 87m bw
Radio messages are received from Mars, the content of which cause a religious revival.

Over-talkative science fiction with religious and propagandist elements (make love not war, etc.). Poor handling scuppers what potential it has (which isn't much).

p: Donald Hyde, Anthony Veiller for UA
w: Anthony Veiller, John L. Balderston
play: John L. Balderston, John Hoare
d: Harry Horner
ph: Joseph Biroc
m: Mahlon Merrick
ed: Francis D. Lyon
ad: Charles D. Hall
Peter Graves, Andrea King, Orley Lindgren, Herberg Berghof, Walter Sande, Marvin Miller, Willis Bouchey, Morris Ankrum, Richard Powers, Bayard Veiller

Red Sonja

USA/It 1985 93m Metroclor Panavision
Red Sonja sets out to retrieve a powerful talisman from an evil queen and to avenge the death of her sister.

Conan-style sword and sorcery. Wooden script and acting, but it occasionally looks good, despite itself.

p: Christian Ferry for MGM/UA/Famous Films
exec p: Dino de Laurentiis
w: Clive Exton, George MacDonald Fraser
books: Robert E. Howard
d: Richard Fleischer
ph: GIUSEPPE ROTUNNO
m: ENNIO MORRICONE
ed: Frank J. Urioste
pd/cos: DANILO DONATI

sp: John Striber, Albert Whitlock
sound: Les Wiggins, Amelio Verona
action d: Vic Armstrong
Brigitte Nielsen, Arnold Schwarzenegger (as Conan), Sandahl Bergman, Paul Smith, Pat Roach, Ronald Lacey, Ernie Reyes, Jr.

Reeve, Christopher (1952-)

American actor, best known for playing Superman/Clark Kent in four movies. Began his career in summer stock, after which he appeared in the TV soap *Love of Life*. On Broadway in 1976 he appeared in *A Matter of Gravity* (playing Katharine Hepburn's grandson). Made his film debut in 1978 in *Gray Lady Down*, after which he was chosen to play the Man of Steel. His other credits include *Deathtrap*, *Monsignor*, *Switching Channels*, *Noises Off* and *The Remains of the Day*. A riding accident which left him paralysed from the neck down ended his acting career, since when he has turned to writing, directing and cartoon vocals.

Genre credits:
Superman (1978), *Superman 2* (1980), *Somewhere in Time* (1980), *Superman 3* (1983), *Superman IV: The Quest for Peace* (1987 – also co-story/2nd unit d)

Reeves, Keanu (1964-)

American actor who, after brief appearances in the likes of *Flying*, *Youngblood* and *Dangerous Liaisons*, shot to stardom in *Bill and Ted's Excellent Adventure* in 1988, though he wouldn't hit superstar status until *Speed* in 1994. In as many misses as hits, his other credits include *Permanent Record*, *Point Break*, *My Own Private Idaho*, *Bram Stoker's Dracula*, *Much Ado About Nothing*, *Little Buddha* and *A Walk in the Clouds* and *Speed 2: Chain Reaction* (1996).

Genre credits:
Bill and Ted's Excellent Adventure (1988), *Bill and Ted's Bogus Journey* (1991), *Johnny Mnemonic* (1995)

Reitherman, Wolfgang (Woolie) (1909-1985)

American animator, long with Disney, where he animated, sequence-directed or directed many of the studio's cartoon features, all of which he produced following Disney's death until his own retirement in 1981. He began with the company in 1933 as an animator in the shorts department (his first short was a sequence in *Funny Little Bunnies*, released in 1934) and went on to co-animate such features as *Snow White and the Seven Dwarfs* (animating the magic mirror), *Pinocchio* (co-animating Jiminy Cricket), *The Reluctant Dragon* and *Saludos, Amigos*. He won a Best Animated Short Oscar for *Winnie the Pooh and the Blustery Day* (1968). His son Bruce provided the voice of Mowgli in *The Jungle Book* as well as vocals for *Winnie the Pooh and the Honey Tree*.

Genre credits:
Snow White and the Seven Dwarfs (1937 – co-animator), *Pinocchio* (1940 – co-anim), *Fantasia* (1940 – co-anim), *Dumbo* (1941 – co-anim), *The Reluctant Dragon* (1941 – co-anim [Reitherman also briefly appears as himself]), *Saludos, Amigos* (1943 – co-anim), *Fun and Fancy Free* (1947 – co-anim), *Ichabod and Mr Toad* (1949 – co-anim),

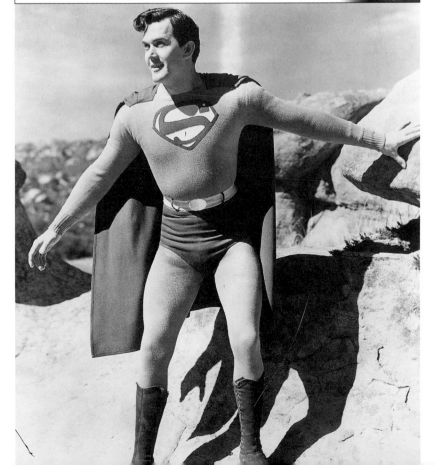
George Reeves looks a little uncertain of his footing as Superman in *Superman and the Mole Men* (also known as *Superman and the Strange People*), which was released both theatrically and shown on television as two episodes of the 50s series.

Cinderella (1950 – co-anim), *Alice in Wonderland* (1951 – co-anim), *Peter Pan* (1953 – co-anim), *Lady and the Tramp* (1955 – co-anim), *The Truth About Mother Goose* (1957 – short – co-d), *Sleeping Beauty* (1959 – sequence d), *Goliath II* (1960 – short – d), *101 Dalmatians* (1961 – co-d), *Aquamania* (1961 – short – d), *The Sword in the Stone* (1963 – d), *Winnie the Pooh and the Honey Tree* (1966 – d), *The Jungle Book* (1967 – d), *Winnie the Pooh and the Blustery Day* (1968 – p/d), *The Aristocats* (1970 – co-p/d), *Robin Hood* (1973 – p/d), *The Rescuers* (1977 – p/co-d), *The Many Adventures of Winnie the Pooh* (1977 – compilation – co-d), *The Fox and the Hound* (1981 – co-p)

Reitman, Ivan (1946-)

Canadian producer, director and occasional composer, best known for the two *Ghostbusters* comedies and such Arnold Schwarzenegger vehicles as *Twins*, *Kindergarten Cop* and *Junior*. He began his directorial career in 1970 with the short *Columbus of Sex* (aka *My Secret Life*), which he also produced and scored. He then produced films for David Cronenberg and David Fruet before hitting the big time in 1978 with *National Lampoon's Animal House*, which he co-produced.

Genre credits:
Spacehunter: Adventures in the Forbidden Zone (1983 – exec p), *Ghostbusters* (1984 – p/d), *Ghostbusters 2* (1989 – p/d), *Junior* (1994 – p/d), *Spacejam* (1996 – exec p)

The Reluctant Astronaut

USA 1967 101m Technicolor
A hayseed janitor working at a rocket site finds himself in orbit.

Juvenile comedy, poorly done.

p: Edward T. Montague for Universal

w: Jim Fritzell, Everett Greenbaum
d: Edward Montague
ph: Rexford Wimpy
m: Vic Mizzy
md: Joseph Gershenson
ed: Sam E. Waxman
ad: Alexander Golitzen, William P. De Cinces
Don Knotts, Arthur O'Connell, Leslie Nielsen, Joan Freeman, Jesse White

---

The Reluctant Dragon

USA 1941 72m bw/Technicolor
Robert Benchley tries to interest Walt Disney in an animated version of *The Reluctant Dragon*, and in doing so gets a guided tour of the studio.

Fairly fascinating mixture of live action, animation and behind the scenes know-how.

p: Walt Disney
w: Ted Sears, Al Perkins, Larry Clemmons, Bill Contrell, Harry Clark
story: Kenneth Grahame
live action d: Alfred Werker
animation d: Hamilton Luske, Ford Beebe, Jim Handley, Erwin Verity
ph: Bert Glennon, Winton C. Hoch
m: Frank Churcholl, Larry Morley
ed: Paul Weatherwax
ad: Gordon Wiles
sound: Frank Maher
ROBERT BENCHLEY, Frances Gifford, Buddy Pepper, Nana Bryant, Claude Allister, Billy Lee, Alan Ladd, Barnett Parker, Walt Disney, Wolfgang Reitherman

---

Rennie, Michael (1909-1971)

British actor best remembered by genre fans for playing the alien Klaatu in *The Day the Earth Stood Still*. Following experience as a salesman, he began breaking into films as an extra or stand-in in the 30s, making his official debut in *Conquest of the Air* in 1935 (though the film wasn't released until 1940). His other credits include *Secret Agent*, *Bank Holiday*, *Trio*, *The Robe*, *The Rains of Ranchipur*, *Third Man on the Mountain* and *Subterfuge*. He was also well known on television in the 50s in *The Third Man*.

Genre credits:
The Man Who Could Work Miracles (1936), *The Day the Earth Stood Still* (1951), *The Lost World* (1960), *Cyborg 2087* (1967)

Repo Man

USA 1984 92m DeLuxe
A young punk becomes involved in the repossession racket and finds himself on the trail of a car containing three radio-active aliens in its trunk.

Generally engaging mixture of black comedy, science fiction, satire and mayhem. Definite cult material.

p: Jonathan Wacks, Peter McCarthy for Universal/Edge City
exec p: Michael Nesmith
w/d: ALEX COX
ph: Robby Muller
m: Steven Hufsteter, Humberto Larriva, Iggy Pop
ed: Dennis Dolan
ad: J. Rae Fox, Lynda Burbank
cos: Theda Deramus
sp: Robby Knott
sound: Don Fick
stunt co-ordinator: Eddie Hice
Harry Dean Stanton, Emilio Estevez, Tracey Walter, Olivia Barash, Sy Richardson, Susan Barnes

---

The Rescuers

USA 1977 77m Technicolor
Two members of the Mouse Rescue Aid Society join forces to rescue a little girl who has been kidnapped by an arch villainess known as Madame

Medusa.

Lively cartoon feature. By no means a classic, but all rather likeable. A sequel, *The Rescuers Down Under*, followed in 1990.

p: Wolfgang Reitherman for Walt Disney
exec p: Ron Miller
w: Larry Clemmons, Ken Anderson
books: Margery Sharp
d: Wolfgang Reitherman
songs: Carol Connors, Ayn Roberts, Sammy Fain
m: Artie Butler
ed: James Melton, Jim Koford
ad: Don Griffith
sound: Herb Taylor
voices: Bob Newhart, Eva Gabor, Geraldine Page, Joe Flynn, John McIntire, Jim Jordan

The Rescuers Down Under

USA 1990 77m Technicolor Dolby
Bernard and Miss Bianca save a young Australian boy who has been kidnapped by an evil poacher.

Brilliantly animated cartoon feature, let down only by its uninspired storyline.

p: Thomas Schumacher for Walt Disney/Silver Screen Partners IV
w: Joe Ranft
d: Hendel Butoy, Michael Gabriel
m: Bruce Broughton
ed: Michael Kelly
ad: Maurice Hunt
voices: Bob Newhart, Eva Gabor, George C. Scott, John Candy, Tristan Rogers, Adam Ryen, Wayne Robson, Frank Welker, Peter Firth, Billy Barty

Return from Witch Mountain

USA 1978 93m Technicolor
Two children with supernatural powers outwit some crooks.

Routine latter-day Disney adventure, a few marks up on its predecessor, *Escape to Witch Mountain*, but only a few.

p: Ron Miller, Jerome Courtland for Walt Disney
w: Malcolm Marmorstein
d: John Hough
ph: Frank Phillips
m: Lalo Schifrin
ed: Bob Bring
ad: John B. Mansbridge, Jack Senter
cos: Chuck Keehne, Emily Sundby
sp: Eustace Lycett, Art Cruickshank, Danny Lee, Joe Hale
sound: Herb Taylor, Ron Ronconi
Bette Davis, Christopher Lee, Ike Eisenmann, Kim Richards, Jack Soo, Denver Pyle, Dick Bakalyan

The Return of Captain Invincible

Australia 1982 91m Eastmancolor Panavision
Having been forced into the wilderness because of the McCarthy with hunts, Captain Wilderness makes a comeback in the 80s when his old enemy, Mr. Midnight, resurfaces with a new dastardly plan.

Obvious spoof with musical numbers, whose over-the-top style soon becomes tiresome. No *Rocky Horror Picture Show*, that's for sure.

p: Andrew Graty for Seven Keys/Willara
w: Steven E. De Souza, Andrew Gaty
d: Philippe Mora
ph: Mike Malloy
m: William Motzing
ed: John Scott
pd: David Copping
Alan Arkin, Christopher Lee, Kate Fitzpatrick, Bill Hunter, Michael Pate, John Bluthal

The Return of Captain Nemo

USA 1978 123m colour TVM
The old captain is brought back to life to save the world.

Limp fantasy adventure re-edited from a TV mini series which came in 50-minute segments.

p: Arthur Weiss for Warner/CBS
exec p: Irwin Allen
w: Norman Katkov, Preston Wood, Robert C. Dennis, William Keys, Robert Bloch, Mann Rubin, Larry Alexander
d: Alex March
ph: Paul Rader
m: Richard La Salle
ed: Bill Brame
ad: Eugene Lourie
cos: Paul Zastupnevitch
Burgess Meredith, Jose Ferrer, Burr de Benning, Tom Hallick, Warren Stevens

The Return of Jafar

USA 1994 66m Technicolor Dolby
Evil Vizier Jafar escapes from the lamp in which he has been imprisoned and returns to avenge himself against Aladdin.

Pacy, gag-filled, made-for-video sequel to *Aladdin* which shouldn't disappoint fans of its predecessor, despite the fact that Robin Williams doesn't provide the voice of the Genie this time round. A television series followed.

p: Tad Stones, Alan Zaslove for Disney/Walt Disney Television Animation
w: Kevin Campbell, Mirith Is Colao, Steve Roberts, Dev Ross, Bob Roth, Jan Sternad, Brian Swelin
story: Duane Capizzi, Douglas Langdale, Mark McCorkle, Robert Schooley, Tad Stones
d: Toby Shelton, Tad Stones, Alan Zaslove
songs: Alan Menken, Randy Petersen, Kevin Quinn, Dale Gonbed, Michael Silversher

m/md: Mark Watters
ed: Robert S. Berchard, Ellen Orson
sound: Stephen Flick
voices: Brad Kane, Jason Alexander, Jeff Bennett, Jonathan Freeman, Liz Callaway, Val Bettin, Dan Castellaneta (as the Genie), Linda Larkin, B. J. Ward, Frank Welker

Return of the Jedi

USA/GB 1983 132m DeLuxe Panavision Dolby

The Rebel Alliance confront a slug-like villain named Jabba the Hutt as well as their old enemy Darth Vader.

The third episode in the "central" *Star Wars* trilogy is by far the weakest. However, despite a plot which contains few surprises, the big budget does show and the special effects are of the high quality expected of the series. As with *Star Wars* and *The Empire Strikes Back*, a special anniversary re-issue appeared in 1997 with improved sound and effects and a couple of new sequences, most notably the climax which has been considerably refashioned.

p: Howard Kazanjian, Robert Watts, Jim Bloom for TCF/Lucasfilm
exec p: George Lucas
d: Richard Marquand
ph: Alan Hume
m: John Williams
ed: Sean Barton, Marcia Lucas, Duwayne Dunham
pd: Norman Reynolds
cos: Aggie Guerard Rodgers, Nilo Rodis-Jamero
sp: RICHARD EDLUND, DENNIS MUREN, KEN RALSTON, PHIL TIPPET (aa)
sound: Ben Burtt
make-up effects: Phil Tippett, Stuart Freeborn
Mark Hamill, Harrison Ford, Carrie Fisher, Billy Dee Williams, Anthony Daniels, Peter Mayhew, Sebastian Shaw, Ian McDiarmid, Frank Oz, James Earl Jones (voice), Dave

Prowse, Jeremy Bulloch, Alec Guinness, Kenny Baker, Michael Pennington, Denis Lawson

Return to Oz

USA 1985 110m Technicolor

Unable to sleep after her previous adventures in Oz, Dorothy is sent for shock treatment by her Aunt Em, only to find herself back in Oz again.

Technically adroit but unnecessarily melancholy and slow starting sequel to the 1939 classic. A distinctly misguided and expensive venture, it failed to appeal to its intended audience, though discerning fantasy fans may appreciate its production values.

p: Paul Maslansky for Walt Disney/Silver Screen Partners
exec p: Gary Kurtz
w: Walter Murch, Gill Dennis
books: L. Frank Baum
d: Walter Murch
ph: David Watkin
m: David Shire
ed: Leslie Hodgson
pd: Norman Reynolds
Fairuza Balk (as Dorothy), Nicol Williamson, Jean Marsh (as the Wicked Witch), Emma Ridley, Piper Laurie (as Aunt Em), Matt Clark

Revell, Graham

New Zealand-born composer now working chiefly in America. Made his scoring debut with the Australian thriller *Dead Calm* in 1989. His other scores include *Spontaneous Combustion*, *The People Under the Stairs*, *Boxing Helena* and *Body of Evidence*.

Genre credits:
The Crow (1994), *No Escape* (1994), *Streetfighter* (1994), *Mighty Morphin Power Rangers – The Movie* (1995), *Strange Days* (1995), *The Crow: City of Angels* (1996),

Spawn (1997)

Revenge of the Creature

USA 1955 85m bw 3D

The Gill Man is captured and put on show in a Florida acquarium. But guess what? He escapes and causes the expected havoc.

Run-down sequel to the *Creature from the Black Lagoon*. Strictly for drive-ins. A second sequel, *The Creature Walks Among Us*, followed in 1956.

p: William Alland for Universal
w: Martin Berkeley
d: Jack Arnold
ph: Charles S. Welbourne
md: Joseph Gershenson
ed: Paul Weatherwax
ad: Alexander Golitzen, Alfred Sweeney
cos: Jay A. Morley, Jr.
make-up effects: Bud Westmore
sound: Leslie I. Carey, Jack Bolger
John Agar, Lori Nelson, John Bromfield, Robert B. Williams, Nestor Pavia, Ricou Browning (as the Creature), Clint Eastwood

Revenge of the Stepford Wives

USA 1980 96m colour TVM

Stepford's secret is discovered by a lady journalist.

Not so much a sequel to *The Stepford Wives*, more of a replay. Quite tolerable, nevertheless.

p: Scott Rudin for NBC
exec p: Edgar J. Scherick
w: David Wiltse
d: Robert Fuest
ph: Ric Waite
m: Leonard Rosenthal
ed: Jerrold L. Ludwig
ad: Tom John
Sharon Gless, Arthur Hill, Julie Kavner, Don

Johnson, Audra Lindley, Mason Adams

Reynolds, Norman

British art director/production designer who has won Oscars for his work on *Star Wars* (1977 – with John Barry and Leslie Dilley) and *Raiders of the Lost Ark* (1981 – with Leslie Dilley). His other credits include *Lucky Lady*, *The Incredible Sarah*, *Young Sherlock Holmes*, *Empire of the Sun*, *Avalon* and *Alive*. He began his career as an assistant art director at MGM's British arm in Boreham Wood.

Genre credits:
The Little Prince (1974 – ad), *Star Wars* (1977 – co-ad), *Superman* (1978 – co-ad), *Superman 2* (1980 – co-ad), *The Empire Strikes Back* (1980 – pd), *Raiders of the Lost Ark* (1981 – co-ad), *Return of the Jedi* (1983 – pd), *Young Sherlock Holmes* (1985 – aka *Young Sherlock Holmes and the Pyramid of Fear* – pd), *Return to Oz* (1985 – pd), *Alien 3* (1992 – pd)

Richardson, John

British special effects technician, an Oscar winner for his work on *Aliens* (1986 – with Robert Skotak, Stan Winston and Suzanne Benson).

Genre credits:
Phase IV (1973 – sp), *The Little Prince* (1974 – co-sp), *Rollerball* (1975 – co-sp), *The People That Time Forgot* (1977 – co-sp), *Moonraker* (1979 – co-sp), *Superman* (1978 – co-sp), *Aliens* (1986)

Richardson, Sir Ralph (1902-1983)

Celebrated British stage actor whose film appearances became increasingly eccentric as he aged. On stage from 1920, he came to prominence in the 30s at The Old Vic. He began his film

career in 1933 in *The Ghoul*. His following credits included *Bulldog Jack*, *South Riding*, *The Four Feathers*, *The Fallen Idol*, *The Heiress*, *Richard III*, *Oscar Wilde*, *Long Day's Journey into Night*, *Tales from the Crypt* (as the Devil) and *Greystoke: The Legen of Tarzan, Lord of the Apes*. He directed one film, *Home at Seven* (aka *Murder on Monday*) in 1952.

Genre credits:
Things to Come (1936), *The Man Who Could Work Miracles* (1936), *The Bed Sitting Room* (1969), *Alice's Adventures in Wonderland* (1972), *Rollerball* (1975), *Watership Down* (1978 – voice), *Time Bandits* (1981 – as God), *Dragonslayer* (1981)

Richter, W. D. (1945-)

American writer and director with a penchant for fantasy and horror themes. His writing credits include *Nickelodeon*, *Dracula*, *Brubaker* and *All Night Long*, whilst his work as a director includes *Needful Things*.

Genre credits:
Invasion of the Body Snatchers (1978 – w), *The Adventures of Buckaroo Banzai Across the Eighth Dimension* (1984 – co-p/d), *Big Trouble in Little China* (1986 – co-w), *Late for Dinner* (1991 – co-p/d)

Ringwood, Bob

British costume designer with a number of large-scale genre pictures to his credit, most notably the Batman films.

Genre credits:
Dune (1984 – cos), *Batman* (1989 – co), *Batman Returns* (1992 – co-cos), *Alien 3* (1992 – co-cos), *Demolition Man* (1993 – cos), *Batman Forever* (1995 – co-cos), *Santa Claus: The Movie* (1985 – cos)

Ripper, Michael (1913-)

British character actor who began his career in rep in 1924. Broke into films in 1935 with *Twice Banned*, which he followed with countless minor roles in the likes of *Prison Breaker*, *The Heirloom Mystery* and *If I Were Boss*, often as a crook, cabby or comic relief. Best known for his brief appearances in seemingly all of the Hammer horrors, either as a coachman or bait for their various monsters. Other films include *The Belles of St. Trinian's*, *Blue Murder at St. Trinian's*, *Geordie*, *Richard III*, *Sink the Bismarck* and *No Sex Please, We're British*. Horror credits include *The Revenge of Frankenstein*, *The Mummy*, *The Brides of Dracula*, *The Curse of the Mummy's Tomb*, *Plague of the Zombies*, *The Reptile*, *Scars of Dracula*, *The Creeping Flesh* and *The Revenge of Billy the Kid*.

Genre credits:
X – The Unknown (1956), *Quatermass 2* (1957 – aka *Enemy from Space*), *The Lost Continent* (1968)

The Road Warrior

see Mad Max 2

Robin Cook's Invasion

see Invasion (1997)

Robin Hood

USA 1973 82m Technicolor
Robin Hood rescues Maid Marion from the wiles of Prince John and the Sheriff of Nottingham.

Adequately animated but rather poorly scripted cartoon feature with too much talk and too little action.

p: Wolfgang Reitherman for Walt Disney

w: Larry Clemmons, Ken Anderson
story: Larry Clemmons
d: Wolfgang Reitherman
m: George Bruns
ly: Floyd Huddleston
ed: Tom Acoster, Phil Nelson
ad: Don Griffith
sound: Herb Taylor
voices: Peter Ustinov, Terry-Thomas, Brian Bedford, Monica Evans, Phil Harris, Pat Buttram, Roger Miller, Carole Shelley, George Lindsey, Andy Devine

Which way to the beach? Commander Christopher Draper (Paul Mantee) attempts to save some of his equipment in the surprisingly good *Robinson Crusoe on Mars*, a futuristic variation on Daniel Defoe's 1719 literary classic.

Robinson, Bernard (1912-1970)

Distinguished British art director and production designer, noted for his contributions to countless Hammer horrors, to which he brought both visual flair and a sense of Victorian clutter. Educated at the Liverpool School of Art, he began his film career as a draughtsman at Warner's Teddington studios, but quickly graduated to art director in 1939 for British Lion. During the war he became a camouflage and decoy expert, after which he returned to films with the likes of *The Shop at Sly Corner*, *Carve Her Name with Pride* and *Reach for the Sky*. He joined Hammer in 1956, staying with them until 1969. His credits for them include *The Curse of Frankenstein*, *Dracula*, *The Mummy*, *Curse of the Werewolf*, *The Phantom of the Opera*, *The Reptile*, *Dracula Has Risen from the Grave* and *Frankenstein Must Be Destroyed*.

Genre credits:
X – The Unknown (1956), *Quatermass 2* (1957 – aka *Enemy from Space*), *The Damned* (1963 – aka *These Are the Damned*), *Quatermass and the Pit* (1967 – aka *Five Million Years to Earth*)

Robinson Crusoe on Mars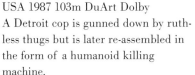

USA 1964 110m Technicolor Techniscope
An astronaut stranded on Mars learns that he is not quite alone...

Interesting, sometimes eerily effective variation on the Defoe classic. Certainly a lot better than its title might suggest.

p: Aubrey Schenck for Paramount/Devonshire
exec p: Edwin F. Zabel
w: Ib Melchior, John C. Higgins
novel: Daniel Defoe
d: Byron Haskin
ph: Winton C. Hoch
m: Van Cleave
ed: Terry Morse
ad: Hal Pereira, Arthur Lonergan
sp: Lawrence Butler, Farciot Edouart
sound: Harold Lewis, John Wilkinson
Paul Mantee, Adam West, Vic Lundin, Mona the Woolly Monkey

Robinson, Glen

American special effects technician, an Oscar winner for his work on *Earthquake* (1974 – with Albert Whitlock and Frank Brendel), *The Hindenburg* (1975 – with Albert Whitlock and Peter Berkos) and *Logan's Run* (1976 – with L.B. Abbott and Matthew Yuricich). Began his career as an assistant to John P. Fulton in the mid-60s.

Genre credits:
The Bamboo Saucer (1967 – co-sp), *Logan's Run* (1976 – co-sp), *Demon Seed* (1977 – co-sp), *Meteor* (1979 – co-sp)

Robocop

USA 1987 103m DuArt Dolby
A Detroit cop is gunned down by ruthless thugs but is later re-assembled in the form of a humanoid killing machine.

The Six Million Dollar Man meets *The Terminator* in thus ultra violent futuristic comic strip for adults which was slickly and humorously enough done to take a lot of money. It was followed by *Robocop 2* (1990), *Robocop 3* (1993) and a TV series.

p: Arne Schmidt, Edward Neumier for Orion
exec p: Jon Davison
w: Edward Neumier, Michael Miner
d: PAUL VERHOEVEN
ph: Jost Vacano
m: Basil Poledouris
ed: Frank J. Urioste
pd: William Sandell
cos: Erica Edell Phillips
sp: Phil Tippett, Peter Kuran
robot design/make-up effects: ROB BOTTIN
sound: Robert Wald
sound effects: Stephen Flick, John Pospisil
stunt co-ordinator: Garry Combs
2nd unit d: Mark Goldblatt
2nd unit ph: Rick Anderson
Peter Weller, Nancy Allen, Dan O'Herlihy, Ronny Cox, Kurtwood Smith, Miguel Ferrer, Robert Do Qui, Ray Wise, Felton Perry, Paul McCrane

Robocop 🛸

USA 1994 96m colour Dolby TVM
Robocop goes after a mad scientist who is using human brains to develop a giant computer to control Detroit.

Acceptable feature-length pilot for the TV series. Certainly no worse than the two big screen sequels.

p: J. Miles Dale for Skyvision/Rysher TPE/Risel/Robocop Productions
exec p: Stephen Downing, Brian K. Ross, Kevin Gillis
w: Michael Miner, Edward Neumeier
d: Paul Lynch
ph: William Gereghty
m/md: Jon Stroll, Kevin Gillis
theme: Basil Poledouris
ed: Gary L. Smith
pd: Perri Gorrara
cos: Linda Kemp
robocop design: Rob Bottin
sp: Michael Kavanaugh
sound: David Lee
2nd unit d: J. T. Scott
2nd unit ph: John Dyer

stunt co-ordinator: Marco Bianco
Richard Eden, Yvette Nipar, Blu Mankuma, Sarah Campbell, Andrea Roth, David Gardner, Cliff De Young, John Rubinstein

Robocop 2

USA 1990 118 DuArt Dolby
Robocop fights a powerful drugs baron who later finds himself transformed into a fearsome robot.

Little more than an expensive retread of the first movie, with little new to offer of its own. Slickly enough done, but it seems to go on forever.

p: Jon Davison for Orion
exec p: Patrick Crowley
w: Frank Miller, Walon Green
story: Frank Miller
d: Irvin Kershner
ph: Mark Irwin
m: Leonard Rosenman
ed: William Anderson
pd: Peter Jamison
sp: Phil Tippett
make-up effects: Rob Bottin
Peter Weller, Nancy Allen, Dan O'Herlihy, Tom Noona, Belinda Bauer, Gabriel Damon, Galyn Gorg

Robocop 3

USA 1991 (released 1993) 103m DuArt Dolby
Robocop joins a rebellion to help the poor of Detroit from being evicted from their homes by a giant Japanese corporation who want to develop the land.

By the numbers sequel of little abiding interest, whose US release was held up for over two years owing to the financial problems of Orion.

p: Patrick Crowley for Orion
w: Frank Miller, Fred Dekker
d: Fred Dekker
ph: Gary B. Kibbe

m: Basil Poledouris
ed: Bert Lovitt
pd: Hilda Stark
cos: Ha Nguyen
sp: Jeff Jarvis
make-up effects: Rob Bottin
Robert John Burke (as Robocop), Nancy Allen, Rip Torn, Mako, Robert Do Qui, Jill Hennessy, John Castle, Stephen Root, Daniel Von Bargen, Shane Black

Robot Monster

USA 1953 63m bw 3D
A man dressed in a monkey suit and a deep sea diver's helmet with a TV antenna on top of it invades earth with orders to conquer it.

Zero budget shlocker, ludicrous enough to make it of interest to fans of the truly awful.

p: Phil Tucker
w: Wyoff Ordung
d: Phil Tucker
ph: Jack Greenhalch
m: Elmer Bernstein (yes, *The* Elmer Bernstein!)
ed: Merrill White
George Nader, Claudia Barrett, Selena Royale, John Mylong, Gregory Moffett, Pamela Paulson, George Barrows

Rock-a-Doodle

USA/Eire 1991 74m Technicolor
A barnyard rooster goes to the city and becomes a rock and roll singer when the other animals lose their faith in his ability to bring up the sun.

Foolishly plotted cartoon feature which very quickly becomes a chore to watch, despite the short running time. Strictly for the under-fives.

p: Don Bluth, Gary Goldman, John Pomeroy for Goldcrest/Sulliva-Bluth
exec p: George A. Walker, Morris F. Sullivan
w: David N. Weiss

story: Don Bluth, David N. Weiss, John Pomeroy, T. J. Kuenster, David Steinberg, Gary Goldman
d: Don Bluth, Gary Goldman, John Pomeroy
songs: T. J. Kuenster
m: Robert Folk
ed: Bernard Caputo, Fiona Trayler, Lisa Dorney, Joe Gall
pd: Dave Goetz
sp: Fred Craig
voices: Glenn Campbell, Christopher Plummer, Eddie Deezen, Phil Harris, Sandy Duncan, Ellen Greene, Charles Nelson Reilly, Toby Scott Ganger

---

Rocket to the Moon

GB 1967 96m Technicolor Panavision

In Victorian times, P. T. Barnum and his friends plan to send the first manned rocket to the moon.

Silly but engaging all-star fantasy romp in the manner of *Those Magnificent Men in Their Flying Machines* (hence its alternate title, *Those Fantastic Flying Fools*). Let down only by overlength.

p: Harry Alan Towers for Jules Verne Productions
w: Dave Freeman, Peter Wellbeck (Hary Alan Towers)
novel: Jules Verne
d: Don Sharp
ph: Reg Wyer
m: Patrick John Scott, Ron Goodwin
ed: Ann Chegwidden
ad: Frank White
cos: Carl Toms
sp: Les Bowie, Pat Moore
Burl Ives, Jimmy Clitheroe, Terry-Thomas, Dennis Price, Judy Cornwell, Gert Frobe, Lionel Jeffries, Daliah Lavi, Troy Donahue, Hermione Gingold, Stratford Johns, Graham Stark

---

The Rocketeer

USA 1991 108m Technicolor Panavision Dolby

In 1938, a handsome young aviator combats a group of fifth columnists with the aid of a backpack which enables him to fly.

Handsomely mounted superheroics with excellent period detail and lively effects sequences. It does get a little too silly in its later stages, but otherwise is superior adventure hokum in the best *Indiana Jones* tradition. Sadly, its poor performance at the box office meant that the planned sequels were cancelled.

p: Lawrence Gordon, Charles Gordon, Lloyd Levin for Walt Disney/Levin Company/Silver Screen Partners IV
w: Danny Bilson, Paul de Meo
story: Danny Bilson, Paul de Meo, William Dear
comic strip: Dave Steven
d: JOE JOHNSTON
ph: HIRO NARITA
m: JAMES HORNER
ed: Arthur Schmidt
pd: JIM BISSELL
cos: MARILYN VANCE-STRAKER
sp: KEN RALSTON
sound: Thomas Causey
make-up effects: Rick Baker
stunt co-ordinator: M. James Arnett
2nd unit d: Ken Ralston, M. James Arnett
2nd unit ph: Frank Holgate, Rexford Metz
animation: Mark Dindal, Jim Beihold, Phil Phillipson
titles: Saxon/Ross
Bill Campbell, Jennifer Connelly, Alan Arkin, Timothy Dalton, Paul Sorvino, Terry O'Quinn (as Howard Hughes), Ed Lauter, James Handy, Tiny Ron, Robert Guy Miranda, Jon Polito, Eddie Jones

---

The Rocky Horror Picture Show

GB 1975 101m Eastmancolor

A young couple take refuge in a creepy castle during a thunderstorm, only to discover that their host is a mad transvestite scientist on the verge of creating life. It also transpires that his assistant, Riff Raff, is an alien from outer space.

High camp rock musical horror spoof whose legion of followers has turned it into *the* cult phenomenon on the late-night circuit. Mildly amusing for those in the mood, though most may now wonder what all the fuss is about, especially as it becomes rather tedious after the first 40 minutes. It is energetically performed, nevertheless.

p: Michael White for TCF
exec p: Lou Adler
w: Richard O'Brien, Jim Sharman
d: Jim Sharman
ph: Peter Suschitsky
songs: Richard O'Brien
m/md: Richard Hartley
ed: Graeme Clifford
ad: Brian Thomson, Terry Ackland-Snow
cos: Sue Blane
sp: Wally Veevers, Colin Chilvers
sound: Keith Grant, Ron Barron, Bill Rowe
ch: David Toguri
make-up: Peter Robb-King
TIM CURRY (as Frank N. Furter), Susan Sarandon (as Janet), Barry Bostwick (as Brad), Richard O'Brien (as Riff Raff), Jonathan Adams, "Little" Nell Campbell, Meatloaf, Peter Hinwood, Patricia Quinn, CHARLES GRAY (teaching The Timewarp), Christopher Biggins, Koo Stark, John Marquand, Mark Johnson

---

Roddenberry, Gene (1921-1991)

American writer, producer and executive (real name Eugene Roddenberry), working mostly in television, where he created such series as *The Lieutenant* and, of course, *Star Trek* and *Star Trek: The Next Generation*, both of which were later turned into a lucrative film series, although Roddenberry's input into these decreased as the franchise grew (he also acted as executive consultant for the 1973 animated *Star Trek* series). A fighter pilot during the Second World War and, later, an airline pilot (for Pan Am), he also worked as a policeman, which served him well on his first television writing assignment, creating stories for *Dragnet* in the mid-50s. He then wrote for such television shows as *West Point*, *Highway Patrol*, *Have Gun Will Travel*, *Dr. Kildare* and *The Naked City* (sometimes using the pseudonym Robert Wesley). The *Star Trek* films aside, his only other theatrical feature credit is for *Pretty Maids All in a Row*, which he wrote and produced.

Genre credits:
Genesis II (1972 – TVM – w/p), *The Questor Tapes* (1973 TVM – co-w), *Planet Earth* (1974 TVM – co-w/story/exec p), *Star Trek – The Motion Picture* (1979 – p), *Star Trek II: The Wrath of Khan* (1982 – co-exec p), *Star Trek III: The Search for Spock* (1984 – consultant), *Star Trek IV: The Voyage Home* (1986 – consultant), *Encounter at Farpoint* (1987 – TVM – co-exec p [feature-length pilot for *Star Trek: The Next Generation*]), *Star Trek V: The Final Frontier* (1989 – consultant), *Star Trek VI: The Undiscovered Country* (1991 – consultant)

Roeg, Nicolas (1928-)

Distinguished British cinematographer who began his career as an assistant in 1950 on *The Miniver Story*. He later worked as an operator on such films as *Island in the Sun*, *The Sundowners* and *The Trials of Oscar Wilde*, becoming a cinematographer proper in 1961 with *Information Received*. He

Producer Gene Roddenberry (back centre) poses with (left to right) director Robert Wise, William Shatner, DeForest Kelley and Leonard Nimoy during a break in filming *Star Trek: The Motion Picture*.

photographed the second unit for David Lean's *Lawrence of Arabia*, which he followed with such films as *Doctor Crippen*, *The System*, *The Masque of the Red Death*, *A Funny Thing Happened on the Way to the Forum* and *Far from the Madding Crowd*. He turned to direction with *Performance* in 1970 (with Donald Cammell), which he followed with *Walkabout*, *Don't Look Now*, *Bad Timing* and *Insignificance*, etc.

Genre credits:
Fahrenheit 451 (1966 – ph), *Casino Royale* (1967 – co-2nd unit ph), *The Man Who Fell to Earth* (1976 – d), *The Witches* (1990 – d)

Rollerball

USA/GB 1975 129m Technicolor Panavision

In the future, the star player of a violent ball game becomes a national hero.

Well choreographed action sequences go for little when the story (such as it is) comes to nothing and the point (obvious from the start) is never practised by its preachers. All rather dated by now and hellishly overlong.

p: Norman Jewison for UA
w: William Harrison
d: Norman Jewison
ph: Douglas Slocombe
md: Andre Previn
eds: Anthony Gibbs
pd: John Box

cos: Julie Harris, Ron Postal
sp: Sass Bedig, John Richardson
sound: Derek Ball, Gordon K. McCallum
2nd unit d/stunt co-ordinator: Max Kleven
James Caan, John Houseman, Ralph Richardson, Maud Adams, John Beck, Moses Gunn, Pamela Hensley, Shane Rimmer, Burnell Tucker, Burt Kwouk, Robert Ito

---

Romero, Cesar (1907-1994)

Latin-American actor, perhaps best known to fantasy fans for playing The Joker in TV's *Batman*, a role he repeated for the 60s film version. A former dancer, he was in films from the early 30s, among his credits being *The Shadow Laughs*, *Clive of India*, *Charlie Chan at Treasure Island*, *Coney Island*, *Deep Waters*, *Vera Cruz*, *Skidoo* and *Lust in the Dust*. He also portrayed the Cisco Kid in a handful of second feature numbers (*The Cisco Kid and the Lady*, *Lucky Cisco Kid*, *Romance of the Rio Grande*, *Ride on*, *Vaquero*, etc).

Genre credits:
The Lost Continent (1951), *Sergeant Deadhead* (1965 – aka *Sergeant Deadhead the Astronaut*), *Batman* (1966), *Latitude Zero* (1969 – aka *Ido Zero Daisakusen*), *The Computer Wore Tennis Shoes* (1970), *Now You See Him, Now You Don't* (1972), *The Strongest Man in the World* (1974)

Rooney, Mickey (1920-)

Diminutive American actor (real name Joe Yule, Jr.), best known for playing Andy Hardy in a series of popular second features in the 30s and 40s. Also for teaming with Judy Garland in a string of musicals, including *Strike Up the Band*, *Babes in Arms* and *Babes on Broadway*. Began his stage career in 1922 at the age of two, appearing in his parents' vaudeville act. He began his film career at the age of six in a series of short comedies under the name Mickey McGuire. After further stage experience he returned to films in 1932 with the name Mickey Rooney, making a strong impression three years later as Puck in *A Midsummer Night's Dream*. His other credits include *Captains Courageous*, *Boys' Town* (for which he won a special Oscar), *The Adventures of Huckleberry Finn*, *Young Tom Edison*, *National Velvet*, *Baby Face Nelson*, *Breakfast at Tiffany's*, *The Black Stallion*, *Leave 'em Laughing* (TVM), *Bill* (TVM), *Silent Night, Deadly Night 5: The Toymaker* and *The Legend of O.B. Taggart* (which he also wrote). He is also known for the stage musical *Sugar Babies*, in which he has appeared on and off since 1979.

Genre credits:
A Midsummer Night's Dream (1935), *The Atomic Kid* (1954 – and p through Mickey Rooney Productions), *Francis in the Haunted House* (1956), *Journey Back to Oz* (1974 – voice), *Pete's Dragon* (1977), *Arabian Adventure* (1979), *The Fox and the Hound* (1981 – voice), *The Care Bears Movie* (1985 – voice), *Erik the Viking* (1989), *Little Nemo: Adventures in Slumberland* (1990 – voice), *The Magic Voyage* (1992 – voice)

Rootes, Maurice

British editor who worked for Hammer in the 50s. He later cut a couple of Ray Harryhausen's stop motion fantasy adventures. His other credits include *Stolen Face*, *The Last Page* (aka *Man Bait*), *Blood Orange* (aka *Three Stops to Murder*), *The Gambler and the Lady*, *Face the Music* (aka *The Black Glove*) – all of them for Hammer – and *Krakatoa – East of Java*.

Genre credits:
Four-Sided Triangle (1952), *Spaceways* (1953), *Jason and the Argonauts* (1963), *First Men in the Moon* (1964)

Rosenberg, Max J.

American producer who, with his partner, writer and producer Milton Subotsky, founded Amicus Films in Britain, which gave Hammer a run for their money from the mid-60s to the early 70s. They began a trend for compendium horrors with the *Dead of Night*-style *Dr. Terror's House of Horrors* in 1965 and followed it with several other compendiums and shockers, including *Torture Garden*, *The House That Dripped Blood*, *Asylum* and *Vault of Horror*. They also produced the two big screen Dr. Who adventures.

Genre credits:
Dr. Who and the Daleks (1965 – co-p), *Daleks – Invasion Earth, 2150 A. D.* (1966 – co-p), *The Terrornauts* (1967 – co-p), *They Came from Beyond Space* (1967 – co-p), *The Mind of Mr. Soames* (1969 – co-p), *The Land That Time Forgot* (1974 – co-p), *At the Earth's Core* (1976 – co-exec p)

Rosenman, Leonard (1924-)

American composer, an Oscar winner for his music direction of both *Barry Lyndon* (1975) and *Bound for Glory* (1976). Began scoring films in 1955 with *The Cobweb*, which he followed with *East of Eden* and *Rebel Without a Cause*, both of which starred James Dean. His other credits include *The Chapman Report*, *A Man Called Horse*, *Race with the Devil*, *An Enemy of the People*, *Making Love* and *Cross Creek*.

Genre credits:

Fantastic Voyage (1966), *Countdown* (1967), *Beneath the Planet of the Apes* (1969), *Battle for the Planet of the Apes* (1973), *The Lord of the Rings* (1978), *Star Trek IV: The Voyage Home* (1986), *Robocop 2* (1990)

Rudyard Kipling's The Jungle Book

see The Jungle Book (1994)

Runaway

USA 1984 100m Metrocolor Dolby

In the near future, a robotics expert discovers an industrialist's warped plan to flood the market with dangerous micro chips.

High tech science fiction thriller. Good use of gadgetry, but a little cold-hearted.

p: Michael Rachmil for Tri-Star/Delphi
w/d: Michael Crichton
ph: John A. Alonzo
m: Jerry Goldsmith
ed: Glenn Farr
pd: Douglas Higgins
cos: Betsy Cox
sp: John Thomas
sound: Rob Young
robot designs: David Duranci
stunt co-ordinator: Dick Ziker
2nd unit ph: Peter Donen
Tom Selleck, Cynthia Rhodes, Gene Simmons, Kirstie Alley, Stan Shaw, Joey Cramer, G. W. Bailey

---

Running Against Time

USA 1990 96m CFIcolor TVM

A college professor uses a fellow professor's time machine to travel back to 1963 to prevent President Kennedy's assassination and, subsequently, America's involvement in the Vietnam war during which his brother was

killed, but things don't go accordingly to plan.

Despite a few longueurs, this is a reasonably engaging variation on *Back to the Future*, though it purposefully creates a paradox simply so it can have a happy ending.

p: David Roessell for MTE/Coastline/Finnegan-Pinchuk
exec p: Pat Finnegan, Sheldon Pinchuk
w: Stanley Shapiro, Robert Glass
novel: Stanley Shapiro
d: Bruce Seth Green
ph: Brian R. R. Webb
m: Don Davis
ed: Heather MacDougall
pd: Barry Robison
cos: Joan Hunter
sound: Itzhak Magal
Robert Hays, Catherine Hicks, Sam Wannamaker, James Distefano, Brian Smiar, Tracy Fraim

---

The Running Man

USA 1987 101m Technicolor Dolby

In the future, a framed convict finds himself the chief attraction on a violent TV game show.

Slow starting action thriller which picks up speed as it goes along.

p: Tim Zinnemann, George Linder for Braveworld/HBO
w: Steven E. de Souza
novel: Stephen King
d: Paul Michael Glaser
ph: Thomas del Ruth
m: Harold Faltermeyer
ed: Mark Roy Warner, Edward A. Warschilka, John Wright
pd: Jack T. Collis
cos: Robert Blackman
sp: Larry Cavanaugh, Bruce Steinheimer
sound: Richard Bryce Goodman
2nd unit d/stunt co-ordinator: Bennie Dobbins
add ph: Reynaldo Villalobos

ch: Paula Abdul
Arnold Schwarzenegger, Maria Conchita Alonso, Yaphet Kotto, Jim Brown, Richard Dawson, Jesse Ventura, Dweezil Zappa, Mick Fleetwood

---

Russell, Chuck (Charles)

American writer who successfully turned to direction, most notably with the Jim Carrey comedy *The Mask*. His other directorial credits include *A Nightmare on Elm Street Part 3: The Dream Warriors* and *Eraser*.

Genre credits:

Dreamscape (1984 – co-w), *The Blob* (1988 – co-w/d), *The Mask* (1994 – d)

Russell, Kurt (1951-)

American actor who began his career as a child at Disney, after which he matured into a seasoned action star in such films as *Tequila Sunrise*, *Tango and Cash*, *Backdraft*, *Tombstone* and *Executive Decision*. He has made several films with director John Carpenter, including two outings as the one-eyed Snake Pliskin.

Genre credits:

The Absent-Minded Professor (1961), *The Computer Wore Tennis Shoes* (1970), *Now You See Him, Now You Don't* (1972), *Charley and the Angel* (1973), *The Strongest Man in the World* (1975), *The Fox and the Hound* (1981 – voice), *Escape from New York* (1981), *The Thing* (1982), *Big Trouble in Little China* (1983), *Escape from L.A.* (1996 – also co-w/co-p)

Salkind, Alexander (1915-1997)

Polish producer on the international scene who, with his son Ilya (1948-) produced the first three Superman movies. His other credits include *The Trial*, *The Light at the Edge of the World*, *The Three Musketeers*, *The Four Musketeers* and *Christopher Columbus: The Discovery*.

Genre credits:

Superman (1978 – co-p), *Superman 2* (1980 – co-p), *Superman 3* (1983 – co-p), *Supergirl* (1983 – co-p), *Santa Claus: The Movie* (1985 – co-p)

Salter, Hans J. (1896-1994)

Prolific German-born composer and music director, in Hollywood from 1938 where he worked on the Universal comedy *The Rage of Paris*. He trained at Vienna's Academy of Music, after which he became the musical director at two European opera houses: The Volksoper in Vienna and the State Opera in Berlin. While in Berlin he also scored a number of early sound films for UFA. Long at Universal, he worked on many of their key horror and science fiction films of the 40s and 50s, often in collaboration (mostly with Charles Previn, Frank Skinner, Paul Desau and Joseph Gershenson), and

often uncredited. His horror scores include *The Mummy's Tomb*, *Frankenstein Meets the Wolf Man*, *The Mummy's Ghost*, *The Invisible Man's Revenge*, *Abbott and Costello Meet Dr. Jekyll and Mr. Hyde* and *The Mole People*.

Genre credits:

Man Made Monster (1941 – aka *The Electric Man* – co-m), *The 5000 Fingers of Dr. T* (1952 – co-m), *This Island Earth* (1955 – co-m), *The Mole People* (1956 – co-m), *The Land Unknown* (1957 – co-m), *The Incredible Shrinking Man* (1957 – co-m)

Sandell, William

American production designer who, after working on a handful of low budget horrors (*The Pack*, *Piranha*, *Blood Beach*) moved on to bigger things in the science fiction genre, including two for director Paul Verhoeven. His other credits include *St. Elmo's Fire*, *Nothing But Trouble*, *Newsies* (aka *News Boys*) and *Outbreak*.

Genre credits:

The Clones (1977), Airplane II: The Sequel (1982), Robocop (1987), Total Recall (1990), The Flintstones (1994)

Sanders, George (1906-1972)

British (but Russian born) actor, the archetypal cad in countless Hollywood films. He won a Best Supporting Actor Oscar for playing Addison de Witt in *All About Eve* (1950) and is remembered for such equally distinguished films as *Foreign Correspondent*, *The Moon and Sixpence*, *The Picture of Dorian Gray* and *Call Me Madam*. After experience in the textile and tobacco industries he turned to the stage and radio, making his film debut in 1936 with *Find the Lady*. He went

to Hollywood later the same year and appeared in *Lloyd's of London*. He is also known for two popular crime series, *The Saint* and *The Falcon*. He committed suicide.

Genre credits:

The Man Who Could Work Miracles (1936), *The Ghost and Mrs Muir* (1947), *From the Earth to the Moon* (1958), *Village of the Damned* (1960), *The Jungle Book* (1967 – voice, as Shere Khan), *The Body Stealers* (1969 – aka *Thin Air*), *Doomwatch* (1972)

Sangster, Jimmy (1927-)

British writer, producer and director who scripted many of Hammer's classic genre films, including *The Curse of Frankenstein*, *Dracula* and *The Mummy*. His first script was for the short *A Man on the Beach* (1956), which was followed by his first full-length screenplay, *X – The Unknown*, in the same year. Turned director with less success in 1970 with *Horror of Frankenstein*. Left Hammer in the mid-70s and went to America where much television work followed. Sometimes uses the pseudonym John Sansom.

Genre credits:

X – The Unknown (1956 – w), *The Trollenberg Terror* (1958 – aka *The Crawling Eye* – w)

Santa and the Three Bears

USA 1970 1970 60m colour

Two baby bears decide to stay awake all winter so as to see Santa Claus at Christmastime.

Tame cartoon feature with live action bookends.

p: Tony Benedict for Pirate World/Mansen

International
w/d: Tony Benedict
live action d: Barry Mahon
ed: Milt Krea
ad: Walt Peragoy
no other credits given

Santa Claus – The Movie

GB/USA 1985 120m Technicolor
Panavision Dolby
Santa Claus thwarts a megalomaniac's
plans to commercialise Christmas.

Expensive fantasy spectacular, a
pleasant enough seasonal offering for
younger audiences, but a little long-
winded and overblown for its purpose.

p: Ilya Salking, Pierre Spengler for Alexander
Salkind
w: David Newman
story: David Newman, Leslie Newman
d: Jeannot Szwarc
ph: Arthur Ibbetson
m: Henry Mancini
ly: Leslie Bricusse
ed: Peter Hollywood
pd: Anthony Pratt
cos: Bob Ringwood
sp: Derek Meddings, Roy Field
sound: David Crozier

2nd unit d: David Lane
add ph: Paul Beeson
ch: Pat Garrett
David Huddleston, Dudley Moore, John
Lithgow, Burgess Meredith, Judy Cornwell,
Jeffrey Kramer, Christian Fitzpatrick, Carrie
Kei Heim, Melvyn Hayes, Don Estelle, John
Barrard

Saturn 3

GB 1980 87m Technicolor Dolby
In the future, a psychotic astronaut
threatens the lives of two research scientists working on a remote moon on
the far side of Saturn with a giant

A visually arresting moment from *Saturn 3*, the direction of which
was taken over by producer Stanley Donen following the dismissal of
the film's original director John Barry. Here, good guys Kirk Douglas
and Farrah Fawcett (both in white) greet bad guy Harvey Keitel, who is
about to make their life hell. Way to go, Harv!

robot he has built.

Slick but ultimately rather silly addition to the space fiction genre of the late 70s. It manages to keep one watching, but is never quite as good as one hopes it will be. The film was originally to have been directed by *Star Wars* production designer John Barry, who was replaced a few days into filming.

p: Stanley Donen for ITC/Transcontinental
exec p: Martin Starger
w: Martin Amis
story: John Barry
d: Stanley Donen
ph: Billy Williams
m: Elmer Bernstein
ed: Richard Marden
pd: Stuart Craig (and John Barry)
cos: Anthony Mendleson
sp: Roy Field, Wally Veevers, Peter Parks, Colin Chilvers
sound: Gerry Humphreys, Derek Ball
add ph: Robert Paynter
2nd unit d: Eric Rattray
Farrah Fawcett, Kirk Douglas, Harvey Keitel, Ed Bishop

Savage

USA 1995 91m colour Dolby

A young man, thought to be responsible for the murder of his wife and son, escapes from a mental hospital two years later and goes savage in the wilderness, where he develops special powers which he uses to track down the killer of his family, who turns out to be a megalomaniacal alien.

Or something like that. A ludicrous and almost incomprehensible ragbag of ideas and situations, barely worth following.

p: Avi Nesher for Hollywood/Mahogony
exec p: Pscal Borno
w: Patrick Highsmith, Peter Sagal
story: Patrick Highsmith
d: Avi Nesher

ph: Peter Fernberger
m: Roger Neill
ed: Michael Schweitzer
pd: Gary Randall
cos: Dan Lester
sp: Joseph Grossberg, Ray McIntyre, Jr., OSC, Freeze Frame, Pixel Magic
sound: Bill Reinhardt
stunt co-ordinator: Scott Leva
fight ch: Oliver Gruner
Oliver Gruner, Kario Salem, Jennifer Grant, Sam McMurray, Kristin Minter, Luke Askew, Herschel Sparber

Sawtell, Paul (1906-1971)

Prolific Polish composer working in America, often in collaboration with Bert Shefter (as noted by co-m below). His many credits include several Tarzan adventures, *The Gay Falcon*, *Inferno*, *Texas Lady*, *Stopover Tokyo* and many horror entries, among them *The Mummy's Curse*, *Jungle Woman* and *Son of Dr. Jekyll*.

Genre credits:

The Black Scorpion (1957 – co-m), *Kronos* (1957 – co-m), *The Cosmic Man* (1958 – co-m), *The Fly* (1958 – m), *It! The Terror from Beyond Space* (1958 – co-m), *The Return of the Fly* (1959 – co-m), *The Lost World* (1960 – co-m), *Jack the Giant Killer* (1961 – co-m), *Voyage to the Bottom of the Sea* (1961 – co-m), *The Last Man on Earth* (1964 – aka *L'Ultimo Uomo della Terra* – co-m), *The Bubble* (1966 – co-m)

Schifrin, Lalo (1932-)

Prolific Argentinian composer and conductor working on the international scene, where his credits include *The Cincinnati Kid*, *Blindfold*, *Cool Hand Luke*, *Bullitt*, *Kelly's Heroes*, *The Four Musketeers*, *The Eagle Has Landed*, *The Amityville Horror* and all of the Dirty Harry films, not to mention such

TV themes as *Mission: Impossible* and *Mannix*. A noted jazz composer and arranger, he worked for Xavier Cugat as an arranger and Dizzy Gillespie as a pianist and composer in the 50s. His first American score was for *Rhino* in 1964, though prior to this he had composed music for *El Jefe* in Argentina in 1957 and *Les Felins* (aka *Joy House*) in France in 1964.

Genre credits:

Way, Way Out (1966), *THX 1138* (1970), *Earth II* (1971 – TVM), *The Neptune Factor – An Undersea Odyssey* (1973 – aka *The Neptune Disaster*), *Return from Witch Mountain* (1978), *The Cat from Outer Space* (1978),

Schneer, Charles H. (1920-)

American producer, long associated with the effects films of Ray Harryhausen, with whom he later shared producer chores. He has also produced such diverse films as *I Aim at the Stars*, *Half a Sixpence*, *The Executioner* and *Land Raiders*.

Genre credits:

It Came from Beneath the Sea (1955), *Earth vs. the Flying Saucers* (1956), *Twenty Million Miles to Earth* (1957), *The Seventh Voyage of Sinbad* (1958), *The Three Worlds of Gulliver* (1960), *Mysterious Island* (1961), *Jason and the Argonauts* (1963), *First Men in the Moon* (1964), *The Valley of Gwangi* (1968), *The Golden Voyage of Sinbad* (1973 – co-p), *Sinbad and the Eye of the Tiger* (1977 – co-p), *Clash of the Titans* (1981 – co-p)

Schoedsack, Ernest B. (1893-1979)

American writer, producer, director and cinematographer who, with his partner Merian C. Cooper (whom he met in Poland in 1920), made a number of documentaries in the 20s (*Grass*, *Chang*) before going on to make a series of spectacular big budget features, including *The Four Feathers* and, of course, the legendary *King Kong*. He began his film career as a cameraman for comedy producer Mack Sennett, which led to his becoming a combat cameraman during World War One. His other credits include *Rango*, *Long Lost Father*, *The Most Dangerous Game* (aka *The Hounds of Zaroff*), *The Last Days of Pompeii* and *Outlaws of the Orient*.

Genre credits:

King Kong (1933 – actor/co-p/co-d), *Son of Kong* (1933 – d), *Dr. Cyclops* (1939 – d), *Mighty Joe Young* (1949 – d)

Schumacher, Joel (1942-)

American director who began his career as a window dresser for Bonwit Teller in New York before becoming a costume designer (*Bananas*, *The Last of Sheila*, *Interiors*, *Blume in Love*), then a screenplay writer (*Sparkle*, *Carwash*). His other directorial credits include *St. Elmo's Fire*, *The Lost Boys*, *Cousins*, *Dying Young*, *Falling Down* and *The Client*.

Genre credits:

Sleepers (1973 – cos), *The Incredible Shrinking Woman* (1981 – d), *Flatliners* (1990 – d), *Batman Forever* (1995 – d), *Batman and Robin* (1997 – d)

Schwarzenegger, Arnold (1947-)

Muscle-bound, heavily accented German-born action star who, after winning the Mr. Universe and Mr. Olympia contests (five and seven times each respectively) inevitably broke into

films, though his debut, *Hercules in New York* (as Arnold Strong) in 1969, is perhaps best forgotten. He retired from body building in 1980, by which time he'd already made *The Long Goodbye* (as Arnold Strong again), *Stay Hungry*, *Pumping Iron*, *The Villain* (aka *Cactus Jack*) and *The Jayne Mansfield Story* (TVM – as Mickey Hargitay). He was also a millionaire by this time thanks to shrewd business investments, primarily in real estate. He became a star in 1982 with *Conan the Barbarian*, securing his position in 1984 with *The Terminator*, which he followed with such action fare as *Commando*, *Raw Deal* and *Red Heat*. He has also tried comedy with mixed results (*Twins*, *Kindergarten Cop*, *Junior*, *Jingle All the Way*). An American citizen since 1983, he married John F. Kennedy's niece, TV presenter Maria Schriver, in 1986. So far he has directed one film, *Christmas in Connecticut* (1992 – TVM). His other credits include *True Lies* and *Eraser*.

Genre credits:

Conan the Barbarian (1982), *Conan the Destroyer* (1984), *The Terminator* (1984), *Red Sonja* (1985 – as Conan), *Predator* (1987), *The Running Man* (1987), *Total Recall* (1990), *Terminator 2: Judgement Day* (1991), *The Last Action Hero* (1993), *Junior* (1994), *Batman and Robin* (1997 – as Mr. Freeze)

Sci-Fighters

Canada 1996 90m Kodak Ultra Stereo
In 2009, a Boston cop tracks down an infected con who has escaped a penitentiary on the moon.

So-so actioner with incidental sci-fi trimmings and a plot borrowed from *The Quatermass Experiment*. Archetypal video fodder.

p: Danny Rossner, Murray Shostak for

Cinetel/Workin' Man
exec p: Ed Shapero, Mark Balsam
w: Mark Sevi
d: Peter Svatek
ph: Barry Gravelle
m: Milan Kymlicka
ed: Jean-Marie Drot
ad: Michael Devine
cos: Claire Nadon
sp: Denis Mondion
make-up effects: Adrian Morot
sound: Gabor Vadnay, Luc Budrias
stunt co-ordinator: Dave McKeown
titles: PMT Video (!)
Roddy Piper, Jayne Heitmeyer, Billy Drago, Larry Day, Tyrone Benskin, Richard Raybourne, Donna Sarrasin, Karen Elkin

Scott, Elliot

British production designer on the international scene, with credits for Pal, Spielberg, Lucas, Zemeckis and Henson. His other credits include *Evil Under the Sun*.

Genre credits:

Tom Thumb (1958 – ad), *Children of the Damned* (1963 – ad), *The Warlords of Atlantis* (1978 – pd), *Arabian Adventure* (1979 – pd), *Dragonslayer* (1981 – pd), *Indiana Jones and the Temple of Doom* (1984 – pd), *Labyrinth* (1986 – pd), *Who Framed Roger Rabbit?* (1988 – pd), *Indiana Jones and the Last Crusade* (1989 – pd)

Scott, John (1930-)

British composer and jazz saxophonist who began his career arranging for the Ted Heath Band. Later, at EMI, he also arranged for the likes of Tom Jones and The Hollies, and also played on a number of film soundtracks before scoring his first film, *A Study in Terror*, in 1965. His other work includes *The Long Duel*, *Trog*, *Antony and Cleopatra*, *Craze*, *Symptoms*, *Hennessy*, *The Hostage Tower*,

Greystoke: The Legend of Tarzan, Lord of the Apes and *The Deceivers*. He also scored several documentaries for undersea explorer Jacques Cousteau (*Cape Horn*, *The Channel Islands*, *Parc Oceanique Cousteau*, *Papua New Guinea*, etc.).

Genre credits:
Rocket to the Moon (1967 – aka *Jules Verne's Rocket to the Moon/Those Fantastic Flying Fools/Blast Off*), *Doomwatch* (1972), *The People That Time Forgot* (1977), *The Final Countdown* (1980), *Inseminoid* (1980), *King Kong Lives* (1986)

Scott, Ridley (1937-)

Celebrated British director who, after experience as a designer for the BBC, turned to directing episode television, most notably the police drama *Z Cars*. Through his own company, Ridley Scott Associates, he then began directing television commercials (such as the Hovis ads) which were noted for their slickness. He made his theatrical debut with *The Duellists* in 1977, but it wasn't until two years later that he came to world attention for directing the box office hit *Alien*. His credits since include *Someone to Watch Over Me*, *Black Rain*, *Thelma and Louise*, *1492*, *White Squall* and *G.I. Jane*. He is the brother of director Tony Scott (*The Hunger*, *Top Gun*, *Beverly Hills Cop 2*, *True Romance*, *The Crimson Tide*, etc.), with whom he took over Britain's Shepperton Studios in 1994.

Genre credits:
Alien (1979), *Blade Runner* (1982 – a director's cut of which was released in 1991), *Legend* (1985)

Screamers

Canada 1995 106m colour Dolby
In 2078, murderous robots which have the ability to evolve threaten the mining colony of Sirius.

Yet another mining colony on a distant planet finds itself at risk from something nasty. Despite a reasonable budget, the results are a little dull this time round thanks to a surplus of chat, though some of the effects aren't bad.

p: Tom Berry, Franco Battista for Triumph/Fuji Eight/Fries/Allegro
exec p: Charles W. Fries
w: Dan O'Bannon, Miguel Tejad-Flores
story: Philip K. Dick
d: Christian Duguay
ph: Rodney Gibbons
m: Normand Corbeil
ed: Yves Langlois
pd: Perri Gorrara
sp: Chiodo Bros., Ernest Farino, Richard Ostiguy
screamers designed by: Deak Ferraud, Jim Bandsuh
make-up effects: Adrien Morot
stunt co-ordinator: Michael Scherer
2nd unit ph: Keith Young, Bruno Phillip
sound: Richard Nichol
Peter Weller, Roy Dupuis, Andy Lauer, Jennifer Rubin, Charles Powell, Ron White, Jason Cavalier, Liliana Komorowska, Michael Caloz

---

Scrooge ☕

GB 1935 78m bw
Ebeneezer Scrooge is visisted by three ghosts on Christmas Eve who convince him to reform his miserly ways.

Very tolerable early version of the oft told tale. Also see under *A Christmas Carol*.

p: Julius Hagen, John Brahm for Twickenham
w: Seymour Hicks, H. Fowler Mear
novel: CHARLES DICKENS
d: Henry Edwards
ph: Sidney Blythe, William Luff
m: W. L. Trytel

ed: Jack Harris, Ralph Kemplen
ad: James A. Carter
cos: L. and H. Nathan
sound: Benjamin Honri
Seymour Hicks, Donald Calthrop, Oscar Asche, Maurice Evans, Athene Seyler, Marie Ney, Barbara Everest, C. V. France

---

Scrooge ☕☕

GB 1951 86m bw
A miser decides to reform his ways after ghostly visitations on Christmas Eve.

Perhaps the most faithful adaptation of the Dickens novel, with an engaging central performance and some nicely judged cameos. Alastair Sim would later provide the voice of Scrooge for a 1971 animated version of the story under the title *A Christmas Carol*, whilst the film's editor, Clive Donner, would direct a TV movie of the story in 1984, also under the title *A Christmas Carol*.

p: Brian Desmond Hurst for Renown
exec p: George Minter
w: Noel Langley
novel: CHARLES DICKENS
d: BRIAN DESMOND HURST
ph: C. PENNINGTON RICHARDS
m: RICHARD ADDINSELL
md: Muir Mathieson
ed: Cliver Donner
ad: RALPH BRINTON
cos: Doris Lee, Constance da Pinna
sound: W. H. Lindup
narrator: Peter Bull
ALASTAIR SIM, Mervyn Johns, Jack Warner, Michael Hordern, George Cole (as the young Scrooge), Hermione Baddeley, Miles Malleson, Peter Bull, John Charlesworth, Glyn Dearman, Hattie Jacques, Richard Pearson

---

Scrooge

GB 1970 113m Technicolor Panavision

Generally lively musical remake. A little long, and with songs that tend to go in one ear and out the other, but the acting is vigorous and the production solid enough.

p: David B. Orton, Robert H. Solo for Cinema Center/Waterbury/National General
w/m/ly/exec p: Leslie Bricusse
novel: CHARLES DICKENS
d: Ronald Neame
ph: OSWALD MORRIS
md: Ian Stone, Herbert W. Spencer
ed: Peter Weatherley
pd: Terry Marsh
cos: Margaret Furse
sp: Wally Veevers
sound: John Cox, Jock May
ch: Paddy Stone
make-up: George Frost
titles: Ronald Searle

ALBERT FINNEY, Edith Evans, Kenneth More, ALEC GUINNESS, Michael Medwin, David Collings, Laurence Naismith, Kay Walsh, Roy Kinnear, Molly Weir, Anton Rodgers, Gordon Jackson, Graham Armitage, James Cossins, Paddy Stone, Geoffrey Bayldon, Suzanne Neve

The Secret Garden

USA 1949 92m bw/Technicolor

An orphan leaves India for Yorkshire to live with her mysterious uncle. Once at his home she discovers a secret garden which has been locked up for ten years...

Rather enjoyable adaptation of the popular Edwardian novel, with lavish production values and just the right atmosphere. Ideal for children.

p: Clarence Brown for MGM
w: Robert Ardrey
novel: Frances Hidgson Burnett
d: FRED M. WILCOX

ph: RAY JUNE
m: Bronislau Kaper
md: Andre Previn
ed: Albert J. Kern
ad: CEDRIC GIBBONS, URIE MCCLEARY
cos: Walter Plunkett
sp: Warren Newcombe, A. Arnold Gillespie
sound: Douglas Shearer

MARGARET O'BRIEN, Dean Stockwell, Brian Roper, Herbert Marshall, Gladys Cooper, Elsa Lanchester

The Secret Garden

USA 1987 96m colour TVM

Uninspired TV remake with none of the charm of the 1949 version.

p: Steve Simmons for Rosemont Productions
exec p: Norman Rosemont
w: Blanche Hanalis
novel: Frances Hodgson Burnett
d: Alan Grint
ph: Robert Paynter
m: John Cameron
ed: Keith Palmer
pd: John Stoll
ad: Brian Ackland-Snow
cos: Diana Holmes
sound: Brian Simmons
2nd unit ph: Jeff Paynter

Gennie James, Barret Oliver, Jadrien Steele, Michael Hordern, Billie Whitelaw, Derek Jacobi, Colin Firth, Julian Glover, Lucy Gutteridge, Carmel McSharry, Pat Heywood

The Secret Garden

GB/USA 1993 101m Technicolor Dolby

Sometimes cold but carefully mounted version of the Hodgson Burnett story with strong production values throughout.

p: Fred Fuchs, Fred Roos, Tom Luddy for American Zoetrope/Warner
exec p: Francis Ford Coppola
w: Caroline Thompson

novel: Frances Hodgson Burnett
d: AGNIESZKA HOLLAND
ph: Roger Deakins
m: Zbigniew Preisner
ed: Isabelle Lorente
pd: STURAT CRAIG
cos: Marit Allen
sp: John Evans and others
sound: Leslie Shatz, Lora Hirschberg, Drew Kunin
titles: Nina Saxon

Kate Maberly, Maggie Smith, Heydon Prowse, Andrew Knott, John Lynch, Laura Crossley, Irene Jacob

Semple, Jr., Lorenzo

American screenplay writer whose credits include *Pretty Poison*, *Papillon*, *The Parallax View*, *Three Days of the Condor*, *Hurricane* and a handful of fantasy projects.

Genre credits:
Batman (1966), *King Kong* (1976), *Flash Gordon* (1980)

Seven Faces of Dr. Lao

USA 1964 100m Metrocolor

A mysterious Chinaman brings his circus to a remote western town and teaches the inhabitants a thing or two.

Mild pantomime for family audiences, stagily presented, with the interest primarily focused on the star's various disguises.

p: George Pal for MGM
w: Charles G. Finney from his novel
d: George Pal
ph: Robert Bronner
m: Leigh Harline
ed: George Tomasini
ad: George W. Davis, Gabriel Scocgnamillio
make-up effects: WILLIAM TUTTLE (special aa)
sp: Jim Danforth, Wah Chang, Paul B. Byrd,

Ralph Rodine, Robert R. Hoag
TONY RANDALL, Barbara Eden, Arthur
O'Connell, John Ericson, Lee Patrick, Noah
Beery, Jr., Minerva Urecal, Peggy Rea, John
Qualen

The Seventh Voyage of Sinbad

USA 1958 89m Technicolor Dynamation

Sinbad sails to an island populated by monsters in order to find a roc egg which will restore his fiancée to her normal size, from which she was reduced by a mad magician.

Patchy though sometimes quite lively fantasy adventure whose greatest asset is its rather splendid trick work. It was followed by two sequels: *The Golden Voyage of Sinbad* (1973) and *Sinbad and the Eye of the Tiger* (1977).

p: Charles H. Schneer for Columbia/Morningside
w: Kenneth Kolb
d: Nathan Juran
ph: Wilkie Cooper
m: BERNARD HERRMANN
ed: Edwin Bryant, Jerome Thoms
ad: Gil Perrando
sp: RAY HARRYHAUSEN
sound: John Livardy
titles: Bob Gill
Kerwin Mathews, Kathryn Grant, Torin Thatcher, Richard Eyer, Alec Mango

The Shadow

USA 1994 107m DeLuxe Dolby

A former criminal, now a caped vigilante, attempts to save 1930s New York from being destroyed by a descendant of none other than Genghis Khan.

Sometimes eye-catching but otherwise disappointing attempt to revive a character previously popular in a 30s radio series and a 1940 film serial. It proved to be one of several superhero

flicks made during this period that quickly crash-landed at the box office.

p: Martin Bregman, Willi Baer, Michael S. Bregman for Universal
exec p: Louis A. Stroller, Rolf Deyhle
w: David Koepp
d: Russell Mulcahy
ph: Stephen H. Burum
m: Jerry Goldsmith
ed: Peter Honess
pd: Joseph Nemec III
cos: John Mollo
Alex Baldwin, John Lone, Penelope Ann Miller, Peter Boyle, Ian McKellen, Tim Curry, Sab Shimono, Joseph Maher, Andre Gregory, Jonathan Winters

The Shaggy D.A.

USA 1976 93m Technicolor

With the aid of a magic ring, a lawyer turns himself into a dog and rounds up some crooks.

Unremarkable Disney romp, a belated sequel of sorts to *The Shaggy Dog*.

p: Bill Anderson for Walt Disney
exec p: Ron Miller
w: Don Tait
novel: Felix Salten
d: Robert Stevenson
ph: Frank Phillips
m: Buddy Baker
ed: Bob Bring, Norman Palmer
ad: John B. Mansbridge, Perry Ferguson
cos: Chuck Keehne, Emily Sundby
sp: Eustace Lycett, Art Cruickshank, Danny Lee, Peter S. Ellenshaw
sound: Herb Taylor, Frank Regula
titles: Guy Deel, Stan Green, Ed Garbert
2nd unit d: Arthur J. Vitarelli
Dean Jones, Tim Conway, Suzanne Pleshette, JoAnne Worley, Vic Tayback, Dick Van Patten, Keenan Wynn, Richard O'Brien

The Shaggy Dog

USA 1959 101m bw

A young boy finds himself trans-

formed into a dog after reading the inscription on a magic ring.

Mild Disney caper in the tried and tested manner, one of the studio's few in black and white. It was followed by *The Shaggy D. A.* (1976), *The Return of the Shaggy Dog* (1987 – TVM) and a remake, *The Shaggy Dog* (1994 - TVM).

p: Bill Walsh for Walt Disney
w: Bill Walsh, Lillie Hayward
novel: Felix Salten
d: Charles Barton
ph: Edward Colman
m: Paul Sawtell
Fred MacMurray, Jean Hagen, Tommy Kirk, Cecil Kellaway, Annette Funicello, Tim Considine, Kevin Corcoran, Alexander Scourby

The Shaggy Dog

USA 1994 96m colour TVM

An encounter with a magic ring turns an unsuspecting teenager into a dog.

Wholly unremarkable and quite pointless remake of the 1959 movie, which wasn't that great to begin with.

p: Joseph B. Wallenstein for Walt Disney/Zaloom-Mayfield
exec p: George Zaloom, Les Mayfield, Scott Immergut
w: Bill Walsh, Lillie Hayward, Tim Doyle
d: Dennis Dugan
ph: Russ Alsobrook
m: Mark Mothersbaugh, Denis M. Hannigan
ed: Jeff Gourson
ad: Peter Clemens
cos: Tom Bronson
sp: Magic Box Inc.
sound: Jacques Nosco
Scott Weinger, Ed Begley, Jr., Sharon Lawrence, James Cromwell, Jon Polito, Jeremy Sisto, Jordan Blake Warkol, Sarah Lassez

The Shape of Things to Come

Canada 1979 96m colour TVM

A colony on the moon is threatened by renegade robots from outer space.

A flat and tediously scripted production, nothing really to do with H. G. Wells. In a bid to cash in on the *Star Wars* boom the film was released theatrically in some countries outside the US.

p: William Davidson for Scott/CFI/Torrington
exec p: Harry Alan Towers
w: Martin Lager
d: George McCowan
ph: Reginald H. Morris
m: Paul Hoffert
ed: Stan Cole
pd: Gerry Holmes
sp: Wally Gentleman

Jack Palance, Carol Lynley, Barry Morse, Nicholas Campbell, Eddie Benton, John Ireland, Mark Parr, Ardon Bess

Shatner, William (1931-)

Canadian actor, known the world over for playing Captain James Tiberius Kirk in the *Star Trek* television and film series. Began his career on local stage and radio which led to a season at the National Repertory Company in Ottowa. He later moved to New York, where he made his first television appearances in the 50s, which eventually led to his film debut in *The Brothers Karamazov* in 1958. Until *Star Trek* came along in 1966, Shatner's film career consisted of minor appearances in *Judgement at Nuremberg*, *The Intruder* and *The Outrage*, etc. Once the TV series folded he appeared in countless TV movies and series, and such films as *Big Bad Mama*, *The Devil's Rain* and *Kingdom of the Spiders* before the franchise was resus-citated for the big screen (of which he directed episode V). His other TV work includes the series *T.J. Hooker* (several episodes of which he directed) and *Rescue 911*. He is now also a successful science fiction writer, most notably of the Tek series (*Tek War*, *Tek Lords*, *Tek Lab*, *Tek Vengeance*, *Tek Secret*, etc.) which were turned into a television series, four episodes of which were feature-length.

Genre credits:
The Sole Survivor (1969 – TVM), *Star Trek* (1979), *Star Trek II: The Wrath of Khan* (1982), *Airplane: The Sequel* (1982 – spoofing his Kirk image), *Star Trek III: The Search for Spock* (1984), *Star Trek IV: The Voyage Home* (1986), *Star Trek V: The Final Frontier* (1989 – also co-story/d), *Star Trek VI: The Undiscovered Country* (1991), *Tek War* (1994 – aka *Tek War: The Original Movie* – actor/novel/co-exec p/d), *Star Trek: Generations* (1994), *Tek War: Teklords* (1994 – actor/novel/co-exec p), *Tek War: Tek Lab* (1994 – actor/novel/co-exec p), *Tek War: Tek Justice* (1994 – ator/co-exec p)

Shayne, Robert (1910–1992)

American actor (real name Robert Shaen Dawe) who cropped up in a handful of minor genre pictures. Made his movie debut in 1934 in *Keep 'em Rolling* following experience as a reporter. His other credits include *Shine on Harvest Moon*, *The Neanderthal Man*, *Spook Chasers* and *How to Make a Monster*.

Genre credits:
Tobor the Great (1954), *The Giant Claw* (1957), *Kronos* (1957), *Teenage Caveman* (1958 – aka *Out of the Darkness*), *Son of Flubber* (1963)

She ☺

USA 1935 89m bw

Old documents lead an explorer and his friends to a mysterious Arctic country ruled by a queen who cannot age.

Occasionally striking if somewhat reshaped version of the Haggard novel in the manner of the same producer's *King Kong*. Of interest chiefly for its art direction.

p: Merian C. Cooper for RKO
w: Ruth Rose, Dudley Nichols
novel: H. Rider Haggard
d: Irving Pichel, Lansing G. Holden
ph: J. Roy Hunt
m: MAX STEINER
ed: Ted Cheesman
ad: VAN NEST POLGLASE, AL HERMAN
cos: Aline Bernstein, Harold Miles
sp: Vernon L. Walker
sound: John L. Cass
sound effects: Walter Elliott
ch: Benjamin Zemach

Randolph Scott, Nigel Bruce, Helen Gahagan (as She – her only film), Helen Mack

She ☺

GB 1965 105m Technicolor Hammerscope

Explorers discover a remote colony in Africa governed by a queen who cannot die unless she falls in love...

Claustrophobic, ill-adapted Hammer remake lacking the sense of mystery of its predecessor. A few moments of interest along the way, but the sluggish pace is self-defeating. A sequel, *The Vengeance of She*, followed in 1968.

p: Michael Carreras for Hammer/Associated British
w: David T. Chantler
novel: H. Rider Haggard
d: Robert Day
ph: Harry Waxman
m: JAMES BERNARD
md: Philip Martell

ed: James Needs, Eric Boyd-Perkins
ad: Robert Jones, Don Mingaye
cos: Carl Toms
sp: George Blackwell, Les Bowie
sound: Claude Hitchcock, A. W. Lumkin
make-up: Roy Ashton
associate p: Aida Young
ch: Cristyne Lawson
cam op: Ernest Day
make-up: John O. Gorman, Roy Ashton
Ursula Andress, Peter Cushing, Bernard Cribbins, Christopher Lee, John Richardson, Andre Morell, Rosenda Monteros, The Oo-Bla-Da Dancers (!)

Shefter, Bert

Prolific Russian-born composer, often in collaboration with Paul Sawtell (as noted by co-m below). His credits include *Danger Zone*, *M*, *She Devil*, *Cattle Empire* and *The Christine Jorgensen Story*.

Genre credits:

The Black Scorpion (1957 – co-m), *Kronos* (1957 – co-m), *The Cosmic Man* (1957 – co-m), *It! The Terror from Beyond Space* (1958 – co-m), *The Return of the Fly* (1959 – co-m), *The Lost World* (1960 – co-m), *Jack the Giant Killer* (1961 – co-m), *Voyage to the Bottom of the Sea* (1961 – co-m), *The Last Man on Earth* (1964 – aka *L'Ultimo Uomo della Terra* – co-m), *The Curse of the Fly* (1965 – m), *The Bubble* (1966 – co-m)

Sherman, Richard M. (1928-)

American songwriter who, with his brother Robert B. (1925-), won two Oscars for *Mary Poppins* (1964), for best song score and best song, *Chim Chim Cheree*. They have contributed many single songs and whole song scores to many more movies since, a good deal of them for Walt Disney, among them *The Parent Trap*, *Summer Magic*, *The Happiest*

Millionaire and *The One and Only Genuine Original Family Band*. Non-Disney work includes *Tom Sawyer*, *Huckleberry Finn* and *The Magic of Lassie*, all of which they also scripted (the latter with Jean Holloway).

Genre credits:

The Absent-Minded Professor (1961 – song), *Moon Pilot* (1962 – song), *The Sword in the Stone* (1963 – songs), *Winnie the Pooh and the Blustery Day* (1963 – songs), *Mary Poppins* (1964 – songs), *Winnie the Pooh and the Honey Tree* (1965 – songs), *The Jungle Book* (1967 – co-songs), *Chitty Chitty Bang Bang* (1968 – songs), *The Aristocats* (1970 – songs), *Bedknobs and Broomsticks* (1971 – songs), *Snoopy, Come Home* (1972 – songs), *Charlotte's Web* (1973 – songs), *The Slipper and the Rose* (1976 – co-w/songs), *Little Nemo: Adventures in Slumberland* (1990 – songs)

Sherman, Robert B.

see Sherman, Richard M.

The Silencers

USA 1995 96m Foto-Kem
A secret service agent teams up with a friendly alien to prevent further aliens from taking over the earth via interdimensional travel.

Surprisingly lively variation on the old, old story, with plenty of spectacular action to keep one watching (though ultimately, perhaps one exploding car crash too many).

p: Richard Pepin, Joseph Merhi for PM
w: Joseph John Barmettier
story: Joseph John Barmettier, Richard Preston, Jr., William Applegate, Jr.
d: Richard Pepin
ph: Ken Blakey
m: Louis Febre
ed: Chris Worland
pd: Gregory Martin

cos: Lisa Dyehouse
sp: Steve Rundell
sound: Mike Hall
stunt co-ordinator: Cole S. McKay
associate p: Jack Scalia
Jack Scalia, Dennis Christopher, Carlos Lauchu, Lucinda Weist, Stephen Rowe, Terri Power, Clarence Williams III, Charles McDaniel

---

Silent Running

USA 1971 90m Technicolor
On board a spaceship carrying the last of earth's flora and fauna, a technician rebels when orders are given to destroy the cargo.

Curious mixture of science fiction and ecology, quite charmingly put together and now something of a cult item. It also has some interesting credits.

p: Douglas Trumbull for Universal
exec p: Michael Gruskoff
w: Deric Washburn, Michael Cimino, Stephen Bochco
d: DOUGLAS TRUMBULL
ph: Charles F. Wheeler
m: Petere Schickele
ed: Aaron Stell
ad: Wayne Smith, Richard Alexander
cos: Anne Vidor
sp: DOUGLAS TRUMBULL, JOHN DYKSTRA, RICHARD YURICICH
sound: Charles Knight, Richard Portman
BRUCE DERN, Cliff Potts, Ron Rifkin, Jesse Vint, Mark Persons, Steven Brown, Cheryl Sparks, Larry Wisenhunt

---

Silvestri, Alan (1950-)

American composer, a graduate of Boston's Berklee College of Music. Began scoring films in 1976 with *Las Vegas Lady*, though he is perhaps best known for his scores for the films of director Robert Zemeckis, which include *Romancing the Stone*, the

Back to the Future trilogy, *Who Framed Roger Rabbit?*, *Death Becomes Her*, *Forrest Gump* and *Contact*. He has also scored many action films for producer Joel Silver. His other credits include *The Amazing Dobermans*, *Clan of the Cave Bear*, *Delta Force*, *Father of the Bride*, *Ricochet*, *Richie Rich* and *The Quick and the Dead*.

Genre credits:

Back to the Future (1985), *Flight of the Navigator* (1986), *Predator* (1987), *Who Framed Roger Rabbit?* (1988), *My Stepmother is an Alien* (1988), *The Abyss* (1989), *Back to the Future Part II* (1989), *Back to the Future Part III* (1990), *Predator 2* (1990), *Ferngully: The Last Rainforest* (1991), *Super Mario Bros.* (1993), *Judge Dredd* (1995), *Contact* (1997)

Sinbad and the Eye of the Tiger

GB 1977 113m Metrocolor

Sinbad helps a princess break a spell which has turned her brother into a baboon.

Predictable fantasy adventure with only the trick effects to recommend it to anyone but children.

p: Charles H. Schneer, Ray Harryhausen for Columbia/Andor
w: Beverly Cross
story: Beverly Cross, Ray Harryhausen
d: Sam Wanamaker
ph: Ted Moore
m: Roy Budd
ed: Roy Watts
pd: Geoffrey Drake
sp: RAY HARRYHAUSEN
sound: George Stephenson, Douglas Turner
Patrick Wayne, Taryn Power, Jane Seymour, Margaret Whiting, Patrick Troughton, Kurt Christian, Nadim Sawalha, Damien Thomas, Bruno Barnabe, Bernard Kay, Salami Coker,

Peter Mayhew

Sinclair, Ronald

American editor of low budget entries, mostly for AIP and Roger Corman. His other credits include *Five Guns West*, *Apache Woman*, *Swamp Woman*, *Oklahoma Woman*, *Machine Gun Kelly*, *Premature Burial*, *The Raven* and *The Haunted Palace* – all for Corman!

Genre credits:

The Day the World Ended (1956 – ed), *The Viking Women and the Sea Serpent* (1957 – ed), *Invasion of the Saucer Men* (1957 – aka *The Invasion of the Hell Creatures* – co-ed), *Dr. Goldfoot and the Bikini Machine* (1965 – aka *Dr. G and the Bikini Machine* – co-ed), *Sergeant Deadhead* (1965 – aka *Sergeant Deadhead the Astronaut* – co-ed)

Singer, Marc (1948-)

Muscle-bound American actor, best known for the *Beastmaster* movies. He began his film career in 1974 with *Things in Their Season*, which he has since followed with the likes of *Go Tell the Spartans*, *For Ladies Only* (TVM), *Body Chemistry* and *Sweet Justice*. His TV work includes appearances in such series as *The Contender*, *V* and *Dallas*.

Genre credits:

The Beastmaster (1982), *High Desert Kill* (1989 – TVM), *Dead Space* (1991), *Beastmaster 2: Through the Portal of Time* (1991)

Siodmak, Curt (1902-)

German writer and director, in America from 1938 following experience in his home country as a journalist and screenplay writer, most notably of *People on Sunday* (aka *Menschen am Sonntag*) which he co-wrote with

Billy Wilder. His American credits include *Her Jungle Love*, *Aloma of the South Seas*, *Berlin Express*, *Tarzan's Magic Fountain* and several horror titles, among them *The Invisible Man Returns*, *The Wolf Man*, *I Walked with a Zombie*, *House of Frankenstein* and *The Devil's Messenger*. He is also the author of *Donovan's Brain*, which has been filmed as *The Lady and the Monster*, *Vengeance* and *Hauser's Memory*.

Genre credits:

F.P.1 (1933 – co-w), *The Tunnel* (1933 – aka *Der Tunnel* - co-w), *Non-Stop New York* (1937 – co-w), *The Magnetic Monster* (1953 – co-w/d), *Riders to the Stars* (1953 – w), *The Creature with the Atom Brain* (1955 – w), *Earth vs. the Flying Saucers* (1956 – story)

Slave Girls from Beyond Infinity

USA 1987 76m Foto-Kem

On a distant planet, a group of bikini-clad girls are hunted down like animals by an evil lord.

Stupid svariation on *The Most Dangerous Game* (aka *The Hounds of Zaroff*) with plenty of attractive babes for the six-pack crowd.

p: Ken Dixon for Titan
w/d: Ken Dixon
ph: Ken Wiataak, Tom Calloway
m: Carl Dante
md: Jonathan Scott Bogner
ed: Bruce Stubblefield, James A. Stewart
ad: E. Scott Morton
sp: Mark Wolf, John Eng
sound: Rick Fin, Paul Bacca
make-up effects: John Buechler, Joe Reader
Elizabeth Clayton, Don Scribner, Cindy Beale, Brinke Stevens, Carl Horner

---

Sleeping Beauty

USA 1958 75m Technicolor Technirama

A beautiful princess is put to sleep by a wicked witch but is later awakened by the kiss of a handsome prince.

Stylish sequences don't quite atone for the lacklustre script of this animated feature, though this probably won't matter too much to younger audiences.

p: Walt Disney
w: Erdman Penner, Joe Rinaldi, Winston Hibler, Bill Peet, Ted Sears, Ralph Wright, Milt Ganta
story: Charles Perrault
d: Clyde Geronimi, Eric Larson, Wolfgang Reitherman, Les Clark
songs: Erdman Penner, Tom Adair, Sammy Fain, Winston Hibler, Ted Sears, Jack Lawrence, George Bruns
m: Tchaikovsky
md: George Bruns
ed: Roy M. Brewer, Jr., Donald Halliday
pd: Don da Gradi, Ken Anderson
sp: Ub Iwerks, Eustace Lycett
sound: Robert O. Cook
voices: Mary Costa, Bill Shirley, Verna Felton, Eleanor Audley, Barbara Joe Allen, Taylor Holmes, Bill Thompson, Barbara Luddy

The Slipper and the Rose

GB 1976 146m Technicolor Panavision

Cinderella eventually gets to the ball with the help of her fairy godmother.

Beautifully set and costumed all-star musical version of the famous children's story, scuppered by lifeless handling and a hellishly overlong running time. Moments of charm do survive, though.

p: Stuart Lyons for Paradine
exec p: David Frost
w: Bryan Forbes, Richard M. and Robert B. Sherman
d: Bryan Forbes

ph: TONY IMI
songs: Richard M. and Robert B. Sherman
md: Angela Morley
ed: Timothy Gee
pd: RAY SIMM
cos: JULIE HARRIS
sp: Ray Capel
sound: Bill Daniels, Gordon K. McCallum
ch: Marc Breaux
titles: Robert Ellis
Richard Chamberlain, Gemma Craven, Kenneth More, Michael Hordern, Edith Evans, Annette Crosbie, Margaret Lockwood, Christopher Gable, Julian Orchard, Lally Bowers, John Turner, Roy Barraclough, Peter Graves, Gerald Sim, Geoffrey Bayldon, Valentine Dyall, Andre Morell, Wayne Sleep

Slipstream

GB 1989 101m Eastmancolor Dolby

Some time in the not too distant future, an adventurer and two cops try to bring in a wanted man for a reward, but their task is not an easy one.

Long, slow, relentlessly boring and unimaginative would-be fantasy epic which never begins to take off. Something of a mistake for all concerned.

p: Gary Kurtz for Entertainment Film Productions
w: Tony Kayden
d: Steven M. Lisberger
ph: Frank Tidy
m: Elmer Bernstein
ed: Terry Rawlings
pd: Andrew McAlpine
cos: Catherine Cook
sp: Brian Johnson
sound: Ivan Sharrock, Gerry Humphreys, Dean Humphreys
sound ed: James Shields
stunt co-ordinator: Eddie Stacey
2nd unit ph: Terry Cole
Mark Hamill, Bob Peck, Bill Paxton, Kitty Aldridge, Eleanor David, Ben Kingsley, F.

Murray Abraham, Robbie Coltrane, Murray Melvin

Slocombe, Douglas (1913-)

Distinguished British cinematographer, a former photo journalist who began his film career photographing documentaries, newsreels and propaganda films. In 1944 he began a long association with Ealing, first as an operator on such films as *Champagne Charlie*, then as a cinematographer on *Painted Boats* (aka *The Girl on the Canal*), *Dead of Night* (co-photographed with Stan Pavey), *Hue and Cry*, *It Always Rains on Sunday*, *Saraband for Dead Lovers*, *The Lavender Hill Mob*, *Mandy* and *The Titfield Thunderbolt*, etc. Other major credits include *Freud*, *The L-Shaped Room*, *The Servant*, *The Blue Max*, *Dance of the Vampires* (aka *The Fearless Vampire Killers*), *The Lion in Winter*, *The Italian Job*, *The Music Lovers*, *The Great Gatsby*, *Julia*, *Nijinsky* and *Never Say Never Again*, not to mention the Indiana Jones trilogy.

Genre credits:

The Man in the White Suit (1951), *Rollerball* (1975), *Close Encounters of the Third Kind* (1977 – 2nd unit ph), *Close Encounters of the Third Kind: The Special Edition* (1980 – 2nd unit ph), *Raiders of the Lost Ark* (1981), *Indiana Jones and the Temple of Doom* (1984), *Indiana Jones and the Last Crusade* (1989)

The Small One

USA 1977 15m Technicolor

A young Hebrew boy is forced by his father to sell his small donkey, which he does – to a man named Joseph who uses it to bear his expectant wife Mary to Bethlehem.

Mildly charming cartoon featurette

whose director went on to bigger and better things away from Disney, among them *The Secret of Nimh* and *An American Tail*.

p: Don Bluth for Walt Disney
exec p: Ron Miller
w: Vance Gerry, Pete Young
book: Charles Tzewell
d: Don Bluth
songs: Don Bluth, Richard Rich
m: Robert F. Brunner
ed: James Melton
voices: Sean Marshall, William Woodson, Olan Soule, Hal Smith, Gordon Jump, Joe Higgins

Smith, Jack Martin

American art director, long with Twentieth Century-Fox. An Oscar winner for his work on *Cleopatra* (1963 – with John DeCuir, Hilyard Brown, Herman Blumenthal, Elven Webb, Maurice Pelling and Boris Juraga) and *Fantastic Voyage* (1966 – with Dale Hennesy).

Genre credits:

Voyage to the Bottom of the Sea (1961 – co-ad), *Way, Way Out* (1966 – co-ad), *Fantastic Voyage* (1966 – co-ad), *Planet of the Apes* (1967 – co-ad), *Beneath the Planet of the Apes* (1969 – co-ad), *Escape from the Planet of the Apes* (1971 – co-ad)

Smith, Paul

Hulking American actor, often in villainous roles in such films as *Midnight Express* (as the guard), *Pieces* and *Crimewave*.

Genre credits:

Popeye (1980 – as Bluto), *Dune* (1984), *Red Sonja* (1985)

Smith, Paul J.

American composer, long with Disney and often in collaboration. He won an Oscar for his score for *Pinocchio* (1940 – with Ned Washington and Leigh Harline). Other Disney scores include *Perri*, *Pollyana*, *The Parent Trap* and various True Life Adventures (*Nature's Half Acre*, *Beaver Valley*, *The Olympic Elk*, etc.).

Genre credits:

Snow White and the Seven Dwarfs (1937 – co-m), *Pinocchio* (1940 – co-m), *The Three Caballeros* (1945 – co-m), *Song of the South* (1946 – co-m), *Fun and Fancy Free* (1947 – co-m), *Cinderella* (1950), *20 000 Leagues Under the Sea* (1954 – m)

Smith, Roy Forge

British art director (*Far from the Madding Crowd*, *The Amazing Mr. Blunden*, *The Hound of the Baskervilles*), now working chiefly in America, where he designed the Turtles trilogy.

Genre credits:

Jabberwocky (1977), *Bill and Ted's Excellent Adventure* (1989), *Teenage Mutant Ninja Turtles* (1990), *Teenage Mutant Ninja Turtles II: The Secret of the Ooze* (1993), *Teenage Mutant Ninja Turtles III: The Turtles Are Back... In Time* (1992)

Snow White and the Seven Dwarfs

USA 1937 82m Technicolor

In order to escape her wicked stepmother, Snow White hides in the forest where she is befriended by seven dwarfs.

Dated only by an anthropomorphic cuteness, the world's first animated feature still retains much of its original charm thanks to the excellent characterisations, the brilliant animation and a memorable score, whose highlights include *Whistle While You Work*, *Some Day My Prince Will Come* and *Heigh Ho*. Despite initial industry fears, it went on to break box office records and was consequently much re-released.

p: WALT DISNEY
w: Ted Sears, Otto Englander, Earl Hurd, Dorothy Ann Blank, Richard Creedon, Dick Richard, Merrill de Maris, Webb Smith
story: The Brothers Grimm
supervising d: DAVID HAND
songs: LARRY MOREY, FRANK CHURCHILL
m: Frank Churchill, Leigh Harline, Paul Smith
voices: Adriana Caselotti, Harry Stockwell, Lucille La Verne, Otis Harlan, Scotty Mattraw, Roy Artwell, Billy Gilbert, Pinto Colvig

Solaris

Russia 1972 165m Sovcolor 'Scope

A scientist is sent to investigate a remote space station where a mysterious force has made itself felt.

Long, slow, but almost continuously absorbing think piece.

p: Mosfilm
w: Andrei Tarkovsky, Fredrich Gorenstein
novel: Stanislav Lem
d: ANDREI TARKOVSKY
ph: Vadim Yusov
m: Edouard Artemyev
ad: Mikhail Romadin
Natalya Bondarchuk, Donatas Banionis, Juri Jaarvet, Nikolai Grinko, Anatoli Solonitsyn, Vladislav Dvoryetsky, Sos Sarkissian

Solo, Robert H. (1932-)

American producer whose credits so far include two versions of *Invasion of the Body Snatchers*. He was also

Warner Bros'. president of foreign production in the 70s. His other credits include *The Devils*, *The Awakening*, *Bad Boys* and *Blue Sky*.

Genre credits:
Scrooge (1970), *Invasion of the Body Snatchers* (1978), *Body Snatchers* (1993)

Solyaris see Solaris

Something Wicked This Way Comes

USA 1982 94m Technicolor Panavision Dolby

At the turn of the century, a sinister carnival visits a small American town, and two boys help to destroy its evil owner who is out to get them because they have stumbled across his secrets.

Skilfully made macabre fantasy whose elements come together most satisfactorily. Unfortunately, it failed to find an appreciative audience.

p: Peter Vincent Douglas for Walt Disney/Bryna
w: RAY BRADBURY from his novel
d: JACK CLAYTON
ph: STEPHEN H. BURUM
m: JAMES HORNER (after a score by Georges Delerue was rejected)
ed: Argyle Nelson, Barry Mark Gordon
pd: Richard MacDonald
cos: Ruth Myers
sp: LEE DYER and others
sound: Bob Hathaway
sound effects: Richard R. Portman, David M. Horton
make-up effects: Robert J. Schiffer
JASON ROBARDS, JR., Jonathan Pryce, Shawn Carson, Vidal Peterson, Pam Grier, Diane Ladd, Royal Dano, Angelo Rossitto, Jill Carroll, Tony Christopher, Mary Grace Canfield, Richard Davalos

---

Somewhere in Time

USA 1980 104m Technicolor

A playwright travels back in time to meet a woman whose photograph he has fallen in love with.

Pleasant, quite carefully mounted romantic fantasy with one or two nicely judged moments. Though it didn't fare well at the box office, it later became a television favourite.

p: Stephen Deutsch for Universal/Rastar
w: Richard Matheson from his novel
d: Jeannot Szwarc
ph: Isidore Mankosky
m: JOHN BARRY
ed: Jeff Gourson
pd: Seymour Klate
cos: Jean-Pierre Dorleac
Christopher Reeve, Jane Seymour, Christopher Plummer, Teresa Wright, Bill Erwin, George Voskovec

---

Son of Godzilla

Japan 1967 86m Technicolor

Godzilla protects his (apparently motherless) son from a giant praying mantis and a spider.

Enjoyably ludicrous monster pic which has to be seen to be believed.

p: Tomoyuki Tanaka for Toho
w: Shinichi Sekizawa, Kazue Shiba
d: Jun Fukuda
ph: Kazuo Yamada
m: Masaru Soto
ed: Ryohei Fujuii
ad: Takeo Kita
sp: Sadamas Arikawa, Eiji Tsuburaya
sound: Shin Hatari, Toshiya Ban
Tadao Takashima, Bibara Maeda, Akira Kubo, Akihiko Hirata, Kenji Sahara

---

Son of Kong

USA 1933 69m bw

After the death of Kong, Carl Denham returns to Skull island only to discover another giant ape which later saves him from drowning in a storm.

Rushed sequel made to cash in on the success of *King Kong*. Relentlessly padded and generally disappointing, though the effects have their interest. Nevertheless, even at this length, the results are often tedious to sit through.

p: Merian C. Cooper for RKO
w: Ruth Rose
d: Ernest B. Schoedsack
ph: Eddie Linden, Vernon L. Walker, J. O. Taylor
m: Max Steiner
ed: Ted Cheesman
ad: Van Nest Polglase, Al Herman
cos: Walter Plunkett
sp: WILLIS O'BRIEN
sound: Earl A. Wolcott
sound effects: Murray Spivack
ROBERT ARMSTRONG, Helen Mack, Frank Reicher, John Marston, Victor Wong, Ed Brady, Katherine Ward, Noble Johnson, Clarence Wilson, Lee Kohlmar

---

Soylent Green

USA 1973 97m Metrocolor Panavision

In 2022 a police detective on a murder case discovers the true nature of a synthetic food.

Dated and sometimes rather lacklustre science fiction piece which settles down into just another cop thriller, though it somehow manages to keep one watching, if only to see what the outcome is.

p: Walter Seltzer, Russell Thatcher for MGM
w: Stanley R. Greenberg
novel: Harry Harrison
d: Richard Fleischer
ph: Richard H. Kline
m: Fred Myrow
md: Gerald Fried
ed: Samuel E. Beetley
pd: Edward Carfagno
cos: Pat Barto

sp: Robert R. Hoag, Matthew Yuricich, A. J. Lohman
sound: Charles M. Wilborn, Harry W. Tetrick
stunt co-ordinator: Joe Cannutt
Charlton Heston, EDWARD G. ROBINSON (his last film), Leigh Taylor-Young, Chuck Connors, Joseph Cotten, Brock Peters, Paula Kelly, Stephen Young, Mike Henry, Whit Bissell

Space Jam

USA 1997 87m Technicolor Dolby

Bugs Bunny and his friends face kidnap by aliens who want them for their amusement park, Moron Mountain, but help is at hand in the form of basketball star Michael Jordan.

Pale imitation of *Who Framed Roger Rabbit?*, poorly scripted and with a paucity of genuine jokes. The animation, though slick, also lacks the old style.

p: Ivan Reitman for Warner
exec p: David Falk, Ken Ross
w: Leo Benvenuti, Steve Rudnick, Timothy Harris, Herschell Weingrod
d: Joe Pytka
m: James Newton Howard
Michael Jordan, Wayne Knight, Theresa Randle, Bill Murray, Danny DeVito (voice)

Space Marines

USA 1995 90m Foto-Kem Ultra Stereo

Space marines are sent in to save the crew of a space freighter who have been captured by pirates after the cargo.

The effects aren't at all bad, but otherwise this is standard direct to video fare, with a dull script peppered with the usual violence, explosions and gunfire.

p: Talaat Captan for Green Communications/Republic/Light Year

exec p: Marion Oberauner
w: Robert Moreland
d: John Weidner
ph: Garett Griffin
m: Randy Miller
ed: Brian Chambers, Daniel Lawrence
pd: Natbeh Nazarian
sp: Ronald Schmidt, David Wainstain
sound: Ward Philips
2nd unit d: Randy E. Moore, Robert Moreland
2nd unit ph: Bill Schwarz
stunt co-ordinator: Randy E. Moore
Billy Wirth, Meg Foster, John Pyper-Ferguson, Edward Albert, Cady Huffman, Sherman Augustus, Bill Brochtrue, James Shigeta

Space Master X-7

USA 1958 71m bw Regalscope

A rocket returns to earth carrying a deadly fungus.

Dismal rehash of themes better explored in *The Quatermass Experiment*, with a climax involving much stock footage.

p: Bernard Glasser for Regalscope/TCF
w: George Worthington Yates, Daniel Mainwaring
d: Edward Bernds
ph: Brydon Baker
m: no credit given
ed: John F. Link
ad: no credit given
cos: Clark Ross
sound: Victor Appel
Bill Williams, Lyn Thomas, Robert Ellis, Paul Frees, Joan Barry, Moe Howard, Rhoda Williams

Space Raiders

USA 1983 81m DeLuxe

A young boy finds himself caught up with space pirates.

Low budget space opera, utilising the same effects and score from

Corman's *Battle Beyond the Stars*. Strictly for kids.

p: Roger Corman for Millennium
w/d: Howard Cohen
ph: Alec Hirschfeld
m: James Horner
songs: Murphy Dunne
ed: R. J. Kizer, Anthony Randel
ad: Wayne Springfield
cos: Sarah Bardo
sound: Mark Ulano
make-up effects: Mike Jones
2nd unit d: Mary Ann Fisher
Vince Edwards, David Mendenhall, George Dickerson, Thom Christopher, Drew Snyder, Patsy Pease, Ray Stewart, Bill Boyett, Howard Dayton

Space Truckers

USA 1997 97m colour Dolby

In the future, a space trucker is tricked into transporting a load of deadly bio-mechanical warriors to earth. Unfortunately for him and his two travelling companions, the androids become activated during the journey.

Tongue-in-cheek adventure, quite slickly done on a medium-sized budget, with plenty of humorous winks in the script and some well designed humanoids.

p: Peter Newman, Greg Johnson, Ted Mann, Stuart Gordon for Goldcrest/Internal/Mary Breen-Farrelly Productions
exec p: Guy Collons, Stephen Kay
w: Ted Mann
story: Ted Mann, Stuart Gordon
d: Stuart Gordon
ph: Mac Ahlberg
m: Colin Towns
ed: John Victor Smith
pd: Simon Murton
cos: Anne Bloomfield, John Bloomfield
sp: Brian Johnson, Paul Gentry
make-up effects: Greg Cannom
Dennis Hopper, Stephen Dorff, Debi Mazar,

Charles Dance, George Wendt

Spaceballs

USA 1987 96m Metroclor Dolby

The evil leader of the planet Spaceball determines on stealing the oxygen supply from the neighbouring planet of Druidia, but reckons without the intervention of a maverick space pilot.

Belated spoof on the *Star Wars* cycle. Generally over padded, but with one or two irresistable moments for fans of the director's low-brow humour, the tap-dancing alien being well worth waiting for alone.

p: Mel Brooks, Ezra Swerdlow for MGM/UA
w: Mel Brooks, Thomas Meehan, Ronny Graham
d: Mel Brooks
ph: Nick McLean
m: John Morris
ed: Conrad Buff IV, Peter G. Smith
pd: Terence Marsh
cos: Donfeld
sp: Peter Donen, Apogee
sound: Randy Thom, Gary Rydstrom
stunt co-ordinator: Richard Warlock
titles: Anthony Goldschmidt
Mel Brooks, John Candy, Rick Moranis (as Dark Helmet), Bill Pullman, Daphne Zuniga, Dick Van Patten, George Wyner, Michael Winslow, Ronny Graham, Dom DeLuise (voice), Joan Rivers (voice), John Hurt (gag cameo repeating his chestbursting role in *Alien*)

Spacecamp

USA 1986 105m Technicolor Dolby

Teenagers spending the summer at spacecamp find their newly acquired capabilities tested to the limit when a freak accident launches their shuttle into orbit.

Surprisingly tolerable romp with moments of tension. For no accountable reason it failed to make any headway at the box office.

p: Patrick Bailey, Walter Coblenz for ABC
exec p: Leonard Goldberg
w: W. W. Wicket, Casey T. Mitchell
story: Patrick Bailey, Larry B. Williams
d: Harry Winer
ph: William A. Fraker
m: John Williams
ed: John W. Wheeler, Timothy Board
pd: Richard MacDonald
cos: Patricia Norris
sp: Barry Nolan, Chuck Gaspar
sound: David MacMillan
sound ed: John Leveque
titles: Penelope Gottlieb
2nd unit ph: Robert Jessup, Jack Cooperman
Kate Capshaw, Lea Thompson, Tate Donovan, Leaf Phoenix, Kelly Preston, Larry B. Scott, Tom Skerritt

Spacehunter: Adventures in the Forbidden Zone

USA 1983 108m Metrocolor 3D Dolby

A space adventurer attempts to rescue three earthlings held captive on a barren planet by a mutant, and is joined in his quest by a young girl who is more of a hindrance than a help.

Fairly lively but wholly predictable and familiar adventure, one of several films shot in 3D in the early 80s. When it's shown on television sharp-eyed viewers of the film will notice that, in an early scene showing the spaceship carrying the three earthlings crash-landing, a car can be seen parked at the top left of the picture. Some of the effects scenes were filmed outdoors in a car park, and this gaffe somehow slipped through!

p: Don Carmody, John Dunning, Andre Link for Columbia
exec p: Ivan Reitman
w: David Preston, Edith Ray, Dan Goldberg, Len Blum
story: Jean Lafleur (the original director), Stewart Harding
d: Lamont Johnson
ph: Frank Tidy
m: Elmer Bernstein
ed: Scott Conrad
pd: Jackson de Govia
cos: Julie Weiss
sp: Dale Martin, Fantasy II
sound: Richard Lightstone
make-up effects: Thomas Burman
Peter Strauss, Molly Ringwald, Ernie Hudson, Andrea Marcovici, Michael Ironside

The Spaceman and King Arthur

GB 1979 93m Technicolor

An astronaut and his lookalike robot travel back in time to the court of King Arthur.

Elementary variation on *A Connecticut Yankee* with jokes on the thin side. But plenty of familiar faces.

p: Ron Miller for Walt Disney
w: Don Tait
d: Russ Mayberry
ph: Paul Beeson
m: Ron Goodwin
ed: Peter Boita
ad: Albert Witherick
cos: Phyllis Dalton
sp: Cliff Culley
sound: Claude Hitchcock, Ken Barker
stunt co-ordinator: Vic Armstrong
Denis Dugan, Jim Dale, Kenneth More, John le Mesurier, Ron Moody, Rodney Bewes, Robert Beatty, Sheila White, Reg Lye, Pat Roach, Cyril Shaps

Spaceways

GB 1953 74m bw

A scientist is accused of murdering his faithless wife and her lover and disposing of their bodies in a satellite rocket.

Interesting idea, but a very dull film.

p: Michael Carreras for Exclusive
w: Paul Tabori, Richard Landau
radio play: Charles Eric Maine
d: Terence Fisher
ph: Reg Wyer
md: Ivor Slaney
ed: Maurice Rootes
ad: J. Elder Wills
sp: The Trading Post, Les Bowie
sound: Bill Salter
ass d: Jimmy Sangster
Howard Duff, Eva Bartok, Michael Medwin, Philip Leaver, Alan Wheatley, Andrew Osborn

Spawn

USA 1997 97m colour Dolby

A former government assassin is sent to hell where he is made to do the bidding of the devil back on earth, but he eventually manages to turn the tables.

Incoherent and often repulsive superhero fantasy in the MTV manner, whose flashy camera work and plethora of effects fail to compensate for the lack of storytelling abilities.

p: Clint Goldman for New Line/Todd McFarlane Entertainment
exec p: Todd McFarlane, Alan C. Blomquist
w: Alan McElroy
comic strip: Todd McFarlane
d: Mark A.Z. Dippe
ph: Guillermo Navarro
m: Graeme Revell
ed: Michael N. Kune
pd: Philip Harrison
cos/make-up: Kurtzman, Nicorette & Berger EFX group
sp: Steve Williams, ILM
John Leguizamo, Michael Jai White, Martin Sheen, Theresa Randle, Nicol Williamson, D.B. Sweeney, Miko Hughes, Sydney Beaudoin, Melinda Clarke

Species

USA 1995 108m DeLuxe DTS Stereo

A shape-shifting alien escapes from a research institute and goes on the run in the guise of a beautiful young woman.

Tired, over-talkative, not to mention wholly predictable variation on *Alien* and *The Thing* which nevertheless did remarkably well at the box office.

p: Frank Mancuso, Jr., Dennis Feldman for MGM/UA
exec p: David Streit, Lee Orloff
w: Dennis Feldman
d: Roger Donaldson
ph: Andrzej Bartkowiak
m: Christopher Young
ed: Conrad Buff
pd: John Muto
cos: Joe I. Tompkins
sp: Richard Edlund
sound: Jay Boekelheide
make-up effects: Steve Johnson
alien design: H. R. Giger
titles: Dan Perri
stunt co-ordinator: Glenn Randall, Jr., Max Kleven
Ben Kingsley, Michael Madsen, Forest Whitaker, Alfred Molina, Marg Helgenberger, Natasha Henstridge

Spiderman

USA 1978 74m colour TVM

A special serum enables a young reporter to scale buildings and catch spies.

Lame pilot for a short-lived series, some episodes of which were cobbled together and released theatrically outside America under the titles *Spiderman Strikes Back* (1978) and *Spiderman: The Dragon's Challenge* (1979).

p: Edward J. Montague for Columbia
exec p: Charles Fries, Dan Goodman
w: Alvin Boretz
d: E. W. Swackhamer
ph: Fred Jackman
m: Johnnie Spence
ed: Aaron Stell
ad: James Hulsey
cos: Frank Novak
sp: Don Courtney
sound: Marty Bolger
stunt co-ordinator: Fred Waugh
Nicholas Hammond, David White, Thayer David, Michael Pataki, Hilly Hicks, Lisa Eilbacher, Dick Balduzzi

Spiderman Strikes Back

USA 1978 96m colour TVM

Spiderman averts a criminal's plans to blow up Los Angeles with an atomic bomb.

Unbearable feature-length re-edit from the TV series.

p: Ron Satlof, Robert Janes for Columbia
exec p: Charles Fruis, Daniel B. Goodman
w: Robert Janes
d: Ron Satlof
ph: Jack Whitman
m: Stu Phillips
ed: David H. Newhouse, Erwin Dumbrille
ad: Bill McAllister
cos: Bernie Pollack, Anne Laune
sp: Don Courtney
sound: Robert Miller
stunt co-ordinator: Fred Waugh
Nicholas Hammond, Robert F. Simon, Michael Pataki, Chip Fields, Joanna Cameron, Randy Powell, Robert Alda

Spiderman: The Dragon's Challenge

USA 1979 96m colour TVM

Spiderman saves a visiting Hong Kong businessman from assassins.

More artless adventures strung together from the TV series.

p: Don McDougall for Columbia
exec p: Charles Fries, Dan Goodman

w: Lionel Siegel

d: Don McDougall

ph: Vince Martinelli

m: Dana Kaproff

ed: Edwin Dumbrille, Fred Roth

ad: Julian Sacks

cos: Robert Moore, Dodie Shepard

sp: William Schirmer

sound: Robert Sheridan

2nd unit d/stunt co-ordinator: Fred Waugh

Nicholas Hammond, Robert F. Simon, Ellen Bry, Ted Danson, Myron Healey, Chip Fields, Rosalind Chao, Benson Fong, Richard Erdman

Spielberg, Steven (1947-)

Commercially successful American writer, producer, director and executive, responsible for a string of blockbusting action and adventure films which caused him to be dismissed by serious critics, though more recently he has displayed a more mature side with such films as *The Color Purple*, *Empire of the Sun* and *Schindler's List*, the last of which which finally won him Best Director and Best Picture Oscars. His genuine understanding of all things cinematic has occasionally been squandered a little too freely (*1941*, *Hook*), but when in top form (*Jaws*, *Close Encounters of the Third Kind*, *Raiders of the Lost Ark*, *E. T.*) his films can transport millions. Into making home movies from an early age, Spielberg went professional in 1969 (after studying film at California's State College) with the short *Amblin*, a name he later used for his production company, founded in 1984 with producers Kathleen Kennedy and Frank Marshall. Several episode segments (*Night Gallery*, *Columbo*) and TV movies followed at

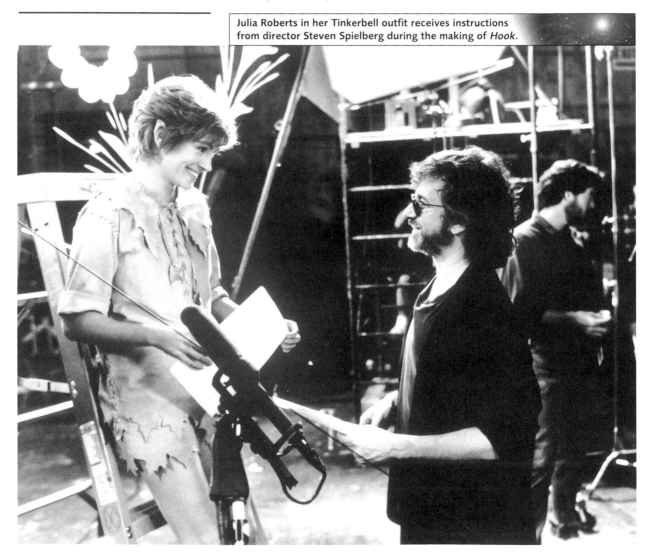

Julia Roberts in her Tinkerbell outfit receives instructions from director Steven Spielberg during the making of *Hook*.

Universal, climaxing with the acclaimed thriller *Duel* (released in theatres outside America), leading to his big screen directorial debut, *The Sugarland Express*, which he followed with *Jaws*. And the rest, as they say, is cinema history, his latest venture being Dreamworks SKG, a new studio which he created with producers Jeffrey Katzenberg and David Geffen. Its first film was *The Peacemaker* in 1997.

Genre credits:
Close Encounters of the Third Kind (1977 – w/d), *lose Encounters of the Third Kind – The Special Edition* (1980 – w/d), *Raiders of the Lost Ark* (1981 – d), *Twilight Zone: The Movie* (1983 – co-p/co-d), *Indiana Jones and the Temple of Doom* (1984 – d), *Gremlins* (1984 – co-p/actor), *Back to the Future* (1985 – co-exec p), *The Goonies* (1985 – co-exec p), *An American Tail* (1986 – co-exec p), *Innerspace* (1987 – co-exec p), *The Land Before Time* (1988 – co-exec p), *Who Framed Roger Rabbit?* (1988 – co-exec p), *Indiana Jones and the Last Crusade* (1989 – d), *Always* (1989 – co-exec p/d), *Back to the Future Part II* (1989 – co-exec p), *Back to the Future Part III* (1989 – co-exec p), *Gremlins 2: The New Batch* (1990 – co-exec p), *Dreams* (1990 – aka *Akira Kurosawa's Dreams* – exec p), *An American Tail: Fievel Goes West* (1991 – co-exec p), *Hook* (1991 – co-exec p/d), *Jurassic Park* (1993 – co-p/d), *The Flintstones* (1994 – exec p/presenter [as Steven Spielrock]), *Balto* (1995 – exec p), *The Lost World: Jurassic Park* (1997 – co-p/d), *Men in Black* (1997 – exec p)

Splash
USA 1984 105m Technicolor Dolby
The owner of a Manhattan fruit market is saved from drowning off Cape Cod by a mermaid, and she follows him home to New York.

Bright fantasy comedy, agreeably scripted and gamely performed. A well timed hit for the newly formed Touchstone arm of the Disney organisation. A TV movie sequel, *Splash, Too*, followed in 1988.

p: Brian Grazer for Touchstone
exec p: John Thomas Lenox
w: Lowell Ganz, Babaloo Mandell, Bruce Jay Friedman
story: Brian Grazer
d: RON HOWARD
ph: Don Peterman
m: Lee Holdridge
ed: Daniel P. Hanley, Michael Hill
pd: Jack T. Collis
cos: May Routh
TOM HANKS, DARYL HANNAH, John Candy, Eugens Levy, Dody Goodman, Shecky Greene, Bobby di Cicco

Splash, Too
USA 1988 96m colour TVM
A mermaid and her human boyfriend set up house in New York.

Dismal sitcom-style tele-sequel, of which the less said the better.

p: Mark V. Ovitz for Walt Disney
w: Bruce Franklin Singer
d: Greg Antonacci
ph: Fred J. Koenekamp
m: Joel McNeely
ed: Dennis M. Hill, Bob Wyman
ad: Raymond G. Storey
Todd Waring, Amy Yasbeck, Donovan Scott, Noble Willingham, Dody Goodman, Doris Belack, Barney Martin

The Spy Who Loved Me
GB 1977 125m Eastmancolor Panavision
When a megalomaniac plans to take over the world from his undersea base, James Bond joins forces with a female Russian spy so as to destroy his empire.

Lavish Bond adventure, the best of the Moore Bonds, with exotic locations, splendid sets, superb action sequences and one of the most breathtaking pre-credit stunts ever filmed. Responsible for reviving the then flagging series, it was also the first to depart entirely from the original novel – only the title is used.

p: ALBERT R. BROCCOLI for UA/Eon
w: Christopher Wood, Richard Maibaum
novel: Ian Fleming
d: LEWIS GILBERT
ph: CLAUDE RENOIR
m: MARVIN HAMLISCH
ly: Carole Bayer Sager
ed: JOHN GLEN
pd: KEN ADAM
ad: Peter Lamont
cos: Rosemary Burrows, Ronald Paterson
sp: DEREK MEDDINGS
sound: Gordon Everett, Gordon K. McCallum
stunt co-ordinator: Bob Simmons
2nd unit d: John Glen, Ernest Day, Willy Bogner
underwater ph: Lamar Boren
titles: MAURICE BINDER
ski stunt: RICK SYLVESTER
Roger Moore, Barbara Bach, Curt Jurgens, Richard Kiel (as Jaws), Caroline Munro, Walter Gotell, Bernard Lee, Lois Maxwell, Desmond Llewellyn, Geoffrey Keen, George Baker, Edward de Souza, Sydney Tafler, Valerie Leon, Shane Rimmer, Jeremy Bulloch

The Stand
USA 1994 4x96m colour TVM
Survivors of a man-made virus band together to fight against an evil force.

Initially intriguing blend of fantasy and horror. Unfortunately, the plot meanders rather too much, the music score is poor and the pace often sags (episode three is mind-numbingly tedious). Just about worth a look for King devotees.

The U.S.S. *Enterprise* glides majestically into view in *Star Trek: The Motion Picture*.

p: Mitchell Galin for Laurel/Greengrass
exec p: Richard P. Rubinstein, Stephen King
w: Stephen King from his novel
d: Mick Garris
ph: Edward Pei
m: W. G. Snuffy Walden
ed: Pat McMahon
pd: Nelson Coates
cos: Linda Matheson
sp: Lou Carlucci
sound: Rick Schexnayder
make-up effects: Steve Johnson's XFX Inc.
2nd unit d: Peter McIntosh
2nd unit ph: Ian Fox
stunt co-ordinator: Dan Bradley
Gary Sinise, Rob Lowe, Molly Ringwald, Jamey Sheridan, Ed Harris, Kathy Bates, Laura San Giacomo, Ruby Dee, Ossie Davis, Miguel Ferrer, Corin Nemec, Matt Frewer, Ray Walston, Aedam Storke, Bill Fagerbakke, Peter Van Norden, Shawnee Smith, Stephen

King, Sam Raimi, John Landis, Tom Holland

Star Trek: The Motion Picture ☽☽

USA 1979 132m Metroclor Panavision Dolby

When a mysterious alien force threatens earth, the starship *Enterprise* and her crew set out to discover its origin.

Big screen version of the popular 60s television series, with all the old familiar faces on board. Impressive technical effects and an intriguing if obviously padded story make it good enough fun for aficionados. It was followed by many sequels (listed chronologically here).

p: Gene Roddenberry for Paramount
w: Harold Livingstone

story: Alan Dean Foster
original series created by: GENE RODDENBERRY
d: Robert Wise
ph: Richard H. Kline
m: JERRY GOLDSMITH
ed: Todd Ramsey
pd: Harold Michelson
cos: Bob Fletcher
sp: DOUGLAS TRUMBULL, JOHN DYKSTRA, RICHARD YURICICH
sound: Tom Overton
sound effects: Dirk Dalton, Joel Goldsmith, Alan S. Howarth, Frank Serafine, Francisco Lupica
consultant: Isaac Asimov
William Shatner, Leonard Nimoy, DeForest Kelley, Stephen Collins, Persis Khambatta, James Doohan, George Takei, Walter Koenig, Nichelle Nichols, Majel Barrett, Mark Leonard, Grace Lee Whitney, Billy Van Zandt

---

Star Trek II: The Wrath of Khan

USA 1982 114m Movielab Panavision
Dolby

Kirk and his crew find themselves at the mercy of their old enemy Khan, an evil spacelord out for revenge.

Patchy sequel, a continuation of one of the original TV episodes. Harmless fun for devotees, many of whom seem to regard it as the best in the film series.

p: Robert Sallin for Paramount
exec p: Gene Roddenberry, Harve Bennett
w: Jack B. Sowards
story: Harve Bennett, Jack B. Sowards
d: Nicholas Meyer
ph: Gayne Rescher
m: JAMES HORNER
ed: William P. Dornisch
pd: Joseph R. Jennings
sp: ILM
William Shatner, Leonard Nimoy, DeForest Kelley, Ricardo Montalban (as Khan, recreating his original television role), Nichelle Nichols, Walter Koenig, James Doohan, George Takei, Paul Whitfield, Ike Eisenmann, Bibi Besch, Kirstie Alley, Merritt Butrick, Nicholas Guest

Star Trek III: The Search for Spock

USA 1984 100m Technicolor Panavision
Dolby

The crew of the *Enterprise* learn that though Spock is dead, his spirit lives on in a rejuvenated body...

A silly and singularly unimaginative entry in the series. A lot more style and originality were needed if its absurd plot was going to work.

p: Harve Bennett for Paramount/Cinema Group
w: Harve Bennett
d: Leonard Nimoy
ph: Charles Correl
m: James Horner
ed: Robert F. Shugrue
pd: John E. Chilberg II
cos: Robert Fletcher
sp: Ken Ralston
sound: Gene S. Cantamessa
sound effects: Frank Serafine
William Shatner, Leonard Nimoy, DeForest Kelley, James Doohan, Walter Koenig, George Takei, Nichelle Nichols, Judith Anderson, Robin Curtis, Merritt Butrick, Christopher Lloyd, James B. Sikking

Star Trek IV: The Voyage Home

USA 1986 119m Technicolor Panavision
Dolby

Captain Kirk and his crew travel back to the 20th century to rescue two hump-backed whales, the only creatures able to communicate with a deadly probe from outer space.

Lively addition to the franchise, with plenty of pace and invention. A pleasant surprise after the banality of number three.

p: Harve Bennett for Paramount/ILM
exec p: Ralph Winter
w: Steve Meerson, Peter Kirkes, Harve Bennett, Nicholas Meyer
story: Leonard Nimoy, Harve Bennett
d: Leonard Nimoy
ph: Don Peterman
m: Leonard Rosenman
ed: Peter E. Berger
pd: Jack T. Collis
cos: Robert Flectcher
sp: Ken Ralston
sound: Gene S. Cantamessa, Terry Porter, Dave Hudson, Mel Metcalfe
sound effects: Mark Mangini
titles: Dan Curry, Harry Moreau
William Shatner, Leonard Nimoy, DeForest Kelley, James Doohan, George Takei, Walter Koenig, Nichelle Nichols, Catherine Hicks, Mark Leonard, Robin Curtis, Robert Ellenstein, John Schuck, Brock Peters, Scott de Venney

Star Trek V: The Final Frontier

USA 1989 107m Technicolor Panavision
Dolby

Captain Kirk and the crew of the *Enterprise* are coerced into searching the galaxies for The Supreme Being by a Vulcan lord.

A good looking, fairly light-hearted adventure for the crew, with a little more intelligence to it than some of the previous episodes.

p: Harve Bennett for Paramount
exec p: Ralph Winters
w: David Lougherby
story: William Shatner, Harve Bennett, David Lougherby
d: William Shatner
ph: Andrew Laszlo
m: Jerry Goldsmith
ed: Peter Berger
pd: Herman Zimmerman
ad/cos: Nilo Rodis-Jamero
sp: Bran Ferren
sound: David Ronne
special make-up: Kenny Myers
titles: Barry Hyman
2nd unit d: Robert Carmichael
William Shatner, Leonard Nimoy, DeForest Kelly, James Doohan, Walter Koenig, Nichelle Nichols, George Takei, David Warner, George Murdock, Laurence Luckinbill

Star Trek VI: The Undiscovered Country

USA 1991 109m Technicolor Panavision
Dolby

Kirk and his crew are accused of assassinating a Klingon ambassador on the eve of peace talks, but they fight to clear their name.

Top: Jonathan Frakes (Riker) and Patrick Stewart (Captain Picard) pose for the cameras during a break from filming *Star Trek: First Contact*. Below: Frakes gets back to the business at hand.

Watchable but rather slow moving conclusion to the first wave of films which takes a long time to get to an inevitable solution. Affection for the cast helps to maintain interest.

p: Ralph Winter, Steven-Charles Jaffe for Paramount
exec p: Leonard Nimoy
w: Nicholas Meyer, Danny Martin Flinn
story: Leonard Nimoy, Lawrence Konner, Mark Rosenthal
d: Nicholas Meyer
ph: Hiro Narita
m: Cliff Eidelman
ed: Ronald Roose
pd: Herman Zimmerman
cos: Dodie Shepard
sp: ILM, Scott Farrar
sound: Jeffrey J. Haboush, Michael Herbick, Greg P. Russell
2nd unit d: Steven-Charles Jaffe
2nd unit ph: John V. Fante
make-up effects: Edward French, Richard Snell, Greg Cannom

William Shatner, Leonard Nimoy, DeForest Kelley, James Doohan, Walter Koenig, Nichelle Nichols, George Takei, Kim Catrall, Mark Lenard, Brock Peters, Grace Lee Whitney, Christopher Plummer, David Warner, John Schuck, Rosana De Soto, Iman, Christian Slater (uncredited cameo)

Star Trek: Generations

USA 1994 118m DeLuxe Dolby
Captain Kirk and Captain Picard join forces to prevent a scientist's plans to destroy half the galaxy so as to be able to reach a mysterious ribbon of energy known as The Nexus.

Slickly handled adventure which marked the changeover from the old *Star Trek* crew to the new one, though audiences unfamiliar with the television series *Star Trek: The Next Generation* may find some of the in-jokes mystifying.

p: Rick Berman for Paramount
exec p: Bernie Williams
w: Ronald D. Moore, Brannon Braga
story: Ronald D. Moore, Brannon Braga, Rick Berman
d: David Carson
ph: John A. Alonzo
m: Dennis McCarthy
ed: Peter Berger
pd: Herman Zimmerman
cos: Robert Blackman
sp: ILM
sound: Thomas D. Causey
stunt co-ordinator: Bud Davis
make-up: Michael Westmore

Patrick Stewart, William Shatner, Malcolm McDowell, James Doohan, Walter Koenig, Whoopi Goldberg, Jonathan Frakes, LeVar Burton, Brent Spiner, Gates McFadden, Marina Sirtis, Michael Dorn, Alan Ruck

---

Star Trek: First Contact

USA 1996 111m DeLuxe Dolby
Captain Jean-Luc Picard and his crew travel back in time to prevent the Borg from colonising earth.

Just as *Star Trek II: The Wrath of Khan* is a follow-up to an episode of the original *Star Trek* television series, this movie is a sequel to an episode of *Star Trek: The Next Generation*. Consequently, those who haven't followed the series might be a little mystified as to what's going on. Despite good effects work, the film is rather dull and over-talkative anyway and doesn't rank among the best, though fans will no doubt disagree.

p: Rick Berman for Paramount
exec p: Martin Hornstein
w: Brannon Braga, Ronald D. Moore
story: Rick Berman, Bannon Braga, Ronald D. Moor
d: Jonathan Frakes
ph: Matthew F. Leonetti

m: Jerry Goldsmith
add m: Joel Goldsmith
ed: John W. Wheeler
pd: Herman Zimmerman
cos: Deborah Everton
sp: ILM

Patrick Stewart, Jonathan Frakes, Brent Spiner, Levar Burton, Michael Dorn, Gates McFadden, Marina Sirtis, Alfre Woodard, James Cromwell, Alice Krige

---

Star Wars

USA/GB 1977 121m Technicolor
Panavision Dolby
A long time ago in a galaxy far, far away, a farm boy, a maverick space pilot and two robots helped a rebel princess escape the wiles of an evil warlord and destroy his death star.

Upon its release this quickly became the biggest box office grosser in movie history, not only managing to bring back the family to the cinema, but heralding a new era in movie science fiction, as well as considerably advancing the art of special effects technology. In itself it's a fast, imaginative and visually exciting adventure with its roots firmly planted in the Saturday morning serials of the 30s and 40s. An industry of toys, book and video games followed in its wake, making it an event of social as well as cinematic importance, though if it's just colourful, escapist entertainment you're after it satisfies those criteria too. It was followed by *The Empire Strikes Back* (1980) and *The Return of the Jedi* (1983). A special 20th anniversary re-issue of the film appeared in 1997 with improved sound and effects and a handful of new sequences, most notably in the space port of Mos Eisley, which now includes a previously excised encounter with Jabba the Hutt. Likewise, *The Empire Strikes Back* and *Return of the Jedi* received a sound and effects brush-up. This re-issue of

Before and after. Artoo-Detoo and See Threepio discover that the streets of Mos Eisley are now populated with digitally created creatures in the special 20th anniversary edition of *Star Wars*.

Star Wars made well over $130m in the U.S. alone, thus restoring *Stars Wars* to its rightful place at the head of the list of top money-making movies.

p: Gary Kurtz for TCF/Lucasfilm
w/d: GEORGE LUCAS
ph: GILBERT TAYLOR
m: JOHN WILLIAMS (AA)
ed: PAUL HIRSCH, MARCIA LUCAS, RICHARD CHEW (AA)
pd: JOHN BARRY
ad/set decoration: NORMAN REYNOLDS, LESLIE DILLEY, ROGER CHRISTIAN (AA)
cos: JOHN MOLLO (AA)
sp: JOHN STEARS, JOHN DYKSTRA, RICHARD EDLUND, ROBERT BLALACK, GRANT MCCUNE (AA) and others
sound: DON MACDOUGAL, RAY WEST, BOB MINKLER, DEREK BALL (AA)
sound effcts: BENJAMIN BURTT, JR. (AA)
make-up effects: Stuart Freeborn, Rick Baker, Douglas Beswick
2nd unit ph: Carroll Ballard, Tak Fujimoto, Rick Clements, Robert Dalva
titles: Dan Perri
MARK HAMILL, HARRISON FORD, CARRIE FISHER, ALEC GUINNESS, PETER CUSHING, Anthony Daniels, Kenny Baker, Peter Mayhew, Dave Prowse, James Earl Jones (voice), Phil Brown, Shelagh Fraser, Jack Purvis, Eddie Byrne, Dennis Lawson, Don Henderson, Jeremy Sinden, Graham Ashley

Star Wars, Episode IV: A New Hope see Stars Wars

Star Wars, Episode V: The Empire Strikes Back see The Empire Strikes Back

Star Wars, Episode VI: Return of the Jedi
see Return of the Jedi

Starcrash

It 1979 97m colour
Two rebels are recruited to destroy an evil spacelord's hideaway.

Abysmal space opera with cheap effects and all the expected clichés on hand. *Star Wars* it wasn't.

p: Nat Wachsberger, Patrick Wachsberger
w: Lewis Coates (Luigi Cozzi), Nat Wachsberger, R. A. Dillon
d: Lewis Coates (Luigi Cozzi)
ph: Paul Beeson, Roberto D'Ettorre
m: John Barry
ed: Sergio Montanari
pd: Aurelio Crugnolla
sp: Ron Hays
Christopher Plummer, Caroline Munro (as Stella Star), Marjoe Gortner, David Hasselhoff, Joe Spinell, Judd Hamilton, Robert Tessier, Hamilton Camp (voice)

Starflight One

USA 1982 96m colour TVM
The world's first hypersonic passenger plane meets with disaster on its maiden voyage.

Hackneyed mixture of *Airport* melodramatics and *Star Wars* hardware. Intolerable.

p: Peter Welson, Arnold Orgolini
exec p: Henry Winkler, Allan Mannings
w: Robert Malcolm Young
story: Peter R. Brooke
d: Jerry Jameson
ph: Hector Figueroa
m: Lalo Schifrin
ed: John F. Link II
pd: David L. Snyder
cos: Carolina G. Ewart
sp: John Dykstra
sound: Bud Alper
Lee Majors, Hal Linden, Ray Milland, Lauren Hutton, Gail Strickland, George DiCenzo, Robert Webber, Terry Kiser

Stargate

USA 1994 122m Technicolor Dolby
An Egyptologist finds himself transported across the galaxies to a mysterious planet after deciphering the code on an ancient gateway.

Big budget science fiction epic which unfortunately jettisons the mysticism of its first hour for standard action climaxes in the second. It certainly looks good throughout, however, and benefits enormously from Arnold's score.

p: Joel B. Michaels, Oliver Eberle, Dean Devlin for Le Studio Le Canal + /Centropolis/Carolco
exec p: Mario Kassar
w: Dean Devlin, Roland Emmerich
d: Roland Emmerich
ph: KARL WALTER LINDENLAUB
m: DAVID ARNOLD
ed: Michael J. Duthie, Derek Brechin
pd: HOLGER GROSS
cos: Joseph Porro
sp: Kit West, Patrick Tatopoulos, Kleiser-Walczak
sound: David Ronne
Kurt Russell, James Spader, Jaye Davidson, Viveca Lindfors, Alexis Cruz, Mili Avital, John Diehl, Leon Rippy

The Starlost: Deception

USA 1982 96m colour TVM
In 2790, the crew of a 5,000-mile long spaceship find their lives in danger from a mysterious force.

Astonishingly inept and set-bound rubbish, stitched together from episodes of a TV series so cheap-looking that it makes the worst episodes of *Dr. Who* look like *Gone with the Wind*.

p: William Davidson for Glenn-Warren
exec p: Douglas Trumbull, Jerry Zeitman
w: Arthur Heinemann, Norman Klenman
d: Joseph L. Scanlon, Ed Richardson
ph/m/ed: no credits given

cos: Shirley Mann
sp: Douglas Trumbull
sound: Wally Harris
Keir Dullea, Gay Rowan, Robin Ward, Ed
Ames, Angel Tomkins

Starman

USA 1984 115m Metrocolor Dolby
An alien stranded on earth is helped by
a Wisconsin housewife and takes the
form of her dead husband.

Amiable science fiction story which
quickly turns into a road movie, for a
pleasant change concentrating more on
the relationship between the earthling
and the alien rather than whizz-bang
special effects.

p: Larry J. Franco, Barry Bernardi for
Columbia/Delphi
exec p: Michael Douglas
w: Bruce A. Evans, Raynald Gideon
d: JOHN CARPENTER
ph: Donald M. Morgan
m: Jack Nietzche
ed: Marion Rothman
pd: Daniel Lomino
cos: Andy Hylton, Robin Michael Bush
sp: Roy Arbogast, Bruce Nicholson, ILM
make-up effects: Dick Smith, Stan
Winston, Rick Baker
sound: Tommy Causey
2nd unit d/visual consultant: Joe Alves
2nd unit ph: Steve Poster
stunt co-ordinator: Terry Leonard
JEFF BRIDGES, Karen Allen, Charles Martin
Smith, Richard Jaekel, Tony Edwards, Robert
Phalen

Stay Tuned

USA 1992 86m Technicolor Dolby
A suburban couple find themselves
trapped inside their television.

Amusing fantasy comedy which
keeps moving, not outstaying its welcome, though it's at its best when spoofing particular styles and programmes.

p: James G. Robinson for Warner/Morgan
Creek
w: Tom S. Parker, Jim Jennewein
d/ph: Peter Hyams
m: Bruce Broughton
ed: Peter E. Berger
pd: Philip Harrison
cos: Joe I. Tompkins
sp: John Thomas, George Erschbamer
sound: Ralph Parker, Daryl Powell
John Ritter, Pam Dawber, Jeffrey Jones, Bob
Dishy, Heather McComb, David Thom

Stein, Herman (1915-)

American composer, long at Universal,
where he worked on a handful of 50s
science fiction movies, often in collaboration and often uncredited. His non-
genre films include *Girls in the Night*,
The Black Shield of Falworth, *The Far
Country* and *No Name on the Bullet*.

Genre credits:
It Came from Outer Space (1953 – m), *The
Creature from the Black Lagoon* (1955 – co-
m), *Revenge of the Creature* (1955 – co-m),
This Island Earth (1955 – co-m), *The
Creature Walks Among Us* (1956 – co-m),
The Incredible Shrinking Man (1957 – co-m)

Stein, Ronald

Prolific American composer with a
penchant for low budget science fiction
and horror films. He began composing
for films in 1955 with *Apache Woman*
for Roger Corman. He followed this
with *Oklahoma Woman*, *The
Gunslinger*, *The Undead*, *She Gods of
Shark Reef*, *Thunder Over Hawaii*,
Sorority Girl, *Atlas*, *The Premature
Burial*, *The Terror* and *The Haunted
Palace* – all for Corman. His other
credits include *The Legend of Tom
Dooley*, *Requiem for a Gunfighter*, *Jet
Attack*, *Suicide Commandos*, *Reform
School Hellcats*, *Spider Baby* (aka
Spider Baby or The Maddest Story

Ever Told/ The Liver Eaters),
Dementia 13 (aka *The Haunted and
the Hunted*), *Getting Straight*, *The
Rain People* and *Razzle Dazzle*.
Genre credits:
The Day the World Ended (1955), *The
Phantom from 10 000 Leagues* (1955), *It
Conquered the World* (1956), *Attack of the
Crab Monsters* (1956), *Not of This Earth*
(1956), *Invasion of the Saucer Men* (1957 –
aka *The Invasion of the Hell Creatures*),
Attack of the 50-foot Woman (1958), *The
Last Woman on Earth* (1960), *The
Underwater City* (1961)

The Stepford Wives

USA 1974 115 TVCcolor
Having moved to an exclusive com-
muter village outside New York, a
young housewife discovers that the
menfolk have had their wives replaced
by replicants and that she is the next
on the list.

Glossy thriller which works pretty
well, sustaining its intentions through
to the end. Slick late-night viewing. It
was followed by three television
sequels: *Revenge of the Stepford
Wives* (1980), *The Stepford Children*
(1987) and *The Stepford Husbands*
(1996).

p: Edgar J. Scherick for Palomar/Fadsin
exec p: Gustave Berne
w: William Goldman
novel: IRA LEVIN
d: BRYAN FORBES
ph: Owen Roizman
m: Michael Small
ed: Timothy Gee
pd: Gene Callahan
cos: Anna Hill-Johnstone
sound: James Sabat
KATHERINE ROSS, PAULA PRENTISS,
Nanette Newman, Peter Masterson, Patrick
O'Neal, Tina Louise, William Prince, Dee

Wallace, Kenneth McMillan

The Stepford Children

USA 1987 96m colour TVM

The title really tells all about this tired third installment, which has the Stepford men replacing their brats with super intelligent replicants.

d: Alan Levi

Barbara Eden, Don Murray, Tammy Lauren, James Coco, Ken Swofford, Richard Anderson

Stephen King's The Lawnmower Man

see The Lawnmower Man

Stevens, Leith (1909-1970)

American composer, long with Paramount, where he worked on three of producer George Pal's key 50s science fiction films. Conducting from the age of 16, he joined CBS radio in 1930 and entered films in 1942 with *Syncopation*. His other credits include *The Wild One*, *The James Dean Story*, *Julie* and *A New Kind of Love*.

Genre credits:

Destination Moon (1950), *When Worlds Collide* (1953), *The War of the Worlds* (1953), *World without End* (1956)

Stevenson, Robert (1905-1986)

British director, long with Disney, where he directed several of their key live action fantasy films, most notably *Mary Poppins* and *The Love Bug*. Following experience as a journalist, he began his film career as a writer in 1930 with *Greek Street*. He co-directed his first film *Happy Ever After* (with Paul Martin) in 1932, which he followed with *Falling for You* and *Jack of All Trades* (aka *The Two of Us*), both of which he co-directed with Jack Hulbert. His solo career kicked off with *Tudor Rose* (aka *Nine Days a Queen*) in 1935 and was followed by such projects as *The Man Who Changed His Mind* (aka *The Man Who Lived Again*), *King Solomon's Mines* and *A Young Man's Fancy*. In 1939 he went to Hollywood under contract to producer David O. Selznick who loaned him out (but never personally used him) to direct such films as *Tom Brown's Schooldays*, *Jane Eyre* and *Dishonoured Lady*. He worked for RKO from 1949 on *Walk Softly, Stranger* and *My Forbidden Past*. He also did much television work in the 50s before moving to Disney where his first film was *Johnny Tremain*, released in 1957. His other Disney credits include *Old Yeller*, *Kidnapped*, *That Darn Cat* and *One of Our Dinosaurs is Missing*.

Genre credits:

F.P.1 (1933 – co-w English language version only), *Non-Stop New York* (1937), *Darby O'Gill and the Little People* (1959), *The Absent-Minded Professor* (196), *In Search of the Castaways* (1961), *Son of Flubber* (1963), *The Misadventures of Merlin Jones* (1963), *Mary Poppins* (1964), *The Monkey's Uncle* (1965), *The Gnome-Mobile* (1967), *Blackbeard's Ghost* (1967), *The Love Bug* (1968), *Bedknobs and Broomsticks* (1971), *Herbie Rides Again* (1973), *The Island at the Top of the World* (1974), *The Shaggy D.A.* (1976)

Stewart, Patrick (1940-)

Respected British character actor with a background in Shakespeare, though he is now better known as Captain Jean-Luc Picard in *Star Trek: The Next Generation* and its movie spin-offs. His other credits include *Antony and Cleopatra*, *Hedda*, *Excalibur*, *Robin Hood: Men in Tights* and *Jeffrey*.

Genre credits:

Excalibur (1981), *Dune* (1984), *Lifeforce* (1985), *Encounter at Farpoint* (1987 – TVM [feature-length pilot for *Star Trek: The Next Generation*]), *Emissary* (1993 – TVM [feature-length pilot for *Star Trek: Deep Space Nine*]), *The Pagemaster* (1994 – voice), *All Good Things* (1994 – TVM [feature-length conclusion to *Star Trek: The Next Generation*]), *Star Trek: Generations* (1994), *The Canterville Ghost* (1996 – TVM), *Star Trek: First Contact* (1996)

Stine, Clifford

American cinematographer and special effects technician who worked on a couple of key science fiction films in the 50s. His other credits include *Abbott and Costello Meet the Mummy*, *Monster on Campus* and *The Thing That Couldn't Die* (all dealing with special effects).

Genre credits:

It Came from Outer Space (1953 – ph), *Abbott and Costello Go to Mars* (1953 – ph), *This Island Earth* (1954 – ph/co-sp), *Tarantula* (1955 – sp), *Francis in the Haunted House* (1956 – sp), *The Incredible Shrinking Man* (1957 – sp), *The Land Unknown* (1957 – co-sp), *The Monolith Monsters* (1957 – sp), *The Deadly Mantis* (1957 – sp), *The Brass Bottle* (1963 – ph)

Strange Days ⊙

USA 1995 145m DeLuxe Dolby

During the last days of 1999, an ex-cop makes a living by selling virtual reality "clips" showing robbery and rape which his clients can then experience for themselves via a special headset.

However, his racket is disturbed when he is supplied snuff clips by a killer whose identity he subsequently attempts to discover.

Overlong thriller with the usual glum view of the future, a virtual reality story that is fast becoming a cliché and a dull hero. Things do pick up after a slow start, though basically the film is little more than an old-fashioned murder mystery with sci-fi trimmings and plenty of violence. A shorter running time would certainly have made for a better film.

p: James Cameron, Steven-Charles Jaffe for TCF/Lightstorm
exec p: Rae Sanchini, Lawrence Kasanoff
w: James Cameron, Jay Cocks
story: James Cameron
d: Kathryn Bigelow
ph: Matthew F. Leonetti
m: Graeme Revell
ed: Howard Smith
pd: Lilly Kilvert
sp: Terry Frazee
sound: Gary Rydstrom, Jeff Wexler, David Ronne
2nd unit d: Phil Pfeiffer, Steven-Charles Jaffe
2nd unit ph: Phil Pfeiffer
stunt co-ordinator: Doug Coleman
Ralph Fiennes, Angela Bassett, Juliette Lewis, Glenn Plummer, Tom Sizemore, Vincent D'Onofrio, Michael Wincott

Strange Invaders 🛸
USA 1983 93m DeLuxe
An entymologist searching for his missing ex-wife discovers that her home town has been taken over by aliens and that she is one of them.

Tongue-in-cheek low budgeter apeing the Corman quickies of the 50s – and all the better for it.

p: Walter Coblenz for Orion
exec p: Michael Laughlin
w/d: Michael Laughlin
ph: Louis Hovarth
m: John Addison
ed: John W. Wheeler
pd/cos: Susanna Moore
sp: PSE
sound: Lon E. Bender, Peter Shewchuk
associate p: Joel Cohen, Richard Moore
2nd unit ph: Zoltan Vidall
Paul Le Mat, Nancy Allen, Louise Fletcher, Diana Scarwid, Fiona Lewis, Kenneth Tobey, Michael Lerner, June Lockhart, Joel Cohen

The Strange World of Planet X
GB 1957 75m bw
A scientist's experiments with magnetic fields cause insects to mutate into giant maneaters.

Talkative schlocker with (when they finally appear) some pretty dismal monsters.

p: George Maynard for Eros/Artistes Alliance
w: Paul Ryder
novel: Rene Ray
d: Gilbert Gunn
ph: Joe Ambor
m: Robert Sharples
ed: Francis Bieber
ad: Bernard Sarron
cos: Irma Birch
sp: Anglo-Scottish Pictures
sound: Cecil Mason
Forrest Tucker, Gaby Andre, Martin Benson, Hugh Latimer, Alec Mango, Wyndham Goldie, Dandy Nicholls, Richard Warner

Stranger from Venus
GB 1954 75m bw
An alien from Venus arrives on earth in an attempt to deter Man from experimenting with atomic power.

Low budget programmer, not as bad as some, but in no way comparable to *The Day the Earth Stood Still* despite the same star and story.

p: Burt Balaban, Gene Martel for Princess/Rich and Rich
w: Hans Jacoby
story: Desmond Leslie
d: Burt Balaban
ph: Kenneth Talbot
m: Eric Spear
ed: Peter Hunt
Patricia Neal, Helmut Dantine, Derek Bond, Cyril Luckham, Willoughby Gray, John le Mesurier, Nigel Green, Marigold Russell

Strock, Herbert L. (1918-)
American writer, director and editor with a penchant for low budget horrors, among them *I Was a Teenage Frankenstein*, *Blood of Dracula* and *How to Make a Monster*.

Genre credits:
The Magnetic Monster (1953 – ed), *Riders to the Stars* (1954 – ed/co-p), *Gog* (1954 – ed/d), *The Crawling Hand* (1963 – co-w/ed/d)

Subotsky, Milton (1921-1991)
American writer and producer who began his career making documentaries and industrial films, which he wrote, directed and edited. This led to a stint with the US Army's Signal Corps Photographic Centre as an editor during World War Two. Experience as an "ideas man" for impressario Billy Rose and work as a sales manager for a distribution company followed, though it was in television (where he'd already had experience in 1941) that he finally began to make inroads as a writer in 1949. In 1953 he met distributor Max J. Rosenberg while working on the children's TV series *Junior Science* (which he wrote and produced and which Rosenberg financed) and the two decid-

ed to go into partnership, the outcome of which was *Rock, Rock, Rock* (1957), a musical exploitation item modelled after the success of the previous year's *Rock Around the Clock* that they produced together and which Subotsky wrote. This eventually led to Subotsky and Rosenberg forming Amicus Pictures in Britain in 1965, which gave Hammer a run for its money with a series of chillers and *Dead of Night*-style horror compendiums, such as *The House That Dripped Blood*, *Asylum*, *Vault of Horror* and *From Beyond the Grave*. Subotsky left Amicus in 1975 and went on to produce either solo or with others, but pretty much remained in the fantasy/horror genre, though the results of his efforts were more variable.

Genre credits:

Dr. Who and the Daleks (1965 – w/co-p), *Daleks – Invasion Earth, 2150 A. D.* (1966 – w/co-p), *The Terrornauts* (1967 – co-p), *They Came from Beyond Space* (1967 – w/co-p), *The Mind of Mr. Soames* (1969 – co-p), *The Land That Time Forgot* (1974 – co-p), *At the Earth's Core* (1976 – co-exec p), *The Martian Chronicles* (1979 – TVM – co-p), *Lawnmower Man* (1992 – aka *Stephen King's The Lawnmower Man* – co-p)

Suburban Commando

USA 1991 90m DeLuxe Dolby
An extra-terrestrial bounty hunter is ordered to take a vacation for six weeks and finds himself stranded on earth at the home of an architect and his family.

Dumb blend of science fiction and comedy action, aimed at youngsters, who turned it into a minor box office hit.

p: Howard Gottfried for New Line
exec p: Hulk Hogan, Kevin Moreton, Deborah Moore

w: Frank Capello
d: Burt Kennedy
ph: Bernd Heinl
m: David Michael Frank
ed: Terry Stokes
pd: Ivo Cristante
cos: Ha Nguyen
sp: Jeffrey Ohun
sound: Walter Holyman
stunt co-ordinator: Dave Cass, Jake Crawford
2nd unit d: Dave Cass
Hulk Hogan, Christopher Lloyd, Shelley Duvall, Roy Dotrice, JoAnn Dearing, William Ball, Larry Miller, Jack Elam, Michael Faustino

Sukman, Harry

American composer with several scores for producer Ivan Tors to his credit.

Genre credits:

Gog (1954), *Riders to the Stars* (1954), *Around the World Under the Sea* (1965), *Genesis II* (1972 – TVM)

Super Mario Bros.

USA 1993 104m Technicolor Dolby
Two Brooklyn plumbers cross into another dimension to save a princess.

Expensive but overly raucous live action version of the popular video game. Not really a movie.

p: Jake Eberts for Lightmotive/Allied Filmmakers/Cinergi
w: Parker Bennett, Terry Runte, Ed Solomon
d: Rocky Morton, Annabel Jankel
ph: Dean Semler
m: Alan Silvestri
ed: Mark Goldblatt
pd: David L. Snyder
cos: Joseph Porr
sp: Christopher Woods
sound: Steve Maslow, Gregg Lanaker
2nd unit d: James Devis, Dean Semler
2nd unit ph: James Devis
stunt co-ordinator: Warren Stevens

Bob Hoskins, John Leguizamo, Dennis Hopper, Samantha Mathis. Fisher Stevens, Fiona Shaw, Richard Edson

Supergirl

USA/GB 1984 124m Technicolor Panavision Dolby
Supergirl travels to earth from her home in inner space to retrieve a life-giving orb, only to discover it to be in the hands of an arch villainess.

Tongue-in-cheek nonsense on a big budget, a few marks up on *Superman III* and with improved special effects. A badly timed flop at the box office, though.

p: Timothy Burrill for Tri-Star
exec p: Alexander Salkind, Ilya Salkind
w: David Odell
d: Jeannot Szwarc
ph: Alan Hume
m: JERRY GOLDSMITH
ed: Malcolm Cooke
pd: Richard MacDonald
cos: Emma Porteous
sp: DEREK MEDDINGS, ROY FIELD
sound: Derek Ball, Robin Gregory, Guido Reidy
sound effects: Brian Mann
titles: SHELDON ELBOURNE
Helen Slater, Faye Dunaway, Peter O'Toole, Brenda Vaccaro, Mia Farrow, Peter Cook, Simon Ward, Marc McClure, Hart Bochner, Maureen Teefy, Sandra Dickinson, David Healy

Superman

USA/GB 1978 142m Technicolor Panavision Dolby
Saved by his parents from the exploding planet of Krypton, a young child is sent across the galaxies to earth where he grows up with incredible powers which he uses to fight evil and save the world from disaster.

Expensive, lavishly mounted big

Christopher Reeve struts his stuff for the 1978 blockbuster *Superman*, a role he returned to a further three times. Tragically, a riding accident in 1995 rendered him paralysed from the neck down.

screen resurrection of a famous 30s comic strip character, crammed with special effects and a plethora of guest stars. The plot drags its heels in places, and on the whole it is perhaps a little too reverential, but it is an otherwise highly entertaining enterprise with enough up on the screen to satisfy most pleasure seekers. It was followed by *Superman II* (1980), *Superman III* (1983), *Supergirl* (1984) and *Superman IV: The Quest for Peace* (1987). There was also a short-lived TV series titled *Superboy* from the same producers.

p: Pierre Spengler for Warner
exec p: Alexander Salkind
w: Mario Puzo, Robert Benton, David Newman, Leslie Newman
comic strip: Jerry Siegel, Joe Shuster
story: Mario Puzo
d: RICHARD DONNER
ph: GEOFFREY UNSWORTH
m: JOHN WILLIAMS
ly: Leslie Bricusse
ed: Stuart Baird
pd: JOHN BARRY
cos: Yvonne Blake, Betty Adamson, Ruth Morley
sp: LES BOWIE, COLIN CHILVERS, DENYS COOP, ROY FIELD, DEREK MEDDINGS, ZORAN PERISIC (aa)
sound: Roy Charman, Norman Bolland, Ronnie Fox Rogers, Ginger Gemmell, Roy Ford, Jack Lowen
stunt co-ordinator: Alf Joint, Vic Armstrong
titles: DENIS RICH
creative consultant: Tom Mankiewicz
2nd unit d: David Tomblin, John Barry, John Glen, David Lane, Robert Lynn
CHRISTOPHER REEVE, Marlon Brando, Gene Hackman (as Lex Luthor), MARGOT KIDDER (as Lois Lane), Ned Beatty, Jackie Cooper, Glenn Ford, Trevor Howard, Jack O'Halloran, Valerie Perrine, Maria Schell, Phylis Thaxter, Terence Stamp, Susannah York, Jeff East, Marc McClure, Sarah Douglas, Harry Andrews, Rex Reed, Larry

Hagman, Larry Lamb, Michael Ensign, John Ratzenberger, Roy Stevens

Superman II

USA/GB 1980 127m Technicolor Panavision Dolby
Superman saves the world from three villains with powers equal to his own.

Expensive, rather fragmentary sequel with plenty of action and special effects, climaxing in a battle of gigantic proportions against the baddies. About half an hour too long, nevertheless.

p: Pierre Spengler for Warner/Dovemead/International
exec p: Alexander Salkind
w: Mario Puzo, David Newman, Leslie Newman
story: Mario Puzo
d: Richard Lester (some scenes by Richard Donner)
ph: Geoffrey Unsworth, Bob Paynter
m: Ken Thorne (using themes by John Williams)
ed: John Victor Smith
pd: John Barry, Peter Murton
cos: Yvonne Blake
sp: COLIN CHILVERS, ROY FIELD, DEREK MEDDINGS
creative consultant: Tom Mankiewicz
Christopher Reeve, Margot Kidder, Gene Hackman, Ned Beatty, Valerie Perrine, Jackie Cooper, Jack O'Halloran, Susannah York, Clifton James, E. G. Marshall, Marc McClure, Terence Stamp, Sarah Douglas, Shane Rimmer, John Ratzenberger

Superman III

USA/GB 1983 122m Technicolor Panavision
An industrialist builds an enormous computer to take over the world and destroy Superman.

Slackly written and directed addition to the series with poor effects and an

overdose of "comic" relief from Pryor. Wholesale editing might have helped, but on the whole it's a pleb-pleaser of the worst possible kind.

p: Pierre Spengler for Warner/Dovemead
exec p: Alexander Salkind, Ilya Salkind
w: David Newman, Leslie Newman
d: Richard Lester
ph: Robert Paynter
m: Ken Thorne (using themes by John Williams), Giorgio Moroder
ed: John Victor Smith
pd: Peter Murton
cos: Evangeline Harrison
sp: Colin Chilvers, Derek Meddings, Roy Field
2nd unit d: Dave Lane
Christopher Reeve, Richard Pryor, Jackie Cooper, Margot Kidder, Annette O'Toole, Marc McClure, Robert Vaughn, Annie Ross, Pamela Stephenson, Gavan O'Herlihy, Nancy Roberts, Graham Stark, Bob Todd, Sandra Dickinson, Ronnie Brody

Superman IV: The Quest for Peace

GB 1987 92m Technicolor Panavision
Lex Luthor tries to conquer Superman with his new creation, Nuclear Man.

Tired attempt by the Cannon Group to continue the series, which had already outstayed its welcome. Tolerable enough for younger audiences perhaps, but wholesale pre-release editing is evident throughout and the effects are poor.

p: Menahem Golan, Yoram Globus for Cannon
w: Lawrence Konner, Mark Rosenthal
story: Christopher Reeve, Lawrence Konner, Mark Rosenthal
d: Sidney J. Furie
ph: Ernest day
md: Alexander Courage (using themes by John Williams)
ed: John Shirley

pd: John Graysmark
sp: Harrison Ellenshaw
Christopher Reeve, Gene Hackman, Margot Kidder, Jackie Cooper, Mariel Hemingway, Sam Wanamaker, Jon Cryer, Marc McClure, Mark Pillow (as Nuclear Man), William Hootkins, Jim Broadbent, Clive Mantle, Esmond Knight, Bernard Spear, Susannah York (voice)

Supertrain

USA 1979 96m colour TVM
A killer threatens passengers on board an atomic-powered super train.

Juvenile disaster flick with a distinct paucity of imagination, both in the script and handling. The resultant series quickly crashed.

p: Anthony Spinner for NBC
exec p: Dan Curtis
w: Earle W. Wallace
story: Earle W. Wallace, Donald E. Westlake
d: Dan Curtis
ph: Dennis Dalzell
m: Bob Cobert
ed: Robee Roberts, Bernard Gribble
pd: Ned Parsons
cos: Nolan Miller
sp: Russ Hessey, Gene Polito
sound: Bill Teague
2nd unit d: Eugene Lourie
stunt co-ordinator: Walter Scott
Steve Lawrence, Don Meredith, Char Fontaine, George Hamilton, Stella Stevens, Keenan Wynn, Don Stroud, Robert Alda, Edward Andrews

Suschitzky, Peter (1940-)

British cinematographer, the son of Austrian cinematographer Wolfgang Suschitzky (1912- [*No Resting Place*, *The Vengeance of She*, *Entertaining Mr. Sloane*, *Get Carter*, *Theatre of Blood*, etc.]). Began his career photographing *It Happened Here*, which

was released in 1963 following a lengthy production process. He followed this up with *Privilege*, *Charlie Bubbles* and second unit work on *The Charge of the Light Brigade*. His other credits include *Henry the VIII and his Six Wives*, *That'll Be the Day*, *Lisztomania*, *Valentino*, *Falling in Love* and three for director David Cronenberg (*Dead Ringers*, *Naked Lunch* and *M. Butterfly*).

Genre credits:

The Pied Piper (1971), *The Rocky Horror Picture Show* (1975), *The Empire Strikes Back* (1980), *Krull* (1983), *Mars Attacks!* (1996)

Swamp Thing

USA 1982 92m Technicolor
A scientist working on a top secret formula in the Everglades is turned into a half-human, half-plant monster when his experiment is sabotaged.

Foolish stuff adapted from the *DC* comic strip, ludicrous even by the standards of the genre. A sequel, *Return of the Swamp Thing*, followed in 1989.

p: Benjamin Melniker, Michael E. Uslan for UA
w/d: Wes Craven
ph: Robin Goodwin
m: Harry Manfredini
ed: Richard Bracken
ad: David Nichols, Robb Wilson King
cos: Patricia Bolomet, Bennett Choate
sound: David Dockendorff, John Mack, Bob Deschaine
make-up effects: William Munne
stunt co-ordinator: Ted Duncan
Louis Jourdan, Adrienne Barbeau, Ray Wise, David Hess, Nicholas Worth, Dick Durock (as Swamp Thing)

The Swan Princess

USA 1994 89m Technicolor

A princess is turned into a swan by an evil sorcerer, and her suitor sets out to remedy the situation.

Fairish animated feature, not quite up to Disney's more recent standards, despite being directed by Rich, who co-directed *The Fox and the Hound* and *The Black Cauldron* for Disney. It was followed by *The Swann Princess and the Secret Castle* in 1997, also directed and co-produced by Richard Rich, from a story by himself and Brian Nissen.

p: Richard Rich, Jared F. Brown for Columbia Tri-Star/Rich Animal/International Net
exec p: Jared F. Brown, Sheldon Young
w: Brian Nissen
story: Brian Nissen, Richard Rich
d: Richard Rich
m: Lex de Azevedo
songs: David Zippel, Lex de Azevedo
ed: James Koford, Armetta Jackson-Hamlett
ad: Mike Hodgson, James Coleman
voices: Jack Palance, Michelle Nicastro, Howard McGillin, Sandy Duncan, Steven Wright, John Cleese, Mark Harelik, Liz Callaway, David Gaines, Dakin Matthews

Switch

USA 1991 103m Technicolor Panavision Dolby
A male chauvenist is murdered by three of his disgruntled lovers and reincarnated in the body of a beautiful woman, in which guise he is supposed to win the love of another woman if he is to avoid going to hell.

Fitfully amusing sex-change comedy, better than most of its director's later output, though in no way comparable to his similarly themed *Victor/Victoria*.

p: Tony Adams for Columbia/Tri Star/Odyssey/Regency/HBO/Beco/LP/Cinema Plus
w/d: Blake Edwards

ph: Dick Bush
m: Henry Mancini
ed: Robert Permagent
pd: Rodger Maus
cos: Ellen Mirojnick
titles: Anthony Goldschmidt
Ellen Barkin, Jimmy Smits, JoBeth Williams, Perry King, Lorraine Bracco, Tony Roberts, Lysette Anthony, Bruce Martin Payne, Victoria Mahoney

The Sword and the Sorcerer 💩

USA 1982 99m DeLuxe Dolby

A young prince regains his kingdom from an evil tyrant.

Bloodthirsty but generally lively sword and sorcery adventure which does fairly well by its low budget and is often imaginatively staged. The script needed more work, though.

p: Brandon Chase for Sorcerer/Group One
w: Tom Karnowski, Albert Pyun, John Stuckmeyer
d: Albert Pyun
ph: Joseph Mangine
m: David Whitaker
ed: Marshall Harvey
ad: George Costello
cos: Christine Bowar
Lee Horsley, Kathleen Beller, Simon MacCorkindale, George Maharis, Richard Lynch, Nina Van Pallandt, Jeff Corey, Robert Tessier, Richard Moll

The Sword in the Stone 💩

USA 1963 80m Technicolor

The adventures of the young King Arthur and the magician Merlin.

Tame cartoon feature, in no way comparable to the studio's classics, but with a few lively sequences along the way for younger audiences.

p: Ken Peterson for Walt Disney
w: Bill Peet
novel: T. H. White
d: Wolfgang Reitherman
songs: Richard M. and Robert B. Sherman
m: George Bruns
ed: Donald Halliday
ad: Ken Anderson
sound: Robert O. Cook
voices: Ricky Sorenson, Karl Swenson, Junius Matthews, Martha Wentworth

Sylos, Jr., Paul

American art director with a handful of undistinguished low budget genre pictures to his credit, among them *Billy the Kid vs. Dracula*, *Jesse James Meets Frankenstein's Daughter* and *The Dunwich Horror*.

Genre credits:
The Lost Continent (1951), *Mutiny in Outer Space* (1964), *The Human Duplicators* (1964), *Women of the Prehistoric Planet* (1965), *Cyborg 2087* (1966), *Destination Inner Space* (1966), *Dimension 5* (1966), *Wild in the Streets* (1968)

Szwarc, Jeannot (1939-)

French director working in America, where he got his big break in 1978 with *Jaws 2*, prior to which he had helmed a number of TV movies. His other credits include *Bug*, *Enigma* and *Honour Bound*.

Genre credits:
Somewhere in Time (1980), *Supergirl* (1984), *Santa Claus: The Movie* (1985)

Takei, George (1939-)

American supporting actor, best remembered for playing Mr. Sulu in the television and film series of *Star Trek*. His other credits include *The Green Berets*, *Return from the River Kwai* and *Prisoners of the Sun*.

Genre credits:

Star Trek: The Motion Picture (1979), *Star Trek II: The Wrath of Khan* (1982), *Star Trek III: The Search for Spock* (1983), *Star Trek IV: The Voyage Home* (1986), *Star Trek V: The Final Frontier* (1989), *Star Trek VI: The Undiscovered Country* (1991), *Oblivion* (1994), *Oblivion 2: Backlash* (1995)

Tales of Beatrix Potter

GB 1971 90m Technicolor

A selection of Beatrix Potter's animal tales, as danced by members of the Royal Ballet company.

Careful but inevitably repetitious transposition of the tales into dance terms. There are charming sequences, but one wonders exactly at whom the film was aimed.

p: JOHN BRABOURNE, RICHARD GOODWIN for EMI
w: Richard Goodwin, Christine Edzard
stories: Beatrix Potter
d: Reginald Mills
ph: AUSTIN DEMPSTER
m: JOHN LANCHBERRY
ed: John Rushton
pd/cos: CHRISTINE EDZARD
sp: Tom Howard
sound: Len Abbott
ch: FREDERICK ASHTON
masks: ROTISLAV DOBOUJINSKY
principal dancers: Frederick Ashton, Wayne Sleep, Carole Ainsworth, Sally Ashby, Richard Coleman, Graham Fletcher, Wilfred Babbage

Tales of Hoffmann

GB 1951 127m Technicolor

Hoffmann the poet searches for the ideal woman.

Over-ambitious attempt to create a film told entirely with music and dance, with recollections of the same team's *The Red Shoes*. Despite the talent involved, it eventually suffocates on its own opulence.

p: Michael Powell, Emerich Pressburger for BL/London Films/The Archers/Lopert
w/d: Michael Powell, Emerich Pressburger
ph: Christopher Challis
m: JACQUES OFFENBACH
libretto: Jules Barbier, Dennis Arundell
md: Sir Thomas Beecham
ed: Reginald Mills
pd: HEIN HECKROTH
cos: Ivy Baker, Josephine Boss
sp: E. Hague
sound: Ted Drake, John Cox
ch: Frederick Ashton
ass d: Sydney Streeter
cam op: Freddie Francis
Robert Rounsseville, Moira Shearer, Robert Helpmann, Pamela Brown, Frederick Ashton, Ludmilla Techerina, Ann Ayars, Mogens Wieth, Leonide Massine

Tank Girl

USA 1994 104m DeLuxe Dolby

In the 2033, when water is at a premium, Tank Girl and her friends attempt to prevent a megalomaniac from monopolising the world's water supply.

Disappointing, not to mention irritating, attempt to transfer yet another comic strip character to the big screen. Inanity unfortunately quickly sets in and some of the handling is quite shoddy. Mercifully, any planned sequels failed to materialise following the film's deservedly disappointing run at the box office.

p: Richard B. Lewis, John Watson, Pen Densham for UA/Trilogy
exec p: Aron Warner, Tom Astor
w: Tedi Sarafian
comic strip: Alan Martin, Jamie Hewlett
d: Rachel Talalay
ph: Gale Tattersall
m: Graeme Revell
ed: James R. Symons
pd: Catherine Hardwicke
cos: Arianne Phillips
make-up effects: Stan Winston
Lori Petty, Malcolm McDowell, Ice T, Don Harvey, Naomi Watts, Reg E. Cathey, Scott Coffey, Jeff Kober

Tarantula

USA 1955 80m bw

Scientists experimenting on a new serum infect a tarantula which subsequently escapes into the desert where it grows to an enormous size.

Standard low budget sci-fi-horror for the 50s drive-in market, let down by risible effects work. For connoisseurs of the genre.

p: William Alland for Universal
w: Robert M. Fresco, Martin Berkeley
d: Jack Arnold
ph: George Robinson
md: Joseph Gershenson
ed: William A. Morgan
ad: Alexander Golitzen, Alfred Sweeney
sp: Clifford Stine
make-up: Bud Westmore

Leo G. Carroll, John Agar, Mara Corday, Nestor Piava, Ross Eliott, Clint Eastwood (glimpsed briefly as a bomber pilot)

Taurog, Norman (1899-1981)

American director, an Oscar winner for *Skippy* (1930). Began his career as a child actor on stage, breaking into films at 14. He began directing comedy shorts in 1919, turning to features in 1928 with *The Farmer's Daughter*. His other credits include *The Big Broadcast of 1936*, *The Adventures of Tom Sawyer*, *Girl Crazy*, *Onionhead* and several Elvis Presley musicals (*G.I. Blues*, *Blue Hawaii*, *Tickle Me*, *Double Trouble*, *Speedway*, etc.).

Genre credits:

Visit to a Small Planet (1959), *Dr. Goldfoot and the Bikini Machine* (1965 – aka *Dr. G and the Bikini Machine*), *Sergeant Deadhead* (1965 – aka *Sergeant Deadhead the Astronaut*)

Taylor, Gilbert (1914-)

Distinguished British cinematographer whose list of credits includes such important films as *The Guinea Pig*, *Ice Cold in Alex*, *A Hard Day's Night*, *The Bedford Incident* and *Frenzy*. Began as a camera assistant in 1929 at Gainsborough, becoming an operator after the war on such films as *Fame is the Spur* and *Brighton Rock*. He became a cinematographer in his own right in 1948 with *The Guinea Pig*. His other credits include *Repulsion*, *The Omen* and *Dracula*.

Genre credits:

Dr. Strangelove (1963), *Star Wars* (1977), *Flash Gordon* (1980), *Voyage of the Rock Aliens* (1985)

Teenage Mutant Ninja Turtles 💩

USA/GB/Hong Kong 1990 93m Technicolor

Four mutated turtles with special martial arts fighting skills combat an evil gang leader called The Shredder, who is corrupting the children of New York.

Variably amusing mixture of action, special effects and comedy, adapted from a popular cartoon strip. A surprise runaway success, its merchandising possibilities seemed endless. It was followed by two sequels: *Teenage Mutant Ninja Turtles II: The Secret of the Ooze* (1991) and *Teenage Mutant Ninja Turtles III: The Turtles Are Back... In Time* (1992).

p: Kim Dawson, Simon Fields, David Chan, Graham Cottle for Golden Harvest/Limelight
exec p: Raymond Chow, Gary Propper
w: Todd W. Langen, Robby Herbeck
story: Robby Herbeck
cartoon strip: Kevin Eastman, Peter Laird
d: Steve Barron
ph: John Fenner
m: John DuPrez
ed: William Gordean, Sally Menke, James Symons
pd: Roy Forge Smith
sp: Jim Henson's Creature Shop
sound: Lee Orloff, Steve Maslow, Michael Herbick, Gregg Landaker
Judith Hoag, Elias Koteas, Josh Paris, Michelan Sisti, Leif Tilden, David Forman, Michael Turney, Jay Patterson, Raymond Serra, James Sato, Corey Feldman (voice), Robbie Rist (voice), Kevin Clash (voice), David McCharen (voice), Brian Tochi (voice)

Teenage Mutant Ninja Turtles II: The Secret of the Ooze

USA/Hong Kong 1991 87m Technicolor
The turtles discover the nature of the ooze which mutated them.

Lame, money-grubbing sequel, an embarrassment to sit through.

p: Thomas K. Gray, Kim Dawson, David Chan, Terry Morse for Golden Harvest
exec p: Raymond Chow, Gary Propper
w: Todd W. Langen
d: Michael Pressman
ph: Shelley Johnson
m: John DuPrez
ed: John Wright, Steve Mirkovich
pd: Roy Forge Smith
sp: Jim Henson's Creature Shop
sound: Michael Kilkene
2nd unit d: Terry Leonard
2nd unit ph: Jon Kranhouse
Paige Turco, David Warner, Michelan Sisti, Leif Tilden, Kenn Troum, Marl Caso, Kevin Clash, Vanilla Ice, Francois Chau, Laurie Faso (voice), Robbie Rist (voice), Brian Tochi (voice), Adam Carl (voice), David McCharn (voice)

Teenage Mutant Ninja Turtles III: The Turtles Are Back... In Time

USA/Hong Kong 1992 96m Technicolor
As the titles suggests, the turtles travel back in time to 17th-century Japan in this third installment, where they become entangled in a feudal battle between two dynasties.

So-so conclusion to the series, not quite as bad as episode two (which would be pretty much impossible).

p: David Chan, Thomas K. Gray, Kim Dawson for Golden Harvest/Clearwater
exec p: Raymond Chow
w/d: Stuart Gillard
ph: David Gurfinkel
m: John DuPrez
ed: William Gordean, James Symons
pd: Roy Forge Smith
cos: Christine Heinz
sp: Jim Henson's Creature Shop
sound: Larry Kemp, Lon E. Bender
Elias Koteas, Paige Turco, Stuart Wilson, Sab

Shimono, Vivian Wu, David Fraser, Mark Caso, Matt Hill, Jim Raposa, Corey Feldman voice), Brian Tochi (voice), Robbie Rist (voice), James Murray (voice), Tim Kelleher (voice)

The Terminal Man

USA 1974 107m Technicolor Panavision
After a series of blackouts during which he becomes excessively violent, a computer genius is given an implant to suppress his urges. Unfortunately, it increases them.

Technically competent but otherwise slow and rather boring fantasy thriller.

p: Mike Hodges for Warner
w/d: Mike Hodges
novel: Michael Crichton
ph: Richard H. Kline
m: Bach
ed: Robert L. Woolfe
ad: Fred Harpman
George Segal, Joan Hackett, Richard Dysart, Jill Clayburgh, Donald Moffat, Michael C. Gwynne, James B. Sikking

The Terminator

USA 1984 108m CFIcolor
A cyborg from the future travels in time to the present to terminate the mother of a revolutionary yet to be born.

Pacy, cleverly plotted thriller with plenty of action and narrative drive. It quickly became a cult item and was followed by an even more successful sequel, *Terminator 2: Judgement Day* (1991).

p: Gale Anne Hurd for Orion/Pacific Western/Cinema '84
exec p: John Daly, Derek Gibson
w: James Cameron, Gale Anne Hurd
d: JAMES CAMERON
ph: Adam Greenberg
m: Bred Fiedel

ed: Mark Goldblatt
ad: George Costello
cos: Hilary Wright
sp: Roger George, Frank de Marco, Gene Warren, Jr., Peter Kleinow
sound: Richard Lightstone, Terry Porter, David J. Hudson, Mel Metcalfe
sound ed: David Campling
sound effects: Robert Garrett
make-up effects: Stan Winston
2nd unit d: Stan Winston, Jean-Paul Oulette
stunt co-ordinator: Ken Fritz
titles: Ernest D. Farino
Arnold Schwarzenegger, Michael Biehn, Linda Hamilton, Paul Winfield, Lance Henriksen

Terminator 2: Judgement Day

USA 1991 136m Technicolor Panavision Dolby
A second terminator is sent back in time to assassinate the young John Connor.

Expensive ($88m) sequel with lively action sequences and innovative effects work on which count it broke box office records.

p: James Cameron for Carolco
exec p: Gale Anne Hurd, Mario Kassar
w: James Cameron, William Wisher
d: James Cameron
ph: Adam Greenberg
m: Brad Fiedel
ed: Conrad Buff, Mark Goldblatt, Richard A. Harris
pd: Joseph Nemec III
cos: Marlene Stewart
sp: DENNIS MUREN, STAN WINSTON, ROBERT SKOTAK, GENE WARREN, JR. (AA)
make-up effects: Stan Winston, Jeff Dawn (aa)
sound: Tom Johnson, Gary Rydstrom, Gary Summers, Lee Orloff (aa)
sound effects ed: Gary Rydstrom, Gloria S. Borders (aa)

2nd unit d: Gary Davis
2nd unit ph: Michael A. Benson
titles: Paul Olsen
Arnold Schwarzenegger, Linda Hamilton, Edward Furlong, Robert Patrick, Earl Boen, Joe Morton, S. Epatha, Castulo Guerra, Danny Cooksey

Terror from the Year 5000

USA 1958 74m bw
Scientists working on a time machine inadvertently transport a monster back from the future.

This is Grade Z rubbish. A real schlock fest.

p: Robert J. Guerney, Jr. for AIP
exec p: James H. Nicholson, Samuel Z. Arkoff
w/d: Robert J. Guerney
ph: Arthur Florman
m: no credit given
ed: Dede Allen
ad: Bill Hoffman
sound: Bob Hathaway
Ward Costello, Joyce Holden, John Stratton, Frederic Downs, Fred Herrick

Terror of Mechagodzilla

Japan 1975 88m colour
Godzilla finds himself pitted aginst a giant mechanical version of himself.

Lunatic monster epic in the established Japanese manner.

p: Tomoyuki Tanaka for Toho/Miracle ("If it's a good one, it's a Miracle!")
w: Yukiko Takayama
d: Inoshiro Honda
ph: Mototaka Tomanu
m: Akira Ifukuke
ed: Yoshitami Kuroiwa
sp: Teruyoshi Nakano
sound: Fumio Yanoguchi
Katsuhiko Sasaki, Tomoko Ai, Akihito Hirata,

Katsumasa Uchida, Goro Mutsu, Kenji Sahara

The Terrornauts
GB 1967 75m Eastmancolor

An entire building and the scientists inside it are transported to another planet.

Poor *Dr Who*-style romp on a miniscule budget. Strictly for the kids.

p: Max J. Rosenberg, Milton Subotsky for Amicus
w: John Brunner
novel: Murray Leinster
d: Montgomery Tully
ph: Geoffrey Faithful
m: Elizabeth Lutyens
ed: Peter Musgrave
ad: Bill Constable
sp: Les Bowie, Ernest Fletcher
Simon Oates, Zena Marshall, Charles Hawtrey, Patricia Hayes, Stanley Mendoza, Max Adrian

Thatcher, Torin (1905-1981)

British actor, rembered for playing such villains as Sokurah in *The Seventh Voyage of Sinbad* (1958) and Pendragon in *Jack the Giant Killer* (1962). His other credits include *Great Expectations*, *The Crimson Pirate*, *The Robe*, *Witness for the Prosecution* and *Hawaii*.

They Live

USA 1988 94m DeLuxe Panavision Dolby

In the near future, a wanderer discovers that the world has been infested by aliens who have disguised themselves as humans, and can only be seen for what they really are through special sunglasses.

Promising thriller which works in fits and starts. Good sequences along

The effects may not be too wonderful by today's standards, but the 1954 semi-classic *Them!* still manages a thrill or two. Surely another film ripe for remaking?

the way, though on the whole it doesn't quite come off and certainly isn't among its director's best productions. Perhaps best remembered for a fist fight which seems to go on forever.

p: Larry Franco for Alive
exec p: Shep Gordon, Andre Blay
w: Frank Armitage
story: Ray Nelson
d: John Carpenter
ph: Gary B. Kibbe
m: John Carpenter, Alan Howarth
ed: Gib Jaffe, Frank E. Jimenez
ad: William J. Durrell, Jr., Daniel Lomino
cos: Robin Bush
sp: Roy Arbogast
sound: John Judkins
stunt co-ordinator: Jeff Imada
Roddy Piper, Keith David, Meg Foster, George "Buck" Flower, Peter Jason,

Raymond St. Jacques, Jason Robards III, John Lawrence, Larry Franco

Them! 😶😶

USA 1954 94m bw

Giant ants roam the New Mexico desert as a result of atomic radiation.

Despite unconvincing effects work, this remains one of the better examples of the 50s science fiction genre, tautly scripted and directed throughout, with a tense climax in the storm drains of Los Angeles.

p: David Weisbart for Warner
w: TED SHERMAN, Russell Hughes
story: George Worthington Yates
d: GORDON DOUGLAS
ph: SID HICKOX
m: Bronislau Kaper

md: Ray Heindorf
ed: Thomas Reilly
ad: Stanley Fleischer
cos: Moss Mabry
sp: Ralph Ayers
sound: Francis J. Scheid
EDMUND GWENN, James Whitmore, Joan Weldon, James Arness, Onslow Stevens, Fess Parker

---

Theodore Rex

USA 1996 91m 1995 DeLuxe Dolby

In the future, a lady cop joins forces with a talking dinosaur (!) called Theodore Rex to investigate a murder, which leads them to discover a mad billionaire's plan to launch a missile to start a new ice age.

About as bad as a mainstream genre picture ought to be, this garishly coloured fantasy comedy has to be seen to be believed. Astonishingly, high things were expected of it, though this didn't prevent it from going straight to video in the end, presumably after a lesson had been learned by its makers. Even five-year-olds will feel superior to it.

p: Richard M. Abramson, Sue Baden-Powell for J&M/New Line/Shooting Star Entertainment
exec p: Stefano Ferrari, Jonathan Betuel
w/d: Jonathan Betuel
ph: David Tattersall
m: Robert Folk
ed: Rick Shaine, Steve Mirkovich
pd: Walter Martishius
cos: Mary Vogt
sp: Robert Harbros
dinosaur effects: Criswell Productions, Chris Finch
sound: James E. Webb
stunt co-ordinator/2nd unit d: Ernie Orsatti
2nd unit ph: Michael A. Benson, Peter Demming
puppeteers: Bruce Lanoil, Terri Harden,

Michelan Sisti, Kevin Carlson, James Murray Whoopi Goldberg, Armin Mueller-Stahl, Bud Cort, Juliet Landau, Stephen McHattie, Richard Roundtree, Joe Dallesandro, Jack Rile, George Newbern (voice – as Teddy Rex), Carol Kane (voice)

There Goes the Bride

GB 1980 91m Eastmancolor

On the day of his daughter's wedding, an over-worked ad man dreams up a campaign involving a cardboard cut-out of a 20s flapper – which subsequently comes to life.

1980 was perhaps a little late for a fantasy comedy of this type, especially one so inept. An embarrassment all concerned will no doubt wish to forget.

p: Martin Schute, Ray Cooney for Lonsdale
w: Terence Marcel, Ray Cooney
play: John Chapman, Ray Cooney
d: Terence Marcel
ph: James Devis
m: Harry Robinson
ed: Alan Jones
pd: Peter Mullins
ad: John Siddall
Twiggy, Tom Smothers, Sylvia Syms, Martin Balsam, Phil Silvers, Graham Stark, Broderick Crawford, Jim Backus, Michael Whitney, Geoffrey Sumner, Hermione Baddeley, John Terry

---

They Came from Beyond Space

GB 1967 85m Eastmancolor

Strange meteors from outer space take over the minds of a group of scientists.

Grade Z stuff with an invisible budget, made on the coat-tails of the same producers' *The Terrornauts*, which wasn't that much better.

p: Milton Subotsky, Max J. Rosenberg for Amicus
w: Milton Subotsky

novel: Joseph Millard
d: Freddie Francis
ph: Norman Warwick
m: James Stevens
ed: Peter Musgrave
ad: Don Mingaye, Scott Slimon
Robert Hutton, Jennifer Jaye, Zia Mohyeddin, Bernard Kaye, Michael Gough, Kenneth Kendall

---

The Thief of Bagdad

USA 1924 135m bw silent

In Bagdad, a cunning thief outwits an evil caliph and woos a beautiful princess.

Expensive silent version of the famous story, with top notch production values, eye-catching art direction and interesting trick effects.

p: Douglas Fairbanks
w: Lotta Woods, Douglas Fairbanks
d: RAOUL WALSH
ph: ARTHUR EDESON
ad: WILLIAM CAMERON MENZIES
Douglas Fairbanks, Snitz Edwards, Anna May Wong, Charles Belcher, Julanne Johnston, Etta Lee, Brandon Hurst, Sojin

---

The Thief of Baghdad

GB/USA 1940 109m Technicolor

A deposed king thwarts an evil vizier and rescues a beautiful princess with the help of a young thief.

Marvellous, splendidly colourful box of magic and adventure, brilliantly assembled by a crew of master technicians (despite many production problems). Sets, photography, music, direction and performances all seamlessly combine to provide an exhilarating piece of movie entertainment.

p: ALEXANDER KORDA for London Films
w: MILES MALLESON, LAJOS BIRO

Captain Patrick Hendry (Kenneth Tobey – centre) and his buddies prepare for an encounter with *The Thing*.

d: MICHAEL POWELL, LUDWIG BERGER, TIM WHELAN, Zoltan Korda, Alexander Korda, William Cameron Menzies, Geoffrey Boothby, Charles David
ph: GEORGES PERINAL (AA), OSMOND BORRADAILE
m: MIKLOS ROZSA
ed: WILLIAM HORNBECK, CHARLES CRICHTON
ad: VINCENT KORDA (AA)
cos: OLIVER MESSEL, JOHN ARMSTRONG, MARCEL VERTES
sp: LAWRENCE BUTLER, JOCK WHITNEY (AA), PERCY DAY
sound: A.W. Watkins
associate p: Zoltan Korda, William Cameron Menzies
CONRAD VEIDT, SABU, JOHN JUSTIN, JUNE DUPREZ, REX INGRAM, MILES MALLESON, Mary Morris, MORTON SEL-TEN, Bruce Winston, Hay Petrie, Roy Emerton, Allan Jeayes

The Thief of Baghdad

USA/GB/Fr 1978 96m colour TVM
Inept and unnecessary TV remake which received a theatrical release in Britain. It has none of the style or sparkle of the previous versions.

p: Aida Young for Columbia/Palm
exec p: Thomas M. C. Johnston
w: A. J. Carothers, Andrew Birkin
d: Clive Donner
ph: Denis Lewiston
m: John Cameron
ed: Peter Tanner
ad: Edward Marshall
cos: John Bloomfield
sp: Allan Bryce, Zoran Perisic, John Stears, Dick Hewitt
sound: Michael Sate, Doug Turner
stunt co-ordinator: Peter Diamond
Roddy McDowall, Peter Ustinov, Terence

Stamp, Kabir Bedi, Frank Finlay, Marina Vlady, Ian Holm, Daniel Emilfork, Pavla Ustinov

---

Thin Air see The Body Stealers

The Thing

USA 1951 87m bw
Members of a scientific expedition in the Antarctic find themselves menaced by a monster from another world.

Semi-classic thriller, a little slow to start, but building up to sequences of genuine tension and alarm. A sequel followed in 1982.

p: Howard Hawks for RKO/Winchester
w: Charles Lederer
story: J. W. Campbell, Jr

Raymond Massey takes in a view of the future in the 1936 H.G. Wells-scripted *Things to Come*, many of whose prophecies have since come true. Cue the *Twilight Zone* theme.

d: Christian Nyby
ph: Russell Harlan
m: Dimitri Tiomkin
ed: Roland Gross
ad: Albert S. D'Agostino, John J. Hughes
cos: Michael Woulfe
sp: Donald Steward, Linwood Dunn
sound: Phil Brigand, Clem Portman
Kenneth Tobey, Robert Cornthwaite,
Margaret Sheridan, Bill Self, Dewey Martin,
James Arness (as The Thing)

The Thing

USA 1982 109m Technicolor Panavision
Dolby

A monstrous creature from another world, able to take the form of its victims, is unwittingly let into an isolated Arctic research station, where it consequently runs amok.

Technically adroit, genuinely frightening remake of the 1951 movie, with superior make-up effects. Not for the squeamish, it is now rightly ranked among its director's best work, though at the time of release it was a critically derided box office flop.

p: David Foster, Lawrence Turman, Stuart
Cohen for Universal
exec p: Wilbur Stark
w: Bill Lancaster
story: J. W. Campbell, Jr
d: JOHN CARPENTER
ph: DEAN CUNDEY
m: Ennio Morricone
ed: Tony Ramsey
pd: John L. Lloyd
cos: Ronald I. Caplan, Gilbert Loe
sp: Albert Whitlock, Roy Arbogast
sound: Thomas Causey
make-up effects: ROB BOTTIN
stunt co-ordinator: Dick Warlock
Kurt Russell, J. Wilford Brimley, T. K. Carter,
David Clenon, Richard Dysart, Richard
Masur

The Thing from Another World

see The Thing (1951)

Things to Come

GB 1936 113m bw

Everytown first finds itself facing war in 1940, followed by plague and revolution. The future, however, brings the re-birth of civilisation.

Though inevitably dated in some respects, this nevertheless remains a brilliant montage of effects, action, personal drama, fantasy and prohecy, put together with great style by master technicians.

p: Alexander Korda for London Films
w: H.G. WELLS from his novel
d/pd: WILLIAM CAMERON MENZIES
ph: GEORGES PERINAL
m: ARTHUR BLISS
md: Muir Mathieson
ed: WILLIAM HORNBECK
ad: VINCENT KORDA
cos: John Armstrong, Rene Hubert, The
Marchioness of Queensberry (!)
sp: NED MANN, LAWRENCE BUTLER,
EDWARD COHEN
sound: A.W. Watkins
cam op: Robert Krasker
RAYMOND MASSEY, RALPH RICHARD-SON, Margaretta Scott, Edward Chapman,
Cederic Hardwicke, Sophie Stewart, Derrick
de Matney, John Clements

This Island Earth

USA 1955 86m Technicolor

Research scientists working at a remote institute turn out to be aliens who have come to earth to recruit humans to help them save their planet.

Typical 50sgenre pic, a little slow on the whole, though it does pick up speed as it goes along. Something of a cult favourite, thanks primarily to the delayed appearance of the mutant during the climax. Surprisingly, it was also shot in colour.

p: William Alland for Universal
w: Franklin Coen, Edward G. O'Callaghan
novel: Raymond F. Jones
d: Joseph Newman
ph: Clifford Stein
m: Herman Stein
md: Joseph Gershenson

ed: Virgil Vogel
ad: Alexander Golitzen, Richard H. Reidel
cos: Rosemary Odell
sp: Clifford Stine, David S. Horsley
sound: Leslie I. Carey, Robert Pritchard
Jeff Morrow, Rex Reason, Faith Domergue,
Lance Fuller, Russell Johnson, Robert
Nichols, Karl Lindt, Douglas Spencer, Eddie
Parker (as the mutant)

Thomas, Bill

American costume designer, an Oscar
winner for *Spartacus* in 1960, who did
much work for Disney in the 60s and
70s.

Genre credits:
Moon Pilot (1961), *Babes in Toyland* (1961),
Mary Poppins (1964 – co-cos), *Blackbeard's
Ghost* (1967), *The Love Bug* (1968),
Bedknobs and Broomsticks (1971), *Wonder
Woman* (1974 – TVM), *The Island at the Top
of the World* (1974), *Logan's Run* (1976 -
cos), *Pete's Dragon* (1977), *The Black Hole*
(1979)

Thomas, Henry (1971-)

American actor, remembered for playing the young Elliott in Spielberg's
E.T. (1982). His only other genre credit
is for *Fire in the Sky* (1993). His other
films include *Misunderstood*, *Cloak
and Dagger*, *Valmont*, *Psycho IV: The
Beginning* (TVM – as the young
Norman Bates) and *Curse of the
Starving Class*.

Thomerson, Tim

American actor, best known for playing
Jack Deth in the Trancers series. His
other film credits include *Car Wash*, *A
Wedding*, *Fade to Black*, *Carny*, *Near
Dark*, *Uncommon Valor*, *Rhinestone*
and *Air America*, as well as much tele-
vision work (*Cos*, *The Associates*, *The
Two of Us*, *Sirens*, etc.).

**Exeter (Jeff Morrow) encounters a mutant
in the colourful *This Island Earth*.**

Genre credits:
Metalstorm: The Destruction of Jared Syn
(1983), *Trancers* (1984 – aka *Future Cop*),
Zone Troopers (1984), *Trancers II: The
Return of Jack Deth* (1990), *Dollman* (1991),
Nemesis (1992), *Trancers III: Deth Lives*
(1993), *Dollman vs. Demonic Toys*
(1993), *Trancers IV: Jack of Swords* (1994),
Trancers V: Sudden Deth (1995), *Nemesis
III: Time Lapse* (1995), *When Time Expires*
(1997 – TVM)

Thompson, Brian

Muscular American actor with chis-
elled looks, whose career has mostly
been in the action and horror genres,

his credits taking in *Cobra*,
Commando Squad, *Pass the Ammo*,
Fright Night Part 2, *Hired to Kill* and
Rage and Honour.

Genre credits:
The Terminator (1984), *Nightwish* (1989)
Moon 44 (1989), *Doctor Mordrid* (1990),
Star Trek: Generations (1994), *Dragonheart*
(1996), *Mortal Kombat II: Annihilation*
(1997)

Thompson, Lea (1961-)

American actress with dancing experience, remembered by genre fans for

playing Lorraine McFly (nee Bates) in the *Back to the Future* trilogy. Her other credits include *Jaws 3D*, *Some Kind of Wonderful* and *Dennis the Menace* (aka *Dennis*).

Genre credits:

Back to the Future (1985), *Howard the Duck* (1986 – aka *Howard, A New Breed of Hero*), *Spacecamp* (1986), *Back to the Future Part II* (1989), *Back to the Future Part III* (1990)

Thomson, Alex (1929-)

British cinematographer whose credits include *Dr. Phibes Rises Again*, *Rosie Dixon – Night Nurse*, *The Cat and the Canary*, *Eureka*, *Year of the Dragon*, *Bullshot*, *Track 29*, *The Krays*, *Cliffhanger* and *Hamlet*. Began his career in 1946 as an assistant at Denham, becoming an operator for Nicolas Roeg on such films as *Information Received*, *Nothing But the Best*, *The System*, *Masque of the Red Death*, *A Funny Thing Happened on the Way to the Forum* and *Fahrenheit 451*. He photographed his first film, *Here We Go Round the Mulberry Bush*, in 1967, after which came *The Strange Affair*, *The Best House in London*, *I Start Counting* and *Alfred the Great* (among others), along with second unit work on the likes of *The Man Who Would Be King* and *The Seven Per Cent Solution*.

Genre credits:

Fahrenheit 451 (1996 – cam op), *Superman* (1978 – 2nd unit ph), *Excalibur* (1981), *The Keep* (1983), *Electric Dreams* (1984), *Legend* (1985), *Labyrinth* (1986), *High Spirits* (1988), *Leviathan* (1989), *Mr. Destiny* (1990), *Wings of Fame* (1990), *Alien 3* (1992), *Demolition Man* (1993)

Those Fantastic Flying Fools see Rocket to the Moon

Thumbelina

Eire 1994 87m Technicolor Dolby

A diminutive girl, searching for a similar-sized suitor, is kidnapped by a toad before finding true romance with the prince of the fairies.

Tolerable cartoon feature, well enough animated, but like many of Bluth's more recent productions, the film lacks real charm and the narrative is slack.

p: Don Bluth, Gary Goldman, John Pomeroy for Warner
w: Don Bluth
story: Hans Christian Andersen
d: Don Bluth, Gary Goldman
songs: Barry Manilow, Jack Feldman, Bruce Sussman
m: William Ross, Barry Mainlow
md: William Ross
ed: Thomas V. Moss
pd: Rowland Wilson
sound: Martin Maryska
voices: Jodi Benson, Gino Conforti, Will Ryan, Barbara Cook, June Foray, Kenneth Mars, Gary Imhoff, John Hurt, Carol Channing

Thunder Rock

GB 1942 112m bw

A journalist seeks refuge from the world in a lighthouse on Lake Michigan, where he is haunted by the passengers of a ship who drowned there a century before.

Generally amusing mixture of comedy, drama and politics which gets its various messages across through flashback and fantasy frameworks. Well enough done, though it is beginning to show its age.

p: John Boulting for Charter Films

w: Jeffrey Dell, Bernard Miles
play: ROBERT ARDRAY
d: ROY BOULTING
ph: Mutz Greenbaum
m: Hans May
ed: Roy Boulting, Cliff Boote
ad: Duncan Sutherland
cos: Howard Plesch
sp: Tom Howard, Fred Ford
sound: J. C. Cook
cam op: Jack Hildyard
MICHAEL REDGRAVE, Barbara Mullen, JAMES MASON, Lilli Palmer, FINLAY CURRIE, Frederick Valk, Sybilla Binder, Frederick Cooper, Jean Shepherd, George Carny, Miles Malleson, A. E. Matthews

Thunderbird Six

GB 1968 90m Technicolor Techniscope Supermarionation

With the help of their new vehicle, Thunderbird Six, International Rescue thwart their Nemesis, The Black Phantom.

Second of the big screen adventures derived from the popular television puppet series, though perhaps not quite as lively as the first.

p: Gerry Anderson, Sylvia Anderson for UA/AP/Century 21
w: Gerry Anderson, Sylvia Anderson
d: David Lane
ph: Harry Oakes
m: Barry Gray
ad: Bob Bell
sp: Derek Meddings and others
voices: Sylvia Anderson, Shane Rimmer, Charles Tingwell

Thunderbirds Are Go!

GB 1966 92m Technicolor Techniscope Supermarionation

International Rescue launch into space to rescue a doomed mission to Mars.

Silly but agreeable big screen version

of the popular television series, which even includes a music spot by the puppet versions of Cliff Richard and the Shadows. Ideal for children.

p: Gerry Anderson, Sylvia Anderson for UA/AP/Century 21
w: Gerry Anderson, Sylvia Anderson
d: David Lane
ph: Paddy Seale, Harry Oakes, Ted Fowler
m: Barry Gray
ed: Len Walter, George Randall
ad: Bob Bell, Glenville Knott, Keith Wilson
cos: Elizabeth Coleman, Zena Relph
sp: Derek Meddings and others
models: Ray Brown
sound: Maurice Askew, Ken Scrivener
sound ed: John Peverill, Brian T. Hickin
puppeteers: Christian Glanville, Mary Turner, Judith Shutt, Wanda Webb
voices: Sylvia Anderson, Shane Rimmer, Charles Tingwell, Bob Monkhouse, Ray Barrett, Alexander Davion, Christine Finn, David Graham, Paul Maxwell, Neil McCallum, Cliff Richard, The Shadows

Snooker, anyone? THX:1138 (Robert Duvall) attempts to make a break for it in director George Lucas's debut feature *THX:1138*.

Thunderbirds: Thunderbirds to the Rescue

see Thunderbirds to the Rescue

Thunderbirds to the Rescue

GB 1965 91m colour TVM

Arch villain The Hood attempts to blow up a supersonic plane on its maiden flight, but reckons without the intervention of International Rescue.

Engaging feature-length pilot for the phenomenally successful *Thunderbirds* puppet series, with some action sequences that wouldn't disgrace a live action movie.

p: Gerry Anderson, Sylvia Anderson for Century 21
w: Gerry Anderson, Sylvia Anderson

d: Alan Pattillo
m: Barry Gray
sp: Derek Meddings
voices: Sylvia Anderson, Shane Rimmer, Ray Barrett, David Holliday, Matt Zimmerman, David Graham

THX 1138

USA 1970 95m Technicolor

In a future subterranean society, a man rebels against the system and makes his way to the surface.

Clinical futuristic allegory, falling somewhere between *1984* and *This Perfect Day*. Well made but somehow hard to appreciate, it is now chiefly of interest for the emerging talent involved.

p: Lawrence Sturhahn for Warner/American Zoetrope
exec p: Francis Ford Coppola
w: George Lucas, Walter Murch
d/ed: GEORGE LUCAS
ph: Dave Meyers, Albert Kihn
m: Lalo Schifrin
ad: Michael Haller

cos: Donald Longhurst
sound montages: Walter Murch
titles/animation: Hal Barwood
Robert Duvall (as THX 1138), Donald Pleasance, Don Pedro Colley, Maggie McOmie, Ian Wolfe, Johnny Weissmuller, Jr.

Tim Burton's The Nightmare Before Christmas

see The Nightmare Before Christmas

Time After Time

USA 1979 112m Metroclor Panavision

Jack the Ripper escapes into the future in H.G. Wells' time machine. When the machine returns, Wells gives chase...

Charming fantasy adventure, quite inventively handled.

p: Herb Jaffe for Warner/Orion
w/d: NICHOLAS MEYER
story: Karl Alexander, Steve Hayes
ph: Paul Lohmann
m: MIKLOS ROZSA
ed: Don Cambern

pd: Edward Carfagno
cos: Sal Antonio, Yvonne Rubis
sp: Richard F. Taylor
sound: Jerry Jost
stunt co-ordinator: Everett Creach
MALCOLM MCDOWELL, David Warner (as Jack the Ripper), Mary Steenburgen, Charles Cioffi, Kent Williams, Andonia Katsaros, Corey Feldman

Time Bandits

GB 1981 113m Technicolor Dolby

A schoolboy finds himself travelling through time with a group of dwarves who have plans to steal the treasures of every age.

Imaginative fantasy adventure with ingenious touches and just a few lapses in pace and taste.

p: Terry Gilliam for Handmade
w: MICHAEL PALION, TERRY GILLIAM
d: TERRY GILLIAM
ph: Peter Biziou
m: Mike Moran, George Harrison
ed: Julian Doyle
pd: MILLY BURNS
cos: Jan Acheson, Hazel Cote
sound: Paul Carr, Brian Paxton
DAVID RAPPAPORT, John Cleese, Sean Connery, Craig Warnock, David Warner, Ralph Richardson (as God), Shelley Duvall, Katherine Helmond, Michael Palin, Kenny Baker, Peter Vaughan

Timecop

USA/Canada 1994 98m DeLuxe

A cop whose job it is to patrol time to prevent people from altering the course of history tries to avert a corrupt politician's plans to become president.

Slick, fitfully amusing but rather foolishly plotted adventure which creates more paradoxes than it prevents.

p: Moshe Diamant, Sam Raimi, Robert Tapert for Largo/JVC/Signature/

Renaissance/Dark Horse
exec p: Mike Richardson
w: Mark Verheiden
story: Mark Verheiden, Mike Richardson
comic: Mark Verheiden, Mike Richardson
d/ph: Peter Hyams
m: Mark Isham
ed: Steven Kemper
pd: Philip Harrison
cos: Dan Lester
sp: VIFX, John Thomas and others
sound: Eric Batut
stunt co-ordinator: Glenn Randall
titles: Nina Saxon
Jean-Claude Van Damme, Mia Sara, Ron Silver, Gloria Reuben, Scott Bellis, Bruce McGill

The Time Machine

USA 1960 103m Metrocolor

A Victorian scientist transports himself into the distant future only to discover that the world is ruled by cannibalistic mutants known as the Morlocks.

Engaging fantasy adventure which has dated somewhat. Nevertheless, perhaps the best example of its producer-director's output.

p: George Pal for MGM/Galaxy
w: David Duncan
novel: H. G. Wells
d: George Pal
ph: Paul C. Vogel
m: Russell Garcia
ed: George Tomasini
ad: GEORGE W. DAVIS, WILLIAM FERRARI
sp: Gene Warren, Tim Baer (aa), Wah Chang
sound: Franklin Milton
make-up: William Tuttle
ROD TAYLOR, Yvette Mimieux, Alan Young, Sebastian Cabot, Whit Bissell, Tom Helmore, Doris Lloyd

Jean-Claude Van Damme prepares to do some damage in *Timecop*.

Time Walker

USA 1982 75m DeLuxe

A re-animated mummy proves to be an alien who visited earth 3,000 years ago.

Occasionally atmospheric low budgeter which does quite well by its story.

p: Jason Williams for Byzantine/Wescom
exec p: Dimitri Villard
w: Tom Friedman, Karen Levitt
d: Tom Kennedy
ph: Robbie Greenberg
m: Richard H. Band
md: David Franco
ed: Maria Digiovani, Lucile Jones
ad: Robert A. Burns, Joe Garrity
Ben Murphy, Nina Axelrod, Shari Belafonte-Harper, Kevin Brophy, Royce Alexander, Michelle Avonne, Annie Barbieri, Sam Chew, Jr.

Tippet, Phil

American stop-frame animator, special effects technician and make-up effects artist, an Oscar winner for his work on *Return of the Jedi* (1983 – with Richard Edlund, Dennis Muren and Ken Ralston) and *Jurassic Park* (1993 – with Stan Winston, Dennis Muren and Michael Lantieri). He first came to note for co-animating (with Jon Berg) the chess pieces on board Han Solo's *Millennium Falcon* in *Star Wars*.

Genre credits:

Star Wars (1977 – co-anim), *The Empire Strikes Back* (1980 – co-anim), *Dragonslayer* (1981 – co-sp), *Return of the Jedi* (1983 – co-sp), *Robocop* (1987 – co-sp), *Willow* (1988 – co-sp), *Honey, I Shrunk the Kids* (1989 co-sp), *Robocop 2* (1990 – sp), *Jurassic Park* (1993 – co-sp), *Tremors II: Aftershocks* (1995 – TVM – co-sp), *Dragonheart* (1996 – co-sp)

Tobey, Kenneth (1919-)

American general purpose actor, popular as either a lead or support in 50s science fiction and monster films. Familair to TV audiences in *The Whirlybirds*, he now pops up mostly in cameo roles. His other credits include *Dangerous Venture*, *Davy Crockett – King of the Wild Frontier*, *The Vampire*, *The Great Locomotive Chase*, *Ben*, *Walking Tall* and *Airplane!*

Genre credits:

The Thing (1952), *The Beast from 20 000 Fathoms* (1953), *It Came from Beneath the Sea* (1956), *The Search for Bridey Murphy* (1956), *The Creature Wasn't Nice* (1981 – aka *Spaceship*), *Strange Invaders* (1983), *Gremlins* (1984), *Gremlins 2: The New Batch* (1990)

To Catch a Yeti

Canada 1993 95m colour

A yeti, captured by hunters in the Himalayas, is taken to New York, where it befriends a small girl who determines on returning it to its homeland.

Jaw-droppingly inept "comedy" adventure with one of the most uncon-

vincing monsters in screen history. What Meat Loaf thought he would gain by appearing in this drek is anyone's guess. An embarrassment from beginning to end.

p: Lionel Shenken, Beverely Shenken-Brin for Visual/Dandelion/New World
exec p: Noel Cronin
w: Paul Adam
d: Bob Keen
ph: David Perrault
m: Jack Lanz, Brent Barkman, Carl Lenox
ed: Stewart Dowds, Paul Kirsch
ad: Gerine de Jong
make-up effects: Image Animation, Paul Jones, Martin Mercer
sound: Peter Clements
stunt co-ordinator: Rik Panthera
Meat Loaf, Chantallese Kent, Richard Howlanti, Jim Gordon, Leigh Lewis, Jeff Moser, Mike Panton, Mona Matteo, Kevin Robbin (voice)

Tom and Jerry: The Movie

USA 1993 87m Technicolor Dolby

Tom and Jerry help a little orphan girl usurp her scheming aunt.

Dismal, poorly animated feature-length cartoon based on the classic MGM shorts. Here, Tom and Jerry not only talk (!), but sing (!!) and are friends (!!!). Awful.

p: Phil Roman for Turner/WMG/Film Roman
w: Dennis Marks
d: Phil Roman
songs: Henry Mancini (m), Leslie Bricusse (ly)
m: HENRY MANCINI
sound: Gordon Hunt
titles: Neal Thompson
voices: Richard Kind, Dana Hill, Andi McAfee, Charlotte Rae, Henry Gibson, Rip Taylor, Ed Gilbert, Tony Jay

---

Tomasini, George (1909-1964)

Notable American editor who worked on many of Hitchcock's films, among them *The Wrong Man*, *Vertigo*, *North by Northwest*, *Psycho* and *The Birds*. His other credits include *Wild Harvest*, *Elephant Walk* and *Cape Fear*.

Genre credits:

I Married a Monster from Outer Space (1958), *The Time Machine* (1960), *The Seven Faces of Dr. Lao* (1964)

Tomlinson, David (1917-)

British comedy character actor, remembered for playing Mr. Banks in *Mary Poppins*. On stage from 1935, he entered films in 1940 with *Quiet Wedding*. His other credits include *Sleeping Car to Trieste*, *The Chiltern Hundreds*, *Up the Creek*, *Tom Jones*, *The Liquidator* and *The Fiendish Plot of Dr. Fu Manchu*.

Genre credits:

Miranda (1948), *Mary Poppins* (1964), *City Under the Sea* (1965 – aka *War-Gods of the Deep*), *The Love Bug* (1968), *Bedknobs and Broomsticks* (1971), *Wombling Free* (1977), *The Water Babies* (1978)

Tom Thumb

GB 1958 98m Eastmancolor

A poor woodcutter and his wife are granted three wishes and so ask for a son – but he turns out to be only three inches tall.

Lively fantasy adventure for children, with plenty of music and special effects.

p: George Pal for MGM/Galaxy
w: Ladislas Fodor
d: George Pal

ph: Georges Perinal
songs: Peggy Lee, Fred Spielman, Janice Torre, Kermit Goell
md: Ken Jones, Douglas Gamley
ed: Frank Clark
ad: Elliot Scott
cos: Olga Lehmann
sp: TOM HOWARD (aa)
sound: A.W. Watkins, John Bramall
cam op: Denys Coop
RUSS TAMBLYN, Jessie Matthews, Bernard Miles, Peter Sellers, Terry-Thomas, Alan Young, June Thorburn, Ian Wallace, Peter Butterworth, Peter Bull, Stan Freberg, Barbara Ferris, Dal McKennon (voice)

The Tommyknockers

USA/New Zealand 1993 2x96m colour TVM Dolby

The residents of a small Maine township are taken over by a mysterious force which emanates from a long-buried spaceship.

Watchable nonsense, somewhat typical of its author's output.

p: Jaybe Bieber, Jane Scott for Kongsberg/Sanitsky
w: Lawrence D. Cohen
novel: Stephen King
d: John Power
ph: Danny Burstall, David Eggby
m: Christopher Franke
ed: Tod Feuerman
pd: Bernard Hides
cos: Taryn De Chellis
sp: Kevin Chisnall
sound: Fred Schultz
Jimmy Smits, Mark Helgenberger, John Ashton, Alyce Beasley, Traci Lords, Cliff De Young, Annie Corley, Robert Carradine, Joanna Cassidy

The Tomorrow Man

USA 1995 85m DeLuxe TVM

An android with the ability to morph travels from the future, where man no longer exists, in order to prevent the events which led to this catastrophe, and teams up with a discredited scientist in order to do so.

Mildly amusing pilot for a series that never happened. It certainly could have been worse.

p: Cyrus Yavneh for TCF/3 Arts
exec p: Alan Spencer, Howard Klein
w: Alan Spencer
d: Bill D'Elia
ph: Frank Byers
m: Lance Rubin
ed: Jimmy B. Frazier
pd: Michelle Minch
cos: Bobbie Mannix
sp: Chris Woods, Paul Lombardi
make-up effects: David Miller
sound: Robert Wald
2nd unit d/stunt co-ordinator: Eddy Donno
2nd unit ph: Billy Brao
Julian Sands, Obba Babbatunde, Ray Baker, Tom Knowles, Craig Wasson, Giancarlo Esposito, Sydney Walsh, James Saito

Topper

USA 1937 96m bw

A New York banker finds himself haunted by his two friends, the Kirbys, who have to perform a good deed before they can go to heaven.

Patchy but well cast and played supernatural farce. Its success spawned two sequels: *Topper Takes a Trip* (1938) and *Topper Returns* (1941). There was also a TV series in the 50s starring Leo G. Carroll.

p: Milton H. Bren for MGM
exec p: Hal Roach
w: Jack Jevne, Eric Hatch, Eddie Moran
novel: Thorne Smith
d: Norman Z. McLeod
ph: Norbert Brodine
md: Marvin Hatley, Arthur Morton
ed: William Terhune
ad: Arthur I. Royce
cos: Samuel M. Lange
sp: Roy Seawright
sound: William Randall
CARY GRANT, CONSTANCE BENNETT, ROLAND YOUNG, BILLIE BURKE, ALAN MOWBRAY, EUGENE PALLETTE, Arthur Lake, Hedda Hopper, Virginia Sale

Topper Returns

USA 1941 87m bw

Topper helps a lady ghost discover who murdered her and why.

Third, last and liveliest of the *Topper* comedies, which resolves itself in a spooky house farce with an heiress in jeopardy.

p: Hal Roach for MGM
w: Jonathan Latimer, Gordon Douglas, Paul Gerard Smith
d: Roy del Ruth
ph: Norbert Brodine
m: Werner Heymann
md: Irvin Talbot
ed: James Newcom
ad: Nicolai Remisoff
cos: Royer
sp: Roy Seawright
sound: William Randall
ROLAND YOUNG, JOAN BLONDELL, EDDIE ROCHESTER ANDERSON, Carole Landis, Dennis O'Keefe, BILLIE BURKE, Donald McBride, Rafaela Ottiano, H.B. Warner

Topper Takes a Trip

USA 1938 86m bw

Topper follows his wife, who is attempting to divorce him, to the French Riviera, and is helped by the ghostly Mrs Kirby and her dog.

Fitfully amusing follow-up to *Topper*, helped more by its cast than the script.

p: Hal Roach for MGM

Quaid (Arnold Schwarzenegger) loses his head in *Total Recall*.

w: Eddie Moran, Jack Jevne, Corey Ford
novel: Thorne Smith
d: Norman Z. McLeod
ph: Norbert Brodine
m: Hugo Friedhofer
ed/ad/cos/sound: no credits given
ROLAND YOUNG, Constance Bennett, Billie Burke, Alan Mowbray, Franklin Pangborn, Verree Teasdale, Alexander D'Arcy

Total Recall
USA 1990 109m Technicolor Dolby
In the future, a construction worker haunted by dreams of Mars discovers that he is actually a secret agent who has been brainwashed.

At $70m, one of the most expensive films ever made, not that you'd think it by watching it. A somewhat relentless exercise in comic strip violence and fashionable excess, its sheer extravagance depresses well before the end. Nevertheless, this didn't prevent it from becoming a box office hit.

p: Buzz Feitshans, Ronald Shusett for Carolco
exec p: Mario Kassar, Andrew Vajna
w: Ronald Shusett, Dan O'Bannon, Gary Goldman
story: Philip K. Dick
screen story: Ronald Shusett, Dan O'Bannon, Jon Povill
d: Paul Verhoeven
ph: Jost Vacano
m: Jerry Goldsmith
ed: Frank J. Urioste
pd: William Sandell
cos: Erica Edell Phillips
sp: Eric Brevig, Dream Quest, ILM and others
sound: Nelson Stoll
sound effects ed: Stephen H. Flick
make-up effects: Rob Bottin
2nd unit d: Vic Armstrong
2nd unit ph: Alex Phillips
titles: Wayne Fitzgerald
Arnold Schwarzenegger, Rachel Ticotin, Sharon Stone, Ronny Cox, Michael Ironside, Marshall Bell, Mel Johnson, Michael Champion, Roy Brocksmith, Ray Baker

The Toxic Avenger
USA 1985 76m colour
A nerdy, much-mocked gymnasium janitor is transformed into a monstrous-looking superhero after falling into a barrel of toxic waste.

Determinedly crude and self-mocking low budgeter which succeeded in its bid to become a cult item. It was followed by *The Toxic Avenger Part II* (1989), *The Toxic Avenger Part III: The Last Temptation of Toxic* (1989) and a children's cartoon series.

p: Lloyd Kaufman, Michael Herz for Troma
w: Joe Ritter, Gay Terry, Lloyd Kaufman, Stuart Strutin
story: Lloyd Kaufman
d: Michael Herz, Samuel Weil
ph: James London, Michael Kaufman
m: various

ed: Richard W. Haines
ad: Barry Shapiro, Alexander Masur
make-up: Jennifer Aspinal
Mitchell Cohen, Pat Ryan, Jr., Andree Maranda, Cindy Manion, Jennifer Babtist, Robert Prichard, Mark Torgi, Gary Schneider

Tover, Leo (1902-1964)
American cinematographer who photographed a couple of key science fiction/fantasy films in the 50s. His other credits include *The Snake Pit*, *The Heiress* and *The Sun Also Rises*.

Genre credits:
The Day the Earth Stood Still (1951), *Journey to the Center of the Earth* (1959)

Toy Story 🌀🌀🌀
USA 1995 81m Technicolor Dolby
Woody the Cowboy finds his status as his owner's favourite toy usurped by the arrival of an astronaut called Buzz Lightyear, but the two later join forces to get home when they find themselves lost.

Computer animated feature, brilliantly done, with plenty for adults to enjoy as well as children. A major technical achievement and a deserved box office success.

p: Ralph Guggenheim, Bonnie Arnold for Pixel/Walt Disney
w: Joss Whedon, Andrew Stanton, Joel Cohen, Pete Docter, John Lasseter
d: JOHN LASSETER (special AA)
m: Randy Newman
ed: Robert Gordon, Lee Unkrich
ad: Ralph Eggleston
sound: Gary Rydstrom
voices: TOM HANKS, TIM ALLEN, Don Rickles, John Ratzenberger, Annie Potts, Jim Varney, Wallace Shawn

Toys

USA 1992 122m CFIcolor Dolby

Following a toymaker's death, his army officer brother inherits his factory and turns the output over to military toys.

Every director has his big budget folly, and this overlong whimsy is Levinson's. Worth a look for the impressive production design, but otherwise something of a miscalculation by all concerned.

p: Barry Levinson, Mark Johnson for TYCF/Baltimore
w: Barry Levinson, Valerie Curtin
d: Barry Levinson
ph: Adam Greenberg
m: Hans Zimmer
md: Shirley Walker
ed: Stu Linder
pd: FERDINANDO SCARFIOTTI
cos: ALBERT WOLSKY
sp: Clayton Pinney, Pacific Data Images, Dream Quest and others
sound: Richard Beggs
make-up effects: Rob Bottin, Greg Nelson
stunt co-ordinator: James Arnett
Robin Williams, Michael Gambon, Donald O'Connor, Joan Cusack, Robin Wright, L L Cool J, Jack Warden, Yeardley Smith

Trancers

USA 1984 75m DeLuxe

A detective from 2247 travels back in time to 1985 to track down the leader of a zombie cult called The Trancers.

So-so low budget blend of action, detection and science fiction which rather surprisingly took on cult status and provoked a slew of sequels: *Trancers II: The Return of Jack Deth* (1990), *Trancers III: Deth Lives* (1993), *Trancers IV: Jack of Swords* (1994) and *Trancers V: Sudden Deth* (1995).

p: Charles Band for Empire/Lexyn
w: Danny Bilson, Paul de Meo

d: Charles Band
ph: Mac Ahlberg
m: Mark Ryder, Phil Davies
ed: Ted Nicolau
pd: Jeff Staggs
ad: Christopher Amy
cos: Kathie Clark, Jill Ohanneson
sound: Jonathan Stein
make-up: John Buechler
Tim Thomerson, Helen Hunt, Michael Stefani, Art Le Fleur, Thelma Hopkins, Richard Herd, Anne Seymour, Miguel Fernandez

Trapped in the Sky

see Thunderbirds to the Rescue

The Travelling Companion

Czechoslovakia 1990 96m colour

After the death of his father, a young shepherd travels the countryside and befriends a mysterious stranger who helps him to woo a princess.

Mildly diverting fairytale for younger audiences.

p: Omnia/Slovensky/Sabre/RAIDU/TVE/FR3/ZFD
w: Michael Schulz, Ludvik Raza
story: Hans Christian Andersen
d: Ludvik Raza
ph: Jiri Macak
m: Petr Hapka
ed: Josef Valvsiale
pd: Jindrich Goetz
cos: Evzebie Razova
sound: Pavel Jelinek
Tomas Valik, Fritz Bachschmidt, Matthias Habich, Mapi Galan, Eva Vejmeikova, Marian Labuda, Powel Zednicek

Transatlantic Tunnel

see The Tunnel

Tremors

USA 1989 96m DeLuxe Dolby

A small desert community is attacked by giant meat-eating worms.

Energetic hokum with good effects work. An amusing harkback to the desert-set sci-fi shockers of the 50s.

p: Brent Maddock, S. S. Wilson for Universal/No Frills
w: Brent Maddock, S. S. Wilson
story: Brent Maddock, S. S. Wilson, Ron Underwood
d: Ron Underwood
ph: Alexander Gruszynski
m: Ernest Troost
ed: O. Nicholas Brown
pd: Ivo Cristante
cos: Abigail Murray
sp: Tom Woodruff, Jr., Alec Gillis
sound: Walt Martin
titles: Neal Thompson
2nd unit d: S. S. Wilson
Kevin Bacon, Fred Ward, Finn Carter, Reba McEntire, Michael Gross, Bobby Jacoby, Tony Genaro, Charlotte Stewart

Tremors II: Aftershocks

USA 1995 96m Foto-Kem DTS stereo TVM

Earl Bassett and a buddy travel to Mexico to see off another batch of Graboids which have been threatening an oil field.

Entertaining tele-sequel with excellent effects and a spoofier atmosphere than its theatrical predecessor. Well worth seeking out at the video store.

p: Nancy Roberts, Christopher de Faria for Universal/MCA/Stampede
exec p: Brent Maddock, Ron Underwood
w: Brent Maddock, S.S. Wilson
d: S.S. Wilson
ph: Virgil Harper
m: Jay Ferguson
ed: Bob Ducsay

pd: Ivo Cristante
cos: Rudy Dillon
sp: Phil Tippett, Tom Woodruff, Jr., Alec Gillis, Peter Chesney
sound: Rick Waddell
2nd unit d: Peter Chesney
2nd unit ph: Tony Cutrono
add ph: Chris Taylor, George Hosek
stunt co-ordinator: Noon Orsatti
executive consultant: Gale Anne Hurd
Fred Ward, Christopher Gartin, Helen Shaver, Michael Gross, Marcelo Tubert, Marco Hernandez, Jose Rosario, Thomas Rosales

The Trollenberg Terror

GB 1958 84m bw

A Swiss village is terrorised by aliens who use a radioactive cloud for cover.

Thin *Quatermass*-style horror filler which at least has a go, but is restricted by a low budget and some pretty unconvincing special effects.

p: Robert S. Baker, Monty Berman for Eros/Tempean
w: Jimmy Sangster
story: Peter Key
d: Quentin Lawrence
ph: Monty Berman
m: Stanley Black
ed: Henry Richardson
ad: Duncan Sutherland
sound: Dick Smith
Forrest Tucker, Laurence Payne, Janet Munro, Jennifer Jayne, Warren Mitchell, Frederick Schiller, Andrew Faulds, Stuart Sanders

Tron ☁

USA 1982 96m Techniscope Super Panavision 70

A computer expert finds himself involved in an adventure on the other side of his video screen.

Its innovative computer graphics aside, this rather juvenile adventure

bores well before the end, while being plunged straight into the thick of the story doesn't help matters much, either.

p: Steven Lisberger for Walt Disney
w/d: Steven Lisberger
ph: Bruce Logan
m: Wendy Carlos
ed: Jeff Gourson
pd: Dean Edward Mitzner
Jeff Bridges, David Warner, Bruce Boxleitner, Cindy Morgan, Barbara Hughes, Dan Shoa, Peter Jurdsik, Tony Stephano

Trumbull, Douglas (1942-)

American special effects technician, producer and director who, after experience as an illustrator, began his career working on films for the US Air Force, NASA and Cinerama 360. He worked as one of the technicians on *2001* and, after further experience with effects and as a director, formed his own effects house, Future General, in 1974. He subsequently worked on several key science fiction productions in the late 70s and early 80s before turning his attention to designing motion-controlled fairground rides, such as 'Back to the Future' for Universal.

Genre credits:

2001: A Space Odyssey (1968 – co-sp), *The Andromeda Strain* (1970 – co-sp), *Silent Running* (1971 – co-sp/p/d), *Close Encounters of the Third Kind* (1977 – co-sp), *Star Trek* (1979 – co-sp), *Close Encounters of the Third Kind: The Special Edition* (1980 – co-sp), *The Starlost: Deception* (1982 – TVM – co-exec p/sp), *Blade Runner* (1982 – sp), *Brainstorm* (1983 – p/d)

Tsuburaya, Eiji (1901-1970)

Japanese special effects technician, a

former cameraman, in films from as early as 1919 developing special effects. Early credits include *Chimatsuri*, *Yoma Kidan* and *Kwaidan Yanagi Zoshi*, though he is perhaps best remembered for his work on the Godzilla films of the 50s and 60s.

Genre credits:

Godzilla (1954 – aka *Godzilla, King of the Monsters/Gojira*), *Rodan* (1956 – aka *Radan*), *The Mysterians* (1957 – aka *Chikyu Boeigun*), *The H-Man* (1958 – aka *Bijyo To Ekitai*), *Varan the Unbelievable* (1958 – aka *Daikaiju Baran*), *The Secret of the Telegian* (1960 – aka *Denso Ningen*), *The Human Vapour* (1960 – *Gasu Mingen Dai Ichi-Go*), *Mothra* (1961 – aka *Mosura*), *The Last War* (1961 – aka *Sekai Dai Senso*), *Gorath* (1962 – aka *Yosei Gorasu*), *King Kong vs. Godzilla* (1962 – aka *Kingu Kongu Tai Gojira*), *Attack of the Mushroom People* (1963 – aka *Matango, Fungus of Terror/Matango*), *The Lost World of Sinbad* (1963 – aka *Samurai Pirate/Daitozoku*), *Atragon* (1963 – aka *Atragon the Flying Sub/Kaitei Gunkan*), *Mothra vs. Godzilla* (1964 – aka *Godzilla vs. the Thing/Mosura Tai Gojira*), *Dagora the Space Monster* (1964 – aka *Uchu Daikaiju Dogora*), *Ghidrah the Three-Headed Monster* (1964 – aka *Sandai Kaiju Chikyu Saidai No Kessen*), *Frankenstein Conquers the World* (1965 – aka *Furankenstein Tai Baragon*), *Daiboken* (1965), *Invasion of the Astro Monsters* (1965 – aka *Monster Zero/Battle of the Astros/Kaiju Daisenso*), *War of the Gargantuas* (1966 – aka *Sanda Tai Gailah/Furankensteın No Kaiju*), *Godzilla vs. the Sea Monster* (1966 – aka *Ebirah, Horror of the Deep/Namkai No Dai Ketto*), *King Kong Escapes* (1967 – aka *Kingu Kongu No Gyakushu*), *Son of Godzilla* (1967 – aka *Gojira No Musuko*), *Destroy All Monsters* (1968 – aka *Kaiju Soshingeki*), *Latitude Zero* (1969 – aka *Ido Zero Daisakusen*), *Godzilla's Revenge* (1969 – aka *Oru Kaiju Daishingeki*)

Tsukamoto, Shinya (1960-)

Japanese actor, writer, editor, art director, cinematographer and director (practically a one-man army), responsible for the startling Tetsuo series.

Genre credits:

Tetsuo: The Iron Man (1990 – aka *Tetsuo* – actor/w/co-ph/ed/ad/d), *Hiruko the Goblin* (1990 – w/co-ph/ed/ad/d), *Tetsuo II: The Bodyhammer* (1991 – actor/w/co-ph/ed/ad/d)

Tubby the Tuba

USA 1977 82m colour

Tubby the Tuba envies the other instruments in his orchestra because they get to play the beautiful melodies whilst all he gets to play is the same old oom-pah oom-pah.

Adequately mounted animated version of the popular children's story which should delight younger audiences.

p: Alexander Schure for New York Institute of Technology
w//story/ly/narrator: Paul Tripp
d: Alexander Schure
animation supervisor: John Gentilella
m: George Kleinsinger
md: Lehman Engel
additional songs: Ray Carter
ed: Nat Greene
sound: Al Stegmeyer
voices: Dick Van Dyke, Pearl Bailey, Ruth Enders, Hermoine Gingold, Jack Gilford, Ray Middleton, Jane Powell, Cyril Ritchard, David Wayne

Tully, Montgomery (1904-)

British writer and director of undistinguished low budgeters, among them *Murder in Reverse*, *The Glass Cage*

and *Who Killed the Cat?* Began his career in 1929 directing documentaries before turning to features in the mid-40s.

Genre credits:

Escapement (1958 – aka *The Electronic Monster* – d), *The Terrornauts* (1967 – d), *Battle Beneath the Earth* (1967 – d)

The Tune

USA 1992 69m colour

A composer has trouble finishing a hit song.

Offbeat cartoon with amusing touches for those who can appreciate its director's style.

p/d: Bill Plypton
story: Bill Plympton, Maureen McElheron, P.C. Vey
m: Maureen McElheron
ed: Merril Stern
sound: Phil Lee
voices: Marty Nelson, Maureen McElheron, Daniel Neiden, Emily Bindiger, Chris Hoffman

The Tunnel

GB 1935 94m bw

Having successfully tunnelled the Channel in 1940, an engineer plans to to tunnel to America, but he is beset by financial skullduggery.

An interestingly dated extravaganza with solid production values. One for genre buffs.

p: Michael Balcon for Gaumont
w: L. DuGarde Peach, Clemence Dene
novel: Bernard Kellerman
story: Curt Siodmak
d: Maurice Elvey
ph: Gunther Krampf
md: Louis Levy
ed: Charles Frend
ad: E. Metzner

cos: Marianne, Schiaparelli, Strassner
sound: M. Rose
Richard Dix, Leslie Banks, George Arliss, Madge Evans, C. Aubrey Smith, Helen Vinson, Walter Huston, Basil Sydney, Jimmy Hanley

Tuntke, William

American art director, with Disney in the 60s before going freelance in the 70s.

Genre credits:

Son of Flubber (1962 – co-ad), *The Misadventures of Merlin Jones* (1963 – co-ad), *The Monkey's Uncle* (1964 – co-ad), *Mary Poppins* (1964 – co-ad), *The Andromeda Strain* (1970 – ad)

Tuttle, William

American make-up artist who won a special Oscar for George Pal's *The Seven Faces of Dr. Lao* (1964). He also created the Morlocks for Pal's *The Time Machine*. Long with MGM, he worked on countless films, among them *The Bad and the Beautiful*, *Pat and Mike*, *Julius Caesar*, *Cat on a Hot Tin Roo* and *Gigi*. His later credits include *Necromancy*, *What's Up, Doc?*, *Young Frankenstein*, *Silent Movie* and *The Fury*.

Genre credits:

The Time Machine (1960), *The Seven Faces of Dr. Lao* (1964), *The Power* (1968)

Twelve Monkeys

USA 1995 130m Eastmancolor DTS stereo

A lady psychiatrist attempts to determine whether one of her patients is mentally unbalanced or, as he claims, a time traveller from the year 2035, out to discover the cause of a virus which wiped out 99 percent of the human race in 1997.

Lengthy but reasonably engrossing saga about the survival of man both as a race and an individual, told in its director's usual in-your-face style. The story is based on the French short *La Jetée* (1962).

p: Charles Roven for Universal/PolygramClassico/Atlatas
exec p: Robert Cavallo, Gary Levinsohn, Robert Kosberg
w: David Peoples, Janet Peoples
d: Terry Gilliam
ph: Roger Pratt
m: Paul Buckmaster
ed: Mick Audsley
pd: Jeffrey Beercroft
cos: Julie Weiss
sp: Vincent Montepusco
sound: Jay Meagher
Bruce Willis, Madeleine Stowe, BRAD PITT, Christopher Plummer, Jon Sedda, Vernon Campbell, Joseph Melito, Michael Chance, Bill Raymond, Fred Strother, Bob Adrian, David Morse, Carol Florence, Simon Jones, Michael Walls

Twentieth Century Fox (TCF)

Formed in 1935 following a merger between Twentieth Century Pictures and the Fox Film Corporation, TCF is known for a wide variety of productions which range from musical blockbusters such as *The King and I* and *The Sound of Music* to the *Home Alone* comedies. The studio's contribution to the science fiction genre is also major and include the *Star Wars*, *Alien*, *Fly* and *Planet of the Apes* franchises, not to mention such classics as *The Day the Earth Stood Still*.

Genre filmography:
Just Imagine (1930), *The Blue Bird* (1940), *The Day the Earth Stood Still* (1951), *The Rocket Man* (1954), *Spacemaster X-7* (1958), *The Fly* (1958), *Journey to the Center of the Earth* (1959), *Return of the Fly* (1959), *The Wizard of Baghdad* (1960), *The Lost World* (1960), *The Day Mars Invaded Earth* (1962), *The Earth Dies Screaming* (1964), *Curse of the Fly* (1965), *Space Flight IC-I* (1965), *Fantastic Voyage* (1966), *Batman* (1966), *Dr. Dolittle* (1967), *Planet of the Apes* (1968), *Beneath the Planet of the Apes* (1969), *Escape from the Planet of the Apes* (1970), *Conquest of the Planet of the Apes* (1972), *Battle for the Planet of the Apes* (1973), *Zardoz* (1974), *The Blue Bird* (1976 – remake), *Alien* (1979), *Star Wars* (1977), *Wizards* (1977), *Damnation Alley* (1977), *The Boys from Brazil* (1978), *Quintet* (1979), *The Empire Strikes Back* (1980), *The Return of the Jedi* (1983), *Aliens* (1986), *The Fly* (1986 – remake), *The Fly II* (1989), *Alien 3* (1992), *Alien Resurrection* (1997)

Twenty Million Miles to Earth

USA 1957 82m bw

An American rocketship returning from Venus crashes into the Mediterranean and a fisher boy rescues a cannister which contains a monster.

Inept, low budget monster pic with a few amusing moments for lovers of inept, low budget monster pics.

p: Charles H. Schneer for Columbia/Morningside
w: Bob Williams, Chris Knopf
story: Charlott Knight
d: Nathan Juran
ph: Irving Lippmann, Carlos Ventigmilia
md: Mischa Bakaleinikoff
ed: Edwin Bryant
ad: Cary Odell
sp: Ray Harryhausen
sound: Lambert Day
William Hopper, Joan Taylor, John Zaremba, Frank Puglia, Tito Vuolo, Thomas B. Henry

Twenty-Thousand Leagues Under the Sea

USA 1954 122m Technicolor Cinemascope

A Victorian scientist and his two friends are shipwrecked by a sea monster which turns out to be a futuristic submarine.

Well-remembered though flabbily directed Disney version of the popular Jules Verne novel. Strong performances, good underwater work and a famous battle with a giant squid keep one watching. Two television remakes appeared in 1997, with the part of Captain Nemo being played by Ben Cross and Michael Caine.

p: Walt Disney
w: Earl Felton
novel: Jules Verne
d: Richard Fleischer
ph: Franz Planer
m: Paul Smith
ed: Elmo Williams
ad/set decoration: John Meehan, Emile Kuri (aa)
cos: Norman Martien
sp: Ub Iwerks, John Hench, Josh Meador (aa), Peter Ellenshaw, Ralph Hammeras
sound: C. O. Slyfield, Robert O. Cook
2nd unit d: James Havens
underwater ph: TILL GABBANI
Kirk Douglas, JAMES MASON (as Captain Nemo), PAUL LUKAS, Peter Lorre, Ted de Corsia, Robert J. Wilke, Carlton Young

Twilight Zone – The Movie

USA 1983 101m Technicolor Dolby
Four tales of the imagination, based on the cult science fiction series of the 60s.

At best a rather bland concoction, lacking the wit, style and intelligence of the original series. The last episode is certainly the best, but the whole enterprise is a considerable disappointment from these talents.

p: Steven Spielberg, John Landis, Frank Marshall, Kathleen Kennedy, Michael J. Finnel, George Folsey, Jr., Jon Davison for Warner
w: John Landis, George Clayton, Josh Rogan, Richard Matheson
d: John Landis, Steven Spielberg, Joe Dante, George Miller
ph: Stevan Larner, Allen Daviau, John Hora
m: Jerry Goldsmith
ed: Malcolm Campbell, Tina Hirsch, Michael Kahn, Howard Smith
pd: James D. Bissell
make-up effects: Rob Bottin, Craig Reardon, Michael McCracken
narrator: Burgess Meredith
Dan Aykroyd, Albert Brooks, Scatman Crothers, Vic Morrow (who was killed during filming), Bill Quinn, Kevin McCarthy, JOHN LITHGOW, Kathleen Quinlan, Dick Miller, Jeremy Light, Abbe Lane, Donna Dixon, Martin Garner

---

2001: A Space Odyssey 🪐🪐🪐🪐

GB 1968 141m Metrocolor Super Panavision

At various stages of existence, Man discovers several mysterious black monoliths. Meanwhile, on board a spaceship bound for Jupiter, the computer controlling the mission has a "mental" breakdown and tries to murder all the crew.

A technically brilliant and thought-provoking piece of film-making with excellent effects and many striking moments. A genre milestone, it continues to grow in stature despite the intervening years. *2010: Odyssey Two* followed in 1984.

p: Victor Lindon for MGM
exec p: Stanley Kubrick
w: STANLEY KUBRICK, ARTHUR C. CLARKE
novel: ARTHUR C. CLARKE
d: STANLEY KUBRICK
ph: GEOFFREY UNSWORTH, JOHN ALCOTT
m: Johann Strauss and others (after a commissioned score by ALEX NORTH had been rejected)
ed: RAY LOVEJOY
pd: TONY MASTERS, HARRY LANGE, ERNIE ARCHER
ad: JOHN HOESLI
cos: Hardie Amies
sp: STANLEY KUBRICK (AA), DOUGLAS TRUMBULL, WALLY VEEVERS, CON PEDERSON, TOM HOWARD
sound: A. W. WATKINS, H. L. BIRD, J. B. SMITH
sound ed: Winston Ryder
KEIR DULLEA, Gary Lockhart, William Sylvester, Leonard Rossiter, DOUGLAS RAEN (as the voice of HAL 9000), Margaret Tyzack, Sean Sullivan, Frank Miller

---

2010: Odyssey Two 💩

USA 1984 114m Metrocolor Panavision Dolby

A joint Soviet-American expedition is sent to Jupiter to discover what became of the *Discovery* mission nine years earlier.

Inevitably disappointing when compared to its predecessor, this long awaited and much publicised sequel lacks the power and mysticism of the original, despite the excellent opportunities offered by the book. Taken on face value, however, it looks good and the special effects are fine.

p: Peter Hyams for MGM/UA
w/d: Peter Hyams
novel: ARTHUR C. CLARKE
ph: PETER HYAMS
m: David Shire
ed: James Mitchell
pd: ALBERT BRENNER
cos: Patricia Norris
sp: RICHARD EDLUND
sound: Dale Strumpell, Gene Cantamessa, Michael J. Kohut, Aaron Rochin, Carlos de Larios, Ray O'Reilly
sound ed: Richard L. Anderson
stunt co-ordinator: M. James Arnett
make-up: Michael Westmore
Roy Scheider, John Lithgow, Helen Mirren, Bob Balaban, Keir Dullea, Madolyn Smith, James McEachin, Dana Elcar, Douglas Raen (as the voice of HAL 9000), Arthur C. Clarke (gag cameo)

One of the many groundbreaking special effects featured in Stanley Kubrick's *2001: A Space Odyssey*, arguably the finest science fiction movie ever made.

Undersea Kingdom

USA 1936 12x15m episiodes bw

A naval hero travels by submarine to the lost city of Atlantis where he helps to usurp Unga Kahn and his Volkites.

Silly but lively serial stuff with hilariously dated hardware. Chapter titles include *Beneath the Ocean Floor*, *Arena of Death* and *Revenge of the Volkites*.

p: Nat Levine for Republic
w: John Rathmeil, Maurice Geraghty, Oliver Drake
story: Tracy Knight, John Rathmeil
d: B. Reeve Eason, Joseph Kane
ph: William Nobles, Edgar Lyons
md: Harry Grey
ed: Dick Fantl, Johseph H. Lewis, Helene Turner
Ray "Crash" Corrigan, Lois Wilde, Monte Blue, William Farnum, Booth Howard, C. Montague Shaw, Lee Van Atta

Unearthly Stranger

GB 1963 78m bw

A research scientist discovers that his wife is an alien.

Better than average low budget sci-fi/horror with a few neat touches.

p: Albert Fennell for Anglo Amalgamated/Independent Artists
exec p: Julian Wintole, Leslie Parkyn
w: Rex Carlton

story: Jeffrey Stone
d: John Kirsch
ph: Reg Wyer
m: Edward Williams
md: Marcus Dods
ed: Tom Priestley
ad: Harry Pottle
cos: Vi Murray
sound: Simon Kaye, Ken Cameron
Mark Davidson, Gabriella Licudi, Patrick Newell, Jean Marsh, Warren Mitchell

Universal

Though now one of the biggest film companies in the world, Universal began as something of a family affair. Founded in 1912 by German-born Carl Laemmle, the studio churned out all manner of films during the silent period, one of their most popular stars being the romantic idol Rudolph Valentino. Also under contract was Lon Chaney who starred in several of the studio's early brushes with horror, though it wasn't until the early 30s that they became identified with the horror genre following the success of *Dracula* and *Frankenstein*. A close brush with bankruptcy occurred in the mid-30s, from which the studio was rescued by a string of musicals starring Deanna Durbin. More horror helped to keep the coffers filled during 40s, as did a series of comedies starring Abbott and Costello, who went on to spoof the studio's monsters in the 50s. More recent hits have included *Jaws*, *E. T.* and *Jurassic Park*, all of which were directed by Steven Spielberg, and the *Back to the Future* franchise, which he co-executive produced.

Genre filmography:
The Invisible Ray (1935), *Flash Gordon* (1936 – serial), *Flash Gordon's Trip to Mars* (1938 – serial), *Buck Rogers* (1939 – serial), *Flash Gordon Conquers the Universe* (1940 – serial), *Man Made Monster* (1941 – aka *The Electric Man*), *It Came from Outer Space* (1953), *This Island Earth* (1954), *The Land Unknown* (1957), *The Monolith Monsters* (1957), *The Incredible Shrinking Man* (1957), *The Forbin Project* (1970 – aka *Colossus: The Forbin Project*), *The Andromeda Strain* (1970), *Silent Running* (1971), *Battlestar Galactica* (1978 – TVM), *Buck Rogers in the 25th Century* (1979 – TVM), *Somewhere in Time* (1980), *The Incredible Shrinking Woman* (1981), *The Thing* (1982), *Back to the Future* (1985), *Back to the Future II* (1989), *Back to the Future III* (1990), *Jurassic Park* (1993), *The Flintstones* (1994), *The Lost World: Jurassic Park* (1997)

Universal Soldier

USA 1992 102m Technicolor Dolby

Two dead Vietnam soldiers are turned into humanoids, but one of them goes haywire.

Expensive but brain dead actioner with an over-plus of unintentional laughs.

p: Allen Shapiro, Craig Baumgarten, Joel B. Michaels for Carolco
exec p: Mario Kassar
w: Richard Rothstein, Christopher Leitch, Dean Devlin
d: Roland Emmerich
ph: Karl Walter Linenlaub
m: Christopher Franke
ed: Michael J. Duthie
pd: Holger Gross
cos: Joseph Parro
sp: Kit West
sound: David Chornow
make-up effects: Larry M. Hamlin, Michael Burnett
2nd unit d: Vic Armstrong
2nd unit ph: Dan Turrett
Jean-Claude Van Damme, Dolph Lungdren, Ally Walker, Ed O'Ross, Jerry Orbach, Leon Rippy, Tico Wells, Ralph Moeller, Robert Trevor, Gene Davis, Drew Snyder

Unknown World

USA 1951 74m bw

Scientists preparing for life in a post-atomic age drill beneath the earth's crust and discover a giant cavern thousands of miles below the surface.

Tame low budget entry. *Journey to the Center of the Earth* it ain't.

p: J. R. Rabin, I. A. Block for Lippert Pictures
w: Millard Kaufman
d/ed: Terrell O. Morse
ph: Allen G. Siegler, Henry Freulich
m: Ernest Gold
pd/sp: J. R. Rabin, I. A. Block, V. Von Mulldorfer
sound: Marshall Pollock
Victor Kilian, Bruce Kellogg, Otto Waldis, Jim Bannon, Marilyn Nash, Dick Cogan, Tom Handley

Unsworth, Geoffrey (1914-1978)

Distinguished British cinematographer whose visual flair has added immeasurably to such films as *A Night to Remember*, *Northwest Frontier*, *Becket*, *Half a Sixpence*, *The Assassination Bureau*, *Cromwell*, *A Bridge Too Far* and *The First Great Train Robbery*, not to mention Kubrick's *2001*, which he co-photographed with John Alcott. He won Oscars for his work on *Cabaret* (1972) and, posthumously, *Tess* (1980), which he co-photographed with Ghislain Cloquet. He began his career in 1932 at Gaumont British before becoming an operator for Technicolor, in which capacity he worked on such films as *The Four Feathers*, *The Thief of Bagdad*, *The Life and Death of Colonel Blimp* and *A Matter of Life and Death*. He became a lighting cameraman in his own right with *The Laughing Lady* in 1946.

Genre credits:
The Thief of Bagdad (1940 – cam op), *A Matter of Life and Death* (1946 – cam op), *2001: A Space Odyssey* (1968 – co-ph), *Alice's Adventures in Wonderland* (1972 – ph), *Zardoz* (1973 – ph), *Superman* (1978 – ph), *Superman II* (1980 – co-ph [utilising scenes shot for *Superman*])

Upworld

USA 1993 (made 1988) 84m DeLuxe Dolby

A young cop teams up with a gnome for a top secret undercover case.

Dire buddy movie which makes *Turner and Hooch* look like a classic. Despite the directorial credit, the effects are pretty variable.

p: Robert W. Cort, Scott Kroopf, Pen Densham, Richard Lewis for Lightning Pictures/Interscope Communications/Trilogy
w: Pen Densham, John Walsen
story: Pen Densham
d: Stan Winston
ph: Bojan Bazelli
m: Richard Gibbs
ed: Marcus Manton
pd: Marcia Hinds
2nd unit d: Jack Gill
Anthony Michael Hall, Jerry Orbach, Claudia Christian, Eli Danker, Mark Harelik, Robert Z'Dor

The Valley of Gwangi

USA 1968 95m Technicolor Dynamation

Cowboys discover prehistoric monsters in a valley in Mexico and catch one for their wild west show, but it escapes and goes on the rampage.

Flatly made and routinely scripted monster adventure with only the trick effects to hold one's interest. Originally intended as a Willis O'Brien project after his success with *King Kong*.

p: Charles H. Schneer for Warner/Morningside
w: William E. Bast, Julian More
d: James O'Connelly
ph: Erwin Hillier
m: Jerome Morros
ed: Henry Richardson
ad: Gil Parrondo
sp: RAY HARRYHAUSEN
sound: Malcolm Stenai
titles: Antonia Saura
Richard Carlson, Laurence Naismith, James Franciscus, Gila Golan, Freda Jackson, Dennis Kilbane

Van Damme, Jean-Claude (1961-)

Belgian actor (real name Jean-Claude Van Varenberg), dubbed by the press as "the muscles from Brussels". A kickboxing and karate champion, he began his career at the low budget end of the action/exploitation market with a part in *Missing in Action* in 1984, having moved to America in 1981. He gradually rose to stardom via such vehicles as *Rue Barbara*, *No Retreat, No Surrender*, *Bloodsport* and *Black Eagle*. He has also co-written several of his scripts, among them *Kickboxer*, *Lionheart* (aka *AWOL*) and *Double Impact*. His other credits include *Death Warrant*, *Nowhere to Run* and *Hard Target*.

Genre credits:
Cyborg (1989), *Universal Soldier* (1992), *Timecop* (1994), *Streetfighter* (1995)

Vance-Straker, Marilyn

American costume designer who has worked on many of Walter Hill's movies (*48 Hours*, *Streets of Fire*, *Brewster's Millions*, etc.). Her other credits include *Pretty Woman*, *Die Hard*, *The Untouchables*, *Die Hard 2* and *Hudson Hawk*.

Genre credits:
Predator (1987), *Predator 2* (1990), *The Rocketeer* (1991)

Vaughn, Robert (1932-)

American actor, perhaps best known for playing Napoleon Solo in *The Man from U.N.C.L.E.* and Harry Rule in *The Protectors*, both of them on television. He made his film debut with a small part in *The Ten Commandments* in 1956, after which he gradually rose to stardom, appearing in such films as *The Young Philadelphians* (aka *The City Jungle*), *The Magnificent Seven*, *The Caretakers*, *Bullitt* and *The Towering Inferno*. More recent credits include *Transylvania Twist*, *Witch Academy*, *Dust to Dust* and *Visions*.

Genre credits:
Teenage Caveman (1958 – aka *Out of the Dark*), *The Mind of Mr. Soames* (1969), *Starship Invasions* (1977), *Demon Seed* (1977 – voice), *Battle Beyond the Stars* (1980), *Hangar 18* (1980), *Superman III* (1983)

Veevers, Wally (? -1983)

British special effects technician who began his career working for Alexander Korda. He died whilst in the midst of working on *The Keep*.

Genre credits:
Things to Come (1936 – co-sp), *Satellite in the Sky* (1956 – sp), *Day of the Triffids* (1962 – sp), *Dr. Strangelove: Or How I Learned to Stop Worrying and Love the Bomb* (1963 – sp), *2001: A Space Odyssey* (1968 – co-sp), *Superman* (1978 – co-sp)

Verhoeven, Paul (1938-)

Dutch director who, after working as a teacher for many years, began making documentaries which in turn led to features in his home country, among them *Spetters* and *The Fourth Man*. He moved to Hollywood in 1985 and has enjoyed commercial success with a variety of projects, most notably *Robocop* and *Basic Instinct*, though he came a cropper with the misogynistic *Showgirls*. His films usually draw critical comment for their excessive violence.

Genre credits:
Flesh and Blood (1985 – also co-w), *Robocop* (1987), *Total Recall* (1990), *Starship Troopers* (1997)

Verne, Jules (1828-1905)

French novelist and playwrite whose first novel, *Five Weeks in a Baloon*, was published in 1863. He followed this with such science fiction and fantasy classics as *Journey to the Centre of the Earth*, *20,000 Leagues Under the Sea*, *Master of the World*, *From the Earth to the Moon* and *Mysterious Island*, not to mention such non-genre works as *Around the World in Eighty Days*, *Michael Strogoff* and *The Light at the Edge of the World*. His fantasy subjects have been filmed many times.

Filmography:
A Trip to the Moon (1902 – aka *Le Voyage Dans la Lune*), *20,000 Leagues Under the Sea* (1907 – aka *Vingt Milles Lieues Sous les Mers*), *Journey to the Centre of the Earth* (1909 – aka *Voyage au Centre de la Terre*), *20,000 Leagues Under the Sea* (1954), *From the Earth to the Moon* (1958), *Journey to the Center of the Earth* (1958), *Mysterious Island* (1960), *In Search of the Castaways* (1961), *Rocket to the Moon* (1967 – aka *Jules Verne's Rocket to the Moon/Those Fantastic Flying Fools/Blast Off!*), *Captain Nemo and the Underwater City* (1969), *L'Isola Misteriosa e il Captain Nemo* (1974 – aka *Mysterious Island of Captain Nemo*), *Where Time Began* (1976), *The Amazing Captain Nemo* (1978 – TVM), *Monster Island* (1980 – aka *The Mystery of Monster Island*)

Vice Versa

GB 1947 111m bw

A Victorian schoolboy and his stern father find themselves in each other's shoes having made a wish with a magical stone.

Deliciously witty fantasy comedy with lively performances and delightful detail. Jolly good fun. A remake followed in 1988.

p: Peter Ustinov, George H,. Brown for Rank/Two Cities
w/d: PETER USTINOV
novel: F. Anstey
ph: Jack Hildyard
m: Anthony Hopkins
md: Muir Mathieson
ed: John D. Guthridge
ad: Carmen Dillon
cos: Nacha Benois
sp: Henry Harris
sound: W. Barnes-Heath, L. E. Overton
ass d: Michael Anderson
ROGER LIVESEY, ANTHONY NEWLEY, JAMES ROBERTSON JUSTICE, Kay Walsh, Petula Clark, Joan Young, David Hutcheson, Vida Hope, James Hayter, Harcourt Williams, Alfie Bass

Vice Versa

USA 1988 98m colour

With the aid of a magical skull, an 11-year-old boy exchanges places with his father, much to the surprise of both.

Lively update of a story previously filmed in 1947, with plenty of easy laughs for those in the mood. One of several age-reversal comedies released at the time (also see *Big*, *Like Father, Like Son* and *18 Again!* etc).

p: Dick Clement, Ian La Frenais for Columbia
exec p: Alan Ladd, Jr.
w: Dick Clement, Ian La Frenais
novel: F. Anstey
d: Brian Gilbert
ph: King Baggott
m: David Shire
ed: David Garfield
pd: Jim Schoppe
Judge Reinhold, Fred Savage, Corinne Bohrer, Swoozie Kurtz, David Profal, Jane Kaczmerek, Gloria Gifford

Vickers, Mike

British composer, a former member of Manfred Mann, who contributed to a handful of 70s films, among them *Please, Sir!* and *Dracula A.D. 1972*.

Genre credits:
At the Earth's Core (1976), *Warlords of Atlantis* (1978)

The Viking Women and the Sea Serpent

USA 1957 70m bw

A group of Viking women set out to discover what has become of their husbands, who went on an expedition three years earlier.

Lunatic low budget fantasy adventure with poor effects and no attempt at historical accuracy whatsoever. Consequently, quite enjoyable in the Golden Turkey manner.

p: Roger Corman for AIP/Malibu
exec p: James H. Nicholson, Samuel Z. Arkoff
w: Lawrence Louis Goldman
story: Irving Block
d: Roger Corman
ph: Monroe P. Askins
m: Albert Glasser
ed: Ronald Sinclair
ad: Bob Kinoshita
cos: Gwen Fitzer
sp: Jack Rabin, Louis De Witt, Irving Block
sound: Herman Lewis
ch: Wilder Taylor
Abby Dalton, Susan Cabot, Brad Jackson, Richard Devon, June Kenney, Betsy Jones-Moreland, Gary Conway, Jay Sayer

Village of the Damned

GB 1960 78m bw

Women in a small English village simultaneously give birth to offspring whose origins are from another planet.

Clever low budget thriller which makes the very most of its situation. A minor classic, smartly put across.

p: Ronald Kinnoch for MGM
w: STIRLING SILLIPHANT, WOLF RILLA, GEOFFREY BARCLAY
novel: JOHN WYNDHAM
d: WOLF RILLA
ph: GEOFFREY FAITHFULL
m: Ron Goodwin
ed: Gordon Hales
ad: Ivan King
cos: Eileen Sullivan
sp: Tom Howard
sound: A. W. Watkins, Cyril Swern
2nd unit ph: Gerald Moss
GEORGE SANDERS, Barbara Shelley, Michael Gwynn, Martin Stephens, Laurence Naismith, Peter Vaughan

Village of the Damned

USA 1995 98m Eastmancolor DTS Stereo

All the women in the township of Midwich find themselves simultaneously pregnant with children who grow up with mysterious powers.

Passable video fodder, not quite as bad as some make out, but otherwise a pointless and unnecessary remake lacking the effect of the original.

p: Michael Preser, Sandy King for Universal/Alphaville
w: David Himmelstein
novel: JOHN WYNDHAM
d: John Carpenter
ph: Gary K. Kibbe
m: John Carpenter, Dave Davies
ed: Edward Warschilka
pd: Rodger Maus
sp: Bruce Nicholson, ILM
sound: Thomas Causey
make-up effects: KNB
2nd unit d: Jeff Imada
2nd unit ph: Arthur K. Botham
Christopher Reeve, Kirstie Alley, Mark Hamill, Linda Kozlowski, Michael Pare, Meredith Salenger, Pippa Pearthree, John Carpenter

Virtuosity

USA 1995 105m DeLuxe Dolby

In 1999, an ex-cop tracks down a computer-generated killer who has managed to enter the real world.

Standard futuristic chase thriller, little more than another video game posing as a movie.

p: Gary Lucchesi for Paramount
w: Eric Bernt
d: Brett Leonard
ph: Gale Tattersall
m: Christopher Young
ed: Rob Korbin, B. J. Sears
pd: Nilo Rodis
sp: N2 Communications
Denzel Washington, Kelly Lynch, Russell

Crowe, Louise Fletcher, Stephen Spinella, William Forsythe

Vitarelli, Arthur J.

American second unit director working almost exclusively for Disney, for whom he helmed additional sequences for many of their live action movies.

Genre credits:

The Absent-Minded Professor (1961), *Blackbeard's Ghost* (1967), *The Love Bug* (1968), *The Computer Wore Tennis Shoes* (1970), *Bedknobs and Broomsticks* (1971), *Million Dollar Duck* (1971), *Herbie Rides Again* (1974), *The Island at the Top of the World* (1974), *The Shaggy D.A.* (1976), *Herbie Goes to Monte Carlo* (1977)

Visitors of the Night

Canada 1995 91m DeLuxe TVM

In a small township where mysterious patterns have been appearing in the local crops, a woman and her daughter have strange dreams about being captured and experimented upon by aliens...

Basically little more than a distaff version of *Fire in the Sky*. No great shakes, but better than you might think, with the alien sequences at the end worth hanging on for (or fast forwarding to!).

p: Marilyn Stonehouse for Pebble Hut/ACI
exec p: Anne Daniel, Richard L. O'Connor
w: Michael J. Murray
d: Jorge Montesi
ph: Philip Linzey
m: Micky Erbe, Maribeth Solomon
ed: Pia Di Ciaula
ad: Andree Brodeur
cos: Margaret Mohr
sp: John Camptens
make-up effects: Steve Johnson
Markie Post, Stephen McHattie, Candace Cameron, Dale Midkiff, Pam Hyat, Susan

Hogan

Vogel, Virgil

American editor turned director who, after helming a number of unremarkable theatrical features turned to directing TV movies (*The Return of Joe Forrester*, *Law of the Land*, *Longarm*, etc.).

Genre credits:

This Island Earth (1954 – ed), *The Mole People* (1956 – d), *The Land Unknown* (1957 – d), *Invasion of the Animal People* (1960 – aka *Terror in the Midnight Sun* – co-d)

Von Harbou, Thea (1888-1954)

German novelist and screenwriter known primarily for her collaboration with the director Fritz Lang, to whom she was married, which ended when Lang went to Hollywood in 1934 and she stayed behind as the Nazi party's official screenwriter. Her other screenplay credits include *Dr. Mabuse*, *Phantom*, *The Testament of Dr. Mabuse*, *M* and *A Woman of No Importance*. She also directed two films: *Elisabeth Und der Narr* and *Hanneles Himmelfahrt*.

Genre credits:

Die Nibelungen (1924 – co-w), *Metropolis* (1926 – co-w/novel), *Die Frau Im Mond* (1929 – aka *The Woman in the Moon/By Rocket to the Moon* – story/co-w)

Von Sydow, Max (1929-)

Swedish actor (real name Carl Adolf Von Sydow), noted for his work with director Ingmar Bergman (*The Seventh Seal*, *Wild Stawberries*, *The Face*, *The Virgin Spring*, *Through a Glass Darkly*, *The Winter Light*, etc.).

Since appearing as Jesus in *The Greatest Story Ever Told* in 1965 he has turned up in all manner of international productions, often bringing a note of much-needed dignity. His other credits include *Hawaii*, *Three Days of the Condor*, *The Exorcist* (as Father Merrin, the exorcist), *Exorcist II: The Heretic*, *Never Say Never Again* (as Blofeld), *Hannah and Her Sisters* and *Pelle the Conqueror*.

Genre credits:

The Ultimate Warrior (1975), *Flash Gordon* (1980 – as Ming the Merciless), *Judge Dredd* (1995)

The Voyage of the Viking Women to the Waters of the Giant Sea Serpent

see The Viking Women and the Sea Serpent

Voyage to the Bottom of the Sea 🛸

USA 1961 105m DeLuxe Cinemascope

The crew of an atomic-powered submarine help save the world from a belt of radiation.

Mildly diverting though somewhat slackly handled underwater adventure, the success of which inspired the popular television series.

p: Irwin Allen for TCF/Windsor
w: Irwin Allen, Charlesa Bennett
d/story: Irwin Allen
ph: Winton C. Hoch
m: Paul Sawtell, Bert Shefter
ed: George Boemler
ad: Jack Martin Smith, Herman A. Blumenthal
cos: Paul Zastupnevich
sp: L. B. Abbott
sound: Alfred Bruzlin, Warren B. Delaplain
underwater ph: John Lamb

Walter Pidgeon, Joan Fontaine, Robert Sterling, Peter Lorre, Barbara Eden, Regis Toomey, Frankie Avalon, Henry Daniell, Michael Ansara

Walas, Chris

American make-up effects artist who, with Stephen DuPuis, won an Oscar for his work on *The Fly* (1986), which led to his directing the sequel. His other work as a make-up artist, mostly in collaboration, includes *Scanners*, *House II: The Second Story*, *The Kiss* and *Arachnophobia*. He has also directed another film, *The Vagrant*.

Genre credits:

Galaxina (1980), *Raiders of the Lost Ark* (1981), *Caveman* (1981), *Gremlins* (1984), *The Fly* (1986), *The Fly II* (1989 – d/make-up effects), *Naked Lunch* (1991)

Walker, Shirley

American composer, conductor and orchestrator, long associated with the film scores of Danny Elfman (she orchestrated and/or conducted *Batman*, *Dick Tracy*, *Nightbreed*, *Darkman* and *Scrooged*, etc). Her other scores include *Memoirs of an Invisible Man* and the television series *The Flash*.

Genre credits:

Batman (1989 – conductor), *Dick Tracy* (1990 – cond), *Scrooged* (1990 – cond), *Toys* (1992 – md), *Batman: Mask of the*

Phantasm (1993 – m), *Escape from L.A.* (1996 – co-m), *Asteroid* (1997 – TVM – m)

Wallace, Dee (1949-)

American actress (also known as Dee Wallace Stone), best known for playing the mother in Spielberg's *E. T.* She entered films after experience as a teacher and a dancer. Her other credits include *The Hills Have Eyes*, *The Howling*, *Cujo*, *Shadow Play* and *Popcorn*.

Genre credits:

The Stepford Wives (1975), *E. T.* (1982), *Critters* (1986)

Walsh, Bill (1918-1976)

American writer and producer, long with Walt Disney, for whom he penned and produced some of their best live action films. He began his association with the studio in the 50s, writing and producing television programmes before moving on to features. His other credits – all for Disney – include *Davy Crockett – King of the Wild Frontier*, *Bon Voyage*, *That Darn Cat*, *The World's Greatest Athlete* and *One of Our Dinosaurs is Missing*.

Genre credits:

The Shaggy Dog (1959 – co-w/p), *The Absent-Minded Professor* (1961 – w/associate p), *Son of Flubber* (1962 – co-w/co-p), *The Misadventures of Merlin Jones* (1963 – story), *The Monkey's Uncle* (1964 – story), *Mary Poppins* (1964 – co-w/co-p), *Blackbeard's Ghost* (1967 – co-w/p), *The Love Bug* (1968 – co-w/p), *Bedknobs and Broomsticks* (1971 – co-w/p), *Herbie Rides Again* (1974 – w/p), *The Shaggy Dog* (1994 - TVM - co-w [based on his 1959 screenplay])

War Games

USA 1983 113m Metrocolor Dolby

A teenage computer whiz accidentally taps into America's defence programme.

Slick-looking adventure thriller which certainly keeps one watching whilst it plays.

p: Harold Schneider for MGM/UA
exec p: Leonard Goldberg
w: Lawrence Lasker, Walter F. Parkes
d: John Badham
ph: William A. Fraker
m: Arthur B. Rubinstein
ed: Tom Rolf, Michael Ripps
pd: Angelo Graham
sound: Willie D. Burton
visual consultant: Geoffrey Kirkland
Matthew Broderick, Dabney Coleman, Ally Sheedy, John Wood, Barry Corbin, Kent Williams, Irving Metzman, Eddie Deezen

War of the Worlds

USA 1952 85m Technicolor

Invaders from Mars threaten to take over the earth, but are eventually destroyed by common germs.

Well remembered but poorly assembled spectacular in ghastly colour, further hampered by a soggy script, lifeless characters, pedestrian direction and unconvincing effects with plenty of visible wires. Despite its reputation, the plain matter of the fact is that it has dated very badly.

p: George Pal for Paramount
w: Barre Lyndom
novel: H. G. Wells
d: Byron Haskin
ph: George Barnes
m: Leith Stevens
ed: Everett Douglas
ad: Hal Pereira, Albert Nozaki
cos: Edith Head
sp: Gordon Jennings, Wallace Kelley, Paul K.

Lerpae, Ivyl Burks, Jan Domela, Irmin Roberts (aa)
sound: Harry Lindgren, Gene Garvin Gene Barry, Ann Robinson, Les Tremayne, Bob Cornthwaite, Sandra Giglio, Lewis Martin, Housley Stevenson, Jr., Paul Frees

Warburton, Cotton

American editor, long associated with Walt Disney, for whom he cut many live action features, winning an Oscar for his work on *Mary Poppins* (1964).

Genre credits:
The Absent-Minded Professor (1961), *Moon Pilot* (1961), *Son of Flubber* (1962), *The Misadventures of Merlin Jones* (1963), *The Monkey's Uncle* (1964), *Mary Poppins* (1964), *The Love Bug* (1968), *The Computer Wore Tennis Shoes* (1970), *Bedknobs and Broomsticks* (1971 – co-ed), *Now You See Him, Now You Don't* (1972), *Herbie Rides Again* (1974), *Freaky Friday* (1976), *Herbie Goes to Monte Carlo* (1977), *The Cat from Outer Space* (1978)

Ward, Burt (1945-)

American actor, best remembered as Robin in TV's *Batman*, whose film appearances have been occasional. He now also runs an effects house called Logical Figments.

Genre credits:
Batman (1966), *Robochick* (1989), *Robot Ninja* (1989)

Warlords of Atlantis

GB 1978 96m Technicolor
Victorian scientists find themselves transported to the lost city of Atlantis whilst testing out a submarine.
　Risibly scripted monster pic with grotty effects, somewhat typical of its producer and director's output. For under-fives only.

p: John Dark for EMI
w: Brian Hayles
d: Kevin Connor
ph: Alan Hume
m: Mike Vickers
ed: Bill Blunden
pd: Elliot Scott
sp: John Richardson, George Gibbs
Doug McClure, Peter Gilmore, Shane Rimmer, Lea Broadie, Michael Gothard, Cyd Charisse, Daniel Massey, Ashley Knight, John Ratzenberger, Donald Bisset, Derry Power, Hal Galili

Warlords of the 21st Century see Battletruck

Warner Bros.

Formed in 1923 by brothers Jack L., Harry M., Albert and Sam, the studio was known in the late 20s for producing the first talkie, *The Jazz Singer*, and in the 30s for its gangster melodramas and Busby Berkeley-choreographed musicals. Larger scale musicals followed in the 60s, including *My Fair Lady* and *Camelot*, whilst more recent big earners have been the *Lethal Weapon* and *Batman* franchises.

Genre filmography:
Jack and the Beanstalk (1952), *The Illustrated Man* (1968), *A Clockwork Orange* (1971), *The Terminal Man* (1974), *The Amazing Captain Nemo* (1978), *The Swarm*

This is apparently called a Zaarg, and is one of the many highly convincing monsters featured in *Warlords of Atlantis*.

(1978), *Time After Time* (1979), *Altered States* (1980), *Gremlins* (1984), *The Goonies* (1985), *Innerspace* (1987), *Batman* (1989), *Gremlins 2: The New Batch* (1990), *Batman Returns* (1992), *Batman Forever* (1995), *Batman and Robin* (1997)

Warner, David (1941-)

British actor with much stage experience. He made his film debut in 1963 in *Tom Jones*, though it was his role in *Morgan – A Suitable Case for Treatment* that made him a star. He now works in Hollywood primarily as a supporting actor in films often unworthy of his talents. His other credits include *The Bofors Gun*, *Straw Dogs*, *From Beyond the Grave*, *The Omen* (in which he was memorably decapitated), *The Thirty-Nine Steps*, *The Company of Wolves*, *The Unnameable Returns* and *Necronomicon*.

Genre credits:
Time After Time (1979 – as Jack the Ripper), *Time Bandits* (1981), *Star Trek V: The Final Frontier* (1989), *Star Trek VI: The Undiscovered Country* (1991), *Teenage Mutant Ninja Turtles II: The Secret of the Ooze* (1991), *Wild Palms* (1993 – TVM)

Warren, Gene

American special effects technician, an Oscar winner for *The Time Machine* (1960 – with Tim Baar). His son, Gene Warren Jr won an Oscar for his work on *Terminator 2: Judgement Day* (1991 – with Dennis Murren, Stan Winston and Robert Skotak).

Genre credits:
Tom Thumb (1958 – co-sp), *The Time Machine* (1960 – co-sp), *Master of the World* (1961 – co-sp), *The Power* (1968 – co-sp)

Warren, Norman J.

British director with a penchant for gorily over-stated low budget horror films, among them *Satan's Slave* and *Terror*. A former assistant director and commercials editor, he began directing in 1965 with the short *Fragment*. Two sexploitation dramas followed (*Her Private Hell* and *Loving Feeling*) along with various commercials. His other credits include *Gunpowder* and various pop videos.

Genre credits:
Prey (1977 – aka *Alien Prey*), *Outer Touch* (1979 – aka *Spaced Out*), *Inseminoid* (1980 – *Horror Planet*), *Bloody New Year* (1986 – aka *Time Warp Terror*)

The Water Babies

GB/Poland 1978 92m Technicolor
In 1859, a young chimney sweep flees when wrongly accused of theft, falls into into a river and finds himself in a strange underwater world.

Flat, insufficiently imaginative Victorian fantasy, lacking the charm of the same director's *The Railway Children* or *The Amazing Mr. Blunden*. Mild compensations can be found in the live action bookends; the animated mid-section doesn't work at all, though.

p: Peter Shaw for Ariadne/Studio Miniatur Filmowych
w: Michael Robson, Lionel Jeffries, Dennis Norden
novel: Charles Kingsley
d: Lionel Jeffries
ph: Ted Scaife
m/md: Phil Coulter
songs: Bill Martin, Phil Coulter
ed: Peter Weatherley
pd: Herbert Westbrook
cos: Phylis Dalton
sound: Cyril Collixck, Otto Snell
make-up: Harry Frampton

James Mason, Bernard Cribbins, Tommy Pender, Samantha Gates, Billie Whitelaw, Joan Greenwood, David Tomlinson and the voices of Lance Percival and Jon Pertwee

Watership Down

GB 1978 92m Technicolor Dolby
After a vision of destruction, a colony of rabbits leave their warren and go in search of a new home, but their trek is not an easy one.

Particularly tedious and bloodthirsty version of a much-loved novel whose general air of doom and gloom makes for poor family viewing.

p: Martin Rosen for Nepenthe/Watership
w/d: Martin Rosen
novel: Richard Adams
m: Angela Morley, Malcolm Williamson
song: *Bright Eyes*, MIKE BATT
ed: Terry Rawlings
sound: Bill Rowe
voices: John Hurt, Richard Briers, Zero Mostel, Roy Kinnear, Ralph Richardson, Denholm Elliott, Hannah Gordon, Harry Andrews, Nigel Hawthorne, Simon Cadell, Michael Hordern, John Bennett, Joss Ackland

Waterworld

USA 1995 135m DeLuxe DTS Stereo
In the future, when the polar ice caps have melted and the earth has been covered by water, a nameless mariner helps a young woman and a girl with a mysterious tattoo on her back discover the whereabouts of Dryland.

Thinly plotted but elaborately staged epic with a plethora of often excitingly staged action highlights. Production problems saw its budget rise to an unrecoupable $200m, however, which caused much negative reaction in the press at the time.

p: Charles Gordon, John Davis, Kevin

Costner for Universal/Gordon Company/Davis Entertainment Company/Lict and Mueller
exec p: Jeffrey Mueller, Andrew Licht, Ilona Herzberg
w: Peter Rader, David Twohy
d: Kevin Reynolds
ph: Dean Semler
m: James Newton Howard
ed: Peter Boyle
pd: Dennis Gassner
cos: John Bloomfield
sp: Michael J. McAlister
sound: Keith A. Webster
stunt co-ordinator: R. A. Rondell
2nd unit d: David Ellis, Mickey Gilbert
2nd unit ph: Gary Capo
titles: Pittard Sullivan Fitzgerald
underwater ph: Pete Romano
Kevin Costner, Jeanne Tripplehorn, Dennis Hopper, Tina Majorina, Michael Jeter, Zakes Mokae, Chaim Jeraffi, Ric Aviles

---

Watkins, Peter (1937-)

British writer and director who began his career in television, where he directed the brilliant *Culloden* and the banned *War Game*. His other film credits include *Edvard Munch*, *Fallen* and *Evening Land*.

Genre credits:
Privilege (1967 – co-w/d), *The Peace Game* (1969 – aka *Gladiatorerna* – co-w/d), *Punishment Park* (1971 – co-wd)

Watts, Roy

British editor with a handful of fantasy credits to his name, including two for Ray Harryhausen.

Genre credits:
Quest for Love (1971), *The Golden Voyage of Sinbad* (1973), *Sinbad and the Eye of the Tiger* (1977)

Weaver, Sigourney (1949-)

American star actress (real name Susan Alexandra Weaver) who, after brief appearances in *Annie Hall* and *Madman*, shot to international stardom in 1979 as Ripley in *Alien*. She earned a Best Actress Oscar nomination for repirising the role in the sequel. Her other credits include *The Year of Living Dangerously*, *Ghostbusters*, *Working Girl*, *Gorillas in the Mist*, *Ghostbusters II*, *1492*, *Dave* and *Death and the Maiden*.

Genre credits:
Alien (1979), *Ghostbusters* (1984), *Aliens* (1986), *Ghostbusters II* (1989), *Alien 3* (1992), *Alien Resurrection* (1997)

Webster, Ferris (1916-)

Distinguished American editor who has worked on such prestige productions as *The Picture of Dorian Gray*, *Father of the Bride*, *Lili*, *Cat on a Hot Tin Roof*, *The Manchurian Candidate*, *Seven Days in May* and several for director Clint Eastwood (*High Plains Drifter*, *The Gauntlet*, *Bronco Billy*, etc).

Genre credits:
Forbidden Planet (1956), *The Satan Bug* (1964), *Seconds* (1966)

Sigourney Weaver's Officer Ripley gets a little too close for comfort to the alien in *Alien³*.

Weird Science

USA 1985 94m Technicolor

Two teenage boys create their ideal woman with the aid of their home computer.

Juvenile wish fulfilment fantasy in the John Hughes manner. It should satisfy its intended audience.

p: Joel Silver for Universal
w/d: John Hughes
ph: Matthew F. Leonetti
m: Ira Newborn
ed: Mark Warner, Christopher Lebenzon, Scott Wallace
pd: John W. Corso
cos: Marilyn Vance

Anthony Michael Hall, Ilan Mitchell-Smith, Kelly Le Brock, Bill Paxton, Suzanne Snyder, Judie Aronson, Robert Downey, Robert Rusler

---

Welch, Bo

American production designer whose work includes such diverse films as *The Accidental Tourist*, *Grand Canyon*, *Wolf* and several for director Tim Burton.

Genre credits:

Beetlejuice (1988), *Edward Scissorhands* (1990), *Batman Returns* (1992)

Weller, Peter (1947-)

American actor, perhaps best known for playing Robocop in the first two movies. Much stage experience before turning to the big screen. His other credits include *Tell Me What You Want*, *Shoot the Moon*, *Blue Jeans Cop*, *Cat Chaser* and *The New Age*.

Genre credits:

Of Unknown Origin (1983), *The Adventures of Buckaroo Banzai Across the Eighth Dimension* (1984), *Robocop* (1987), *Leviathan* (1989), *Robocop 2* (1990), *Naked Lunch* (1991), *Screamers* (1995)

Wells, H. G. (1866-1946)

Celebrated British novelist whose filmed works include *Kipps* (also as the musical *Half a Sixpence*), *The History of Mr. Polly* and *The Invisible Man*, which provoked a handful of sequels. Filmed science fiction/fantasy works include *The Man Who Could Work Miracles*, *The Island of Dr. Moreau* (also as *Island of Lost Souls*), *Things to Come*, *The War of the Worlds* and *The Time Machine*. A former draper's assistant, he later turned to science, biology and journalism before finally finding lasting success as an author. Despite his prestige, he personally adapted only two of his own works for the screen.

Filmography:

The First Men in the Moon (1919), *The Island of Lost Souls* (1932), *The Man Who Could Work Miracles* (1936 – and co-w), *Things to Come* (1936 – and w), *The War of the Worlds* (1952), *The Time Machine* (1960), *The First Men in the Moon* (1964), *The Twilight People* (1972), *Food of the Gods* (1976), *The Island of Dr Moreau* (1977), *The Shape of Things to Come* (1979 – TVM), *Island of Mutations* (1979), *Food of the Gods II* (1989), *The Island of Dr Moreau* (1996)

West, Kit

American special effects technician, an Oscar winner for his work on *Raiders of the Lost Ark* (1981 – with Richard Edlund, Bruce Nicholson and Joe Johnston).

Genre credits:

Raiders of the Lost Ark (1981 – co-sp), *Return of the Jedi* (1983 – co-sp), *Dune* (1984 – co-sp), *Young Sherlock Holmes* (1985 – aka *Young Sherlock Holmes and the Pyramid of Fear* – co-sp), *Universal Soldier* (1992 – sp)

Westmore, Bud (1918-1973)

American make-up artist (real name Hamilton Adolph Westmore), part of the Westmore make-up dynasty founded by his father George and continued by himself and his brothers Monty, Perc, Ern, Wally and Frank. Long with Universal, his many credits include *The Devil Bat's Daughter*, *Abbott and Costello Meet Frankenstein*, *Abbott and Costello Meet Dr Jekyll and Mr Hyde*, *Man with a Thousand Faces* (in which he re-created many of Lon Chaney's famous make-ups), *The Mole People*, *The Night Walker* and *Skullduggery*.

Genre credits:

Mr Peabody and the Mermaid (1948), *Francis* (1949), *It Came from Outer Space* (1953), *The Creature from the Black Lagoon* (1953 – co-make-up), *Revenge of the Creature* (1954), *This Island Earth* (1954), *Tarantula* (1955), *The Monolith Monsters* (1957), *The Land Unknown* (1957), *The Brass Bottle* (1963)

Westmore, Wally (1906-1973)

American make-up artist (real name Walter James Westmore), brother of Bud, Monty, Frank and Perc. Long at Paramount, where he worked on such films as *Dr Jekyll and Mr Hyde* and *Alias Nick Beal*.

Genre credits:

Island of Lost Souls (1932), *When Worlds Collide* (1951), *The War of the Worlds* (1953), *Conquest of Space* (1955), *The Space Children* (1958), *Visit to a Small Planet* (1959), *Robinson Crusoe on Mars* (1964)

Westworld

USA 1973 89m Metrocolor Panavision
Guests at a futuristic holiday resort
peopled by robots find their lives in
danger when things go wrong.

A novel idea, smartly enough put
together, with signs of wit and originality, though the low budget does show.
Futureworld followed in 1976, whilst
the writer-director's later novel
Jurassic Park proved to be a variation
on the same theme.

p: Paul N. Lazarus III for MGM
w/d: MICHAEL CRICHTON
ph: Gene Polito
m: Fred Karlin
ed: David Bretherton
ad: Herman Blumenthal
cos: Richard Bruno, Betsy Cox
sp: Charles Schulthies, Brent Sellstrom
sound: Richard Church, Harry W. Tetrick
stunt co-ordinator: Dick Ziker
Yul Brynner, Richard Benjamin, James Brolin,
Norman Bartold, Alan Oppenheimer, Dick
Van Patten, Steve Franken, Linda Scott,
Victoria Shaw

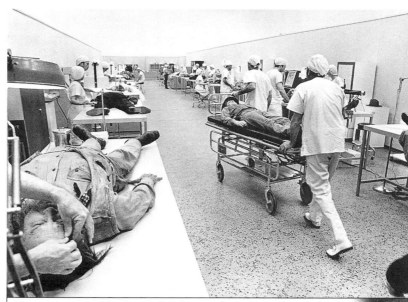

The robots are repaired ready for the next day's shooting in Michael Crichton's excellent *Westworld*, his predecessor to *Jurassic Park*.

When Dinosaurs Ruled the Earth

GB 1969 100m Technicolor
A prehistoric girl escapes sacrifice and
befriends a small dinosaur.

Childish but occasionally lively prehistoric nonsense, let down by its low
budget and some poorly integrated studio work.

p: Aida Young for Hammer/Warner
w/d: Val Guest
ph: Dick Bush
m: Mario Nascimbene
md: Philip Martell
ed: Peter Curran
ad: John Blezard
cos: Carl Toms
sp: Jim Danforth, Allan Bryce, Roger Dicken,
Brian Johncock

John Blane (James Brolin) and Peter Martin (Richard Benjamin) watch as Yul Brynner's supposedly dead robot gunslinger is dragged from the saloon in Michael Crichton's *Westworld*.

sound: Kevin Sutton
2nd unit ph: Johnny Cabrera
narrator: Patrick Allen
Victoria Vetri, Patrick Allen, Robin Hawdon,
Imogen Hassall, Patrick Holt, Sean Caffrey,
Magda Konopka, Carol Hawkins, Drewe
Henley

When Worlds Collide

USA 1951 83m Technicolor
When it is discovered that a planet is
careering towards earth and that
destruction is inevitable, a millionaire
builds a rocketship to help save 40 people.

Naive science fiction, somewhat typical of its producer. Routine production and a talkative script will make it tolerable only for devoted genre fans.

p: George Pal for Paramount
w: Sidney Boehm
novel: Philip Wylie, Edwin Balmer
d: Rudolph Mate
ph: John F. Seitz, W. Howard Greene
m: Leith Stevens
ed: Arthur Schmidt, Doane Harrison
ad: Hal Pereira, Albert Nozaki
cos: Edith Head
sp: Gordon Jennings, Harry Barndollar (aa), Farciot Edouart
sound: Gene Mwerritt, Walter Oberst
Richard Derr, Barbara Rush, Peter Hanson, John Hoyt, Larry Keating, Judith Ames, Stephen Chase, Hayden Rorke, Frank Cady

---

Where Time Began

Sp 1976 86m colour

A professor and his friends embark on an expedition to the centre of the earth and encounter many strange sights along the way.

Poorly scripted and dubbed but otherwise quite lively fantasy adventure, based on Jules Verne's *Journey to the Centre of the Earth*. Should please younger audiences.

p: J. Piquer Simon for Almena/International Showcase
w: John Melson
novel: Jules Verne
d: J. Piquer Simon
ph: Andres Berengeur
m/ly: Juan Carlos Calderon, John Melson, J. J. Garcia Cafh
pd/sp: Frank Propsper
Kenneth More, Pep Munne, Yvonne Sentis, Frank Bana, Jack Taylor, Lone Fleming, George Ridaud

---

Whitlock, Albert (1915-)

Distinguished British matte painter and special effects technician who won Oscars for his work on *Earthquake* (1974 – with Frank Brendel and Glen Robinson) and *The Hindenberg* (1975 – with Glen Robinson). Working on both sides of the Atlantic, he has also contributed to several films for Alfred Hitchcock (*The Man Who Knew Too Much*, *The Birds*, *Marnie*, *Torn Curtain*, *Topaz*, *Frenzy*, *Family Plot*) and Mel Brooks (*High Anxiety* [in which he also briefly appears], *History of the World, Part One*). His other credits include *The War Lord*, *Thoroughly Modern Millie*, *Diamonds Are Forever*, *The Blues Brothers*, *Dracula* and *Missing*.

Genre credits:
The Reluctant Astronaut (1967 – sp), *The Forbin Project* (1969 – aka *Colossus: The Forbin Project* – sp), *The Andromeda Strain* (1971 – co-sp), *Slaughterhouse Five* (1972 – co-sp), *The Day of the Dolphin* (1973 – sp), *The Wiz* (1978 – sp), *Heartbeeps* (1981 – co-sp), *Dune* (1984 – co-sp), *Red Sonja* (1985 – co-sp), *Millennium* (1989 – co-sp), *Never Ending Story II: The Next Chapter* (1990 – co-sp).

Who?

GB 1974 93m Eastmancolor

A scientist is turned into an android after a car crash, but questions are raised as to his true identity.

Unpersuasive nonsense, poorly presented (despite the talent involved) and lacking in humour.

p: Barry Levinson for British Lion/Hemisphere/Mclean
w: John Gould
novel: Algid Budrys
d: Jack Gold
ph: Petrus Schloemp

m: John Cameron
ed: Norman Wanstall
Elliott Gould, Trevor Howard, Joseph Bova, Ed Grover, James Noble, Lyndon Brock

---

Who Framed Roger Rabbit?

USA 1988 103m Metrocolor/DeLuxe
Panavision Dolby

A down-at-heel private eye investigates a murder in Toon Town.

Technically brilliant blend of live action and animation which nevertheless does tend to overwhelm, both visually and aurally. Its sheer novelty value turned it into a box office smash, however.

p: Robert Watts, Frank Marshall for Touchstone/Amblin/Silver Screen Partners III
exec p: Steven Spielberg, Kathleen Kennedy
w: Jeffery Price, Peter Seaman
novel: Gary K. Wolf
d: Robert Zemeckis
ph: Dean Cundey
m: Alan Silvestri
ed: Arthur Schmidt
pd: Elliot Scott, Roger Cain
cos: Joanna Johnston
sp: KEN RALSTON, RICHARD WILLIAMS, EDWARD JONES, GEORGE GIBBS (aa)
sound: Tony Dawe
sound effects ed: Louis Edelman, Charles L. Campbell (aa)
animation d: RICHARD WILLIAMS (SPECIAL AA)
add ph: Paul Beeson
2nd unit d: Frank Marshall, Ian Sharp, Max Kleven
BOB HOSKINS, Christopher Lloyd, Joanna Cassidy, Stubby Kaye, Alan Tilvern, Charles Fleischer (voice – as Roger), Kathleen Turner (voice), Mel Blanc (voice), Amy Irving (voice), Lou Hitsch (voice)

Wilcox, John (1905-1984)

British cinematographer who, in the 60s, photographed a number of horror films for cinematographer-turned-director Freddie Francis, among them *Nightmare*, *The Evil of Frankenstein*, *The Psychopath* and *The Skull*. His other credits include *The Mouse That Roared*, *Where's Jack*, *The Last Valley* and *Legend of the Werewolf*.

Genre credits:
Dr Who and the Daleks (1965), *Daleks – Invasion Earth 2150 A.D.* (1966)

Wild Palms

USA 1993 1x96m 3x50m (varying formats) colour TVM

In the near future, a megalomaniac attempts to take over the world via interactive television.

Overstretched but very slickly produced fantasy drama which generally keeps one watching, if only to find out what it's all about. A great hit with the *Twin Peaks* crowd.

p: Michael Roman for Ixtlan/Greengrass
exec p: Oliver Stone
w/cr: Bruce Wagner
d: Peter Hewitt, Keith Gordon, Kathryn Bigelow, Phil Joanu
ph: Phedon Papamichail
m: Ryuichi Sakamoto
ed: Patrick MacMahon
pd: Dins Danielson
cos: Judianna Makovsky
sp: Pacific Data Images
sound: Don Summer
stunt co-ordinator: Ernie Orsatti
James Belushi, Robert Loggia, Kim Cattrall, Angie Dickinson, Ernie Hudson, Dana Delany, David Warner, Robert Morse, Brad Dourif, Bebe Neuwirth, Nick Mancuso, Ben Savage.

The Wild Women of Wongo

USA 1958 87m Pathecolor

A tribe of sex-starved prehistoric women go in search of men.

Unintentionally hilarious romp in which all the women have modern hair-dos, wear bikinis and speak with Brooklyn accents. A golden turkey indeed.

p: George R. Black for Jaywall/Tropical
w: Cedric Rutherford
d: James L. Wolcott
ph: Harry Walsh
m: no credit given
ed: David L. Cazelt
Jean Hawkshaw, Johnny Walsh, Ed Fury, Mary Ann Webb, Rex Richards, Cande Gerrard, Adrienne Bourbeau

Williams, John (1932-)

Celebrated American composer, conductor and musical director, an Oscar winner for *Fiddler on the Roof* (1971 – musical director), *Jaws* (1975), *Star Wars* (1977), *E. T.* (1982) and *Schindler's List* (1993). He trained at the Juilliard School of Music, after which he became a jazz pianist. He began scoring for television in the late 50s, which he followed with work as an orchestrator and film composer from the early 60s (*I Passed for White*, *Diamond Head*, etc.). Now associated with the films of producer George Lucas and directors Steven Spielberg and Oliver Stone, he remains the most important and influential film composer of his generation, many of his themes having entered the public consciousness. Other key scores include *The Reivers*, *The Cowboys*, *The Poseidon Adventure*, *The Towering Inferno*, *The Eiger Sanction*, *Earthquake*, *Family Plot*, *Jaws 2*, *1941*, *Born of the Fourth of July*, *JFK*, *Home Alone* and *Nixon*.

Genre credits:
Star Wars (1977), *Close Encounters of the Third Kind* (1977), *Superman* (1978), *The Empire Strikes Back* (1980), *Raiders of the Lost Ark* (1981), *E. T.* (1982), *The Return of the Jedi* (1983), *Indiana Jones and the Temple of Doom* (1984), *Spacecamp* (1985), *Indiana Jones and the Last Crusade* (1989), *Always* (1989), *Hook* (1991), *Jurassic Park* (1993), *The Lost World: Jurassic Park* (1997)

Williams, Richard (1933-)

Canadian animator and title designer (*A Funny Thing Happened on the Way to the Forum*, *The Charge of the Light Brigade*, *What's New, Pussycat?*, *The Return of the Pink Panther*, *The Pink Panther Strikes Again*, etc). He won two Oscars for *Who Framed Roger Rabbit?* (1988); one for best effects (with Ken Ralston, Edward Jones and George Gibbs), the other a special achievement award as director of animation. His excellent animated short *A Christmas Carol* (1971) also won a best animated short Oscar. His long-in-the-works feature *The Thief and the Cobbler* was eventually taken out of his hands, though. It was completed by others and released as *Arabian Knight* in 1995. He has also animated many commercials.

Genre credits:
The Little Island (1955 – d), *Casino Royale* (1967 – titles), *A Christams Carol* (1971 – short – p/d), *Raggedy Ann and Andy* (1977 – d), *Who Framed Roger Rabbit?* (1988 – co-sp/animation d), *Arabian Knight* (1995 – aka *The Thief and the Cobbler* – d)

Williams, Robin (1951-)

American comedy actor and stand-up comedian who first found fame on TV with *Mork and Mindy*. He turned to films with variable success at first, but his persistence has since paid off, especially with dramatic roles in such films as *The World According to Garp*, *Good Morning, Vietnam*, *Dead Poets Society* and *Awakenings*.

Genre credits:

Popeye (1980), *The Adventures of Baron Munchausen* (1989 – uncredited gag cameo), *The Fisher King* (1991), *Hook* (1991 – as Peter Pan), *Aladdin* (1992 – voice), *Ferngully: The Last Rainforest* (1992 – voice), *Toys* (1992), *Being Human* (1994), *Jumanji* (1996), *Aladdin and the King of Thieves* (1997 – voice, as the Genie)

Willow

USA/GB 1988 121m DeLuxe Panavision Dolby

A young dawrf and a warrior hero rescue a baby princess from the clutches of an evil queen.

Expensive but derivative fantasy adventure with the expected action highlights and effects that go with a big budget. A technician's rather than an actor's film.

p: Nigel Wooll for MGM/Lucasfilm/Imagine Entertainmen
exec p: George Lucas
w: Bob Dolman
story: George Lucas
d: Ron Howard
ph: Adrian Biddle
m: JAMES HORNER
ed: Daniel Hanley, Michael Hall
pd: Allan Cameron
cos: Barbara Lane
sp: Dennis Murren, Michael McAlister, John Richardson, Phil Tippett
sound: Ben Burtt, Ivan Sharrock, Gary Summers, Shawn Murphy
sound ed: Richard Hymns
2nd unit d: Michael Moore
2nd unit ph: Paul Beeson

3rd unit ph: Paul Wilson
ch: Eleanor Fazan
titles: Ray Mercer
stunt co-ordinator: Gerry Crampton
fight ch: Bill Hobbs
Val Kilmer, Joanne Whalley, Warwick Davis (as Willow), Billy Barty, Jean Marsh, Patricia Hayes, Pat Roach, Gavan O'Herlihy, Phil Fondacaro

Willy Wonker and the Chocolate Factory

USA/Bavaria 1971 100m Technicolor

A young boy wins one of five golden tickets for a trip to a magical chocolate factory.

Enjoyable and generally imaginative musical with a nice line in malicious humour and an eccentric role for its star. Good fun for kids and adults alike.

p: David Wolper, Stan Margulies for David Wolper Productions
w: ROALD DAHL from his novel
d: Mel Stuart
ph: Arthur Ibbetson
songs: Leslie Bricusse, Anthony Newley
md: Walter Scharf
ed: David Saxon, Mel Shapiro
ad: HARPER GOFF
cos: Helen Colvig
sp: Logan Frazee
sound: Karsten Ullrich, Dick Portman
ch: Howard Jeffrey, Betty Walberg
GENE WILDER, JACK ALBERTSON, Peter Ostrum, ROY KINNEAR, Aubrey Woods, Tim Brooke-Taylor, David Battley, Julie Dawn Cole, Leonard Stone, Denise Nickerson, Paris Themmen, Ursula Reit, Michael Bollner, Diana Sowle

The Wind in the Willows

GB 1996 83m Technicolor Dolby

Mr. Toad's penchant for driving (and crashing) expensive motor cars gets him into all sorts of scrapes. Luckily, his friends Rat, Mole and Badger are at hand to rescue him.

Lively, generally charming live action version of the Kenneth Graham classic, with the odd musical number thrown in for good measure. Ideal video viewing for all the family.

p: John Goldstone, Jake Eberts for Allied Filmmakers
w/d: Terry Jones
book: Kenneth Graham
ph: David Tattersall
songs: John DuPrez, Terry Jones, Dave Howman, Andre Jacquemin
m: John DuPrez
ed/2nd unit d: Julian Doyle
pd/cos: Jasmes Acheson
sp: Peter Chiang, Peter Hutchinson
make-up/hair: Jan Sewell
sound: Andre Jacquemin, Bob Doyle
2nd unit ph: Luke Cardiff
stunt co-ordinator: Marc Boyle
Terry Jones, Steve Coogan, Eric Idle, Antony Sher, Nicol Williamson, Stephen Fry, Bernard Hill, John Cleese, Julia Sawalha, Michael Palin, Nigel Planer, Victoria Wood, Robert Bathurst, Don Henderson, Keith-Lee Castle, Richard James

The Winged Serpent

see Q: The Winged Serpent

Wings of Fame

Netherlands 1990 108m Agfacolor Dolby

A writer and a film star find themselves in the afterlife, unable to leave a luxury hotel – until, that is, their earthly fame diminishes.

Dull and dreary looking take on an old wheeze.

p: Laurens Geels, Dick Maas for First Floor Features
w: Otakar Votocek, Herman Koch
d: Otokar Votocek

ph: Alex Thomson
m: Paul van Brugge
ed: Hans van Dongen
pd: Dick Schillemans
ad: Peter Jansen
cos: Yan Tax
sound: George Bossaers, Ad Roest
Peter O'Toole, Colin Firth, Marie Trintignant, Maria Becker, Walter Gotell, Gottfried John, Ellen Umlauf, Andrea Ferreol

Winnie the Pooh and a Day for Eeyore

USA 1983 35m Technicolor
Winnie the Pooh and his friends forget Eeyore's birthday.

Tame addition to Disney's ongoing Pooh series.

p: Rick Reiner for Walt Disney
w: Peter Young, Steve Hullett, Tony L. Marino
books: A. A. Milne
d: Rick Reiner
m: Steve Zuckerman
voices: Hal Smith, Laurie Main, Ralph Wright, John Fielder, Will Ryan, Paul Winchell

Winnie the Pooh and the Blustery Day 🍯🍯

USA 1963 32m Technicolor
(aa Best Animated Short)
Winnie the Pooh and his friends find themselves caught up in a blustery storm.

Charming animated featurette with just the right approach to the material. The best of the Disney Poohs.

p: Walt Disney
w: Larry Clemmons, Julius Svendson, Ralph Wright, Vance Gerry
books: A. A. Milne
d: Wolfgang Reitherman
m: Richard M. and Robert B. Sherman
md: Buddy Baker

narrator: Sebastian Cabot
voices: STERLING HOLLOWAY, Paul Winchell, John Fielder, Clint Howard, Howard Morris

Winnie the Pooh and the Honey Tree 🍯

USA 1965 25m Technicolor
Pooh's yearning for honey gets him into all kinds of trouble.

Engaging cartoon short, ideal viewing for youngsters.

p: Walt Disney
w: Larry Clemmons, Ralph Wright, Xavier Atencio, Ken Anderson, Vance Gerry, Dick Lucas
books: A. A. Milne
d: Wolfgang Reitherman
m: Richard M. and Robert B. Sherman
md: Buddy Baker
narrator: Sebastian Cabot
voices: STERLING HOLLOWAY, Howard Morris, Junius Matthews, Bruce Reitherman, Hal Smith

Winston, Stan

Celebrated American make-up and effects artist, an Oscar winner for his work on *Aliens* (1986 – with Robert Skotak, John Richardson and Suzanne Benson), *Terminator 2: Judgement Day* (1991 – with Dennis Murren, Gene Warren, Jr. and Robert Skotak, Jr.) and *Jurassic Park* (1993 – with Dennis Murren, Phil Tippett and Michael Lantieri). He began his film career in 1969 as a make-up trainee for Walt Disney. He first came to attention in 1973 when he won an Emmy (with Rick Baker) for his work on the TV movie *The Autobiography of Miss Jane Pittman*. He has also directed two films: *Pumpkinhead* (for which he also co-authored the story) and *Upworld* (aka *A Gnome Named Gnorm*). His other credits include

Mansion of the Doomed, *W. C. Fields and Me*, *Dead and Buried*, *The Monster Squad*, *Interview with the Vampire* and *The Relic*.

Genre credits:
Gargoyles (1974 – TVM), *The Wiz* (1978), *Heartbeeps* (1981), *The Thing* (1982 - additional effects), *Something Wicked This Way Comes* (1983), *Starman* (1984), *The Terminator* (1984 – also co-2nd unit d), *Aliens* (1986 – also 2nd unit d), *Invaders from Mars* (1986), *Alien Nation* (1988), *Leviathan* (1989), *Predator 2* (1990), *Edward Scissorhands* (1990), *Terminator 2: Judgement Day* (1992), *Batman Returns* (1992), *Jurassic Park* (1993), *Tank Girl* (1994 – co-sp), *Congo* (1995), *The Island of Dr. Moreau* (1996), *The Lost World: Jurassic Park* (1997 – co-sp)

Wise, Robert (1914-)

American producer and director who won Oscars for both producing and directing *West Side Story* (1961 – co-directed with Jerome Robbins) and *The Sound of Music* (1965). A former editor, he began his career at RKO in 1933 and worked on many of the studio's top productions, among them *The Hunchback of Notre Dame*, *Citizen Kane*, *The Magnificent Ambersons* and *All That Money Can Buy*. He began directing in 1944 with *The Curse of the Cat People* (co-directed with Gunther Frisch). His first solo effort, *Mademoiselle Fifi* followed the same year. His subsequent credits have taken in such wide-ranging films as *The Set-Up*, *Executive Suite*, *The Haunting*, *Sand Pebbles*, *Star!* and *The Hindenberg*, as well as three key science fiction films. He made his acting debut at the age of 82 in *The Stupids*.

Genre credits:
The Day the Earth Stood Still (1951 – d), *The Andromeda Strain* (1970 – p/d), *Star Trek –*

The Motion Picture (1979 – d)

The Witches ☺

USA/GB 1990 91m Eastmancolor
A young boy and his grandmother manage to dispatch an evil witch and her cronies before they succeed with their plan to turn all the children in England into mice.

Engagingly macabre fantasy for youngsters who like a scare or two.

p: Mark Shivas for Warner/Lorimar
exec p: Jim Henson
w: Allan Scott
novel: Roald Dahl
d: Nicolas Roeg
ph: Harvey Harrison
m: Stanley Myers
ed: Tony Lawson
pd: Andrew Sanders
cos: Marit Allen
sp: Jim Henson's Creature Shop
sound: Peter Sutton, Gerry Humphreys
2nd unit d/ph: John Palmer
sp ph: Paul Wilson
Anjelica Huston, MAI ZETTERLING, Jasen Fisher, Rowan Atkinson, Brenda Blethyn, Jane Horrocks, Anne Lambton, Charlie Potter

Within the Rock

US/GB/Fr 1996 84m Foto-Kem Dolby
In 2019, miners working on Galileo's Child, a moon they are tunnelling into in a bid to destroy it before it collides with earth, accidentally release an alien buried there in a sealed chamber launched from the planet Trillium some two million years earlier.

As a low budget *Outland/ Alien/ Inseminoid* hybrid, a lot better than you might think. Adequate late night video fodder.

p: Stanley Isaacs, Scott McGinnis, Robert Patrick for Le Monde/360 Entertainment/Prism

Director Robert Wise takes to the air to achieve a shot for his understated science fiction thriller *The Andromeda Strain*, the first film to be based on a novel by Michael Crichton.

exec p: John Fremes, Barry Collier, Barbara Javitz
w/d/make-up effects: Gary T. Tunnicliffe
ph: Adam Kane
m: Rod Gammons, Tony Fennell
ed: Roderick Davis
pd: Dorian Vernacchio, Deborah Raymond
cos: Kristin M. Burke
sp: Corbitt Design
sound: John Brasher, Marty Hutcherson, Ezra Dweck
stun co-ordinator: Scott Ateah
2nd unit d: Coleson Hammond
2nd unit ph: Mark McGinnis
Xander Berkeley, Caroline Barclay, Bradford Tatum, Brian Krause, Barbara Patrick, Michael Zelniker

The Wiz

USA 1978 134m Technicolor Panavision
Misconceived and over-inflated all-black version of the classic fairytale with New York locations. Hellishly overlong and with very few rewards.

p: Robert Cohen for Universal/Mowtown

exec p: Ken Harper
w: Joel Schumacher
d: Sidney Lumet
ph: Oswald Morris
songs: Charlie Smith
md: Quincy Jones
ed: Dede Allen
pd/cos: Tony Walton
sp: Albert Whitlock
ch: Louise Johnson
Diana Ross, Michael Jackson, Nipsey Russell, Ted Ross, Lena Horne, Richard Pryor (as the Wiz), Mabel King, Theresa Merritt

The Wizard of Oz
☺☺☺☺

USA 1939 102m Technicolor/bw
An unhappy Kansas girl runs away from home and is whisked away by a cyclone to a magical land where she has adventures with a scarecrow, a tin man and a cowardly lion.

One of the screen's genuine all-time-great classics, this colourful musical benefits especially from memorable performances, splendid art direction and bouncy tunes. A delightful piece of entertainment which endears itself to every new generation which discovers it.

p: Mervyn LeRoy for MGM
w: Noel Langley, Florence Ryerson, Edgar Allen Wolfe
novel: L. Frank Baum
d: VICTOR FLEMINBG (and KING VIDOR – bw prologue/epilogue)
ph: HAROLD ROSSON (and ALLEN DAVEY – bw prologue/epilogue)
songs: HAROLD ARLEN, E. Y. HARBURG (AA, BEST SONG, *Over the Rainbow*)
md: HERBERT STOTHART (AA)
ed: BLANCHE SEWELL
ad: CEDRIC GIBBONS, WILLIAM A. HORNING
cos: ADRIAN
sp: ARNOLD GILLESPIE
sound: DOUGLAS SHEARER
ch: Bobby Connolly
make-up: JACK DAWN
JUDY GARDLAND, FRANK MORGAN, RAY BOLGER, JACK HALEY, BERT LAHR, BILLIE BURKE, MARGARET HAMILTON, Charley Grapewin, Clara Blandick, Pat Walshe

Wonder Man
USA 1945 97m Technicolor
The ghost of a brash nightclub comedian returns to persuade his shy twin brother to avenge his murder.

Familiar star antics which might have been more palatable had it not been for his incessant mugging. Good colour, though.

p: Sam Goldwyn
w: Don Hartman, Melville Shavelson, Philip Rapp, Jack Jevene, Eddie Moran
story: Arthur Sheekman
d: Bruce Humberstone
ph: Victor Milner, William Snyder
songs: Sylvia Fine, Leo Robin, David Rose
md: Ray Heindorf, Louis Forbes
ed: Daniel Mandell
ad: Ernst Fetge. McClure Capps
cos: Travis Banton
sp: John P. Fulton, A. W. Johns
sound: Fred Lau
ch: John Wray
Danny Kaye, Vera-Ellen, Virginia Mayo, Steve Cochran, S. Z. Sakall, Otto Kruger, Ed Brophy, Richard Lane, Natalie Schaefer, Allen Jenkins

Wonder Woman
USA 1974 74m colour TVM
Wonder Woman goes undercover to work for the CIA.

Dismal comic strip heroics, not even laughably bad. The format was later revamped by another studio (with Lynda Carter in the title role) with reasonably popular results.

p: John G. Stephens for Warner/ABC
exec p: John D. F. Black
w: John D. F. Black
d: Vincent McEveety
ph: Joseph Biroc
m: Artie Butler
ed: Gene Ruggiero
ad: Phillip Bennett
cos: Bill Thomas
sound: no credit given
stunt co-ordinator: Joe Hooker
Cathy Lee Crosby, Ricardo Montalban, Kaz Garas, Andrew Prine

Judy Garland's Dorothy Gale encounters Jack Haley's Tin Man and Ray Bolger's Scarecrow in the timeless musical fantasy *The Wizard of Oz*.

The Wonderful World of the Brothers Grimm

USA 1962 134m Technicolor Cinerama
The story of the German fairy tale writers, interspersed with several of their stories.

Overlong and rather dull fantasy biopic with just a couple of sequences with the required style and brightness. Youngsters may tire of it well before the end.

p: George Pal for MGM/Cinerama
w: David P. Harmon, Charles Beaumont, William Roberts
story: David P. Harmon
d: George Pal, Henry Levin
ph: Paul C. Vogel
songs: Bob Merril
m: Leigh Harline
ed: Walter Thompson
ad: George W. Davis, Edward Carfagno
cos: Mary Willis (aa)
sp: George Warren, Wah Chang, Tim Barr, Robert R. Hoag
sound: Franklin Milton
ch: Alex Romero
Laurence Harvey, Karl Boehm, Claire Bloom, Barbara Eden, Walter Slezak, Oscar Homolka, Martita Hunt, Russ Tamblyn, Yvette Mimieux, Jim Backus, Beulah Bondi, Terry-Thomas, Buddy Hackett, Otto Kruger, Arnold Stang

Wordsworth, Richard (1915-1993)

British character actor, the great-great-great grandson of the poet Wordsworth. On stage from 1938, he didn't make his first film until 1955. However, this was Hammer's *The Quatermass Experiment* (aka *The Creeping Unknown*) in which he played the doomed astronaut, Victor Caroon, for which he is still remembered. His other credits include *The Man Who Knew Too Much*, *The*

Camp on Blood Island, *The Revenge of Frankenstein*, *The Curse of the Werewolf*, *Lock Up Your Daughters* and *Song of Norway*.

Wynn, Ed (1889-1966)

American character comedian who began his career in Vaudeville. Also a stage producer, radio personality and TV star, he appeared in films throughout his career, beginning with *Rubber Heels* in 1927, though it was in old age that he was most successful on the big screen in films such as *The Diary of Anne Frank*, *Mary Poppins* and *That Darn Cat*.

Genre credits:
Alice in Wonderland (1955 – voice), *Cinderfella* (1960), *The Absent-Minded Professor* (1961), *Babes in Toyland* (1961), *Son of Flubber* (1962), *Mary Poppins* (1964), *The Gnome Mobile* (1967)

Wynn, Keenan (1916-1986)

American actor, the son of comedy character actor Ed Wynn and the father of screenwriter Tracy Keenan Wynn. Much stage and radio experience in the 30s, after which he turned to films in 1942 with a small part in *Me and My Gal*. His other credits include *The Clock*, *Ziegfield Follies*, *Royal Wedding*, *Kiss Me, Kate*, *It's a Big Country*, *Around the World Under the Sea*, *The Great Race*, *Once Upon a Time in the West*, *Pretty Maids All in a Row*, *The Devil's Rain*, *Best Friends* and *Black Moon Rising*.

Genre credits:
Angels in the Outfield (1954 – aka *Angels and the Pirates*), *The Glass Slipper* (1955), *The Absent-Minded Professor* (1961), *Son of Flubber* (1962), *Dr Strangelove* (1963), *Finian's Rainbow* (1968), *The Monitors*

(1969), *Herbie Rides Again* (1974), *The Shaggy D.A.* (1976), *Laserblast* (1976), *The Last Unicorn* (1982 – voice), *People from Another Star* (1986)

Wynorski, Jim (1950-)

American writer and director with a penchant for all manner of exploitation items. A former campaign manager for Doubleday, he became a TV production assistant in 1980, which he followed with promotional work for Roger Corman's trailer department. He began writing screenplays for Corman in 1981 with *Forbidden World*, which he followed with *Sorcoress* and the teen sex comedy *Screwballs*. He finally turned to direction in 1986 with *Lost Empire*. His other credits include *Big Bad Mamma II*, *Hollywood Scream Queen Hot Tub Party*, *Hard to Die*, *Body Chemistry II*, *Little Miss Zillions* (aka *Home for Christmas*), *Chopping Mall*, *Transylvania Twist*, *Sorority House Massacre II*, *976 Evil: The Return*, *Ghoulies IV* and *Body Chemistry III*.

Genre credits:
Forbidden World (1981 – aka *Mutant* – w), *Sorcoress* (1982 – w), *The Lost Empire* (1986 – w/d), *Not of This Earth* (1988 – d), *Return of the Swamp Thing* (1989 – d), *Dinosaur Island* (1994)

X The Unknown

GB 1956 81m bw

Whilst on training exercises in Scotland, the army unearths a strange force which feeds off radioactive energy.

Overpadded variation on *The Quatermass Experiment*, let down by poor effects work and a restricted budget. Genre addicts may enjoy the clichés.

p: Anthony Hinds for Hammer/Exclusive
w: Jimmy Sangster
d: Leslie Norman
ph: Gerald Gibbs
m: James Bernard
md: John Hollingsworth
ed: James Needs
ad: Bernard Robinson
cos: Molly Arbuthnot
sp: Jack Curtis, Les Bowie
sound: Jock May
production manager: Jimmy Sangster
Dean Jagger, Edward Chapman, Leo McKern, William Lucas, John Harvey, Peter Hammond, Michael Ripper, Anthony Newley, Michael Brook, Marianne Brauns

Xanadu

USA 1980 93m Technicolor

A record cover designer is helped by the muse Terpsichore to open a roller disco (!).

Unbelievably flimsy and instantly dated youth musical which plays like a 90-minute record promo. It has to be seen to be believed.

p: Lawrence Gordon, Joel Silver for Universal
w: Richard Christian Danus, Marc Reid Rubel
d: Robert Greenwald
ph: Victor J. Kemper
songs: Barry de Vorzon, John Farrar
m/md: Barry de Vorzon
ed: Dennis Virkler
pd: John W. Corso
cos: Bobbie Mannix
sp/titles: Robert Greenberg
Olivia Newton John, Gene Kelly, Michael Beck, James Sloyan, Dimitra Arliss, Katie Hanley, Fred McCarren, Sandahl Bergman, Lynn Latham

Yagher, Kevin

American make-up effects artist who began his career by making Halloween masks. Started his film career in 1983 as an assistant to Greg Cannom on such films as *Dreamscape*, *The Last Starfighter*, *Friday the 13th Part IV*, *Cocoon* and the Michael Jackson video *Thriller*. He went solo in 1985 with *A Nightmare on Elm Street Part II: Freddy's Revenge*, since when he has worked on such movies as *Child's Play* (and its two sequels), *The Seventh Sign*, *Glory*, *Man's Best Friend* and *Getting Even with Dad*. In 1995 he turned to direction with *Hellraiser: Bloodline*, having already directed two episodes of TV's *Tales from the Crypt* (*Lower Berth* and *Strung Along*). He also designed the Cryptkeeper for the series and directed all the wraparound segments.

Genre credits:
Dreamscape (1984 – assistant), *The Last Starfighter* (1984 – assistant), *Cocoon* (1985 – assistant), *The Hidden* (1988), *Bill and Ted's Excellent Adventure* (1988), *Radio Flyer* (1992), *Honey, I Blew Up the Kid* (1992)

Yates, George Worthington (1901-)

American writer, perhaps best remembered for writing the story for the giant ant shocker *Them!* His other credits include *Frankenstein 1970*, *Earth vs. the Spider*, *Attack of the Puppet People* and *Tormented*.

Genre credits:
Them! (1954 – story), *It Came from Beneath the Sea* (1955 – story/co-w), *Conquest of Space* (1955 – co-adaptation), *Earth vs the Flying Saucers* (1956 – co-w), *The Flame Barrier* (1958 – story/co-w)

Yellow Submarine

GB 1968 87m DeLuxe

The Beatles help save the kingdom of Pepperland from invading Blue Meanies.

Interestingly designed cartoon feature which does nevertheless outstay its welcome fairly early on. Psychedelia freaks may have a field day.

p: Al Brodax for King Features/Apple
w: Lee Mintoff, Al Brodax, Jack Mendleshon, Erich Segal
story: Lee Mintoff
d: George Dunning, Jack Stokes, Robert Balser
live action d: Dennis Abey

songs: THE BEATLES
md: George Martin
ed: Brian J. Bishop
ad: Heinz Edelman
sound: Hugh Strain
voices: Paul Angelis, John Clive, Dick Emery, Geoff Hughes, Lance Percival (the Beatles themselves are only heard singing the film's songs)

You Only Live Twice
🍲🍲🍲

GB 1967 117m Technicolor Panavision

When an American space rocket is hijacked over Japan, James Bond is sent to investigate, only to find his old enemy Blofeld behind the operation.

Slam bang Bond adventure with the expected mixture of gadgets, girls and exotic locations, plus some impressive production design and a plethora of well-staged action sequences. Tongue-in-cheek fun on a big budget.

p: Harry Saltzman, Albert R. Broccoli for UA/Eon
w: Roald Dahl
novel: Ian Fleming
d: LEWIS GILBERT
ph: FREDERICK A. YOUNG
m: JOHN BARRY
ly: Leslie Bricusse
title song sung by: Nancy Siantra
ed: PETER HUNT, THELMA CONNELL
pd: KEN ADAM
cos: Eileen Sullivan
sp: John Stears
sound: John Mitchell, Gordon K. McCallum
2nd unit d: Peter Hunt
2nd unit ph: Bob Huke
aerial ph: John Jordan
underwater ph: Lamar Boren
stunt co-ordinator: Bob Simmons
ass d: William P. Cartlidge
Sean Connery, Akiko Makabayashi, Tetsuro Tamba, Teru Shimada, Karin Dor, Lois Maxwell, Bernard Lee, Desmond Llewellyn, Charles Gray, DONALD PLEASENCE (as

Blofeld), Alexander Knox, Robin Bailey, Burt Kwouk, Shane Rimmer

Young, Christopher

American composer who studied music with film composer David Raksin at UCLA. Began his career providing synth scores for low budget horror films (*Pranks*, *The Power*, etc.) after which he graduated to fully-fledged symphonic soundtracks (*Hellraiser*, *Hellbound: Hellraiser II*, etc.). His other credits include *A Nightmare on Elm Street Part 2: Freddy's Revenge*, *Haunted Summer*, *Bat-21*, *The Dark Half*, *The Vagrant*, *Jennifer 8* and *Dream Lover*.

Genre credits:

Barbarian Queen (1985 – co-m), *Invaders from Mars* (1986), *Desert Warrior* (1987 – aka *Wheels of Fire*), *The Fly II* (1989), *Species* (1995), *Virtuosity* (1995)

Young Sherlock Holmes 🍲

USA 1985 105m Technicolor Panavision Dolby

In their first case together whilst still at school, Holmes and Watson link a series of murders to an Egyptian sect hidden in the depths of London.

An agreeable enough concept is unfortunately let down by too weak a mystery plot and an over-emphasis on special effects, making the whole enterprise seem like an Indiana Jones adventure rather than the pastiche it set out to be. Effort is evident throughout, however, and the period detail is fine, though the intended sequels did not materialise when the film failed to perform as expected at the box office.

p: Mark Johnson for Paramount/ILM/Amblin
exec p: Steven Spielberg, Kathleen Kennedy, Frank Marshall

w: Chris Columbus
d: Barry Levinson
ph: STEPHEN GOLDBLATT
m: BRUCE BROUGHTON
ed: Stu Linder
pd: NORMAN REYNOLDS
cos: Raymond Hughes
sp: Kit West, Dennis Murren, Stephen Norrington
sound: Paul Bruce Richardson
2nd unit d: Andrew Grieve
2nd unit ph: Steven Smith
narrator: Michael Hordern
Nicholas Rowe, Alan Cox, Sophie Ward, Anthony Higgins, Susan Fleetwood, Freddie Jones, Nigel Stock, Patrick Newell

Young Sherlock Holmes and the Pyramid of Fear
see Young Sherlock Holmes

Yuricich, Matthew

British special effects technician and cinematographer working in America, an Oscar winner for his effects work on *Logan's Run* (1976 – with Glen Robinson and L. B. Abbott). His best work has been in association with Douglas Trumbull. His other credits include *Die Hard* and *Mission: Impossible*.

Genre credits:

Silent Running (1971 – co-sp), *Soylent Green* (1973 – co-sp), *Close Encounters of the Third Kind* (1977 – effects ph), *Star Trek* (1979 – co-sp), *Close Encounters of the Third Kind – The Special Edition* (1980 – effects ph), *Blade Runner* (1982 – co-sp), *Brainstorm* (1983 – ph), *Bill and Ted's Bogus Journey* (1991 – sp), *Event Horizon* (1997 – co-sp)

ZPG: Zero Population Growth

see Zero Population Growth

Zadora, Pia (1954-)

Pouting American actress and singer who started her career as a juvenile in the delightfully awful *Santa Claus Conquers the Martians* in 1964 in which she played Grimar. Her other credits include *Butterfly*, *The Lonely Lady* and *Hairspray*, along with one more genre appearance in *Voyage of the Rock Aliens* (1987).

Zardoz

GB 1973 105m DeLuxe Panavision
In the future, a Brutal finds his way into the Vortex where he encounters Eternals, Apathetics and Renegades.

Despite some occasionally arresting visual qualities, this is a highly pretentious and self-indulgent would-be fantasy which never begins to make any sense, never mind entertain. The title is derived from *The Wizard of Oz* (geddit?).

p: John Boorman for TCF/John Boorman Productions
w/d: John Boorman
ph: Geoffrey Unsworth
m: David Munrow
ed: John Merritt

pd: Anthony Pratt
cos: Christel Kruse Boorman
sound: Gerry Johnston
Sean Connery (wearing a ludicrous and unsuitably abbreviated costume), Charlotte Rampling, Sara Kestleman, John Alderton, Niall Buggy, Jessica Swift

Zavitz, Lee

American special effects technician who won an Oscar for his work on *Destination Moon* (1950).

Genre credits:
Destination Moon (1950 – sp), *From the Earth to the Moon* (1958 – sp), *On the Beach* (1959 – sp), *Captain Sinbad* (1963 – co-sp)

Zehetbauer, Rolf

German production designer on the international scene who won an Oscar for *Cabaret* (1972). He also designed two fantasy films for director Wolfgang Petersen – *The Never Ending Story* and *Enemy Mine* – as well as *Das Boot* (aka *The Boat*). His other credits take in *Twilight's Last Gleaming*, *Brass Target*, *Lili Marleen* and *Lola*.

Genre credits:
The Never Ending Story (1984), *Enemy Mine* (1985), *The Never Ending Story III* (1994)

Zemeckis, Robert (1952-)

American writer and director who made his directorial debut in 1978 with *I Wanna Hold Your Hand*, which he wrote with his most frequent collaborator Bob Gale, with whom he went on to script *1941* for Spielberg and *Used Cars*, which he also directed. He hit the big time with *Romancing the Stone* in 1984, which he followed up with the even more successful *Back to the Future*, again written with Gale (as were the sequels, which Gale also co-produced). Since then he has become one of Hollywood's most sought after directors, winning an Oscar for helming *Forrest Gump* (1994). His other credits include *Death Becomes Her*.

Genre credits:
Back to the Future (1985 – co-w/d), *Who Framed Roger Rabbit?* (1988 – d), *Back to the Future II* (1989 – co-story/d), *Back to the Future III* (1990 – story/d), *Contact* (1997 – co-p/d)

Zero Population Growth

GB/USA/Sweden 1971 96m Eastmancolor
In the future, child-bearing is banned by the authorities in an attempt to control the population growth, but a young couple conspire to have a baby.

A promising idea is scuppered by flat handling and the usual bleak, totalitarian view of the future.

p: Thomas F. Madigan for Sagittarius
w: Max Erlich, Frank de Felita
d: Michael Campus
ph: Michael Reed
m: Jonathan Hodge
ed: Richard C. Meyer, Dennis Lanning
pd: Tony Masters
cos: Jytte Paby, Margit Brandt
sp: Derek Meddings
sound: no credit given
add ph: Mikael Salomon
Oliver Reed, Geraldine Chaplin, Diane Cilento, Aubrey Woods, Bill Nagy, Don Gordon

Zimmer, Hans (1957-)

German composer and synth player, working in Britain and America. A former member of The Buggles, he began his film career as an assistant to composer Stanley Myers, with whom he co-scored *Moonlighting*, *The Nature of the Beast* and *Insignificance*, etc. He went solo with *A World Apart* in 1987, which he followed with such projects as *Burning Secret*, *The Fruit Machine*, *Rain Man*, *Driving Miss Daisy* and an abundance of action scores, among them *K2*, *Backdraft*, *True Romance* and *Crimson Tide*. He finally won an Oscar for scoring Disney's *The Lion King* (1994). He is now the music supervisor for Dreamworks SKG.

Genre credits:
Radio Flyer (1992), *Lifepod* (1993 – TVM – co-m), *Batman: Mask of the Phantasm* (1993 – synth player only), *The Lion King* (1994), *Muppet Treasure Island* (1996), *The Preacher's Wife* (1996), *The Borrowers* (1997 – music p only)

Zsigmond, Vilmos (1930-)

Hungarian cinematographer who won an Oscar for *Close Encounters of the Third Kind* (1977). His other credits include *Deliverance*, *The Sugarland Express*, *Obsession*, *The Deer Hunter*, *Heaven's Gate*, *Blow Out*, *Bonfire of the Vanities*, *Maverick* and *The Ghost and the Darkness*.

Genre credits:
The Time Travellers (1964), *The Monitors* (1967), *Close Encounters of the Third Kind* (1977 – co-ph), *Close Encounters of the Third Kind – The Special Edition* (1980 – co-ph)

Top left: Peter Fonda in *Futureworld*
Top right: The filming of *The Quatermass Xperiment* that shot Hammer Films to fame
Centre: Keith Barron and Doug McLure fleeing monsters in *The Land that Time Forgot*
Bottom right: James Olson's face guard in *The Andromeda Strain*
Bottom far right: A scene from the 'ecological' *Silent Running*